THE ASSOCIATION FOR SCOTTISH LITERARY STUDIES

NUMBER TWENTY

THE ASSOCIATION FOR SCOTTISH LITERARY STUDIES

ANNUAL VOLUMES

1971 James Hogg, *The Three Perils of Man*, ed. Douglas Gifford.
1972 *The Poems of John Davidson*, vol. I, ed. Andrew Turnbull.
1973 *The Poems of John Davidson*, vol. II, ed. Andrew Turnbull.
1974 Allan Ramsay and Robert Fergusson, *Poems*, ed. Alexander M. Kinghorn and Alexander Law.
1975 John Galt, *The Member*, ed. Ian A. Gordon.
1976 William Drummond of Hawthornden, *Poems and Prose*, ed. Robert H. MacDonald.
1977 John G. Lockhart, *Peter's Letters to his Kinsfolk*, ed. William Ruddick.
1978 John Galt, *Selected Short Stories*, ed. Ian A. Gordon.
1979 Andrew Fletcher of Saltoun, *Selected Political Writings and Speeches*, ed. David Daiches.
1980 *Scott on Himself*, ed. David Hewitt.
1981 *The Party-Coloured Mind*, ed. David Reid.
1982 James Hogg, *Selected Stories and Sketches*, ed. Douglas S. Mack.
1983 Sir Thomas Urquhart of Cromarty, *The Jewel*, ed. R. D. S. Jack and R. J. Lyall.
1984 John Galt, *Ringan Gilhaize*, ed. Patricia J. Wilson.
1985 Margaret Oliphant, *Selected Short Stories of the Supernatural*, ed. Margaret K. Gray.
1986 James Hogg, *Selected Poems and Songs*, ed. David Groves.
1987 Hugh MacDiarmid, *A Drunk Man Looks at the Thistle*, ed. Kenneth Buthlay.
1988 *The Book of Sandy Stewart*, ed. Roger Leitch.
1989 *The Comic Poems of William Tennant*, ed. Alexander Scott and Maurice Lindsay.
1990 Thomas Hamilton, *The Youth and Manhood of Cyril Thornton*, ed. Maurice Lindsay.

SPAIN AND PORTUGAL Showing major places mentioned
in *CYRIL THORNTON* and notes
(from DAVID G. CHANDLER *Atlas of Military Strategy*, LONDON 1980)

THE ASSOCIATION FOR SCOTTISH LITERARY STUDIES

GENERAL EDITOR—DOUGLAS S. MACK

Thomas Hamilton

The Youth and Manhood
of
Cyril Thornton

Edited by
Maurice Lindsay

THE ASSOCIATION FOR SCOTTISH LITERARY STUDIES
ABERDEEN
1990

First published in Great Britain, 1990
by The Association for Scottish Literary Studies,
c/o Department of English,
University of Aberdeen, Aberdeen AB9 2UB

Introduction and Notes © 1990, Maurice Lindsay

The Association for Scottish Literary Studies
acknowledges subsidy from the Scottish Arts Council
towards the publication of this volume.

ISBN 0-948877-11-1

Typeset at Oxford University Computing Service.
Printed and bound by Bell and Bain Ltd, Glasgow

CONTENTS

Introduction   vii
Acknowledgements   xix
Note on the Text   xx

Volume 1   1
Volume 2   145
Volume 3   293

Notes   443

THE ASSOCIATION
FOR
SCOTTISH LITERARY STUDIES

THE Association for Scottish Literary Studies aims to promote the study, teaching and writing of Scottish literature, and to further the study of the languages of Scotland.

To these ends, the ASLS publishes works of Scottish literature (of which this volume is an example), literary criticism in *Scottish Literary Journal*, scholarly studies of language in *Scottish Language*, and in-depth reviews of Scottish books in *SLJ Supplements*. And it publishes *New Writing Scotland*, an annual anthology of new poetry, drama and short fiction, in Scots, English and Gaelic, by Scottish writers.

All these publications are available as a single 'package', in return for an annual subscription. Enquiries should be sent to:

ASLS
c/o Department of English
University of Aberdeen
ABERDEEN
AB9 2UB

INTRODUCTION

Thomas Hamilton (1789–1842) was the younger son of William Hamilton (1758–1790), surgeon and Professor of Anatomy and Botany in the University of Glasgow. Like his elder brother, who became the Scottish metaphysical philosopher Sir William Hamilton (1788–1856), Thomas was born within the precincts of the Old College, at number one Professors' Court.[1] He was sent south to a school at Chiswick, now a London borough, where he received a classical education. Returning to Scotland, he entered the College at Glasgow in 1803.[2] There, he studied through three winter sessions but left without taking a degree. According to brother William, Thomas had a retentive memory but lacked application. He then entered a Glasgow merchant's warehouse,[3] where doubtless he encountered the prototype of Cyril Thornton's uncle, David Spreull. The mercantile life was not to Thomas Hamilton's liking, however, and in 1810, he obtained by purchase, after the manner of the time, a commission in the 29th (Worcester) Regiment, an odd choice for a Scot, though perhaps it explains why he located the seat of his fictional Thornton family in the Severn Valley.

Hamilton had barely joined, let alone received much training in his new calling, when his regiment was despatched on active service to the Peninsula. There, it played a vigorous part in the victory of Albuera, though Hamilton was wounded by a bullet in the thigh which lamed him for life.

Having sufficiently recovered from his wound to be able to rejoin his regiment, Hamilton saw further active service in the Peninsular War. This was followed by a period of service in Nova Scotia and in New Brunswick during the American War of 1812.

In 1818 his short military career ended, and Hamilton retired on the half pay of a Captain and set himself up as a man of letters at 5 Darnaway Street, Edinburgh, quickly becoming a friend of the publisher William Blackwood, a regular member of the Blackwood group and a fairly frequent contributor to Blackwood's 'Maga'. One of his contributions, a somewhat sarcastic review of 'Dunluce Castle', a feeble enough poem by Edward Quillinan, resulted in the author challenging his reviewer to a duel: but the two men reached an understanding, became friends and, later, neighbours in the Lake District, to which Hamilton moved soon after his second marriage.[4] Like most of the Blackwood group, Hamilton featured in 'Christopher North''s *Noctes Ambrosianae* where he was Ensign O'Doherty, although this was a pseudonym he was made to share with Dr Maginn.

In 1820, Hamilton married. When Sir Walter Scott's son-in-law, John Gibson Lockhart — who had helped found *Blackwood's Magazine*, with Hogg and Wilson writing the *Chaldee Manuscript* — moved with his

family to London to edit the Tory *Quarterly Review*, he let Chiefswood, his
cottage adjacent to Abbotsford, to Hamilton and his wife, who seem to
have spent the summer months (May to November) in the Borders,
returning to Edinburgh during the winter. Soon after he first moved in,
Hamilton wrote to Lockhart on 24 June 1825,[5] thanking him for
sending the cellar key. 'I cannot possibly think of dislodging your wine',
Hamilton protested:

> Indeed, my own stock is so small as to make it matter of
> indifference where it is kept ... I can easily enter into your
> feelings about Chiefswood. We are both delighted with it, and
> the kindness shewn us by all the neighbours is far greater than
> we as interlopers could possibly have looked for. I hope when
> you and Mrs Lockhart return to it, you will not find it much
> injured by our occupancy ... Offer Annette's [Hamilton's
> wife] kind regards to Mrs Lockhart and hoping you will hate us
> as little as possible for enjoying all the pleasures of Chiefswood
> in your absence
>
> > I remain and am
> > my dear Lockhart,
> > Most sincerely yours
> > Thomas Hamilton

He was not always to remain so.

Hamilton's nearest neighbour was, of course, the Laird of Abbotsford, and in his *Journal*,[6] on 2 July 1826, Scott records: 'Mr. and Mrs.
Hamilton from Chiefswood, present inhabitants of Lockhart's cottage,
dined and spent the night with us which made the society pleasant. He is
a fine soldierly looking man though affected with paralysis. His wife a
fine good humourd little woman. He is supposed to be a writer in
Blackwood's magazine. Since we were to lose the Lockharts we could
scarce have had more agreeable folks'.

The friendship deepened and over the next three years there are
entries chronicling dinners and breakfasts both at Abbotsford and
Chiefswood, a fishing expedition and another, with Mrs Hemans, to
Yarrow. Scott read the 'new and interesting volumes' of *Cyril Thornton*
on 13 May 1827, on one of his depressed days when his 'gay thoughts
strangely mingled with those of dismal melancholy'.

Scott's daughter, Anne, writing[7] to her sister, Sophia, in July 1826,
told her: 'The Hamiltons and we meet almost every day. We generally
meet either at Chiefswood or here in the evening and take long walks.
They are famous walkers and they are people whom I like extremely.
As she has no carriage I generally call for her to make visits. Both are
pleasant, but I must own that I get on much better with Mr Hamilton'.

Blackwood visited Chiefswood on more than one occasion, and Scott
noted in his *Journal* entry for 31 July 1826: 'Blackwood the bookseller
came over from Chiefswood to breakfast'. Sir William Hamilton also

visited his brother that summer and Thomas took Sir William round to Abbotsford to meet Scott on 1 September.

It is not precisely clear when Hamilton began to draft *Cyril Thornton*. Much of the material developed in the first two of its three volumes is autobiographical, and there are hints in letters[8] in the Blackwood archive in the National Library of Scotland suggesting that he may have begun researching his *Annals of the Peninsular Campaign* at about the same time, leaving it to be finished later, much of it being written at Chiefswood after the publication of the novel. He regularly reported progress on *Cyril Thornton* to Blackwood, though most of Hamilton's letters are only partially dated, the year usually omitted, and the publisher's replies have not survived.

On 20 January 1826,[9] Hamilton wrote to Blackwood from 5 Darnaway Street: 'I send you a few sheets of Cyril Thornton to look at and should be obliged to you for any remarks that occur to you. I am not at home in my Scotch having never tried that before', adding that if he could finish an article he was writing for an encyclopedia, 'I think I should get on swimmingly'.

Later in the year,[10] writing from Chiefswood, he provides a progress report. 'I am getting on with my book again after a considerable interval of idleness and am now approaching fast the end of the second volume. What is to me of more consequence than my actual progress in writing is that I think I have now the programme of the whole book fairly before me and can see my way to the end. The ending is melancholy, and I am not quite sure that the cause is fully adequate to the effect, but I think it is out of the common run and that, in these days of imitation, is in itself something'.

During the autumn he reports again[11]: 'Since you last saw Cyril's Memoirs I have finished the second volume and have done about a third of the third volume. This frosty weather agrees with me and I am getting on quicker and better than I have done all summer. When I come to town in December I hope to bring the book with me nearly completed, it will certainly be finished early in January. I leave it entirely to your judgment to decide on the most advantageous time to begin advertizing it in Maga ... Let me hear any literary news you have. We shall be in town early in December, when I shall wait on you in the Sanctum with an enormous bundle of MS'.

Probably at this point (or a little earlier, during the late summer — all the letters are undated) Blackwood apparently became worried about the proposed melancholy ending. Hamilton at first showed some resistance to the criticism of his design:[12] 'I send you some more MS, which will let you more into the plot than you now are. I quite agree with you that a happy termination to a work of this kind is most popular, but without changing the whole scope and conception of the work, and I think weakening its effect, it could not be done. Yet I think the general tone will not be considered melancholy. I wish to avoid that as much as possible. Let the first advertisement state only in 3 vols without specifying the size till I see into what length my remaining materials are likely to fall. Let me know your opinion of what I send and point out any flaws you may detect in the narrative. We shall be in town in three weeks ... Pray keep my authorship a profound secret. Wilson[13] may know. Nobody else ...'

Blackwood probably applied further pressure, and, this time, Hamilton capitulated.[14]

Since I wrote you last I have been considering the matter and trying to conform the story of the book to your suggestions about a happy ending. I find the thing can be done if under all the circumstances which I will state to you it is judged best. Now the case is this. The ending I have had in view from the commencement of the book is certainly what is called melancholy. He [Cyril] is killed in storming St Sebastians, and would afford, I think, a striking conclusion, in the description of his grave in a grove of cork trees in the neighbourhood of the city. With this catastrophe to the story I have no doubt the book as a mere object of criticism would be better and have a stronger impression on the reader. But if from your experience you think what is called a happy ending would have any material effect in promoting the sale, or rather if you think the melancholy one would impede the sale to any great extent, I will not hesitate to give up my own judgment and model it after the bad taste of lady novelists and womanish readers. I should like to know your jugdment on this matter as soon as possible, as the story requires to be moulded somewhat differently as I advance by the conclusion intended. In event of your being for a happy ending he must marry Laura Willoughby and the finale will all together I think be rather humdrum. The point therefore for your decision I think is briefly the following. Whether in your jugdment as a bookseller a worse book with a happy concl-usion, will be apt to sell better, than a better book with a melancholy termination ... I am sure you ought to make money of Cyril Thornton for it has cost you a world of trouble.

Blackwood, whose authors were by no means always as malleable, opted for the worse book with the happy ending.

Hamilton must have worked fast, for on 9 January 1827 Blackwood was able to write to his son that he was 'printing a splendid and first-rate novel, "Cyril Thornton". It is by Captain Hamilton, but this you must not mention to anyone. It is, I think, superior to either "Marriage" or "The Inheritance"'. On 1 July, Blackwood promised his son:[15] '"Cyril Thornton" you will be quite delighted with in all its parts. Everybody likes it, but it has not yet sold so extensively as it deserves; it is, however,

sure to go off. In this number of "Maga" there is a long review of it by
Professor Wilson'; and on 15 August, 'I hope you will have received the
box of books containing "Cyril Thornton", "Napoleon"[16] etc., before
this reaches you. It is most popular, and I have sold 1300 copies of it. If
times had been better, it would have sold double or treble this quantity'.

Two days before Blackwood thus enthused about the book to his son,
Hamilton, on 13 August, had himself written to his publisher on the
subject of sales.[17]

> I am glad to find by your last letter that Cyril had taken
> something of a start in London. I hope it will continue. I have
> had some conversation on the subject with Lockhart, who says,
> that one cause of the heaviness of the sale is its not having been
> *paragraphed*, and that one paragraph is worth a dozen advertise-
> ments. This is as much as to say that the mass of the public are
> idiots who can be gulled by a puff. L. also says that Colburn
> has completely revolutionised the book trade with regard to all
> light literature, and that Murray's books have not sold of late
> because he will not puff and paragraph like Colburn. I merely
> mention this to let you know his opinion. My own interest
> about the matter has fallen nearly to zero. By the by Lockhart
> tells me he read a review of Cyril in the *Atlas Newspaper*
> accompanied by *a personal description* of the Author! Can you
> contrive either to buy or borrow this paper for me, having some
> curiosity to know the cut of my own gib when transferred to
> print.[18]

While it is difficult to put a year to many of Hamilton's letters where
there is no mention of external circumstances, it appears that his wife's
health was already giving him cause for concern; for in the same letter he
explains that he has 'literally done nothing a couple of months past from
having been kept in a continual state of anxiety abt Mrs Hamilton who
has been all summer very unwell indeed. Whenever this impediment is
removed, which I trust ... it will be soon, I shall be able to get on at a
swimming rate'. It was, indeed, removed soon, but only temporarily, for
his wife died some months later. By 31 December, a year or so later, he is
telling Blackwood, [19] 'Have you heard I am going to be married? Get
Lockhart to write an *epithalamium*'.

Much of Wilson's unsigned review in the July 1827 issue of *Blackwood's Magazine* consists of a precis of the story, such as the clients of
Reader's Digest are accustomed to in our own day. There are, however,
some pseudo-critical observations, embedded in Wilson's vague and
pompous verbiage.[20]

> This is the Story of a Life, and we do not know that we ever
> read any piece of fictitious biography with a stronger feeling of
> all its chief transactions being founded in truth. Its power lies in
> its reality. The reader, every leaf he turns, becomes better and

> better and better acquainted — not with an abstraction — a
> shadow — but with a living flesh-and-blood man and gentle-
> man.

Towards the end of twenty double-column pages of such tedious ful-
someness, Wilson avoids pronouncing any verdict.

> When we like a book, we laud it, without any of those base
> 'ifs' and 'buts' that take away all grace of commendation, and
> leave the mind balancing between praise and censure. When
> we dislike a book, our worst enemies will allow, that we
> condemn it to the heart's content of all reasonable people. We
> daresay that these three volumes are full of faults, and that, if all
> carefully picked out by some sharp-sighted, nimble-fingered
> critic, partial to such employment, they would fill a bushel ...
> He goes backwards and forwards ... from England to the
> Peninsula, we think, or elsewhere on leave of absence, when we
> are hardly prepared for such proceedings; and provided the
> reasons of his change of place are sufficient to his own judgment
> and feelings, he cares little about those of the critical world ...
> On some parts of his life he dwells too long — and on others too
> shortly — unmindful of proportion ...

Wilson then ends with a dissertation on phrenology and another on
architecture, concluding with the observation that 'people's lives, it
would appear to us, are, in a great measure, self-constructed — or by the
Fates'. The readers of the 'Maga' in July 1827 must have been hard put
to it to discover whether Wilson was commending the book or condemn-
ing it.

Even the author himself was in doubt. Wilson, he complained to
Blackwood, though giving him abundant praise,[21] had behaved not as
a friend should. 'The criticism of the book may be true or false, it matters
little which, but I shall not attempt to conceal from you that I feel the
tone of the greater part of the article to be unpleasant and offensive. It is
written in a tone of familiarity and with an air of patronage which I
cannot but consider to be somewhat out of place'. He particularly
objected to 'insinuations of censure witheld', and reminded Blackwood
that he had written indicating that Wilson voluntarily undertook to do
it. 'Why he volunteered it I now really cannot understand'.

By his next letter,[22] however, Hamilton has recovered his equipoise
and told Blackwood he regretted having raised the matter at all. But
there had also been the initial annoyance of seeing a character called
'Colonel Thornton' appearing in the *Noctes Ambrosianae*, though on
second thoughts Hamilton decided that the bogus Colonel might promote the sale of the book. On the credit side, however, there was praise
from his English friends the Earl of Bradford and his sister, Lady Lucy
Whitmore.[23] Above all, he thanked Blackwood for letting him know
that 'Miss Ferrier[24] likes Cyril. I place much on her opinion'.

No such ambiguities were presented to the author or to the readers of the Whig-orientated *Edinburgh Review*[25] for October 1830, where its reviewer, dealing with a batch of novels, wrote of *Cyril Thornton*:

> It has been published three years, a considerable period in the existence of a novel; and we should not have noticed it now, if we had not thought that it deserved to be remembered much longer. It is one of the best of its class. The style is flowing and nervous, and tolerably correct; the descriptions are graphic, sometimes powerful; the characters for the most part ably drawn. It never falls below mediocrity, and frequently rises considerably above it; and though there is no particular skill shown in the arrangement and developement of the story, it is throughout very interesting.

Then follows a much briefer and more critical account of the story, concluding: 'The author is very successful as a delineator of character. His old Scotch merchant, David Spreull, is worthy of a place in any novel of the last twenty years. The other characters are inferior to this, but cleverly handled nevertheless. His Lady Melicent is perhaps not very consistently drawn; rather too amiable and disinterested at one period to be so heartless at another; but on this point we give him up to be dealt with by his female readers; and if they acquit him, we shall gladly ratify their verdict'.

Enough people, both here and in America, found the book 'interesting' enough for it to remain more or less in print until the 1880s.

In his *Journal* for June 1829, Scott entered: 'I walked over to Huntly Burn, and round by Chiefswood and Janeswood, where I saw Captain Hamilton. He is busy finishing his Peninsular campaigns. He will not be cut out by Napier,[26] whose work has a strong party cast; and being, besides, purely abstract and professional, to the public seems very dull'. *Annals of the Peninsular Campaign* appeared towards the end of 1830. It was written in what might be called plain soldier's English and was well received, though it has long since been superseded by more scholarly accounts.

Hamilton set out for America the following Autumn, this time as a civilian to collect material for his third, and final book, *Men and Manners in America*. The man who once wanted his authorship of *Cyril Thornton* kept secret — probably until he could be sure that it would be well-received by the public — wrote to Blackwood from Baltimore on 1 February 1831:[27] 'You are one of those friends who will I think be glad to hear from me, and to know that I am getting on well and swimmingly among the Yankees. My reception everywhere has been most cordial, and almost less I think on account of my letters than of my authorship ... Everywhere I have met with the greatest kindness and most flattering attention. I almost regret this, for it hampers me a good deal in my project of giving an account of my observations. ... I know also it will be unpalatable and I really cannot bring myself to say what might be unpleasant to the feelings of people who have been so unwearied in their good offices to a stranger. With regard to their form of government and political institutions, the impression they have made on me is most unfavourable. I was always, as you may remember, a bit of a *Whig*; I shall come home a Tory.[28] God defend England from any experimental imitations of American democracy'.

From Washington, Hamilton travelled to Wheeling where he sailed down the Ohio river. After 'a day or two at Cincinnati and Louisville', he sailed on 'the Mississippi down to New Orleans, a *river* navigation of near 2000 miles! I return by the coast south by Charleston and Richmond, then again to New York, then to Niagara, then Canada and Quebec, then New York again and embark for England about September. Such are my plans, but they are so extensive that I am almost afraid to look forward to them'. It was, indeed, for the time a remarkable journey, lasting more than a year.

In the course of his travels he met Joseph Buonaparte, 'a sad dolt and a vulgar beast. I was surprised at this. He hates the English, so I was not introduced'. Joseph had been placed, first, on the throne of Naples by his brother the Emperor, then on the throne of Spain, from which he had been ejected by the British army.

Hamilton's book on America did, indeed, give great offence, and not only to those who had befriended him during his visit. He was, of course, an ex-officer of an army which had been fighting against the United States in 1812, and he was travelling through a country still in the process of shaping itself, a fact for which he made little allowance when complaining of governmental corruption, the differing constitutions of the member States, their penal and scholastic systems, the dress and appearance of American womenfolk in the more remote areas and what he regarded as their linguistic barbarities.

By the time Hamilton's American book had been published he seems to have become disillusioned with Lockhart's later habit of savaging his friends. Writing from Rydal to Blackwood, he remarks: 'You saw, of course, the wretched attack and stupid compliment in the last number of the Quarterly. This is all you can expect from Lockhart. I knew this well from the first therefore I am not deceived'.

After *Men and Manners*, Hamilton confined his authorship to occasional articles for 'Maga', though no longer on military matters since he had presented all his military books to the United Services Club. He kept up his mountain walking. William Blackwood being abroad convalescing from an illness, Hamilton wrote[29] to Robert Blackwood asking him to try and send down a pedometer from 'Adie the optician, or any other good shop ... The price of the pedometer will be £5 or at most £6'. Robert is also informed that 'The Bard', as Hamilton called Wordsworth, had come back from his tour 'in high spirits'.

Increasingly, Hamilton relished the pleasures of a Lakeland gentleman. In the Autumn of 1838 he told Blackwood:[30]

> I was very glad to receive a letter from you from you dated Edinr, not having heard of your return from foreign parts. I trust you have done so completely reestablished in health. Mr Wordsworth told me he saw you somewhere in Italy and gave rather a bad account of your condition at that time. Tell your brother Robert I have been casting about for something for Maga, and only did not answer his last letter because I had hopes of being able to send him an article, but summer came on, bringing with it, its usual fit of inactivity of mind and increased activity of body, and I have done nothing. Tell the Professor we have had great racing on Windermere. Branker's[31] boat had been for some years the bully of the Lake. Nothing cd touch her, and I determined to have a shy at her. With this view I with great trouble carried thro' a subscription for a Cup, and then set to work to build a boat to run for it. My naval architect was Swinburne[32] in whose knowledge of such matters I have great faith. Well the 1st heat came on in July. My boat hardly off the stocks and out of all trim was beat for it without much difficulty. The second heat was sailed for two days ago and the Victoria — so is my boat called — came in first beating Mr Branker's by upwards of four minutes, so the Dolphinites are sadly down in the mouth. The third heat is to take place on this day week. These races excite a great deal of interest in the neighbourhood.

In the winter of 1842, Hamilton and his wife set out for Italy. On 7th December, Hamilton suffered a fatal stroke at Pisa. He lies buried in Florence.

An anonymous obituary notice appeared in *Blackwood's Magazine* vol. LIII, no.328, in February 1843. The writer observed that Hamilton had been 'associated with the Magazine from its commencement', and remarks that

> "Cyril Thornton", which appeared in 1827, instantly arrested public attention and curiosity, even in an age eminently fertile in great works of fiction. With little of plot — for it pursued the desultory ramblings of military life through various climes — it possessed a wonderful truth and reality, great skill in the observation and portraiture of original character, and a peculiar charm of style, blending freshness and vivacity of movement with classic delicacy and grace. The work soon became naturally and justly popular, having reached a second edition shortly after publication: a third edition has recently appeared.

The Youth and Manhood of Cyril Thornton falls roughly into three parts. In the first, the young Cyril comes to study at the College in Glasgow, as the author himself had done. At an early age Cyril had accidentally shot and killed his brother, an accident which alienates him from his father. There is to some degree a guilt parallel with Lockhart's novel *Adam Blair* (1824), though the guilt motif is not fully followed through by Hamilton.

In Glasgow Cyril meets his merchant uncle, David Spreull, who lives in Spreulls Land, in Argyle Street, and who is looked after by Girzy, an outspoken Scots-tongued retainer of a type that persisted well into the twentieth century. Cyril attends a civic reception, and there is an amusing sketch of the Provost and his lady. The kindly, couthy philistinism of all the 'Scotch' characters might seem to some overdrawn, almost to the point of caricature; yet I clearly recall, as a boy in the late 1920s and early 1930s, meeting with my father their linguistically watered-down living counterparts. Even the Scottish Archie Shortridge, though more nearly a caricature when he is made to cut a figure of fun in a Bath ballroom with the five gauche Miss Spreulls later in the book, does represent the way in which many English people still view the rough-spoken Scot in relation to their own fancied smoother urbanity.

In the first section of the book a realistically vigorous depiction of merchant life in the Glasgow of the tobacco lords is re-created. There may be more of sociology in it than high art, but it has the ring of actuality, is amusing, and, above all, eminently readable.

The second section of the book is mainly concerned with Cyril's army experiences serving as an officer in some of the campaigns of the Peninsular War. It may be argued that now and again the novelist so far forgets himself in points of detail as to become the enthusiastic historian. Nevertheless, no other novelist of a period that included Scott, Galt, Hogg, Jane Austen and Susan Ferrier, quite achieved in fiction the sense of war's utter confusion, misunderstanding, cruelty, chaos, and strategic chance that Hamilton unfolds before us in *Cyril Thornton*.

It is in the handling of the third section of the book, which deals principally with love and upper-class English manners, that the book is weakest. This is partly due to our impatience with Hamilton's handling of the prolix upper-class circumlocutions which the manners of the time, or at least its literary conventions, demanded. Hamilton's upper-class characters never use one word if they can find half-a-dozen. When we first meet Laura Willoughby, all seems set for her to become Cyril's bride. Instead, he falls in love with the socially superior charms of Lord Amersham's daughter, Lady Melicent, while at Amersham's country seat, Staunton Court. It could be argued that Lady Melicent's initial warmth of character and, by the standards of the time, encouragement of Cyril, hardly accord with her revulsion at the sight of the returned and wounded hero, the cold suddenness of her decision to marry the richer and more socially acceptable scion of her own class.

At this point, of course, the disappointed hero was intended by the author to return to the army and be heroically killed in action. Under pressure from Blackwood, Cyril instead turns to the by now rather distant figure of Laura Willoughby and marries her, making the novel conform to a regular early nineteenth-century romantic pattern, that of a conventionally resolved triangle.

The Youth and Manhood of Cyril Thornton is thus flawed both in its construction and in the consistency of some of its character-building. Yet for all its faults it remains what Scott called it, 'interesting'; interesting indeed and, more importantly, eminently readable. While those parts of it which deal with the manoeverings of manners perhaps seem somewhat crude and clumsy compared to the handling of similar situations by Jane Austen or even Susan Ferrier (at any rate in *Marriage*, by far her finest novel) Hamilton recreates the atmosphere of the fateful battle that overshadowed the age in which all of them were writing, and brings alive more vividly than any social historian the long-since vanished days of the tobacco lords whose blunt-spoken energies laid the foundations of Glasgow's future industrial success. For these reasons his only novel is still worth our attention more than a hundred and sixty years after it first appeared.

NOTES

1   *Sir William Hamilton* by W.H.S. Morick (London, 1881)
2   Matriculation Album of the University of Glasgow, 1728–58
3   Dictionary of National Biography
4   Edward Quillinan (1791–1851). An Irishman born in Oporto who became a prosperous wine merchant. He married Wordsworth's daughter, Dorothy. He was, according to Matthew Arnold, 'sweet, generous and humane', but an indifferent poet.
5   National Library of Scotland (hereafter N.L.S.) MS 934 / 202
6   *The Journal of Sir Walter Scott* ed. W.E.K. Anderson (Oxford, 1972)
7   See Scott, *Journal* ed. Anderson, p.167 footnote 1.
8   N.L.S. MS 4014
9   N.L.S. MS 4017 / 117
10   N.L.S. MS 4017 / 123
11   N.L.S. MS 4017 / 125
12   N.L.S. MS 4017 / 130
13   John Wilson (1785–1854) wrote under the pen-name of 'Christopher North', and was responsible for the collection of convivial pieces, *Noctes Ambrosianae* (1822–35), 'Nights at Ambrose's', a tavern which stood on the site of the present Cafe Royal in Edinburgh. Though quite without any suitable training or qualifications, he was appointed to the Chair of Moral Philosophy at Edinburgh University, partly at the instigation of Scott.
14   N.L.S. MS 4017 / 127
15   N.L.S. MS D 765035
16   Scott's *Life of Napoleon* (1827)
17   N.L.S. MS 4718 / 162
18   Copies of *The Atlas* newspaper, unindexed, from 1826 to 1869 are held by the British Library.

19 N.L.S. MS 4718 / 162
20 *Blackwood's Magazine*, vol. XXII, no. 129
21 N.L.S. MS 4019
22 N.L.S. MS 4017 / 129
23 Lady Mary Whitmore, sister of the Earl of Bradford, married a Member of Parliament, W.W. Whitmore. The Whitmores lived at Dudmaston Bridge, North Shropshire, where Hamilton was a frequent guest.
24 Susan Ferrier (1782–1854), regarded by some during her lifetime as the Scottish Jane Austen, wrote three novels: *Marriage* (1818), *The Inheritance* (1824) and *Destiny, or The Chief's Daughter* (1831). She became addicted to religion and the two later novels suffer from an increasing tendency on the part of the author to moralize.
25 *Edinburgh Review*, vol. LII, no. 3
26 Sir William Francis Patrick Napier (1785–1860) fought with Sir John Moore at Corunna. He was severely wounded several times during the subsequent campaign. His *History of the Peninsular War* (1828–40) was highly thought of.
27 N.L.S. MS 4029
28 Hamilton claimed to be 'a bit of a Whig', but his journalistic manner and general outlook seem to have been decidedly patrician.
29 N.L.S. MS 4044 / 296
30 N.L.S. MS 4046 / 188
31 According to Mr G.W. Pattinson, the Chairman of the Council of Management of Windermere Nautical Trust, Branker was possibly James Brancker, a wealthy Liverpool sugar merchant who bought Croft Lodge, Clappergate, Ambleside and who in 1828/30 pulled down the house at the head of Lake Windermere to build another. It was described by his friend Hartley Coleridge as being 'in a style which neither Vitruvius, Palladio, Inigo Jones, Piranesi, nor Sir Jeffrey Wyatville ever dreamed of even in a nightmare or under the influence of opium'. He sold the property in 1843.
32 Swinburne. Probably Swinbourne, an artist who spent some time in Italy but c.1839/43 rented Colgarth Hall, on the north side of Lake Windermere, from Bishop Watson of Llandaff. Swinbourne was friendly with both Professor Wilson and Dickens. Mr Pattinson's records show that 'E. Swinbourne of Colgarth in yacht "Norway" raced against Earl Tyrconnell and J. Brancker in 1839'.

ACKNOWLEDGEMENTS

I should like to acknowledge the help of various people in what turned out to be the fairly laborious business of preparing the notes for this edition of *The Youth and Manhood of Cyril Thornton*. Hamilton frequently quoted from memory, not always accurately, adding to the problem of identifying his quotations, a few of which, despite the help of numerous experts, remain untraced.

As so often before I am deeply indebted to the Mitchell Library, in particular Mr Joe Fisher of the Glasgow Room, for help in various aspects of my research. I am also most grateful to Mr S. M. Simpson of the Department of Manuscripts at the National Library of Scotland, who made available to me Hamilton's side of his lengthy correspondence with William Blackwood.

The British Library assisted me over various points, as did the library of the University of Glasgow. Cumbria County Library and the founder of the Windermere Steamboat Museum, Mr George Pattinson, discovered records of Hamilton's boat-racing activities in the Lake District.

For his help with the classical allusions I am much indebted to Professor Ian Kidd of St Andrews University. Help with some of the more abstruse English quotations was freely given by, amongst others, Robin Moffat of the University of Wales College of Cardiff. Mrs Marianne Huhtala kindly kept me right on the French tags liberally scattered through the text. My wife spent many hours tracing the careers of the French military men who feature in the story. To Dr W. R. Aitken I am indebted for much valuable bibliographical information; and to Dr David Hewitt of the University of Aberdeen, and the General Editor of the series, Dr Douglas Mack of the University of Stirling, I am grateful for the time they spent considering whether the text of the first or second editions should be used. The reasons for our decision to use the text of the first edition are given in the Note on the Text.

Finally, I should like to thank my Secretary at The Scottish Civic Trust, Mrs Wilma Bryce, who was much involved in the typing and re-typing of the editorial material.

Note on the Text

The first edition of Thomas Hamilton's *The Youth and Manhood of Cyril Thornton* was published in 1827 by William Blackwood in Edinburgh and by T. Cadell in London; and on its appearance the novel sold reasonably well without being a runaway success. The early months of 1828 found Hamilton anxious for the publication of a second edition; but Blackwood—aware that there were still about five hundred unsold copies of the first edition—was more cautious. As the Blackwood Papers in the National Library of Scotland show, an exchange of letters followed in which Hamilton's air of gentlemanly detachment masks some rigorous probing for commercial advantage. In the event Blackwood, having paid five hundred guineas for the rights to the two thousand copies of the first edition, agreed to purchase the copyright of the novel for a further three hundred guineas. A second edition appeared in 1829; and thereafter successive Blackwood reprints of the second edition kept *Cyril Thornton* before the public for much of the nineteenth century.

The text of the second edition contains numerous changes. As frequently happens with reprints, small errors are corrected—and other small errors are introduced. In addition, the second edition is more formal than the first in matters of presentation: for example, money is written in words rather than figures, and foreign-language phrases appear in italic type rather than roman. There are other, more substantial changes; sentences are re-cast, for example, and short passages are removed. Thus in the eighth chapter of volume one, the first edition describes a meal with Galt-like relish; and the second edition makes cuts that tone down what may have seemed the vulgarity of this passage.

It is not clear who was responsible for such changes. Some are so substantial that it is difficult to believe that they are not authorial. On the other hand, we know that in the 1820s Blackwood employed D.M. Moir to make extensive changes to *The Last of the Lairds*, and he employed Robert Hogg to undertake a similar task on James Hogg's *The Shepherd's Calendar*.[1] It may be that Blackwood, feeling that he had paid a generous price for the purchase of the copyright of *Cyril Thornton*, employed someone like Moir or Robert Hogg to spruce up his new property before its second edition appeared; or it may be that Hamilton, wishing to respond to a generous settlement by his publisher, decided to give the work the benefit of an authorial revision. Indeed, both these things may have happened.

In the absence of the author's manuscript, the first edition of 1827 is the earliest surviving version of the text. It is difficult to perceive any sustained artistic purpose in the revisions made for the second edition; and it is not possible to discriminate between changes made by the author, those made by the publisher, and those made by the printer. The present edition, therefore, reprints the first edition, the version which reflects Hamilton's original creation.

The first edition is not reprinted exactly as it stands. Self-evident printer's errors (for example 'wlll' for 'will', and 'gounpunished' for 'go unpunished') are corrected silently. In addition to such cases the following alterations have been made in an attempt to correct what appear to be errors by the printer. The reading of the present edition is followed by the reading of the first edition.

p.	8, l.43	sea. / sea."
p.	20, l.25	Plenissime / Plenissume
p.	20, l.26	est. / 'st.
p.	20, l.28	semel / simitu'
p.	72, l.24	Auchintorlie / Auchintulie
p.	94, l.12	persons / person
p.	104, l.33	à la sauce / au sauce
p.	155, l.45	fathers' / father's
p.	175, l. 3	rely on / rely, on
p.	236, l.44	Pæans / Pœans
p.	263, l. 8	monstrari et dicier, / monstrari, et dicier
p.	285, l.27	*savoir vivre* / *sçavoir vivre*
p.	377, l.42	Miss Austen / Miss Austin
p.	385, l.27	calmly." / calmly.
p.	407, l.35	effect an entrance / affect an entrance

However, some errors appear to be Hamilton's (or perhaps Thornton's) rather than the printer's: and these are allowed to stand. For example, the Madrid garrison is said to be governed by 'General Bellegarde' in the first edition, and this is corrected to 'General Belliard' in the second. Presumably the mistake arose because Hamilton had never seen the name written, but had only heard it. Be that as it may, the mistake is appropriate to the fiction: Thornton is a man who gives up education for the army, and we would not expect him to consult works of reference before committing himself to paper.

DH; DM

1 Ian A. Gordon, *John Galt: the Life of a Writer* (Edinburgh, 1972), 78-83; and Douglas S. Mack, 'Hogg, Blackwood, and *The Shepherd's Calendar*', in *Papers Given at the Second James Hogg Society Conference (Edinburgh 1985)*, ed. Gillian Hughes (Aberdeen, 1988), 24-31.

Have I not heard great ordnance in the field,
And heaven's artillery thunder in the skies?
Have I not, in a pitched battle, heard
Loud 'larums, neighing steeds, and trumpets clang?
                                        Shakespeare

CHAPTER I

—— The hopes
That were but in conception, now have birth,
And what was but idea till this day,
Hath put on essence.
Challenge for Beauty.

THE stock of which I have the honour to be a scion, is one of ancient descent and spotless blazon. Though untitled, its dignity had always been baronial; and the frequency with which the names of my ancestors occur in the county records, as filling offices of provincial trust and dignity, shows their influence to have been considerable. While it is due to truth and my progenitors to state thus much, I am quite ready to confess that our family-tree has produced no very distinguished fruit. Its branches have never been pendent with the weight of poets, heroes, statesmen, or philosophers. " If they have writ our annals right, " births, marriages, and deaths, the sale or purchase of land, the building of a house, or a donation to the parish church or county hospital, were generally the only events sufficiently salient, to afford footing even for the partial eloquence of a family historian. But if I have little reason to boast, I certainly have none to blush, for my ancestors. They were English gentlemen, fulfilling with propriety the duties of their situation, generally respectable in their relations to society, and leaving, when dead, nothing either " to point a moral, or adorn a tale. "

My grandfather was a courtier and a man of expense. He married an earl's daughter, whose habits and tastes were even more expensive than his own, and engaged in several ruinous contests for the representation of the county. The natural consequences followed. Part of the family estate was sold, heavy mortgages incurred on the remainder, and when, in the course of nature, the succession devolved on my father, he found himself in possession of little more than the wreck of a magnificent estate. Of my grandmother, who survived her husband many years, I have a distinct and vivid recollection. I remember a stately old lady, in an oreille-d'ours-coloured silk gown, with a pyramidal head-dress, an enamelled snuff-box in her hand, and a ponderous gold equipage at her girdle. I remember, too, the insidious delight taken both by my brother and myself in getting behind her chair, and tugging at the lace lappets, which depended from the apex of her coiffure. She died, and I was allowed to join in paying the last duties to her remains. The pomp and splendour with which the earthly tabernacle of my grandmother was restored to its kindred elements, made a prodigious impression on my young imagination. The hearse, in all its plumed and melancholy grandeur; the crimson velvet coffin, with its gilt escutcheons; the sable mutes, and the long and sombre procession, contributed to people my mind with ideas to which till then it had been a stranger. There is something wild and shadowy in death to the imagination of a child. It is surrounded by a certain dim grandeur and awful solemnity, which perhaps his very ignorance of its nature, tends rather to increase than diminish. He reads in the countenances around him, that something of dread and terror has befallen them. He learns that a being, from infancy familiar to his eyes, and at whose approach, perhaps, they ever brightened, shall meet them no more—that he is gone to a far-distant land, from which he never will return. He knows this, and he knows, likewise, that this is *not all*. There is something still beyond, with which his understanding vainly strives to grapple. Death is an abstraction too pure for the comprehension of a child; and when, in the gradual dawning of his intellect, it becomes intelligible, he finds that the dispersion of the mist which obscured the summit of the mountain has added nothing to its splendour and sublimity. For myself, while the funeral pageant of my grandmother impressed me with feelings of respect for her when dead, of which when living I had been far from betraying any symptoms, I likewise drew from it my first lesson of the transient nature of human glory, by observing how speedily she was forgotten.

My father was a man of retired habits and reserved manners. I have already stated, that, on the death of my grandfather, it had been found necessary to sell a large portion of the family estates. This was a severe blow to my father's pride, and one, I think, from which he never afterwards recovered. At no period of his life had his taste led him into expensive pursuits, nor had he launched into any expenditure unsuited to the liberal establishment, which the world considered it fitting for a person of his station and expectations to maintain. The portion of his fortune which still remained to him, was amply sufficient for the supply of all the comforts, and even elegancies of life; yet the dismemberment of his hereditary property was not the less severely felt by a person of his temperament, because it involved no curtailment of his own personal enjoyments. The wound rankled in his mind, and a change in his character was thenceforward visible to all. Before this event, my father had been accustomed to move among the magnates of the land, with that due feeling of consequence and equality which belonged to his birth and fortune. He had entered life with the feelings of a high-born English gentleman, knowing his proper station in society, and neither betraying petty jealousy of his equals, nor kibing the heels of his superiors. It was now different. From the loss of property the loss of influence was inseparable. He was no longer selected as the foreman of grand juries, or the chairman of quarter sessions. His hall, at Michaelmas and Ladyday, was no longer crowded with the throng of tenants, who came to pay their rents, or solicit forbearance. "Like angel visits, few and far between," they now came singly in; and though the steward still received them throned as formerly in his elbow-chair, and with all his former solemn courtesy, the life and bustle of the scene was gone;—

"'Twas Greece, but *living* Greece no more."

Poor Humphreys felt it to be so, and locked his slender receipts in his bureau, with an air of less consequence, than had sat well upon him in better and brighter days. And thou, too, Jacob Pearson, thou paragon of butlers, thou best and worthiest of all the ministers of Bacchus! thy occupation, too, was gone. Where were those vollies of corks, which, like the fire of hostile armies, came quick and frequent on the ear? Where the gurgling and delightful sound of liberated liquor, full of sweet promise to the thirsty souls, who waited with bashful anxiety for thy approach? Alas, it was no longer heard. Thy visage was as rubicund, thy paunch as portly, as in former days; but where was the laughing sparkle of thine eye, thy ponderous alacrity of motion, the jest that circulated with the tankard, the hospitable jocularity that gave, like nutmeg, a racy flavour to its contents? These, alas, were gone too. Since that sad period, thine eye has been dull, thy motions heavy, and the cork of thy wit has been undrawn.

It is not in all cases that the uses of adversity are sweet. In my father's they certainly were not so. He became irascible and morose, and jealous of those small attentions and trifling distinctions in society, to which birth affords, probably, the best claim, but to which wealth is the surest passport. In attempting to conceal even from himself the mortifying fact, that he was now become a much less considerable person than formerly, he assumed an air of austerity in his own family, and of dogmatism in society. He refused the county hunt access to his fox-covers, became litigious about the extent of his manorial rights, cut the vicar for saluting him with a familiar nod, and succeeded in getting himself almost unanimously voted, both the worst neighbour, and the most disagreeable man, in the county. Henceforth my father's life was embittered by a series of difficulties and disappointments, petty indeed in their nature, but not on that account less galling to a mind so morbidly sensitive as his. He imagined himself slighted, and knew himself to be disliked. He was probably both; but the cause was to be found, less in his change of circumstances than of character. At all events, there still remained attached to the family a sort of prescriptive influence and respect, which, like other prejudices, may decay slowly, but cannot be suddenly eradicated.

Of my mother I have not yet spoken: I would now do so. She was the daughter of a dignitary of the church, and brought with her little accession either of blood or of fortune. But she brought what was better, and more valuable than these, an excellent understanding, and an affectionate heart. She had been a beauty in her youth, and, during two seasons which she spent at Bath with her father, her charms had been the object of general homage and admiration. Circumstances of which I have acquired a knowledge, induce me to believe that her marriage with my father had been one rather of prudence than of love. If this was so, it belied the common prediction with regard to such marriages, for the union was not an unhappy one. It was indeed impossible, I think, to know my mother in the intimate relations of domestic life, and not to love her. While her conduct as a wife and mother was truly exemplary, her cheerfulness and benevolence of disposition tended greatly to soothe and soften the inequalities, to which my father's spirits were habitually subject; and she threw around her an elegance and refinement, of which the whole establishment unconsciously partook. The fruit of this union was two sons and two daughters. Of the former I was le cadet. My brother Charles was two years older, Jane one year younger than myself, and I was ten years old when little Lucy (for so I must still call her) was born, at a time when my mother's age rendered any further addition to her family extremely improbable. However, the little visitant was not the less cordially welcomed, on account of the unexpectedness of her arrival. She was the darling and the plaything of us all; and if any of the family were in danger of being spoiled by indulgence, it was little Lucy.—Dearest sister, how do thy infant beauties, and thy joyous frolics, mingle unbidden with the sadder memories of my youth! They run like silver threads through the woof of the dark tissue of my life. I look back on them as to a green and sunny spot, which perhaps shows brighter because seen through a long and darkened vista of intervening years. Read, Lucy, these Memoirs of your brother's life. You will find in them much of error, perhaps more of suffering; but from you, at least, he will meet pardon for the one, and for the other sympathy.

CHAPTER II

They grew in beauty, side by side,
  They fill'd one house with glee ;
Their graves are sever'd, far and wide,
  By mount, and stream, and sea.
The same fond mother bent at night
  O'er each fair sleeping brow ;
She had each folded flower in sight—
  Where are those dreamers now ?

                                        F. HEMANS.

READER, if you have ever travelled from Avington to Mountford, about
a mile beyond the village of Edgehill, near where the road to Spixley
branches off to the right, you may probably have remarked an ancient,
and rather venerable-looking gate, the pillars of which are surmounted
by two rampant lions. The dexter of these royal animals has suffered
considerable mutilation ; the effacing fingers of time, or violence, having
deprived him of whatever personal decoration might have resulted from
the ornamental appendages of paws and tail. His antagonist has been
more fortunate, and still retains one paw, with which he appears in the
act of taking snuff; an indication of taste for the enjoyments of civilized
life undoubtedly somewhat startling and anomalous. Be this as it may,
the gate in question forms the entrance to an avenue about a mile long,
winding gradually up a gentle acclivity, and flanked on either side by a
row of lime-trees of uncommon luxuriance and beauty. In the distance,
you may catch, as you advance, occasional glimpses of a house through
the intervals of the trees, which is marked by its lofty peaked roof, and
clustered chimneys, to belong to the era of Queen Elizabeth. You will
not admire the building, but you will admire, I think, the situation in
which it stands ; the wooded hill that rises behind it, the mazy Severn,
which flows a little to the right, the village church visible in the distance,
and Cromar wood, that fills the left of the landscape, from which the
cuckoo and ring-dove delight to send forth sweet music. This, reader, is
Thornhill Manor, the spot where I was born, and where the intervening
years of my infancy and youth flew rapidly away.

  With the occurrences of those years I shall not swell my narrative.
The joys and sufferings of a child are too minute and evanescent to
afford matter for the grave records of maturer years. Their shadowy
remembrance is food for midnight dreams, but eludes the glare of
waking noonday contemplation.

  It had been the intention of my father to superintend the education of

my brother and myself, a task for which his talents and acquirements
well fitted him; but the unsettled state of his spirits, and the extreme
mental depression to which he was occasionally subject, soon compelled
him to resign the task. The charge of our education, therefore, was
committed to Dr Lumley, the rector of a parish in a neighbouring
county, between whom and my father there had subsisted an early
friendship. They had been companions at college; and though, in after
life, their intimacy had decreased, I believe they still did continue to
entertain a mutual regard. At all events, my father was not unfortunate
in his substitute. Dr Lumley was a good scholar, and an excellent man;
and whatever deficiency of early acquirement I have had since occasion
to lament, is attributable not to the fault of the master, but the negligence of the pupil. The Doctor had a son, whose age nearly coincided
with that of Charles. William Lumley was a young man of a quiet and
studious disposition, ardent in his pursuit of learning, but taking little
pleasure in those active recreations, which, to persons of his age, are
generally so attractive. This was perhaps a favourable circumstance for
Charles. The superior advancement of Lumley excited his emulation,
and called into action those new energies and exertions, which were
necessary to prevent his being distanced in the race by so formidable a
competitor. We were not the only pupils whom Dr Lumley admitted
into his family. No. There was Jack Spencer, the best-natured and
giddiest of God's creatures, now known as one of the best officers of the
navy. There, too, was Dick Sutton, with his round and stupid face, and
look of self-satisfied dulness. He began Latin with a fair wind, got
through his accidence with flying colours, but ran a-ground at " propria
quæ maribus. " There he stuck. Human exertion could get him no
further, and further he never went, I'll answer for it, till this hour. Dick is
now one of the most popular of our parliamentary orators, a ponderous
debater on matters of finance, eloquent on Catholic Emancipation, and
overpowering on the Corn Laws.

For myself, I was not a dunce, but I found little pleasure in study. My
energies were only fully excited by athletic exercises, and the sports of
the field. In leaping, running, and vaulting, I had no competitors. In
horsemanship my supremacy was disputed; and, to settle our rival
claims to superiority, we rode steeple chases on our ponies, and though
these generally ended in the bouleversement of both horses and riders, it
is to these early trials of nerve and prowess that I owe the skill and
confidence as an equestrian, from which I have in after life derived
much pleasure and advantage.

There was too a pack of harriers in the neighbourhood, with which,
on holidays, we were suffered to hunt. How our hearts bounded at the
cry of the huntsman, and the music of the dogs! the trumpets of the
seraphim would to our ears have sounded less sweet: there was a halo
around us, a glory on earth and in the sky. After all, how vulgar and

miserable is the intoxication of the bottle, when compared with that of the hunting-field! How perfect is the concentration of soul —of all energies, both mental and physical—of heart and purpose, in the all-absorbing pursuit! Hunting is your true leveller. In the field, all distinctions of youth and age, of rank and fortune, are forgotten. The old man feels the blood of youth once more dancing in his veins; the boy anticipates the slow progress of nature, and at once swells into a man.

In such scenes and occupations years passed away. Charles was now sixteen, and my father determined to send him to the University. He had always been his favourite son, and, independently of his claims as the future head of the family, destined to bear its honours, and transmit them to posterity, his qualities were fully sufficient to justify such a preference. Charles was indeed a universal favourite. I have known, I think, young men of greater talent, and of equal goodness of heart, but I have never known any upon whom nature had so visibly stamped the signet of kindness and benevolence; in whom vivacity of temper was so perfectly amalgamated with gentleness of disposition. The attachment which had subsisted between Charles and myself, was strong as the love between brothers ever was or can be. With me, he had never attempted to assume the privilege or authority of an elder brother. We had associated as friends and equals, yet his maturer mind had not failed to exercise its natural influence in guiding and directing mine. We had never been divided, but

> " Still had slept together,
> Rose at one instant, learn'd, play'd, ate together,
> And wheresoe'er we went, like Juno's swans,
> Still we went coupled and inseparable. "

In my character and disposition there was but little similitude to his. I was not, like Charles, the idol of my companions; and while every eye brightened at his approach, I felt that mine was regarded with indifference. I had not, like him, the innate and spontaneous power to conciliate attachment; and, in the little circle of my playmates, I knew that my absence occasioned no regret, my presence no joy. But these wide differences of character did not in any degree diminish our attachment, and we had grown together, in sun and shower, like two young trees intertwining their branches, and ignorant of the support they mutually afforded, until one has been suddenly removed.

The current of my life had hitherto glided on smooth and unruffled, and the separation from Charles, which was now about to take place, was the first sorrow of my youthful and happy heart. William Lumley, too, was going to the University, and in a month, he and Charles were to set out together. They were attached to each other, and rejoiced in the knowledge, that in the new and busy scene, in which they were about to mingle, they would not cease to be companions.

Dr Lumley's reports of my application and advancement, I imagine, had not been very favourable. I manifested, on all occasions, the strongest predilection for a military life, and entreated Dr Lumley to make my wishes on this subject known to my father. Never shall I forget the glowing interest with which I read the history of the campaigns of the Great Gustavus, Prince Eugene, and Lord Peterborough. I followed the course of their armies on the map; I drew plans of the battles, and modelled little fortresses, on the principles of Vauban.

In a town about twenty miles distant, I had accidentally heard that a review of the troops of the district was to take place. With what deep, but silent anxiety, did I expect the appointed day! I was too apprehensive of being prevented from gratifying my curiosity, to communicate my intentions to any one. At length the day came, and the dawn of morning found me mounted on my horse, and proceeding, with a beating heart, to the scene of action. It may be conceived what effect the imposing spectacle of pomp and parade, which I there witnessed, was likely to produce on my excited spirit. It added fuel to the flame that already burned within me, and what Lord Peterborough and Gustavus had begun, the spectacle of this review completed.

My father, however, was not disposed to offer any vehement objection to my entering on a military life. His own views with regard to me had been directed to the bar; but finding I was neither suited, by character or inclination, for that profession, it was determined I should become a soldier, and that the two years which were to intervene before my obtaining a commission, should be spent in preparatory studies at the Military Academy at Marlow. When Charles, therefore, quitted Doctor Lumley's, I also returned to Thornhill, where it had been arranged that I should remain a few months, after his departure for the University. On taking our leave of the worthy Doctor, "we shed some natural tears, but wiped them soon." In that moment, we even loved Mrs Lumley, and received her parting benediction with softened hearts, and an oblivion of all the petty annoyances, of which the over-anxiety of that worthy lady with regard to our outward elegance of deportment, had sometimes been the cause.

Warm welcome awaited us at Thornhill. The old Lions seemed to regard us with looks of peculiar benignity as we passed the gate, where our sisters were waiting our arrival. Jane locked her arms in ours as we walked onward to the house, and little Lucy bounded by our side, with a heart full of buoyancy and glee.

> No fountain, from its native cave,
>   E'er tripp'd with foot so free;
> She was as happy as a wave
>   That dances on the sea.

CHAPTER III

> *M.*   Will you follow?
> *Hel.* Even where fate leads me — we are all her slaves,
> And have no dwellings of our own.
> *M.*   Yes — graves.
>
> *Royal King and Loyal Subject.*

THE period of Charles's departure for College now rapidly approached, and nothing else could be talked or thought of in the family. All hands were busy, and everything around gave note of preparation. My mother was engaged in issuing, and the housekeeper in executing, orders for a copious supply of every imaginable comfort; Jane, in marking his linen with her own hair, and making little keep-sakes, that might recall her often to his memory. Even little Lucy would not be idle, and might be seen seated with unwonted gravity, assiduously employed in hemming his pocket-handkerchiefs. By my father he had been summoned to two long audiences in the library, and had been furnished with suitable directions and advice, for his guidance in the new circumstances of the life on which he was about to enter. For myself, I haunted him like his shadow. We rode and walked together, talked of our little griefs and glowing hopes, and bound ourselves by solemn promise to maintain a frequent and regular correspondence.

There was heaviness in every heart, but most of all in mine. It was now October, and Charles was to return home, for the summer vacation, in June. The very days were counted, and the length of his absence computed to an hour; but I would then be gone, and years might elapse before we again embraced in brotherhood and love. Our separation seemed long and limitless, for to a boy the future is an eternity, the past a point.

Thus did all things go on, until the day preceding that fixed for his departure. There is nothing in that day that is not burned deeply and indelibly on my memory. The morning dawned in clouds. Volumes of deep red vapour obscured the rising of the sun, and seemed to presage a day of rain and storm; but at ten o'clock they began to disperse, and before the sun had attained his meridian, the sky was clear, and he shone forth in all his summer brightness and glory.

After discussing several plans of amusement for the day, it was at length agreed by Charles and myself that we should take our guns, and ramble out into the fields, less for the sake of killing game, than to enjoy each other's society once more, on the eve of so long a separation as that which impended over us. It was not without difficulty that I obtained

Charles's consent to this project. My father had always been peculiarly apprehensive of accidents from loaded fire-arms, and was peremptory in his injunctions that we should never join the same shooting party, though he had no objections to our singly accompanying the keeper. But on this occasion we could not bear to be divided, and I prevailed on Charles to consent on that morning to the first deliberate breach of our father's commands. Bitter indeed were the fruits of our disobedience, and deeply has it been atoned for by both.

Our intentions were, of course, kept secret, and we did not summon the keeper to attend us, but sallied forth alone, conversing, as we went, of the thoughts by which our hearts were stirred, and the hopes that shed a radiance on the future.

Thus had an hour or two passed on. We had fired several shots, but this occasioned little interruption to our colloquy. The dogs again pointed. With boyish eagerness I cocked my gun, and advanced towards the spot. It was necessary to pass a hedge. Charles leaped it, and I held his gun while he did so. I then returned it to him through the hedge, and was in the act of passing my own, which he waited to receive. It was cocked. His head was close to the muzzle—a twig caught the trigger— and the contents were lodged—in his brain.

He fell, but uttered no sound. For a moment I stood silent and motionless; then I called on Charles, and entreated him to answer me. All was silent. A dreadful presentiment of evil arose within me; and, unable longer to bear the torture of suspense, by a convulsive spring I leaped the hedge, and stood trembling beside him. He lay with his face on the ground, and there was blood on the grass. I called—I shouted aloud for assistance, and uttered wild shrieks in the helplessness of my agony. A ray of hope that the wound might not be mortal, dawned for a moment on my heart. I knelt down beside him, and raised tenderly and softly his drooping head. Then hope gave place to despair, for, through the bloody clusters in his golden hair, I saw a frightful opening in his forehead, and I knew that death would not be cheated of his victim. There was still a gurgling in his throat, and a slight quivering in his limbs, that showed life was not yet extinct. His eyes were fixed and lustreless. O God! how did the iron enter into my soul, as I gazed on them! I threw myself on the ground beside him, bound his head with my handkerchief, and, supporting him in my arms, his head rested on my bosom. I kissed his livid lips and bloody cheeks, and talked to him wildly and fondly, and adjured him, by the blood of our Redeemer, to grant me some sign of his forgiveness. He died, and gave no sign. The pulsation of his heart became every moment feebler and less frequent, the convulsive action of the muscles gradually ceased, and my arms no longer embraced a living brother, but a cold and rigid corpse.

How long I remained in this situation I know not, for despair, like joy, takes no note of time; but I imagine it must have been for some hours. The concentration of agony and horror contained in that brief space, might be diluted into centuries of ordinary misery.

At length I observed some labourers passing at a distance. I rose, and attempted to call them, but my throat was parched and powerless, and I could produce no sound. I made a signal, and they approached. What they saw spoke too plainly, to require from me an explanation, which I was incapable of giving. They procured a blanket at a neighbouring cottage, and bore the body towards Thornhill. I almost mechanically followed, and was only roused from my stupor by our approach to the house. At sight of that, I thought on the misery I had brought on its inmates, and of the horror with which I should be regarded there as my brother's murderer. Faces that till now had ever been lighted up with love, seemed to scowl on me with hatred ; and I imagined myself driven forth, by those dear to me as my heart's-blood, with curses and execrations. Such ideas poured like a flood of fire upon my soul, and uttering a cry of torture, I fled into the neighbouring wood.

It was evening. The night set in dark and stormily, and with heavy rain. My garments were soon drenched ; but I heeded it not, knew it not. I rushed into the middle of the wood, and cast myself on the ground. I attempted to pray, but I could not. I thought myself a thing accursed of God and man, a helpless and devoted castaway, without hope or refuge. Fiendish faces glared on me from behind the trees, and strange and terrible voices were borne on the wind. Then would the scene change, and I thought myself a thing heaving on the mountainous billows of the ocean, and that I sought for death amid the waters in vain, for I bore a charmed life, and could not die. This too passed away, and I lay in a loathsome pit, with creatures unutterably loathsome. There the toads spit upon me, and the lizards gazed on me with their sparkling eyes, and crawling things defiled me with their slime. Then peals of wild and horrid laughter sounded in my ears, and I saw my brother's face all ghastly and grinning, and he called me murderer and fratricide. Worn out as I was I could not rest. There was a voice within, that cried for ever, On, on, and I could not but obey the behest. I plunged through the thickest parts of the underwood, and found a strange delight in being gored and lacerated by the thorns.

Such are the glimmerings which my memory affords me, of the sufferings of that fearful night. At length I thought myself dying. My limbs became gradually numb and stiff, and I drew breath with difficulty. In the expectation of death, my mind became calmer. There was consolation in the idea, that I should not survive the dreadful deed that I had done, and that, when my parents witnessed the terrible expiation of my crime, they would forgive—perhaps weep for me. I wished to die a penitent at my father's gate, and I made an effort to return to the house. More I know not. But I have since learned that I was found insensible in the morning, on the steps of the vestibule, with the countenance of death, and eyeballs red with blood.

Weeks passed away, of which I know and remember nothing. I had a brain fever. The struggle was a long and severe one; and so trembling was the vibration of the balance between life and death, that a hair in either scale would have decided the preponderance.

At length I awoke as from a deep sleep. I gazed on the objects around me, but could recognise none of them, and I again closed my eyes, and endeavoured to arrange the confused multitude of ideas, that thronged tumultuously on my mind. By slow degrees I succeeded. I remembered as familiar things, the bed on which I lay, the furniture, the pictures, the distant spire seen through the window; and I knew my mother, who sat watching by my pillow. She was dressed in the deepest mourning, and gazed on me with looks such as never beam but from a mother's eye. She had observed a change in the expression of my countenance, and hope, almost dead within her, revived once more to cheer and animate her heart. I looked on her long in silence. At length the words, "Oh, my dear mother," faltered from my lips, and I attempted to embrace her; but the effort was too great for me, and my arms dropped powerless by my side. She saw at once that my mind was restored. For a moment she seemed endeavouring to subdue her emotion; then she bent over me, and warm tears fell on my face as she pressed her quivering lips to mine, and I heard her breathe the words, "My poor boy, my Cyril; thank God, I have yet a son! thou, at least, art restored to me." I clasped my feeble arms around her neck, and joined my tears with hers. They were refreshing tears, and I was calmed and relieved by them. But my mother feared the effect of any strong agitation on my newly-awakened mind, and once more kissing me, she retired from the bed. Then I saw her kneel, and she prayed a prayer of thanksgiving to God, under whose terrible dispensations she had not been left utterly destitute and bereft.

CHAPTER IV

There was a time, when meadow, grove, and stream,
The earth, and every common sight,
To me did seem
Apparell'd in celestial light,
The glory and the freshness of a dream.
It is not now as it hath been of yore.
WORDSWORTH.

My recovery was slow, and spring was fast verging into summer, before my returning strength enabled me to exchange the atmosphere of a sick chamber for the pure air of heaven. Those only who, like me, have lain for months on a sick-bed, and who, like me, have recovered at the moment when all nature seems simultaneously bursting into new life and activity, and wears her most beautiful and joyous aspect, can understand the feelings of delight which I experienced on my release from captivity. Then indeed there seemed

" A glory in the grass, and splendour in the flower, "

and the symphony of angel choirs could not have fallen more melodiously on my ear, than did the carolling of the birds in the greenwood. The minutest objects of Nature rose in my eyes into consequence and beauty. To me, in all her works, she was instinct with voice, and with them all I held sweet communing.

" The daffodils,
That come before the swallow dares, and take
The winds of March with beauty ; violets dim,
But sweeter than the lids of Juno's eyes,
Or Cytherea's beauty, "

had all deep hold on my affection ; and when, as the summer advanced, I saw them wither, I felt for them as friends of my bosom, and almost wept for their decay.

As I walked forth, my mother and sister, with anxious assiduity, supported my tottering steps, and guided them to the favourite haunts of my childhood. Little Lucy, too, would take my hand with infantine caresses, and lead me to her little flower-garden, to see the cowslips and anemonies, and the nest which the green-linnet had built in her favourite rosebush. But I better loved to wander forth alone, amid the singing of birds and the blossoming of flowers, to yield up my spirit to the pervading impulses around me, and in the lonely communion of my own thoughts, to add another voice to the general unison of nature. For I felt that " impulses of deeper birth " came to me in solitude, and I loved to gather

> " The harvest of a quiet eye,
> That broods and sleeps on his own heart. "

My strength now rapidly returned, and I was soon able to mount my favourite horse, and thus to render my exercise more varied and continuous. But my mind by no means regained its healthful tone with equal rapidity. The bow had been so strongly bent as to injure its elasticity, and it could not speedily return to its natural curvature. The exhilarating influence, too, of external nature, gradually diminished as the objects became more familiar to my eye, and a mental torpor was gradually stealing over my faculties. The memory of Charles was too strongly connected with the scene around me. Everything was associated with his image ; animate and inanimate nature were alike full of him. His idea would not pass away, and though my grief now was neither passionate nor vehement, it was becoming what was perhaps still worse, a deep and rooted sentiment, acting with permanent influence on my character.

It would have been well if the fatal consequences of my disobedience had been confined wholly to myself. But it was not so. In the shrunken form, the ashy cheek, and hollow eye of my mother, there might be read a dreadful tale of grief and suffering. Nor was it the less apparent that she strove to conceal it from every eye. She wished not to cloud the hearts of those she loved, by making them partakers in her sorrow. She smiled, but her smiles, though kind and benignant as ever, were no longer those of gladness. She ministered comfort to others, while it was but too visible that the canker-worm was gnawing at her own heart.

Jane's grief, too, was intense. But how transient is the cloud of sorrow on a youthful brow !

> " The tear down childhood's cheek that flows
> Is like the dewdrop on the rose ;
> When next the summer wind comes by,
> And waves the bush, the flower is dry. "

And so was it with my sisters. The blow that at first stunned them with its violence, left on their young and buoyant hearts no permanent marks, and in a few weeks a tender and softened memory was all they retained of their lost brother.

With my father it was different. Like a stroke of God's lightning had the blow descended on his head, and the consequences were at first terrible. He rolled in the dust—he grieved, and would not be comforted. Dreadful and agonizing were the pangs he suffered, till at length he lay exhausted by the intensity of his anguish,

" And shew'd no signs of life, save his limbs quivering. "

Then, in the bitterness of a wounded spirit, he uttered curses on the author of his bereavement. Oh, how witheringly did they fall on my mother's heart! She knew that, till then, her cup of misery had not mantled to the brim. She knelt at his feet, and implored, vainly implored, him to recall the dreadful words. Then she told him, what as yet he knew not, of my danger, of my madness. In the agony of her despair, she brought him to my bed. My father heard there the sounds of suffering and delirium that burst from me, and he gazed on my fiery eyeballs and haggard countenance. Then only it was, that he recalled the dreadful curse he had invoked, and with a penitent and softened heart, bedewed my temples with his tears.

Yet I believe he never perfectly forgave me. On my recovery, his manner towards me was kind, and unmarked by any of that austerity to which I had been accustomed. He studiously avoided any recollection which might disturb that mental tranquillity, so essential to the complete restoration of my health. Still there was ever about him something of coldness and constraint, that told me I could never more be the object of his love. I knew and felt this. My mother, with affectionate earnestness, endeavoured to combat this growing dislike, and to turn the current of his affection into its natural channel. Never surely was there a warmer or more impassioned advocate. She directed his view to all that was good and praiseworthy in my character, and enlarged on those qualities and talents, which appeared to her partial eyes to give large promise of future distinction. But in vain. There was a barrier that could not be surmounted, and the place which Charles had filled in my father's heart was destined to remain for ever in abeyance.

In order to dissipate my dejection, my father wrote to request that William Lumley would pay us a visit. He came, and his presence had a temporary effect in raising my spirits. It was much to have a friend to whom I could unburden my heart, and talk of Charles. He, too, had loved him; we mingled our tears together, and I felt that grief loses half its bitterness by participation. But his stay was necessarily short. He was obliged to return to College; and on his departure, my mother feared that I should once more relapse into my former depression. I was therefore encouraged to mingle in society, and to visit those families in the neighbourhood where I might meet companions of my own age. This, too, was done, and Jane and I spent, as I remember, a fortnight at Sir John Willoughby's. Sir John was member for the county, and resided about ten miles from Thornhill. Lady Willoughby and my mother had contracted a friendship in early life, which, exceeding the ordinary duration of female friendships, continued unabated till the close of theirs. To this circumstance it may perhaps be attributed, that, while my father had become generally unpopular in the county, no cessation

of the friendly intercourse of the families had taken place. Sir John's only
son, Frank Willoughby, was a young man rather above my own age, of
high animal spirits and kind heart. I had always felt towards him a
strong regard, probably because he was the only one of all our acquaintance who had betrayed a preference for my society over that of Charles.
I condemned his taste, and yet I loved him for it. To cure me of my
melancholy, the society of Frank did much, but the bright eyes of his
sister Laura more. She was a pretty and elegant girl, about two years
younger than myself, with bright blue eyes, and I thought the sweetest
smile in the world. I had known her from childhood, for she had often
visited my sisters at Thornhill; but it was then for the first time that her
charms burst upon me, and I felt emotion in beholding them. Then I
think it was, that the first glimmerings of love dawned in my bosom, and
I made my purest and earliest offering at the shrine of beauty. Certain it
is, that her image dwelt with me during an absence of several years,
unconnected, it is true, with any passionate attachment, but still the
object of fond and pleasing recollection.

The benefit which I derived from my visit at Middlethorpe was too
obvious to escape notice at home, and the family physician recommended that I should quit Thornhill for a longer period. I accordingly
received one morning, soon after my return, a summons from my father
to attend him in the library, where he communicated in due form his
intention of sending me without delay to the University of Glasgow. Of
such a seminary I had at that time never heard, and as this resolution
may perhaps excite in my readers as much surprise as it did in me, I shall
state, briefly as possible, the reasons which I believe to have led to its
adoption. In the first place, I was just fifteen, and that was considered
too early an age to enter at either of the English Universities. In the next
place, two sons of Lord ———, a friend of my father, had been for
several years at Glasgow, and Lord ———, for whose judgment my
father entertained great deference, was warm in his praises of the
advantages they had derived from their course of study in that learned
seminary. My father, too, when abroad, had formed an acquaintance
with Professor R———, then tutor to a distinguished nobleman, and had
been impressed with a very favourable opinion of his talents and character. But there was another cause, which had probably a greater influence on his decision than either or all of those already mentioned, and
which, from its important bearing on this narrative, will require to be
elucidated at somewhat greater detail.

In the cursory notice I have already given of the family of my mother,
I did not think it necessary to state that my grandmother was of Scottish
origin. Such, however, was the fact. That lady was a daughter of Spreull
of Balmalloch, in Dumbartonshire, a family well known in that county,
though it is probable that its fame has not much extended beyond it.
Several generations back, the head of this distinguished house had

possessed barely property enough to entitle him to the rank and precedence of a *Cock Laird*. By the parsimony of its possessors, however, the estate had gradually increased. It was to this hereditary quality, indeed, that the Spreulls owed their elevation from the rank of humble cottars to that of bein and comfortable lairds ; and could the skulls of the successive owners of Balmalloch be submitted to the inspection of Mr Combe or Dr Poole, they would either discover in them an uncommon development of the organs of Caution and Covetiveness, or Phrenology would at once be overthrown. At all events, the estate throve apace in their hands ; and by small additions of a " park " on this side, and a " pendicle " on that, which the necessities of their less prudent neighbours induced them to dispose of, it gradually rose to be an estate of some note in the county, and the family of Spreull were suffered to mingle with others of older standing and baronial rank. Thus did matters stand, when my grandfather, a captain of dragoons, who served in Scotland somewhere about the middle of last century, married the blooming Miss Rebecca, or, as she was more commonly called, Miss Becky Spreull. This lady had two brothers, one of whom succeeded to the paternal property, and the other, having too much spirit to remain at home in the contemned and subordinate capacity of " Jock, the laird's brother, " was sent forth with very trifling advantages to " push his fortune " in the world. With this view the old laird procured him admission into the office of Sandy Swanston in Glasgow, a douce and cosie trader, who united, as was common in those days, the business of a wholesale importer of sugar and tobacco, with the profits of dealing in the same articles by retail. In this situation, did David Spreull succeed in rendering himself both useful and agreeable to his employer, and in a few years it became only necessary that he should advance a small capital, to procure a very advantageous share in the business. His father was now dead, and he was naturally led to solicit this accommodation from his brother the laird. The application was an unsuccessful one. The laird was married, and had a family to provide for, and rather unceremoniously informed his brother, in reply to his request, that he had other uses for his money, and " devil a bawbee " he need ever expect from him. The resentment excited in my grand-uncle David by this truly fraternal epistle, was naturally very strong, and put a stop to all intercourse between the brothers. In this state did matters remain for many years, without advances on either side.

At length, however, the reputation of David's wealth penetrated even to Balmalloch, and the laird thought it prudent and advisable to effect, if possible, a reconciliation. But all such attempts failed. David Spreull was immovable ; and now when, as he said himself, he was " well to do in the world, " he would never forget nor forgive the unbrotherly and unchristian manner in which he had been treated in the time of his necessity. Even the grouse, and the red-deer hams, the flitches, and the salt-butter, which he annually received from Balmalloch, effected no mitigation of his resentment. He received them indeed, but with expressions of his contempt and dislike for the givers, returned no thanks, and burned the epistles by which they were generally accompanied, unread. With his sister, my grandmother, he had maintained an occasional correspondence, and on her death, he had written to my mother, a letter of affectionate condolence. His commercial transactions were now very widely extended, and the accounts of his wealth, and of his estrangement from his brother and his family, were naturally considered very interesting intelligence at Thornhill. Any advances from so important a person were, of course, " to be gratefully received, and thankfully acknowledged. " His letters were answered with profuse assurances of regard, and expressions of anxious hope, that, some time or other, he might be induced to visit Thornhill, where every heart was prepared to afford him a warm and cordial welcome. Such, at least, is the general style of letters to rich old bachelors from aspirant legatees, and to this I have no reason to suppose, that those in question formed any exception. At all events, they were not without effect. A passenger and his luggage were one day deposited by the London mail at the ancient gate I have already commemorated, and this passenger was no other than my uncle David. He spent a week with us. I was then about four years old, and recollect something of an elderly gruff-looking personage, who dandled me on his knee, and spoke in a dialect which I could not understand. The impression he left on the family, was that of his being a very singular and eccentric character. Among other oddities, I have heard it narrated, that he sadly puzzled old Pearson, the butler, by calling for a glass of Glenlivet ; and fairly posed my father after dinner, by expressing a wish to be indulged with a bowl of toddy, a liquor, eo nomine at least, not familiar to any member of the establishment.

Between our family and that of Balmalloch, little or no intercourse had been maintained, and that little had been confined to a formal notification of births, marriages, and deaths, perhaps occasionally garnished with a few of those cheap expressions of civility, which mean, and which are intended to mean, nothing.

After reading this long preliminary statement, it will probably be seen, that the resolution of sending me to Glasgow, was the effect of a more recondite policy than might at first have been apparent. On my part, the business of preparation went merrily on. I was chiefly occupied in making arrangements for the comfortable provision, during my absence, of my horses and dogs. By my father, I was particularly enjoined to fail in no demonstration of respect and regard towards my uncle, and to have recourse on all proper occasions, to his experience and advice. Many cautions, too, did I receive on the score of extravagance ; and, ignorant as I then was, either of the value or necessity of money, I promised, without regret or scruple, that my expenses should be confined within the narrowest limits my father might impose. At length, all was finished ; and duly furnished with letters to my uncle and Professor R——, in whose family I was to become an inmate, I took a mournful and affectionate leave of my family ; and, attended by a steady servant, stepped into the north mail, and on the third morning from my departure, found myself safely arrived at the place of my destination.

CHAPTER V

——I'll view the manners of the town,
Peruse the traders, gaze upon the buildings,
And wander up and down to view the city.
Comedy of Errors.

" AND this, " said I to myself, as I gazed from the window of my inn, on the crowd and bustle in the street below—" this is Glasgow!—this the chosen seat of Science and the Muses—this the academic quiet, in which the mind of youth is to be nursed in the calm abstractions of Philosophy! " There was, indeed, rather a ludicrous contrast between the ideas I had conjured up, and the scene before me; and I could scarcely regard it without smiling. In the centre of the street, waggons, loaded with merchandize of different sorts, passed without intermission : and on the trottoirs, two opposing torrents of passengers were pouring along with extreme rapidity, and with looks full of anxiety and business. Of these some would occasionally stop for a moment's conversation, on which a loud and vulgar laugh mingled anon with the prevailing dissonance, and added unnecessarily to the general cacophony. Their gait and gestures, too, were singularly awkward and ungainly, and differed not only in degree, but in character, from anything I had seen before.

In the crowd before me, the actors seemed rigidly to adhere to the directions given by Plautus, for clearing a passage through a street encumbered by a population inconveniently dense.

" Plenissime eos, qui adversum eunt, aspellito,
Detrude, deturba in viam : hæc hic disciplina pessima est.
Currenti, properanti, haud quisquam dignum habet decedere.
Ita tres semel res agendæ sunt, quando unam occeperis:
Et currendum, et pugnandum, et jurgandum est in via. "
Merc. Act I. s.2.

The scene, however, had at least the charm of novelty ; and the spirit and animation which pervaded it, were sufficient to invest it with interest in my eyes. I had indulged some time in contemplation before my attention was recalled to the business of the day. My first step was to remove to the house of Professor R——; and with this view I ordered the waiter to procure a hackney-coach. This, however, I discovered was a luxury of which Glasgow did not boast ; and dispatching my servant with the porters and baggage, I resolved leisurely to explore my way on foot. Having received from my landlady, a person of very portly dimensions, all requisite information with regard to the geography of the University, I set forth on my walk. For the first time in my life did I now mingle in the tumult of a great city. It is true I had been in London; but I was then a child; and when pent up in a carriage, and whirled rapidly through the streets, I felt myself an isolated thing, and formed no unit in the busy crowd around me. It was not, therefore, without some degree of mental excitement, that I now for the first time mingled in the throng, and threaded the devious mazes of the living labyrinth, in which I found myself involved. Every sense was alive to the demonstrations of industry and activity, which presented themselves on all sides; and the clink of hammers, and loud creaking of machinery, mixing with the busy hum of men, formed a strange amalgamation of sound to ears like mine, hitherto accustomed only to the voice of simple nature.

At length, the appearance of an ancient and venerable building, informed me that I stood in presence of the University. There is certainly something fine and imposing in its proud and massive front. It seems to stand forth in aged dignity, the last and only bulwark of science and literature, among a population by whom science is regarded but as a source of profit, and literature despised. On passing the outer gate, I entered a small quadrangle, which, though undistinguished by any remarkable architectural beauty, yet harmonized well, in its air of Gothic antiquity, with the general character of the place. This led to another of larger dimensions, of features not dissimilar; and having crossed this, a turn to the left brought me to a third, of more modern construction, which was entirely appropriated to the residence of the Professors. There was something fine and impressive in the sudden transition from the din and bustle of the streets which surround it, to the stillness and the calm which reign within the time-hallowed precincts of the University. I seemed at once to breathe another and a purer atmosphere; and I thought in my youthful enthusiasm, that here I could cast off the coil of the world and its contemptible realities, and yield up my spirit to the lore of past ages, where I saw nothing round me to intrude the idea of the present.

When I arrived, Professor R. was at home, and received me in his library. He was a person about sixty years of age, in a periwig of rather ancient construction, and dressed in a silk robe de chambre, which, from its texture and grotesque pattern, appeared to be of foreign manufacture. With the easy manners of a finished gentleman, he led me into conversation, probed insensibly the extent of my acquirements, and sketched for me the plan of study which he thought it advisable for me to pursue. The term or session of the College, he told me, had not yet commenced, and recommended my devoting the intervening period, to previous preparation with a private tutor. Having arranged these preliminaries, and taken possession of my apartments, I next turned my thoughts to my uncle, and finding that the Professor perfectly agreed in the propriety of my waiting on him without delay, I once more set forth in search of his habitation. The discovery was attended with little difficulty, for his name and his dwelling were familiar to all from whom I requested information; and I had only to answer the question, " Is't his house or his countin'-house ye're axin' for, " to have my steps immediately directed in the proper channel. The domicile of Mr Spreull was situated in one of the great thoroughfares of the city, and was approached by a stair, which, being the common property of all the tenants of the same mansion, was, as might naturally be expected, offensively dirty.

My appeal to the door-bell was answered by a female servant, without covering to foot or leg, and in other respects not very nice in her person, who testified, by a broad stare, that the apparition of a morning visitor was by no means regarded as a common occurrence by the establishment. My English accent and her Scotch one, did not contribute to make us mutually intelligible, and when, to my inquiry, " if Mr Spreull was at home, " she answered, " What's your wull? " I felt rather at a loss to understand whether this periphrasis involved a negative or an affirmative. My question therefore was again repeated, and I at length succeeded in eliciting the equally laconic, but more intelligible response, " He's no in. " Considering any further colloquy with this damsel to be useless, I was about to withdraw, when a brisk and bustling matron came forward, exclaiming as she advanced, " Gang ben, ye tawpy, and let me speak to the gentleman. " I afforded her the opportunity she desired, by stating that I called in the hope of finding Mr Spreull. " I ettle ye're a stranger here, sir, or ye wad, nae doubt, ha'e kent it was no very likely that Mr Spreull wad be at hame at this time o' day. "

" If Mr Spreull is at present abroad, will you be good enough to inform me at what time I shall be likely to find him at home? "

" It wants, " said she, glancing her eye at a venerable-looking clock that stood ticking in the passage, " it wants fully twa hours o' his dinner-time; he'll no be at hame afore then; and when he does come hame, " added she significantly, " he doesna like to be disturbit. But if ye'll just step to the counting-house, ye'll be sure to find him there, if he's no upon the Change; and, " added she, again looking at the clock, " it's no likely he'll be there at this time o' day. "

I thanked the good dame for her information; but considering the alternative of his being upon Change when I called at the counting-house as at least possible, I requested her to mention, on his return, that his nephew Cyril Thornton had called to pay his respects, and deliver personally a letter from his mother.

" An' are ye Maister Ceeral Thornton, " exclaimed she, " the young gentleman my maister expecks to come down frae England? Troth, had I been ordinar kenspeckle, I might ha'e gathered as muckle frae yer English tongue, forbye yer likeness to the faimily. Surely I was beglamoured a' thegither, no to ha'e kent ye at yince. Will ye no step ben, and rest ye a bit? Weel I wat, my maister will be glad to see you. "

I courteously declined the hospitable invitation of the worthy matron, alleging as an excuse, my intention of proceeding immediately in
search of my uncle; and wishing her a good morning, I again set forward
with that purpose.

Mr Spreull's counting-house was in the Tron-gate, and formed part
of a large tenement which he had originally built, and which, from this
circumstance, was generally known by the patronymic of " Spreull's
Land. "

Of this building, however, he occupied but a small portion, the rest
being divided among a very numerous body of tenants, as appeared by
the variety of painted names with which both sides of the outer entrance
were adorned. Among these the following notice, printed in large
yellow letters, on a black ground, made no undistinguished figure—
" David Spreull & Co., first door right hand. " I advanced in the
direction indicated, and entered a chamber where about a dozen clerks
appeared very diligently engaged in business. In answer to my inquiries,
I was informed, that there was at that moment a gentleman with Mr
Spreull, but that it was not probable the interview would last long, and
he would, in a minute or two, be at liberty to receive me. The anticipations of the clerk were correct, for I had not kept my station above the
time indicated, before a person passed me from an inner apartment, and
immediately afterwards I heard the following directions issued in a loud
and harsh voice, from within:—" Fergus, enter a sale of the fifty hoggits
of muscovado sugar, marked L. T. by the Mary Jane, to MacVicar,
MacFarlane, and MacNab, at ninety-four, two months and two
months. " I was now desired to " walk ben, " and, doing so, found myself
at once in the presence of my uncle.

He was engaged in writing, and did not at first look up. I had thus an
opportunity afforded me of examining his person, which I did with no
small curiosity. He was a man whose age it was not easy to determine
from his appearance. Judging from his grey hair and wrinkled forehead,
I had set him down at seventy-five, but when he turned upon me his
quick and penetrating eye, I felt inclined to admit that he *might* be ten
years younger. He was certainly a hale man, and bore about him no
mark of decrepitude. The features of his face were coarse, and his nose,
in particular, far transcended, both in length and diameter, the ordinary and vulgar limits of nasal protuberance. His countenance was
strongly marked throughout by shrewdness and intelligence, and the
curvature of his upper lip, and an habitual contraction of the eye-brows,
gave indication of a temper at once irascible and pertinacious. Such at
least were the conclusions I had come to, when my observations were
suddenly cut short by their object, who, regarding me with a cursory
and careless glance, thus addressed me : " Oh, you're from Mr Muckle-
hose. Just tell him from me, that I cannot agree to a total loss in the case

o' the Hercules. There's a claim o' salvage, and nae mair. I told him sae
yesterday at the coffee-room, and there's nae use in his bothering me
with messages about the matter. My mind's made up.—Good morning
to you. "

Having said this, he once more resumed his writing; and I remained
silent for a minute or two, partly from surprise at being thus addressed,
and partly in the hope that a second glance might correct the error into
which he had fallen with regard to my character and business. Of this,
however, there seemed little prospect. He appeared utterly insensible of
my presence, and I at length determined to make myself known to him
without further delay.

" Sir, you mistake. I—— "

" What the deevil, sir, are you there yet? " exclaimed the old gentleman, his eye kindling with passion—" I mistake, do I? Baldy Muckle-
hose will find, however, the mistake lies wi' him, if he thinks the Glasgow
underwriters are to accept a total loss, for what, at Lloyd's, is considered
only a case o' salvage. "

" Permit me, sir, to inform you— "

" No, sir, I want none of your information. You can inform me of
nothing in the business, that I do not know better than either yourself or
your employer. So, be good enough to stop your thrapple, and steek the
door ahint you. I've other use for my time than to stand argol-bargoling
wi' you. "

So saying, he again commenced writing, and I could scarce refrain
from laughing at the ridiculous position in which I was placed. Perceiving all the difficulties which opposed themselves to a verbal explanation,
I determined to bring about an eclaircissement by the delivery of my
mother's letter. He received it in silence, and, having glanced over its
contents, hastily rose and advanced towards me, extended a huge hard
and bony hand, and, grasping mine, administered a shake, which, in the
length of its duration, and the vehemence of its pressure, gave evidence
of a cordial welcome. " Ye're welcome to Glasgow, Mr Cyril—I'm
happy, very happy, to see you. Ye've grown a braw big callant since I
saw you last, that's now ten years past at Martinmas; but you'll no mind
me, for you was then just a wee bit toddlin' thing, wi' great red cheeks,
and twa wee shining een glaikin' out ower them. To an old man like me,
Mr Cyril, ten years are no just sae lang as they are to you; and it seems
almost like yesterday that I dandled you on my knee. But I maunna
forget to speir after your lady-mother; I hope she's keeping stout, and no
suffering mair than we maun a' expect to do as we advance in years. "

The old gentleman still kept my hand pressed in his while he uttered
this kind and voluble address, yet it was done with the same unbending
rigidity of feature, which had struck me on my first entering the apartment. His face had apparently been modelled into one expression, by
the unvaried and habitual action through life of one dominant feeling

and excitement, till it had lost the power of change, and, like sculptured stone, the look once impressed on it was to be for ever ineffaceable. But though my grim-visaged uncle possessed not the power of smoothing his wrinkled front, or of relaxing at will the hard contraction of his facial muscles, still there might be discovered, in the milder and more softened expression of his eye, indication of warm and kindly feeling. It required some time to answer all his inquiries with respect to my family, but having done so, he proceeded.

" So ye've come down here to be a colleeginer. It's a lang gait to gang for learning. But after a', I am no sure that you could ha'e done better. Our Colleges here are no bund down like yours in the south by a wheen auld and fizzionless rules, and we dinna say to ilka student, either bring three hundred pounds in your pouch, or gang about your business. We dinna lock the door o' learning, as they do at Oxford, and Cambridge, and shut out a' that canna bring a gouden key in their hand, but keep it on the sneck, that onybody that likes may open it. But where are ye gaun to bide ? "

" With Professor R——, at the College. "

" Weel, from all I ken myself or have heard tell o' him, he's a douce and discreet person ; and your father hasna chosen amiss. It's no very often that we forgather, but he's a weel-faurt and pleesant man, without muckle o' the Dominie aboot him ; at ony rate, he's far afore that heavy tike, Professor ———, wha's little better than a haveril, and has stocked his mind so extraordinar weel wi' science and philosophy, that he has no room left in't for common sense. And there's Principal ———, I never heard a screed o' a sermon frae him that was worth a button, and he's nae mair fit to haud the candle to Dr Balfour or Dr Porteous—— "

Here our colloquy was interrupted by the entrance of a person with a face full of business, who, pulling out of a huge coat-pocket several samples of cotton and tobacco, began a conversation in which I could be expected to take neither interest nor participation. Mr Spreull took advantage of the first pause in the dialogue to turn to me, and said, " It's no often, God knows, that I meet friends, no to say relations, and it would be a slighting o' his mercies no to be kind to them when I do sae ; but you're auld enough to ken, Mr Cyril, that business must be attended to. So I'll let you gang now, gin you'll promise to tak pat-luck wi' me the day. You'll get poor fare, but if I hae got a right inkling o' your heart, blood's thicker than water, and you'll put up for one day with a bad dinner and an auld man's cracks. "

Though this invitation, like many other passages of the preceding conversation, was at that time by no means superfluously intelligible, yet I contrived to pick up the drift of it, and answered by a ready acceptance. I then took my departure, having arranged that I should call on my uncle at his place of business precisely at a quarter to four o'clock, and accompany him to his house.

CHAPTER VI

He was not taken well; he had not dined:
The veins unfill'd, the blood is cold, and then
We pout upon the morning, are unapt
To give or to forgive; but when we have stuff'd
These pipes, and these conveyances of our blood,
With wine and feeding, we have suppler souls,
Than in our priest like fast.

Coriolanus.

Qu. Troth, he uses his uncle discourteously now. Can he tell what I may do for him? He knows my humour: I am not so usually good; 'tis no small thing that draws kindness from me; he may know that an he will.

A Trick to catch the Old One.

BEFORE returning to the College, I determined to gratify my curiosity by seeing something of the Lions of Glasgow; and, committing my footsteps to chance, I wandered for a considerable time about the city. I visited the Gallowgate and the Saltmarket, mused with a curious eye on the Doric beauties of the Brig-gate and the Goosedubs, and admired the romantic vista of the Candleriggs, terminating in the Ram's-horn Church, the graces of whose architecture harmonize so perfectly with the classic euphony of its name. Thus interestingly occupied, the time sped unheeded, and the hour of four sounded from the College steeple, before I had effected those changes in my habiliments which the dirty condition of the streets had rendered necessary. Roused by this intimation, I completed my toilet as expeditiously as possible, and set forth on my engagement; but ere I was able to reach the place of rendezvous, another half hour had elapsed. In the outer apartment of the place of business, so crowded in the morning, I now found only one clerk, who, "like a brotherless hermit, the last of his race," sat with blank and disconsolate aspect, probably ruminating on the more enviable occupation, in which his colleagues were then engaged, and counting the minutes till he should be set at liberty by their return. My uncle was by no means in the same bland and benevolent humour in which I had parted from him in the morning. He was pacing the apartment as I entered with long and irregular strides, and his arms immersed to the elbows in coat-pockets, about the size of a bushel measure. The expression of his countenance spoke at once the state of his feelings. There was a compression of the lips, an unusual contraction of the brows and sparkle of the grey eyes beneath them, that portended a hurricane. He did not

notice me on my entrance, and I had some time to collect myself for a patient endurance of the pitiless pelting of the storm that was evidently brewing in the horizon. He brushed close past me several times, without giving the smallest indication of his being aware of my presence; but at length, stopping full in my front, he thus sardonically addressed me.—
" So, sir, ye've condescended to come at last. Ca' ye this a quarter to four o'clock? " said he, pulling out a gold chronometer of uncommon dimensions. " Look at that, sir, " said he, holding it up, " it wants just seventeen minutes to five by the Tolbooth clock. I suppose ye dinnered wi' the Professor afore ye set out, for ye couldna reckon on getting onything wi' me at this time o' day. But maybe they're yer English fashionable hours, and ye thought it vulgar, perhaps, ay, vulgar, that's what ye ca't, to dine at—— "
" I really beg your pardon, sir; I am very sorry I have detained you; but I was walking about the town, and was not aware of the lateness of the hour, till—— "
" Ye wasna aware o' the lateness o' the hour? But ye ought to ha'e been aware o't, sir. Is my stamach, that's as boss as a drum, to pay the penalty o' your negligence? It's weel we ha'e some o' the same blood in our veins, or I wadna ha'e pardoned this. But dinna, in time to come, lippen ower muckle even to *that*, or ye'll maybe find ye're leaning against a slap. There's them wi' as muckle o' my blood that I ha'ena forgi'en, no, and what's mair, winna forgi'e, till I or they are laid in the kirkyard. "
His voice fell towards the close of the sentence, and he pronounced it in a deep and hollow tone. In a moment he was silent. His former train of thought and emotion seemed to be suddenly changed; and when he again spoke, it was in a softened and milder voice.
" But there's enough said, and maybe mair than was needfu'. After a', ye was in a strange place, and exactness is maybe no to be expeckit in a callant like you. Sae come awa', for Girzy will think I'm lost a'thegither, " said he, putting on a broad-brimmed quaker-looking hat; " we've lost mair time already than there was occasion for. "
We went forth accordingly, and, on reaching the street, I was desired by my uncle to " cleek oxters. " Sanscrit was not more unintelligible to me than these words; but observing that he extended his arm to receive mine, I understood the signal, and obeyed the mandate. We walked at the rate of five miles an hour, and of course soon reached the house. As we turned the last corner, I observed the head of Girzy protruded from the window, evidently in anxious expectation of her master, and watching to receive the earliest notice of his approach. Girzy received us on the landing-place of the stair, and inquired, with apparently much solicitude, into the cause of the present most unwonted breach of regularity.
" I began amaist to think, " said she, " that ye had just gane hame wi' Provost Shortridge or Collector M'Nair, as ye did yince about seven years ago, without sendin' me word. But that was no very likely neither.

God grant he's no dead, says I to mysel; he surely canna ha'e faun down in the dead-thraws, like Bailie Wallace, or just gane aff in a pluff like puir Doctor M'Corkadale, or—— "

Over how wide a field the conjectures of Girzy might have extended cannot now be ascertained; for my uncle, to whom the last gratuitous suppositions seemed by no means agreeable, cut them short by stating, that he had been detained by business, and that I had accompanied him home, for the purpose of partaking of his repast, which he desired might be served up without delay. The expression of her countenance evidently showed that this was very unexpected intelligence to the worthy matron, who betrayed considerable symptoms of being what is termed in nautical phrase " taken aback. " Thinking it more politic, however, to conceal her discomfiture, she turned towards me with a smiling aspect, and said, " We're very glad to see you, sir, though I'm fear't yer denner will no just be sae good as it might ha'e been, if Mr Spreull had tell't me ye war comin'. "

" Haud yer peace, and let it be sair't immediately, " interrupted her master, as we entered the parlour; " I have been tormented wi' a yirnin' for these twa hours; and here, bring me a candle to gang down to the cellar. "

While he was thus engaged, I had leisure to examine the apartment. It was of small dimensions; the furniture it contained was of antique construction, and had evidently seen better days, but the room bore altogether an air of snugness and comfort. On a chair before the fire hung a duffle wrapper, and a Kilmarnock nightcap, chequered in various diagonal divisions of blue and scarlet; and a pair of morocco slippers, the primitive colour of which was now undistinguishable, rested against the fender. From these circumstances, it was tolerably apparent, that the comforts of the master were not neglected by his establishment. A table was laid for dinner, with a cloth by no means rigorously clean, and the few appurtenances displayed on it, were not remarkable for nicety or elegance. On opposite sides of the fireplace, stood a large black-hair sofa, and an old-fashioned, high-backed easy-chair, from which conveniences it might be inferred as probable, that the owner was occasionally in the habit of indulging in an evening nap. One end of the room was occupied with a book-case, the shelves of which were tenanted to the utmost extent of their capacity. Among the works it contained, in the cursory glance I had time to throw over them, I recognised Swift's Works and De Foe's, the Tatler, Spectator, and Rambler, Smollett's Novels, a translation of Rabelais, the Institutes of Scottish Law, Burke's Letters on a Regicide Peace, an odd volume of Hume's History, and a considerable body of Calvinistic divinity. Over the chimney-piece hung a portrait of Mr Pitt.

In making the preceding observations, my attention was occasionally diverted from its more immediate object, by hearing, through the open door, the following monologue in the kitchen.

"Lord saf us! what's to be done? Here he's brought the young Englishman to denner, and there's naething, guid or bad, in the hoose, but some cauld beef, and the kail that wasna suppit at yesterday's denner. If he had but sent me yae hauf hour's notice, I could hae gotten a gigot of mutton, and had things a wee decent. But there's nae use in talking about it.—Jenny, clap on yer mutch, and rin awa ower to Thamson, the flesher in the Stockwell, and bring hame a pund o' minched collups in yer brat, and bring twa tippeny tarts frae Baxter the baker's, and bid him charge them in the buik; and mind ye dinna staun' clashin' wi' a wheen o' thae idle ne'er-do-weel hizzies at the West-port well, but gang stracht there and back, and mak haste, or ye shall never pit yer ugly neb inside o' this door again, I can tell ye that."

My uncle soon returned from the cellar, charged with a bottle in each hand, which gave, in externals, a promise of antiquity, not afterwards belied by their contents. Having decanted a bottle of choice old Madeira, and deposited it on the " chimley lug, just to tak the air aff o't, " he next proceeded to doff his external habiliments, and to invest himself in the wrapper, night-cap, and slippers, laid out for him by the providence of Girzy. A more grotesque figure cannot well be imagined, than that now presented by the old gentleman; and, notwithstanding the respect, approaching to awe, with which he had inspired me, I ventured to indulge in a laugh, loud enough to attract his attention. Coleridge's description of the Ancient Mariner was not inapplicable to his figure, and to this day I never read the following passage of that beautiful and transcendently imaginative poem, without thinking of my uncle David—

> " I fear thee, ancient mariner,
> I fear thy skinny hand;
> And thou art *long, and lank, and brown,*
> As is the ribb'd sea-sand. "

The comfort of his domestic integuments, and of his easy-chair, had apparently contributed to his good-humour, for he was not offended at the rather impertinent liberty I had assumed. " So you're laughin' at your uncle in his night-gown and coul? I dare say they're no very bonny; I'm sure they're auld enough; but when ye come to be an auld bachelor like me, Cyril, (which God grant, for your ain sake, may never be,) ye'll care as little aboot the look o' things then as I do now. But I wonder what the deevil keeps Girzy wi' the dinner; this is no like her for ordinar; it's noo on the chap of sax.—Ay, come awa, " said he, addressing Girzy, who that moment entered, carrying a tureen, " it's nine hours since a morsel has passed my thrapple, and I'm sair forfachten for want o' something. "

Girzy deposited the tureen on the table, and supplied us with plates from before the fire. One of these my uncle filled to the brim with broth, and handed across the table to me, informing me, at the same time, that he had only sent me " a very few. " He then helped himself in the same proportion, that is, to the full extent of the capacity of the dish, and seizing on a " farel " of oatmeal cake, which lay in a bread-basket by his side, he fell to work with the voracity of a famished wolf. Girzy was too well aware of the deficiencies of the repast, and too sensitively apprehensive of a stigma being thrown by these deficiencies on the character of the establishment, in which her own was so materially involved, not to make an effort to palliate and excuse them.

" Really, " said she, addressing herself to her master, who was too much absorbed in eating to pay any attention to her, " really it's no blate o' Mrs Ross, the henwife, that lives oot at Partick ; wad ye believe it, she has neither sent me the turkey nor the pair o' howtoudies I ordered frae her last week, though she tell't me I might lippen to gettin' them, on the word o' an honest woman. As for Thamson the flesher, the man's gane clean demented a'thegither. Didna he gang and send the loin o' veal and the kidneys I ordered there mysel yesterday's blessed day, to Spreull the grocer's, in Gibson's Wynd ? Sae the tae thing wi' the tither has left the hoose sae bare o' provisions, as it's a shame and a disgrace for a gentleman's hoose to be. Ye maun just thole the day wi' some cauld beef and some minched collups, which was what I had gotten for yersel, afore I kent o' Maister Thornton. "

My uncle chanced to finish his plate of broth, as the matron pronounced the last sentence of her apologetical oration, and becoming then, for the first time, aware that her clapper was in motion, lost no time in stopping it, by desiring her gruffly, " To haud her gaffin, and rax the Madeira; " with both of which mandates, Girzy, having accomplished her business of explanation, willingly complied. Her injunctions to Jenny against dilatoriness on her errand, appeared to have produced good effect on that damsel ; for the minced collups and the tarts made their appearance in good season, and were done due honour to by both of us. My appetite, like my uncle's, was pretty sharp, and when the cloth was removed, after cheese, I felt every internal evidence of having made a good dinner. It was much to the satisfaction of Girzy that I did so on the present occasion ; and her attention to my wants was really quite overpowering.

" That's no a gude slice o' the beef ye're sending Maister Thornton, " she would say to my uncle; " send him a bit nearer the bane. " Or addressing me, " Tak a few mae o' the collups, they'll no hurt ye.—Lord saf us, ye're no done !—Just tak ae spoonfu' mair; at your age, yer teeth's langer than yer baird. Weel, if ye'll no try the collups again, ye maun tak a tart, " continued she, on hospitable thoughts intent, shovelling, at the same time, a whole one upon my plate, nolens volens, and again placing it before me. Luckily, in the present case, it happened to be *volens* ; and the tart was duly dispatched, with as much facility of deglutition, and appearance of relish, as Girzy herself could desire.

The table being cleared, and wine glasses placed before us, Girzy put the interrogation,—" What bowl are ye for? " and being answered " Number seven, " soon after made her appearance with a China bowl capable of containing about a gallon, which, with lemons, sugar, and a bottle of rum, was placed before her master.

" Ye'll maybe no like punch, " said my uncle to me, " and if sae, ye'll just drink on at the Madeira; or there's a bottle o' claret out ower there, " pointing to a corner of the room, " gin ye like it better. Make yourself quite free, and ca' for whatever ye like; if it's no to be had *in* the house, it's to be had *out* o' the house, and that's the same thing. "

I assured him in reply, that I would take advantage, if required, of the liberty he thus gave me; but as I had never tasted punch, it was necessary that I should do so, to enable me to act as a conscientious judge in the case.

The office of mingling the discordant elements of punch, into one sweet and harmonious whole, is perhaps the only one which calls into full play, the sympathies and energies of a Glasgow gentleman. You read, in the solemnity of his countenance, his sense of the deep responsibility which attaches to the duty he discharges. He feels there is an awful trust confided to him. The fortune of the table is in his hands. One slight miscalculation of quantity,—one exuberant pressure of the fingers,— and the enjoyment of a whole party is destroyed. With what an air of deliberate sagacity does he perform the functions of his calling! How knowingly he squeezes the lemons, and distinguishes between the Jamaica rum, and Leeward Island, by the smell! No pointer ever nosed his game with more unerring accuracy. Then the snort and the snifter, and the smacking of the lips, with which the beverage, when completed, is tasted by the whole party! Such a scene is worthy of the pencil of George Cruikshank, and he alone could do justice to its unrivalled ridicule.

Even in my uncle there was something of all this apparent. An anxious nicety in the compounding of the liquor, as if he considered it necessary to his character as a punch-maker, that it should meet my approbation. If so, the old gentleman was gratified, for I had no sooner tasted its contents, than I expressed my full and unhesitating resolution of what is called in Glasgow, " sticking to the bowl. " Under its exhilarating influence, a freer and less constrained intercourse was soon established between us. I felt perfectly at ease, amused my saturnine companion with school-boy anecdotes, and we became, in short,

> " A pair of friends, though I was young,
> And Matthew seventy-two. "

Young as I was, I soon discovered my uncle to be a person of much natural shrewdness, and considerable acquired knowledge, with a memory well stored with local anecdotes, which were rendered more piquant and amusing, by a certain broad and caustic humour, with which they were invested by the narrator.

Our conversation was interrupted by the entrance of Girzy, who approached the table with a wine glass in her hand, and thus addressed her master.

" I'm just come to ask for a preein o' the bowl, to drink the health o' Maister Ceeral there. Ye ken it's no for the punch, for I keep the keys o' the gardevin, and I can tak what I like, and you neither ken nor care ; but it's noo twa-and-twenty years come Candlemas, that I've keepit your hoose, and I never saw kith or kin o' yours within the door till this blessed day. Sae here's till ye, Maister Ceeral, " said she, raising to her lips the glass which her master had filled a bumper ; " here's till ye, and ye're hairtily welcome to yer uncle's hoose ; I ken ye are sae, though he's maybe no had the grace to tell ye as muckle. And here's till you, too, sir, I houp ye'll be kind to yer nevoy, noo ye've gotten him doon here, and no be snappin' him up sae short as ye do folks for ordinar, for he doesna ken yer ways yet ; and, " added she, lowering her voice to a confidential whisper, " he's as nice and canty a callant as ever I clappit een on, and no pridefu' aboot his meat. "

" Are ye gaun to stand there a' night, yelpin' in our lugs ? " exclaimed my uncle, with impatience, on finding Girzy's harangue was extending beyond its due limits ; " gang and get the tea maskit, and send it ben when I ring for't. " Exit Girzie. " It's a sad thocht, Cyril, that, single or married, there's nae escapin' frae the deavin' o' a woman's tongue. I've a' my life been shy o' yokin' to with ony o' them, and resolved first and last, baith to live a bachelor and die one ; but you see, after a', I've made little profit o't. That Girzy's a bell whose clapper never lies ; and the warst is, she kens I canna want her, though the disturbance she gies me's beyond description. But there's still a thocht mair in the bowl, " added he, " and there's yae toast we maun drink in a bumper ; so take aff your dribblet, and put in your glass. "

I did so.

" Here's the health o' your father, and your leddy mither ; your brith—na, yer sisters. "

" And may God Almighty bless them, " exclaimed I, a little elevated by what I had drank.

" Amen ! " ejaculated my uncle, as he raised his glass.

" In giving the toast, " continued he, " the name o' puir Charles just cam', without thinking, to my lips, though I ken he's dead ; weel I wat, his death maun hae been a waesome loss to your parents. I mind him weel when I was at Thornhill ; he was the gleggest and the funniest wee chiel' that ever gladdened my een ; and yet, for a' that, he would often put his wee hand in mine, and walk out wi' me quite quietly and doucely, just as if the bairn likit the company o' an auld man like me.

And he would tell me about his powney, and his dows, and fleech wi' me to gang and look at them, and happy was the wee man when I gaed wi' him. I wat he wasna like you, little sinner as ye was, that would never bide wi' me twa minutes on end, but come todlin ahint me, and pook me by the coat-tails, and then rin awa' laughin', as fast as your twa fat legs wad carry ye. An' yet ye was a blithe and winsome bairn, too, though I'll no say but I likit him the best. An', wae'e me, he's gane! Is't no strange, that Death shuld tak' a young and gleesome creature like that, and leave an auld man like me? But the ways o' Providence are no to be accounted for. Oh, but it gars me grue to think on him!"

The old gentleman was not much accustomed to the melting mood; and there was a striking, perhaps to an indifferent spectator, a ludicrous contrast, between the warmth and tenderness of feeling displayed in the matter spoken, and the gruff and saturnine expression with which it was delivered. An occasional huskiness and tremor was discernible in his voice; and he found it necessary several times to clear his throat, with a cough so loud and sonorous, as to prove that his difficulty of utterance did not originate in the feebleness of his lungs.

"But there's yae part, " continued he, after a short pause, "there's yae part o' the letter ye brought me, that I dinna very weel understand; and I wad like to hae't redd up to me, for I've an unco interest about a' that concerns your family. "

So saying, he produced from his pocket a letter, folded in the shape in which letters of business are usually preserved, and bearing the following indorsation:—

Thornton, Mrs Elizabeth.
Thornhill, 22d September 18—.
Concerning son Cyril, and sundries;
Received 27th September 18—;
Answered————

And having adjusted his "specs, " read aloud from it, the following extract:

"You have, of course, received intimation of the terrible infliction with which it has pleased God to visit this family. The dreadful accident by which we had to deplore the loss of one son, long left us little ground on which we could found a hope for the preservation of the other. I thank God, however, he is at length restored to us———. "

"Now, " my uncle continued, "though I kent, wae's me, that puir Charles was dead, afore I got your leddy mither's letter, yet I never heard tell o' the awfu' accident she speaks about, nor how your life cam amaist to be despaired o', and it would be a great satisfaction to me to hear a' the sad story; for Charles had wun himsell into my heart, in a way I never tell't naebody when he was leevin', for fear o' settin' folk a bletherin'. But, noo he's dead, it's nae matter. It often seemed strange to mysell, that his figure haunted me like a ghaist. It's true, I seldom thocht on him by day, yet he was aye present in my dreams at night, wi' his blue e'en, and his gowden hair, lookin' up sae douce and sweetly in my face; for his looks differed a hantle frae yours, and he had neither your black curly pow, nor your dark e'en. It wad be a sad pleasure to me, to hear how the bonny innocent cam by his death. "

My uncle had been too much engrossed with his own feelings, to think at all of mine. I sat writhing in my chair, as he spoke. Every word had been torture. I felt the blood rush in volumes to my head, and my temples throb almost to bursting, and then, by a sudden revulsion, it was again thrown back upon my heart, and lay a load upon my lifesprings. But this subsided. What I had drank, though far too little to disturb the serenity of an older and sounder head, was yet enough to act as a strong stimulus to a brain which, like mine, had scarcely recovered from the effect of recent inflammation. I was spurred on to comply with my uncle's wishes, by a strange and unnatural excitement, and I narrated, with a shuddering and shrinking heart, the circumstances of the fatal story. I stood while I spoke. As first, the wild energy of my manner seemed to strike him with surprise, but as my narrative approached the horrid catastrophe, he, too, became overpowered by emotion, and starting from his chair, came and clasped me in his arms,—" Say nae mair, Cyril,—for the love o' God, sae nae mair.—I ken, I see, I understand a' noo. " And he kissed my forehead, and as I looked on him, I saw the tears roll down the furrowed channels of his cheeks.

Scott and Wordsworth, both undoubtedly high authorities in everything connected with the human heart, agree that there is something more than ordinarily moving in " the tears of bearded men." It was perhaps fortunate, in the dangerous state of excitement in which I then was, that those of my uncle served in some degree to divert the current of my emotion.

" Ay, " said he, observing my gaze fixed on him, " ye may see I'm greetin'. I'll no deny't; but it's no for him, it's for you. "

And he once more pressed me in his arms.

" Poor Cyril! it wants nae words to tell me how your life cam to be amaist despaired o'; yet blessed be Providence ye've been sparet, and come safely through your awfu' trials. Ye may believe me, " said he, wiping his eyes, " these are the first draps that through a lang life have wat my e'en. I have never kent the blessing of a tear sin my mither's death, and then I was just saxteen year auld; and I little thocht that onything could have gart me greet in my auld age.

" But here's that born deevil, Girzy, " said he, suddenly passing his handkerchief across his eyes, and perking his face instantly into its usual austere expression, " I wadna that she fund me yammerin' this gait, for a thousand pounds.—What, in Satan's name, brings ye here, when there's naebody wants ye? " said my uncle, with more than usual asperity; "I tell't ye I would ring for tea when we wantit it, —wasna that aneuch? But ye maun aye be interruptin' a' rational conversation, with the sound of yer gab, and the sight o' yer ill-faured neb."

"Ye ken ye tell't me to mask the tea," responded Girzy, with meekness, "and it's been maskit this hauf hoor, and it's now amaist cauld; sae I cam to see gin ye hadna forgotten't a'thegither."

"Weel, tak awa' the bowl, and bring't in; onything's better than your clack."

Girzy accordingly set to work in removing the punch-bowl and its appliances, and replacing them with the tea-tray. She soon showed, however, that her attention was not wholly engrossed by the operation in which she was engaged; for, after looking for a moment at her master, she exclaimed,—

"Lord preserve us, Mr Spreull, what's the matter wi' yer e'en? — they're as red as a boiled labster. Ye surely canna hae gotten the opthalmy in them, that the Hielanders brought hame frae Egypt wi' them? Ye just look, for a' the world, as if ye had been greetin'."

"It's a strange thing," rejoined her master, rather astounded at this shot in the bull's-eye,—"it's really an astonishing thing, that a man canna get a grain o' ause in his e'e, without its being made matter o' remark by an idle limmer like yoursell. Me greet indeed! Fesh the tea ben, and let me hear nae mair o' sic nonsense."

The tea soon made its entrée, garnished with a plate of "cookies," and a saucerfull of Girzy's own jam; and these being all duly partaken of, I prepared to take my leave.

"Ye maun just wait awee," said my uncle, "I canna let you gang hame, in a strange town, by yourself.—Girzy, send Jenny to tell Sanders MacAuslan to come here frae the office directly, for he maun see Cyril safe hame to the College."

In vain did I protest, that I knew the way perfectly, and would infinitely prefer walking alone, to being placed under Sanders Mac-Auslan's protection. Entreaties and protestations were of no avail; and I was obliged to submit. At length Sanders arrived; but I found my annoyances did not end here.

"Ye'll just wrap this aboot yer craig," said Girzy, approaching me with a huge old greasy-looking comforter in her hand, and applying it officiously to my throat, and blocking up my mouth with a triple entrenchment of woollen.

"And here's my big-coat," said Mr Spreull, seizing me at the same moment by the arms, and pushing them successively into the sleeves of an upper Benjamin, under the weight of which I could scarcely move.

"The streets are wat the night," said Girzy, coming again to the attack, "and ye'll no gang hame without my pattens." This was too much; and finding my only hope of escape consisted in flight, I watched my opportunity,—bolted through the door, with all the rapidity which the weight of my accoutrements would allow of,—and, in spite of the oppression of my comforter and upper Benjamin, reached the College in safety.

CHAPTER VII

" ——Here science rears
Her proud emblazon'd front on high, and here
By these time-darken'd pillars, and beneath
These reverend colonnades, in distant times,
Did sages send those words of wisdom forth,
Which circled all the echoes of the land,
And yet are in our ears. "

The Principal, an Epic Poem.

A FEW weeks passed away, and the courts of the College, formerly deserted and silent, were instinct with life and bustle. The session had now commenced, and nearly two thousand students crowded its halls. These were principally the sons of merchants and tradesmen of the city, and natives of the north of Ireland, of the very lowest order of the people, who came generally in a state of miserable destitution, to qualify themselves in the speediest and cheapest manner for the functions of the ministry. The leavening of English in this promiscuous assemblage was comparatively small, and chiefly furnished by the dissenters, who were compelled to seek in the more liberal establishments of Scotland, that access to knowledge and instruction, from which they were legally excluded by the great seminaries of their native land. There were also a few Englishmen of a higher class, who were placed like myself under the more immediate guidance and tuition of some particular professor, and in whose family they were received as inmates.

Educated as I had been in comparative privacy and seclusion, the scene in which I now mingled was naturally fraught with powerful interest. I entered with ardour the new field of honourable contention that was opened to my exertions, and received all the advantage which is invariably found to result, from the collision of youthful minds and the successful excitement of emulation. Learning now dropped the forbidding mask which she had hitherto worn in my eyes, and appeared adorned in graces which I had never imagined her to possess. In short, I entered, in jockey phrase, for all the University plates and sweepstakes for which I was qualified, and though generally not first in the race, I always saved my distance, and was more than repaid by the vigour of limb and elasticity of muscle which I permanently acquired from my exertions, even when unsuccessful in the struggle.

I feel a melancholy pleasure in looking back on the eminent persons who then shed a lustre on the University, and to whose kindness and instruction I have been so deeply indebted. Many years have passed, and they all, with one exception, sleep in the grave. May I be pardoned if I venture to embody in these Memoirs my own youthful impression of men, whose names have at least outlived their generation, and whose memory is yet warmly cherished in the hearts of thousands? They are now beyond the reach of praise or censure, but I would speak of them only in a spirit of reverence and love.

Of Professor R—— I have already transiently spoken. He was certainly a person of elegant accomplishments, and, as a man of the world, stood unrivalled among his colleagues. It must be a rare circumstance, that an obscure northern university can number in its members, a person who like him was qualified to shine in a more conspicuous, if not a higher sphere. Of the depth of his learning it is not for me to speak; but I believe it was his ambition rather to be distinguished as a poet and a polite writer than as a scholar — that he would have preferred the character of the Addison to that of the Porson of his age. Perhaps this bias of his inclinations proceeded from a knowledge of his own powers, and he chose that walk in which he was qualified to shine, in preference to one which he could have pursued with little prospect of distinguished success. If so, he did wisely. In the " Characters of Shakspeare's Plays, " he has left behind him a work which may serve as a model of elegant and philosophical criticism, and which, notwithstanding all that has since been written on the subject, still maintains its place in our literature. In poetry he was less successful. What, in the present day, can be said of a Rondeau on a Rose, or an Idyllium on a Lady knitting? He wrote a play, too, which, if I remember rightly, was damned; if not, it should have been so. His mind was essentially unpoetical. He could not disembody his spirit, and quicken with it the beings of a new creation. His soul was chained to its tenement, and bore about it too plainly the marks of scholarship and criticism. It was not the soul of a poet, but of Professor R——.

No person could have filled the Chair of Humanity with greater usefulness and success. His mind was thoroughly imbued with the beauties of Roman literature; and he was happy in the mode of communicating his instruction: though it must be confessed, that a gentleman distinguished, as he was, for the elegance and refinement of his manners, was not the person best calculated to maintain a constant subordination in the crowd of turbulent and vulgar boys by whom he was surrounded. Mr R——, I think, was somewhat of a misogynist; at all events, he was not partial to female society, and seldom mingled in it. He was a bachelor; and there were rumours afloat among the students, of an attachment to a Russian princess, when he resided at Petersburgh with Lord——, which was believed to have occasioned the celibacy of his future life.

In large and mixed society, he was perhaps a little formal and precise. It may be, that he disliked the general tone of society in Glasgow, and it probably was so. But of a small and select circle, he was the life and the ornament. I look back with pleasure and gratitude to those hours of familiar intercourse which I enjoyed as an inmate of his family, when, vailing the high claims of his age and character, he appeared only as the companion and the friend.

The Greek Chair was filled by Professor Y——. He it was who made the strongest and most vivid impression on my youthful mind, and it is his image which is still imprinted there, the most deeply and ineffaceably. That he was a profound and elegant scholar, I believe has never been denied. No master ever ruled with more despotic sway the minds of his pupils. None ever possessed the art of communicating his knowledge so beautifully and gracefully,—of transfusing the glowing enthusiasm of his own mind into that of his audience. Over every subject to which his great powers were devoted, did he cast a mantle of grace. From him a dissertation on the Digamma, or a Greek particle, became instinct with interest. His mind was the real philosopher's stone : it transmuted all baser metals into gold. I cannot analyse his character, and examine its separate elements. He appears to me only one grand and majestic whole, and as such only can I consider him. The admiration which he inspired in my youth, still remains undiminished; it enters vitally into my idiosyncrasy; it is part and parcel of me, and must remain with me till I die. Nothing could be more captivating than the eloquence with which he treated of the liberty, the literature, and the glory of ancient Greece, while tears of enthusiasm rolled down his cheeks. He was naturally a great and effective orator ; and had his powers been called into action in a different field, he might have added something to our scanty and imperfect records of national eloquence. It has always seemed to me, that his mind bore some resemblance to that of Burke. It possessed, I think, though perhaps in a smaller degree, the same vivid and creative power, and delighted in the same prodigal diffusion of intellectual riches. Like Burke, too, he felt all the influence of the spells he cast on others, and his own heart trembled at the images of dread or beauty which he conjured up from the depth of his imagination. Professor Y—— was scarcely known as an author. I believe he published nothing but a Continuation of Johnson's Criticism on Gray, a jeu d'esprit rather too voluminous to be very happy, and a translation of the Odes of Tyrtæus.

This is probably not exactly the portrait I should have drawn of this eminent person had I known him in maturer years, and been capable of exercising a cooler and more discriminating judgment on his character ; but such is the impression he left on me, and that impression is indelible.

Under Professor J—— I was initiated in the more simple and elementary principles of metaphysics, and the year in which I became his pupil, I have ever looked back upon as the greatest intellectual era of my life. Until Mr J— assumed the Chair of Logic, I believe the studies of the class had been exclusively devoted to the acquisition of the Aristotelian philosophy, a branch of knowledge not in itself very generally useful, and in the mode of teaching it not fraught with any peculiar advantage to the student. Of all men, Professor J—— is perhaps most entitled to be called a *radical reformer*. He saw at a glance the deficiency of the system which till then had existed. He knew that the means were everything, and the end comparatively nothing; that it was little to acquire a knowledge of the philosophy of Aristotle, but all in all to bring into full action and development, the dormant faculties of youthful minds. He did not hesitate, therefore, at once to overthrow the whole system followed by his predecessors, and to introduce a course of study in its place, marked throughout by practical good sense, and an extensive and thorough knowledge of the human mind. No success was ever more brilliant and decided, and I believe I may safely say, that the Logic Class is now admitted by all who have, like myself, experienced its benefit, to be paramount in importance to every other in the circle of academical study.

Professor J——, I believe, has outlived his contemporaries, and still survives. Like the last oak of the forest, he stands the sole relic of a generation which has passed away. He too is soon destined to fall, but surely not unhonoured.

It was no common advantage to enjoy the instruction of persons so distinguished as those I have already mentioned. But my hours were not wholly devoted to study.

A young Englishman, however moderately graced with the advantages of birth or fortune, is always an object of attraction to the female circles of Glasgow. But when, as in my case, he united the character of being heir-apparent to a fine English estate, to that of being heir-presumptive to a rich old uncle, it was not likely that he should be suffered to languish in obscurity. It was therefore not long that I was destined to "waste my fragrance on the desert air;" I soon rose into request among civic dignitaries and mercantile magnates. All mothers with marriageable daughters courted my society. It is true, in Glasgow, morning visits are neither fashionable nor convenient, and these Professor R—— informed me I must not look to have. But the gentlemen generally sent their cards by their office porters, along with the invitations of their wives, and I was not at that time disposed to attach much importance to points of punctilio. One visit, however, does occur to my memory.

I was busily engaged one morning in writing in my own apartment, when the door was opened, and my servant announced, " Mr Archibald Shortridge, jun. " I looked up from my paper, and beheld a young gentleman enter, with his hat in one hand, and the other thrust into his breeches-pocket. He was dressed in leather breeches, and jockey boots, a checked cotton neckcloth, and a short green jacket. *A priori*, he displayed a prodigious number of gaudy under-waistcoats, and a ponderous bunch of seals depended from what looked like part of a jack-chain, converted into gold by some chance touch of the philosopher's stone. *A posteriori*, he was adorned by the protrusion from his pocket of a Belcher handkerchief, which dangled in graceful negligence to his knee, thus affording relief to what he probably considered the comparative tameness of his personal scenery in that quarter. He entered with an air of swagger, and making me an awkward bow, he jerked himself into a chair with what was evidently intended to pass for elegant *nonchalance*. It was apparent, however, that the booby laboured under considerable embarrassment in having to address a stranger; and it was not until he had crossed and uncrossed his legs several times, adjusted his neckcloth, and run his fingers through his hair, that he gave any articulate signals of his presence. At length, however, he did so. After a few preliminary observations on the weather, he informed me, that the object of his visit was to present an invitation to dinner, for the Friday following, and stated, that his father would have had the pleasure of calling on me, had his time not been entirely engrossed by his numerous official duties. To these civilities I made an answer as polite as the occasion required, and, in a few minutes, it was evident enough that the evanescent bashfulness of my visitor had entirely disappeared. He sat picking his teeth, lolled in a negligent attitude in his chair, and occasionally diversified the charms of his conversation by spitting on the floor. He first talked of College and the Professors, bespattering them all with his vulgar abuse; and then changing his topic to my uncle,—

" Have you seen Mr Spreull lately? " he proceeded; " you found him a queer chap, I take it—a crabbit auld chiel'? "

" Perhaps you are not aware, Mr Shortridge, that the person you speak of is my uncle. "

" Oh, I'm perfectly aware o't; and I wish I had just such another. But he's a rough diamond, as we used to say in Manchester, when I was there in Lees, Cheatham, and Company's counting-house, and he's better kent here by the name of Auld Girnegogibby than by his own. What lots of cash he has, to be sure! Do you know, Peter MacCormick tells me, he has never less than thirty thousand pounds lying in Robin Carrick's Bank. By Jupiter, I wish I had his name at the tail of a ten-shilling stamp. "

I was now thoroughly disgusted with my visitor, and I think it probable my countenance gave some intelligence of the character of my feelings; if so, it was, or appeared to be, unnoticed.

" The Provost and he are hand in glove, but he never visits at our house now; and what's devilish odd, the very sight of me puts him in a passion. To be sure I quizz him a little now and then; but he's slow at a joke, and I dare say never found that out. I offered to dine with him about three months ago, on a day my father was engaged to him, but all the answer I got was, that when he wanted my company he would ask it. He's got a capital cellar of wine too, I'm told, and has some fine Grenada rum that's been about seventy years in bottle. "

I had become so tired of this style of conversation, that in order to communicate my feelings in what I thought the least offensive way, I took up the pen that lay before me on the table, and gave evident signs of a desire to resume my occupation.

" Oh, I see you're busy, so I'll not interrupt you, " at length said my companion, taking the hint and rising to depart; " but don't forget next Friday at five, and I'll take care to warn some capital fallows to meet you, just to give you a spunk of the way we carry on the war in Glasgow. " And so saying, with an air of perfect self-complacency, Mr Archibald Shortridge, junior, took his departure.

This dapper and facetious personage was no other, as the reader has of course discovered, than the son and heir-apparent of the Lord Provost of Glasgow, or, as it is more commonly designated in the west of Scotland, " the second city of the Empire. " The invitation was of course accepted ; but the dinner of so distinguished a civic dignitary deserves a new Chapter, and it shall have one.

CHAPTER VIII

Dinner is on table.
My father desires your worship's company.
Merry Wives of Windsor.

Give me a good dinner, and an appetite to eat it, and I will be happier than the mightiest potentate which this world can produce, surrounded by his satellites, and rioting in the indulgence of immeasurable power. Satisfied in this respect, I should pass my time in unalloyed happiness, and pity those whom fate had excluded from a similar enjoyment, as the victims of chance, and the slaves of misery.

DR JOHNSON.

ON the day, and precisely at the hour indicated, I was at the door of the Lord Provost. His house was situated in a small square, of a sombre and dreary aspect, the centre of which, instead of being as usual laid out in walks and shrubbery, was, with true mercantile sagacity, appropriated to the more profitable purpose, of grazing a few smoky and dirty-looking sheep. It was certainly not pleasant to approach the house of feasting amid the plaintive bleatings of these miserable starvelings; but there was no time to be sentimental, and, like the Lady Baussiere, I passed on. On being admitted into the hall, I was received by two servants in the Royal livery, a circumstance of magnificence for which I was certainly not prepared. The truth was, however, as I have since discovered, that a male domestic formed no part of the ordinary establishment of the Lord Provost, and these were a couple of the City Guard, or, as they were more generally called, "Town's Officers," admitted *pro loco et tempore*, to assume the functions of livery servants. I was in the act of divesting myself of my hat and greatcoat, when I heard the following question put in a bawling voice from the landing place of the stair above.

"Hector, what ca' ye him?"

"I ettle he's a young Englishman frae the College," answered Hector.

"I carena' whare he's frae," returned the other, "but I want his name. Didna I tell baith you and Duncan, to cry oot a' the names to me, that they may be properly annoonced?"

Hector lost no time in rectifying his mistake, and I speedily heard my name reverberated in a voice like thunder, through every corner of the mansion. The person from whose lungs this immense volume of sound proceeded, was a large stout man with a head like a bull's, and a huge carbuncled nose. His dress bespoke him to belong to the same corps with his brethren below, and he was in fact no other than the person who officiated as town-crier, commonly known by the familiar *soubriquet* of Bell Geordy. His duty of announcing the guests being somewhat analogous to his usual avocation, he appeared to discharge it *con amore*, and proclaimed every successive arrival in the same monotonous and stentorian tones, in which he was accustomed to give public intimation of the arrival of a cargo of fresh herrings at the Broomielaw. Bell Geordy, too, was a wit, and did not scruple occasionally to subjoin in an under tone, some jocular remark on the character or person of the guests as he announced them.

The drawing-room into which I was ushered, was evidently an apartment not usually inhabited by the family, but kept for occasions of display. The furniture it contained was scanty, but gaudy; the chairs were arranged in formal order against the walls; and there were flower-stands in the windows, displaying some half-dozen scraggy myrtles, and geraniums, with leaves approaching to the colour of mahogany. The room was cold; for the fire, which had evidently been only recently lighted, sent up volumes of smoke, but no flame; and when I looked on it, I remembered to have passed a dirty maid-servant on the stair, with the kitchen bellows in her hand. On my entrance, I found I was the first of the party; and before the attention of the reader is distracted by the arrival of fresh guests, it may be as well to seize the present opportunity of introducing him to the Lord Provost and his family.

His lordship was a little squab man, with a highly-powdered head and a pigtail, and an air somewhat strutty and consequential. His visage was a little disfigured by the protrusion of an enormous buck-tooth, which, whenever his countenance was wreathed into a smile, over-shadowed a considerable portion of his under-lip. One of his legs, too, was somewhat shorter than the other, which, when he walked, occasioned rather a ludicrous jerking of the body, and did by no means contribute to that air of graceful dignity which he was evidently desirous of infusing into all his motions. He was dressed in a complete suit of black velvet, and bore conspicuously on his breast the insignia of his civic supremacy. His lady was a stiff and raw-boned-looking matron, hard in feature, and somewhat marked by the small-pox. She wore a yellow silk-gown, adorned in front with a Scotch pebble brooch, about the size of a cheese-plate, and on her head a green turban, from which depended on one side a plume of black ostrich feathers. The two daughters, Miss Jacky and Miss Lexy, displayed their young and budding charms by the side of the parent-flower. Neither had the smallest pretension to good looks; but of their character, nothing immediately betrayed itself to the spectator, beyond a certain air of self-complacency, with which they occasionally regarded their pink dresses. There, too, was Mr Archibald Shortridge, junior, with his carroty head, and his great red ears, his mouth perked up as if about to whistle, and his mutton-fists in his breeches-pockets, straddling before the fire, with the tails of his coat below his arms, to prevent all possible obstruction to the radiation of the heat. I was welcomed by his lordship with an air of dignified hospitality, saluted with a nod by his son, introduced to, and benignantly received, by the Lady Provost and the young ladies.

The sound of the door-bell now became more frequent, and Bell Geordy's powers were called into full and active employment. I shall venture, even at the risk of being considered a romancer, (a character which more than any other I despise,) to give a specimen or two of the facetious manner in which this functionary discharged the duties of his office. As thus:—Door-bell rings—drawing-room door opens—Bell Geordy, in a loud, slow, and sonorous voice, " Doctor Struthers. " In a low and suppressed key, " Hech, but he's a puir stick in the poopit. " Again:—Preparation as before. Bell Geordy—" Miss Mysie Yule. " In a lower tone, " She's right aneuch to come here, for I'm thinkin' there's no muckle gaun' at hame. " Forté—" Major Aundrew MacGuffin. " Piano—" Wi' the happety-leg.—Maister Saumel Walkinshaw.—I'se warrant he'll carry awa' a wame-fu'. "

In vain did the Lord Provost, whose ear these unseemly comments occasionally reached, express his disapprobation of the indecorum, and authoritatively direct him to confine his speech to the mere annunciation of names. Bell Geordy's wit was not thus to be trammelled, especially when he observed it generally followed by a grin and titter through the assembly. Everybody, indeed, appeared to enjoy those jokes which were cut at their neighbours' expense, without reflecting that their own appearance had probably given rise to similar witticisms.

At length the company were all assembled, and dinner, after a dreary interval of expectation, announced. The ladies, in solemn dignity, led the way, singly and unescorted by the gentlemen. I observed some little scuffling among the dowagers about precedence, and occasionally a poke of the elbow given and returned with interest, and my ear sometimes caught a contemptuous snorting, like that of a frightened horse, which proceeded from some of those ladies, who, defrauded by their more active competitors of what they considered their proper place in the cortège, were compelled unwillingly to figure in the rear. The indignation of Mrs M'Corkadale, indeed, (the widow, I presume, of the poor doctor whose fate has been commemorated by Girzy,) was too vehement to be confined to mere pantomimic expression; and as she passed, I overheard the following soliloquy:—" Set her up, indeed, to walk before me! Does she think folk hae forgotten that her grandfather was a tailor on the tae side, and a flunky on the tither—that her father was naething but a broken baxter—and that she hersel was brought up in the Aumshouse?—My certy, but she's no blate! "

The sight of the dinner-table, however, and the savour of the steaming viands, had a soothing effect in calming for the nonce, all effervescences of temper, and restoring mental equanimity to the ruffled matrons. The dinner, if not elegant, was plentiful. Corned-beef and greens at the top; roast sirloin at the bottom; ham and boiled mutton, *vis à vis*, at the sides; and goose and turkey at the opposing corners. Dr MacTurk said grace, and the worthy divine's solicitations for a blessing were no sooner concluded, than the guests, with one accord, cried havoc, and commenced the work of destruction. Hector, Duncan, and Bell Geordy, felt that now was the tug of war, and trotted about the table with unwieldy alacrity, perspiring at every pore. " Duncan, a clean plate. "—" Geordy, fetch me a platefu' o' white soup. "—" Hector, rin for some o' the turkey. Get twa or three slices o' the breest. Mak haste, or the best o't will be gane, " were the sounds which on all sides met the ears of the assiduous triumvirate. At length the choler of Bell Geordy was roused by the number of simultaneous demands for his services; for, though acting as chief ministering angel on the occasion, patience was not numbered among his angelic attributes; and, standing stock-still, he exclaimed in a loud and angry voice, " What for do ye sit there, craik, craikin' a' at yae time? Ye ken weel aneuch I can sair but yin at yince, " wiping the dew from his forehead as he spoke. " Tak my word, ye'll come nae speed by't; and he that craiks the loudest shall be last sair't. "

The voice of the enraged Provost, who ordered him instantly to hold his peace and resume his services, silenced any further appeal on the part of Bell Geordy, who returned to his functions, but with a dogged air, and more leisurely than before.

Partial repletion had now blunted the edge of the hunger of the party, and voracity was reduced to appetite. Conversation commenced, and jocular remarks were heard and laughed at in the intervals of eating. I had the honour of sitting next Miss Jacky Shortridge, who, having spent a year at Mrs Blenkinsop's seminary for young ladies, at Doncaster, considered herself quite *au fait* in the manners of the best society in England. She expressed her regret, that those of her native city were deficient in that polish and elegance indispensable to a person of refined tastes and English education; that so few families in Glasgow kept carriages; that the theatre was so badly attended; and expressed strong hopes that " Pa " would allow her to spend next winter with her aunt, married to a cornfactor in Leith, who, of course, could introduce her to the first society in Edinburgh. The language of the Glasgow people she considered quite shocking to any person who had spent a year at Doncaster, and acquired the true attic pronunciation inculcated in Mrs Blenkinsop's academy. Miss Jacky too, was particularly kind and press-ing in her attention to my wants.—" Let me help you to some of thir collups. "—" Thae patties I can recommend. "—" Take a bit of yon turkey. "

My attention was soon diverted from my fair neighbour to a fat and jolly-looking person at the upper end of the table, who, from the comic twinkle of his eye, and a certain buffoonery of manner, I concluded to be a sort of privileged joker and a wit. His good things, of whatever character they might be, were proved by the expectation that sat on the countenances of those around him, and the guffaws by which they were followed, to be well adapted to the taste of his audience. Deglutition paused whenever this merry and obese personage gave symptoms of being pregnant with a joke ; and an elderly lady, who, relying on her age and constitutional gravity, ventured to neglect this precaution, paid the penalty of her rashness, in being nearly choked while in the act of eating, from the sudden and uncontrollable laughter into which she was thrown, by an unexpected explosion of his wit.

On the right of the Provost, sat a person who seemed to divide the admiration of the company with the " stout gentleman " at the other end of the table. His walk indeed was different. He did not attempt those broad and trenchant witticisms, in which lay the principal strength of his rival, but confined himself to story-telling, a department in which he shone without a competitor. In the narratives themselves I found little interest and no point, and had they been told by a less skilful narrator, would probably, even in Glasgow, have been considered flat and insipid. The principal charm of the performance appeared to consist in the invincible gravity with which incidents, at once coarse and trivial, were detailed, and the unrelaxed solemnity of visage maintained by the speaker, while laughter, loud and vehement, shook the sides of his auditors. To me all this was new, and I listened with curiosity, though not yet neophyte enough to participate in the enjoyment which it evidently diffused among the rest of the company.

The dinner was not, as is usual with such entertainments, served up in a succession of courses, and was without any of those little agremens which the middle classes in England consider necessary to their comfort. Sweets and solids simultaneously garnished and loaded the board, and, when removed, were succeeded by the wine and the dessert. The gentlemen now began to show evident signs of anxiety for the departure of the ladies, who on their part appeared by no means disposed to afford them the gratification they desired. In vain did the Lord Provost recur to the facetious expedient of drinking the health of the ladies in the character of " the outward bound, " and indicate his wishes by significant winks to his better half. The ladies openly expressed their intention of awaiting the introduction of the punch-bowl, and partaking of its contents, and they were at length only driven from their strong-hold by some coarse and indelicate jokes of Mr Mucklewham (the fat personage already mentioned), which indicated only too plainly the prudence and propriety of an immediate retreat.

The ladies were no sooner gone than Bell Geordy made his appearance, bearing a bowl of extraordinary dimensions, which he deposited on the table. Lemons, sugar, limes, rum from Jamaica, and the Leeward

Islands, soon followed, and expectation sat on every brow. It was not a
matter of easy arrangement by whom these ingredients were to be
mingled. The Lord Provost called on Mr Walkinshaw, but Mr Walkinshaw could not think of officiating in presence of so superior an artist as
Mr Mucklewham. Mr Mucklewham modestly yielded the pas to Major
MacGuffin; Major MacGuffin begged to decline in favour of Mr
Pollock; Mr Pollock in favour of Dr MacTurk, and Dr MacTurk once
more pushed the bowl to Mr Mucklewham, who, after many bashful
excuses, was at length prevailed on to "handle the china." I have
already noticed the solemnity and entire absorption of mind with which
this portion of the Bacchanalian rites is uniformly celebrated in Glasgow, but it was now for the first time that I became witness of the fact.
When the beverage had been duly concocted, at least an half hour
passed, during which the merits of the punch formed the sole topic of
conversation in the party. On this subject, even the most taciturn and
obtuse members of the company waxed eloquent. Whether the liquor
was too strong or too sweet, whether it would be improved by another
" squeeze of a yellow, " or an additional lump of sugar, became topics of
animated and interesting debate, in which all but myself took part.

Every improvement which human ingenuity could devise with
regard to the punch, having been at length suggested, the business of
drinking commenced in good earnest, each replenishing of the glasses
being prefaced by a loyal or patriotic toast by the Lord Provost. The
King, the Queen, the Prince of Wales, " the Trade of Clyde, " having
been drunk in bumpers, the current of conversation ws gradually
diverted into other channels. They were channels, however, in which
the bark of my understanding was little calculated to swim. The state of
the markets, the demand for ginghams, brown sugar, cotton, logwood,
and tobacco, were matters on which my interest was precisely equal to
my knowledge. There were jokes, it is true, and, judging from their
effect, good ones; but they were so entirely local, and bore a reference so
exclusive to people of whom I knew nothing, and manners of which I
really desired to know nothing more, that I found some difficulty in
contributing the expected quota of laughter, to the general chorus of my
more hilarious companions. My situation, indeed, was tiresome enough,
but I endured it for an hour or two, before I quitted the party, then
waxing deep in their cups, and joined the ladies in the drawing-room.
On my entrance there, it was pretty evident that I was considered an
unwelcome intruder. The female guests were gone, and the Lady
Provost had, in the assurance that none of the gentlemen would be
tempted to forsake the charms of punch for those of coffee and female
society, divested her head of its former splendid garniture, and substituted a cap of very homely pretensions in its room. Miss Jacky was
seated in front of the fire with her feet on the fender, apparently half
asleep, and Lexy was busily engaged in repairing a garment, which, on

my entrance, was hastily thrust under a chair, and obscured as much as possible from observation. The appearance of a gentleman in the drawing-room was indeed a novelty, and, under the circumstances, not a very pleasing one. After partaking, therefore, of a dish of cold tea, and exerting myself for some time to keep up a languid conversation, I wished the ladies good night, and departed.

As I retrod my way to the College, I reflected on the novel scene and characters I had just quitted, and when my head was on my pillow, the contrast rose strongly between that society in which I had recently mingled, and the calm and quiet elegance of my beloved home. In my dreams that night, I returned to Thornhill. My mother came forth to embrace me, with love beaming from her pale countenance, and even the welcome of my father was kind. There, too, was Jane with her dove-like eyes, and little Lucy, than whom

> No dolphin ever was more gay,
> Upon the tropic sea,

as, with beating heart and glowing cheeks, she ran to cast herself into my arms.

Such were the visions of the night; they were broken only by the sound of the College bell, which recalled me unwillingly to the more material world in which I was destined to move. After dressing by the cold hazy twilight of a winter's morning, I hurried across the College courts, more than ancle deep in snow, to my class. I was too late. Prayers were over, and the lecture had begun. The Professor lowered his huge eye-brows on me as I entered, and in a moment all my pleasing dreams were forgotten.

CHAPTER IX

Winc. And what's this Delaval?
Wife.   My apprehension
Can give him no more true expression,
Than that he first appears a gentleman,
And well conditioned.

English Traveller.

AT breakfast, Professor R—— appeared curious to know what impression had been made on me by the society into which on the day previous I
had for the first time been introduced. He laughed at the description I
gave of it, but said it was perhaps scarcely fair to judge entirely of the
society of Glasgow by the specimen I had already seen. " In this city, "
he said, " there are two circles. Of the one, which includes the great
majority of the mercantile and manufacturing aristocracy, I need say
nothing, since you are already, from actual observation, tolerably
qualified to judge for yourself. But there is another, a smaller circle, to
which you have not yet been introduced. It consists principally of those
who have united a taste for literature with the pursuits of business, and
have not merged all the higher powers of a rational being, in the
manufacture of muslins or the importation of tobacco. The individuals
of whom this circle is composed, are of course comparatively few, and,
like their neighbours, are not untinged with some ludicrous peculiarities. These are fair game, and may be laughed at; yet you will find that
in many essential points, they rise superior to the general body of society
by which they are surrounded. It is in this circle alone that the Professors
of the University ever mingle, and though not much in the habit of
frequenting it myself, I will take care, if your curiosity is not yet satiated,
to procure you an introduction. "

I thanked the Professor for his offer, and I accepted it; nor did I
neglect, during my residence in Glasgow, frequently to take advantage
of the introduction he was good enough to afford.

Nothing, I think, tends more to open the understanding, and enlarge
the mind, of a young man just entering on life, than an opportunity of
observing the manners, and tracing the prevailing current of thought, in
classes of society different from his own. In this will be found the most
efficacious antidote to that narrow bigotry, and those exclusive modes of
thinking, which seldom fail eventually to impair the understanding, by
circumscribing its exercise and expansion. Of minds originally endowed
with equal strength, his will be found best prepared to take a useful share
in the business of the world, of whom it can be said, that

" Mores hominum multorum vidit et urbes. "

But I would speak only of myself, and I know of no more useful branch of education to which I have been indebted, than that which I studied at the supper parties and coteries of the Glasgow dowagers.

The only companion with whom at this period my intercourse at all approached to intimacy, was Charles Conyers, who, like myself, was an inmate in the family of one of the Professors. He was a young Irishman, whom the death of his parents had freed, at an early age, from all moral control and guidance, and who had grown up from infancy to the verge of manhood, in the almost unlimited indulgence of every caprice. His guardians considered it their duty to protect his fortune, not to form his character, and suffered their ward to plunge into premature dissipation, if not without remonstrance, at least without any effectual restraint. It was, in truth, only owing to his own naturally generous disposition, that Charles Conyers had not become entirely a profligate. His very boyhood had been sullied by the precocious adoption of the vices of maturer age ; and he had attained a proficiency in loose and dissolute acquirement, apparently inconsistent with his years. With all this, however, he had not, as might have been expected, grown up into a cold and heartless rake. Far from it. He possessed all the elements of a fine and noble character ; and he displayed, when circumstances called it forth, a warmth and tenderness of feeling certainly incompatible with innate depravity of heart. To me he particularly attached himself; and there was a charm in the openness and gaiety of his disposition, which I found it impossible to resist. He was the very soul of whim and frolic, and possessed in perfection that peculiar humour and vivacity indigenous to the Emerald Isle. It is probable, that under other circumstances, this intimacy might have been attended by bad consequences. In Glasgow it was not so. Both Conyers and myself were framed of very ductile materials, and if our intercourse occasionally involved me in scrapes, and led me into situations certainly of very doubtful propriety, my influence with him was at least sufficient to prevent his lapsing into any of those grosser excesses, which he knew I could not but regard with disgust.

It is perhaps an advantage to Glasgow, as a seminary of education, that it affords none of the appliances of elegant dissipation. Nowhere else does Vice meet the eye so perfectly denuded of those external decorations with which Refinement too often succeeds in hiding her deformity. She there appears not as a young and captivating female, rich in guilty and seductive blandishments, but as a haggard and disgusting beldame. To be dissipated in Glasgow, one must cease to be a gentleman. He must at once throw off all the delicacy with which nature or education have invested him, and become familiar with the squalid haunts of low and loathsome debauchery. Youth cannot do this. At that age even the

visions of sensual enjoyment are mingled and connected with high intellectual excitement. In the very strength and ardour of his passions, there is safety. He contemplates the glowing pictures of love and beauty, which teem in his imagination; and he is guarded as with a sevenfold shield from the assaults of gross and vulgar pollution. In Glasgow, therefore, young and inexperienced as I was, my intimacy with Conyers had no tendency to produce an injurious effect on my character. To him, perhaps, it was of some benefit; for my principles, if not strong, were unshaken; and though I loved him, I was not blind to his errors.

Conyers was destined for the army, and spoke with enthusiasm of his prospects. In the passion for a military life, our hearts beat in unison. The sleeping embers within me were once more fanned into a flame, which burned even more fiercely than before. I was again agitated by doubts and apprehensions lest the wish nearest to my heart might meet the opposition of my father. It is true, he had formerly given his consent that I should become a soldier; but a sad change of circumstances had since taken place, and I was now an only son. It was probable, more than probable I thought, that my father's sentiments might have altered with regard to my future destination; and most fervently did I deprecate this the only contingent misfortune, which appeared in my imagination to cast a shadow on my prospects.

The father of Conyers was an officer of rank, who had served with distinction in the American war; and I listened with intense interest to the narratives of broil and battle with which he had been wont to amuse the childhood of his son. He told me tales of Washington, of Burgoyne, and of Cornwallis,—of ambuscades in the passes of the deep eternal forests, and of the destruction of gallant armies by enemies whom they could not see, and consequently could not resist. And then Wolfe and the siege of Quebec! What would I not have given to have stood but for a brief space, sword-girt by his side, on the red heights of Abraham! He spoke, too, of Minden and its field of glory, where the pride of France was humbled, and her banners trodden in the dust, till the battle rose before me, and I saw the dragoons charge on with harquebuss and gleaming sabres over the dying and the dead.

"Down with the Fleurs de Lis, and wave the banner of St George! Bravo the Green Horse! The Enniskillings are plunging on through the morass on the right—God prosper them!—There go the gallant Evelyn's brigade!—The enemy wavers!—Charge home, in the name of Old England!—Now the Guards take them on the left flank!—Hurrah! the field is our own, and a sun of glory that shall never set, is gleaming on the arms of my country!"

It is with a smile on my lips, yet with something of melancholy in my heart, that I recall these sallies of strong though boyish enthusiasm. The glow of feeling which produced them soon faded, and is long since gone. It comes but once in the spring of life, and never lingers long.

In this manner was it that the communion of our hopes and wishes added mutually to their intensity. Towards one point did all the aspirations of my spirit converge. In one absorbing desire were garnered all my powers and energies; and opposed to this, I felt that even filial duty and obedience would be but as dust in the balance. God might change my purpose—man could not shake it.

CHAPTER X

Braken. Why looks your grace so heavily to-day ?
Clarence. Oh, I have spent a miserable night,
So full of ugly sights, and ghastly dreams,
So full of dismal terror, was the time.
Richard III.

NEITHER my studies nor amusements, in whatever degree I was engrossed by them, had the effect of rendering me less attentive to my uncle. As
our intercourse became more intimate and frequent, I was able to
penetrate the rough husk of his character, and discover many estimable
and even amiable qualities, for which the world had never given him
credit. It was owing to the circumstances in which he had been placed,
that the better feelings of his nature had remained dormant, while its
lower and baser principles had been called into habitual exercise.

David Spreull had entered life penniless and friendless. He had been
left to jostle his way through a crowd of scheming and designing men,
ever prompt to betray the unwary, and turn their neighbour's weakness
to advantage. Trade, when combined with poverty, narrows the heart,
while it sharpens the understanding. It had this effect upon my uncle.
To compete with such rivals as I have described, it was perhaps necessary to adopt their weapons ; but the deeper energies of his character had
led him further. In all the arts of money-making, he had overtopped his
instructors ; and though rigid in his adherence to the established code of
mercantile morality, had left no means of acquisition unemployed, in
advancing the one great object of his life. Among those around him, he
had the character of being sharp in trade ; that is, one who considers all
advantages fair in a bargain, and who is known to be as incapable of
defrauding a creditor, as of forgiving a debtor. All his successes had
been the produce of cold, dispassionate calculation, of deeper forecast
than was possessed by those around him, and of a steady and un-
deviating adherence to the course prescribed by his own interest, wherever it might lead. Cut off, too, from his family and relations, by distance
on the one hand, and unkindness on the other, his heart had no object
which might fill the void of its affections. Unconsciously, perhaps, he
had long sought for something to love, but he had not found it ; and the
warm feelings thus repulsed from without, remained only in a state of
deeper concentration within. Thus had his heart become soured ; and all
nobler and better principles of action, if not eradicated, were at least
blunted by long inertion. He was not,—I am sure he was not, a miser ;
yet the habitual desire of acquisition still governed his character, and to

amass wealth continued the sole object of his age, as it had been of his youth. His life had been passed in a crowded city, yet he had lived a solitary man, and he knew and felt himself to be so.

Such was the character, and such the circumstances, of my uncle, when I arrived in Glasgow. There was something about him to me so new and original, as at first to excite my curiosity and interest. These soon ripened into attachment; and the old man was gratified to find himself, for the first time in his life, the object of disinterested regard, in spite of that external repulsiveness, of which he could scarcely be unconscious. There was something, perhaps, in the youthful artlessness of my deportment towards him, which bore with it convincing test-imony that my attentions had their origin in no sinister motive. He felt this; and I soon became to him an object of regard and interest, which till then he had never known. There was a native though uncultivated power of intellect about him, which induced me often to court his society. I dined with him frequently; and though my visits to the counting-house were generally considered idle interruptions of business, and sometimes treated as such, even these troublesome attentions were, I believe, not unacceptable. Nor was it uncommon, that after business hours, he would consent to take in my company the unusual relaxation of a saunter in the Green, or a walk down the banks of Clyde, to the pretty and rural village of Govan.

Girzy, too, regarded me with complacency, and was most strict in her injunctions that I should always give her previous intimation of my intention to dine with my uncle. " When ye're gaun to tak your denner wi' us, " said she,—" and the oftener ye do that, the mair welcome ye'll be,—just gie me three or four hours' notice, and gin there's onything better than anither in the toon o' Glasgow, my certy but ye shall hae't. But dinna come stravaigin' in aboot four o'clock, takin' folk a' by surprise as ye did afore, and allowin' nae time to mak things nice and comfortable, as I ken you English aye like to hae them. " By giving her the desired promise, " I calmed her fears, and she was calm, " though I believe I was never very rigid in my observance of it.

These dinner parties were occasionally much enlivened by the pres-ence of Conyers, who was gifted with strong powers of humour, and a certain light-hearted jocularity, which frequently forced even the satur-nine visage of my uncle to relax into a smile. He was not slow in establishing himself in the good graces of the old gentleman, who was always pleased whenever I could prevail on him to form an addition to our party. On one of these occasions an occurrence took place which merits prominent record in this portion of my narrative.

One evening, when Conyers and myself had partaken of Girzy's good cheer, and my uncle was sedulously engaged in the task of the scientific mixture of a second bowl of punch, a letter was brought in and placed on the table, to await his leisure for perusal. He was apparently unwilling to disturb the social enjoyments of the festive board, by the introduction of business. " It maun be by the Greenock mail, " said he, " which is later than usual to-night. I daresay it's just frae that sumph Bailie M'Phun, about the twa puncheons o' rum that leakit oot on board the Lord Melville, and cam hame little better than twa empty casks, and yet the Custom-house folk want to charge duty on them, the same as they had come hame fu'. I'm makin' the punch the now, and canna be fashed to put on my specs; sae, Cyril, as your een are baith younger and better than mine, ye may read it, and gie me an inkling o' the contents, which will do just as weel as if I read it mysel. " I obeyed the old gentleman's directions, and taking the letter, read aloud as follows :—

" *To* DAVID SPREULL, ESQ. MERCHANT,
Spreull's-land, Trongate, Glasgow.

" *Auchterfechan Manse.*

" DEAR SIR,

" I AM commissioned by his inconsolable widow, to communicate the mournful intelligence of the death of your worthy brother, the Laird of Balmalloch, which took place last night, at seventeen minutes past eleven o'clock. For a week before his death, he had suffered sorely from a diaray, which wasted him down to a perfect skeleton, and left nothing for Death at last but a mere rickle o' bones. His spirit, poor man, passed away easily, for he lay in a dwam for many hours, from which he only wakened to find himself in Abraham's bosom. This is a gruesome loss to his wife and childer; but I am glad to say they are supported by Providence under this sad dispensation, and submit to it with a resignation most edifying to behold. You being the nearest male relation, Mrs Spreull begs you will sign the funeral letters for next Tuesday, and make any arrangements you think proper. I remain ever, your sincere and sympatheesing friend,

" Dear Sir,
" ARCHIBALD M'CRAIK. "

While I was engaged in reading this letter, my uncle was silent. When his ear first caught the intimation of the death of his brother, his frame was shaken by a sudden and convulsive tremor; the lemon, which he was in the act of squeezing, dropped into the punch-bowl, and he threw himself back in his chair, where he remained immovable, with his face covered with his hands. We both saw that he was greatly agitated, and felt as if either sound or motion on our part, would have been an unwarrantable intrusion on his sorrow. The perfect stillness of the apartment was broken only by the breathing of my uncle, which was thicker and more laborious than usual. A few minutes passed in this manner. At length, raising himself in his chair, and stretching forth a hand to each of us, he said, " Gang your ways hame, my bonny lads, the house o' mourning is no the place for you. I wad be alane the night. Cyril, ye may call to-morrow morning, gin ye like; I'll be able to speak to you then, which I canna do now. Sae good night, and may God bless you baith. " Having thus given us our valediction, he once more covered his face, and relapsed into his former attitude.

We departed quickly and silently as possible, but had scarcely reached the passage, when we were assailed by the watchful Girzy. " Lord saf us, Maister Ceeral, ye're no awa ? ye surely canna hae finished the bowl already ? and ye've no gotten yer tea yet—it's a' just ready to gang ben, sae just stap back, and I'll hae't maskit in a minute. I really think it's no that kind o' Mr Spreull to let you awa this frosty night, wi' sae little either o' meat or drink to keep out the cauld.—Maister Conyers, I houp it's no you that's takin' him awa at thae untimeous hoors ? Ye'll just bide whare ye are, and get yer tea, like good laddies, afore ye pit yae fit out ower the door the night. I ken weel, you young men may gang to waur places than ye're in the now, and I maun tak' a mitherly charge o' ye baith, " said she, locking the outer door and securing the key in her pocket; " Na, na, ye maun just bide a wee. "

This resolute determination of Girzy, who was probably rather annoyed that the " *cookies* " she had provided for tea should be left untasted on her hands, knowing, though no logician, that " *de non apparentibus, et de non existentibus, eadem est ratio,* " drew forth an explanation of the cause of our sudden departure. She no longer, on hearing this intelligence, opposed our egress, but gave vent to her surprise in sundry ejaculations connected with the melancholy event. " Hech, and the Laird's dead at last !—Weel I wat, death micht hae taen a haurl o' them that cou'd hae been warse spared !—I'se warrant Mr Spreull will be gaun' to the funeral, and the snaw lyin' on the ground.—Hech, sirs, we should be a' mindfu' o' our latter end, baith auld and young ! " and Girzy looked towards Conyers and myself, as if to intimate that the wisdom of this moral aphorism was intended for our especial benefit.

On the following morning I called on my uncle according to his desire. I was met at the door by Girzy, who informed me that he was still in bed. She had, she said, " been maist driven oot o' her five senses, by the gruntin' and grainin' he had keepit up a' night; it was awsome to hear till him, puir man, pechin' and sighin' wi' his sair trouble. An' a' this blessed day, " said she, " neither bite nor sup has gane ower his thrapple; but what's mair extraordinar, he's ordered me no to set fit within his chamber door; sae when I want to ken aboot him, I'm just obliged to keek through the key-hole—but at ony rate, I'll tell him ye're here. "

So saying, in violation of the express injunction of her master, she ventured to enter his chamber, and inform him of my arrival, trusting, perhaps, for the pardon of her disobedience, to the agreeable intelligence of which she supposed herself the bearer. I was soon directed to enter, and found my uncle, as Girzy's information had led me to anticipate, in bed. He stretched forth his hand to me as I approached, and having ordered Girzy " to steek the door on the outside, " he desired me to "ease myself, " at the same time pointing to a high-backed elbow-chair that stood near to the bed. His head was enveloped in a Kilmarnock night-cap, the hue of which had once perhaps been a bright scarlet, but which had then certainly degenerated into a dark and dingy crimson. His face was more than usually gaunt and cadaverous, and from the heaviness of his eyes, and the absence of that *vivida vis*, by which his countenance was generally marked, it was not difficult to perceive, that he had passed a night of mental suffering and agitation.

" Ye're a kind laddy, Cyril, " said he, " ye're a kind and good laddy, to come and sit at the bedside o' a crabbit and cankered auld man. "

I, of course, disclaimed any merit on this score, and expressed my sympathy for the loss he had sustained, and by which he seemed so deeply affected.

" Maybe, " rejoined he, " the death o' an auld man, aboon threescore and ten, can hardly be called a loss, to a brither that hadna seen nor spoken to him, for mair than forty years. Death has now separated us for ever ; but there was a separation between us worse than death while he lived. We were brithers, Cyril, but ye may be ken we were never friends. The strife o' blood relations is no like the enmity of ither folk. It cuts deeper, and the wounds it leaves are cankered and ill to cure. I needna tell you how our difference began, though till now I have aye thocht the wyte o't didna lie wi' me. Nae matter for that now. Yet, as God knows my heart, had I been in his place, and he left like me, a penniless and younger brother, we might have lived and died in love and charity. "

As he said this, the old man turned from me in the bed, seemingly in strong emotion, and a silence of some minutes ensued. I assured him of my sincere sympathy in his sorrow, but requested him not to dwell on a subject which occasioned such deep agitation.

" It's a relief to me to speak, " rejoined he, " and my heart feels easier when disburdened of its load. To naebody on this wide earth but you hae I ever spoken o' my troubles. May you never feel, Cyril, the pangs and the reproaches under which I now suffer, from the dourness of my own heart. He was unkind, but I was hard and unforgiving. Nay, were he even now to appear before me in the flesh, I fear I might still turn from him in anger. But he is gone before his Maker, where I must shortly follow him, and resentment canna reach beyond the grave, though mine, God forgive me, has followed him till his. "

Here his voice was again choked, and he turned himself once more toward the wall and was silent. I too was agitated. There is a blind propensity in our nature, to participate in deep emotion of any kind, and I felt its influence at that moment. To a spirit so perturbed, I felt it would be impertinent in me to offer either condolence or consolation. I took the old man's hand, and pressed it in mine; and when, after a considerable interval, he again turned towards me, I saw that the veins of his forehead were turgid, and his eyes bloodshot. For some hours I sat by his bed-side, and he became gradually calmer, and the storm by which he had before been so powerfully stirred, at length subsided.

The task of making the necessary arrangements for the funeral devolved upon him, and I think he experienced relief from having it in his power to offer this, the last and only tribute to his departed brother.

By his dictation, I wrote to Bailie Cleland all suitable directions with regard to the conduct of the funeral; and letters of invitation having been prepared by one of the clerks, and signed by my uncle, were dispatched to all the friends of the family. It was likewise arranged, that on the Monday following, we should set out for Balmalloch in a mourning coach, in order to attend the obsequies of the Laird.

CHAPTER XI

But when return'd the youth? The youth no more
Return'd exulting to his native shore;
But fifty years elapsed, and then there came
A worn-out man.

CRABBE.

With easy roads he came to Leicester,
And lodged in the Abbey.

Henry VIII.

IN a few days, the shock occasioned to my uncle by his brother's death, in a great measure subsided. His sorrow, if it did not pass away, was at least calm and silent, and the tortures of self-reproach, under which he had at first suffered so deeply, gradually softened into feelings of melancholy regret. He did not again speak on the subject of his brother; little change was observable in his deportment, and his countenance gave no indication of internal suffering.

On the morning fixed for our departure, I breakfasted with Mr Spreull, and the meal was scarcely concluded, when the arrival of the mourning coach, which was to convey us to our destination, was duly announced. The vehicle in question was one of preposterous dimensions, apparently crazy from age, and drawn by two long-tailed black horses, which would have done no discredit to the team of the Newcastle waggon. The driver was a red-faced and facetious-looking person, suitably clad in sables, and mounted on a coach-box decorated by a hammer-cloth of black calico. The work of packing the baggage in the carriage now commenced, under the special superintendance of Girzy and myself. Mine consisted only of a small portmanteau, and was easily disposed of. This was not the case, however, with my uncle's. I could scarcely refrain from laughing, when my servant and Sanders Mac-Auslan appeared laboriously descending the narrow stairs, bearing with difficulty between them an enormous hair-trunk, about the size of a meal-girnel, fortified at every corner with iron plates, and the letters D. S. conspicuously traced in brass nails on the lid. Honest Jehu stood aghast at this unlooked-for addition to his load, and appeared sorely puzzled as to the mode in which the transit of this ponderous appendage was to be effected.

While we were yet engaged in such meditations as may be supposed to have occupied Mr Belzoni when he first contemplated the removal of the Memnon, our cogitations were interrupted by the appearance of my uncle, who came to inspect the travelling arrangements.

" Deevil tak the woman, " exclaimed he, exasperated at the heavy marching trim in which the faithful Girzy was about to dispatch him ; " why, here's baggage enough for a regiment of heavy horse. Do ye think, born tawpy as ye are, that I'm gaun a voyage to the Indies ? Why, that kist's about half freight for an American lumber-ship. Just tak it back, and pit me up a change o' linen in a napkin. I declare the woman's little better than a bedlamite ! "

Against the execution of these orders Girzy strongly entered her protest. She declared she would on no account allow him to travel at this season of the year, so slenderly provided with necessaries as he desired. To do so, she said, would be a wilful tempting of Providence. Who could tell that he might not be seized with one of those attacks of cramp in the stomach, to which he was so liable. He might get wet and require a change of clothes. He might——But it is unnecessary to follow Girzy through all her supposed cases of contingent misfortune. She concluded, however, by positively declaring, that the things could not now possibly be unpacked ; but were that even practicable, the trunk contained not one iota that could be spared. As a proof of this, she said it contained " only nine couls, a dizen sarks, fifteen—— "

" Nine couls, and a dizen sarks ! " exclaimed my uncle, impetuously interrupting her ; " do ye think, gowk, gomeril, and idiot, as ye are, that I can use nine couls, and a dizen sarks in twa days ! But there's nae use in speaking to a senseless tawpy, that can neither understand reason nor common sense; " and he walked away in anger, leaving Girzy mistress of the field, and still determined to carry into full execution her schemes for the comfort of her master. After some delay, the trunk, which had been the subject of so much perplexity and contention, was with difficulty placed on the roof of the coach, where it was secured by about twenty yards of new rope, which Saunders M'Auslan provided for the occasion. This addition gave the vehicle a singular and picturesque appearance, which on the journey did not fail to attract abundance of attention.

At length the carriage was reported ready. Peter (for such was the coachman's name) had already mounted the box, and my servant who was to accompany us, stood with his hand on the carriage door, ready to enclose us in its lugubrious cavity. But the cares and importunate anxieties of Girzy still impeded our departure. She had succeeded by her eloquence, in prevailing on my growling companion, to invest his legs in a huge pair of galligaskins of her own knitting, and to encase his higher regions in the greatcoat and comforter, from which I had on a previous occasion suffered so severely. Fortunately for me, the establishment boasted no duplicates of the latter articles, but this was not the case with regard to the galligaskins. A second pair was speedily produced, with which I was forced to decorate my person, as the only condition of my peaceable departure. The invention of Girzy, too, was not slow in discovering a succedaneum for a greatcoat, in her scarlet duffle cloak, which, without unnecessary parlance, she threw across my shoulders, and tied carefully in front. Making a merit of necessity, I submitted with a good grace, and in this trim proceeded to the carriage, aware that I should there speedily enjoy the means of ridding myself of these encumbrances, without obstruction. Girzy, followed by Jenny, descended to the street to see us seated in the carriage. Before we were suffered to enter it, however, its scanty appliances for comfort underwent a rigid examination. "Hoot, tout," exclaimed Girzy, feeling the seat-cushions as she spoke, "this will never do! Jenny, rin up and fesh twa cods frae the bed;—just wait awee," continued she, addressing my uncle, "for ye ken sharp banes and hard brods are but ill neebours."

Here the old gentleman lost all patience, and his eyes glittered with passion.

"As I've a soul to be saved," exclaimed he, in a voice more than usually gruff and discordant; "as I've a soul to be saved, if either you or her, that's sumph enough to do your bidding, offers to come near me wi' cods, or ony ither sic nonsense, ye shall fin' the weight o' my staff on your crown.—Come awa, Cyril, loup in, for the woman wad rouse the corruption of Job himsel."

I obeyed, and was instantly followed by my uncle.

"Will ye no hae a blanket to keep your legs warm?" inquired Girzy, still perseveringly intent on her unwelcome demonstrations of kindness, and poking her head into the carriage as she spoke.

"Steek the door, and be d—d to you," was the only answer vouchsafed to her query; and the coach at length getting fairly into motion, Girzy's parting injunction, "Poo up the glasses, for the wind's snell," was half drowned by the rattling of the wheels as they whirled over the causeway.

We were four hours in reaching Dumbarton, but the scenery through which our road lay was so beautiful, that I did not regret the slowness of our progress. In my journey down, I had passed the border after night-fall; and as the mail reached Glasgow by day-dawn on the following morning, I had till now seen nothing of Scotland, but that city and its vicinity.

Every object, therefore, of the landscape around me possessed the charm of novelty, in addition to its own natural attractions, and I now for the first time gazed on scenery, than which the most vivid creations of my youthful fancy were not more impregnated with beauty.

I had never seen before, and I have never seen since, any river which for natural beauty can stand in competition with the Clyde, along the northern bank of which our journey lay. Never did stream glide more gracefully to the ocean, through a fairer region. The scenery of the Thames above London is occasionally beautiful, but the beauty is of a tamer and less striking character. It is one which I, at least, can regard without any deep or lofty emotion, which never haunts me in my dreams, nor rises unbidden to my memory in distant lands. There Art divides the palm with Nature, and the latter must be satisfied to wear but half the diadem.

For the first few miles of our journey, the scenery, though rich, was not peculiarly striking. The surface of the country was varied only by gentle undulations, like the bosom of a summer sea, when the wind which agitated its waters has died away. But as we advanced, the hills became gradually more lofty ; rugged and precipitous rocks gave occasional variety to the scene, and everything indicated our approach to a more mountainous and sterile country. At length the Castle of Dumbarton, on its pyramid of solid rock, rose in stern grandeur to the view, and on our arrival at the Inn, I was not sorry to learn that a halt of two hours was considered necessary, as an opportunity was thus afforded me of visiting this ancient and interesting fortress. Finding my uncle by no means disposed to join in the excursion, I sallied forth alone, and by the assistance of the parish " Betherel, " who acted likewise in the capacity of Cicerone to strangers visiting the Castle, found no difficulty in the gratification of my curiosity. Not the least interesting object that I beheld that morning, was the sword of the stalworth and heroic Sir William Wallace ; and, unable as my feeble arms were to wield it aloft, I yet felt pleasure in grasping its massive hilt, and repeating the beautiful invocation of John Finlay, beginning—

" Thou sword of true valour, though dim be thy hue,
And all faded thy flashes of light. "

The view from the summit of the Castle was beautiful and extensive. On the opposite side of the Firth was Greenock and its forest of shipping, the shore studded with villas, and far down, and scarce distinguishable to the eye, the blue mountains of Bute mingled with the horizon. Roseneath Castle, and its beautifully wooded isthmus, formed a prominent object of the nearer landscape ; and high up among the clouds, towering in solitary grandeur, rose the snowy peak of Benlomond. But I had little time to bestow on objects of mere pictorial beauty, and aware of the irritable disposition of my companion, hurried back to the Inn, fearing that my protracted absence might in some measure have disorganized the arrangements for the journey.

On my arrival, however, I fortunately found this had not been the case. My uncle was placidly engaged in reading the newspapers ; and the steeds being declared by the driver to be sufficiently refreshed, we once more entered the mourning coach, and set forward on our journey.

Our course now diverged from its former direction into the interior of the country, and we caught occasional glimpses of the river Leven, a beautiful and rapid stream, immortalized in tuneful song. My uncle,

who had been silent and abstracted during the first part of our journey,
now became more communicative. It is true, he had no great taste for
the sublime and beautiful; and the objects to which he was generally
anxious to direct my attention, were not those in which I was inclined to
feel the greatest interest. " That, " said he, pointing to a large building
on the banks of the Leven, — " that is the printfield of Tod and
Shortridge; and there, aboot a mile ayont it, are the works of Dal-
quhurn. Now ye get a keek o' a yellow house through the trees; that's
Cordale, just a wee paradise o' a place, where the shrubs and the grass
are clippit twice a-week, and the plants against the wa', just look as if
they were kaimed and brushed every morning. Mony a funny and a
happy day hae I spent there in auld times. "

We now approached Loch-Lomond; and as we did so, I became
more occupied with the remarkable objects which presented themselves
as we advanced, and less attentive to my uncle's details. The influence of
the scene, however, was not wholly unfelt even by him.

The old gentleman became silent, and gazing across the waters,
embedded in the vast amphitheatre of hills, kept his eyes fixed on the
rugged side of Benlomond, as if the more distant and sterner features of
the scene were more congenial to his spirit than the softer beauties of the
nearer landscape.

Evening was now fast approaching, and our progress had been so
slow, that it was declared by Peter impossible to reach the point of our
destination within the compass of anything like " timeous hoors. " It was
judged necessary, therefore, that we should pass the night at Luss, and
set out at an early hour on the following morning for Balmalloch, which
was still thirteen miles distant.

Night had set in before we reached the inn of Luss. The family were
evidently unprepared for so unwonted a circumstance as the arrival of
guests after night-fall, at this season of the year. A Scottish country inn
is but a bad house of entertainment at any time; but, taken at such a
disadvantage, the probable cheer of guests unexpected as we were, may
be safely calculated at a point not far transcending zero. When questioned with regard to his accommodations, the landlord was evidently at
a nonplus, and confessed the poverty of his larder with more ingenuous-
ness than is at all customary with his more southern brethren, when
occasionally involved in a similar dilemma. We were not disposed,
however, to be very exorbitant in our demands; and understanding that
the bill of fare consisted only of eggs and a rasher, directions were
instantly given for their expeditious preparation.

We were at first ushered into the kitchen, where the family were
assembled round a large peat fire, until another apartment could be
prepared for our reception. This was soon done by a smart and pretty-
looking girl, whose activity and exertions for our comfort were noticed
favourably by my companion, who patted her on the back, and saluted

her with the endearing appellation of " a braw sonsie lassie. " Her speedy appearance with the supper tended to increase still more the benignity of his regards, and he observed to me in a whisper, " My troth, Cyril, but that's a clever quean. "

Never was meal dispatched with greater relish. The old gentleman tossed over, as with a pitchfork, about a dozen of eggs and a couple of pounds of bacon, with incredible dispatch; and the sharpness of the mountain air made me almost regard with envy his unparalleled facility of deglutition. I followed him, however, if not *passibus æquis*, at least with a pertinacity and endurance of appetite, more than sufficient to save my distance; and though I only ranked second in the race, it certainly was not *longo intervallo*. With respect to potables, we had no reason to complain. Ale, porter, and the genuine " mountain-dew, " were all that heart could desire in such a situation, and with these the landlord's cellar was copiously furnished.

With such appliances to good fellowship, we grew mutually communicative and agreeable, and I had fairly got into the middle of a lecture on drags, bag-foxes, covers, double ditches, and five-barred gates, notwithstanding sundry signals of somnolency exhibited by the old gentleman; when he at length interrupted my discourse by observing, " What's a' that ye've been speaking about, Cyril, for the last half hour? for, to say the truth, I've been sae overcome wi' drowsiness, I havena heard yae word ye've been saying. Just begin wi' your story again, and tell me a' about it. "

Under such circumstances, this obliging invitation was declined, and the chambermaid was summoned to show us to our sleeping apartments. This was a summary proceeding; for the damsel aforesaid, on receiving our directions, merely opened the doors of what had till now appeared to be two closets in the wall of the supper-chamber, and informed us, that in these crevices we were to find our accommodation for the night. This arrangement appeared neither to surprise nor discomfit my uncle, who directed his trunk to be brought up to the apartment. This, however, was found impracticable. In the first place, it would have been an operation of extreme difficulty to remove it from the elevated position it at present occupied, on the roof of the coach. In the second place, we were assured that the stair was considerably too narrow to afford a passage for this unwieldy appendage. The old gentleman, therefore, was obliged to content himself with uttering a few hearty curses on Girzy and her officiousness, and to receive from my portmanteau such temporary accommodation as its comparative poverty could afford. These matters were soon arranged; the beds were apparently clean, and the loud and sonorous snoring of my companion soon gave evidence of his being wrapt in slumber.

By sunrise we were again upon the road. I beheld his first rays gild the summits of the mountains, and watched his increasing altitude, till the bosom of the Loch at once received and reflected the full glory of his effulgence. It was a sight of memorable beauty. Our route lay along the margin of the Loch, till we reached Tarbert; but here we struck into another and less-frequented road, which wound for several miles through the deep and solitary passes of the surrounding mountains. I never travelled on a more execrable road. Large masses of granite were scattered on its surface, and opposed most unpleasant and dangerous obstruction to the passage of a carriage; and it was intersected at numerous points by small mountain streams, which had worn deep channels in its bed. With such obstacles, our progress was necessarily slow, and to ease our bones, which already ached with the jolting they had endured, we determined to proceed on foot to Balmalloch, which was distant but a mile or two.

Every object that now presented itself, appeared linked in my uncle's mind with the recollections of his youth. As we proceeded, he pointed out to me the rivers where he had delighted to fish,—the woods in which he hunted the roe,—the hills where he had shot the ptarmigan, or chased the wild deer. An absence of half a century had apparently blunted no feeling, obliterated no early association. He had quitted these scenes, a poor and almost friendless boy, he now returned to them an aged and a wealthy man. It is true, there had been a dreary interval between, which, perhaps, he would then willingly have forgotten. But it could not be. The objects he beheld around him, were all indissolubly united with the memory of youthful vigour, and enjoyment unalloyed by the worldly cares and anxieties, which, in later and less happy days, had preyed on his heart. His youth and age were not " bound each to each, by natural sympathy; " there appeared nothing in the scenes around him, to link together those distant periods of his life, to connect the thoughtless and happy boy, with the infirm and grey-headed visit-ant of these mountain regions. The objects he again beheld, could not but suggest to him the contrast of what he then was, and what he had been in former days, nor fail to embitter the consciousness of present feebleness with the memory of past power. How forcibly and how naturally are the melancholy associations of youth remembered in age, expressed in the following stanzas of Wordsworth:—

> " Down to the vale this water steers,
>   How merrily it goes!
> 'Twill murmur on a thousand years,
>   And flow, as now it flows.
>
> " And here, on this delightful day,
>   I cannot choose but think,
> How oft a vigorous man I lay
>   Beside this fountain's brink.

" Mine eyes are dim with childish tears,
　My heart is idly stirr'd,
For the same sound is in mine ears,
　Which in those days I heard.

" Thus fares it still in our decay;
　And yet the wiser mind
Mourns less for what it takes away,
　Than what it leaves behind. "

Perhaps I am fanciful in attributing to the old gentleman such feelings as I have now attempted to describe; for certainly he did not express them. I could only observe, as he gazed around him, an uneasy wandering of the eye, and certain sudden and abrupt pauses in his hurried and animated descriptions of the different objects that presented themselves as we advanced.

We now approached a small village, or what, in the vernacular language of the country, is termed a Clachan. Every ragged urchin in the place was abroad to see us pass. Their mothers, too, desisted for a while from their household occupations, and peeped forth on us from door or cranny, and aged grandsires, seated on stone benches by the road, or supporting their tottering limbs with a staff, respectfully vailed their bonnets, and saluted us in Gaelic. The sound seemed for a moment to stir the heart of my uncle like the blast of a trumpet. On hearing it, he stopped suddenly short, drew a long breath, and made an answer in the same language. I thought he gazed on the aged countenances around him, as if trying to recognise among them some of the " old familiar faces" he remembered in his youth. No signs of recognition, however, took place on either side, and having passed the Clachan, the road entered a very thriving plantation, which, I was informed, constituted part of the " policy" of Balmalloch. A rude gate, formed of wood covered with the bark, admitted us to an approach of a few hundred yards in length, which led directly to the house.

It was a dark stone building, of that order of architecture which Highland lairds appear to consider most akin to beauty, and rose in the majestic form of an inverted chest of drawers. Slow as our progress had been, we had outstripped the coach, and consequently, the family had not yet received notice of our approach. The door of the mansion stood open; but my uncle, who apparently did not wish to take advantage of the facility of entrance thus afforded, preferred giving notice of our presence by a sonorous application of his walking-stick. The signal was speedily answered by a female servant in mourning, who, on receiving intimation of our names, ushered us into a small parlour, and retired to give information of our arrival to her mistress. On her departure, my uncle cast a quick and hurried glance round the apartment, and then retiring to a window, stood there, either occupied in silent meditation, or in gazing on the objects without.

After a short interval, the maid again made her appearance, and said her mistress would be happy to receive us up stairs. We were accordingly ushered up to the apartment of the ladies. On our entrance, we were received by the mistress of the house, who removed a white handkerchief from her eyes, and addressed my uncle in plaintive accents:—

" I'm happy to see you at Balmalloch, Mr Spreull, and you too, Mr Thornton. Oh, but this is a hard and a sair dispensation upon us a'! A sair bereavement, Mr Spreull, for his poor widow and children; but it is aye a comfort, as Dr M'Craik says, that he has exchanged this sinfu' world for anither and a better, though, hech sirs, it's a waesome loss to them he's left ahint him in this vale of tears! "

To this lachrymatory address the old gentleman felt it incumbent on him to make some reply; and while he was engaged in delivering his tribute of condolence, I had time to glance round the apartment and observe the company. Mrs Spreull appeared to be a hale and florid old lady, whose health had by no means suffered from her recent affliction; and having said and done on the occasion all that she considered suitable and becoming, her five daughters next came forward to welcome their relatives. The epithet *young*, applied by their mother to these ladies, appeared to me exceedingly gratuitous. In truth, they constituted a series of mature virgins, of whom the youngest could scarcely be under thirty, nor the oldest less than fifteen years her senior. As they successively greeted their uncle, Mrs Spreull announced their names. " That's Peggy, your auldest niece. She's been sair fashed a' this bygane winter wi' the lumbago. That's Jean, my second daughter; and that's David, your namesake; and that's Archy; and that's Thomasina, the youngest, she's aye been reckoned the very image of you; and the poor Laird used to like her the best for that reason. "

The masculine names of some of these ladies occasioned, on my part, some surprise. But I was afterwards informed that it is by no means uncommon, especially in the Highlands, to bestow on girls the name of any male relative, whom it may be considered prudent to propitiate by such an incongruous demonstration of respect.

Mrs Spreull now requested a private audience of my uncle, with the view of speaking " anent the funeral ceremonial, " the time appointed for which was now at hand. The old folks accordingly retired, leaving us younger ones, who were all included in the general appellation of " bairns, " alone in the apartment. I entered into conversation with my fair cousins. I found that all of them were good-natured, and several not wanting in a certain rustic intelligence. The melancholy circumstances of the family, of course, imposed restraint both upon the manner and the matter of our intercourse. It was frequently interrupted, too, by the entrance of female servants, who whispered, generally loud enough to be heard, some new and pressing necessity of the establishment, or un-expected misfortune in the kitchen. Each of these messages occasioned the exit of one of these matronly virgins, who, judiciously, had not deemed it necessary to merge their attentions to the living in their duties to the dead. My uncle did not return, and conceiving that my presence, in the pressure of these household duties, might be an inconvenient restraint, I begged permission to retire to my apartment, in order to arrange my toilet previous to the melancholy ceremony, the hour of which the striking of the house-clock announced to be at hand.

CHAPTER XII

Let such honours
And funeral rites, as to his birth and virtues
Are due, be first perform'd.
                    DENHAM's *Sophy*.

ON descending, I found my uncle in the large apartment destined for the
reception of the funeral guests, a few of whom had already assembled.
The chairs were closely ranged round the room, in order to afford as
much accommodation as possible to the large party who were expected
to grace the funeral of the Laird. The sideboard supported a cold round
of beef, and a mutton-ham, flanked by whisky on one side, and wine on
the other. My uncle occupied the chair nearest the door, and I was
directed to fill the one immediately on his right. He rose from his seat,
and bowed on the entrance of every new guest, who now arrived in such
numbers as speedily to throng the apartment. Unaffected as I was by
any strong regret for the death of a person whom I had never seen, it was
not entirely without curiosity that I regarded the scene around me. A
deep silence, broken only by an occasional cough or blowing of the nose,
reigned in the apartment. Every countenance was moulded into a most
lugubrious expression ; and in moving to their seats, the guests walked as
if treading on eggs. All eyes were bent on the ground, and not a whisper
of conversation was suffered to enliven the general and pervading gloom
of the meeting. The silence was first broken by one of the undertaker's
men, who entered, and pronounced in a sonorous voice, " The Rev. Dr
M'Craik of Auchterfechan will ask a blessing. "

This call was obeyed, and a long prayer repeated by the Doctor ; after
which, wine, and whisky, and biscuits, were circulated round the apartment by the servants. Suddenly the stillness which had reigned till now
was changed into clamour and vociferation. " Mr Spreull, your good
health. "—" Your good health, Mr Thornton, " burst from a hundred
voices at once, in every variety of loud and discordant intonation.
" Drumshinty, here's to ye. "—" Garscud, your health. "—Glen-
" scadden, better health to your wife. "

When the noise and bustle had in some degree subsided, following the
example of my uncle, I rose, and bowing round the room, drank the
health of the assembled guests. Many of these had come from a considerable distance, and now gave proof of the sharpness of the mountain air,
by the ferocity of their attack on the solids displayed on the sideboard.
Of these assailants, I was one. We had neglected the precaution of
breakfasting at Luss before starting, and since last night's supper my

abstinence had been unbroken. It would have been indecorous in my uncle to have betrayed any symptoms of appetite on so mournful an occasion; though, from the occasional direction of his glances towards the theatre of action, it struck me he would, under other circumstances, have been well satisfied to become a participator in our labours.

The repast was briefly dispatched, and another minister, whose designation I cannot recall, was called on to return thanks. This he did in a pithy prayer and exhortation; after which, preparations immediately commenced for the progress to the churchyard. This was not distant above a mile, and the procession was on foot.

The body was carried on the shoulders of six stout Highlanders, and the piper of the family played a coronach, or lamentation for the deceased, as we advanced, which, wakening the echoes of the high and solitary hills through which we passed, had a solemn and impressive effect. My uncle, with little apparent indication of deep emotion, followed his brother's head to the grave. The other pall-bearers were myself and the Lairds before-mentioned of Lamlash, Garscud, Drumshinty, and Glenscadden. As we passed, the whole population of the neighbourhood appeared to line the road, a procession so splendid being evidently no every-day occurrence. The shepherd vailed his bonnet and looked down on us bare-headed from the hill, and the lambkins of his flock, which had sportively approached the road, as if to gaze on the passing wonder, darted off on our approach, half in fear, half in the wildness of their glee, to their bleating dams in the uplands.

The church towards which our steps were directed, stood the solitary tenant of a mountain glen. It was a small, rude, and unornamented structure, built of the masses of granite which had fallen from the rock, or been gathered from the bed of the stream. It was only distinguishable from an ordinary dwelling-house, by the projection of a small belfry from the roof, and the absence of all external sign of human habitation. The churchyard, in the midst of which it stood, was surrounded by a low wall, or rather what is called in Scotland a "drystane dyke," and contained few external marks to denote it a place of sepulture. Few of the graves could boast a headstone, and fewer still an inscription, and but for the obtrusive pretensions of a large obelisk-shaped monument, erected, as the stone bore testimony, by an inconsolable widow of the neighbourhood to her beloved and lamented husband, it presented nothing to arrest the casual glances of the passer by.

In this unpretending receptacle, the burying place of the Spreulls was separated from those of the meaner parishioners, only by an iron railing, and its site was plainly indicated by the new-dug grave. Within its precincts did we deposit the remains of the Laird of Balmalloch, with that absence of all ceremony in which rigid presbytery delights. Neither in advancing across the church-yard to the grave, nor when the tressels were removed, and we finally committed the body to the gaping earth, could I detect any visible accession of emotion in the countenance or deportment of my uncle. But when this last duty was performed, and as a parting mark of respect, the company had uncovered, and stood bareheaded for a brief and mournful space, and the death-music, if I may so call it, of the clods rattling on the coffin, broke harshly the surrounding silence, then, and then only, did I observe a convulsive shudder pass over the frame and the countenance of the old gentleman. It seemed to come suddenly as a shock of electricity, and to pass like one, for in an instant it was gone, and he stood calm, rigid, and unmoved as before.

We remained, as is the custom, in the church-yard, till the grave-diggers had completed their task, and then turned homeward. My uncle walked alone, and as I did not think proper at such a time to intrude my society on him, I was not displeased to have an opportunity of gratifying my curiosity by entering into conversation with some of the Highland lairds as we returned to Balmalloch. There was no want of cordiality in the address of these gentlemen.

" A sad office ye've come upon, Mr Thornton, " said Mr Lamont of Drumshinty, rather a hard-featured old gentleman, with a powdered head and an enormous queue ; " I didna expect to have laid Balmalloch in the mouls for these ten years to come. Why, it's just a fortnight come Friday since he dined at the half-yearly meeting at Dumbarton—I never saw him better in my life, nor make a better use of baith glass and knife and fork. Neither he, Auchintorlie, nor myself, went to bed afore twa in the morning, though Balmalloch, to be sure, for twa or three hours before that, just sat in his chair and dozed like a peerie. Poor man, he's really a loss to the country, and his worthy widow must find a sair want o' him. "

In these sentiments the other lairds appeared very cordially to join, and I gathered from the context of the dialogue, that my deceased relation was one of those very worthy persons, whose character admits of praise in the gross, but affords no prominence sufficiently tangible for eulogium in the detail.

On our return to the house, it was not difficult to discern that arrangements were making for a splendid banquet. The savoury steams of roast and stew, mingled with other less prominent culinary odours, pervaded the mansion from the cellar to the attics, and the whole establishment were evidently engaged in active preparations for the entertainment of a large party. A funeral in the less populous districts of Scotland, is always followed by a feast, and the walls, which in the morning heard but the voice of grief and wailing, at evening generally echo the sounds of Bacchanalian merriment.

While the guests were amusing themselves, some by conversing in the drawing-room, (if a small and rather rudely-furnished apartment may be so called,) and others by strolling into the fields, and examining the condition of the cattle and the barn-yard, I received a message from my uncle, to desire my presence at the ceremony of opening the will.

On obeying, I found the ladies of the family, my uncle, Dr M'Craik the parish minister, and Mr MacFie, the writer from Dumbarton, all assembled, and ready to proceed to business. The grief of the ladies appeared to have sustained some accession since I last saw them. They were all decorously seated with handkerchiefs at their eyes, and frequent sobs and long-drawn sighs gave evidence of the intensity of their sorrow. Mr MacFie now proceeded to open the scrutoire of the deceased, and search for the important document in question. After some rummaging among charters of infeftment, instruments of sasine, heritable bonds, account sales of cattle and black-faced sheep, it was discovered and read aloud. It directed, in case of the testator dying without male issue, that the estate of Balmalloch should be sold, and the interest of the proceeds equally divided among his daughters: To his widow he bequeathed an annuity of three hundred a-year, in addition to the sum to which she was already entitled by her marriage-settlement. The trustees appointed by the testator, were Provost Aulay MacAulay of Dumbarton (probably a descendant of the very amusing personage commemorated by my friend Galt;) his brother David, to whom, in token of forgiveness of his unchristian and unbrotherly conduct, he bequeathed his bamboo cane and horn snuff-box, adorned by a Scotch pebble on the lid; and his old friend, Peter Murdoch of Glasgow, a very worthy and influential merchant of that city, to whose use the sum of five guineas was directed to be appropriated, for the purchase of a mourning-ring. The laird, it appeared, died rich. An inventory of his property found among his papers, showed it to amount to something over £15,000, exclusive of the estate, which might be expected to produce nearly double that sum. Altogether, therefore, my fair cousins were to be regarded as heiresses, perhaps the greatest in the whole county of Dumbarton, a distinction, on which it would argue more than female humility, to suppose they did not pride themselves.

The business of reading the will being concluded, another, almost equally important, succeeded on the tapis. It was now the hour of dinner, and on our return to the drawing-room, we found the party assembled in tolerable force. It consisted chiefly of those persons of whom mention has already been made, a considerable body of lairds, whose names I have forgotten, the doctor, and man of business.

The dinner was plentiful, and well suited to the character of the guests. The ladies, of course, did not appear, and the honours of the table were performed by my uncle, by whose orders I acted as croupier. Unluckily the primary duties of the office thus imposed on me, consisted in carving a huge round of beef, on which the demands of the company were more numerous and frequent than my strenuous exertions were capable of supplying. My toil indeed seemed "never ending, still beginning, " for my tormentors returned pertinaciously to the charge, and round of beef was voted by the whole party as the *ne plus ultra* of good living, especially when garnished, as in the present case, with the decorative adjuncts of turnips and cabbage.

" Bless me, " at length said an old red-faced gentleman on my right, laying down his knife and fork after the discussion of four platefuls of beef,—" bless me, Mr Thornton, ye're getting nae dinner — I've but a small appetite and am doing nothing, so pray let me assist you and take that round off your hands. "

I did not hesitate a moment in accepting this welcome offer of assistance, and gladly consigned the remains of the dish to the care of my ruby-visaged neighbour. With regard to my own dinner, the board was all before me where to choose, and really choice was not very difficult at an entertainment which could boast salmon of the very finest quality, and profusion of grouse, ptarmigan, and black game. These were luxuries, however, too common in this quarter to be much prized, and in the estimation of the present company, evidently yielded the pas to dishes of much lower pretension, and more vulgar name.

While dinner was on the board, and the servants remained in the apartment, everything went on with regularity and decorum. My uncle did the honours of the table with a degree of propriety and good-breeding, for which, to say the truth, all I had hitherto seen of him had not prepared me. From a coarse and vulgar humourist, habituated to the unrestrained indulgence of every whim and peculiarity, he was now become a finished gentleman of the old school; equal in all respects, superior in some, to the best of those by whom he was surrounded.

There does, or perhaps rather there *did*, exist in Scotland a strong and undisguised dislike between the landed and the mercantile interests. The former, of course, consider their trading rivals as beings of an inferior caste, and are inclined to regard both them and their pursuits with a contempt and aversion which they are at little pains either to qualify or conceal. The latter feeling, if not the former, is not unreturned by the men of trade, who profess themselves equal in all respects to their acred antagonists, and are little disposed to conciliate them by any supererogatory demonstrations of respect. Little intercourse, therefore, is generally kept up between these bodies ; the pride of the traders feeling sorely outraged by the aristocratic haughtiness of the lairds, and the lairds waxing very wroth at the vulgar and ostentatious luxury affected by their purse-proud rivals. I mention this for the purpose of showing, that on the present occasion my uncle had rather a difficult part to play, in presiding at an entertainment composed of country gentlemen, and in which he was the only person present connected with the pursuits of commerce.

The first toast given from the chair of course was the King. The Laird of Arncraik then proposed the health of Mrs Spreull, and the ladies of the family, to which toast my uncle returned thanks, and expressed his acknowledgments to those gentlemen who had conferred honour on the family, by their attendance on the funeral of his deceased brother.

These formal preliminaries being passed, the meeting soon began to assume something of a more hilarious character. The bottles circulated rapidly, the solemn circumstances connected with the entertainment were forgotten, and the funeral banquet might easily have been mistaken by an uninitiated observer, for a marriage feast.

Nothing pleases a boy so much, as to find himself placed among men, in a situation of some consequence and authority. I felt this on the present occasion, filling, as I did, the important office of vice-president or croupier. My spirits became elevated, I drank bumpers, acted as toast-master, pushed about the bottles, and proposed fining more than one individual in a bumper, for filling on a heeltap. These sallies were well received, and drew on me the eulogiums of many of the party, who began to fear, that they would not find in the example of my uncle either a stimulus or excuse, for that excess to which they were desirous of extending their potations; and were glad, therefore, to avail themselves of my example on the occasion. Much discourse on the prices of black cattle, many discussions on the state of county politics, and facetious stories at the expense of eccentric and unpopular neighbours, were interrupted by my noisy and obtrusive discharge of my functions. I made speeches, and roared catches of songs, slapped elderly gentlemen on the back, called them hearty old cocks, and was guilty of a thousand extravagances, the offspring of a brain heated by powerful and unwonted stimulants.

Suddenly I remember my sight grew dim, and there was a loud rushing as if of many waters in my ears. The room, the company, table, bottles, glasses, all danced before my eyes, and were whirled rapidly round as if in a vortex. A deadly sickness came over me, and a cold and clammy perspiration stood on my forehead. I rose and staggered to the door, followed by the smiles of the old stagers, who probably anticipated such a finale to the part I had been playing. With difficulty I reached the passage, on which I met one of the maids, whom I dispatched for my servant, but before he arrived I had fallen insensible on the stair.

When I came again to my recollection, I found myself in the apartment of the ladies, who were kind and assiduous in their attentions. One held a smelling-bottle to my nose, another bathed my temples with cold water, and the old lady had just denuded me of my neckcloth, and was opening my shirt-collar. I had been sick, very sick, and was altogether in a most pitiable predicament. In a short time, however, I recovered sufficient muscular power to enable me, with the assistance of Coker (my servant), to reach my own apartment, where that trusty functionary, after assisting me to undress, deposited me in bed for the night.

Before I fell asleep, I remember the sounds of carousal were loud in my ears. The more seasoned vessels of the party below had now begun to feel the effects of the stimulus, under the influence of which I had succumbed, and the mingled noise of mirth and angry disputation echoed through the mansion. It came, however, softened by distance, like the fitful howlings of the wind, or the voice of the waves bursting afar off on the shore, acting as an efficacious somnolent on senses already stupified by over-excitement.

I slept like a top, and woke, as usual in such cases, with a parched throat and a burning brow. The morning sun shone brightly through my casement, and I determined to cool my fever by a walk before breakfast, and the enjoyment of the mountain breeze. I dressed, therefore, as quickly as possible, and descended the stair. The family were not yet risen, or at all events were not visible, and I encountered no one but the house-maid, busy in her matutinal vocation.

I was tempted *en passant* to take a cursory peep at the dining-room, which had been the scene of my last night's follies. It exhibited certainly a most deplorable spectacle. The relics of the carousal still remained unremoved. Everything was in confusion. The table was covered with jugs, bottles, and glasses, some partially filled, and many broken. A dish or two with the remains of salt herrings, and a vagrant fragment or two of oat-cake, showed of what the supper had consisted. The chairs, some overset and otherwise injured in the fray, were scattered round the apartment, which was redolent of a certain disgusting odour of debauchery, to be felt, not described : an effluvium particularly offensive to one, whose present feelings induced him to regard the orgies of the preceding night with disgust and nausea. Prostrate on the floor, with the hearth-rug rolled under his head for a pillow, lay one of the party fast asleep, snoring loudly. Another, wrapped in a tartan cloak, lay stretched on several chairs, which served him for a couch. He stared at me with a vacant look, and muttered some unintelligible sounds, which showed that his faculties had not yet fully emerged from their eclipse.

To look on such objects was to behold dissipation *in puris naturalibus*, to catch drunkenness in dishabille. The scene carried with it a sort of obtrusive morality, not at such a moment very pleasant, and I gladly turned from it, to sally forth into the pure air of the morning.

The scenery around Balmalloch was wild and beautiful. The house stood near the foot of a mountain called The Cobbler, from some fantastic resemblance in its outline, certainly not obvious to an uninitiated eye. Near it there were other smaller and wooded hills, and a mountain stream which flowed through a deep and lonely dell, the precipitate and lofty banks of which were clothed with the birch and alder. Moutain scenery, in addition to its own natural and inherent beauty, was armed in my eyes with all the charms of novelty. It seemed as if now for the first time I learned to form conception of the sublimities of nature. I joyed in the acquisition of a new sense, and felt that an enlargement of my faculties had been coetaneous with my visit to Balmalloch.

I had spent fully two hours in wandering in the valleys, and on the hills, before I thought of returning to breakfast. Exercise had new-strung my nerves, and given more than its wonted edge to my appetite before I reached the house. I found the ladies in the breakfast-room, and a considerable congregation of the guests. It was impossible to meet the former without emotions of humiliation and shame, for the condition in which I had been indebted to their good offices on the night before. I stammered something of an apology, which they appeared to consider very unnecessary, and treated the whole affair as a trifle.

Their good nature afforded some relief to my sensibility on this subject, and enabled me to turn my attention from myself to those around me. In none of them were there observable any marks of indisposition, proceeding from the excesses of the preceding night. It is true, the eyes of several of the elderly gentlemen were a little bloodshot, but this symptom was accompanied by no apparent diminution either of appetite or vivacity.

The appearance of none of the party, however, had improved by their night's sojourn. Little attention had been devoted to the toilet; many had evidently not washed, none had undergone the super-erogatory decoration of shaving. Their clothes, too, were unbrushed, and from the wool adhering to them, it was evident that several of the wearers had gone to bed without the ceremony of undressing.

But the breakfast!—Who has not heard of a Scotch breakfast? No one. But till now I had never beheld that (in England) trivial meal in all its native glory and attraction. Surely even the mouth of Apicius or Dr Kitchiner might venially water at the following bill of fare. Kipper, herrings fresh from Loch Long, pickled trouts, venison and mutton hams, cold grouse and ptarmigan, oat cakes, barley and flour scones, a large tureen of milk porridge (which appeared in considerable request), several kinds of sweetmeats, and a huge vessel charged with the genuine mountain dew. Could the eccentricity of human appetite devise any useful or agreeable addition to a banquet composed of such ingredients? I imagine not—to me, at least, it appeared that

" The force of fancy could no further go. "

But such a breakfast is a thing to dream of, not to describe; to be treasured up and survive unfading in the memory, not to be obtrusively emblazoned by pen or pica.

Suffice it, therefore, that due honour was done to the repast; that saddle-horses were brought to the door, and the tramontane guests gradually departed, singly or accompanied, till my uncle and myself were once more the only guests in Balmalloch.

CHAPTER XIII

They say this town is full of cozenage,
As—nimble jugglers that deceive the eye,
Disguised cheaters, prating mountebanks,
And many such like libertines of sin.
Comedy of Errors.

——Thou now exact'st the penalty,
Which is a pound of this poor merchant's flesh.
Merchant of Venice.

THE day succeeding the funeral was spent by my uncle, in obtaining minute and accurate information relative to the state of the deceased Laird's affairs, and concerting the future arrangements of the family. In all matters of business and accounts, he was particularly clear-sighted and acute, and a few hours' application sufficed to furnish him with all the requisite information. Towards Mrs Spreull and her daughters, his manners and deportment were uniformly benevolent, and unmarked by any of those exacerbations of temper to which he was habitually liable. He showed an anxiety to contribute, by every means in his power, to their comfort, and assured them, his best exertions would in no circumstances be wanting, for the promotion of their interest. Still, I could not but remark, that in his intercourse with these ladies, there was a calmness in his manner, and an utter absence of that warmth and cordiality with which from the first he had distinguished me. To me, who knew him, it was evident, that he considered himself engaged in the performance of a duty which he was called upon sacredly to discharge, but that he was not urged on to this, by any strong sentiment of personal regard. In truth, the old gentleman was not partial to the fair sex, and had an uncommon aversion to all elderly single ladies, a designation under which his nieces were not without some claim to be included. Yet there was nothing about them calculated to excite aversion. Good-natured they certainly were, perhaps a little vulgar and outré. But ridicule can only be attracted by pretension, and that quality was scarcely predicable of my fair cousins, as I saw them at Balmalloch.

While my uncle was busied in the examination of papers, I mounted a pony which had enjoyed a sinecure since the death of the Laird, and rode forth to enjoy, if possible, a more extended view of the beautiful scenery in the neighbourhood, than had come within the scope of my morning's ramble. Ignorant of the geography of the country, I left the choice of road to the taste and sagacity of the pony, and really the beauties of the one he selected, left me no reason to regret this proceeding. Nothing, I imagine, can be much more sublime than the valley of Glencroe, up which my steed directed his steps; in after life, at least, I have seen no spot which so powerfully excited my imagination. Scenery of features more desolate and gigantic — more indomitable to the influence of man—on which Nature has set more legibly the seal of eternal barrenness—where is it to be found?

Perhaps I have dwelt altogether too long on this short visit to the Highlands, unmarked as it must be to the reader, by any peculiarity of interest, and disproportioned in importance to many of the future scenes in which I must be called on to act and suffer. Yet these are the portions of my life on which most I delight to dwell. They are armed with no sting,—they recall no melancholy remembrance,—no deep and poignant regret—such as are too inseparably linked with many of the busier and more active parts of my career. Bear with me, then, I pray you, gentle reader, when you find me dull and prosy, and inditing, for your punishment, long stories ending in nothing. I am given, I confess it, to a little tediousness and prolixity; yet, for the life of me, I can tell my story but in one way, and that way is my own.

The remainder of the day and evening, on my return to Balmalloch, passed heavily enough, notwithstanding the expressive glances of Miss Thomasina's eyes, and the lavished blandishments of her smiles. I remembered brighter eyes, and sweeter smiles, and was proof to the fire of her artillery. The next morning was fixed for our departure; and after partaking of another breakfast, similar in its attractions to the one already described, my uncle's huge trunk was once more elevated to the roof of the coach, and bidding adieu to the family at Balmalloch, we set out on our return.

The journey was attended with nothing remarkable; my uncle, between his naps, was comparatively pleasant and companionable, and we reached Glasgow shortly after dark. During the greater part of the last stage he had been involved in a sound slumber, to which I afforded no interruption, and it was not till we had passed the long and hideous suburbs by which Glasgow is on all sides surrounded, that his ideas were recalled by the flickering of the lamps, and the noise and jolting of the vehicle, as it leisurely advanced over the rough and ill-paved streets. There was apparently something congenial to the old gentleman's disposition, in the busy hum of men. His habits and predilections were strictly urbane; there was nothing rural in his cast of thought, and the noise and bustle of the city, (considerable even at so late an hour,) seemed to act as an instant stimulus in recalling his energies, and concentrating his ideas. The absence even of a day or two, appeared sufficient to invest the accustomed objects which he again beheld, with additional interest and novelty. As we passed, he gazed earnestly into every shop, and seemed as if endeavouring to read in the countenances of the pedestrians who thronged the streets, whether any occurrence of importance had taken place during his absence.

The stopping of the carriage, at length indicated the completion of our journey. I cast my eyes upwards to the windows of the house, but all was veiled in darkness. The head of the faithful and attentive Girzy was not visible, as I expected it would have been, and not even the glimmer of a taper was discernible in the interior. The coachman descended from his box, and assisted us to alight, while my servant ascended the stair, to give notice to my uncle's dilatory domestics, of our arrival. On being released from durance vile (for vile durance travelling in such a vehicle literally was), we followed his steps, and found him battering loudly at the portal of the dwelling, without any signal being afforded of the presence of inhabitants within. " What's a' this ? " vociferated my uncle as we gained the landing place of the stair. " What's come ower thae twa neer-do-weel kimmers, in the deevil's name ? Are they fou' or asleep ? Haud awa, " said he addressing the servant, " haud awa, and let me try to wauken up the guid-for-naething hizzies. I'se warrant I'se mak' them hear on the deaf side o' their heads. " So saying, he advanced to the door, and accompanied a sonorous application of the knocker with such ejaculations as the following, uttered in a key loud enough to have awakened the dead:—" Girzy, I say Girzy, open the door, ye limb o' Satan ! are we to be keepit here standin a' night on the stairhead, while ye're dosing like a tap ? come and open the door directly, ye buckie of Belzebub. " To this emphatic adjuration no answer was returned, and a similar address to Jenny produced no greater effect.

It was now evident that both the females in question had evacuated the premises, and the anger of my uncle exceeded all bounds. In truth, his wrath was not without some shadow of excuse. Instead of a comfortable reception in his own house, to be denied admission altogether, and kept standing both cold and hungry on a common stair, when he reasonably calculated on enjoying the full restoration of his domestic comforts, might have afforded apology for an unusual excitation of bile, in a person neither very choleric nor easily irascible. Provoking as the situation was, it was necessary to devise some expedient to mitigate its inconvenience. The first idea that suggested itself, was that of breaking open the door, and effecting forcible entrance. But *cui bono ?* The house was untenanted, the fires probably extinguished, and the keys of everything, whether esculent or potable, in Mrs Girzy's pocket. This project, therefore, was speedily abandoned, and, after considerable deliberation, it was determined that the luggage should be deposited in a neighbouring shop, while we proceeded in quest of a comfortable supper to a tavern. My servant was directed to hover round the premises, and give the errant housekeeper the earliest possible notice of our return, and the inconvenience which her absence had occasioned. These arrangements being effected, we set forth in search of the Regency Tavern, (my uncle's favourite house of entertainment,) his indignation finding vent in frequent ebullitions by the way.

It is an old proverb, and I have generally found it a true one, that misfortunes never come single, and the occurrences of this evening afforded no contradiction to the truth of the adage. We had not advanced above the length of a street or two, and my uncle had just got into the middle of a long and hearty imprecation on Girzy, and denunciation of those "deevil's cantrips" which had led her abroad at so unseasonable an hour, when we encountered a fat, jolly-looking person, who immediately accosted my companion—"Bless me, Mr Spreull, is this you? a sight o' you in the streets at this time o' night, is a thing no seen yince in a twalmonth. I thocht ye had been awa *plantin* the Laird yer brither in the mouls." This address, the irreverent tone of which, it may be presumed, was not much in accordance either with his temper or feelings, still afforded an opening for the narrative of Girzy's delinquency too favourable to be neglected. On learning that we were bound for the Regency, Baillie Lapslie (for so was this jolly gentleman designated,) immediately volunteered to join the party, an offer which my uncle, anxious to learn all the news, accepted.

Our supper was a good one, Mrs Golder, the landlady, civil and assiduous in her attentions, and Baillie Lapslie made several efforts at wit, which showed at least his inclination to be facetious. Whether the irritation of my uncle might or might not have yielded to a combination of such agrémens, is, and must ever remain a moot point; for a new cause of discomposure was speedily interposed to prevent the restoration of his mental equanimity.

"Well, Baillie," said my uncle, while engaged in the act of compounding his first tumbler, "ye maun tell us a' the news. How did cottons go off at Wednesday's sale? are boweds looking up, and rum selling with more spirit than it did last week?—Is there anything in the Tontine list about the David Spreull, of whose arrival at Demerera I expected to hear before now? I ettle the underwriters are beginning to shake in their shoon about her. Four months since she left Greenock, and naething either seen or heard tell o' her sin syne. Sorry would I be that ony ill had happened to her, though, in point of loss, I'm safe enough, for she's weel ensured, baith ship, freight, and cargo."

"In regard to news," returned Baillie Lapslie, "there's no muckle o' ony kind, and little or no variation in the markets frae last week; sugars may be a shade higher, and cottons a thocht lower, but nae change worth the mentioning. At the coffee-room this morning, naething was talked of, but the stoppage o' Penny and Trotter, wha, they say, will not pay a shilling in the pound."

"Penny and Trotter!" exclaimed the old gentleman, in a loud and angry voice, his eyes flashing fire, and vehemently striking the table with his clenched fist,—"Penny and Trotter bankrupts—ay, that's what they may ca' them in the Gazette,—but thieves, rogues, and swindlers, is what I'll take care they shall be ca'ed everywhere else. Let them try to get a certificate frae me—let them see whether I'll agree to their discharge—let them come, wi' pitifu' speech and long faces, yammerin and fleechin about their wives and young families, wi' their offers o' composition o' yin, twa, three, ay, or even ten shillings in the pound, and see what comfort they'll get frae me. "

I had never before seen his evil passions called so fully into play as at this moment. All the bitterness of his nature seemed to be collected in order to be discharged at once on the unfortunate Penny and Trotter. So unexpectedly had this violent ebullition broken forth, and so apparently uncalled for did it appear, that something of the ludicrous involuntarily mingled with it in my imagination. If I smiled however, it was un-observed, and I remained a silent spectator of a scene in which I had no inclination to take a part. The Baillie soon made rejoinder, though apparently somewhat awed by the deep and vehement excitement his intelligence had raised in the old gentleman.

" Hoot, Mr Spreull, ye shouldnae tak on sae, although ye are maybe in for a thousand or twa ; ye ken sic things maun happen in trade, and are just to be tholed by us a'. Your losses at yae time, ye ken, are made up for by your profits at anither ; an' weel I wat sic a loss might have fa'en on them that's less able to bear it than yoursel, had it been a thousand for every hunder. "

" For losses in the fair way of business, " replied the other, " I lay my account wi' them like ither folk, and can bear them as weel as my neighbours ; but to be cheated, robbed, and swindled by a fair-faced and dishonest scoundrel, is what I am called upon to bear neither by British law nor Christian morality ; and baith Mr Penny and Mr Trotter will maybe find, to their cost, they could not have selected a worse subject for siccan an imposition, than David Spreull. "

" Lord bless us ! " rejoined the Baillie, who did not appear more than myself to comprehend the gist of my uncle's accusations, " I'm sorry to hear ye talk in that dour and bitter way, aboot the poor folk. What waur are ye aff in the present business than fifty mair, less able to bear their losses than yoursel ? Penny and Trotter hae stoppit payment, and ye're a creditor o' the concern, which, if a' that's said be true, is no likely to make much return. There's naething extraordinar in a' this, though a body would think, frae the violent and flytin' way ye speak o' them, they had clappit a pistol to your breast and robbit you on the highway. "

" Clappit pistol to my breast and robbit me, say ye ? " vehemently rejoined my uncle—" to do that requires spirit and courage, and these puir miserable deevils have none. Wad ye even chiels like thae, wha come to swindle you wi' a smooth tongue and a girnin gab, to a fair and open robber who demands yer siller on the King's highway ? *He* comes at least in his real character of an open enemy, and perils baith life and soul for the miserable pittance he gains by his unprofitable trade. Such a man I neither hate nor despise; and whatever means I may think myself bound to take for the recovery or preservation of my property, he has my best wishes to escape from the gallows in this world, and the deevil's claut in the next."

"Weel, weel," exclaimed the Baillie, perceiving all contention on this matter to be hopeless, and willing, at least, to know the simple facts of the case, " it's weel ken't, Mr Spreull, that there's no a langer head in the toon o' Glasgow than yer ain; and trying to cheat you, is like suppin' kail wi' the deil, it needs a lang spoon no to come aff second best. But you forget that neither Mr Thornton nor I, ken ony of the particulars of the case."

Upon these, at last, Mr Spreull condescended to enter, and it soon appeared that the head and front of the offending of Messrs Penny and Trotter, consisted in incurring a debt of three thousand pounds to the old gentleman only a few days before, when it was scarcely possible to suppose them ignorant of their impending insolvency. This, to say truth, was provoking enough, but perhaps would not so vehemently have excited the old gentleman's passions, had the deception not involved, besides pecuniary loss, an imputation on his sagacity, and exposed him to the mortification of having it known to the world that he had been duped. To a man of his substance, indeed, the loss did not carry with it any serious inconvenience, and it is but justice to state, what I afterwards learned, that in this case, according to the old Scottish saying, " his bark was waur than his bite," and that his better feelings did not suffer him to carry his threatened vengeance into effect.

Instruments so ill in tune as my uncle, the Baillie, and myself, could not be expected to produce a very harmonious concert, and the excellent Glenlivet of the Regency wasted its powers in vain. At length the party broke up, and having wished the Baillie good night, I accompanied the old gentleman home, in order to see him once more installed in his domicile. All the way he spoke not a word, and we were ascending the stair, when Girzy, now on the alert, appeared on the landing-place, bearing a candle to light our steps. Aware of the advantage of offensive operations in a case like the present, she determined to carry war into the camp of the enemy, and lost no time in coming to the scratch.

"Weel, I'm glad to see you hame again, baith o' ye," said she, as we advanced, " though yin wad hae expeckit better things frae a man o' your years, than to be takin' folk by surprise at this gate. Couldna ye hae just drappit me a line to let me ken ye war comin' the night, and I might hae had a gude comfortable supper ready for you and Mr Ceeral? But this is no the first time ye hae sair't me sae, and I maun e'en say it's really a daft-like proceeding."

This fire of Girzy's stern chaser was answered, as might be expected, by a whole broadside from her enraged antagonist, who, taking advantage of his heavier metal, poured in both shot and shell with such destructive energy, that the Girzy bomb lay at length a mere log upon the water, much damaged both in hull and rigging, yet disdaining to strike her colours. In the course of the engagement, however, the facts of the case were elicited, which were briefly these.

Girzy's talents as a "howdie" were held in much estimation by a large circle of matronly acquaintance, and as we are naturally partial to that pursuit in which we excel, Girzy by no means shunned any opportunity that offered for the display of her obstetrical talents. In the present instance she had been induced to desert her post, by a pressing message from the wife of Deacon Dinwiddie, stating that she had just been "ta'en wi' her thraws," requesting a visit from her friend, and expressing much apprehension that she was destined to "hae a sair time o't." Girzy could not resist this golden opportunity for the exercise of her skill, and seized it with all the avidity of a dilettante practitioner. She had not gone forth, however, on the exercise of her high vocation, without issuing special injunctions to Jenny to remain a close tenant of the house during her absence, and desiring that she might receive the earliest information in case her master should arrive in the interval. No sooner, however, was Girzy's back turned, than Jenny sallied forth to hear the "clash o' the toon," from her companions at the West-port Well. Such were the causes of this domestic uproar, which threatened to involve consequences of the most serious nature to the whole of Mr Spreull's establishment.

"An' what business hae ye to be concerned in any such matters? are there no doctors eneugh in the town, without your setting up for a howdie? think ye it's a guid reason to gie a man, when he's just come aff a journey baith cauld and hungry, and finds his ain door steekit in his face, that he maun cool his cuits on the stair-head, because Mrs Dinwiddie's ta'en wi' her thraws?—the deevil thraw baith you and her! But it's just as weel that ye should understand yae thing, that my housekeeper's no to be trotting after every kittling wife in the parish, and gin ye canna mak up your mind to mind your ain business, and leave the care of cleckin' wives to ither folk, ye had better just pack up your duds and seek a place that will suit you better, for here ye shall not stay, ye may just tak that in your lug."

At this, as it appeared to Girzy, unprovoked and gratuitous threat, she waxed wroth.

"Na, Mr Spreull," exclaimed the indignant matron, "gin ye want to part wi' an auld,—ay, and though I say it that shouldna say't, a gude servant, ye hae just to say the word, and I'se warrant ye shall soon hae a toom house o' me. Just speak, and in hauf an hour's time, I promise you I'se darken yer doors nae mair; and gin this is a' that's come o' twenty years hard and faithfu' service,—for takin' tent o' ye baith day and night—in health and sickness,—for guidin', and managin', and scrimpin' a' things to save yer substance,—if this be a' the thanks I'm to get for a' my service, I here tak Maister Ceeral to witness, that I'm ready to shake the dust frae aff my feet at yer door, and rather die in the aulmshoose than eat the bread, even for anither day, o' sae doure, cauld-hearted, and thankless a maister. "

"What for do ye gang on like a gomeril at this gait?" rejoined her master, not a little taken aback by this unexpected effervescence of female spirit; " wha wants ye to gang gin ye like to stay——— "

"What for do I gang on, ask ye," interrupted Girzy, determined to keep her vantage ground, " what for do I gang on at this gait? — rather tell me what for is a' this stramash?—What for do you come hame like a fury, wi' yer een on a low, and a voice louder than Bell Geordy's, and tell an auld servant to gang her gait, because she happened to be no just in the hoose when ye arrived at an unexpected and untimeous hour frae the country? Oh, Mr Spreull, but ye're a doure and a hard man, and that a' the warld says o' ye. But fare ye weel; for a' that's come and gane, " here she softened her voice, " I wadna part wi' ye in ill bluid; there, tak the keys, " producing, at the same time, a large bunch, and extending her hand with them towards her master, " there, tak the keys, ye'll find a' things right; and fare ye weel, for beneath your roof-tree I shall na sleep anither night. "

Whether Girzy really intended to take her departure, or whether this was merely a rhetorical artifice, is beyond my fathom to determine. But the very idea of such an event, so utterly unlooked for, was evidently not a little appalling to my uncle. If artifice it was in Girzy, never was artifice better supported by external demonstrations of truth. She had assumed, in the course of her speech, a stately port and demeanour, to her unwonted. A look of high resolve sat throned on her brow, as she stretched forth her hand with the keys to her astonished master.

"What, in God's name, Girzy, mak's ye speak such haevers as ye've been bletherin' for the last five minutes, and what for do ye keep raxin' the keys, as if I wanted them frae ye? Gie us nae mair o' your clishma-clavers, but gang ben the house, and gin ye dinna think better o't in the morning, I'se warrant you'll find nae objections on my part to your seeking for another place. "

Perceiving, now, that the contest was likely to terminate without any important results, and observing both parties to manifest an inclination for peace, on the footing of the *status ante bellum*, I took an early opportunity of withdrawing from the field, and returned to my quarters in the College.

CHAPTER XIV

Farewell ! a word that hath been, and must be.
                                              BYRON.

Now lords and earls, and all their sweeping train,
And garters, stars, and coronets appear.
                                              POPE.

IN youth, with all its gaiety and excitements, " time passes o'er us with a
noiseless lapse ; " and his course is swift and trackless as that of a bird.
Spring was now gone, and it was summer. The halls of the College were
once more deserted, and I, too, made preparation for departure.

The first of May is the day fixed by immemorial usage in the
University, for the distribution of the prizes : a day looked forward to
with " hopes, and fears that kindle hope, " by many youthful and ardent
spirits. The great hall of the College on that day certainly presents a very
pleasing and animated spectacle. The academical distinctions are bestowed with much of ceremonial pomp, in presence of a vast concourse of
spectators, and it is not uninteresting to mark the flush of bashful
triumph on the cheek of the victor,—the sparkling of his downcast eye,
as the hall is rent with loud applause, when he advances to receive the
badge of honour assigned him by the voice of his fellow-students. It is
altogether a sight to stir the spirit in the youthful bosom, and stimulate
into healthy action faculties which, but for such excitement, might have
continued in unbroken slumber. Of such distinctions, irregular as my
habits of study had been, I was a partaker. In some of my classes I stood
first,—in all I carried off some mark of successful application ; and, in
now looking back on the year which I spent in the College of Glasgow, I
cannot but refer to it, the acquisition of that love of literature, which has
never died within me, and in which I have found a relief and a resource,
under circumstances when its place could not have been otherwise
supplied.

Of my family I have of late said little, yet they were but seldom absent
from my thoughts, and with the different members of it I kept up a
constant intercourse by letter. My father seldom wrote to me, and when
he did, his letters betrayed little of that affectionate feeling which might
be expected to breathe in the confidential intercourse of a parent, and an
only son. His letters were indeed neither harsh nor unkind, but they
were cold and stately, and in character those of a monitor rigid in the
performance of a duty, more than of a father, whose hopes were
garnered up in the object he addressed. From my mother I heard more

frequently, but writing was an exertion to which she was frequently unequal, and my principal correspondent was Jane. In the letters of that dear sister, nothing that interested me, was too insignificant to find a place. She gathered information from the grooms and keeper of my stud and kennel, which she faithfully embodied (bating a few technical mistakes,) in her epistles. She told me of Hecuba, my favourite old mare, and enlarged on the colour and beauty of her foal, which little Lucy fed daily in the paddock. She spoke, too, of Don and Ponto,—of Ariel, my little spaniel, petted and caressed by all, for the sake of her absent master. The accounts which I received from Jane of my mother's health, though unfavourable, did not excite in me any alarm. Nor did either Jane or my father appear to feel such. She had, I was told, become more feeble, but a trip to Brighton was meditated, and the sea-breezes would restore her strength. She suffered from a severe cough; but this the warmth of the approaching summer would remove. Her spirits, too, were good, and her letters betrayed no symptom of the languor of disease. It is not the character of youth to anticipate evil. Death is then regarded as a distant, though inevitable event, to whose dreaded approach we shut our eyes and stop our ears, till his chariot-wheels are at hand, and he already thunders at the gate.

In this situation did matters stand, when, at the conclusion of the College session, I wrote to my father to learn his wishes as to my motions. My friend Conyers was about to visit one of his guardians in Yorkshire, an old fox-hunting squire, where he was to remain till a cornetcy of dragoons had been obtained for him. We proposed a tour by the Lakes, and he pressed me to accompany him on his visit, before returning to my own family. I mentioned this scheme to my father, and requested his consent. He gave it, but desired that I would take advantage of my being in Yorkshire to offer a visit to our relation the Earl of Amersham, with whom, from the seclusion in which my father had spent the latter years of his life, little intercourse, during my remembrance, had been maintained. To the advantages which might arise from keeping up this connexion, he was not insensible. The Earl was ministerial in his politics, and had a borough or two at command; and therefore he was, at least, a person worth courting, by a young man just about to enter the world, with fewer friends and smaller fortune than was desirable. My mother wrote accordingly to the Countess, with whom she had at one period of her life been intimate, informing her that she could not hear of my being in Yorkshire without feeling anxious that I should become personally known to relations, for whom both she and my father entertained so perfect a regard.

Preliminaries being at length settled for our departure, Conyers and myself set forth on our excursion, with light and joyous hearts. My parting with my uncle was to me an affecting one. Before I rose to say farewell, at our last interview, we had been conversing for about an hour. I had laid before him with perfect openness and sincerity my hopes and prospects, for I then regarded him only as a warm and faithful friend. He could scarcely be expected to approve of my partiality for a military life, but he had knowledge enough of character to perceive that my inclinations were not to be controlled on this matter, and he did not seriously attempt it.

"Weel, Cyril," said he, "since ye will be a sodger, and are fool enough to gang to be shot at for twa or three shillings a day, when ye might stay at hame and do far better, it's needless for me to try and reason you out o' what I see ye've set your heart on. But gang where ye like, ye'll hae the prayers o' an auld man for the blessings o' Providence on your head. May God's mercy be a fence and a buckler to you in the day of battle, and his grace ever guide you and protect you in the perilous course of life on which you are about to enter."

Here the old man was silent, the expression of his face was stern and unmoved as ever, but my own heart sympathetically told me of all that was working in his. Tears gushed from my eyes as I rose to bid him adieu. I endeavoured,—but I could not speak. He grasped my hand in his, with a strong and yet somewhat tremulous pressure. For a minute there was silence, but the old man became gradually calmer, and thus spoke :— "Farewell, Cyril, farewell; it's like that on this side o' the grave we may never meet again. Yet I may live to hear o' your well-doing, and that will be to me the best and maist joyfu' tidings I can hear in this world. Gang,—but mind while I live, gin ye want a friend to help you in time of need, ye hae yin in your auld uncle that will no forsake you in your trouble. Gang,—and an auld man's blessing be on your head, and his prayers shall follow for your happiness and prosperity, wherever it may please God that your lot may be cast." As he spoke, he laid his hand solemnly on my head, then embracing me, he turned suddenly from me. I rushed, much moved, from the apartment, and in a moment found myself—in the arms of Girzy. Before I succeeded in extricating myself from this unpleasant predicament, I had undergone the penalty of several kind kisses, while I felt her arms clasping my neck with such a gripe, as that with which a vulture seizes a lamb. "Just promise to come back again," said the worthy creature with red eyes and in a choking voice—"Just promise to come back and see us again, and I'll let you gang."

"Yes, yes," I answered, anxious to escape, and quite overcome by this unexpected prolongation of the scene—"Yes, and may God bless you;" and by a sudden effort I released myself from her grasp, and effected my escape.

No cure for mental depression is so efficacious as travelling. My heart was heavy when, seated in the Carlisle mail *vis à vis* to my friend Conyers, we whirled rapidly through the Gallowgate, and bade a long, probably an eternal farewell to Glasgow. With reverted eyes I gazed upon the lofty towers of the Cathedral, till, by the increasing distance, they could no longer be distinctly traced in the dense canopy of smoke which overhung the city. My attention, however, was soon engrossed by the new objects which were constantly presenting themselves as we advanced, and long before we reached Hamilton, " my bosom's lord sat lightly on its throne, " and my spirits were light and buoyant as the air I breathed.

Never did I pass a more delightful week than that which we spent in the neighbourhood of the lakes, in exploring their transcendent scenery. Amidst such objects, and at such an age, was it possible for beings, with hearts young and unoppressed by the cares of the world, to be otherwise than happy? We required no artificial stimulus,—no extraneous excitement, to goad on our fancy to enjoyment. " The common air, the earth, the skies, " were in themselves all sufficient. They gave us *then*, what millions, did I possess them, could not purchase *now*. In youth happiness is cheap, but the enjoyments of a jaded spirit must be dearly bought, and when bought, are vapid.

On quitting the lakes, a day's journey brought us to the house of Squire Parkyns, who received both his ward and myself with a hearty welcome. He was a gentleman of a good estate and a justice of the quorum, a warm-hearted and well-meaning man, and marked by that devotion to field-sports, " which is the badge of all his tribe, " but I should imagine one of the most unfit persons in the world to be entrusted with the guardianship of a young man. His wife, Conyers told me, had been dead many years, and he had lost an only son, whose skull had been fractured by a fall from his horse, when out hunting. The old man's spirits had long succumbed under this latter blow, but they had again recovered, and, notwithstanding he had three daughters married in the neighbourhood, he preferred keeping what he called " bachelor's hall, " to again submitting his establishment to female management and control. To a jovial old spirit like this, the society of Conyers and myself was not unpleasing. We admired and praised his stud, listened to his sporting anecdotes, and in all disputes about hunting or shooting, deferentially chose him as our umpire. In three days we drank him into a fit of the gout, and in three more, I received a letter from Lord Amersham, expressing in courtly phrase his thanks for the proposed visit, and the delight which both he and Lady Amersham would feel in receiving at Staunton Court the son of his old and valued friend.

After receiving this communication, I spent a week in the society of Conyers and the old Squire, before I could bring myself to think of taking my departure. Even then I was induced more than once to uncord and unpack my trunks, when all prepared for a start, and to add another day to the duration of my sojourn. With regard to Conyers, our characters amalgamated wonderfully, and a strong mutual regard had grown up between us. Of all the men I have ever known, Conyers, I

think, possessed in the greatest degree the power of conciliating attachment. He was indeed a fine and generous creature, and the gaiety of his
spirit, the openness of his disposition, and his entire recklessness of self,
were enough to disarm the censure of the most rigid moralist on his
failings.

At length we parted, but there was no tinge of melancholy in our
adieu—we embraced, vowed friendship, and bade farewell, with all the
warmth and sincerity, yet with all the light-heartedness of youth. We
were about to enter on the same profession, to encounter the same
dangers, to mingle in the same world. We were to meet frequently, and
were destined to pass many happy days in each other's society—we were
but to enjoy the pleasures, to pluck the rose of life; and as for its
thorns,—we thought not—knew not of them.

And so we parted.—The Gazette shortly after informed me that
Charles was appointed to a cornetcy of dragoons in a regiment then
stationed in Ireland. Soon after joining, he wrote me in ecstasies of his
new profession, entreating me to procure, if possible, a commission, then
vacant in the regiment. But it was yet dubious whether my father would
consent to my becoming a soldier. In any case it was very certain, that
my preference for a particular regiment would be treated by him as a
mere boyish whim, and disregarded as such. Under present circumstances, therefore, I felt and knew the obstacles to the accomplishment of
my wishes to be insurmountable. Years of separation elapsed. Our
correspondence, regular at first, became gradually less frequent, as the
pleasures and business of the world thickened around us, and more
deeply engrossed our thoughts; and long before we again met, it had
been altogether discontinued.

On parting from my friend and the old Squire, I had thirty miles to
travel before reaching Staunton Court, the seat of my noble relatives.
Hitherto I had mixed but little in society, and that little only in the
character of a boy. The dignity of a grown man—a gentleman—which I
had known only by anticipation, I was now for the first time to enjoy;
and it was not without a sense of novel dignity, that I felt myself about to
take part in a scene, which, even to my own imagination, seemed worthy
of the actor. Still it was with some palpitations of the heart,—some more
than wonted misgivings of my own power of pleasing, that I beheld the
gates of the lodge thrown open at my approach, and thought, as the
carriage wound along the stately and serpentine approach, that the
wished-for moment was at hand.

The park was extensive, and stocked with the finest timber. Large
herds of deer were cropping the pastures, or reclining in the shade.
Everything around gave indication of magnificent antiquity,—of a
residence which in my imagination well befitted one whose ancestors
had bled in the Crusades—a descendant of those noble barons who
gained, at their sword's point, the great and enduring charter of their

country's freedom. The hand of wealth indeed was everywhere visible, but with none of that tinsel ornament and gewgaw profusion, which marks the splendour of a *nouveau riche*.

An approach of three miles brought us at length in sight of the house. It was a large and massive pile of building, of a quadrangular form, and showing, in its style of architecture, that picturesque peculiarity, by which the works of Inigo Jones, our English Palladio, are so generally distinguished. The house had originally been surrounded by a moat, but that was now dry, and planted with flowers and shrubs of singular beauty and luxuriance. Across this was thrown a bridge of light and graceful construction, terminated by an arch, over which the arms of the family, surmounted by an earl's coronet, were cut in high relief, and supported on either flank by a ferocious dragon, displaying all the exuberance of tail and tusk with which heralds usually rejoice to adorn their fabulous creations. Beneath, the motto, " *A gladio et per gladium,* " was emblazoned in golden characters, and harmonized well with my own ideas of the chivalrous dignity of baronial tenure.

On descending from the carriage, I entered a circular hall of spacious dimensions, the roof of which ascended to the full height of the building, and was lighted by a cupola in the centre. The walls were wainscoted and hung with pictures, and on a pedestal in the centre stood a statue of Charles the Second, who, in the days of his adversity, had found both welcome and safety within the walls of Staunton. I was ushered across this magnificent apartment through a troop of liveried menials, and, after ascending a short marble staircase, adorned and perfumed by a double row of beautiful exotics, entered the library, which I found untenanted. The groom of the chambers then informed me that neither Lord nor Lady Amersham were at home, and requested to know whether I chose any refreshment after my journey. To this I answered in the negative, and the attendant, making a polite bow, quitted the apartment. Thus left alone, and perhaps a little daunted by the pomp and ceremony by which the scene around me was invested, I seated myself in an easy chair, and once more gave the reins to my fancy.

I pictured to myself the owner of this splendid demesne. " Undoubtedly, " I said, " he is a person of lofty carriage and finished elegance of manner; proud, for how can he be otherwise?—but his is a generous pride, ever veiled in courtesy to his equals, and kindness to his inferiors. Raised by his wealth and station above the petty cares and anxieties by which meaner men are agitated, he is liberal, nay, munificent in his ideas, with a hand open as day to melting charity. He is a hero,—for the blood of the noblest chivalry of England flows in his veins. He is a patriot,—for he cannot forget the country to which he owes so much. He is loyal,—for his station marks him out as a hereditary bulwark of the throne. "

In this manner did my imagination run on, adding new colours to the picture it had drawn, till the owner of the mansion seemed to stand before me, invested with every possible grace and excellence.

" And I am now, " thought I, " to appear in the presence of this noble and transcendent personage. With what an air of deference and respect must I address him, and what impression can I, a raw, ignorant, and untutored boy, expect to make on one whose taste and talents, must, at a glance, lay bare to him the whole extent of my deficiencies? I shall at least do my best, " resolved I, and, rising from my chair, advanced towards a pier glass, in front of which I began to practise such bows and deferential modes of address, as appeared to me best suited to so formidable an introduction. In order to derive all possible benefit from this preparatory rehearsal, I judged it right to suit the word to the action, addressing myself first in the character of Lord Amersham, and then framing a fitting answer in my own.

" Mr Thornton, " said I, as his lordship's mouth-piece, assuming at the same time an air of graceful dignity, mingled with much kindness and condescension, " I am delighted to have the honour of welcoming you for the first time to Staunton Court. Believe me, I sincerely rejoice in this opportunity of cultivating an acquaintance which circumstances have long, too long, delayed.—Lady Amersham, let me present to you our relation, Mr Cyril Thornton. Lady Melicent, I beg to introduce your cousin. "

" My lord, " replied I, in my own character, making, as I spoke, a profound obeisance, " do me the honour, I pray your lordship, to accept my very sincere thanks for your kindness and condescension. To Lady Amersham and my fair cousin I—— "

Here I was interrupted by a half-suppressed titter in the apartment, a sound at that moment more dreadful to my ear than would have been that of the explosion of a mine beneath my feet, or the hissing of a Boa Constrictor beneath the drawing-room table. I stood for an instant as if transfixed, my head bent forward in the act of addressing my noble host, and my right hand extended to receive the friendly pressure of his palm. At length, assuming the courage of despair, I determined to know the worst at once. I raised my head, and, looking round, beheld two young ladies, who had evidently been witnesses of my absurd exhibition. Fancy a youth of acute, nay, almost morbid sensibility, placed in such a situation, and it is possible, barely possible, if you are a person of strong imagination, that you may form some inadequate idea of the spiritual torture I then suffered. If anything in this world can afford a good apology for suicide, it is undoubtedly such a detection as that of which I was the subject. Luckily neither pistol, razor, nor pen-knife presented themselves, nay, not a bodkin, or I verily believe that instant had terminated my mortal career. From the top of my head to the sole of my foot, I had a pulse throbbing like a sledge-hammer in every inch. My eyes stared wildly round, in the hopeless effort to find some avenue of escape. I would have given my inheritance for a snug birth in the coal-cellar, or have paid down a handsome difference to have changed situations with Daniel in the lions' den. I would have caught at a cell in the Inquisition, or the dungeon of Baron Trenck, and have thought the penalty a light one, compared to the agonizing horror of such a detection. Never did Ghost, Gorgon, or Chimæra, appear so terrific to human eyes, as did the vision of these two elegant and blooming girls at that moment to mine.

They stood near the fire-place, shawled and bonnetted, as if just returned from a walk. One of them was curiously reconnoitring me with an eye-glass, and the other, with her handkerchief at her mouth, was evidently endeavouring to suppress a laugh, in which she was not wholly successful. What could I do? To prolong the ridicule of my situation, by continuing to stand before the mirror, was impossible; to advance or retire, equally dreadful. Which evil I at length preferred, whether I rushed on Scylla or Charybdis, my mind was in too great a state of confusion to enable me now to recollect.

" What a very odd person! " observed one of my fair tormentors, in a half whisper.

" Yes, a delightful original, " replied her companion; and, making a strong effort to resume her gravity, she advanced, and thus addressed me: " Since chance has thrown us together, there is, I think, no reason to wait for a formal introduction. Some expressions of your soliloquy which we accidentally overheard, sufficiently betrayed that you are Mr Cyril Thornton, who has been, I know, an expected guest for some days. Mr Thornton, let me introduce you to Miss Pynsent—Miss Pynsent, Mr Thornton. "

In reply to this address, delivered with the most perfect self-possession, and an air of grace and high breeding, the union of which was remarkable in one evidently so young, I stammered out some inquiries for Lord and Lady Amersham, bowed, and, I suppose, looked like a blockhead. I am very sure I felt like one. The ice, however, was now broken; and though, in a case like the present, it cannot exactly be said that " ce ne que le premier pas qui coûte, " it is certainly true that the premier pas is, out of sight, the most painful and difficult, and each succeeding one becomes comparatively easy. The young lady was lively and animated, and did not suffer the conversation to languish; and I might have hoped that my folly had been either overlooked or forgotten, had I not observed that a look of laughing intelligence was occasionally interchanged between the fair companions.

" Come, Julia, " at length said the lady Melicent, " our malapropos intrusion has already too long interrupted the rhetorical studies of Mr Thornton, " at the same time rising to depart; " we must get rid of these odious walking habiliments—Mamma and Lady Pynsent are gone to call at Feversham Park, " continued she, addressing me, and looking at her watch. " It is now half-past four o'clock, and we do not dine till seven, so you still have two hours to practise oratory ; but should you tire of that, and choose a turn in the park, you will probably meet papa at the farm, to which any one will direct you. *Au revoir* ; pray do not forget to introduce into your speech, something peculiarly elegant about your *fair cousin.* " So saying, she linked her arm in that of her sister grace, and with the lightness of sylphs they glided out of the apartment.

She spoke with a wicked archness of look, and there was a laughing devil in her eye, by no means soothing to my irritated sensibilities, and when left alone, I for some time paced the apartment with long and irregular strides, reflecting, in no enviable mood, on the ridiculous figure I must have cut before those very persons in whose eyes I was most anxious to make a favourable impression. It may be imagined, I had no inclination to resume the exercise in which I had been so unseasonably interrupted. I determined, therefore, on a stroll in the park, and to effect my introduction to Lord Amersham, in case I should encounter him in my walk.

The air and exercise tended to calm my spirits, and somewhat to restore the self-composure, of which my unfortunate debut in the library had so utterly deprived me. There is something in the very aspect of nature—in its simplest sounds and commonest features—soothing and delightful. They seem as if intended to act as an oblivious antidote to those mental perturbations which are generated by the cares and anxieties of artificial life. For such wounds, nature has provided a simple medicament, which the united experience of mankind proves to be efficacious. The citizen retires to his box at Hackney or on Champion-hill, and the lawyer " babbles of green fields, " at his villa in Kent or Hertfordshire. They are conscious of the effect, though perhaps ignorant of the cause. They feel that the thousand tight-drawn ligaments which bind them to the world are for the moment loosened,—the shackles fall from their limbs, and they draw from the bosom of nature that simple nourishment, which strengthens and braces them again to undergo the repetition of their daily toils.

Of this restorative power, I felt in my ramble the full medicinal efficacy. The park was fine and extensive. The venerable oaks cast their shadows broader as the sun sunk in the horizon, on the greensward beneath them and around. The birds were carolling their vespers, and the deer that stood on a neighbouring eminence tossing high their branchy foreheads, showed like creatures embedded in the purple glory of the sky.

Occupied with the scene around me, I had forgotten my purpose of seeking Lord Amersham, till warned of the necessity of returning to the house, by the sound of the first dinner-bell. I had turned for that purpose, and was leisurely retracing my steps to the mansion, when I observed a person of rather outré appearance approaching hastily in a

diagonal direction, evidently with the wish to overtake me. I accordingly waited for his approach, and as he advanced, had time to take a pretty
accurate observation of his person.

He was dressed in a jacket of bottle-green, garnished with buttons of
mother-of-pearl, of dimensions unusually large. His nether integuments
were of dark plush, and over his legs, which were exceedingly clumsy
and unshapely, he wore gaiters, the under part of which was of cloth,
and the upper of dingy-coloured leather. His beaver was of a drab-
colour, distinguished by an unusual latitude of brim, and bearing
evident marks of long exposure to the vicissitudes which mark our
climate. In his hand he carried a long pole, terminating at its lower
extremity in a weeding-hook. His figure was round and squab, of
ungainly proportions, and marked, when in motion, by a singular
jerking of the body and limbs, producing altogether rather a ludicrous
effect. His face and head were large. The former slightly pitted by the
small-pox, and displaying features coarse and apparently unsuited to
each other, constituting just such a contenance as one might be supposed to form, were he to select a feature from each of his ugly acquaintances, and huddle them altogether into one visage. Judging from the
tout ensemble, he might be park-keeper or farmer; one probably well to
do in the world, and in his obesity furnishing at once a practical
illustration and comment, on the " scope and tendency of Bacon. "

Curious to know what such a person could want with me, and taking
compassion on the exertions which his pursuit evidently cost him, I
stopped my walk, which at first I had only slackened, till he came up.
For some seconds he was unable to speak, and stood panting for breath
to enable him to commence his address.

" Mr Cyril Thornton, I presume ? " said this grotesque personage. I
bowed in acquiescence, and without pausing, he proceeded. " Beg ten
thousand pardons, that you should have been left so long alone.—
Delighted to see you at Staunton.—Saw your carriage pass, and guessed
it was you, but was so busy with Sam Brown, (my farm bailiff,) that I
could not escape a moment to welcome you. We farmers, Mr Thornton,
as you will probably know by and by, are literally *adscripti glebæ*; we
must follow the plough, and trust to the good-nature of our friends to
forgive omissions. You must come to-morrow, and see my farm; I'll
show you stock worth the seeing. But let us move on now, for the
dinner-bell has rung, and we have no time to stand chattering. "

This voluble address was so rapidly enunciated, that I found it
impossible to hitch in any thing in reply; and as we proceeded towards
the house, the Earl, for he it was, still continued to talk.

" Hope you left your family quite well ?—Your mother is a charming
woman,—first saw her at a ball at Bath, two, three, four, five and twenty
years ago,—turned the heads of all the young men in those days. Your
father, too, a most worthy and excellent person, and my particular

friend. But oh! I forget, you're not from Thornhill; I think I heard you were at school, at— at— at— Manchester?"

"At the College of Glasgow, my Lord," interrupted I, rather piqued at the mistake, and unwilling to be mistaken for a Manchester school-boy.

"Oh, ah, Glasgow was it?—my memory is so bad, and I am apt to make a sad jumble when talking of those—as Mr Pitt called them, 'great emporiums of commerce,'—Leeds, Sheffield, Glasgow, Manchester.—I knew you were at one or another of them, though not exactly certain which. Glasgow, eh? Then you're from Scotland, and must tell me all about the Scotch farming,—the succession of crops, and all that.—Scotch black-faced sheep too, capital mutton, but devils for leaping fences,—not so good on the huggins as Leicestershire, and coarse in the fleece. Notwithstanding all you've seen in Scotland, flatter myself you'll like our farming in Yorkshire. To-morrow morning you must come to the farm and see my new patent threshing-machine—nine-horse power, and managed by a boy."

We now reached the house, and the necessity of speedy preparations for dinner, occasioned an abrupt termination to be put to the conversation. I retired, accordingly, for this purpose, and when engaged in the operations of the toilet, could scarce refrain from smiling, when I remembered how ludicrously all my anticipations of the person, manners, and character of Lord Amersham had been at variance with the fact.

CHAPTER XV

If love ambitious sought a match of birth,
Whose veins bound richer blood than Lady Blanch ?
King John.

LORD AMERSHAM, to whom in the latter part of the last chapter I have introduced my readers, had been bred a soldier. Possessing rank, fortune, title, high connexions, and parliamentary influence, his rise in his profession had been impeded by none of those obstacles which men in ordinary circumstances always find it difficult, often impossible, to surmount. He rose rapidly to be a General, and without encountering either the hazards of the field, or the vicissitudes of climate, obtained his full share of the solid pudding, as well as of the empty honours of his profession—a regiment of dragoons, and the insignia of the Bath.

Of such a distribution of rewards in a society constituted as ours, it were vain and perhaps impolitic to complain. Of late years, perhaps, the military profession, of all others, is the one in which distinguished merit can with least justice complain of being treated with neglect ; and while this is so—while the system is admitted on all hands to work practically well, we may safely permit a few of its honours to be diverted,—if you will have it so,—from their natural and legitimate channel, into another, which, if it does not equally enrich and fertilize the soil, at least adds something to the general tone and splendour of the landscape.

There was certainly nothing in Lord Amersham's character to indicate any intention of nature to mould him into a great military commander. He was a person, nevertheless, of very tolerable talents, and by no means deficient in any of the ordinary acquirements befitting his rank. Unfortunately he was of a disposition insatiably restless and bustling, and made a point of never suffering his faculties to subside into a state of quiescence. With less of real business than falls to the share of any ordinary mortal, he contrived to spend his life in a flurry. His mind was always on the tread-mill, continually working, but seldom with any visible result ; or, to use a better-sounding simile, Lord Amersham was a planet revolving eternally in the same orbit, and presenting itself to the gaze of the astronomer in a very limited variety of phases. His lordship, in short, was generally something of a bore, and when talking of his favourite pursuits, was apt to be rather too prolix in his reasonings, and minute in his enumeration of details, and when once fairly set a-going on his favourite hobby, would gallop on for a couple of hours on end, to the great enjoyment of himself, and the equal annoyance of his company. There was something indeed almost ludicrous in the strong contrast

which existed between his mind and body—the one ever bustling and
active, the other heavy and inert; and it seemed to an observer passing
strange, that so small a spirit should be able to stimulate into almost
constant action a mass of matter so large and unwieldy. In the absence of
other more important avocations, Lord Amersham had betaken himself to farming, and by applying all his ingenuity to its practical details,
had succeeded, I believe, in discovering and carrying into practice
several agricultural improvements.

There was but one misfortune in the life of Lord Amersham, which
had occasioned him any deep and permanent regret—the want of a
male successor to his hereditary honours and estates. It is true, there was
nothing in the tenure by which these were held, to prevent their
descending to his daughter; but it was galling to reflect, that the
far-descended line of which he was the head, would cease in his person to
boast a male representative, and that the titles and wide demesnes
which had been attached to it for centuries, would probably, by devolv-
ing on a female, become the appanage of some other and perhaps less
noble family. The anticipation of such an event was not unaccompanied
by pain, and had long been felt as a serious deduction from their
happiness, both by Lord and Lady Amersham. To the latter it is now
time the reader should be introduced.

In her youth Lady Amersham had been a beautiful woman, and was
still a fine one. She was tall and of a stately person, bearing herself with a
demeanour dignified and imposing. The expression of her countenance
was perhaps too deficient in softness to be pleasing, and there was a
coldness almost approaching to hauteur in her manner, especially in
mixed company, which showed her fully aware of her own claims in
society, and rigid in exacting a due observance of them in others. Where
Lady Amersham, however, had any object to gain, or where she wished
to make a favourable impression, no one possessed in a greater degree
the power of doing so. No one could unbend more gracefully, and cast
aside for a season that air of distance and repulsive dignity, by which all
nearer approach was precluded from those whose claims to such a
distinction were at all apocryphal. Bred in the precincts of a court, and
accustomed through life to move in the very highest circles of ton, she
was an able and experienced tactician in all the underhand manœuvres
and expedients which are necessary to preserve the effulgence of even
the brightest star in the hemisphere of fashion, from occasional obscuration. Over Lord Amersham she exercised an influence greater than he
was perhaps aware of. Her power however was rather felt than seen;
and while she threw no obstacle in the way of his indulgence in his
favourite bucolical pursuits, she succeeded in bending his inclinations to
her own, by securing his consent to a house in Grosvenor-Square, and at
least four months per annum of a town life. That there were amiable
traits in Lady Amersham, I have reason to know; and though feared

and disliked by her rivals in the great world, there was in her character a certain splendid munificence, and generous kindness of heart, which made her beloved by her inferiors.

The pride and ambition of both parents naturally centered in their only daughter; and in truth she was a creature in whom parental partiality required little apology for feeling pride. Lady Melicent de Vere was then about sixteen years of age, and rising into the pride of womanhood. Her figure was rather below than above the common height, but moulded in a symmetry which might have afforded a model for the sculptor. Her features were neither Roman nor entirely Grecian, but belonged to a certain nondescript medium, which might almost, according to the fancy of the observer, be included in either. I know not whether, if examined by a rigid critic, her face might have been considered analytically beautiful; but nothing could exceed the brilliancy of her dark eyes, or the fascination of her smile; and her countenance was lit up with so much spirit and vivacity, as to render it doubtful whether features more classically regular, might not have somewhat injured the charm of its expression. Unaccustomed to restraint, and habituated from her infancy to be the object of admiration, she had acquired a self-confidence somewhat precocious, and moved in society with all the ease and grace " which marks security to please. " Such was the Lady Melicent as she now rises to my memory, in recurring to the period of my visit to Staunton Court.

Having dispatched the duties of the toilet, as expeditiously as possible, I descended, and found a portion of the dinner-party already assembled in the drawing-room. Lady Amersham, though somewhat stately, was kind, made many obliging inquiries respecting my mother and sisters, and introduced me to the assembled circle. This consisted, imprimis, of Lord and Lady Pynsent, people perfectly *comme il faut*, polite and personable, in short, just such people as one would *a priori* suppose to possess a tenement in St James's square, or expect to meet at a reputable dinner-party in Piccadilly or Park Lane. Along with these came Mr Horace Pynsent, their son, an ensign in the Guards, and their daughter Miss Pynsent, a very pretty and accomplished young lady, not unmarked by something of that paleness, and, if I may so write, that conventional manner and expression, which an early subjection to the restraints of a town life seldom fails to substitute for the natural vivacity of youthful spirits.

Next in order came Sir Cavendish Potts, Knight, Commissioner of the Victualling Office, Clerk of the Pipe, &c. &c. Sir Cavendish had begun the world as an inferior clerk in one of the public offices, with a salary somewhat less than a hundred a-year. By dint of constant assiduity, and vigilance in seizing every opportunity of making himself useful to his superiors by little extra-official services, he had gradually risen to the enjoyment of the lucrative and distinguished offices above mentioned.

Sir Cavendish was now become a person of some importance, but his exertions did not slacken with his elevation. The same qualities to which he owed his worldly advancement, likewise procured his admission to the coteries of the beau-monde. He was the favourite of all dowagers of quality, arranged the programme of all grand entertainments, and superintended the execution of the details; was assiduous in procuring rich partners for sedentary young ladies, and danced himself, when occasion required, with the plain ones; knew all that was said or done, in every house, in every fashionable street or square in the metropolis, and was, in short, a very encyclopedia of anecdote, an inexhaustible calendar of scandal and tittle-tattle.

Of course, therefore, he was a favourite with the ladies; as for their husbands, he had always a full budget of politics at their service. He visited the prime minister, and was hand in glove with his under secretary; had always news, of the authenticity of which there could be no doubt, though he was not at liberty to mention his authority; knew of every meeting of the cabinet, and the result of its deliberation five minutes after it broke up. In the sporting world, his information was no less accurate and extensive. He could tell you off-hand the latest odds on the Derby, knew exactly the condition of all the horses, and would mention in a confidential whisper the name of the winner.

Such and so distinguished a person was Sir Cavendish Potts, who, at the season of the year when it was " impossible to live in town, " annually diffused his visits among his noble friends in the country. In this catalogue raisonné, I think I have included all the members of the party.—No, there was a Miss Cumberbatch, a person who seemed to fill a sort of nondescript situation, and to hold a sort of nondescript rank, in the ménage. She could scarcely be called a friend, for neither Lady Amersham nor her daughter admitted her to the privileges which such a title would imply, while she was evidently treated with more consideration than would probably have been conceded to a person in the rank of a governess in such an establishment. With no distinct duties to perform, she seemed to hold her situation in the family, on the difficult and precarious tenure of being not only generally useful, but generally agreeable. Miss Cumberbatch was an extraordinary adept in working lace, and unusually skilful in embroidery; possessed great taste in dress, and was quite unrivalled in the scientific adjustment of drapery; did the honours of the breakfast-table with due propriety, and was always ready, when called on, to supply music, and favour the company with a song. Such were part, and but a small part, of Miss Cumberbatch's qualifications. Add to these, she could fill a place on a sofa, and, on a look from Lady Amersham, be conveniently instrumental in breaking off a tête-à-tête, where Lady Melicent was engaged in one, with a person whom the prudent mother did not think sufficiently entitled to such an honour. With regard to Lord Amersham, she was an excellent listener, never yawned nor betrayed lassitude during the recital of the most tedious story, and had always a smile or an exclamation of wonder ready to introduce at the proper time and place. Miss Cumberbatch was therefore a decided favourite with his Lordship, who found in her an auditor whose patience his utmost loquacity could not exhaust.

Lord Amersham had not yet descended to the drawing-room when I entered, and when he did so, I confess it was not without surprise that I witnessed the metamorphosis he had undergone since our rencontre in the park. I now beheld an elderly gentleman, not much indebted to nature certainly, but exceedingly recherché in his dress, and bearing about him the visible impress of distinction. He wore his hair highly powdered, and curled in a manner so complicated, as evidently to have required the skill of no ordinary friseur. His clothes were made to fit as tight as possible, apparently with the view of diminishing to the utmost the bulk of his figure. In his shoes, and at the knee of his inferior garments, (to use a delicate periphrasis,) which were white, he wore gold buckles, and his upper regions were adorned by the star and riband of the Bath, decorations to which, as they were considered indicative of military distinction, he was particularly partial. The dinner-bell had sounded some minutes before his Lordship appeared. He entered with hasty steps, which shook the apartment at every foot-fall, and trotting up (for walking it certainly was not) to Lady Pynsent, he proceeded to hand her to the dining-room, uttering, with uncommon volubility, as he advanced, a profusion of apologies for having kept the company waiting so long. To these Lady Pynsent did not apparently pay much attention, for, turning towards her son, then engaged in conversation with Sir Cavendish, she thus addressed him :—

"Now, Horace, if Lady Melicent does you today the honour of accepting your arm, be less awkward than yesterday, and mind you don't tear her flounce again by your carelessness. For such an offence you could scarcely expect even from her sweet temper a second forgiveness. "

This, of course, was a pretty intelligible hint to the young gentleman what part he was expected to take in the ceremonial, and he approached, with an air of unhesitating self-complacency, to offer his services. They were playfully rejected.

"No, " replied Lady Melicent; " I must not have my sweet temper put again to so early a proof. You may practise to-day with Miss Cumberbatch, and if she reports you to have shown yourself a tolerable proficient in the duties of a carpet-knight, I may perhaps once more put your skill to the test.—Mr Thornton, it is time we relations should become better acquainted, and I therefore appoint you my Chevalier for the day, hoping you will take warning by the fate of your predecessor, and demean yourself in your office with all manner of grace and propriety. "

Mr Pynsent, though evidently rather mortified, did not venture to disobey; Lady Melicent, laughing, took my arm, and we descended to the dining-room.

I sat beside her at dinner, and this fact may perhaps serve as an excuse for my inability to give any satisfactory detail of the entertainment. Let the reader take for granted, therefore, that it was a sumptuous one; that the courses appeared and vanished in due order of succession; that the routine of the table was conducted with as much ceremony and minuteness of observance as might have satisfied the most vulgar parvenu; and that not one of the party compromised his reputation by the enormity of calling for porter.

At first, I felt a little embarrassed by the vivacity of my fair neighbour. The events of the morning recurred rather unpleasantly to my recollection, and I was inclined to regard her with somewhat of those feelings which Faust entertained, rather unreasonably, towards the devil, after the conclusion of his bargain with that legitimate and infernal potentate.

When seated at table, therefore, I was silent, or, when absolutely called on to speak, my remarks were trite and common-place. " This is really very intolerable, " at length said Lady Melicent, addressing me; " I chose you for my esquire to-day, because I really expected you to turn out the most amusing person in company, and here you have actually sat out the fish and soup without speaking a syllable, or at least only such syllables as could just have been as well spoken by my macaw. Now, this will never do. You must really get up something smart and entertaining another time, that is, in case, " glancing at me at the same time a look of playful malice, " in case all your speeches, like those of this morning, require a previous rehearsal. "

" Nay, on that point I must sue for mercy, though I fear it is impossible to expect it from one whose perceptions of the ludicrous are so strong as those of the Lady Melicent. Yet a generous warrior does not trample on a fallen foe. "

" Do not trust too much to my generosity in a case like the present; the story is too good a one to be lost, and must positively be told some time or other. Your only chance of escape is to conciliate my compassion, and that can only be done by a full confession. Begin, then; I am ready to hear all you can allege in mitigation of punishment. "

I felt great relief in having an opportunity thus afforded me of getting rid of at least some of the ridicule I had incurred, and proceeded to tell the story of my disaster, glozing and suppressing the stronger and more ridiculous features of the case, and joining in the laugh at those which I found it impossible for my ingenuity to overcome.

" Well, then, I spare you for the present, " said Lady Melicent, " not for your own sake, but because there is nobody here to whom I should have any pleasure in telling the story. Lord Pynsent would hear it with polite gravity; her ladyship with an affected smile; Mr Pynsent would adjust his cravat, and call you an extraordinary person; but not one of them would listen to it *con amore*, or indulge in a hearty laugh at your expense. Sir Cavendish perhaps might, but then the anecdote would spread at once through all the world of fashion, and you would be a ruined man. Now, we are to have a large party next week for York races, and I believe I shall keep it in petto till then. "

" Nay, that would be malice prepense, a refinement of cruelty, of which I think, nay, I am sure, Lady Melicent is incapable. "

" Nay, you don't know that; but, at all events, remember I am not the sole depositary of the secret. Miss Pynsent is a witness as well as myself, and must likewise be wooed to silence; not a very easy task, I can tell you, for we women, though paragons in everything else, are not particularly remarkable for secrecy. Now, I should be glad to know how you can expect to interest her in your favour? "

" Through the kind intercession of the Lady Melicent. "

" So you would attempt to gain one woman by means of another? Do you think *this* a plan very likely to be successful? "

" Yes; I am sure I could not possibly select a fairer or a more eloquent advocate, and in your hands I willingly rest my cause. "

" Well, I will try what can be said for you, for I really did feel compassion for you. Never did man look more desperately stupified than you, on discovering we had been witnesses of your soliloquy! Why, you would have made a capital study for Hamlet on the entrance of his father's ghost, your hair on end, " like quills upon the fretful porcupine; " your eyes half starting from their sockets, and fixed as if by the gaze of a basilisk; your mouth open, your limbs stiff as those of Niobe.— But, come, I see you are rather sore on the subject, and I won't laugh at you. Let us try something else. Have you brought no amusing details with you from Scotland? You really look like a person who possessed the faculty of second sight; do afford us a small specimen of your talents in that line. Of course, you are familiar with ghosts, wraiths, and all beings of that description, and were apparelled in the plaid, bonnet, and other appendages of Scottish costume, delightfully uncomfortable and picturesque. Pray begin, therefore; for, in satisfying my curiosity, you will have a tolerably long task to perform, I assure you. "

Stimulated by the piquant badinage of my charming cousin, which was perhaps somewhat aided in its operation by a glass or two of champagne, I ceased to be the mute and changeling I had hitherto appeared, and shone forth, if not with native brilliancy, at least with the reflected lustre of another and a brighter planet. I seemed to inhale excitement in the very air I breathed. There was a delightful exhilaration in the bare idea of being the sole object of attention to a creature so radiantly captivating, whose smiles would probably ere long become the object of contention to the highest and noblest of the land. My faculties enjoyed their full swing, and all the finer powers of intellect and fancy with which nature had endowed me, awoke as from a slumber, and came at that moment to my aid. In short, if I did not succeed in making myself agreeable, it was because nature had denied me the means of being so; for unquestionably I made the effort under a combination of the most favourable circumstances. Our tête-à-tête had been too animated and too long to escape the notice of Lady Amersham, who at length thought it prudent to break the chain of our conversation, which appeared in her eyes somewhat too continuous and engrossing. It is true, my acquaintance with her daughter had been too recent, and I was altogether a person of too humble pretensions, to excite any apprehensions, at least any serious ones, in her ladyship. To her, I believe, it seemed as impossible that Lady Melicent should form a *liaison* with Cyril Thornton, a commoner, and heir to an estate of some two or three thousand a-year, as that she should elope with the butler, or establish a sentimental correspondence with the Irish Giant; but she systematically disapproved of anything approaching to a monopoly of her daughter's smiles, and " *divide et impera* " was the maxim by which her policy was governed. Her ladyship took occasion, therefore, to address to me certain questions, which made it necessary that I should enter, in reply, into considerable details, and at the same time skilfully contrived to engage Lady Melicent in conversation with Mr Pynsent. Having thus succeeded in her object, I found myself, for the first time, at liberty to turn my attention to the general conversation of the table.

Distinguishable above all other voices was that of Sir Cavendish Potts, shrill in tone, and scattering επεα πτεροεντα on all manner of subjects, from a change in the Cabinet to the *faux pas* of an alderman's wife, and never missing an opportunity of insinuating a compliment to his noble host and hostess. Among his other qualities, Sir Cavendish was something of a gourmand, and distinguished for his goût in all matters of the table.

" Nothing can be more exquisite, " said he, at the same time depositing his fork, " than this *fricandeau à la sauce piquante.* Bertrand's dishes have certainly a peculiar character one never meets with anywhere else. When I was at Grimsthorpe, about a month ago, Colonel Haviland, no very great judge, you know, praised his Grace's dinners as being quite superior to all others.— 'Why, no,' said the Duke, 'the dinners are but barely tolerable, and a very few things in them perhaps are really done well; but, Colonel, if you can only manage to get me Lord Amersham's cook, I may perhaps have some chance of meriting your compliment.' I agreed with him, that, under no other circumstances could it be possible for his Grace's entertainments to rival those of your lordship. "

" Yes, " said Lord Amersham, " Bertrand is really very great in his line, though I think he sometimes carries the display of his powers a little too far. No such thing as a plain joint ever comes to table. The venison is generally stuck all over with cloves and pepper-corns; and I have given up all hope of ever tasting my own mutton, so thoroughly disguised is it by Bertrand's sauce and spiceries. "

"The skill of Bertrand, " said Lord Pynsent, "seems like the philosopher's stone,—it turns everything into gold. "

"Ay, just so, " replied Lord Amersham; "but then the baser metals are of use likewise, and I wish Bertrand would not insist in applying the Rosicrucian process to my Southdown. By the by, I have got a new cross, with which I intend astonishing Mr Coke of Holkham when he comes next month. Such fleece and such mutton! I wish my old friend, John Duke of Bedford, had been alive; how delighted he would have been! I remember when he was last at Staunton, a short time before he died, we walked together over my farm; he was prodigiously taken with it, and said, 'Lord Amersham, you are undoubtedly the first farmer in England!' But about my new sheep, they are a mixture of the Welsh, Leicestershire, and Southdown, with a dash of the Angola and Merino. Lord Pynsent, if you would like a Ram, there is one at your service; it will improve your breed amazingly. Your lordship is almost the only person to whom I would have offered such a thing. I assure you, to nobody but your lordship—— "

Lord Pynsent here cut short his brother peer by professing his grateful acceptance of this magnificent donation.

While the Earl was thus copiously disserting on his favourite topic, Sir Cavendish had transferred his attention to the ladies, whom he was amusing by recounting the most recent fashionable *on dits*, describing Lord Pentonville's new house, and the splendid establishment which Lady Jane St Lawrence was about to acquire, by becoming the bride of a certain Mr Blackmore, a wealthy Oriental, who had recently returned with heavy pockets and disordered liver from Bengal. For myself, I found little opportunity for conversation with Lady Melicent during the rest of dinner, and what did pass between us, was of that light and general kind, which, when the words cease to vibrate on the ear, passes away and is forgotten. Mr Pynsent, too, was assiduous in his attentions, and divided her notice; and though my vanity told me I had no reason to shrink from competition with such a rival, still in affairs of love I had a vague consciousness that the battle is not always to the strong, and that Mr Pynsent, heir to a coronet, possessed advantages to which I could lay no claim.

The dinner was succeeded by the dessert, the dessert by the departure of the ladies, and the gentlemen were left to the unrestrained enjoyment of their own masculine dulness. With its cause likewise fled my inspiration. A lassitude crept over me—I was thoughtful and absent, and anxious only for the moment which should bring with it an adjournment to the drawing-room. Lord Amersham, apparently attributing my reserve to boyish shyness, endeavoured to draw me into conversation;

talked of hounds and horses, and other topics calculated to operate as excitements to youthful eloquence. Lord Pynsent, too, was kind and urbane, introduced me particularly to the notice of his son, and gave me an invitation to his house in town. The young gentleman, who, till now, had eyed me askance, and considered it impossible that a person whose coat was evidently made by a country tailor, could be worthy of any notice on his part, now deemed it necessary to make some advances to an acquaintance, and addressed me in a few condescending remarks. My answers were dictated by a spirit as cold and aristocratic as his own, and the conversation, after languishing through a succession of vapid and uninteresting observations and replies, died at length a natural death from mere exhaustion of matter.

The wished-for moment, however, came at last, and we adjourned to the drawing-room. When we entered, Lady Melicent was singing to her own accompaniment on the harp. Her voice, even an indifferent auditor must have admitted to be charming; to me it was the voice of an angel sounding in celestial music from the spheres. Her figure, as she bent forward to the instrument, was fine, and something even of poetical grace seemed to be shed over and around her. The song was the hymn of the Venetian Mariner, a wild, beautiful, and simple air, which it might soothe the most troubled spirit to hear borne by the sea-breeze at the close of twilight, over the sleeping waters of the Adriatic. The low and tremulous swell with which the words " Oh Santissima, oh Purissima ! " were murmured at the commencement of the song, the almost sublime altitude and volume of voice with which she gave sound to the increasing fervour of praise and adoration as it advanced, are at this moment in my ears, like the voice of a departed spirit, fainter yet the same.

I stood mute and motionless, scarcely daring to breathe till the music ceased, and she arose from the instrument. The enchantment which bound me, then changed its character without losing its power. Leaning on the arm of Sir Cavendish, and laughing as she advanced, she passed me without a look, and seated herself beside Miss Pynsent on an opposite ottoman. The knight stood before them, apparently engaged in the narration of some amusing anecdote, which succeeded in drawing forth abundance of wreathed smiles from his fair auditors. But the mothers, not the daughters, were the more peculiar objects of his attentions ; and he soon retired, leaving the field open to more youthful competitors. Mr Pynsent succeeded him, and, seated beside Lady Melicent, all hopes of a nearer approach on my part seemed for the present cut off.

I sat ruminating on a fauteuil, my eyes fixed with a half vacant stare on an equestrian portrait of one of the family progenitors, by Vandyck. It was a noble picture—the attitude bold and commanding, the costume gorgeous and graceful, and the horse,—nothing could be finer. It was such a horse, as, according to the description of Job, might be supposed to " say unto the trumpets, ha, ha ! and to laugh at the strength of the armed men. "

Not one scintilla of approbation, however, did this splendid performance extract from me. My organs of perception were in full activity, but
the connexion between these and the mind was broken; I saw and did
not see. Engrossed by my own thoughts, I was yet perfectly free from all
moodiness and mental depression. It has been truly said by Godwin,
that our waking dreams are those of activity and power, our sleeping
ones of passive sufferance. Mine were dreams of glory and pride, of
happy love and gratified ambition, and perhaps not less baseless and
ridiculous than that of Alnaschar in the eastern story. Be their character, however, what it might, they were abruptly broken by the sound of
my name pronounced by Lady Melicent. I started up, the Guardsman
was gone, and she beckoned me to approach, pointing at the same time
to a stool in front of the sofa, which stood nearly equidistant from herself
and Miss Pynsent. The signal was obeyed with joyful alacrity.

" Really, Mr Thornton, " said she, addressing me in a tone of playful
raillery, " this will never do. You are fast acquiring the character of a
dull, stupid, and disagreeable person. Since you entered the drawing-
room, you have not uttered one syllable, but have sat like Patience on a
monument, in an arm-chair, as fixed and immovable as the picture you
have been staring at. To punish you, I retract the half promise I gave
you at dinner, to interest Miss Pynsent in your favour, so far as to keep
the secret of your morning's exhibition, and leave you to advocate your
own cause. Nay, do not be alarmed, my dear Julia, at the idea of a
tête-à-tête—I only go for a moment to speak to papa, and I assure you,
he is not quite so bad as he appears—a little stupid and silent at first, but
he improves a good deal on nearer acquaintance. "

So saying, she tripped away, leaving me to perform a task for which I
felt little inclination.

In a drawing-room the distance of a yard or two constitutes for some
purposes a solitude as complete as one could enjoy in the very centre of
the great desert of Zahara; and left alone with Miss Pynsent, there was
quite privacy enough to be disagreeable, that is, to make us feel
mutually awkward, and at the same time to impose the necessity of
immediate advances to conversation. Lady Amersham, Lord and Lady
Pynsent, and Sir Cavendish, were engaged in a *partie carrée* at cards, and
Lord Amersham, who had hitherto amused himself in overlooking the
game, and criticising the play of all parties, was now half reclining with
his daughter on a *chaise longue*, her beautiful arm encircling his neck, and
her countenance affording a strong contrast in juxtaposition to his
indented and hard-featured visage. Mr Pynsent was seated at a remote
table, apparently deeply engaged in the studying a portfolio of prints of
military costume. From the party thus variously occupied, there appeared no immediate hope of any seasonable interruption to our interview, and I felt obliged, *invita Minerva*, to set seriously about the task of

E

making myself agreeable. There can be nothing more cloudy and unhopeful than the first dawn of conversational intercourse between a town-bred lady and a young gentleman born and educated in the country, who has never even approached within eyeshot of the metropolis. Between such persons there appears no channel of approximation. The opera, balls, parties, and Hyde Park, are cut off on the one hand, and all matters of provincial interest are equally a dead letter on the other. Still when two people, however different in habit and ideas, are anxious to be agreeable, the means of accomplishing their object will rarely be found wanting. In the most dissimilar characters there will be found, on nearer view, some points of contact, some coincidences of sentiment and feeling, some unison of tastes, solid enough to serve as the foundation of such a light and fragile superstructure of regard, as is requisite for the purposes of pleasant intercourse in society. With this hypothesis, at least, my own experience coincided. The awkwardness of first address was at length surmounted, and the conversation of Miss Pynsent and myself became easy and agreeable. The young lady was, fortunately, fond of poetry and romance, and talked enthusiastically, and not ungracefully, of Marmion, the Pleasures of Hope, and the Mysteries of Udolpho. Coincidence or difference of opinion on these subjects, naturally led to the introduction of others equally interesting. In short, when an interruption to our colloquy did at length occur, it found me sailing with a fair breeze on smooth waters, and was received with none of that thankfulness with which, at an earlier moment, it would have been welcomed. In return for the apparent partiality which had led to an hour's tête-à-tête with their daughter, both Lord and Lady Pynsent regarded me with eyes of favour, and were profuse in their civilities. The secret of all this perhaps was, that though in a matrimonial point of view, I was infinitely beneath the acceptance of a person of the very high pretensions that attached to the Lady Melicent; yet, in the eyes of the world, I was by no means an ineligible match for Miss Pynsent, without fortune, and the eldest daughter of a tolerably numerous family. So probably thought Lord and Lady Pynsent, who were apparently resolved that no want of encouragement on their part should diminish the chance of their procuring an unexceptionable establishment for their daughter. Of such views, however, if such did exist, I was entirely unconscious, and was disposed, in my ignorance of the world, to attribute the very favourable *accueil* which I experienced from both parents, either to disinterested benevolence on their part, or to uncommon powers of prepossession on mine.

Thus did the first evening of my sojourn at Staunton pass away; and when, on retiring to my chamber, I cast a retrospective glance on the day just closed, I found I could regard it altogether with a degree of tranquil complacency, far greater than the character of some of its occurrences might have led me to anticipate. The long excitement and consequent exhaustion of my spirits, soon brought their natural restorative, and when slumber that night descended on my eyelids (need I say it?) the Lady Melicent was in my dreams.

CHAPTER XVI

Fancies and notions he pursues,
Which ne'er had being but in thought,
And, like the Grecian artist, views
The image he himself has wrought.
                                              PRIOR.

——Who comes from the chamber?
It is Azrael, the angel of death.
                                              THALABA.

MY sojourn in the world of dreams continued till the sound of the
morning-bell recalled me to the perception and the consciousness of
grosser and more material entities. Few moments were necessary to
restore my senses to their wonted activity, and I sprung up to prepare for
participation in the pleasures and business of that less visionary world of
which I again found myself a denizen. My preparations, however, were
made with less facility than usual. The duties of the toilet were protracted for a space considerably transcending the limits ordinarily found
sufficient for their due discharge. I was uncommonly fastidious about
the adjustment of my hair, displayed through the interstice of my
waistcoat an unwonted superfluity of frill, and, after many unsuccessful
experiments, remember of being eventually by no means satisfied with
the tie of my cravat. On descending, I found the party (with the
exception of Lady Amersham, who seldom appeared till considerably
later in the day,) assembled in the breakfast-room. Lord Amersham, in
his morning habiliments, exhibited the same grotesque figure which had
excited my astonishment the day before at our meeting in the park.
After breakfast, which he dispatched as hurriedly as possible, his lordship addressed many apologies to Lady Pynsent for his speedy departure.

"Your ladyship will, I hope, excuse me, but we farmers, Lady
Pynsent, cannot neglect our calling, or our calling will neglect us; the
eye of the master must overlook, as the proverb goes, or the plough will
speed badly. If your ladyship only knew the torrent of business I have to
encounter.—In the first place, my wool; I have to receive offers for that,
and sell to the best bidder—never show favour or affection in a case of
that sort—all fair and above board—sealed offers, and the highest
carries the day. Then comes Tompkinson with contract for two steam
engines, thirty-horse power, to set the coal-mines a-going. People may
talk of the Golconda mines as much as they please, but none are so

valuable, you may take my word for it, Lady Pynsent, as the black diamond mines. Then I have to superintend the preparation of my two-bout ridges, an original invention of my own; no succession of crops necessary—wheat—wheat for ever, and the soil never exhausted—fresh as after the first crop. Quite a new era in farming—expect to be awarded the gold medal at the next meeting of the Agricultural Society. Mr Coke is jealous as the devil of my success, and Sir John Sinclair pretends to undervalue it. Sir John is a Scotchman, so no wonder. But your ladyship must not seduce me to stand tittle-tattling a moment longer. I must endeavour to carry off Lord Pynsent, however.—Lord Pynsent, is your lordship inclined this morning for a walk to the farm? You know t'other day we were interrupted by the rain, and I had not time to show you half my lions. "

As an excuse for declining the proffered honour, Lord Pynsent pleaded the fact of having that morning received important letters, which required to be answered by return of post.

"Well, then, young gentlemen, " said Lord Amersham, addressing Mr Pynsent and myself, " I must lay an embargo on you. One of you is a fighting man already, and the other, I dare say, would give his ears to become one; but the time will come at last, when, like me, you will imitate Cincinnatus, and turn your swords into ploughshares, and the sooner you begin to prepare for the change the better. As for you, Mr Thornton, I want you to be able to tell your father all about my improvements, for I know he has a taste for farming. Come along, come along—not a moment to spare. Good morning, au revoir, ladies; necessity, you know—dire necessity "—And, without finishing the sentence, his lordship waddled out into the hall, and, having seized his long weeding-hook, and ensconced his cranium in the broad-brimmed drab-coloured hat already commemorated, we set out for the farm.

Most probably, good reader, you are not a farmer, and have not the smallest curiosity to be troubled at length with the details of the many inventions and improvements with which on that morning we were made acquainted. Suffice it, therefore, that it was proved by his lordship to demonstration, that the simplest operations of husbandry might be performed, if need were, by very complicated machinery; that capital, to almost any extent, may be expended on the soil, without any adequate return; and, lastly, that farming by a nobleman on a great scale, however strong his partiality for the business may be, is, of all modes of employing an estate, the most unprofitable. Such are the principal corollaries that appeared to flow naturally from an involuntarily minute inspection of Lord Amersham's home farm. At the commencement of my task, I was not without hopes of effecting my escape, after cursorily examining the more prominent wonders of the scene, and Mr Pynsent with some difficulty did so, pleading an engagement to drive Lady Amersham in her pony-chair. But his success only seemed to increase the obstacles to mine. In short, all my hopes and efforts proved alike abortive, and, making a merit of necessity, I submitted with the best grace I could to the penance that awaited me. Had I been merely called on to admire luxuriant crops, and specimens of mechanical ingenuity, the task might have been dull, but not positively unpleasant. But this was by no means all. Lord Amersham's experiments extended to the animal as well as the vegetable creation. There was a huge, bloated, scrofulous-looking animal, stall-fed on rape and oil-cake, its limbs tottering under its unnatural and prodigious weight. A sight more thoroughly disgusting it is scarcely possible to conceive; yet this was called, par excellence, "the Staunton Ox," to which the gold medal had been awarded by the Agricultural Society! Then there were pigs, the very sight of which was almost enough to justify a man for turning Jew, and making the abjuration of bacon a part of his religion. And sheep too—but enough.

My patience was completely exhausted by the occupation of the morning, which seemed to me interminable. We returned to the house just in time to dress for dinner. The party assembled in the drawing-room was the same as on the preceding day. I had taken my situation beside Lady Melicent, in order to watch the opportunity, when dinner should be announced, of offering myself as her escort. In this I was baffled. Whether Lady Amersham perceived my intention, I know not, but she decreed me the unwelcome honour of supporting her to the dining-room, and the Lady Melicent followed, leaning on the arm of Sir Cavendish. At dinner I sat next Miss Pynsent, who had thrown off much of that *retenu* of manner in conversing with me, which had rather predominated at our first interview. She was amiable, modest, frank, and unaffected, and never descended to the use of those vulgar arts of captivation, which, in the present day, even demoiselles of high caste do not always scruple to employ.

To a young man whose feelings are fresh, and yet unblunted by worldly experience, there is a charm even in the most unimpassioned intercourse with the other sex. Woman! To him how vast a charm is comprised in the narrow compass of a word! In this single abstraction, unconnected it may be with any individual reality, are united all his purest dreams of happiness, all his brightest conceptions of imaginary beauty. With it no thought of grossness or sensuality comes to contaminate his fancy or his heart. This is at once the portion and the penalty of greyhaired debauchery, the wormwood which mingles in the cup of pleasure, changing the sparkling contents of the goblet to bitterness and poison.

Whether from accident or design, I enjoyed but few opportunities of particular conversation with Lady Melicent. When these did occur, she maintained towards me the same light and *riant* manner with which I had been originally delighted. Still, charming as it was, I should have been better pleased had she exchanged it for one more congenial to the sentiments of which I was myself conscious. It was a manner that expressed no feeling, and gave an apparent denial to my fondly-cherished hopes of having created in her heart a strong impression in my favour. But what right had I to expect that anything in our trifling intercourse had, or could have, inspired such sentiments, in one accustomed to receive, and to neglect, homage as deep, and admiration more flattering, than mine? None; and yet the disappointment was not the less deeply felt, because it was unreasonable. Who is there, in whom youthful vanity has not excited such hopes, to whom it has not occasioned such disappointments? If such a person exists, he is a being cold and calculating, dull of heart and fancy. Poet, Hero, or Patriot, he can never be. Philosopher—yes, in the modern sense of the term, he *may* be a philosopher. But, with such a one I have no communion of spirit; our lot and our portion have been cast apart; let him close this book, nor listen further to the confession of follies which he will despise, of frailties for which his heart can afford no sympathy.

There was one person in company, of whom after a formal introduction to the reader, I have yet said nothing. I mean Miss Cumberbatch, who was generally seated at a small embroidery-table apparently engrossed by her work, and was seldom called on to take any share in the conversation or proceedings of the party. The neglect with which she was treated, tended in no small degree to excite my compassion. She was *in* the party but not *of* it, a solitary person even when mingling in the crowded vortex of society. Miss Cumberbatch was still in the prime of life; in manner she was distant and reserved, and spoke and moved with that unvarying precision and propriety, which seemed to indicate that every thought and motion had been decided on and selected as that best suited to her character and circumstances. There was, in short, a good deal of the automaton about her, her manners were obviously artificial, she courted no notice, and received little, and " *noli me tangere,* " was pretty legibly expressed in her air of self-concentration and retirement.

There was nothing in all this very tempting to a nearer approach, but a degree of curiosity mingled with my compassion, and I repeatedly took advantage of circumstances to engage her in conversation. My attempts in this way, though not absolutely repulsed, were coldly received; my questions elicited only monosyllabic replies, my best jokes were " damned with faint smiles, " my very cleverest observations barely assented to " with civil leer. " In short, like the north pole, there was a frozen barrier around her, which I had not enough of Captain Parry about me to attempt very perseveringly to penetrate. Under such unpromising circumstances, my efforts gradually slackened, and at length resigning a task so apparently hopeless, Miss Cumberbatch remained, as formerly, solitary and unnoticed.

The first few days of my stay at Staunton were passed with little

variation to distinguish them from those already described. I occasionally walked and rode with Lady Melicent, but never alone. Her manner
towards me remained unchanged; and though I did flatter myself she
felt a preference for my society over that of Mr Pynsent, mingled
perhaps with some degree of personal regard, yet of this preference and
partiality I could detect no unequivocal or palpable demonstration.
The quiet tenor of affairs, however, was soon about to undergo a change.
The week following was that of York races, and Staunton Court was
then to be the rendezvous of a large and distinguished party. All was to
be bustle and gaiety, and the anticipated pleasures and arrangements
became matter of eager speculation to the younger part of the circle. In
these projections of future enjoyment, I was a warm participator. The
expected scene was armed with too many attractions, both accessory
and intrinsic, to fail in exciting a strong interest in a mind susceptible as
mine was of every external stimulus. The charm too was rendered more
powerful, from the knowledge that the pleasures, to which with so much
boyish eagerness I looked forward, would be heightened by the smiles
and the society of her by whom my thoughts were engrossed. In this
mutable world hope constitutes our greatest, might I not almost say our
only enjoyment. At all events I was happy. There appeared in my
horizon no cloud to shadow either the present or the future. Above and
around, all was brightness and sunshine, and time flew by " on rapid,
rapid wings. "

The expected day came at last. Splendid equipages were seen in the
intervals of the trees, gliding like meteors through the park, and sounding titles were pronounced loudly in the vestibule. The establishment
were evidently immersed in the bustle of preparation for the reception of
guests of no ordinary consequence, and my eye encountered servants in
sumptuous and strange liveries, as I passed through the hall. Captivated
by the pomp and circumstance of the scene, in which I flattered myself I
was about to play no undistinguished part, I went forth into the park to
indulge in the luxury of solitary reflection, and seek an escape in rapid
motion, for the preternatural activity of an excited imagination. An
hour or two's smart exercise had in some degree produced the desired
effect, the tumult of my thoughts had subsided, the flush had left my
cheek, and my steps were again turned toward the house. The walk I
followed, led in a rectangular direction to the principal approach, and
as I advanced with leisurely steps, my attention was attracted by the
appearance of a carriage, plain and without servants, and forming
altogether rather a contrast to the gayer equipages with which my eye
had recently become familiar. The smoking flanks of the horses, and
their nostrils covered with foam, gave indication that the journey of the
traveller had been performed with unusual speed; and the frequent and
loud crack of the whips of the postilions, alternating with the voice of the
cuckoo from the distant trees, and the nearer song of the linnet, formed a

discord unpleasing to the ear, and broke harshly the sweet unison of nature's music. It passed within a few yards of me, but its progress was suddenly arrested by a loud voice from within, calling vehemently on the postilions to stop. They obeyed the mandate, the door of the carriage flew open, and I saw before me, Humphreys, my father's steward. My first emotion was that of surprise and pleasure, and I ran towards the old man and shook him cordially by the hand. Suddenly my heart was chilled by terrible forebodings, and I started back from him, for I felt he was the ill-omened messenger of fearful tidings. For a minute there was silence. I had no words to ask of what dreadful news he was the bearer, but I looked upon him with keen and fixed gaze, endeavouring to read the dreadful secret in his countenance. That was heavy and mournful, and haggard with sleepless travelling. At length I could bear the agonies of suspense no longer, and exclaimed, " Tell,—Oh, tell me, I conjure you, what has happened! Who is dead? My father, mother, Jane, Lucy? Speak, say whose loss I am to deplore, I can bear anything but suspense. Speak, as you hope for God's mercy, speak, and speak quickly! "

" I have a heavy and grievous task to perform, my dear young master, " began the old man, while the tears stood in his eyes.

In a voice of impatient agony I interrupted him.

" Who? Who? Who? Quick—tell me but the name! " and I grasped him roughly by the arm as I spoke.

" My honoured lady, your mother "—

" Is dead! " exclaimed I, striking my clenched hands violently against my forehead.

" No, not dead, " replied he, raising his grey lustreless eyes to my face. " When I left Thornhill she was ill, but not dead. "

" But she is dying? "

" Life is in God's hands, " said the old man, " he gives and he takes away. "

" But is there no hope? " said I, relieved at the same time by a gush of tears and a convulsive sob; " is this dreadful, this fatal blow inevitable? "

" Humanly speaking, yes. The physicians have declared her past hope, and her recovery, if God wills she should recover, can owe nothing to the assistance of man. "

Stupified by the intelligence, I stood for some time in a state of helpless distraction. " And am I never more to see, to embrace her, to receive no parting kiss, no dying blessing! "

" Yes, my dearest young master, if God so wills it, you may yet see and embrace your angel-mother. It is for this purpose I am come; it is in obedience to her anxious and dying wish, that she may yet live to embrace and to bless her beloved,—her only son. But time is short and life uncertain; we must be speedy. "

" Enough, " I exclaimed with sudden increase of energy; "in ten minutes I shall be prepared to return with you to Thornhill;" and springing into the carriage, I directed the postilions to proceed directly to the house.

In the space of a minute or two, the carriage had drawn up at the portal, and in little more, I had issued orders to my servant for instant departure. My spirits had become more calm and collected; I felt there was an awful duty for me to perform, and the hope of once more pressing my beloved mother in my arms, of soothing by my presence her last moments, roused me to exertion. Precious as time was, I felt it was proper that I should not depart without seeking a moment's interview with Lord or Lady Amersham, and explaining the cause of my abrupt departure. I rung for a servant, and inquired for Lord Amersham.

" His lordship is not within. "

" Lady Amersham? "

" Lady Amersham has gone out airing with the Marchioness of Uttoxeter in her pony phaeton. "

" The Lady Melicent? "

" The Lady Melicent is at home. "

" Then go and present to her this note, " said I, seizing the writing materials that stood on the table, and writing the following words on a slip of paper,—" I am obliged instantly to depart—I wished to have seen Lord or Lady Amersham, but find it is impossible. Will Lady Melicent honour me with an interview of one moment, when I will endeavour to speak (for I cannot write) of the misfortune which has occasioned this singular request?—Cyril Thornton. "

I was not long kept in suspense, for, in a minute or two after my note had been dispatched, Lady Melicent entered the apartment.

" What is this, Mr Thornton? " said she, starting when she beheld the altered expression of my countenance; " what has happened to make you leave us so abruptly? Your father—your mother—your sisters, I hope, are well—no family misfortune—— "

" Yes, a sad one—I have received intelligence by a messenger, informing me that my mother is dying, and that instant departure affords my only chance of yet seeing her alive. I have taken the liberty of soliciting this interview, to request you will offer my sincere thanks to Lord and Lady Amersham for their kindness.—To *you*, Lady Melicent, to *you* —pardon me, I am confused by this dreadful blow, and cannot say what I ought—think all I should feel, in bidding you farewell, and— believe I feel it. "

She was moved, and there was moisture in her eyes, as she replied,—

" I feel,—I deeply feel for you, " she said, holding out her hand at the same time, which was instantly pressed in mine.—" For my father and mother, as well as for myself, I may say, you carry with you our sympathy and best wishes for your happiness; and, as a relation,—I may add "—here she hesitated, and a slight flush rose to her cheek as she spoke,—" our kind remembrance and regard. On an occasion like this, I would not delay you an instant—Farewell, farewell. " The last word was spoken in so low a tone as to be scarcely audible, and as she pronounced it, she half averted her head. " Farewell! " I exclaimed, lingering on the word, and aware it must be the last ; and raising her fingers to my lips, which she made no effort to withdraw, I rushed from the apartment, and in a moment after felt myself whirled rapidly through the park on my return to Thornhill.

CHAPTER XVII

The voices of my home! I hear them still!
They have been with me through the dreamy night,—
The blessed household voices, wont to fill
My heart's clear depths with unalloy'd delight!
I hear them still unchanged,—though some from earth
Are music parted; and the tones of mirth,—
Wild silvery tones, that rang through days more bright,
Have died in others, yet to me they come,
Singing of boyhood back,—the voices of my home!
                                                                    Forest Sanctuary.

WE travelled in silence. My grief could brook no communion, and my
aged companion, worn out alike by the agitation of his spirits and the
fatigues of his journey, sought in sleep, deep though interrupted, the
refreshment necessary for his exhausted frame. I was pleased at this. The
presence of a human eye seemed an intrusion on the sacredness of my
sorrow, and I felt that solitude was freedom. We journeyed with all the
speed that money could command. Day gradually faded into darkness,
the long night-hours passed away, and the glorious sun was once more
abroad in the firmament. But these changes passed unheeded. External
nature was to me a blank — my eyes saw only the image of my dying
mother—the sound of her sweet and feeble voice was in my ears—the
hope of once more beholding her alive, of soothing her last moments by
my presence, occupied and engrossed my heart. We approached Thornhill in the evening of the following day, and I beheld once more the
familiar objects of my youth. Under circumstances how sad and melancholy was I again restored to them!

As we passed through the adjacent village, I looked from the
carriage, perhaps expecting to discover in the countenances and deportment of the inhabitants, traces of that sorrow and sympathy which the
loss of so kind a benefactress might be expected to inspire. No change
was discernible—the business and the pleasures of humble life were
proceeding as usual, the sound of revelry and merriment was heard from
the little inn in the market-place, groups of ragged urchins were at play,
and the labourers, after the toils of the day, were singing merrily as they
returned from the hay-field. I could not bear to look on this scene of
tranquil happiness, and closing my eyes, and throwing myself back in
the carriage, opened them not till we had entered the avenue to Thornhill.

The day, which had been a fine one, had set in clouds, and the wind roared loudly among the trees. The ravens sailing homeward to their rookery amid the tall chestnut-trees, rose and descended in their course, as if tempest-tost on airy billows, and, uttering their harsh notes, seemed birds of evil omen. I listened for the cooing of the ring-dove, in which I had formerly delighted, but it came not from the wood ; and even the multitude of smaller songsters were mute. To me all nature seemed joined in one mournful presage.

The house now rose upon my view, canopied by a dark thunder-cloud, so low that it seemed almost to rest upon the roof. In a minute more all my dreadful fears would be resolved into certainty. I wished, and yet I feared to know the worst, and I sat in awful stillness, waiting the arrival of the moment that was to end my suspense. We approached the front of the house, and the windows were closed. The smoke from the chimney tops alone gave indication that it was tenanted by living beings. At length the carriage stopped, and I stood once more on my paternal threshold.

Nearly a minute elapsed before the signal of my arrival was answer-ed, and that minute seemed to me an age. The door was opened at last by old Jacob Pearson, whose countenance was lit up by a mournful smile on beholding me. I rushed instantly into the hall, exclaiming, " My mother—how—where is my mother ?—I must see her instantly ! "

" Alas ! you cannot see her, but my master — "

" O God, she is dead ! " exclaimed I, tottering into a chair, and covering my face with my hands. Jacob was silent, and I knew the truth. I remained for some time in a state of helpless stupefaction,—how long I know not.

When I regained my senses, I felt the pressure of little fingers on my temples, and of warm kisses on the cold hands by which my eyes were still covered. I looked up, and it was little Lucy smiling on me, yet with eyes red with weeping. I snatched her to my arms, and covered her with my tears and kisses. Strangely constituted is the human heart !—As I gazed on the beauty, and felt the infantine caresses of this innocent and simple child, the burden of my grief became less grievous, and I was soothed and comforted. And Jane, too, had left her station by the death-bed, and came to welcome her brother. She was pale, and worn by long watching in the sleepless hours of the night ; but her sorrow was calm and resigned. Few words were interchanged at this mournful meeting, and encircling my orphan sisters in one fond embrace, our tears were mingled in silence, and we prayed together to that Being, by whom the prayers of an afflicted and bruised spirit are never dis-regarded.

The passionate turbulence of my grief thus passed away, and from the meek, though suffering resignation of my sister Jane, I learned to bend before the blow which had fallen so heavily upon us, and implicitly to submit to His inscrutable decrees, in whose hands are the issues of life.

My heart was softened by suffering; and when I gazed on Jane and Lucy, bereaved and motherless by the same sad dispensation, I felt how little it became me to indulge in violent and selfish grief, with those around me whose loss had been great as my own.

By Jane I was informed of all the particulars connected with the last moments of our dear departed parent; that the progress of her complaint, which was an inflammatory one, had been unusually rapid; that, in the endurance of the deepest bodily suffering, her mind had been serene, and her patience exemplary; that, aware of the fatal termination which was fast approaching, she had expressed a wish to press her son yet once again to her bosom; that the last efforts of her expiring strength had been to write a letter to myself, containing her parting injunctions; that she had uniformly spoken of me with the warmest affection, and with her latest breath bequeathed me her blessing. I learned also, that the grief of my father, on learning the fatal character of my mother's complaint, had been intense; that, since her death, he had secluded himself from his family, in the solitude of his own apartment, where he sorrowed as one that had no hope.

Such was the outline of the details I received, connected with the sad event, and they carried with them consolation. That my mother's last wish of again beholding me had not been gratified, I felt comforted in thinking, was not attributable to any want of exertion on my part. All I could wish to know,—that she had loved me to the last, blessed me, and prayed for me,—I had now learned. Exhausted as I was by fatigue, strong mental emotion, and want of sustenance, (for two days had elapsed since I had taken food,) Jane grew alarmed at the visible ebbing of my strength, and entreated me, with loving earnestness, to take the refreshment evidently so needful, and retire to rest. But rest I felt was impossible, till I had visited the chamber of death, and gazed on all that yet remained to us of our beatified mother. I wished to go alone, but Jane entreated to accompany me, and little Lucy would not be denied. Clinging together, as if for mutual support, and with palpitating hearts, we entered the apartment, and our footsteps were as soft and noiseless, as if we had indeed feared to disturb the sleep of the dead. On the bed, which was surrounded by wax-lights, lay the cold and inanimate remains of our beloved mother. The expression of the countenance was calm and tranquil, and the death-agony had passed over it without leaving any traces of its violence on the features. Yet the repose I beheld was evidently not that of sleep; on every lineament the signet of death was too visibly impressed, to be mistaken even for a moment. The body was wrapped in a winding-sheet of white satin, and the thin pale hands were crossed upon the breast. The coffin stood open at the foot of the bed, waiting for its inmate, and recalled the sad recollections of how soon even these poor relics were to be taken from us for ever. While these remained to us, it seemed as if our lost parent were not wholly gone, and while I gazed on them, I felt all the truth of the sentiment, (and what heart in such circumstances has not felt it?) so beautifully embodied in the words of Charles Wolfe—

If thou wouldst stay, even as thou art,
All cold and all serene—
I still might press thy silent heart,
And where thy smiles have been.
While e'en thy chill bleak corse I have,
Thou seemest all mine own;
But there, I lay thee in the grave,
And now—*I am alone!*

I stood for a short space with my sisters, gazing on the mournful sight before us; then gently withdrawing my arms, I advanced alone to the bed, and bending forward, imprinted the last kiss of filial love on the cold hard lips of my beloved mother, and watered her face with my tears. Then kneeling, with Jane and Lucy by my side, we made our common prayers to the throne of Grace, for comfort and support in this hour of trial.

At length we left the chamber, and when we separated for the night, sleep profound and tranquil visited my eyelids.

I forbear to dwell on the recollections connected with my mother's death. My father remained secluded, even from the society of his family, and was not present at the funeral. A week had elapsed since my return to Thornhill, and yet I had not been admitted to his presence. I felt this estrangement deeply, the more so perhaps, that I appeared to be its exclusive object. To his daughters he had certainly never been a fond father, and it was evident that the place which Charles had filled in his affections, was destined to be occupied by no successor. They, however, were occasionally admitted to the privacy of his apartment, and Jane was frequently employed in reading to him, till the utter exhaustion of her strength occasioned the intermission of her task. The ban was extended to me alone, and it seemed as if, by my mother's death, the only link that had bound us together, had been snapped in twain.

Time, however, which, in all cases of sorrow, is the best and most efficacious physician, brought to my father's grief its natural healing effects, and after an interval of some weeks, he once more quitted his habits of rigid solitude, and betook himself to his ordinary avocations. But there were few of these in which the loss of my mother was not sensibly felt. She was in a manner entwined with all his pleasures and pursuits. In a thousand unknown and imperceptible ways, she had contributed to his comfort; and the verdure which she had scattered on his path, and the flowers with which she had adorned it, were perhaps only first discovered, when the hand that spread them was gone for ever. His, therefore, was a loss neither to be supplied nor forgotten. It was recalled to him in every occupation—in health and sickness, in solitude and society. To his temper, unfortunately, affliction brought no healing balm—it came like the toad, ugly and venomous, but bore no jewel in its head. In early life he had been an ambitious man, and, by the loss of fortune, his schemes of ambition had been blighted. In bitterness of spirit he had withdrawn himself from society, and sought for happiness in study and retirement, and the quiet enjoyments of domestic life. Of these enjoyments my mother was the very life and essence, and with her, they too perished. He had suffered much—dispensations heavy to bear had been laid upon him—he had felt the terrible smiting of an almighty arm, but from its inflictions he had not risen "a wiser and a better man." To me he had ever been an object rather of fear than affection. I had wished to love him, but could not; for, even in the case of parent and child, bound together as they are by nature's closest and most powerful ligaments, love, to exist at all, must be reciprocal.

When we met, his reception of me was cold and embarrassing. Since he last saw me, I had studied, and with some distinction, at College. My mind had been opened and enlarged—I had laid up some trifling stores at least, of liberal and useful knowledge; and my father was himself a man of elegant taste and literature, well qualified to discern and appreciate the extent of my acquirements. Whatever change in these respects, however, was discernible, he regarded without interest, and to him my mind was destined to remain a sealed volume, the contents of which he cared not to know. We were, in short, as two planets kept separate by a repulsive power, which, while it prevented the possibility of nearer approach, unfortunately was not opposed to an unlimited divergence.

My father's ideas of family government, were evidently of the most despotic kind. He was little disposed in any case to mitigate the harshness of command, in proportion to the advancement in years and knowledge of those who were subject to his sway. Least of all in mine. To me his authority was always put forward in its most offensive form; and even in instances where the slightest intimation of his wishes would have been sufficient to guide and regulate my conduct, he preferred to govern by the exercise of command, rendered only more offensive because it was felt to be gratuitous.

My temper too was high, and how long I might have submitted to such unreasonable despotism without deviating into rebellion, unfurnished with stronger motives to obedience, than my own perception of the propriety of filial submission could supply, fortunately remained untried. In the letter which my mother had addressed to me on her death-bed, she made it her solemn and parting injunction, that I should under all circumstances comport myself towards my father with reverence and obedience, and that no harshness of treatment, no act of injustice, however marked on his part, should induce me to throw off my allegiance to my only parent.

The behest of a dying mother, was not, could not be disobeyed, by a spirit yet bleeding for her loss; and thus my rebellious heart still continued to yield a proud obedience to the stern mandates of parental authority.

With peculiar emphasis too, had my mother consigned my sisters to my especial care and support. She entreated that I would guard and watch over them with more, if possible, than even brotherly anxiety, and that in every alternation of circumstances, I would prove their stay, their guardian, their protector, their friend. I read the letter alone and on my knees, and it seemed as if the voice of the dead might yet be listened to by mortal ear. I felt the magnitude of the trust thus confided to me, and I invoked the curses of God upon my head if ever I neglected or betrayed it.

A month or two had elapsed, and the current of affairs at Thornhill had subsided into the channel in which it seemed hereafter destined to flow. It was evident that the health of my father had suffered considerably, yet little change was visible in his habits and deportment. But his temper was subject to more frequent and violent exacerbations. He mingled less frequently than formerly in the family circle, over which his presence never failed to cast a gloom, and his favourite and grey-haired domestics were treated with an austerity and harshness, to which they had been unaccustomed.

What his views were relative to myself, I had not yet learned, nor had I made known to him my own wishes with regard to the choice of a profession. Meanwhile the languid monotony of my life was becoming daily more intolerable. It is true, I had my dogs and my horses, and my amusements were now a matter of too great indifference to my father to become the objects of restraint. But it was neither the season for hunting nor shooting, and I felt certain " prophetic swellings in my breast, " which told me I was destined for higher things, than to become a mere

" Fishing, hawking, hunting country gentleman. "

In the society of my sisters, to whom I had now become the chief object of attachment, I felt indeed a never-failing resource. I read aloud to Jane, while engaged in her work, heard the lessons of little Lucy, and played with her at Blindman's Buff, rode and walked with both, and amused them with descriptions of Scottish scenery and manners, their Highland relations, and the eccentricities of our rich uncle the Glasgow merchant. But such placid enjoyments are better suited to the decline of life than its commencement. To a mind youthful and ardent, which pants for the full exercise of its powers and passions, they are but as dew-drops on the mane of the sleeping lion, glittering and beautiful in themselves, but which he shakes from him unheeded, when he rouses himself to action. My schoolfellows and companions had already gone abroad into the world. William Lumley was at Oxford, and about to take his Bachelor's degree; Conyers was a dragoon, and Jack Spencer had entered the navy and fought at Aboukir. And was I alone, in this busy and bustling world, to remain idle and inactive? Was I to drag on a life of thraldom and insignificance, subject to the whims and humours of a cold and capricious father? My very soul revolted at the thought. No! I would go forth and play such a part as became me, in the great theatre of the world. An ancient and honourable name should be illustrated by my achievements. I would seek my father. I would lay open to him the whole bent and passion of my soul, inform him of my resolutions, enforce their reasonableness, refute his objections, and if he still persisted in refusing his consent, I would shake the dust from my feet as I quitted his threshold, go forth unaided and alone, enter as a volunteer in a regiment abroad, and with no sign "save men's opinion and my own good sword," would win my way to honour and distinction. Such were the visionary projects of youthful enthusiasm. Luckily I was not driven to receive practical proof of their futility.

While I was endeavouring to arrange my ideas for an eclaircissement, and hesitating whether I should solicit an interview verbally or by a letter, I received one morning a message from my father, commanding my presence in the library. My heart throbbed violently, for I felt the long-looked-for moment was come, in which the character of my future prospects, perhaps the happiness of my life, was to be decided. Endeavouring, therefore, to concentrate my ideas as much as, in the agitation of my thoughts, was possible, I proceeded to the conference, filled with the deepest anxiety for its result. When I entered the library, my father was seated at a table, engaged in writing, but on my entrance he rose, and having twice paced the apartment, remained standing in front of the fire-place. Then turning towards me, and looking at me for the first time, he said, " Be seated. " I obeyed.

" I have sent for you, sir, " continued he, " because I think the time has at length arrived when it is fitting we should come to a mutual and clear understanding. You are a young man, and have your way to make in the world. Have you thought of a profession? "

" Long and deeply. "

" And, of course, feel that your own knowledge and experience are of themselves perfectly competent to decide your choice? Is not this so? "

There was something of a sneer discernible on his countenance as he spoke, and I did not answer. He went on.

" You say you have considered the subject of your future profession long and deeply—coolly and dispassionately had been better words, and more to the purpose. You had once a boyish inclination for the army. Does this still continue, or has some newer whimsy supplanted it?—Speak, sir. "

" My sentiments are still unchanged. I feel that for no other profession has nature qualified me. In a military life are centered all my hopes and wishes, and my heart tells me I must be a soldier or nothing. "

" So, I thought as much ; and since I now understand your views and intentions, it is fitting you should understand mine. Mark well, sir, what I am about to say to you, for every syllable of it concerns you deeply. When Dr Lumley formerly communicated to me your wishes in regard to a profession, I need not tell you I had *two* sons, and *you* were the younger. As such, you could expect but a slender provision, and the military life is one in which poverty is perhaps attended with fewer evils and privations than any other. I did not, therefore, think it necessary to oppose your inclinations. Since then, you know how the aspect of this family has been changed. Deep and sad changes have occurred. Your elder brother is no more, and of his death *you* were the cause. I do not mean to accuse you—the *innocent* cause, if you will—but still by that very hand, " pointing as he spoke, and slightly shuddering, " he received his death ; and when you returned, I saw it—yes, I saw it—red with his blood. Nay, I would not willingly wound your feelings, " observing my emotion, " but I have often thought, and cannot but still think, how much sorrow and suffering had been spared us all, had it but pleased God that you had never breathed, or had been mercifully snatched from us in the cradle. — Compose yourself. "

I had indeed need of composure. Had I been stretched on the rack, I feel convinced my sufferings would have been less acute than those I endured during this harsh and unfeeling address. As he uttered it, I kept my eyes fixed on his countenance, as if with all my energies collected to brave the storm. Not once, even when his words pierced deepest, did I withdraw them. At one moment, it seemed as if he quailed beneath their gaze, for he turned his face half from me, and looked upon the ground. I endeavoured, with all my strength, to be calm, and my face, I believe, was so ; but beneath, every nerve and muscle of my body seemed heaved into distinct and separate action, which I had neither the power to command nor to repress. My frame shook as if with an ague. My father betrayed signs of vehement emotion, both in speech and gesture, and the composure he prescribed to me, was evidently not unwanted by himself. He paced several times up and down the apartment, and then confronting me, in his former station, he resumed :—

" You are now an only son, and probably expect to enter on life with greater advantages and higher prospects than before. The world, of course, look on you, and you perhaps look upon yourself, as the heir to this estate. Indulge not in such a delusion. It is but justice to let you know your real situation. While another child of mine survives, Thornhill will never be yours. Such is my determination ; and if you view it calmly and aright, you ought not, you cannot, wish it otherwise. You have been made the instrument of divine vengeance on your family.

Would you accept reward for this? Through your murderous negligence your brother lost his life. Would you, could you, turn fratricide to
profit, and take wages for your brother's blood? Think you, wealth thus
acquired would come to you unburdened by a curse? Or could you for a
moment drown, amid its poor pitiful enjoyments, the remembrance of
the price you paid for them? Believe me, in this respect, at least, I am not
unjust to you, and doubt not that you would cast from you, as a
loathsome thing, fortune so detestable and unhallowed in its acquisition. Were it otherwise, I should disown you for my son, and spurn you
from my threshold. But enough. Expect nothing from me but the
provision you were originally entitled to as a younger son. You now
know the footing on which you will enter the world. Whatever your
inclinations may be, in regard to your future pursuits, I will not oppose
them. But ponder well before you decide. In the church there is a living
in my gift, to which, if you take orders, you may reasonably look
forward. In the army, I can assist you little. In this matter, however, I
wish not to influence you; let the decision be your own. At present
retire, and at some other time I will be glad to learn the issue of your
deliberations. "

I did not immediately obey the mandate to depart, but remained
with my eyes still rivetted on the speaker, for some time after he
concluded his address, partly from a desire to be certain that I had now
heard *all*, and partly, that from the agitation of my mind I did not at first
feel my physical energies to be equal to the required task of locomotion.
These, however, soon returned, and rising slowly from my chair, I
bowed low to my father, and left the room.

My face felt heated, and my head overcharged with blood. I could
not endure the atmosphere within doors, and seizing my hat, went forth
into the air. About a gunshot in rear of the house, there rises a hill of
considerable eminence, and wooded to the summit, on which stands a
turret commanding a beautiful and extensive view of the neighbouring
country. There, if there is a breath of wind stirring, you are sure to meet
with it, and it was to this spot I bent my steps. During my walk, the scene
which had just passed appeared but as a dream. I had a distinct idea of it
as a whole, but I could not resolve it into its component parts, as one
may perfectly remember the contour and expression of a face, though
utterly unable to describe the features of which it is made up. But the
influence of the cooler atmosphere in which I had fixed my station, soon
restored my memory to its wonted powers. I reflected long and deeply
on the extraordinary address to which I had recently listened. I analyzed it in my mind, and endeavoured to recall, if possible, the very words
he had spoken. I did this, I think, on the whole, calmly and deliberately.
Resentment I certainly did feel; but not that resentment which seeks to
pervert the motives of its object. I passed in review all my conduct to my
father, from my very infancy. Towards him I stood acquitted, for I felt

that the natural promptings of my heart had been to love and duty. What, then, had I done, that the greatest and most terrible misfortune of my life, under which even my reason had suffered temporary obscuration, should thus be cruelly recalled, and made matter of insidious and malignant charge? What heart but my father's could have done this? Was it not enough to disinherit me, and, by so doing, affix in the eyes of the world a stigma to my name, without adding insult and outrage to injury, torture to injustice? He could plead no provocation, no passion, no chafing of the blood, to palliate the cowardly ferocity of this most assassin-like attack. No, it was made coolly and deliberately; and, with premeditated malice, a vital part had been selected for every stab.

The mere loss of fortune affected me but little, and though I felt internal consciousness that the privation was unjust, yet worldly advantages had entered too little into my calculations of happiness, to occasion any very strong or poignant disappointment by their loss. The views of youth are seldom interested; the value of wealth is learned only by experience, and experience I had none. The inheritance of my fathers was about to pass from me, but in the possession of my sisters, I felt I could regard it without envy. It was against the cruel and implacable spirit which my father had betrayed towards me, that my whole soul rose in arms. The ocean, it seemed to me, could not separate us more widely than we were destined thenceforward to be divided. There was a gulf between us, which, once passed, like the Stygian river, could never be recrossed. The ties of filial love and reverence seemed to be unloosed for ever, and the shackles of parental bondage to have fallen from my limbs.

And it was so. From that hour I was free and independent. My father saw in my calm and stately bearing, that his authority had passed away, and never afterwards attempted to control my actions. His manner towards me was more considerate and conciliating than formerly, and when, in a few days, I informed him, that my preference for a military life was decided and immutable, he received the communication in silence, and bowed his acquiescence.

CHAPTER XVIII

Love is a thing to which we soon consent,
As soon refuse,—but sooner far repent.
Thracian Wonder.

In those times,
Of all the treasures of my hopes and love
You were the exchequer. They were stored in *you.*
English Traveller.

BEFORE the interview with my father, the particulars of which have been already narrated, my chief source of anxiety had arisen from the dread of opposition on his part to my own resolute determination to become a soldier. That cause of apprehension had been now removed, and my mind was tranquillized by the knowledge, that in the attainment of this, the chief object of my wishes, I should have no further obstructions to overcome. My father, I was aware, had taken the necessary steps to procure me a commission, and I calmly waited the arrival of the moment, when I should be called from my retirement, to start forward in the high career, for which I imagined myself to be destined. Time, too, which softens the human heart, and mitigates its fiercest passions, had not failed to exercise its salutary influence on mine. The bitterness of feeling, which the harsh and unkind conduct of my father had at first excited, gradually subsided. His health was bad ; the objects dearest to him had been snatched away ; he was a man of dilapidated fortunes and blighted hopes ; and to these causes I was disposed to attribute much of that unfeeling moroseness by which his character was marked. His love I had never possessed, and I had long known it ; of his strong aversion I *now* knew myself to be the object. Yet my heart was not formed long to be the depository of unkind feelings towards an only parent. There, indeed, my resentments had been stored ; there I imagined them to be safely treasured ; but when I endeavoured to recall them,—they were gone. The perusal of my mother's letter, too, again did much. It was ever carried in my bosom, and when I looked on it, I felt a relenting of the spirit, and the injustice of my father was forgiven.

In the establishment at Thornhill, the death of my mother had created a void not easily to be supplied. She had in fact been, as it were, the mainspring of the machine, by which each separate part was in-directly impelled and regulated. The superintendence of all domestic arrangements, and the education of my sisters, had been her peculiar provinces, and in these her loss was irreparable. Jane was now sixteen, and, under the tuition of her mother, had almost grown up into an elegant and accomplished woman. In point of acquirement, she was perfectly qualified to conduct the education of her younger sister; but it was perhaps scarcely reasonable to expect, in a girl of her age, the steadiness and energy of character necessary for such a task. To maintain a constant control over little Lucy, indeed, was no easy matter. Never was there a creature of gayer and more buoyant spirit.

She was as sportive as the fawn,
That, wild with glee, across the lawn,
Or up the mountain springs.

No shadow lingered in her path, and she went on, rejoicing in the wild revelry of her own innocent and happy heart.

Jane's health, too, was delicate; she was a creature too fragile to bear a heavy burden, and the new duties which were about to devolve on her, as the future mistress of the establishment at Thornhill, would, to one so young and inexperienced, be of themselves sufficient, without the addition of those necessarily allied to the education of her sister.

It was, however, not without mixed feelings of surprise and regret on our part, that my father, after perusing a letter one morning at the breakfast-table, informed us that we might expect in a few days the arrival of a lady, who was to form a permanent addition to our domestic circle. She was, he said, a person of good family, amiable and accomplished, intended to fill the double role of companion to Jane, and governess to little Lucy. The anticipation of such an addition to our family party, was at first by no means pleasant. But, on more mature consideration, I felt inclined to admit the propriety of the step taken by my father. Jane's spirits were variable, and required occasionally a degree of support, which neither my father nor Lucy, though from different causes, were capable of affording. In the society of a person of her own sex, this alone could be found; and I could not, on reflection, disapprove of an arrangement, which, if my father's statement might be believed, provided her with a companion in every respect eligible.

I remember one day, about the time when my sisters were anxiously expecting the arrival of this new inmate, with mingled feelings of dread and curiosity, I had just returned from a ride, and was dismounting from my horse, when a post-chaise drove up to the door. The vehicle seemed loaded externally with an unusual quantity of luggage, for the commodious conveyance of which it seemed ill calculated. An enormous black-leather trunk was fastened to the back part of the carriage by a voluminous complexity of rope, the summit was crowned by a gigantic band-box, and in front of the vehicle, the driver, instead of a dickey, was seated on a trunk, which seemed from its dimensions twin-brother to that behind. To catch a glimpse of the person who was the owner of so much worldly possession, was impossible, for nothing in the inside of the carriage was discernible but a confused mass of baskets, bonnet-boxes, and other appurtenances of a female traveller. The door of this uncomfortable receptacle, however, at length opened, and, after a world of miscellaneous articles had been removed by the united activity of the servants and the driver, to my infinite astonishment, I beheld descend from the vehicle—Miss Cumberbatch. This circumstance was so unexpected, that I at first imagined she was merely the bearer of some message from Lady Amersham; but a second glance at the confused multitude of packages which half filled the hall, most of which were addressed, in large characters, to "Miss Cumberbatch, Thornhill Park," convinced me she was the true Amphytrion, the real and genuine governess, of whose arrival we were in expectation. I approached her, therefore, and claiming the privilege of former acquaintance, begged to be allowed the pleasure of conducting her to my sisters' apartment, and introducing her to them. My offer was, of course, politely accepted, and the duties it imposed on me duly discharged. The eyes both of Jane and Lucy were naturally directed with some anxiety towards a person on whose character and qualities so much of their future comfort was likely to depend. The latter, I observed, eyed her askance. To her she came in the character of a governess, and the à priori ideas she had formed of the duties attached to that office, seemed by no means to prepossess her in favour of the person by whom it was to be filled. But the scrutiny of deeper physiognomists than either Jane or Lucy might have been baffled by the countenance of Miss Cumberbatch. It seemed the face of one long a stranger to strong emotion of any kind; whose passions, whatever they had been, were become torpid through continued inaction. But whether this unruffled placidity was the gift of art or nature, whether it was transient or unchangeable, it might have puzzled Lavater himself to determine. Her deportment, however, was in all respects marked by strict propriety; her manners, if not prepossessing, were at least far from repulsive; and even the prejudices of little Lucy gradually gave way, when she found her governess was not *quite* so disagreeable as she had expected. In fact, there was nothing in her external appearance to provoke either ridicule or dislike. Jane, too, was pleased with her new companion, and even the half aversion with which she had inspired me at Staunton Court, gave place to more kindly feelings. In short, after the arrival of Miss Cumberbatch, everything went on at Thornhill, if possible, more smoothly than before.

It may be as well, once for all, to inform the reader how Miss Cumberbatch came to make her appearance so unexpectedly in the circumstances already described. The truth was, my father had written to Lady Amersham, requesting her Ladyship's assistance in the weighty matter of procuring a person requisitely gifted for the situation. Lady Amersham, perhaps not averse to get thus easily rid of a dependent, for whose services she had little further occasion, or, to adopt a more charitable supposition, really believing Miss Cumberbatch to be well qualified to discharge the necessary duties, had recommended that lady to my father in the strongest terms. The latter did not hesitate in offering her an advantageous engagement, and Miss Cumberbatch arrived safely and in due season, with bag and baggage as before described.

My narrative has now reached a point, when I am called upon to record events of a somewhat different character, from any which have yet found place in these Memoirs. I would they might be omitted, but it cannot be; their recollection is too darkly and deeply interwoven with my story to be passed over in silence.

I have already said that in the walks of my sisters I was generally their companion. These were frequently directed to a cottage in the neighbourhood, of which there was apparently no other inhabitant than a young and beautiful girl, whom Jane occasionally employed in little works of embroidery and needle-work. In appearance and manners, she was certainly considerably above the common order of cottagers' daughters, and there was a settled melancholy on her countenance, evidently not its natural expression, which could not be regarded, or at least on my part certainly was not regarded, without compassion. The gloom and depression under which she laboured, were clearly not constitutional, for the gleams of a spirit naturally light and joyous, broke occasionally forth, and, like those of a winter's sun, seemed brighter by contrast, with the heaviness and obscurity by which they were preceded and followed. But Mary Brookes (for such was her name) did not dwell in the cottage alone. She lived with her father, a rude and violent man, of whose character report did not speak very favourably in the neighbourhood. Isaac Brookes was sprung of respectable parents, and had commenced life in a station somewhat above that which he now occupied. He had been a farmer, but he was an imprudent man, given to irregular habits, and had not thriven in the world. His stock was distrained for rent, and he was ejected from his farm. Henceforward his hand was raised against every one, and the hand of every one was raised against Isaac Brookes. In this contest, as might be expected, he had come off worst. Many were the bruises and buffetings he had to endure, and he endured them with bitterness of heart, and a reckless spirit. In his more prosperous days he had married, and his wife, it was said, had fallen a victim to his harshness and brutality. She died, and left him the father of a daughter. Willing to be relieved of such a burden, Isaac had consigned her to the care of his wife's sister, who reared the infant, and loved her as her own child. This aunt had been for many years a housekeeper in a nobleman's family, and when unfitted by the infirmities of age for further service, had retired to a neighbouring cottage, and passed the days of her declining life in comfort, on a pension allowed her by her former master. By her had Mary Brookes been instructed in all this aged matron was qualified to teach; and the accomplishments which she thus acquired, were the objects of envy and admiration to the village maidens. When on the verge of womanhood she had lost her kind protectress. Her pension ceased at her death, and Mary was obliged to seek a home in the cottage of her father. It was indeed a home very different from the one she quitted. Isaac Brookes was still a widower, and his temper had become ferocious from poverty and disappointment. Deprived of all the comforts to which she had hitherto been accustomed, and treated by her father with cruelty and neglect, it is not to be wondered, that her spirits sunk under a change of circumstances so sudden and severe. Her sorrow, though deep, was silent and unobtrusive; if she wept, her tears were shed when no eye beheld them; if she sighed, it was in the solitary desolation of her heart, when there was no human ear to listen.

Such was the situation of Mary Brookes, when, with my sisters, I first visited her father's cottage. A creature more interesting it is difficult to conceive. Her figure was tall, and its natural grace was perhaps rendered more remarkable by the simplicity of her dress, and the air of retiring modesty visible in every look and gesture. Her face was pale, but when she spoke there was a suffusion in her cheek, as if the sound of her own sweet voice had made her fearful—

> " A maiden never bold
> Of spirit—so still and quiet, that her motion
> Blush'd at itself. "

To me she seemed a being, whom, to gaze upon, was necessarily to love, who would find sympathy in every heart, and support in every arm. But it was not so. The punishment of the father had been extended to the daughter, and she was friendless. Who would show kindness or protection to the daughter of Isaac Brookes? To whom could she look for comfort or support in her sufferings and trials? To none. The superiority of attraction she possessed rendered her an object of dislike to the mothers, and of jealousy to the daughters; for it is always peculiarly galling to be excelled by the unfortunate. From my sisters, it is true, she received all the kindness and consolation which they were prompted by their own feeling hearts to bestow. And I too,—think of the beauty and distress of this fair creature—of her meekness in suffering—of her fragile frame gradually sinking under the heavy burden that was laid upon her, and think whether every generous impulse of my soul was not awakened in her behalf. Alas for poor human nature, that the indulgence of even our best and purest feelings should lead but to guilt and error!

In the company of Jane and Lucy, I paid several visits to the cottage of Isaac Brookes. Of him we saw nothing, for he uniformly left home in the morning, and never returned till night; and Mary was left sad and solitary the live-long day, to the cheerless task of lace-making or embroidery. The strength of the spells she had cast around me daily increased; her image haunted me by night and by day, yet never was the thought of injuring a creature, so innocent and defenceless, even for one instant harboured in my soul. No, in all my dreams, and they were wild and countless, the Searcher of hearts knows that

" I never tempted her with word too large ;
But, as a brother to a sister, show'd
Bashful sincerity, and comely love. "

One day I visited the cottage alone, charged with a message from Jane, and I found Mary seated as usual at her work; but her eyes were heavy and bloodshot, and she was evidently under the influence of deep depression. There was nothing in the circumstances of my visit to alarm the most scrupulous delicacy, far less to excite apprehension in one so simple and confiding as this poor girl. She saw—she could not but see—that I was deeply interested by her distress, nay, that could the pouring out of my blood have contributed to restore her to happiness, it would have been shed as water. Poor Mary! her heart leaped up within her at the voice of kindness, long a stranger to her ear; and while she listened to the words of pity and of comfort with which I sought to soothe her,

" She could not bear their gentleness,
The tears were in their bed. "

Most true is the old adage, that pity is akin to love. The stream of one passion flows into another so imperceptibly, that the point of union cannot be discovered, and we glide onwards with the current, insensible alike of our own progress, and of the direction in which we are carried, till we strike on some sunken rock, and are left perhaps to float a shattered wreck upon the waters.

Day after day were my steps directed to the cottage, and anxiously did Mary watch in her innocence and simplicity for the accustomed hour, when her solitude would be cheered by my presence, her heart gladdened by my voice. From her own lips I listened to the story of her griefs. She told me her father pressed her to a hateful marriage with a gamekeeper on a neighbouring estate, a rude and violent man, whom she detested. That on her acceptance of his addresses depended her father's safety and continuance in this country; for, on this condition alone, had Pierce agreed to quash a prosecution for poaching, in which conviction was certain. Her tears flowed fast as she spoke, for her heart was torn by conflicting emotions. By a sudden impulse I caught her in my arms, and kissed the moisture from her cheeks, which in an instant glowed like crimson. She started back from my embrace with the offended dignity of maiden modesty, and I knelt down, and, invoking God to witness the purity of my intentions, vowed to guard and to protect her with a brother's love. And thus her fears were calmed; but alas, from that moment our fate was sealed.

The frequency of my visits to Brookes's cottage afforded, as might be expected, matter for village gossip, too interesting to be overlooked, and it became necessary that our interviews should be arranged with secrecy and caution. The heart of every woman tells her, almost instinctively, of the close affinity between guilt and concealment, and that of Mary shrank from it with fear and trembling. But she was young, inexperienced, and, above all—she loved. Our place of rendezvous was the tower on the hill already mentioned, and there we met at midnight, in silence and secrecy. Night after night these visits were repeated, and there did we linger till the dawn of morning-twilight gave the signal for departure. The Being who alone knew our weakness, knows likewise with what purity of purpose we trode the brink of the precipice to which our steps had brought us. Need I go on? The tale of guilty love, of hearts alike deceiving and deceived, has been often told. We were but weak and erring creatures—at length caution slept—Mary ceased to be virtuous—and the reproaches of my own heart told me I was a seducer.

CHAPTER XIX

Oh, County Guy, the hour is nigh—
The sun has left the lea,
The orange flower perfumes the bower,
The breeze is on the sea ;

The lark, his lay who trill'd all day,
Sits hush'd his partner by ;
Breeze, bird, and flower, they know the hour—
But where is County Guy?

Quentin Durward.

ON the night following I was again at the tower, but the hour of tryste passed, and Mary came not. It was a moonless summer's night, and the air was sultry and oppressive. For long hours did I sit watching for the sound of her footsteps, in the path that wound along the hillside, and start at every rustling of the leaves made by the fox, as he stole through the bushes towards his earth in the furze cover,—but Mary came not, and the night passed in solitude and sadness. I lingered till the day at length dawned ; and the song of the birds that came forth to carol their sweet matins in the sunrise, warned me that my hopes were vain, and I sought my pillow with worn spirits and an anxious bosom. My dreams were wild and dreary, and I woke only to encounter the fierce upbraidings of offended conscience. A lovely, friendless, innocent, and defenceless creature had trusted herself to my honour and protection, and I had plunged her in irretrievable ruin. What need was there to add new and more intolerable anguish to the griefs of one already desolate and oppressed ? Why select as a victim, the most innocent, the most confiding, the most unhappy of her sex ? In vain did I attempt to " lull the still small voice, " by pleading that I too had fallen unwarily into the snare. The pitfall was not dug in my path—I had sought it—I had voluntarily courted the temptation under which I fell. Had I not sworn, and called on the Deity to witness my truth, to love her but with a brother's love, and to guard her honour stainless and immaculate ? She had trusted me. To her innocent and unsuspecting heart, my promises had been as those of gospel truth. She had clung to them with woman's faith. In them she had embarked all that belonged to her in this world, her innocence— and she had been betrayed. What was it now to say, that I had over-rated my strength, or to deplore the fatal consequences of my ungoverned passions ? Are not the consequences of his guilt lamented even by the most selfish and hardened sinner, when the enjoyments it afforded him are past? But what could avail regret, however bitter? The victim had fallen—the altar had been desecrated by the sacrifice, and the immolation of innocence had been completed. "Vile seducer! unprincipled betrayer of confiding love! Like Cain, shalt thou be branded among men, and go down into the grave with the guilt of perjury on thy soul." Never till now had I felt the bitterness of an upbraiding conscience, and it goaded me to the quick. There is no extremity of bodily suffering I would not have preferred to the mental agonies I then endured. I strove to escape from my own reflections, but could not—like the wretch, who feels in his quivering flesh the flames by which he is surrounded, and attempts escape in vain, for he is chained to the stake.

And Mary too, where was she? Might she not have been driven to some act of despair, and might not even the guilt of murder be added to my already dark catalogue of crimes! Was I not once more to see, and comfort her, to join my tears with hers, to tell her how much her very weakness had endeared her to my heart? I was indeed full of anxiety on her account, but I feared to venture to the cottage, for I knew my visits there were watched, and guilt is ever full of many fears. My steps were directed, therefore, to a part of the park, from which it was overlooked, and there did I sit for hours gazing on its thatched roof, and the little garden that lay between it and the road, neglected and full of weeds. The sun had gone down ere I quitted my station. No living being had approached the house, no smoke rose from its chimney top—it seemed tenantless and deserted. Sick of soul, did I return to Thornhill; I shrank from society—the caresses even of little Lucy were become hateful and distressing. I pushed her rudely from me, and while the tears started up into her large and blue eyes at my unkindness, I retired to solitude and suffering, in my own apartment. Night came, and the stars again saw me at my watch-tower on the hill-top. They rose and disappeared, but Mary's footstep had not gladdened my ear, nor her tall and slender form delighted my eye. Heavily did the sun appear that morn to raise his disk above the dark curtain of the clouds, and less than usually jocund, methought, was the jubilee of living nature in his return. I did not return home, but roamed onward through the woods, and selecting the path that led to where the shadow of the dark green pines was deepest and least pervious, I cast myself on the ground, and listened to the melancholy sound of the waterfall, that ascended from the glen. It was noon ere I reached Thornhill; a letter had come for me by the post, and I knew it was from Mary. I thrust it hastily into my bosom, rushed up stairs to my apartment, and having secured my chamber-door from the possibility of intrusion, I opened it with a trembling heart. It was indeed from Mary, and gave melancholy evidence that her spirit, which till now had borne up against sorrow and misfortune, was at length broken. It contained no reproaches, she upbraided me not with my broken faith. She had foolishly, she said,—almost wickedly loved, where love was hopeless, and a dreadful punishment had followed her offence. She said that all thought of happiness had fled for ever, and she now knew herself to be a creature alike alienated from God, and despised by man. She told me, too, that her father now treated her with more harshness and cruelty than ever; that he even threatened her life, if she refused to pay the price of his safety by marrying Pierce; and what could she do?—her heart was broken, and she knew not. She concluded by wishing me farewell for ever. We could never meet again. She had been guilty, but her nature would not suffer her to persist in guilt. Her love would cease only in the grave, it was mine unalienably, indefeasibly mine, yet she desired me to forget her. She was, she said, but a guilty, miserable, and worthless thing, unworthy of a thought, a weed tossed upon the waters, bound by no tie, and destined to be the sport of wind and waves. The letter was written with trembling fingers, and blotted with tears. Shall I attempt to describe the effect it produced on me? No. The feelings of suffering that letter cost me shall still rest undisturbed in their sepulchre, nor shall the grave be called on unnecessarily to open its ponderous and marble jaws, and cast them up again.

Notwithstanding the expressed determination of Mary to see me no more, I felt it was necessary to my peace, that at least another interview should take place. I wrote her a letter of comfort; I accused myself as the sole cause of her misfortune; I assured her of my undiminished, my unchangeable attachment; I entreated her to quit her father's roof, and accept an asylum from me, and I made a solemn vow never to intrude myself unbidden on her presence. Lastly, I conjured her by the love she bore me, to see me once more, to grant me at least the melancholy consolation of bidding her an eternal farewell. I dispatched this letter by a sure channel, and with trembling anxiety awaited the answer. A day, and yet another day passed, and it came not. I could bear the tortures of suspense no longer, and determined at all events to seek an interview. Prudence had hitherto withheld me from visiting the cottage of her father, but my mind was now in too high a state of excitement, to think of prudence. There, therefore, I resolved to seek her. And I did so. My heart beat almost audibly, as I approached the cottage. I lifted the latch, and listened for a moment to catch if possible some signal that the house was still tenanted by her so dear to me. No sound but the monotonous ticking of a clock broke the silence of the dwelling. I advanced slowly and on tiptoe, and through a half-opened door I beheld Mary, with her head bent forward to the table, and her face covered with her hands. A basket with her work lay beside her, but it was evidently untouched. I saw before me the creature whom I had ruined and betrayed; my heart was moved with something of awe and fear, and I almost dreaded to approach. For a moment or two I stood irresolute, and then I called her by her name. Quick as lightning she started up, and gazing on me with a look of wildness, exclaimed, "Oh, why have you come? God help me, my misery needed not this. "

"Yes, God will help you, dearest Mary, " said I; "let not your heart be cast down; accept shelter and protection from one, who would peril body, nay soul, in your defence. " She sank back into her chair as I spoke, and I advanced and knelt before her. "Pardon, pardon the wretch who has betrayed you—mine was the guilt, not yours. Spare your self-reproaches, accuse him who is alone guilty, and who now sues for that pardon from you, which his own conscience can never grant. "

Mary's only reply was a loud shriek; quick and heavy steps were heard on the floor, and, turning round, I beheld Isaac Brookes and Pierce the game-keeper. I was instantly on my feet, and turned to front the intruders. The face of Pierce was black as Erebus, and was marked, I thought, by an almost diabolical malignity. He had lowered the butt of the gun which he carried, to the ground, and he stood, with his arm resting on the muzzle, regarding me with a settled scowl. The face of Brookes, though of a different character, was equally marked by evil passion. Its first expression seemed to be one of unmingled fury; but that soon passed away, and his countenance assumed, as he approached me, a look of sardonic, or rather of malignant suavity, more unpleasant than ungoverned passion, because more difficult to deal with.

"Your servant, young squire, " said he, slightly touching his hat, "I thank you for your kindness to my daughter, and the care you seem to be taking of her; but when your honour thinks of visiting her again, you had better let me know before you come; because if you do not, " and his assumed mildness of expression was changed into a look of deadly determination, "it may hap that evil may come of it, " glancing a look at the same time on Pierce's gun.

"I came, I assure you, " answered I, feeling all the awkwardness of my situation, but making an effort to conceal it, "I solemnly assure you, with no evil intentions towards either your daughter or yourself. My sisters are deeply interested for her, and I——"

"Thank them and you too, " interrupted Brookes; "you are very kind and condescending, and I am grateful, as in duty bound. In return, take one word of advice from me, and that is, neither to write to my daughter, " and he produced at the same time my letter from his pocket, "nor to visit her for the future, if you would live to inherit your father's estate. So, good morning to you, sir.—Come, Mary, why don't you wish the gentleman farewell, that's been so kind to you?—Good morning to you, sir, and I recommend you to think on my advice. "

I left the cottage immediately, and as I passed the door, a peal of hellish laughter from within sounded in my ears.

Baffled in all my hopes, I returned home in no very enviable frame of mind. By my imprudence I had aggravated Mary's misfortunes, and exposed her to ignominy and obloquy. Her father, it was evident, was aware of our correspondence, and was thus furnished with an instrument of fearful power to bend his unhappy daughter to his wishes. I would have periled everything to protect her from the tyranny and violence of her brutal parent. But what *could* I do? Every avenue of communication between us was closed. If I approached the cottage, my steps were watched; if I wrote, my letter would probably be again intercepted by her father; and to incur detection in either case, what was it but to draw down on Mary's head persecution yet more severe, and add new dangers and difficulties to the labyrinth of those in which she was already lost. Now, indeed, all the fearful consequences of my crime were opened to my view. I beheld, in all its extent, the dark and dreary gulf into which, on the stream of passion, we had floated. I saw Mary perishing in the waters, and yet was unable to rescue or assist her.—Such were my first lessons in morality, and they were bitter and severe.

My grief was now of that passive nature which requires only patient endurance, and calls into action none of the more active energies in our nature. It was deep, not vehement; fixed, not loud; and experience tells me that such grief is more difficult to bear, than that which comes suddenly, and like a torrent, upon the heart; which

" Flows like the Solway, but ebbs like its tide ; "

and which, sweeping down with the rapidity and desolation of a whirl-wind, like a whirlwind also passes away. I felt no longer a satisfaction in the solitary indulgence of sorrow, but once more sought society, and strove to extract from it, the only solace that remained for me—the power to *forget*. My sisters were engaged to pay a visit of some duration to a neighbouring family, and I agreed to accompany them. I was absent about a month, and during that period received no intelligence of Mary. Alas! had such intelligence never reached me, I had been comparatively happy, for I learned, on my return to Thornhill, she had become the wife of Pierce. And now did the whirlwind I have spoken of, rage in all its violence within me! I uttered curses and execrations on her father, on Pierce, on myself, nay, even on Mary. Why, I exclaimed in my impious frenzy, had this horrid and accursed deed been suffered by the great Ruler of the world? Why had he not blasted with his lightning the perpetrators of a crime so black and unparalleled? Were those lips that I had kissed—that bosom which had throbbed against my own, to be contaminated by the touch of a low and brutal barbarian? There was almost madness in the thought, and yet it was a thought I was compelled to endure. To flee from it was impossible; it haunted me like my shadow. I saw the look of conscious triumph on the face of the vile minion, as he gazed upon his victim. I saw her flesh creep as he approached, and she shrunk with a shudder from his touch. I could not go on. The picture was too horrible to be voluntarily contemplated; and, to avoid it, I would have plunged into the crater of a volcano. But what was past

F

could not be recalled, and submission to the necessary course of events, is in man not optional, but imperative.

Time passed, and my feelings gradually reverted to their former tone, and I regarded Mary, if possible, with even deeper compassion than before. We had been disjoined by an irreversible fiat, and yet I was loath to think that we had already separated for ever. In a short time I should bid farewell—certainly a long,—possibly an eternal farewell, to Thornhill; and I felt I should depart with a lighter spirit, if I could meet Mary once more. The obstacles to such a meeting seemed almost insurmountable—it was even difficult to convey to her an intimation of my wishes. Project after project was considered and rejected, for the consequences of exciting the jealousy of Pierce were too serious to allow me to adopt any plan which involved even the possibility of discovery. I had at length nearly given up the attempt in despair, when I learned that Pierce had gone to the county town to give evidence in several trials for poaching, and that his presence would be required there for several days. This circumstance was too favourable to my wishes not to be taken immediate advantage of. Pierce's cottage was about two miles off, situated on the estate of which he was keeper. On three sides it was surrounded by a wood, which skirted the little garden behind, and where that did not intervene, approached still more closely to the house. In this wood it was possible to lie concealed, and at the same time to command a view of everything that passed around the dwelling. Having arranged my plans, I wrote a letter to Mary, in which I told her of my approaching departure—that it was necessary to my happiness that I should learn whether there was anything in which I could contribute to her comfort and tranquillity; and above all, that I should receive from her own lips assurance of her forgiveness. I urged with all the eloquence I could command, that in the memory of having thus parted with her in kindness, I could alone hope for consolation when far distant, and conjured her, standing on the verge, as we did, of an eternal separation, not to deny this last, this parting request, to one whom she had once loved, who still loved her. My letter likewise indicated the hour and place of meeting on the following night, and if she agreed to this arrangement, I desired she would give signal of her consent by appearing at the window with a white handkerchief in her hand.

Before sunrise I was at my post, but the execution of my scheme was by no means easy. There were servants about the house, by whom it would have been ruin to be discovered. Of Mary I had only caught a few occasional glimpses as she happened to approach the window, and no opportunity occurred of attracting her observation. At length, however, she came forth into the garden, singing in a voice weak but exquisitely sweet, a song whose mournful cadences seemed breathed from a weary and a bursting heart. Every note of it sank deep into my soul. She had approached nearly to the extremity of the garden, which opened by a small wicket into the wood, when I advanced, crouching as much as possible to avoid all chances of detection, and throwing the letter in her path, retreated hastily to my place of concealment. I feared the suddenness of the surprise might have caused her to scream, but it did not. When she saw the letter, she leant for support against a tree, as if suddenly bereft of strength, but soon recovering, she took it up, and I saw her return with tottering steps to the house. A long interval followed, which was passed by me in a state of restless anxiety. At length she approached the window, her eyes evidently swollen with weeping, and the white handkerchief was in her hand. She pressed it to her bosom and retired. I too, satisfied with the success of my mission, returned to Thornhill, screening myself as much as possible from observation, by directing my steps through the thickest and least frequented part of the wood.

During the remainder of the day my mind was restless and uneasy. Our interview would of necessity be a melancholy one, and I almost regretted having sought it. Mary, I thought, was too weak to support the agitation it must necessarily occasion; and the motives which had induced me almost to force it upon her, I feared were wrong and selfish. But the die was cast, and it was necessary now to stand its hazard; and when night closed in I was on my way to the place of meeting. It was a field distant about a quarter of a mile from Pierce's cottage, in the middle of which stood a group of chestnut-trees of uncommon size and luxuriance, and which, from this circumstance, was distinguished among the country people as " the field of the Five Chestnuts. " It was a green and sunny spot; such a one as the passer-by might pause to gaze upon, before he plunged once more into the dark shadows of the surrounding wood. Here and there a large tuft of broom glittered like a mass of molten gold; but I need not describe it, for after all, it was nothing more than a pretty field, such as one may meet almost anywhere. Why I had selected it as a place of meeting I know not; but here it was, beneath the shadow of the chestnut-trees, that Mary and I were once more to meet, and bid each other an eternal farewell. When I reached the appointed place, my watch informed me that the hour of meeting was not yet come, and throwing myself on the ground, I endeavoured, both for Mary's sake and my own, to acquire fortitude and self-command sufficient to enable me to pass calmly through the approaching trial. The spot where I lay was too much sheltered for the wind to reach it; but the swiftness with which the clouds travelled in the sky, showed its influence to be powerful above. One moment a mass of heavy clouds veiled the moon, and the earth was covered with the curtain of darkness. Anon, they had passed away, and the glorious planet again shone forth in all her brightness. Such was the night, but my observations on the firmament were cut short, by perceiving that my watch already indicated the hour of meeting to have come. I started up,

and taking advantage of the glimpses of the moon, whenever in queenly
royalty she came forth from her canopy of clouds, gazed anxiously
around to watch for the approach of Mary. At length I saw a female
figure at some distance, emerging from the wood. It was she—it was my
once pure and innocent,—my still beautiful Mary. With the swiftness of
a greyhound loosed from his leash, I sprung to meet her. In a moment I
was by her side—my arms were extended to fold her once more to my
bosom, when the report of a gun was heard, and at the same instant I felt
myself wounded. A bullet had passed through my shoulder—I staggered backward a few paces and fell.

The circumstance of being shot, always produces a considerable
confusion in a man's ideas. I have no very clear remembrance of what
passed around me, as I lay on the ground. But a shriek, loud and
piercing as ever gave expression to human anguish, yet seems to tingle in
my ear, when I revert to that moment. Then I heard curses horrible and
blasphemous, uttered in a harsh and dreadful voice; but these became
gradually weaker, till they were at length lost in the distance, and all was
silent.

By degrees I became more clear and collected, and felt desirous, for
the night-air now seemed damp and chill, to return as soon as possible,
and procure surgical assistance for my wound. I rose, though with some
difficulty, for my loss of blood had been considerable; and, stanching the
wound with my handkerchief as well as circumstances would permit,
directed my steps to the neighbouring village, which had the advantage
of including in its population a professor of the healing art. I was weak
and faint, and my progress was slow; but I at length succeeded in
reaching the doctor's house, and, with somewhat more difficulty, in
knocking up the doctor from his comfortable bed. He came rubbing his
eyes, and still apparently half asleep.

"Hey—what—Mr Thornton!—bleeding too!—gun-shot wound;—
not in the thorax or abdomen, I hope—vitals safe, and no matter for
the wings—Is this murder, or robbery, or an affair of honour? Sit down,
my good sir, and let me examine the course of the ball.—Morgan, fetch
my instruments, and the tourniquet in the left-hand drawer of my
anatomical cabinet."

The doctor, as the reader will perceive, was a loquacious man, and I
had no inclination either to share his loquacity, or become the subject of
it. I therefore requested he would dress my wound without further
colloquy, and desired that nobody might be present in the room when
he did so. Morgan was therefore dismissed; and my wound, having been
duly probed and examined, was pronounced, in military phrase, to be
severe, not dangerous. The necessary dressings and ligatures were
applied, and after many assurances that I had made a narrow escape,
the bullet having passed between the coracoid process and the scapula,
luckily without injuring either, the doctor's gig was ordered out to

convey me to Thornhill. On the way thither, I informed him that it was necessary the circumstance of my being wounded should remain secret, and that my illness should be attributed by my family to a severe injury occasioned by a fall from my horse. In case he consented to these conditions, well; if not, I should be under the necessity of employing another practitioner. To this alternative, however, I was not reduced by the doctor's obstinacy. He objected, indeed, to committing his character by telling a direct lie, but he had no objection to furnish indirect corroboration to any statement of mine, however much at variance with the fact. This was enough. Our consciences dove-tailed into each other admirably. I told my own story, the doctor supported it, and it passed current without question or suspicion.

On reaching Thornhill, I was ordered to bed. The exhaustion consequent on loss of blood had been succeeded by a state of feverish excitement, which my conversation with the doctor, and the necessity of arranging some project of concealment, had probably increased. My arrival in such a condition, and stained with blood almost from top to toe, of course created, in the phraseology of the present day, " a great sensation " in the family. Old Jacob Pearson stood aghast when he beheld me, and the alarm of Jane and Lucy was strong, and difficult to be calmed. Even my father, on learning the condition in which I had been brought home, was moved to the display of some share of parental feeling.

My recovery was slow, and my confinement tedious. Everything sisterly love could do to relieve the ennui of a sick-bed, was done, but done in vain. Jane could not now, as formerly, be the confidante of all my thoughts and feelings; secrets impossible to be disclosed weighed heavily on my mind; it bent beneath a burden which could not be lightened or participated, and of which time alone could diminish the oppression. To my sisters I was neither unkind nor ungrateful; I loved them dearly as before; but I felt, and I believe Jane too felt, that the charm which openness of heart had before given to our intercourse was gone. Happy, at least comparatively happy was I, when I could with-draw my thoughts from the past, and fix them on that paradise of fools, the future. Sad and painful remembrances seemed indissolubly linked with every object around me, and the thirsty Hart pants not more ardently for the clear brook, than I did for the arrival of the expected moment, when I should bid a long farewell to my parental mansion. I counted the days,—almost the hours, till it arrived, and to me they seemed an exhaustless calendar. Yet " time and the hour " sped on, and the moment of anticipated happiness came at last.

My wound had healed, and I was again convalescent, when I once more received a summons to attend my father in the library; and never was mandate obeyed with greater alacrity. On my entrance, he pointed to a newspaper on the table, and said : " You will find in the Gazette a notification of your appointment to an Ensigncy in the —— regiment of foot. You would have preferred, no doubt, a commission in the Guards or the Dragoons; but, in your circumstances, I have not deemed it prudent or fair to expose you to unnecessary temptation. Remember you have not become a soldier, like many young men of fortune whom you will meet with in the world, merely for the sake of wearing a handsome uniform, or passing a few years in pleasant society. No. The army must be to you a *profession*, not an amusement; and it is by your success or failure in that, you must expect to sink or swim. In future, trust only to yourself, for from this hour you are your own master. Do not think I am your enemy. You will carry with you my warmest prayers for your success, and whatever I can do to advance your interests will be done cheerfully. With advice I will not trouble you. From any act of dishonour, the blood that flows in your veins will preserve you; and to avoid acts of folly and imprudence, it is necessary to taste the punishment that follows them. It is the price paid for the lessons of experience that in fact constitutes their value; cheapen them, and they are worthless. Depart as soon as may be. Life is too short to be unnecessarily wasted in idleness and inaction. When you come of age, the fortune you are entitled to claim by settlement, will be paid you; till then, you shall have a credit on my banker for all suitable expenses. Go to London, and make the necessary preparations for joining your regiment, which is in America. Write often to your sisters—it will give me pleasure to hear of you through them. Farewell. "

Cold as this may appear, when considered as the parting address of a father to an only son, I was yet moved by the tone of unusual kindness in which it was spoken. My heart was softened, and when he extended his hand, I grasped it between mine, and bathed it with my tears. It seemed as if I were now parting for ever with my only remaining parent.

" Father, " I said, " send me not forth into the world without your blessing. "

" It is yours. May God bless and protect you. "

He withdrew his hand, and left the apartment. My journey required few preparations, and these were soon made. On the following morning, I pressed my weeping sisters in my arms,—imprinted a parting kiss upon their lips, and bade adieu to Thornhill.

Of Mary Brookes I saw, I heard no more; but I have since learned that she died soon after my departure. When I returned to Thornhill several years afterwards, I wished to shed a tear on her grave. But there was no stone to mark its site;—the sexton knew it not,—Mary and her grave were alike forgotten.

END OF VOLUME FIRST.

VOLUME II

CHAPTER I

Now has your well-train'd son mature attain'd
The joyful prime, when youth, elate and gay,
Steps into life, and follows, unrestrain'd,
Where passion leads, or pleasure points the way.
Wonder of a Kingdom.

A CHANGE has come o'er the spirit of my dream. The days of my boyhood have passed away, and I am now a man—participating largely in all the hopes, passions, errors, follies and pursuits which belong to that condition of our being, and about to enter on the part allotted me in the busy scene of life. It has been said that the happiest years of human existence are those of childhood. My own experience would lead me to question this. There is no period of my life, to the contemplation of which I return with greater reluctance than that which is embraced in the preceding portion of this narrative. My horizon had been early darkened by the quenching of its brightest stars. The lines had not always fallen to me in pleasant places, and my slender bark had been destined, from the very commencement of its voyage, to endure the buffetings of wind and wave. It may be, misfortunes like mine are uncommon. But the memory which recalls most vividly the happiness of youthful days, is generally a more faithless record of their sorrows ; and they who delight to dwell on the fragrance of the flower, are always the first to forget the sharpness of the thorn. Who indeed can recall the thousand griefs and anxieties of his early years ? The throng of childish fears and disappointments, by which the sunshine of his young spirit was overcast and shadowed ? The sufferings of youth are indeed more evanescent than those of maturer years, but are they necessarily less acute ? I cannot think so.

I shall not encumber my narrative by any attempt to describe the feelings with which for the first time I entered London. The impression produced by this great mart of the world, is, in all cases I believe, pretty nearly the same ; modified indeed in its intensity by the constitutional temperament of individuals, but varying little in the character of the emotions which it excites.

For the first few days my mind was bewildered by the vastness of the scene, and my conceptions of the character and grandeur of the objects around me were vague and dim. I was incapable of business, and devoting my time to contemplation, I roamed about the streets, regarding everything I saw with wonder. By degrees, however, the charm of novelty wore off, and as my eye became gradually familiar with the splendour and magnitude of the objects among which I moved, new and unknown attractions did not fail to present themselves. Fresh allurements daily started up around me, and spread themselves in my path, and I was beset by temptations to which my natural temperament and acquired habits of self-command were unequal to afford effectual resistance. In short, I was my own master, and in London. Chance brought me in contact with several of my early companions, already deep enough in worldly experience to be qualified to instruct my ignorance, and before I had been a fortnight in town, I had become a thorough adept in metropolitan dissipation.

To a young man in my situation, it is perhaps a misfortune, that in London there is scarcely any length to which dissipation may not be carried without loss of character. An individual forms so small a fraction of the mighty mass, and his proceedings are so much a matter of indifference to those around him, that the check of public opinion, which in smaller societies exerts so salutary an influence, is entirely removed. There is no privacy like that one enjoys in a crowd of a million, and it has been truly said by Dr Johnson, that he who would live perfectly secluded from his fellow men, should make London the theatre of his solitude.

Engrossed by pleasure, I was insensible of the rapidity with which time flew by. The weeks allowed for preparation were gone, when I imagined them to be scarcely commenced. To enable me to prolong my stay, I solicited an extension of my leave, and it was granted. I did not fail to take advantage of the means thus afforded me, of continuing my career in the devious path of vice and error on which I had thus early entered. To advance, required no effort of volition, for I was carried on as it were in a vortex; to retrieve my steps, on the other hand, was difficult, if not impossible. It required the exercise of strong energy,— perhaps, the influence of higher motives than any by which my actions had been ever swayed.

Fortunately, circumstances did not permit that I should remain long enough to become a confirmed *Roué*. The period when it was necessary that I should proceed to join my regiment soon came, and further delay was impossible. I did not regard the necessity thus imposed on me with much regret. The goblet of pleasure, too often quaffed, had already lost something of its savour. The world I was about to explore was to me a new one. In youth, even mere locomotion is allied to pleasure. Change of scene seems but transition of enjoyment, and the landscape gazed on by young eyes, is ever bathed in sunshine.

My military enthusiasm, too, was once more awakened, dreams of ambition mingled in my slumbers, and hopes of future honour and distinction brightened my waking contemplations. I would have instantly set about the work of preparation, but a new and unexpected obstacle presented itself. I had squandered in dissipation the sum allotted by my father to defray the necessary expenses to which I was exposed, and I suddenly found myself in a dilemma for which I was wholly unprepared.

I had no reason to complain of any want of liberality on the part of my father. He had given me a credit on his banker for L.300, a sum more than sufficient to supply my wants on the most liberal scale of expenditure. This by my own folly and extravagance had been already dissipated, before the business of my equipment had commenced. What was to be done? Should I address my father in the character of a penitent prodigal, confess the truth, lay bare the secret of my errors, and, in guise of a humble supplicant, solicit present assistance, and forgiveness of the past?

It mattered not that my heart told me this was the proper course to be adopted—that it became me not now to shrink from the consequences of my guilty weakness—that having planted the tree, it was fitting that I should taste its bitter fruit. There was something within me that instinctively recoiled from such a course. Morally speaking, I felt that I had *no* father. He to whom I owed my existence had never treated me as a son, even in the days of innocent boyhood. From him, situated as I now was, I could expect neither pardon for my folly, nor compassion for my errors. Before him, of all men breathing, the idea of appearing in the garb of penitence and humility was most revolting. I could not bring myself to such a step. I would not bend at his feet. He might *hate*, but he should not *despise* me. Whatever punishment I had drawn down, whatever sufferings my conduct might involve, I would not escape from them by a humiliation so revolting.

Having summarily dismissed the idea of an application for assistance to my father, I continued to ruminate in a somewhat disconsolate mood on the unpromising condition of my affairs. A pocket-book, now nearly empty, and a letter from the Adjutant-General directing me to proceed instantly to Portsmouth, lay on the table before me, and I gazed on them with a vacant yet a rueful eye. I was aware that instant measures were necessary, yet what measures to adopt I knew not. The time demanded action, yet my circumstances seemed to afford no sphere in which action could be beneficial. My reflections on the past, and my anticipations of the future, were alike dark and gloomy. I lamented my folly, I bitterly cursed my own imprudence, I vainly sighed to recall that which was irrevocable.

It may seem strange, that, situated as I was, it was long ere the remembrance of my uncle passed through my mind. At length it came, and my heart was gladdened by the gleam of light with which his idea irradiated the gloomy vista of the future. When I thought on him, all my anxieties were relieved; for I knew the old man loved me, and I remembered his parting injunction, to apply to him under any circumstances in which his friendship could be useful. I felt that the words he had spoken were not those of hollow and unmeaning profession; that the love he bore me was not a mere transient impression, which a few days or months of absence might erase. I carried with me the belief, that in my gruff and ascetic uncle I possessed a friend, whom time could not alter, and on whose regard, in difficulty or danger, I might cast myself in confidence and security.

When the thought of my uncle once occurred to me, my spirits, which for some time had been at zero, suddenly remounted to their usual height; and my path, which but a moment before seemed to lead along a desert, dreary and limitless, was suddenly begirt by flowers, and became verdant and inviting as it had spread before me in the dreams of boyhood. I seized the writing materials that lay before me, and without reflection or delay dispatched a letter to the old gentleman, containing a full confession of my folly, and soliciting his assistance in the difficulties which that folly had occasioned.

I believe there is no explaining the eccentricities of feeling. Disclosures, which to my father nothing less than the rack could have wrung from me, cost me no effort when made to my uncle. To him I at once laid open the whole burden of my errors. I introduced no studied palliations of my conduct, and nothing could be more simple, undisguised, and veracious than the narrative of my unfortunate debut on entering the great world into which I had been cast. Had I been writing to a companion of my own age, I could not have been more sincere, though I might possibly have suppressed some expressions of the regret I could not but feel in taking a retrospective view of my recent career.

Having dispatched my letter, there was the necessary intervention of a week, before, in course of post, an answer could be received. During this interval it was my wish to withdraw myself from the society of my companions; yet in this I did not wholly succeed. Dissipation, in losing its novelty, had already been deprived of half its charm; but the spells of the syren's enchantment, though weakened, were not yet broken. The disease was not cured, though the violence of its paroxysms was diminished. I yielded occasionally to the persuasion of my companions, and retrode the course already familiar to my footsteps. These relapses, however, did not go unpunished. Each unnatural elevation of my spirits was followed by a proportionate depression, and the gallings of self-reproach became daily keener, and more difficult to bear.

I well remember the morning when my uncle's letter arrived. The handwriting, strong, round, and betraying a certain mercantile uniformity in the formation of the characters, I recognised at once. It was some time before I opened the letter, for then doubt and misgiving came over me, and I laid it on the table, to afford time for breath and reflection before I broke the seal. I imagined that reflection would have dispelled all my fears. But this was not so. My mind was shaken by forebodings of evil. The support on which I had most confidently reckoned seemed to sink from beneath me. Even my old uncle had cast me off. When the possibility of this occurred to me, I could bear suspense no longer, and snatching up the letter, read as follows. The writing that first met my eye was not my uncle's.

"*Glasgow, 28th March* 18—

"CYRIL THORNTON, Esq.

"SIR,—We beg to acknowledge receipt of your esteemed favour of 17th current to our Mr D. S. By his desire, we now inclose a bill at sight on Messrs Smith, Payne, Smith, and Co. bankers, London, for L.500, which is placed to your debit. As we observe there are no funds of yours in our hands, we shall be happy to receive, at your earliest convenience, a remittance to balance the debt. We remain,

"SIR,

"Your most obedient servants,

"*Per pro*. David Spreull and Co.

"JOHN FERGUS."

I confess I was at first rather hurt and surprised, to find my confidential letter thus answered by a clerk; but observing in one corner, the letters T.O. in large characters, I turned the page, and found on the other side a letter in the well-known autograph of my uncle.

"MY DEAR LADDIE,

"MANY thanks for your letter, and for thinking of your old uncle in the time of your trouble and difficulty; yet, I'll not deny, that it has cost me a sore heart, and given me much uneasiness on your account. There's dole in the thought that you should, so young, have fallen into such courses as you tell me of in your letter. Three hundred pounds in three weeks! never did I hear of such wasterful expense in all my born days. Fourteen pounds, five and eightpence a day! this would keep the Lord Provost, Bailies, Dean of Guild, and hail Town-Council of Glasgow, in bed, board, and washing for a week! There's an old proverb, Cyril, that a fool and his money are soon parted; and, truly, yours seems to have melted like snaw aff a dyke. I think you must have been sore imposed on by designing folk, that have been galraviching at your expense, for such a sum is not to be fairly spent by a callant like you in any way that I can understand.

"But it little matters to think of the money; could ten times, ay, or fifty times the sum do you any good, it should be forthcoming at a word, and shall be so when you want it, whether I'm living or dead. But I would give you a word of advice for your own sake, my dear Laddie, even though you may think it's no kind to do so in the time of your necessity. Remember, Cyril, you're the last prop and stay of an ancient and respectable house. The eyes of those that love you, are now turned towards you with hope and fear. Quit the evil course of life you have already entered. Be not deceived by the glamour and the temptations of vice, but maintain a douce and correct demeanour before man, and a spirit of humble piety towards God. I can only speak in generals to you, Cyril, anent such matters, for I have had no experience of the class of folk among whom your lot has been cast, and cannot warn you more particularly about the trials you are likely to meet in your path of life. But enter on your profession in a right spirit; take Honour for your compass, and however you may be tossed about by misfortune, by the grace of God both ship and cargo will come safely to port at last. Whenever you want a friend apply to me, and I will always take your doing so a kindness.

"By John Fergus's letter, on the other side, you will observe that a draft for £500 is inclosed; he knows nothing of the why or the wherefore; but I like all money disposed of to be entered in the books of the concern, and therefore I desired John to remit you the bill aforementioned, but never fash your thumb about what he says anent expecting a remittance in return. Now, may God bless and prosper you, my dear Laddie, is the prayer of your affectionate friend and uncle,

"DAVID SPREULL."

I felt warm emotions of gratitude to the kind old man, as I read his letter, the contents of which had at once liberated me from the trammels of difficulties which might have operated injuriously on my future prospects. For the first time in my life I had incurred a pecuniary obligation, yet the novelty neither wounded my pride, nor weighed upon my spirit. I did look to my aged relative as to a father; nay, from my own experience of that relation, I felt as if there was something even more than paternal in his kindness.

So engrossed was I with my uncle's epistle, and the varied associations into which it had led me, that a considerable time elapsed ere I recognised on the table before me another letter addressed to myself. That it was so, indeed, required some patience and deciphering to ascertain, for a more perplexing specimen of cacography than the superscription, it would be difficult to imagine. I took it up, and proceeded to break the seal. No impression was there on the wax, of arms and quarterings, of crests, coronets, or escutcheons of pretence, but a thumb of no ordinary dimensions, had distinctly stamped on it the lines and crossings of its hard and horny cuticle. Having opened this most uninviting epistle, I read as follows :—

"DEER MAISTER CEERAL,

"I fand your letter in yin o' Mr Spreull's pockets this morning, when I tuk his claes frae his bed-side for Jenny to brush; and as he tell't me he had gotten a letter frae you, I could na thole without readin't, that I micht ken a' the outs and the ins o' how ye are, and what ye are aboot.

"Lord bless and preserve me, it's just awsome to think that a braw and canty callant like you should be in a place like London, which, frae a' accounts, is just a perfect sink o' extortion and cheatery, without siller. Mrs Dinwiddie, the deacon's wife, that weel kens the London folk, for she ance leeved there for sax weeks, at a place they ca' Wapping, tells me they're a' naithing better than a set o' reevors, and greedy gleds, that wad rive the very claes aff your back for lucre o' gain; and gin they had their wull o' ye, wad turn ye oot into the streets as naked and bare o' duds, as Adam, afore Eve was tempted by the serpent; yet they wad wile ye by their smooth tongues and fair words to think them o' a turn maist douce and discreet. Foul fa' baith their fause hearts and creeshy gabs!

"Kennin weel aneuch the sort o' folks ye're amang, 'My certie,' thocht I, 'he shall ne'er want siller while I hae ony to the fore.' Sae I just cust on my duffle cloak, and aff I tramps to Robin Carrick's Bank, that had a matter o' fifty-sax pounds o' mine in their hands, which had grown frae less to mair, maist without my kennin hoo, for it was just siller I had nae use or occasion for, and I tell't them at the bank I wanted to send it to London, and they gied me a bill, that ye'll find pinned up in a piece o' muslin in this letter. Sae ye'll just tak' it, and mak' a kirk and mill o't, gin ye like, for it's o' nae use to me, and gin Mr Spreull doesna send you aneuch, just drap me a line or twa, and I'se warrant he shall get little rest night or day till he sends ye mair.

"And ye're gaun to America! waes me but that's a lang gait; tak' care o' yoursel', my braw lad, and mind afore ye gaed awa, ye promised to come and see us again, which God grant may be soon, though, I'm fear't, there's little chance o't at present. Noo, God bless you, Maister Ceeral, and dinna affront me by refusing the siller. Yours, till death,
"GIRZY BLACK.

"P.S.—Mrs Dinwiddie tells me there's a wheen fine dressed madams that gang about the streets in the gloaming wi' paint on their chafts, like hungry lions seeking young men whom they may devour. Gin I had my wull, every yin o' them should be burnt. Noo dinna be ta'en in by their fair outsides, but tak' tent o' your steps and mind ye dinna fa' into their snares, for they're the pitfa's o' Satan. "

Such was the letter of this simple and kind-hearted creature, and it was read with emotions as vivid as that of her master. Of course, I did not accept her proposal of appropriating the hard-earned savings of her service. Robin Carrick's bill was returned with thanks, accompanied by the acknowledgment of a smart gown of snuff-coloured poplin as a remembrance. I mistake, if at her death this gown is not found carefully treasured in her wardrobe.

With pockets thus powerfully reinforced, the work of preparation commenced in good earnest. I was already behind my time, and not a moment was to be lost. Tailors, lacemen, hatters, bootmakers, and

military-accoutrement makers, were all set to work, and in the course of
a few days I found myself prepared to start. The sight of my military
panoply fanned into a flame that ardour, which, though stifled for a
time by other pursuits, had never been extinguished, and taking farewell
of my companions by letter, instead of dining in their company at the
Clarendon, I bolted a tough beef-steak at the " Swan with Two Necks, "
and quitted London by the Portsmouth mail.

We travelled by night, and reached that great naval arsenal betimes
in the morning. I breakfasted in the coffee-room of the inn ; and at the
table next me were a party of young midshipmen similarly occupied. A
set of merrier beings I had never seen ; and, jaded, worn, and blue-
devilled as I was with the life I had recently been leading in town, I
could scarce help envying their light-hearted revelry and glee. Perceiving, perhaps, how little the solitude of my situation agreed with my
inclinations, they invited me, with the frankness by which the address of
sailors is always marked, to join their " mess. " I gladly took advantage
of the proffered kindness, and before the first detachment of rolls and
cold meat had disappeared from the board, (a space of time which
appeared to me incredibly short,) I felt as perfectly at home with my
new associates as if our intimacy had been the growth of years. The
duration of the meal was of unusual length, for my companions breakfasted as if that repast had not been with them an event of regular
occurrence, but a rare contingency, of which they were prudently
determined to take every possible advantage. But even under these
circumstances, breakfast is not interminable, and cannot by human
effort be infinitely protracted. The general quiescence of knives and
forks at length intimated pretty intelligibly that the force of appetite
could no further go, and I was preparing to move, when the youngest of
the party, an urchin apparently not more than ten years old, arrested
my intention, by declaring it was quite impossible to stir without a
" *caulker*, " an expression of opinion in which his companions cordially
joined. The necessary orders were issued ; and the waiter speedily
appeared, bearing a flagon of brandy, of which, though somewhat
startled at this unusual sequence to a breakfast, I did not choose to forfeit
the good opinion of my company by refusing to partake.

Under the guidance of my light-hearted messmates, I visited the lions
of the place. It was impossible to see Portsmouth to greater advantage.
A large fleet was about to sail for the Mediterranean, and all was bustle
and activity in the town. One could not walk the streets without jostling
admirals and post-captains ; and as for other officers, the leaves that
strew the brooks in Valambrosa, were not more numerous. Even to an
uninterested observer, there is something in the sight and sound of naval
preparation peculiarly exhilarating. I was delighted with the wonders of
the dockyard, and examined with a soldier's zeal and curiosity, every
angle of the very perfect fortifications by which Portsmouth is rendered

almost impregnable. Having thus rambled about the place for some hours, my good-natured friends were obliged to return on shipboard, and we parted, not without an interchange of hospitable invitations, and hopes mutually expressed of future meetings.

On reporting my arrival to the Quarter-Master-General, I was delighted to learn that a transport would sail in a few days for Nova-Scotia, in which a passage would be provided for me. The intervening time was no more than was necessary for laying in sea stock, and arranging with my fellow-passengers the requisite preliminaries for the formation of a mess. I therefore lost no time in visiting the ship, and depositing on board, as a measure of precaution against sudden surprise, the heavier and more dispensable part of my baggage, retaining nothing on shore, but what was immediately necessary for present comfort. My trip to Spithead was delightful. For the first time I was now borne on the bosom of the pathless deep. There was a breeze, but scarcely strong enough to ripple the surface of the waters, and the ships lay poised and motionless " above their shadow in the deep, " like mighty winged creatures in the glorious sunshine. As we passed near the Admiral's ship, she fired a salute, and the voice of the great leviathan rent the air with its thunder. To a landsman like myself, the scene was peculiarly striking. Great are the wonders reserved for those, " who go down to the sea in ships, and occupy their business in the great waters. "

The transport allotted for my conveyance to the new world was a small one, and I was by no means enchanted by an inspection of the accommodations to which I was to look forward on the voyage. There were several other officers in the ship, who being of course senior to myself, had taken possession of all the tolerable births, and I had nothing left for it but what is called "swinging a cot " in the cabin. Several of my *compagnons de voyage* being experienced sailors, the task of providing the stores necessary for our common comfort, was by common consent intrusted to them ; and finding nothing sufficiently captivating to induce a longer sojourn in the vessel, I returned immediately on shore, and awaited there the signal for sailing. This did not occur for some time. The wind chopped round to an unfavourable point, and blew so strongly, as to make it impossible for the fleet to quit their anchorage. My time in Portsmouth began to hang heavy on my hands, and I was anxious to be gone. To kill it, I visited Southampton, and the Isle of Wight; but after all it was weary work, and the want of society was one not to be supplied. Every morning I examined the weathercock on the steeple, and endeavoured to flatter myself into the belief, that it veered somewhat nearer to the wished for point; but some old sailor always dashed my hopes, by declaring the wind was as bad as could be, and without the smallest symptom of a change.

Under these circumstances, I determined to tempt fortune by taking a run to town, and tasting once more the goblet of pleasure, of which I had already drank so deeply. Trusting to my good luck, and instigated by the blue devils, I set off for London, with the intention of returning the following day. With " Dundas on the Eighteen Manœuvres " in my hand, I had, as might be expected from the nature of my occupation, fallen asleep in the carriage before we reached Petersfield. By the stoppage of the vehicle, however, I was awakened from my slumber, and on looking out, judge of my horror and surprise, when I perceived by a vane, which rose in golden magnificence from the summit of the stables of the inn, that the wind had changed to the north-east, the very point most favourable to the sailing of the fleet. Of course all intention of prosecuting my journey was at once relinquished, and I returned to Portsmouth with all the speed to which four horses could be stimulated by the promise of unusual largess to the post-boys. From a hill about half way, the sea was distinctly visible, and there was an evident bustle among the shipping. The Commodore had loosed his fore-topsail, and the blue Peter was flying at his maintopmast-head. The report of great guns was heard at intervals, and I regarded these signals of departure with intense anxiety. To be separated from my luggage, to incur censure by my negligence at the very commencement of my career, and to lose the only opportunity which might occur for months, of joining my regiment, was a consummation devoutly to be avoided, yet one which, in my folly, I had voluntarily courted.

There is another hill before you reach Hilsea, from which I again had a glimpse of the sea. The fleet was now unmoored, and preparing to follow the Commodore, who was standing onwards with a light but fair breeze for the Needles. The task of pursuit was now apparently hopeless. How could I expect to overtake a vessel sailing with a fair wind, already three leagues from the shore ? But the conviction which I now entertained of their fruitlessness, did not induce me to slacken my exertions. I arrived at the inn, discharged my bill, and in ten minutes was at the Sally Port, calling loudly for a boat to overtake the fleet. But the Portsmouth boatmen understand their own interest too well to answer immediately to such an invocation. The appearance of a gentleman in my circumstances, is a sort of godsend, which, as it comes rarely, is always prudently made the most of.

" Is it the fleet that sailed two hours ago, under convoy of the Pyramus ? " asked an aged and gigantic mariner, with a queue a yard long, and squirting from him as he spoke about a gallon of tobacco spittle, " why they're out at sea afore now, and will be off Plymouth by the morning. "

" It is precisely because they are gone, that I want to follow them. Will you engage to put me aboard a transport in the fleet ? "

" Why master, d'ye see, that depends on our happening to agree about terms. To be sure I have the fastest sailing yawl 'twixt here and Southampton, and were the fleet off the Lizard at this moment, I would engage to have you safe on board, before they reached the Bay of Biscay. There was a gentleman last month—wasn't there, Tom?—that wanted to get aboard the Ramillies, four hours after she had left the Mother-bank, with a spanking breeze in her quarter, and I had him up with her by the time she got twenty miles t'other side the Needles, and he gave me thirty pounds—didn't he, Tom?" Tom grunted assent. "So master, if so be, you'll give the same, why, I'm your man, and am ready to be off with you in a jiffy."

This demand appeared to me so exorbitant, that I at once refused to comply with it, and endeavoured to make a better bargain with some of the numerous watermen who stood silent spectators of the conference. But they betrayed no inclination to spoil the market, by underbidding their comrade, and I found my only resource was to endeavour, by chaffering, to reduce the demand of this salt-water Shylock within limits somewhat less exorbitant. I urged, therefore, that as upon his own showing the Ramillies had sailed *four* hours before he put off with the gentleman in pursuit, and as the fleet I wished to follow was only alleged to have sailed *two*, of course the demand in the present case, ought only to be half what it had been in the other. But my adversary was a bad logician, and although he admitted my premises, was by no means inclined to subscribe to my conclusion. It is generally impossible to convince a man against his interest, and my choler was so much roused by finding myself the subject of an attempt at imposition so gross and apparent, that I had more than half made up my mind to remain till some future opportunity, and brave the consequences of my negligence. The "aged mariner" had discernment enough to perceive this, for he relaxed by degrees in his demand, and a bargain was at length conclud-ed between us, that for twenty pounds, I and my baggage were to be put safely on board the Alfred transport.

So soon as this agreement had been mutually ratified, preparations were immediately made by the old sailor and his friend Tom to put the yawl in sailing trim. This was soon effected, I leaped on board, and the yawl cut swiftly through the water, at a rate which excited confident expectation of soon overtaking the object of our pursuit. Fortunately the breeze, which had been rather fresh during the day, fell off about sunset, and the light airs that continued to blow during the night, though sufficient to propel with considerable speed a boat constructed expressly with a view to swiftness of motion, were yet insufficient to afford any considerable impetus to more bulky vessels. Still, with every advantage on our side, it was morning before my fears were effectually set at rest, by my finding myself on board the Alfred.

That day is an æra in the life of every man, on which, when land has for the first time faded from his view, he finds himself a wanderer on the trackless ocean. Earth—the dear green earth on which he was cradled, with which his fathers' dust has mingled—on which are centered all his hopes and memories, his fears and his affections—seems to have been blotted out from the vast calendar of Nature. He had watched it from the topmast-head as it gradually sunk in the horizon; he saw the altitude of the mountains slowly lower in the distance; now seen as a cloud afar off, or some transient and fortuitous shaping of the air—visible, yet vague and indistinct. Soon it is but a speck distinguishable only by the mariner, from the dim shadow which is seen to rest above it, and around it. Now it is gone. Creation has lost an element, and the ship moves on through a world of sky and waters, with sails bathed in sunshine, and furrowing with her keel the dark blue waves that play sportively around her, and are dashed back with foamy crest from her prow. I remember my feelings as I beheld all this,—the throng of deep thoughts that moved my heart and my imagination,—thoughts that found no voice, for they were unutterable.

Our voyage was at first smooth and prosperous, and we lay our course without difficulty; but on the banks of Newfoundland we encountered a severe gale, from which we were glad to escape with the loss of topgallant-masts. By another, we were driven from our course almost into the mouth of the St Laurence, off which we narrowly escaped destruction on a reef of rocks. Luckily this concluded our perils, and the latter part of our voyage, like its commencement, was pleasant.

By the account I have already given of my accommodation on board, it will not be supposed, though I set the best face on the matter, and roughed it out tolerably well, that I was at all displeased when the cry of " Land ! " from the mast-head, announced that our destined port was at hand. There is generally nothing very grand or striking in the first appearance of the North American coast. Hills of no remarkable eminence covered with wood, and sloping regularly to the sea, are its almost uniform features. Such at least was the character the continent of the New World presented, when, as if emerging from the deep, I saw it stretch slowly upwards into the sky.

The wind was fair, and we ran down with facility our short remaining distance. In a few hours we entered the beautiful inlet, on the side of which the town of Halifax was situated—passed the island of St George, and before night-fall, the dropping of the anchor gave welcome notice of the termination of our voyage.

CHAPTER II

His addiction was to courses vain,
His companies unlettered, rude, and shallow,
His hours fill'd up with riots, banquets, sports,
And never noted in him any study,
Any retirement, any sequestration,
From open haunts, and popularity.

Henry IV.

AT the period of my arrival at Halifax, the Duke of Kent was Governor and Commander-in-chief over Nova Scotia and its dependencies. Those who have ever served under his Royal Highness, or who remember the mutiny which the severity of his discipline afterwards caused in Gibraltar, will easily understand how little the situation either of officer or soldier under his command, approached to the nature of a sinecure. The duties of the garrison were multiplied to such a degree as to become absolutely oppressive; and when off duty, the men were harassed and exhausted by a course of drilling and field exercise, which no inclemency of the weather was suffered to interrupt. The Duke, too, like most officers who have seen little service, attached an overweening importance to matters of costume, and with an acuteness of observation altogether peculiar, could detect at a glance the smallest deviation from the established cut in a coat, or the unwarranted excess of a button in the gaiters; outrages on military propriety which he never failed to visit with his severest displeasure.

The regiment to which I belonged, formed part of the garrison of Halifax, and my first duty on debarkation was to wait on the commanding officer and report my arrival. Colonel Grimshawe, I found, did not live in barracks, and under the guidance of an orderly corporal, I proceeded to his house, which was easily distinguishable from the surrounding habitations, from being guarded by a sentry.

The Colonel was at home, and I was ushered forthwith into his presence. When I entered, he was seated at a table covered with what were apparently military reports, and engaged in conversation with an officer, whose dress marked him to be the Adjutant, and who remained standing, with an air of deference, near the chair of his superior.

" I beg pardon, sir, " said the Colonel, addressing me, as he perceived I was about to speak; " but I request you will have the goodness to reserve your business for a few moments, when I shall be more at liberty to attend to your communication. " As he spoke, he regarded me with a scrutinizing eye, and, as if the impression I had made on him was not wholly unfavourable, he added with a smile, "in the meantime, I request you will be seated."

In this invitation the Adjutant was not included, and from that circumstance I could not help feeling that it conveyed something of a compliment, since it was evidently one he was not always in the habit of affording to his official inferiors.

While thus disengaged, I enjoyed an opportunity of minutely observing the person under whose immediate command I was about to serve.

Colonel Grimshawe was a man apparently between thirty and forty. His face was slightly marked with the small-pox, and wore that tawny sallowness of complexion, which indicated service in tropical and unhealthy climates. There was something fine and penetrating in his eye; and from the perfect regularity and whiteness of his teeth, his countenance might have passed for handsome, had it not been disfigured by a scar, of what had originally been a harelip, which gave an unpleasant contortion to the mouth. In person he was short, but formed with perfect symmetry and elegance, and there was about him an air of distinction, which marked him out to the most casual observer as a person of high breeding and pretensions. When he spoke, his voice was peculiarly musical and clear, yet in his mode of utterance there was a firmness and decision, which showed him to be one accustomed to command. Such were my first impressions of Colonel Grimshawe, who having finished his conference with the Adjutant, whom he directed to wait for further orders, turned towards me, and with an air of suavity, received my annunciation of my name and rank. In his manner of addressing me, there was no assumption of authority, no air of command. He spoke with graceful ease, welcomed me to the New World, hoped my passage had been a pleasant one, talked laughingly of the course of drilling that awaited me, hinted en passant at the strictness of discipline observed in the —— regiment, and warned me, jocularly, to beware of incurring, by any neglect of military observance, the displeasure of the Duke of Kent. "But," continued he, "we shall not require you to perform any duty till you get fairly out of the hands of Mr Hopkins," pointing to the Adjutant, "to whom I beg to make you known.—Mr Hopkins, you will be good enough to accompany Mr Thornton to the barracks, and introduce him to his brother officers. Request Major Penleaze to inspect his accoutrements, and let him report to me if they are strictly regimental, in order that Mr Thornton may, as soon as possible, be enabled to attend parades. In the meantime, he may be attached to Captain Spottiswoode's company.—Good morning, Mr Thornton, I shall have the pleasure of meeting you at mess, and—I had almost forgotten—Mr Hopkins, let the Quarter-Master find a room in barracks for Mr Thornton immediately.—Good morning, sir," rising from his chair, and slightly bending to my obeisance; "you will find your brother officers, I think, very pleasant." I withdrew with the Adjutant, in whose company I returned to the barracks.

He was a person who had evidently risen from the ranks, as adjutants generally do, and who was innocent as a babe of all knowledge, except that connected with the subordinate details of military discipline. In conversing with him, I found he had now cast off that air of deference and respect which he had assumed in presence of Colonel Grimshawe, and was not a little anxious to appear in my eyes a person of consequence and authority. In addressing me, I thought he assumed a certain air of patronage, which, coming from one whose claims to consideration were more than commonly equivocal, did not incline me to any uncalled for intercourse. The task of introduction which had been imposed on him, however, he duly performed, and speedy means were thus afforded me of getting into more agreeable company. In this respect I had been fortunate in my regiment. The officers of the —— were generally gentlemen both by birth and education, and formed among themselves a society considerably superior to what one expects to meet in the fortuitous intercourse of a military life. For some of them I have never ceased to entertain a cordial regard ; and it pleases me, while narrating the events of this portion of my life, to recall the names and characters of my companions, still vividly imprinted on my memory.

There was honest Jack Popham, the best and laziest of mortals, the acknowledged chieftain of that worthy race distinguished by the expressive title of " the King's hard bargains." He was indeed a hard bargain to the King, but any bargain that deprived them of his society would have been still harder to his brother officers. No one grumbled so loudly at a field-day, or abused more heartily the roster of the Adjutant when he read his name in orders for guard. At one time he stood first for purchase of a company, but on the very eve of a vacancy, his banker became bankrupt, and Popham lost his money, and with it all hopes of promotion for years. Then his heart failed him, officers of much junior standing were passed over him, and from that time forward he had no pleasure in his profession. There was not a soul in the regiment that did not pity him, or who would not wink at his occasionally *shirking* a guard, though his own tour of duty was thereby accelerated. After many years, in which he tasted the bitterness of hope deferred, he was at length promoted to a company ; and on the field of Waterloo there fell not a braver or more generous spirit than Jack Popham.

And Frank Stanhope, my friend, my messmate, and brother ensign, how often have we toiled together on interminable field-days, carrying the colours till our arms ached under their honourable burden !—but *he* sleeps in a watery grave, and I would not speak of *him*.

Why, I know not, but Holford, the Falstaff of surgeons, the most humorous of gourmands, rises next to my memory. Never was there so worthy a prototype of " Fat Jack." In point of wit, indeed, the Doctor must have knocked under to the Knight, but he had enough to set the table in a roar,—more had only been excess. He was the target of all our jokes,—a beau too, and the blooming maidens of Halifax rejoiced in his unwieldy gallantry. Many years have passed since we met, and I know not whether age and campaigning may not have somewhat reduced his bulky volume. I hope not. May he continue fat and jovial as I remember him, and I will answer for it, die when he may, that

> " A merrier man,
> Within the limits of becoming mirth, "

was never buried with book and benison.

And now a crowd starts up before me on which I may not linger. They come like shadows, and like shadows shall they depart. First is Major Warburton, melancholy and gentlemanlike, fond of Shakspeare, and cookery, and a first-rate performer on the flute. Let him pass on, to make way for Denis O'Hara, the inheritor of all his country's blunders, and of more than all its native goodness of heart. Denis had but one fault; he was quarrelsome in his cups, challenged his best friends over night, and apologized to them in the morning. He fought, indeed, several duels, but not with the officers of his own regiment, and on one occasion only had he been known to return his adversary's fire. That shot cost his opponent a leg. He was taken prisoner early in the Spanish war, and died at Verdun.—But I have sadly diverged from the straight line of my story, to which it is fitting I should return.

My reception by my brother officers was cordial, and such as, to the credit of the army, a stranger generally experiences on joining a regiment, to every man of which, a day before, his existence was utterly unknown. The day of my arrival happened to be one on which a large party of strangers dined as guests at the mess. Among the number were two captains of the navy, and several staff-officers. Colonel Grimshawe was in the chair, and discharged the duties of it in a manner which delighted me. For ease and urbanity of manners in such a situation, I would almost place him on an equality with Lord Kinnaird; and those who have witnessed the manner in which his Lordship discharges the duties of chairman at a public dinner, will duly appreciate the extent of the compliment. In the course of the evening he made several speeches, and he spoke with elegance, and without effort. In his eloquence, if I may so speak, there was nothing technical; it smacked neither of the bar, the pulpit, or the senate; it was nothing more than the natural language of a high-born and high-bred English gentleman, adorned with unusual grace of delivery. With me he conversed frequently, not in the tone of a superior, but a companion; and a person who could assume more easily every attribute of a delightful one, I had never met before, and am not quite certain I have ever met since.

This being my first appearance at mess, nearly every officer at table thought it necessary to drink wine with me. The song went round, the goblet flowed, till a late hour, and a severe headach, on the following morning, intimated pretty plainly that I had quaffed, " not wisely, but too well. "

I was not, however, suffered to sleep off the effects of my carousal. While it was yet dark, I was awakened by my servant, who told me it was time to commence dressing for parade.

" Parade! " growled I, in no very complacent humour at being thus disturbed, " why, it's now pitch dark, and I presume the regiment don't parade by candlelight? "

" No, your honour; but the drum beats at seven, and it's now five, and I take it your honour will find two hours little enough to dress in. "

Notwithstanding I had never employed a quarter of the time in dressing before, I thought it as well to be guided in the present case by the experience of my attendant. Quitting my couch, therefore, without delay, I set about the duties of the toilet, though still unable to imagine in what manner the long interval allotted for them was to be filled up. My ignorance was soon enlightened. I had scarcely commenced the business of preparation, when a knock at my chamber-door indicated the presence of some one desirous of admission. I directed him to enter, and a person did so, armed with scissors, comb, and curling-irons.

" Who the devil are you? "

" The hairdresser of Captain Spottiswoode's company, come to cut and dress your honour's hair according to regimental pattern. "

" And pray how can you pretend to cut and dress a gentleman's hair, by the light of a farthing candle? "

" Practice makes perfect, your honour. I've just come from dressing Captain Spottiswoode and Mr Popham; and I powder ten heads in the dark for one in the daylight, since we came here to America. Why, sir, I've soaped, floured, and tied ninety-three, this very morning, without so much as a rushlight. "

" Come, no more talk, but set to work immediately; " and the obedient barber commenced his task without farther delay.

Lord Byron piqued himself on the whiteness of his hands, and I confess I was a little foppish about my hair. I flattered myself it clustered in Hyacinthine curls, not unlike those of the Antinous, and I gave the barber very particular directions to cause as little devastation among them with his shears as possible. He promised to abstain from all gratuitous havoc, and engaged to proceed not a single clip of scissor beyond what was absolutely necessary for the " regimental cut. " Perhaps he did not; but I confess my choler was effectually roused, when, looking in the glass, I beheld the change which this villainous artist had wrought on the external appearance of my cranium. On the back and sides of my head, the hair was shorn close to the skin, now almost literally bare, while the summit was adorned by a top-knot, in shape not unlike the comb of a cock, every individual hair of which the art of the friseur had made to stand on end, like "quills upon the fretful porcupine. " But my metamorphosis did not stop here ; and it was not till after the statutory application of powder and pomatum, that I saw myself completely transmogrified. With feelings somewhat akin to those which a Shetland pony, accustomed to enjoy in all their amplitude the luxury of mane and tail, may be supposed to experience on finding himself suddenly *docked* and *hogged*, did I dismiss the military tonsor, and follow his exit with curses, not loud but deep.

The operations of my toilet, which still remained to be performed, were not of a character calculated to allay the irritation of its commencement. Instead of a neckcloth, my throat was encased in a broad black leather stock, the hard edges of which created an unpleasant irritation about the upper extremity of the windpipe, and leaving the power of only lateral motion to my head, prevented me effectually from bestowing a single glance on the large military boots, which reached above the cap of my knee. Then came my coat, one of Stultze's best and tightest fits, which I very unwillingly buttoned to the very top, on an intimation from my servant that such was " the rule of the regiment. " My queue was then duly inserted by the same trusty functionary in the nape of my neck, taking care that it should protrude exactly nine inches by measurement, such being the regimental length, and on no account to be exceeded or diminished. Sash and sword of course followed, not without some peculiarity in their mode of adjustment, discernible, perhaps, to none but those who possessed in such matters the true military coup d'œil.

Thus caparisoned, I descended to the parade ground, where the men, divided into squads, were undergoing the preparatory inspection of the non-commissioned officers. The regularity and precision with which everything was conducted could not but strike even an inexperienced eye, as affording strong evidence of the high state of discipline of the corps. In a few minutes, the drum beat for general parade, and the officers were instantly seen issuing from their quarters, and repairing each to his appointed post. Mine, of course, was in rear of the company to which I was attached ; and catching as well as I could the true military attitude, I stood with drawn sword and unwonted rigidity of limb.

While thus engaged, I was accosted by an orderly sergeant, who delivered, with due respect, an order from Major Penleaze, desiring my presence in the centre of the square. I immediately obeyed ; and being directed by the Major to stand in the attitude of attention, a minute inspection of my dress and accoutrements took place. Luckily, in the cut of my integuments, the tailor had indulged in no flights of fancy, and displayed a laudable adherence to established pattern. The Major, therefore, had only to suggest some slight changes of adjustment, which, without difficulty, were made on the spot. It was only in altering the position of my hat that I experienced any additional inconvenience. To enable the reader to understand its full extent, I must premise, that there were certain peculiarities of costume, to the rigid observance of which the Duke of Kent attached peculiar importance. One of these consisted in wearing huge three-cornered cocked hats, not fore and aft, as was the general custom of the army, but right athwart from shoulder to shoulder, descending to the eyebrow on the right side, and proportionally rising on the left. Now, my hat unfortunately was rather small, and the consequence of this arrangement was, that my right eye was entirely closed up, and I found myself reduced at once to the condition of Polyphemus. Thus monoculated, I was reported to the colonel as being in a state of sufficient *regimentalism* to make my appearance on parade; and I accordingly, though with ardour somewhat damped, assumed the part allotted me in the succeeding pageant.

The inconveniences from which I at first suffered so severely, however, gradually became more tolerable; and under the tuition of Mr Hopkins, and his deputy the sergeant-major, I was soon enabled to master all the mysteries of manual and platoon.

Once a fortnight the Duke of Kent held a levee, and it was considered indispensable that every officer on first joining should be presented. Aware of the unpleasant consequences which the smallest informality of dress would not fail to incur, I was even more than usually punctilious in its arrangement, and appeared at Government-house harnessed completely *selon les règles*. The building was of wood, and stood upon a height which overlooked the town, commanding a fine view of the sea. There was nothing about it either externally or internally at all allied to magnificence. The rooms were spacious, but plainly furnished, and devoid of all those appliances in which modern luxury delights. No ottomans, no easy-chairs, no chaises longues, with cushions tempting to repose, met the eye. Everything bore evidence of the military plainness, and almost primeval simplicity of its owner's taste, and appeared rather in contrast with the splendid liveries of the servants.

On entering, I found a large party of officers assembled in the audience-chamber, but his Royal Highness had not yet made his appearance. Precisely, however, as the clock struck one, a door communicating with an interior apartment was thrown open, and the Duke came forward, followed by his staff, bowing as he entered to the general obeisance of the company. His conversation was first directed to General Hunter, the second in command, and was afterwards extended to the field-officers as they chanced to attract his notice. The air and appearance of his Royal Highness were certainly in the highest degree military. He wore the undress uniform of a field-marshal, and was distinguished by that well-proportioned amplitude of person, which belongs to all the male branches of the Royal Family. His head was large, but well formed, and on the upper part entirely bald. In his face there was nothing intellectual, yet it displayed a certain massiveness and prominence of feature, well adapted for the chisel, and which Chantrey or Flaxman would have turned to good account. Having made the tour of the circle, and noticed the more prominent individuals who presented themselves, the Duke took his station in the centre, and the presentations commenced. This was by no means so idle a ceremony as it is generally considered; for, as the officers were successively introduced to him, he took occasion to examine them on points of military tactics, and frequently put questions which the embarrassment of those interrogated, evidently showed to be not a little puzzling. My turn at length came, and, advancing into the circle, I was presented by Colonel Grimshawe in the usual form.

" How long have you joined, sir? " inquired his Royal Highness.

" About a fortnight. "

" Are you from Marlow? "

" No. "

" Were you educated at a public school? "

" No. My education has been private. "

" Do you understand geometry and fortification? "

" No. "

" Your sword-belt, sir, comes too much across the body. The breastplate should be more on the left side.—Colonel Grimshawe, let this be attended to in future.—You have commenced drill, of course?—Let me see what progress you have made:—Major Warburton, put Mr Thornton through his facings, and let him march about a little. "

Major Warburton, who seemed to like the ceremony not much more than myself, obeyed; and so annoyed was I at the absurdity of my involuntary exhibition, that it is more than probable some of the movements were not executed with that deftness and precision which his Royal Highness considered of such paramount importance.

" Less shuffling of the heels, if you please, sir.—As you were.—Try him once more, Major. In facing to the right about, there is no occasion to swing your body about like a ship in a storm. "

The word, *March*, was given, and the circle opened to afford me a passage.

On approaching the door, I was more than half inclined to exchange ordinary into double quick, and make my exit without farther ceremony. Strong as the temptation was, however, I resisted it, and went through the remainder of a scene, which, although ludicrous in description, was practically most annoying in the performance.

In one respect, however, my apprehensions were unfounded. This sort of exhibition was too common to become, in my case, the subject of any extraordinary ridicule from my companions; but it will readily be believed, that in future I attended as seldom as possible the levees of the Duke of Kent.

It appeared strange to me, that notwithstanding the fascinating manners of Colonel Grimshawe, he should be unpopular in the regiment. Yet such was the case. He was admitted on all hands to be an excellent soldier, and one ardently devoted to his profession. No charge of partiality or injustice was alleged against him, and, though a rigid disciplinarian, he never unnecessarily harassed those under his command. He had served in the East Indies, in the West, and in Egypt, and with distinction in all. No officer knew his duty better, or was more zealous in the discharge of it.

Singular as the dislike which generally attached to Colonel Grimshawe at first appeared to me, on closer observation I was almost led to join in it. There was certainly something disagreeable in the very marked line which he evidently drew between the commanding officer and the companion, and nothing could be more rapid and unexpected than his transition from one character to the other, and nothing stronger than the contrast thus produced. In a moment the whole expression of his countenance would change, and his tone of playful jocularity be converted into one of unbending authority. No two people could be more different than Colonel Grimshawe in private society, and Colonel Grimshawe on military duty. One day, I remember, we rode together into the country, and the drum for parade sounded before we reached the barracks. I had found him during our ride a most agreeable companion. We parted in perfect good-humour at the barrack-gate, and having changed my dress with all possible expedition, I came on the parade-ground just after the officers had fallen in, and the Adjutant was engaged in collecting the reports. It was natural to expect, that a lapse so venial, and of which he so perfectly understood the cause, would have been passed over. Not so. Colonel Grimshawe summoned me, in a loud voice, to the front of the regiment, and in hearing of the whole battalion, inflicted a severe censure on my dilatoriness, which, if continued, he assured me, would not fail to draw down yet more unpleasant consequences.

It may be supposed that such treatment caused a permanent estrangement in our future intercourse. No such consequence, however, followed. After parade, Colonel Grimshawe came up, and taking me by the arm, conversed as if nothing had happened ; and notwithstanding my irritation, I could not long resist the fascination of his society. As a friend, I certainly did not, and could not regard him ; I knew that for any breach of military discipline I had no lenity to expect ; but I had acquired experience enough to know, that *ainsi va le monde*, and that where it was impossible to turn the current, the best policy was to swim with the stream.

I am here prompted to record an anecdote of the boyish folly of poor Stanhope and myself. We both of us detested the annoyance of wearing powder, and agreed to substitute in place of it a flaxen wig, for the

preparation of which we respectively issued orders to the most fashionable peruquier of Halifax. These were punctually executed, and, enchanted with the ingenuity of the contrivance, we lost no time in having
our heads shaved, and came out in all the honours of our novel head-
gear. We were received with shouts of laughter at mess, and submitted
to all the mirth and banter which our appearance excited, with the most
philosophical *sang froid*. In similar trim, we appeared next morning at
parade, but had scarcely taken our places, when the Adjutant came up,
and dropping his sword, informed us, that it was Colonel Grimshawe's
order, that we should instantly quit the parade, and remain close
prisoners in our apartment until the growth of our shorn locks should
qualify us once more to return to duty. A confinement of six weeks
followed, notwithstanding every effort to shorten its duration, by the
strenuous application of Bear's grease and Macassar oil; and cursing
our own folly, the flaxen wigs were committed to the flames.

Another frolic threatened consequences still more disagreeable.
Stanhope and myself were members of a general court-martial, and, of
course, exempt from duty during its continuance. The court could not
be dismissed until the sentence had been ratified by the crown, and as
this required a voyage to England, we enjoyed a liberty—if idleness can
be called liberty—of some duration.

Since my arrival in Halifax, I had bought a large Newfoundland dog,
which was particularly docile, and had been taught the accomplishment
of walking erect on his hinder legs. Neither of us happened to have any
partiality for Major Penleaze, who was confined at the time by some
slight indisposition, and we determined that Neptune should appear on
parade as that gentleman's representative. A tailor of the regiment was
secretly set to work to provide this new aspirant for military honours,
with a suitable uniform; and having completed our preparations, Neptune, by tuck of drum, made his appearance on parade, in a coat and
epaulets which bore the distinctive mark of a major's rank,—cocked
hat, queue, sword, sash, breeches, and military boots, and advanced
slowly and erect to the centre of the square. The effect was electric.
Discipline and decorum were, for a moment, forgotten; ill suppressed
laughter was heard from the ranks, and the countenances, both of
officers and soldiers, were simultaneously broadened by a grin. Instantly
the voice of Colonel Grimshawe was heard pealing forth like thunder,
and every sign of merriment vanished at the sound. His eyes glared
round as he spoke with an expression almost terrific, and Stanhope and
myself, who stood enjoying the scene from a window, almost began to
repent of our frolic. Colonel Grimshawe formed the line into a hollow
square, and addressed them in a speech. He said the outrage just
perpetrated was one unparalleled in his whole military experience; he
dilated on its enormity, and expressed his own firm purpose to bring the
authors of this flagrant violation of discipline to signal punishment. " I

know not, and I care not, " he continued, " who they are, that have thus cast a tarnish on the character of the ——, which it will require long years of discipline and propriety to wipe away ; but they know me little if they expect an impunity at my hands, which would involve a betrayal of the trust reposed in me by my sovereign. I call upon you, both officers and men, to assist me in discovering these unknown delinquents. Were my own brother concerned in this outrage, and ruin about to wait on his conviction, as there is a God in Heaven, I would strain every nerve to bring him to justice. " Colonel Grimshawe concluded, by expressing his intention of punishing the indecorum of which the whole regiment had been guilty, by a series of extraordinary drills, which he gave orders should commence on the following morning.

Strict inquiries were instantly set on foot to discover the decorators of the dog, against whom the wrath of Colonel Grimshawe was principally directed. My own feelings prompted me to come forward and confess at once the head and front of my offending ; but older and more experienced officers strongly dissuaded me from this step. They assured me it would be wilfully sacrificing, not only my own professional prospects, but those of Stanhope, who would not suffer me to bear alone the consequences of our ill-judged jest ; that Colonel Grimshawe, if we confessed the " *corpus delicti,* " could not, after what had passed, avoid trying us by a court-martial, the issue of which could not be doubtful ; and that, by remaining secret, we violated no law of honour. It is possible, indeed, that Colonel Grimshawe himself, notwithstanding the public display of his indignation, was really not very anxious for a discovery. The storm passed, and though the perpetrators of the foolery were generally known, yet as no legal evidence of guilt beyond that of my being owner of the dog, was elicited by inquiry, no further unpleasant consequences followed. We were generally liked, and our brother officers submitted to the punishment we had brought on them, without resentment towards its authors.

These were happy days.

CHAPTER III

A Captain bold in Halifax, that lived in country quarters,
Seduced a maid————

Miss Baillie.

THE Nova Scotian winter sets in early, and though a season of extreme rigour, brings with it the usual accompaniments of gaiety and festivity, and amusements unknown in more genial climates. Every precaution is taken to prevent the soldier from sustaining injury from the severity of the weather. On duty, the usual regimental cap is exchanged for one of fur, and an additional supply of great-coats and blankets is annually issued. Even the taper limbs of the ladies may be seen enveloped in mocassins and snow-boots, reserving the captivations of foot and ancle for a milder season.

Notwithstanding the severity of the garrison-duty, and the annoying activity of the Duke of Kent, the winter passed happily and cheerfully. We amused ourselves by driving sledges over the snow, and shooting spruce partridges in the woods. Occasionally, when we obtained leave of absence for a week, parties of pleasure were formed to visit Windsor and Annapolis; at which places, our appearance never failed to be the signal of a ball. Halifax, too, was the scene of gaiety. The wealthier part of the inhabitants gave dinners and parties, at which the charms of the fair Arcadians were not exerted in vain.

For myself, I have no idea of a man marrying with the thermometer twenty degrees below zero, when he is liable to be frost-bitten on the very way to the altar, and the ceremony to be delayed until, by the application of snow, vitality is restored. The idea of a bride in worsted stockings, and garments of linsey-woolsey, is not pleasant, and a few months delay, in such circumstances, till the return of milder weather, is, perhaps, excusable. Venus, it is true, rose from the sea, but not amid walrusses and icebergs in the Arctic Ocean.

Luckily for the spinsters of Halifax, my sentiments on this matter were not generally shared by the officers of the garrison, and, ere the return of summer, several tender-hearted captains, and inflammable subalterns, rejoiced in celibacy no longer.

Twice a-week there were evening parties at Colonel Grimshawe's, to which, without any regular invitation, the greater part of the officers had the privilege of *entré*. Of these parties I was a frequent member, and the honours of the mansion were done by a Miss Mansfield, a lady occupying in his establishment a situation certainly of very equivocal propriety. She was a pretty and rather elegant woman, rendered, perhaps, more interesting, from showing, by a hurried nervousness of manner, that she felt deeply the awkwardness of her situation. Everything connected with the establishment, of which she was the head, seemed elegant and *recherché*, and bore about it evidences of a more refined taste, than had yet been indigenous in the colony. The furniture and draperies of the apartments were not only (for America) unusually handsome, but arranged with the utmost exactitude of taste, and it was evident at a glance, that Miss Mansfield was a person, in every respect, far removed from the generality of females reduced, by folly or misfortune, to circumstances unhappily similar. By the guests, it was apparently considered not exactly *comme il faut*, to pay her much attention. All seemed to feel that there was a delicacy in her situation, which any very particular or marked attention would have violated. She was uniformly addressed with respect, but the conversation in which she partook, was always of the most trite and common-place description, and devoid of that ease which naturally arises, when the claims of the person addressed, to respect and consideration, are less questionable than those of Miss Mansfield.

Colonel Grimshawe was partial to whist, and that game constituted the principal source of interest and amusement at these parties. I had never touched a card in my life, and was consequently condemned to remain a spectator. Miss Mansfield, too, did not play, and thus did I frequently find myself almost forced into a *tête-à-tête*, for which I should probably not otherwise have voluntarily sought. In addressing her, I threw off that tone of embarrassing coldness to which she had become accustomed, and spoke with the air of respectful interest, which one naturally assumes in conversation with a lady. She evidently felt this, and was grateful; and for myself, the power of conferring pleasure on one whose situation I sincerely pitied, was too flattering not to be frequently exercised.

My *tête-à-têtes* with Miss Mansfield began at length to excite the notice, and draw forth the banter, of my companions. I was accused of attempting to cut out the Colonel, and some of the older and more prudent advised me to desist from playing so hazardous a game. Both the ridicule and advice were disregarded. I was conscious of no improper motive. I felt that I had too much vanity in my nature, to be captivated by a woman, however charming, who was publicly recognised as the mistress of another man.

The only person by whom my attentions to Miss Mansfield appeared to pass entirely unnoticed, was Colonel Grimshawe. His manner towards me was in no respect changed, and the welcome he continued to afford me, was cordial as before. Towards the victim of his passion, his demeanour had never been marked by any of that delicacy and consideration, which might naturally have been looked for in a person of so much tact and knowledge of the world. He treated her coldly and with indifference, and when anything occurred to ruffle his temper, with unkindness and even harshness. She evidently feared him, and the tears were called up into her eyes, by the sarcastic bitterness with which he frequently addressed her. It was impossible not to compassionate a creature, shackled, as she apparently was, by ties so galling; and it seemed that the very guilt which attached to her,—the very atmosphere of shame in which she moved,—only rendered her the object of deeper pity and commiseration.

Miss Mansfield's history was unknown. No one knew under what circumstances she had lapsed from virtue; whether, from the mere credulity of a nature too innocent and trusting, she had fallen a victim to the arts of some practised and heartless seducer, or whether, led on by her own evil passions, she had voluntarily courted degradation. What I read of her character, at least seemed to indicate the former, and my own feelings inclined me to adopt the more favourable supposition. In the frequently recurring conversations which took place between us, not the most distant allusion was made to her situation. I had no wish to win her heart, and every topic of apocryphal propriety was studiously avoided;—nay, had Colonel Grimshawe himself been auditor to every sentence spoken on either side, I am sure he would have heard nothing to raise either anger or suspicion.

In this situation did matters stand, when the arrival of a packet from England brought notice of my being appointed to a lieutenancy in a West India regiment. My father did not write, and I remained ignorant through what channel the promotion had been obtained. I was at first by no means gratified with my good fortune. It was scarcely probable that for so trifling and unimportant a step I should voluntarily quit a regiment, in which I found myself so pleasantly situated, to exercise the same vocation in a West India corps. Of course, therefore, my object was to effect an exchange, if possible, into the regiment to which I had hitherto belonged, or, failing in that, into some other less objectionable than the one to which I was appointed.

On receiving the first intelligence of my promotion, I considered it a proper compliment to Colonel Grimshawe to wait on him immediately, and after explaining to him the circumstances of the case, request his advice. I lost no time, therefore, in proceeding to his house, where his servant informed me, that being field-officer of the day, he had gone out about an hour before, on the duty of visiting the guards, but that his return was instantly expected. Anxious to have an interview with him as early as possible, I resolved to wait his return, and with that view was shown into an apartment. It was not untenanted. Miss Mansfield was seated at a table; but as her back was partly turned towards the door, it was not till I had advanced and offered the usual salutations, that I perceived she held in her hand a letter, over which she was weeping bitterly. Grief, even in the humblest of human beings, has ever been respectable in my eyes, and in this instance I was unwilling to violate its sanctity. I therefore apologised for my intrusion, and was about to depart, but she looked up, and requested me to remain.

" You see before you, " she said, with choking utterance, " one who, fallen and degraded as she is, would still venture to hope that she has a friend, at least a wellwisher, in Mr Thornton. If I am mistaken in this, alas ! I am friendless. "

" A more sincere wellwisher than myself Miss Mansfield does not possess ; but she will excuse me for suggesting, that in Colonel Grim-shawe—— "

" Oh, talk not, " she interrupted, " of Colonel Grimshawe. You know not,—you cannot know, the cold and heartless being of whom you speak. What woman could bear,—more than woman ever yet bore, from the man she loved, I have borne from him. " And as she spoke she looked up, with sparkling eyes, and threw back the dark ringlets that had fallen over her face. " But, " she added, and her expression softened as she proceeded, " it is not this of which I would speak. True, it is hard to meet with harshness and ingratitude from one for whom we have given up all ; but I have borne it long and patiently, and would still bear it, for (though God knows, not from him,) I have deserved it all. "

I here ventured to interrupt her, for I felt the full awkwardness of my situation, and was unwilling to involve myself, by participating in a confidence, which, it appeared to me, could lead to no beneficial consequences.

" Miss Mansfield will pardon me, " I replied, " for reminding her, that it has only been in the character of Colonel Grimshawe's guest and friend that I have enjoyed the pleasure of her society ; that I am at this moment beneath his roof, and cannot with propriety listen to any communication with which he is unpleasantly connected. If, without infringing on the duty I owe to others, I can in anything serve you, command me ; but it is equally useless and unpleasant to be made the depository of secrets, in which I have no right to participate, or of grievances which I want power to redress. While you remain under the protection of Colonel Grimshawe, my good wishes,—my sincere good wishes for your happiness, are, I fear, all it were proper for me to offer, or (pardon my freedom) for you to accept. "

" Say not so, Mr Thornton, " replied she, casting on me a look at which the heart of the sternest and most ascetic misogynist might have melted : " You are generous—your heart is yet unseared by the world. You will not refuse to stretch forth an arm to rescue a poor sinking creature from the gulf of guilt and error, in which, but for your assist-ance, she is still doomed to struggle. Hear but my story ; read but the contents of this letter "——Here a gush of tears interrupted her utter-ance, and I endeavoured to soothe her, by professing a deep interest in her misfortunes.

G

She told me under what circumstances her connexion with Colonel Grimshawe had arisen. " She was the child, " she said, " the only child, of a respectable tradesman in a garrison town. Her mother had died in her infancy, and she was left the sole prop of her aged father. The usual arts of seduction had been employed for her ruin, and successfully. She quitted her father's roof, and became,—what I saw her. Peace, " she said, " from the moment of this guilty act, she had never known, and the demon of remorse haunted her by night and day. " She placed in my hand the letter which she had that morning received. It was from her father, but not written with his own hand. He too had been smitten, and was become blind and paralytic, a solitary and a heart-broken old man. " He was, " he said, " fast sinking into the grave, and this was probably the last letter she would ever receive from him. He spoke mildly and forgivingly of her errors, and conjured her, by the love of God, and the blood of her Saviour, to turn from the path of destruction in which she had already advanced so far. Of his own sufferings he made light ; it was the knowledge of her situation alone that would imbitter his dying hour. Yet in the folly of his old age, " he said, " he sometimes indulged hopes, that her hand might yet close his sightless balls—that he might once more clasp his daughter in his withered arms. But his time was short, and he now knew such hopes were vain. He bade her farewell forever,— in his agony he had never cursed her,—and he now bequeathed her his blessing and forgiveness. That God would also forgive her, would be his latest prayer. "

It was impossible to read this letter without emotion. The tears streamed rapidly down the cheeks of Miss Mansfield, and my feelings were now thoroughly excited in her behalf. I took her by the hand—

" If your object be to return to soothe the dying hours of a suffering and afflicted parent, there is no exertion of mine you may not command, in so good a cause. Yet I cannot conceive how any necessity for such exertion, on my part, should arise. Miss Mansfield is surely mistress of her own actions, and is at liberty to quit the protection of Colonel Grimshawe whenever—— "

" Perfectly so, " said a voice from behind, " Miss Mansfield is quite at liberty to quit Colonel Grimshawe's protection whenever she thinks proper, and to enter upon that of Mr Cyril Thornton. I beg I may not be suffered to interrupt a conversation so interesting : when, however, the arrangements are concluded, Mr Thornton will perhaps be good enough to honour me with an audience. " So saying, the Colonel, for he it was, left the room, and the door of the apartment closed.

Miss Mansfield was dreadfully agitated. It was now impossible to extract any intelligible communication of her wishes, nor learn in what manner my assistance could be of use. I endeavoured to soothe her by assurances, that in any emergency she might command my services. My consolations were of course brief, for I could not but feel the indelicacy and impropriety of prolonging the interview. Compressing, therefore, as much kindness into as few words as possible, I took my leave, and was immediately ushered into the presence of Colonel Grimshawe.

He was seated at a table, and engaged in sealing letters, of which an orderly sergeant waited to be the bearer. He bowed on my entrance, and rising from his chair, remained standing while the process of sigillation proceeded, and until, by the dispatch of the messenger, we were left alone.

" It is necessary, Mr Thornton, " said Colonel Grimshawe, pointing to a chair, and at the same time occupying one himself, " it is necessary, in the relative position in which we now stand to each other, that we should come at once to a full understanding. Of *your* intentions, indeed, the very unequivocal circumstances attending the interview, which my intrusion, I fear, so disagreeably interrupted, and the expressions I unintentionally overheard, are sufficiently explanatory. Of *mine*, I think as a gentleman and man of spirit, you cannot be wholly unaware. "

" Excuse me, Colonel Grimshawe ; on your views or intentions, in this or any other matter, I have not presumed to speculate ; but I wish at once to state, that I am too well aware of the presumption which appearances in the present case may raise with regard to the nature of my intentions, not to be anxious immediately to remove your suspicions, by the fullest explanation in my power. "

" Nay, nay, Mr Thornton, you mistake me exceedingly, if you suppose me desirous of putting your ingenuity to the rack, to account for circumstances in themselves too simple and palpable to require explanation. I should be unwilling to think meanly of Mr Thornton ; and the task of glozing facts, and twisting evidence, is one which I am very sure he would think it far beneath him to undertake. "

" I have no thanks to offer you, sir, for a compliment so paid, even were I quite certain that in what you have now said, there is not more insinuated than what meets the ear. You are above subterfuge, Colonel Grimshawe ; I would ask is this so or not ? "

" To ask such a question, sir, is a proof that you know little of the person whom you address. I hold myself responsible for the plain meaning of my words, not for that to which they may be perverted by the ingenuity of another. In holding with you the present conference, I treat you as *an equal*, a sufficient proof, I should imagine, that I consider you a gentleman by birth, character, and profession. Are you satisfied on this point ? " I bowed. " Then by your leave I shall proceed to another not less important, and in so doing it is necessary that I should speak plainly.

" Since you joined the regiment under my command, you have frequently done me the honour of visiting this house. You found at the head of my establishment, a lady whom you must have been conscious was *not* my wife. With this lady you have thought proper to form a liaison inconsistent with the return, which, as her protector, I had a right to expect. I do not blame you for this; it was natural, perhaps excusable; at all events it is a common occurrence, and one for which a person of tolerable experience in the world is never unprepared. It is enough that when you voluntarily formed this connexion, you knew the relation in which she stood to me, and did so, with the intention, I presume, of affording me that satisfaction, which under such circumstances I was entitled to demand, and to which, you must have been aware, it was more than improbable I would forego my claim.—You appear anxious to interrupt me; have I stated anything from which you dissent?"

"Had the circumstances been such as you state them, I should at once admit the justice of your reasoning. But I deny the assumption on which it proceeds. Towards Miss Mansfield I have neither professed nor felt any such sentiments as those to which you have alluded. I have never entertained a thought of withdrawing her from your protection, nor of turning the advantages I enjoyed as your guest, to any improper purpose. If there is any one point of my conduct towards that lady, on which you require explanation, I am now ready to give it you."

A bitter and sarcastic smile came over the features of Colonel Grimshawe as he listened to me.

"Pooh, pooh, Mr Thornton, this is not exactly what I expected from you. There are some things, believe me, which may be true, but which are so improbable that a prudent man will not rashly hazard his credit by asserting them as truth. Permit me as a friend, to say that a different part in this comedy, would become you better,—would be more congenial with your age, character, family, and profession."

"On these points, sir, I must take the liberty of judging for myself. I have already twice offered to explain every word or action of mine, connected with Miss Mansfield, to which suspicion can possibly attach. Were I alone concerned, it is sufficient to say, that this offer should not be repeated, and I now only do so for the sake of the lady whose name in this business has been so unfortunately united with mine. If, as I suspect, you have entered on this interview with views of hostility previously decided, it is well. If not, the offer of satisfactory explanation which I now make for the last time, will, for the sake of justice towards an injured female, induce you at least to pause and to examine."

"This is trifling, sir, and you have had, I imagine, experience enough of my character to know, that I am not a person with whom trifling is likely to succeed. When you have lived longer in the world, you will learn that affairs of this nature are not conducted with the deliberation of a Chancery suit, or an act of the legislature. When a gentleman feels and knows himself to be injured, he does not wait for a committee of inquiry to ascertain the precise extent of his wrongs. No. He demands instantly that satisfaction, to which, as a man of honour he is entitled, and which no man of honour will refuse to grant. Am I at length sufficiently intelligible? "

" Perfectly so, and Colonel Grimshawe may rely on finding no backwardness on my part, in gratifying his wishes. "

"Thank you, thank you, Mr Thornton. Less than this, I did not expect from you; more, I could not wish. Had you fortunately belonged to another corps, this tedious, and I fear to you unpleasant conference, might here have found a satisfactory termination. In our circumstances, however, there is still another point necessary to be arranged. That satisfaction will be required by me, and granted by you, is now mutually understood between us, and fortunately this agreement of the principals will considerably lighten the duties of those gentlemen who may be kind enough to act in the character of friends. But before this matter can reach the termination to which we are both anxious it should be happily brought, there is still an obstacle, and no trifling one, to be removed. Short as your military experience has been, I think you must be aware, Mr Thornton, how entirely incompatible it is with the discipline of the service to which we have both the honour to belong, that the commanding officer of a regiment should consent to a hostile meeting with any officer under his immediate command. When you did me the wrong, for which you are about so handsomely to atone, you knew this, or at least should have known it. I am sure you did not,—could not intend, to place me in a situation where I must either bear an injury, to which no man of spirit could tamely submit; or, in doing myself right, forfeit every hope of professional distinction, to which years of tolerably severe service entitle me to look forward. It is necessary, therefore, before the final settlement of our account, that you exchange into another regiment. I have some small interest at the Horse-guards; and should you require its assistance to promote your views in this matter, you may rely on its being fully exerted in your behalf. In your rank and situation in the regiment, you can derive little injury from such an arrangement; what we must both regret, is the delay which I fear it renders indispensable. "

" Having resolved to give Colonel Grimshawe the satisfaction he demands, I am of course prepared to take every step which may be necessary for the accomplishment of this purpose. He cannot, however, have more pleasure in learning, than I have in informing him, that the delay which he anticipates will not occur. I have this morning received a notification of my appointment to a lieutenancy in a West India regiment, which I trust removes all obstacle to an immediate adjustment of our difference. Colonel Grimshawe will find me ready at any moment. "

Having thus spoken, I handed him the letter, containing documentary evidence of what I had asserted. As he perused it, his countenance brightened. " This, " said he, " is indeed fortunate; and you may rely on it, " half smiling as he spoke, " that you shall not be put to the inconvenience of unnecessary delay by any tardiness of mine. I shall take

care that you appear in the orders of to-day, as ceasing to belong to the
———, and in the evening you may expect a message through the medium
of a friend. Of course, feeling as we both do, that any attempt at
mediation would in our circumstances be useless, delicacy to the friends
who will accompany us to the field, will prevent its being made. Excuse
me for having detained you so long ; every thing is now arranged, and
believe me I am quite sensible of my good fortune, in having had, under
these unpleasant circumstances, to deal with a person of honour and
gallantry like Mr Thornton. "

I arose to depart, and acknowledged the compliment by a bow,
which being duly returned by Colonel Grimshawe, the conference
ended.

When I went forth, my mind was under the influence of a crowd of
mingled feelings difficult to describe. I was irritated at the idea of being
forced, it might be, to pay the penalty of life for the seduction of a
woman, whom I was innocent, either by word or action, of having
attempted to seduce. I had been confronted with proofs I knew not how
to rebut, and in spite of all my efforts, had fallen a victim to presumpt-
ions, of whose falsehood I was conscious. In the interview which had just
concluded, I felt I had been contending with a being of superior power,
from whose cold and cutting sarcasms, even with truth on my side, I had
shrunk discomfited. I had been overawed,—overmatched in the war of
words ; and I, a naked and defenceless man, had been urging unequal
combat with an enemy, clad in complete steel, and too skilful not to
profit by his advantage.

And why was this ? Why did I now find myself standing thus exposed
to imminent and deadly peril ? For a woman to whom I had accidentally happened to address a little casual conversation in the ordinary
intercourse of society ! What was Hecuba to me, or I to Hecuba, that I
had incurred such hazard in her cause ?

But mine, I have said, were mingled feelings ; and in the situation in
which I found myself, there was pride mixed up with humiliation. I
knew myself matched with no unworthy antagonist. In encountering
Colonel Grimshawe in the field, it seemed as if there had fallen to me a
golden opportunity of distinction. Colonel Grimshawe, even among
brave men, was noted as a person of the coolest and most determined
courage. He was an experienced duellist, and an unerring pistol-shot.
My pulses beat high, when the thought came over me, that I was the
David destined to smite this Goliath in the forehead. I trod the streets
more proudly, as the circumstances of my approaching conquest became vividly shadowed forth in my imagination. " Thrice is he armed
that hath his quarrel just ; " and I felt that I should go forth to meet him
with pure hands, and in the confidence of an unshrinking heart.

But my time was too precious to be wasted in reveries, however
agreeable. Circumstances required instant action, and it was necessary

in the approaching encounter that I should be provided with a friend. Motives of delicacy prevented my applying with this view to any of my companions of the ——, who were under the immediate command of Colonel Grimshawe. My choice was thus considerably narrowed; and, after some deliberation, I determined to solicit the friendly services of the Baron Reiffenstein, then a captain in a foreign battalion of the 60th regiment, which formed part of the garrison of Halifax. The Baron had been my fellow-passenger to America, and I had had it in my power, by a little trifling assistance, to extricate him from some embarrassments before quitting Portsmouth, which might otherwise have prevented the prosecution of his voyage.

I accordingly directed my steps towards the residence of this personage; and, on arriving there, had the good fortune to find him at home. He was seated on a camp bedstead, in a foraging cap of crimson velvet, adorned by a splendid gold tassel, quietly smoking his meershaum, as I entered.

" Ah! Meinherr Thornton, " he exclaimed, springing up to welcome me, " I am ver clad to see you. I thank you, mein goot sare, that you are so kind to come and visit me in my littel apartment; " and the Baron proceeded to pour forth protestations of personal regard, of which, though rather more vehement and prolix than necessary, I have never had any reason to doubt the sincerity. Having listened to these as long as politeness, and much longer than inclination prompted me, I proceeded to explain the immediate motive of my visit. On learning all the circumstances of the case which I thought it necessary to communicate, the Baron, with the utmost promptitude, declared his acceptance of the proposed office; and had my request been, that he should act, not as second but principal, I do verily believe he would not have been deterred from showing his gratitude, by the vicarious dangers attending such a substitution. The necessary arrangements were soon concluded. It was agreed, that when the time and circumstances of the meeting had been duly settled by the seconds, the Baron was to pass the night in my apartment preparatory to an early start, and that in the meantime he should remain at home prepared to receive the visit of Colonel Grimshawe's friend.

It was near the hour of mess, and I returned to the barracks. I was crossing the square to the entrance which led to my apartment, when the sergeant of my company approached, and submitted the orders of the day to my perusal. Among these I observed the following :—

" R.O.—Ensign Thornton having been promoted to a Lieutenancy in the —— West India regiment, his name will from this day cease to be borne on the strength of the battalion, and that officer will be exempt from further duty.

" JOHN HOPKINS, *Adjt.*——. "

I expected this; and yet it struck through my heart a melancholy feeling. In the dispatch which had been used on the occasion, I thought it would seem to the world as if some tarnish had attached to my character, when it was seen that the earliest possible moment was seized on to get rid of me. At all events, it was the prelude of a separation. In the very spot on which I stood I felt as an intruder, and of the room to which I was returning I was tenant only by courtesy. As I returned the orderly-book to the sergeant, he raised his hand to his cap, and said, " I beg to congratulate you, sir, on your promotion. Wherever you go, I am sure you will carry with you the good wishes of the company for your prosperity. "

I thanked him, and retired to my chamber.

It seemed to me indispensable that I should appear at mess. I was aware, that in the circumstances in which I stood, any perceptible derangement of ordinary habits is sure to be ascribed by all one's " d—d good-natured friends, " to the influence of fear. It was above all things necessary that I should avoid any conduct which could even by possibility admit of such an interpretation. Precisely, therefore, as the bugles rung forth the wonted and welcome tune of " The roast-beef of Old England, " I descended to the mess-room. As I entered, my companions thronged round me, and expressions of congratulation on my promotion, and regret for my departure, were simultaneously pronounced by many voices. I received them with an air of gaiety, little in accordance with my real feelings. At dinner every one drank wine with me, and even those uncongenial spirits with whom I had maintained little intercourse, and no intimacy, now strove, by acts of kindness and attention, to show they parted with me on terms of good fellowship, and with regret.

Notwithstanding the temptation thus afforded me, I abstained from any excess in wine. Indeed, I know not any moment of my life, in which I exercised so thorough a mastery over my own mental emotions, and, by the force of one determined purpose, subdued them so completely as on this occasion. There was not,—I think there was not, discernible in my deportment, any symptom of depression. There was not, I am sure, any appearance of that forced and unnatural vivacity, the effect of strong stimulants acting on agitated nerves, which reveals, perhaps, still more plainly, the secrets of the prison-house within.

My health was toasted in a bumper, preceded by a flattering eulogium, and drank with all the honours. I rose to return thanks. My feelings, hitherto in subjection, now mounted into rebellion, and would not be quelled. My speech was one of impulse. In it I recalled the time, not very distant, when I had come amongst them a stranger, and they welcomed me as a friend. The days I had spent in their society had been the happiest of my life. The fiat of our separation had now gone forth, and I had ceased to be a member of the ———. I was *with* them, but *of* them no longer. Their kindness was imprinted for ever on my memory.

The circumstances of our parting, though gratifying, I could not but feel to be sad, and filling a bumper to the brim, I drank the health of the friends and companions around me. This speech, the first I ever made in my life, was received with thunders of applause. I had not delivered it without strong emotion. My feelings pent up in one channel, had found egress in another, and flowed on in it, with a vehemence proportionate to the power previously exercised for their repression ; and before I concluded, my eyes had filled with tears, and my voice became tremulous and inarticulate.

I had not resumed my seat above a minute, and the storm of approbation which had followed my address, had barely subsided into a calm, when I was approached by a mess-waiter, who whispered that a gentleman wished to see me on particular business in another apartment. I was too well aware of the nature of the summons to lose an instant in obeying it. As I rose from table, my eyes glanced towards Colonel Grimshawe, from a feeling somewhat allied to curiosity. He was engaged in conversation with the officer next him, and apparently altogether unconscious of my motion, and the circumstance which had occasioned it.

The gentleman whom I found awaiting my presence, belonged to the staff of the Duke of Kent, and delivered the message with which he was charged, in a manner as agreeable as its nature admitted. My answer was brief. It conveyed an unqualified acquiescence, on my part, to Colonel Grimshawe's demand of satisfaction ; and for the arrangement of time and place, I referred the bearer to Baron Reiffenstein, intimating, at the same time, my own wishes, that the matter should be brought to a termination as speedily as possible. This, of course, terminated the interview, and I again resumed my place at the mess-table.

The melancholy with which, before my exit, I had contributed, in some degree, to tinge the meeting, had now passed away. Of the jest and merriment, which, with the wine, circled the table, I partook, or, at least, seemed to partake ; and the task of simulation, on my part, became gradually more easy, as the increasing excitation of my companions, proportionably diminished the acuteness of their observation. The song, too, went round, and never was that fine one of Captain Morris, (by far the best modern writer of Anacreontics,) called, I think, " Reasons for Drinking, " better or more affectingly sung than by Stanhope. Till this hour, the following verse, and the deep and melodious intonation of his voice in singing it, have never been forgotten. They slumber in my treasured memories of sweet sounds, often in solitude, awaking in their beauty, and recalling associations, which, though sad, have long ceased to be painful.

> " There's many a lad I've loved is dead,
>   And many a lass grown old ;

And when that lesson strikes my head,
My weary heart grows cold. "

The evening was pretty far advanced, when Colonel Grimshawe quitted the mess. As he passed to the door, our eyes accidentally met. He bowed, but so slightly, that it could scarcely be observed by any other than him for whom it was intended ; and as he withdrew his eyes, I remarked there was a smile on his lips. Owing to the slight distortion of his mouth, the smile of Colonel Grimshawe was unpleasant. On the present occasion, from the working of my fancy, it seemed peculiarly hateful and demoniac, and a curse half rose to my lips as I beheld it.

By his departure, I felt relieved from the necessity of remaining longer in a scene, little suited either to my circumstances or feelings. I soon, therefore, took occasion to escape, and pressing, from a certain solemnity of feeling which at that moment came over me, the hand of Stanhope, as if bidding him a long farewell, I said, in a whisper, " May God bless you, my dear friend, " and darted from the mess-room.

On entering my chamber, I found it filled with a cloud of smoke, so dense as to be quite impervious to the eye, and it was some time before the surrounding objects became dimly visible in the cloudy atmosphere. Seated by the fire, and smoking his Meershaum, with a bottle of claret before him, which I had taken care to provide for his accommodation, was my friend the Baron. From him I learned, that he had definitively arranged with the friend of Colonel Grimshawe, all the circumstances of the meeting. It was to take place on the following morning at day-break, and the theatre of action, which had been selected, was a lake, or tarn, about half a league distant from the town.

I immediately issued orders to my servant to have my sleigh at the Barrack-gate by six in the morning, there to await our coming ; and being aware of no other call for previous action on my part, became a quiet listener to the bloody anecdotes of German duelling, with which the Baron's memory was abundantly fraught. If at this distance of time I may trust my memory, he had been run through the body at least a dozen times, yet always came off victorious ; a circumstance not to be wondered at, considering the blood in his veins, for, by his own account, his father and grandfather had been a pair of Drawcansirs, who, in their day, had slain more enemies, than ever did Roland the Paladin, or Amadis de Gaul.

Having listened patiently for *two pipes* to these interesting narratives, the subject was fortunately changed, by a desire expressed by the Baron to see my pistols. The request came like a thunderbolt. I had no pistols, and, absurd as it may appear, the necessity of providing them never had occurred to me. Luckily the Baron had been more provident, and on learning the state of the case, produced a pair from the pockets of his greatcoat, of most unwieldy dimensions, on the unerring accuracy of which, and the services they had rendered him on sundry previous occasions, he found new subjects for eloquence. Perceiving that I was rather a tyro in such matters, he proceeded to give me such instructions as his experience suggested, explained the attitude in which the smallest front was exposed to the enemy, and conjured me, above all things, to beware of levelling my pistol too high. " The barrel, " he said, " should be allowed to incline in a slight degree downwards. By levelling an inch too high, a shot, even when otherwise well directed, did no execution ; whereas, by erring on the other side, I had every chance of considerably inconveniencing my adversary, by deranging his knee-pan, or lodging a bullet in the calf of his leg. "

Thus did the night wax on, and I entreated my companion, whose eyes became gradually heavy, to make use of my bed, and seek a few hours repose. To the former part of my proposal he strenuously object-ed, nor by any argument could I induce his compliance. " It was necessary, " he assured me, " for the steadiness of my hand in the morning, that I should enjoy a comfortable nap over night. That for himself, he had brought his bearskin, and on that, wrapped in his boat-cloak, and with a portmanteau for a pillow, he would sleep as soundly as on a bed of down. " I ceased to argue the point, and suffering the Baron to make himself comfortable in his own way, a grunting, not unlike that of a plethoric pig, soon informed me that he was as happy as oblivion of all worldly misfortunes could make him.

This was the first moment of solitude I had enjoyed for many hours, and not more grateful is a spring in the burning desert to the thirsty traveller, than was this interval of freedom to me. I sat gazing on the embers of the fire, and reviewed, I think, calmly, all the circumstances of my situation. I knew it was probable I should fall in the approaching encounter, and bethought me whether any duties in this world still remained for me to perform. Property, in the larger sense of the term, I possessed none, and yet I felt desirous of bequeathing some tokens of remembrance, to my sisters and the friends whom I had loved. My will was soon made, and of the numerous testamentary donations which it directed, I remember only that I bequeathed my watch to Conyers, and my sword to Stanhope.

I hesitated at first, whether to write to my father and sisters. But I found at that moment their remembrance clung closely to my heart, and I wished not to quit the world, without bidding them farewell. I wrote therefore a few lines as follows :—

" FATHER,

" The son whom you loved not is no more. His death will bring no dishonour on your name. Sisters, dear sisters, you have no longer a brother. His last thoughts were with you,—his last prayer that Heaven's blessings might fall thick on you. Farewell, eternally farewell. "

Having duly signed, sealed, and superscribed these documents, I determined to follow my friend's advice, and to court sleep for the portion of the night that still remained. The state of extreme tension in which my mind had been kept for many hours, was such as could not be continued without cracking the strings of the instrument, and nature called for some relaxation of the screws. I heaped, therefore, some fresh embers on the fire, and disencumbering myself of a few of my external garments, retired to bed. As my head pressed my pillow, my thoughts were rapid but indistinct, and passed like clouds in a tempestuous sky, racking the face of the firmament with a velocity scarcely diminished, even when the wind that impelled them has died away. My mind was in a state somewhat similar to that so powerfully described by the Opium Eater, as generally occurring after his third or fourth tumbler of "laudanum negus, warm, without sugar." My conceptions by degrees became still more awful and indefinite, and eluding by their very vastness, the grasp of my jaded intellect, at length faded into vacancy, and I was asleep.

CHAPTER IV

Death is a fearful thing.
Isab. And shamed life a hateful.
Measure for Measure.

Oh, I do fear thee, Claudio ; and I quake
Lest thou a feverish life should entertain,
And six or seven winters more respect,
Than a perpetual honour. Darest thou die ?
Ibidem.

To bed ;
Take not away the taper ; leave it burning ;
And if thou canst awake by four o' the clock,
I pray thee call me.
Cymbeline.

THOUGH short, my slumber was refreshing. With the first gleam of returning sense I started hastily from the bed, in the fear that I had overslept my time. I examined my watch by the firelight, and found it still wanted two hours of the time of meeting. The snoring of my companion showed he was still asleep, and with a reference, perhaps, as much directed to my own comfort as to his, I was unwilling to awake him. I could not think of again returning to bed, and seated myself in a chair by the fire.

The excitement of the preceding day had thoroughly abated, and my mind was calm and collected. The circumstances of my situation rose before me, not as formerly, in a hurried and confused crowd, and my eye contemplated them in their real form and natural dimensions. I felt like one conscious of standing on the brink of a precipice, down which, by the grasp of a mighty arm, he may in an instant be hurled headlong. I was awe—not fear-struck ; and if, as I gazed down the fearful and dark abyss that yawned beneath my feet, a shudder came over me, my heart, at least, did not cower, and I stood firm and resolute on the perilous brink.

It is impossible, I think, to contemplate the probability of sudden death, and forget the Being into whose presence it must instantly call us. Yet, in the whirlpool of passion by which my mind had been agitated, I had merged in the anxieties of this world, all thought of the next. I was about to face death, yet had addressed no prayer for mercy and forgiveness, to the Being in whose hands alone, are the issues of life. But on that morning, in the solitary darkness of my chamber, a better frame of mind arose within me, and collecting all my thoughts for this greatest and most important duty of a human being, I knelt in prayer.

My devotions continued till interrupted by the Baron, who, being now broad awake, insisted on the necessity of immediate preparation. My servant, too, soon entered, and before the business of the toilet was completed, announced that the sleigh was already at the gate.

The sun had not risen, yet it was light. The snow lay deep on the ground, and the severity of the cold was such as to require, even in travelling so short a distance, that we should be plentifully wrapped in fur. Every preparation being made, we entered the vehicle and drove off. As we passed rapidly through the town, not a soul was in the streets, and everything was still and noiseless, as in a city of the dead. The face of nature lay hid in snow, as if covered by a winding-sheet, and no moving thing, save the smoke that rose right upwards in long unbroken columns to the clouds, was visible. Even the foot-falls of the horse were without sound, and the tinkling of the small bells which depended from the harness, alone broke the depth of the surrounding silence.

We soon reached the spot of our destination, and were first on the ground. Our only welcome was the shrieking of some half-starved water-fowl, that rose startled from the bulrushes on our approach. Directing the servant to retire with the sleigh to a convenient distance, and divesting ourselves of the furs, by which the freedom of motion would have been disagreeably impeded, we resolved to counteract the effects of the cold by a smart walk on the ice, till the arrival of my antagonist. He gave us little cause to complain of his dilatoriness. The sun, which rose the colour of copper, had showed but a small portion of his disk above the tops of the distant forest, when Colonel Grimshawe and his friend, attended by the fat and facetious surgeon of the regiment, were seen rapidly approaching. They soon came up, and having descended from the carriage, which immediately withdrew, bows were mutually exchanged. No verbal communication passed between Colonel Grimshawe and myself. I observed him with deep, and, I confess, almost fearful interest. There was nothing unusual in his expression, but, as he saluted me, the same detestable smile was on his countenance, which I had observed on the preceding evening. In his manner there was nothing of bravado. There was no air of resolute determination put on for the occasion of display; but the ease and graceful facility of his motions, betrayed to an observant eye, that he had abated no jot of his usual confidence and self-possession.

While the seconds were engaged in measuring the distance on the ice, and arranging the other necessary preliminaries, we continued to walk apart. I will not attempt to deny that the few minutes which thus elapsed were armed with awful terrors. In what train of thought my mind was engaged during that period of inaction, I cannot remember. It should have been devoted to prayer—I hope it was so. But I know well, that when the seconds approached, and requested us to take our ground, my heart ceased to flutter, and I felt no longer that universal quivering of the muscles, with which, but an instant before, my frame was shaken. We were to fire by signal. The weapons were placed in our hands, and the seconds hastily retired. The stentorian voice of the Baron pronounced the word "Fire," and we obeyed. Neither fell. I looked on my adversary with eager interest, to observe if my shot had taken effect. It had evidently not done so. Colonel Grimshawe stood in an easy and negligent attitude; and observing my eyes were turned towards him, he addressed me laughingly—"We have shown ourselves sad bunglers, Mr Thornton, but I hope we shall improve by practice."

I replied only by a bow, and the seconds having advanced and supplied us with a fresh case of pistols, the signal was given, and we again fired.

I instantly felt myself to be wounded, but did not fall. The bullet had entered my thigh, a little below the hip-joint, and I staggered back a pace or two, more, perhaps, from the novelty of the sensation, than from any absolute necessity for such a retrogression. The wound occasioned but little effusion of blood, and, in a moment, recovering my self-possession, I advanced and stood again upon my ground. My friend, the Baron, was immediately by my side, making kind and anxious enquiries into the nature of my wound; and the jolly Doctor, who had remained at a short distance, on a spot conveniently situated for *not* seeing what was passing, next came up, armed with a tourniquet, which, as a measure of precaution, he recommended instantly to be applied.

I did not, however, think proper to subject myself to the immediate exercise of his skill, but requesting him for the present to retire, I informed the seconds that I was ready to go on, and requested that fresh pistols might be furnished. Colonel Grimshawe immediately stated that he was already satisfied, and felt no desire that the affair should be carried further. "Gentlemen," I answered, "it gives me pleasure to learn that Colonel Grimshawe expresses himself satisfied; but *I* am *not* satisfied. In an interview with which he lately honoured me, Colonel Grimshawe thought proper to question the truth of some explanatory statements which I felt called on to make, relative to the circumstances which gave occasion to the present meeting. I insist that, with regard to this matter, we come to an issue on the spot. I insist that Colonel Grimshawe shall retract the imputation he was pleased to cast, not only on the truth of my statements, but on my motives in making them, or that the present meeting shall not terminate here."

Colonel Grimshawe addressed the seconds—"Gentlemen, I join Mr Thornton in requesting that we may be immediately furnished with arms, since it appears our differences are not yet entirely adjusted."

On this appeal the seconds held consultation together, and were evidently inclined to demur to the desire expressed by the combatants, of protracting their hostility. A few words, however, which passed in a whisper between Colonel Grimshawe and his friend, had apparently the effect of changing their opposition, and pistols were again placed in our hands.

The signal was once more given, and I instantly fired. Had I followed the Baron's advice, and levelled my pistol an inch lower, Colonel Grimshawe would have probably finished his mortal career on the spot. The bullet struck his hat, and knocked it off. When he felt himself bareheaded, he smiled, and nodding to me familiarly, exclaimed, " A good shot, " then raising his pistol deliberately, he fired it in the air. He then threw it from him, and advanced towards me. I raised my hat as he approached.

" Mr Thornton, " said he, extending his hand, " you have deprived me of the means of returning your salute. Whatever, in the heat and irritation of our late conversation, may have occurred unpleasant to your feelings, I am most happy, in the presence of these gentlemen, our mutual friends, to retract. There is no one of whose honour I entertain a higher opinion. I trust your wound will turn out neither dangerous nor severe. Let me entreat you will no longer delay to receive surgical assistance. "

After this *amende honorable*, the more gratifying from the character of the person who made it, I could no longer refuse the proffered hand of Colonel Grimshawe ; and the seconds having declared the affair terminated in a manner honourable to both parties, I submitted my wound to such examination and treatment as the Doctor judged immediately necessary. The sleighs were then sent for, and having mounted,— though, from the increasing stiffness of my limb, not without difficulty,— the parties, no longer adverse, returned separately to the town.

My wound occasioned much suffering, and tedious confinement. But it was borne patiently, and accompanied by no depression of spirits. When I remembered the severity of the ordeal through which I had passed, I felt a sensation of pride and self-respect, to which I had before been unaccustomed. My character possessed none of that apathy to danger, miscalled constitutional courage. No man breathing loved life better, or feared to lose it more. Death could not be more terrible, than it was in my eyes, yet I had met it with a courageous front. My weapon of conquest, had been love of honour, not insensibility to danger. In my own eyes, I seemed a perfect Bayard, a chevalier *sans peur et sans reproche*. These, at least, were harmless fantasies, and they were happy ones. Why should they be sneered at by the philosopher, or censured by the moralist ?

I had to undergo a painful operation for extracting the ball. My worthy friend Holford had too much sympathy for the pain he inflicted,— too little of the butcher about him, to perform the operation with dexterity. I begged him to resign the knife to his assistant, and he did so. From that hour I loved him. He became endeared to me by the very pain his awkwardness had inflicted; and though I esteemed him less as a surgeon, I loved him better as a man.

I felt deeply the kindness I experienced during my confinement, from my old brother officers of the ———. Stanhope and Popham, in particular, spent daily many hours by my couch. In fact, my chamber formed a sort of lounging place for all the loquacious and good-natured fellows of the regiment, who came running thither with every morsel of news and tittle-tattle, which it was possible for the imagination of idle men, to devise or set afloat. Sometimes, indeed, I was not without suspicion, that pleasant libels and tales of facetious scandal, were frequently fabricated by my visitors, for my express enjoyment and behoof. It might be so, but no one questioned their authenticity, and they won their laugh, and lived their hour.

Colonel Grimshawe sent regularly to inquire for me, and frequently called. His manner and his deportment towards me, had undergone no change. He was the same delightful person, that in private society I had ever found him. It is meting him but simple justice to state, that his nature was not given to cherish petty malice. Those whom he disliked, he neither sought to circumvent, nor to entrap. His resentments were never treasured in darkness, to explode beneath the feet of some unconscious and sleeping victim. They were displayed in the broad sunlight,— the lowering of the sky gave sufficient indication of the coming storm, and I always felt that there was something about him, at once attractive and repulsive. He was not—he never could be, to me a friend; yet to have been compelled to regard him as an enemy, would have been matter of deep and enduring regret.

During the confinement consequent on my wound, I heard but few and vague particulars regarding Miss Mansfield. She was a person to whom I should have felt gratified in being able to render any service, for her story and the deep flow of natural emotion which accompanied its narration, had powerfully interested the better feelings of my nature in her behalf. She was indeed a wanderer from the paths of virtue, and though, by the unbending rules of society, such a person may be held an outcast on earth, we know that there is more joy in heaven over one repentant sinner, than over ninety and nine of those, whose unswerving, and perhaps untempted virtue, has held on its way victorious and rejoicing. Man knew her error; but God, who can read the heart, alone knew the strength of the preceding temptation, the depth and sincerity of that penitence with which it was afterwards deplored.

I learned, that on hearing the issue of the duel, she had been thrown into an agitation almost amounting to insanity, and that with feelings of deep self-reproach she accused herself as its cause. In a few days, intelligence was brought me that she had sailed for England. Delicacy prevented my inquiring any particulars concerning her from Colonel Grimshawe, and that officer appeared on all occasions studiously to avoid allusions to her name. The whist parties at his house proceeded as usual, and the *hiatus* left by Miss Mansfield, if casually observed, was soon forgotten.

It was a fortunate circumstance, that an officer of my own rank in the ——, was desirous, from peculiar circumstances, of exchanging into another regiment. To me, this seemed to afford a golden opportunity. I panted for nothing more ardently, than to become a denizen of my former corps, and be again restored to those messmates and companions with whom I had already spent many happy days. Yet I feared I should find in Colonel Grimshawe an insuperable bar to the gratification of my wishes. It could not, I imagined, be pleasant, to one wielding as he did, the despotic plenitude of military authority—that his eye should daily encounter one, whom he had suspected at least, of having done him grievous wrong, and who was publicly known to have confronted him in the field. In this, however, I was mistaken. Colonel Grimshawe had too much confidence in himself, and was too conscious of his own power of commanding deference and submission, to be swayed by such motives. He had learned from some of my brother officers, the desire I entertained of returning to the regiment, and voluntarily took occasion to inform me, that so far from opposing such a step on my part, he would feel the greatest pleasure in promoting my views.

Every obstacle being thus removed, I lost no time in concluding the arrangement. The necessary documents, strongly backed by Colonel Grimshawe, were forwarded to England, and before, by the re-establishment of my health, I was again fit for duty, my appointment had appeared in the Gazette, and I was once more restored to the ——, in the character of lieutenant.

After my reappointment, the regiment did not long remain in America. Towards the end of spring we were ordered to Gibraltar. The —— regiment arrived to relieve us, and we embarked in the transports which had brought them to America. In a few days we sailed. Twilight was on the waters when, having emerged with a fair breeze from the bay, we found ourselves on the open bosom of the Atlantic. With a feeling somewhat allied to regret, I watched the land till it disappeared in the darkness. In the morning, it was no longer visible.

Our convoy consisted of the Hyperion and Cyrene, and the fleet, which had been joined by many merchant vessels, amounted in all to about thirty sail. We did not take the direct course to the ultimate point of our destination. A detachment of the regiment was stationed in the Bermuda Islands, and it was of course necessary that we should call there to receive them. That this interruption to our voyage might be as short as possible, orders had previously been sent, directing them to be in readiness for instant embarkation, and it was not the intention of the

Commodore to have anchored. But one of the hurricanes to which that portion of the Atlantic is peculiarly liable, came on, and the transport in which I sailed, and several other ships of the fleet, were so severely damaged as to require considerable repairs before they could with safety proceed on their voyage. All of us suffered severely from the storm. I am not sailor enough to describe either its grandeur or its terrors. The ship staggered like a drunken man, and I saw the foretopsail, the only canvass we carried, rent in shivers from the mast, and floating far away upon the wind. This, at least to a landsman, was unpleasant; but this was not all. A sea that apparently might have overset a mountain, struck the stern of the vessel, and carried away her helm. I shall never forget that moment. Her timbers groaned from the violence of the concussion, she reeled under the shock, and for a time was buffeted about, a mere passive and inert mass upon the waters. Whether our situation was really so perilous as it appeared, I know not. But there were loud shrieks and wailing heard from the women and children, and the fear of death fell with a withering chill on the heart of the stoutest ;—

" The boldest held his breath for a time. "

The peril passed, however, and once more there were grateful hearts and happy looks in the ship. The disappearance of the danger made us almost smile at its consequences, and though not only our persons, but our bedding and baggage were drenched with water, these misfortunes were submitted to without repining.

In such a plight did the sun go down on us ; and when he rose, judge of our delight to find ourselves safely anchored in a smooth and quiet cove of the Bermudas. Never was the eye of the mariner greeted by a sight more beautiful. The little bay in which we were anchored, lay embedded in a cluster of islands covered with cedar-wood. White cottages rose here and there, on the sides of the hills, and on the lower ground were seen at intervals, glimmering through the foliage of the trees. Close to the shore was the town of St George, which though, like most towns, it loses much of its charm on a nearer approach, formed an interesting feature in the landscape, when seen from the anchorage.

The luxury of going ashore just after escaping from a tempest, is great, and scarcely too dearly earned, even by the peril of going to the bottom. At least I thought so at Bermuda. Novelty and curiosity contributed to heighten our enjoyment. The boats were instantly ordered to be lowered, and separating into different parties, as inclination prompted, we set out to explore the beauties of the surrounding scenery.

We asked no information, and took no guide, but wandered onwards through the woods, skirting in our progress many calm and lonely inlets of the sea, and resting, when tired, beneath the shade of the lemon-trees, in some sequestered dell. Peace seemed to brood over these happy islands. Nothing can be imagined more brightly yet more serenely beautiful. An European eye knows nothing of such verdure as it here encounters, nothing of the splendour of shade and sunshine which here blend together in the landscape. In the scenery of the Bermuda Islands, there is nothing at all approaching to the grand or magnificent: No lofty mountains, no frowning and precipitous rocks, no sound of cataract, nor sight of mighty river flowing onwards in its majesty. It seems as if nature had here delighted to cast aside her terrors, and appear only in her smiles.

We spent the day in rambling through the woods, which are intersected by footpaths. The heat was intense, but shaded by the far-extending branches of the cedar-trees, and fanned occasionally by a cool breeze from the sea, we did not feel it oppressive. At evening we returned to the ship, and in the close and sultry suffocation of the cabin, fancy returned, in dreams, to those scenes of pleasant beauty amid which we had so recently wandered.

It was known that the repairs necessary for the ships would occupy some time. We had nothing to do on board, and Stanhope, Popham, and myself, employed a fatigue party to erect a hut in a spot of uncommon beauty. It was composed of branches of trees, and impervious to sun and rain. Here we lived during our sojourn at Bermuda, nor did we return on board, till the blue Peter was seen flying from the mast-head of the Commodore, and the signal-gun for weighing anchor was fired. My memory invests the period thus passed with a peculiar charm. By day we spent our time in sailing about the islands, or exploring new beauties through the neighbouring woods. Often, too, when the heat rendered motion unpleasant, did we lie extended on the fragrant greensward, and

> " Under the shade of melancholy boughs
> Lose and neglect the creeping hours of time ; "

while Stanhope, with a taste and elegance I have never heard equalled, read aloud portions of Scott or Shakspeare, the great master spirits of our national literature. Among these selections, I need scarcely say that the play of " As you Like it, " was one. The scene around us—our own situation as voluntary tenants of the woods, gave extrinsic piquancy to its enchantment, and arrayed it in a charm never destined to fade from the heart or fancy. A new page in the beautiful volume of nature had been opened to our view, no worldly cares oppressed our spirits, and gay and thoughtless as we were, even we

> " In this our life, exempt from public haunt,
> Found tongues in trees, books in the running brooks,
> Sermons in stones, and good in everything. "

CHAPTER V

> With easy course
> The vessels glide, unless their speed be stopp'd,
> By dead calms, that oft lie on these smooth seas,
> While every zephyr sleeps; then the shrouds drop,
> The downy feather, on the cordage hung,
> Moves not; the flat sea shines like yellow gold,
> Fused in the fire; or like the marble floor
> Of some old temple wide; but where so wide,
> In old or later time, its marble floor
> Did ever temple boast as this, which here
> Spreads its bright level many a league around?
> DYER's *Fleece*.

WE left Bermuda under different auspices than had marked our arrival. There was a breeze, but so gentle as to cause no ripple on the sea, which, bright and calm, reflected back the blaze of the meridian sun, like a vast mirror. The motion of the ships, as they glided forth from their isle-girt haven, was almost imperceptible; and they held on their way in silence, only broken at intervals by the musical cry of the sailors, or the flapping of the sails, as the wind occasionally lost something of its power. Nowhere is ocean so lucid and transparent as at Bermuda; and the glorious beauty by which above, all nature was encircled, had penetrated even to its depths. Far down were distinctly visible vast rocks of coral, wreathed into innumerable lovely and fantastic shapes—now rising into lofty mountains, now descending into vales, more beautiful than the fabled Tempé; or spreading into forests never visited by verdure. There were cities, too, in the depths, and towers, and temples, and spires, and pinnacles, and pyramids which shall endure, when those of Egypt have been crumbled into dust. On deck, the heat of the sun was almost overpowering. Yet I could not quit gazing on the scene of entrancing beauty for several hours. Towards evening, the breeze freshened, and a haze came on, by which all distant objects were obscured. To me thenceforward, the Bermuda Isles have been, and must ever be, a dream—a memory.

Our voyage, though a tranquil, was a tedious one. For weeks we lay in a dead calm, scarcely stirred but by the currents of the ocean, which carried us still farther from our destined port. Sometimes, indeed, towards evening and at midnight, a slight breathing of wind was perceptible, which, tired as we were with the monotony of the life thus involuntarily imposed on us, we watched with the alternating anxieties of hope and fear, till towards morning it again died away, and the ship lay hovering over her own beautiful image, almost motionless in the sunshine. Nothing can be conceived more tedious and insipid than our life on board. The heat was so oppressive during the day, as to render it almost impossible to remain on deck, even with the protection of an awning; and the cabin—no baker's oven could be more close and sultry. The atmosphere seemed to have lost all power of propulsion, and

> Day after day, day after day,
> We stuck, nor breath nor motion,
> As idly as a painted ship
> Upon a painted ocean.

In vain did we resort to all the usual and approved expedients for killing time on ship-board. We fished for sharks and dolphins, and tried to stimulate their appetite by every unheard of variety of bait; but our lines lay idly in the water, and neither shark nor dolphin condescended to indulge us even with a nibble. Whist, backgammon, and piquet did much to support us in these untoward circumstances; but even their infinite variety was at length staled by repetition, and they were voted dull and insipid. Doctor Johnson, I think, compares a ship to a prison; had ours afforded a treadmill, I do believe we should have become voluntary labourers from pure ennui.

The influence of the time extended even to the sailors. In such a situation, the duties of the ship were nothing, and they might be seen idly seated in groups on the deck, smoking or " spinning tough yarns " to astonish the admiring soldiers. Some ascended to the main-top for the purpose of enjoying a quiet sleep, unbroken by the pranks or noise of their companions; while others, more musical, were leaning lazily against the tafferel, with arms a-kimbo, listening *erectis auribus* to songs commemorative of Admiral Benbow and the exploits of the Arethusa.

Such was our situation for upwards of a month after quitting Bermuda, and a consequence of this unusual protraction of our voyage, was a deficiency of water in many of the ships of the fleet, which threatened serious consequences to the health of those on board. The Commodore, therefore, judged it necessary that we should put into some intermediate port for the supply of our necessities, and issued fresh orders to the fleet, indicating the island of Palma as the place of rendezvous, in case of separation.

A breeze at length sprung up, and though not very favourable, it at least put a stop to that state of sluggish inaction by which we had so long and so unpleasantly been spell-bound. There was pleasure in the mere motion of the vessel; and though we sailed close-hauled to the wind, and made little actual progress, no music could be more grateful to our ears than the splashing of the waves as the ship cut through them with her prow.

Never shall I forget the delight with which, on a beautiful evening, when smoking our cigars on deck, we saw the signal of " Land visible a-head, " displayed by the Commodore. A cry of pleasure burst from every lip, and crowding up into the shrouds, we endeavoured to ascertain by the evidence of our own senses the truth of the intelligence. But it was in vain. All round the verge of the horizon the azure of the sky was bright and unbroken, and night closed in before our eyes were gratified with the view of our destined port.

In our state of excitement, it was impossible to sleep; and on the following morning, before the first gleam of approaching daylight had dappled the east, we had all assembled on the deck. The sun rose brightly on that morning, but we beheld him not. Not a ray fell upon the waters for leagues around; not a beam even kissed the pendant that streamed above the high top-gallant-mast of the Commodore. An island rose before us, from which a mountain, like a vast pyramid, was seen to stretch high up into the air; and while its unclouded summit glowed resplendent in the sunshine, we still sailed on, immersed in the mighty shadow which it cast far out into the ocean.

The island to which we were approaching was Teneriffe. The wind was unfavourable for Palma, and the Commodore, without signifying his intention, had determined on making the former the place of our temporary sojourn. The appearance of Teneriffe, when seen from the sea, is not prepossessing. To the eye it seems to consist of a congregation of rocky and barren hills, many of them of very considerable eminence, unadorned by any brightness of verdure. Our approach to it was slow. The wind fell away as the sun neared his meridian, and it was evening before we came to anchor in the harbour of Santa Cruz.

On the following morning, the British Consul came on board the Commodore, and was received with a salute. By his agency, measures were instantly adopted for supplying our deficiency of water, and procuring such refreshments for the troops as were afforded by the island.

At Santa Cruz my companions and myself once more enjoyed the luxury of treading on *terra firma*. The town is of considerable extent, and with less appearance of poverty than usually meets the eye in towns of equal population in England. To us, indeed, it possessed a deep though extrinsic interest, in being the spot where Nelson experienced the only failure which marked his glorious career. It was not with vacant eye, that we gazed on the scene of this memorable conflict. The natives pointed out to us the exact spot, where, leading his gallant followers, he had effected a landing, in face of a powerful battery, and captured it with the cutlass and bayonet. The attack then extended to the town, and we saw where, from the windows and terraced roofs of the houses, a deadly and destructive fire had been poured on the assailants, and where he, under whose auspices the 'meteor flag' of England was yet destined victoriously to brave both the battle and the breeze, was carried off maimed, yet, even in defeat—glorious.

In the Cathedral Church, the colours which had been captured from our countrymen on that occasion, were hung up as trophies of victory. They were shown to us with an excusable pride. The Spanish flag was floating proudly over them, and we turned hastily away from a sight, which we found it was impossible to muster resolution of the spirit to gaze on calmly.

As we wandered through the town, the fair Senoras peered forth on us with dark-bright eyes, from casements and lattices, and occasionally let fall a shower of myrtle or orange flowers on our heads as we passed. The weather was too hot for promenading, and we met but few of the higher order of females in the street. But the evening brought them to the Alameda, with all their bravery on, and intent on making unprofitable conquest of the hearts of the English intruders.

Till now I had never enjoyed the opportunity of observing the manners of a foreign people, nor obtained palpable experience of those moral differences, which variance of religion, education, and climate, cannot fail to stamp on the character and habits, both of individuals and communities. This my first specimen was certainly an unfortunate one. I had then seen little of the world—I have now seen more, and a considerable—I may almost say, the principal part of my life, has been passed abroad; but I do not remember anywhere, to have witnessed a dissolution of manners so gross and offensive, as in the Island of Teneriffe. In saying this, I wish not to be understood as applying a censure so broad and unqualified, to the higher classes of society in the island. In them, I was naturally struck, indeed, by a freedom of address, which my experience of foreign manners has since proved to be consistent with the most perfect propriety of conduct, and purity of thought. But in a society where the inferior orders are so entirely depraved, it is impossible, I think, to presume that the gangrene has not spread farther. The different classes of a community are "bound each to each, by natural sympathy," and where there is rottenness at the root of the tree, it would be folly to expect that the sap and vigour of the higher branches, can be unimpaired by the decay. I am quite ready to admit, that there is nothing more intolerant than a young Englishman, sallying forth into the world, full of his own ignorance and *John Bullism*—judging of mankind by his own petty and narrow notions of fitness and propriety—without the capacity of generalization—a mighty observer of effects, and disregarder of causes, and traversing continent and ocean, at once blinded and shackled, by the bigotry and prejudices of his own limited and imbecile intellect. Were I writing a book of travels—were it the object of these volumes to furnish facts for the philosopher, or knowledge to the student, I might, indeed, hesitate before I ventured to enounce a conclusion so decided, on the character of a people, from an intercourse so transient. But I pretend to give, not *facts*, but *semblances*—not an account of things as they really existed, but as they appeared when refracted and modified by the peculiarities of my own reasoning and perceptive powers.

At Teneriffe the supply of water was limited, and our stay, on that account, was necessarily prolonged. In the neighbourhood of Santa Cruz the scenery is barren and uninteresting, and the town presented little variety. Our time, from morn till noon, from noon till dewy eve, hung heavy on our hands, and, without a strong incentive, the heat was too great for exercise on shore. In the evenings, indeed, we generally promenaded on the Alameda, and lavished our most languishing looks and sweetest smiles on the sallow and dark-eyed beauties of the island. Then came the Tertullia, a nightly assembly, open to every one with a propensity for either gambling or dancing. There we generally remained till midnight, and then returned to the ship. But this was stupid enough ; and finding there was no prospect of the fleet sailing in less than a week, a party was arranged, consisting of our worthy Doctor, Stanhope, Popham, and myself, to ascend, or, at least, endeavour to ascend, the Peak. New vigour and animation was at once infused into us by this project. The giant cone of the Peak, which, after the first day, I had regarded with little interest, now excited feelings of anxious expectation, whenever I beheld it towering like a mighty king of earth and ocean, far up into the sky.

Though our excursion was easily decided on, there were considerable difficulties to be overcome in the preparatory arrangements. We made inquiries for guides, but there were none to be found ; for even those born within a league of the mountain, lived from infancy to old age without having ever been induced by the promptings of curiosity to ascend from their native valley into the region of barren grandeur above them. The distance to the Peak was considerable, and as we could not afford to waste any unnecessary time on our excursion, we were anxious to procure animals for our conveyance. This, however, was by no means easy. Neither horse nor mule was to be had for love or money, and it was with extreme difficulty that we at length succeeded in procuring a pair of camels, (which are here, not unusually, employed instead of oxen,) and an ass (or, as it is called in Spanish, a Bourico,) for our baggage, which, after dismissing the former, we intended should accompany us in our ascent as far as should be found practicable. We had the good fortune, too, after being disappointed in all our inquiries, to meet with a person who, we were assured, knew all the passes of the mountain, and who, for a handsome reward, agreed to be our conductor.

These indispensable preliminaries being at length arranged, the following morning, at daybreak, was fixed for our departure ; and carrying with us a stock of provisions, which, on a moderate calculation, might have lasted for a week, the first gleam of dawn found us seated, with high spirits, in the ship's boat, and rowing towards the shore. There we found our guide and the animals destined for our conveyance waiting our arrival. A long interval, however, intervened, before we were fairly *en route*. The party consisted of four, of which two were allotted to each camel, and the provender and baggage were placed on the Bourico.

In the idea of travelling on a camel there was something of barbaric grandeur and orientalism, that gave a piquancy half ludicrous and half imposing to the journey ; and I gazed on the two " ships of the desert, " on board of which we were about to embark, with somewhat more of excitement, than the fear of ridicule allowed me to betray to my companions. Perhaps I may be laughed at even now, when I confess that I never yet could look on the face of a camel, without feeling a tear rise up into my eye. There is something about it so subdued and melancholy—so sad and so submissive—it looks so like a creature for which life has no enjoyment, that when the driver, with a curse and a blow of his cudgel, made those in question kneel down for us to mount, I did almost involuntarily return his curse, and felt inclined to do so with the blow.

To mount, however, was not a matter of a moment. There was a packsaddle, but so hard as to afford to the equestrian (that is not the word, but our language affords nothing nearer,) but an uncomfortable and inconvenient seat. The Doctor and Popham were the first to take up their position. The former disliking the pack-saddle, adjusted his boat-cloak for a cushion, and seated himself on the posterior hump of the animal with his feet resting on the back, immediately behind Popham, whose little figure, from the inconveniently wide divergence of his legs, looked not unlike that of a diminutive Bacchus astride upon a tun. In vain did the driver recommend the doctor to take his seat *selon les règles*, and warn him of the insecurity of the position he had assumed ; the Doctor was obstinate, and lent a deaf ear to the voice of his prudent monitor. The consequence to be expected followed. The camel, in rising to his feet, gave a pretty violent jerk, for which he was unprepared, and the follower of Galen paid the penalty of his obduracy by being pitched from his position and laid sprawling in the dust.

The disaster of our worthy surgeon occasioned a considerable derangement of our plans, for by no persuasion could he be induced to make a second experiment in *camelmanship*, and it was found necessary to remove the baggage from the Bourico, and allot to that animal the heavier, though more dignified task, of carrying the practitioner of medicine. At length, after the delay of more than an hour, our difficulties were finally overcome, and in the fashion already described, we journeyed on slowly towards the Peak.

For my own part, I felt so uncomfortable in the novel mode of conveyance by which we travelled, as to have very little attention to bestow on the character and features of the country through which we passed. I remember, however, that it was generally hilly, bleak, and barren, interspersed here and there with valleys, in which were the only specimens of verdure that met the eye. The road, for almost the whole distance, was one continued ascent, unless when crossing the valleys by which the hills over which we passed were divided into almost parallel ridges. Towards evening, the features of the scenery were materially changed. The ridges of hills across which our route lay, became loftier and more steep, and instead of being bare and stony, like those we had traversed in the early part of our march, were covered to their summit with pinewood. We ascended several of these before we halted for the night, but our progress was arrested by the appearance of one evidently too precipitous for the ascent of the camels, and we therefore determined to proceed no farther till the following morning.

I do not remember ever being more perfectly exhausted than by that day's journey. The motion of a camel, when long continued, is painful and fatiguing to a degree which must be felt to be adequately understood. His walk, for I can speak from experience of no other pace, is entirely different from that of a horse. In moving, he throws forward both legs on a side, by which action he communicates a jerk to his rider sufficiently unpleasant to prevent his for a moment imagining himself on a bed of roses.

We halted for the night in a grove of pine trees, and the preparation of our encampment cost little trouble. Our guide soon collected enough of the fallen branches which the wind had broken from the pine trees to supply us with fuel; and in half an hour we were seated, or rather extended, round a comfortable fire. Tired as we all were, there was no flagging of our spirits, and it was with strong hope of success in attaining the object of our excursion, that after partaking of refreshment and fortifying ourselves against the damps of the night air, by smoking a cigar, we sunk, wrapped in our boat-cloaks, into a profound sleep.

We started on the following morning by four o'clock. The camels had been dismissed on the evening before; but the ass, with the panniers of provision, was still destined to be the companion of our ascent. The first part of our day's journey lay through such forests of pine as we had encountered on the evening of the preceding day, but after a few hours we entered on a region bare and desolate, and differing entirely in character, from any portion of the country we had yet traversed. The earth was dry and calcined, bearing no marks of vegetation, and huge fragments of rock, which had evidently fallen from the higher parts of the mountain, lay scattered up and down. Here the sun, which had already attained its meridian, beat on us with overpowering fervour, and the sand on which we trod was so hot as to be almost insupportable when touched by the hand. In several places, however, we encountered springs, which bubbled up from beneath clear as crystal, and which were cool and pleasant to the taste. Indeed, I know not whether, but for the refreshment they afforded, the strength of any of the party, could have enabled him to surmount the difficulties of this dreary region.

Day had been many hours on the wane, before any change in the scene presented itself, though I imagine on the whole we had not advanced above a league ; but every yard of our progress was laborious. The earth was so finely pulverized as to give way beneath our feet, and from this reason, by an ordinary step, we seldom gained more than a few inches of actual advance. The reflection of the sun too, from the heated sand, was painful to a degree of which I have before or since found no example ; and the leather of our shoes, which had become as hard and inflexible as iron, galled our feet exceedingly, and added another impediment to our progress. The large stones by which this arid and dismal region was interspersed, became gradually more numerous, as we ascended, till at length the sand entirely disappeared, and we crossed a considerable tract of dark-coloured loose stones, covered with a sulphuric encrustation, which were evidently *debris*, from the huge gigantic masses that rose black and frowning above.

At the foot of these rocks we again halted for the night. The Doctor and Popham were both thoroughly knocked up, with the pain and fatigue of their day's journey, and on the following morning declared their inability to proceed farther. Neither Stanhope nor myself were in a much better condition, but having advanced thus far, and endured thus much of fatigue and suffering, we were unwilling to return *re infecta* to meet the jokes and banter of our companions on shipboard.

We slept under the ledge of a rock, which sheltered us from the wind that blew with biting keenness from the north-east. The coldness of the night, like the heat of the day, was extreme. The fever which the latter had engendered during our burning ascent, soon subsided, and was succeeded by a state of debility and languor scarcely less distressing. Our pulses did not *beat*, but *flutter*; and even this was so feeble, as to be scarcely perceptible to the touch. We suffered much, too, from giddiness in the head, and an irritability of stomach, which made us regard with extreme distaste the food necessary for the restoration of our strength. At the great elevation to which we had already attained, the rarity of the atmosphere was so great, that at every inhalation it seemed to cut into the lungs like a sharp instrument.

By a judicious exhibition, however, of brandy and cigars, the pressure of these evils was somewhat lightened ; and having made ourselves as comfortable for the night as circumstances permitted, Stanhope and myself prepared on the following morning, to set forward on our journey.

It was settled that the guide should accompany us in what still remained of the ascent, and that the Bourico and the panniers should remain in our present situation till our return. By no argument could

Popham or the Doctor be induced to become partners of our endeavour to reach a yet higher region than that, to which, with so much difficulty, we had already attained. Taking with them, therefore, a stock of provisions sufficient for the supply of all probable wants, they set out on their return to the ship. As they commenced their descent, fatigued and dispirited, Stanhope and myself, ascending a rock that jutted out somewhat more prominently than those around it, gave them three cheers as a parting salute, and then turning our faces towards the lofty cone which we had still to surmount, commenced the difficult and arduous task of climbing towards its summit.

The first and most serious obstacle that intercepted our advance was the dark and precipitous rocks already mentioned, at the foot of which we had passed the night. There was much toil and danger in the ascent of these vast and almost perpendicular barriers, and we had to search above an hour before we could even discover a place in which the attempt could be made with any prospect of success. Formidable as was the difficulty which they presented, it was overcome; and in safety, though certainly not without peril, we reached the flat surface in which they terminate. Here a change in the character of the scene was again observable. Patches of vegetation were visible, and at intervals a low shrub, which in leaf and character bore a strong resemblance to the Whortleberry, was occasionally seen. I remarked, also, a few specimens of a plant of somewhat larger growth, which I took to be a species of Juniper.

As we advanced, however, vegetation gradually died away, and we again found ourselves on a tract of sand resembling that which we had crossed on the preceding day, but considerably whiter in colour. Through this, dark masses of rock occasionally protruded themselves in fantastic shapes, as if forced upwards by some volcanic action of the mountain. The heat of the sand in this greater elevation was much less than that from which we before suffered so severely, but the insecurity of footing was not diminished, and the difficulties of our progress were enhanced by the increased lightness and pungency of the atmosphere.

We were animated to renewed exertions, however, by observing that we now approached the cone or topmost peak of the mountain, which did not in its apparent elevation, threaten any very serious difficulties in the part of our task, which yet remained unperformed. After an hour, therefore, devoted to rest and refreshment, we recommenced our labours, and ascended the side of the cone with greater facility than we had found in surmounting any portion of our previous journey. Our footing was firm and steady, for there was in that elevated region but little earth, except where, by some projection of the rock, it was prevented from being swept downwards, by the action of the elements.

As we advanced, large fissures in the mountain occasionally presented themselves, from which issued a hot and sulphureous smoke, which, when attempted to be inhaled, produced an overpowering sensation of giddiness and suffocation. It was not till we had advanced within half-a-mile of the summit, that we met with any traces of snow, and then only in occasional deep hollows of the rocks, on the northern face of the cone, which betrayed, I imagined, fewer marks of volcanic action than were discernible on the other sides.

It was precisely at seventeen minutes to four o'clock, (I find the hour carefully noted in my memorandum-book,) that we reached the summit of this celebrated mountain, and looking back with something of pride and self-respect, to the difficulties we had surmounted, we waved our hats triumphantly in the air, and congratulated ourselves on being probably at that moment the most exalted personages on the Globe. The wind, which had been violent, and from which we had suffered considerably on our ascent, had by degrees died away; and before we reached the apex of the cone, the air was so calm, that a feather might have lain unmoved upon its airiest pinnacle. On all sides the sky, from verge to centre, was unclouded, and the wide prospect beneath, found its only limit, in the feebleness of human vision.

For a while we were all eye. As an eagle from his eyrie, did we gaze upon that earth, of which we scarcely at that moment felt ourselves to be denizens. Its hopes, its fears, and its ambitions, what were they to us, when, like twin " giants of the western star, " we looked proudly downward from our " throne of clouds o'er half the world ! "

The view from the summit of the Peak, was certainly fine, though I believe our own enthusiasm lent it much of its charms. Immediately beneath, Teneriffe,—its barren and its wooded hills—its green and fertile valleys—its towns,—Laguna, Oratava, and Santa Cruz, lay stretched out before us like a map. Then the wide expanse of ocean that extended on all sides,—the islands of Palma, Canaria, and Gomera, studding its bosom like gems,—the fleet that lay at anchor in the bay,—the ship in which, through storm and calm, we had been safely wafted thus far through the world of waters,—on all these things, did we gaze long and silently, and with pleasure, perhaps heightened by the remembrance of the dangers and difficulties by which it had been earned.

Our pleasurable sensations were indeed materially diminished, by a continual steam of hot and mephitic vapour which rose from the mountain, and occasioned, besides being generally disagreeable, great irritation in our organs of smell and vision. This exhalation seemed to pervade the atmosphere of every part of the summit; but whether this is generally the case, or whether it was merely owing to the perfect stillness of the air during our visit, we of course had no means of ascertaining.

The object, however, that principally occupied our attention, during our sojourn on the Peak, was a huge crater, or, as it is designated by the natives, *Caldera*, whose diameter at the surface we calculated to be about two hundred yards. This vast volcanic cauldron is in form circular, and descends to a great depth in the mountain, the sides sloping inwards like those of an inverted cone, and covered with a coating of loose stones, with which there is perceptibly a large admixture of sulphur. During our stay, we observed no emission of smoke from the crater, but the air and vapour which rose from it was so hot and sulphureous as to occasion a strong feeling of suffocation when inhaled into the lungs, and the stones, even at the edge, were burning to the touch.

Under all these circumstances, however, we attempted to gratify our curiosity by a descent; but the difficulty of secure footing, the danger of being precipitated downwards involuntarily by the sliding of the stones, and the instinctive conviction that life could not be supported under any increased impurity of the atmosphere, prevented our persevering in an experiment so full of hazard. Altogether, I think, we remained on the summit of the Peak about an hour, and having minutely examined all that to our unphilosophical eyes, appeared worthy of examination, we made preparation for our return to a lower region.

In our descent, we followed a route somewhat different from that by which we had ascended, and in an hour or two, safely reached the spot, where in the morning we had left the Bourico and the baggage. In this portion of our undertaking, there were but few obstacles, and these comparatively trifling, to impede our progress. On coming to the tracts of sand which we had found so much difficulty in ascending, we had only to seat ourselves at the top to be speedily conveyed without effort to the bottom—a mode of travelling at once easy and primitive.

We rested for the night, on the same spot where we had slept the preceding one, and again suffered severely from the extreme coldness of the night air. Betimes, we were again on our journey, and before the increasing heat had become oppressive, we reached a cottage, where, being supplied by its hospitable owner, with abundance of goat's milk, we, with the aid of our own panniers, contrived to make a pretty comfortable breakfast. The fatigue we had undergone during the last three days, was excessive, and at the conclusion of our meal, jaded, and almost worn out, we cast ourselves on the ground, and slept till evening, when we recommenced our travel. The camels were gone; but had that mode of conveyance been within my option, I should infinitely have preferred walking. All night we were on the road, and about eleven o'clock on the following morning, we had the satisfaction once more of safely rejoining our companions in the ship.

Not with our return, however, did our sufferings cease. Our faces were literally flayed, and our feet were so much blistered and inflamed, as to render us quite unable to walk for several days. Of Teneriffe I saw no more, for the fleet sailed before I was sufficiently recovered to go ashore.

CHAPTER VI

I am a soldier, and my craft demands,
That whereso duty calls within earth's compass,
Or the unmeasured scope of fathomless ocean,
I do forthwith obey.

Hydaspes.

WHEN we quitted our anchorage at Teneriffe, the wind, though it could scarcely be called fair, was such as to enable us, when close-hauled, to lie our course. For the first seven days of our voyage we saw no land. On the eighth, we were close under the northern coast of Africa, running pleasantly along, at about the distance of a gun-shot from the shore. On the following morning, we were in the Straits, with wind and current in our favour—Mount Atlas full in view, and the rock of Gibraltar looming in the extreme distance. It was about noon, that, having entered the beautiful but insecure bay, which forms the only harbour of that fortress, the sound of the dropping anchor gave notice, that all the perils of our voyage were at length past.

Nothing, I think, can be more magnificently beautiful than Gibraltar, when seen from the sea. The rock itself, dark, grand, and imposing, marking its fine outline on the upper sky,—the huge craggy precipices, to which even the mountain-goat would fear to climb,—the spots of sunny greenery, brighter by contrast with the barren rocks by which they are encircled,—the houses embowered amid almond-trees and acacias, scattered over the mountain-side, and peeping forth in tranquil beauty from the summits of frowning cliffs, on the scene of wild grandeur outspread above, beneath, and around them,—these surely were features of surpassing beauty. But there were yet others. The high and massive walls, that rise from the sea, bristling with cannon, and beating back the roaring waves that break in harmless thunder on their base,— the town, that stretches out along the narrow level and the lower slopes of the hill—not beautiful certainly, but with something about it of picturesque, when viewed from a distance,—the chambers hewn in the stupendous perpendicular rock, that commands the landward app-roach, as if the very mountain would launch forth its thunders, and pour down destruction on its assailants;—add to all this the associations of siege and battle with which its history,—nay, its very name, is indissol-ubly linked,—remember that it is the prize for which kings have striven, and thousands,—tens of thousands, bled on land and ocean, and you will gaze on Gibraltar, as I did, with admiration, blended, perhaps, in the imagination, with thoughts of higher cast and deeper birth.

We were soon visited by the Pratique Master, who judged quarantine to be unnecessary, and Colonel Grimshawe went immediately ashore to report our arrival to the Governor. On the following morning we landed, and were put in possession, of very small and inconvenient barracks in the town. Our quarters were bad ; the apartments dark, dingy, and detestable, and surrounded on all sides by the unhealthy atmosphere of a crowded and uncleanly population. I know of no town in which so great a multitude of living beings are congregated within such narrow limits, as in Gibraltar. In the discordant elements of which it was composed, I found new matter of interest and observation. There, Turks, Jews, and Christians, men of all climates, and all religions, were mingled in one heterogeneous mass,—led by one motive,—bound but by one link, and animated by the pursuit of one object. In a society thus collected, there was not, and there could scarcely be expected, any general amalgamation of manners. There was not, and could not be, any common point of social union, beyond that arising from casual and temporary proximity, among people differing so widely in everything of thought and action, principle and observance. Each nation, in fact, formed a separate society within itself. Englishmen consorted with Englishmen, and talked politics over Port and Madeira : the Greek, with his richly-embroidered jacket and purple cap, and loosely flowing capote, daily met Greek, without encountering " the tug of war : " the Moor, from the neighbouring coast of Barbary, delighted to waste his leisure hours in smoking and drinking Sherbet in a coterie of kindred barbarians : and the Jews, who constituted not the least numerous, and certainly the wealthiest part of the population, permitted neither Christian nor Mahommedan to become partners of their social communion. To all of these there was but one rallying point—the Exchange. There men, of every shade of faith and colour, united in one common worship, and bent the knee to Mammon.

In such a population as I have described, there was of course much to interest one, whose curiosity like mine was unsated, and to whom that foreign world on which he had so recently entered was yet new. Gibraltar seemed a sort of Parliament, in which every nation had its representative ; and precluded as I then was, both by my profession and the political state of Europe, from enjoying the advantages of foreign travel, I rejoiced in the means thus afforded me of becoming acquainted with the manners and observances of many countries, which I knew it to be more than improbable that I should ever visit.

Gibraltar is a good school for a young soldier. There I was initiated into all the disagreeable arcana of the garrison duty of an extensive and important fortress. Nothing could exceed the strictness with which even the minutest statutory regulation was enforced, nor the severity with which any breach of duty, however slight, was sure to be visited. At the period of our arrival, the garrison was below its usual complement, and consisted only of three regiments. From this cause, the duty was more than usually severe. Every day, at least half the officers of the regiment were either on garrison or regimental duty, and the daily absence of so many of its members impaired, if it did not destroy, the usual spirit and hilarity of the mess. Before our arrival at Gibraltar, I had never mounted guard ; but as my health was good, and I never missed a tour of duty, before we left that garrison, few officers of my standing had mounted so many. And weary work they were. To be cut off for a day—a live-long day from all society, with no engrossing subject to interest or occupy the thoughts,—to become a sort of involuntary Robinson Crusoe for one half of every week, was, to one of my age and naturally high spirits, a penance of no ordinary magnitude. I remember now, the dull and heavy spirit of disgust, with which I used to read my name when it appeared in orders for guard. The very names of these guards are to this hour imprinted on my memory, linked as of yore with all their weary associations of monotonous dulness. There was the Mole, and the Ragged Staff, and the Land-Port, and the Water-Port, and the Queen's Lines, and Bayside, and Europa Point, and Europa Advance, and others which I hold at this moment at my pen's point, though I restrain my fingers. I declare, there is not a chair, or a table, or wooden tressel, in any one of the number, no scrap of writing on the wall or the window-panes, no break in the plaster, or fissure in the earthen floor in these guard-rooms, that I could not recall at this moment, in its own individual form, lineament, and pressure.

Gibraltar, however, possessed one advantage, of which few other garrisons can boast. There was an excellent library for the use of the officers, to the full benefit of which, they were entitled by a trifling subscription. It contained, even at that period, many thousand volumes, and, in truth, constituted a very complete collection of British literature. Of the advantages it afforded I did not fail to profit ; and, in the state of isolation from society, in which I was placed by each rapid revolution of the Adjutant's roster, my enforced solitude, came like the toad, ugly and venomous ; yet not, perhaps, without a jewel in its head.

It is impossible for me to recur to the period of my sojourn in Gibraltar, and yet to say nothing of the governor, General O'Hara. His appearance, indeed, was of that striking cast, which, when once seen, is not easily forgotten. General O'Hara was the most perfect specimen I ever saw, of the soldier and courtier of the last age, and in his youth had fought with Granby and Ligonier. One could have sworn to it by his air and look,—nay, by the very cut of his coat—the double row of sausage curls that projected on either flank of his toupee—or the fashion of the huge military boots, which rivalled in size, but far outshone in lustre, those of a Dutch fisherman or French postilion. Never had he changed for a more modern covering, the Kevenhuller hat, which had been the fashion of his youth. There it was, in shape precisely that of an equilateral triangle, placed with mathematical precision on the head, somewhat elevated behind, and sloping in an unvarying angle downwards to the eyes, surmounted by a long stiff feather rising from a large rosette of black ribbon on the dexter side. This was the last of the Kevenhullers; it died, and was buried with the Governor, for no specimen has since been discovered, and the Kevenhuller hat, like the Mammoth and the Mastodon, has become extinct for ever.

Notwithstanding the strictness of the discipline which he scrupulously enforced in the garrison which he commanded, no officer could be more universally popular, than General O'Hara. In person he had been,—and, though somewhat bent by years, even then was,—remarkably handsome. His life had been divided between the camp and the court, and he had been distinguished in both. He was a bachelor, and had always been noted as a gay man; too gay a man, perhaps, to have ever thought of narrowing his liberty, by the imposition of the trammels of wedlock. General O'Hara had always moved in the very highest circles of society at home; and, notwithstanding an office of considerable emolument, which, I believe, he held in the Household, had dissipated his private fortune, and become deeply involved in his circumstances. It was this cause alone, which had induced him, late in life, to submit to the banishment, peculiarly disagreeable to a man of his habits, attached to the acceptance of the chief command at Gibraltar.

The General was a *bon vivant*, an unrivalled boon companion, one to whom society was as necessary as the air he breathed. He never dined alone, and his hospitality was extended to every rank of the officers in the garrison. In his own house, and, above all, at his own table, he delighted to cast off all distinction of rank, and to associate on terms of perfect equality, with even the humblest of his guests. The honours of the table were done by his staff, and the General was in nothing distinguished from those around him, except by being undoubtedly the gayest and most agreeable person in the company.

It was impossible that one, who had spent a long life in the highest and most distinguished circles of society in England, should be unfurnished with an abundant store of interesting and amusing anecdote; and, in truth, anecdote telling was at once his forte and his foible. His forte, because he did it well—his foible, for, sooth to say, he was sometimes given to carry it into something of excess. He would entertain his guests by the hour, with the scandalous tittle-tattle, which had been circulated at court or the club-houses, some thirty years before, and did more than hint at his own bonnes fortunes among the celebrated beauties of the British court, and the Bona-Robas of France, Italy, and Spain. He sang too—and beautifully. I have seldom heard a finer voice, or one more skilfully managed.

Such was General O'Hara, or, as he was more generally called, the "Old Cock of the Rock;" and no man certainly could be more respected for his rigid yet lenient (for these epithets are far from incompatible,) discharge of his military duties, or more beloved for his engaging qualities as a social companion. For myself, during my sojourn in Gibraltar, I was much indebted to his kindness. The General had been intimately acquainted with my grandfather, who had passed his life in the unprofitable pursuit of court favour. My father he had likewise known in the blossom of his early prosperity, which, alas, was never destined to ripen into fruit. He spoke of both kindly, gave me a general invitation to his table, and was lavish of those petty attentions which cost little to the giver, but which, coming from a person of his station and dignity, are always felt to be flattering by one so far his inferior in age and rank.

Having said thus much of General O'Hara, I would yet say something more, and tell the reader that, before we quitted Gibraltar, he died. There was no hypocrisy in the heavy looks of the soldiers, as they followed his remains to their last earthly tenement. He was, of course, buried with all the military honours due to his high rank. I had never before seen the funeral of a general officer. There was his horse—the well-known charger on which we had all so often seen him mounted—bearing the boots and spurs of his departed master; on the coffin, likewise, lay other mournful insignia—the sword, the sash, and—not the least prominent memorial in the group—the Kevenhuller hat and its tall unbending feather. There I gazed on it for the last time.

The ceremony was altogether very impressive. The troops marched slowly with arms reversed ; the report of minute guns was heard from the bastion, and the colours were displayed half-mast high by all the ships in the bay. When the body had been consigned to the vault, and the service was concluded, loud and successive peals of artillery were heard to reverberate from rock to ocean, the anthem best fitted to grace the obsequies of a gallant soldier.

It is not, or at least was not, the fashion in Gibraltar, for the military to maintain much intercourse with the mercantile part of the population. From the character of the place as an important military fortress, it was necessary that the latter should be in a great degree subject to military regulation, and submit to certain restrictions on their freedom, both of action and motion, which could not fail to prove occasionally galling and unpleasant. It therefore frequently happened, that an officer, in the discharge of his duty, was brought into very disagreeable collision with the inhabitants of the town. No civilian, for instance, after dark, was allowed to approach any sentinel, or military post, without a lantern, and any person infringing this order was liable to be seized and conveyed a prisoner to the nearest guard-house. The alternative in question frequently happened ; and the roughness of treatment which the inhabitants sometimes experienced from the soldiers, created a degree of enmity, which even the subsequent civility of the officer, in case,—which was not always,—he was in the humour to be civil, did not uniformly prove successful in appeasing. I remember being on guard, when a whole party of ladies and gentlemen were apprehended on their return from a ball, and brought prisoners before me. Loud and indignant were they in their invectives against the rude and tyrannical regulations, by which they had been subjected to so unpleasant a process, and most happy was I to regain the solitude of my guard-room, by sending home the vociferous and irate party under charge of a corporal, to prevent their encountering any farther obstruction on their route.

Such causes will naturally account for the little intercourse, and the no little dislike, which existed between the military and the English Oppidans of the place. With foreigners the case was different. They came without the same proud feelings of liberty which animated our countrymen, and they knew from experience, that the strictness of observance required in Gibraltar was little, if at all more severe, than that enforced in every garrison town. Our intercourse with them, therefore, was impeded by fewer obstacles, and I still enjoyed the advantage of gleaning from intelligent foreigners, such information as they could afford.

As I write, a name long forgotten has started to my lips, and fain would flow from my pen. Hamet Sherkin! Honest Hamet! The clouds of oblivion in which thy name and memory have so long been shrouded, fade again from around thee, and I once more behold thee in thy primitive and well-known lineaments. There, right opposite, is thy pleasant, bearded, and mahogany-coloured visage, gazing on me from beneath thy turban of white muslin, and surmounting thy tall brawny figure clad in a tastefully embroidered jacket of purple, waistcoat of bright scarlet velvet, and thy lower man buried in white calico trowsers of superhuman dimensions, which suddenly collapse, and terminate at the knee. Lower still are thy legs—and such legs! Most sinewy and Herculean supporters were they of thy robust frame, modelled in fine proportion, and shining forth, undegraded by a stocking, in their native complexion, something between copper colour and nankeen. Such do I see thee even now. Whether thou still livest, or the grave has closed over thee, I know not, but as the last act of kind and friendly remembrance, I would embody thy name and lineaments in these memoirs. Thou indeed wilt never read them, and their memory may be as short-lived as thine own. It matters not; even in this fragile record shalt thou stand enrolled among my friends.

Hamet Sherkin was a Moor, born somewhere in the neighbourhood of Algiers. He was a merchant, had traded to Bagdad and Aleppo, and, with his fleet of " desert ships, " had voyaged to " Ormus and Tydore. " By his speculations he had early in life amassed a large fortune, with which he returned to his native land. His wealth excited the cupidity of

the emperor, who, on pretence of some political offence, had issued
summary orders for his compendious decapitation. Hamet had fortunately obtained some previous intelligence of these beneficent intentions
of his gracious master; and though by flight he lost one half of his
worldly substance, yet wisely judging that no economy could be judicious, which involved the loss of his head, he at once adopted the
alternative however unpleasant, and succeeded in escaping on board an
English man-of-war then cruising in the offing. Thus banished from his
native land, Hamet had become a sort of citizen of the world, travelling
and trafficking from shore to shore, sojourning in all lands,—affiliating
in none.

The Moors are the only dealers in Gibraltar from whom you can
depend on getting genuine Havannah cigars. It was in our respective
capacities of vender and purchaser of cigars that the acquaintance of
Hamet and myself had its commencement. It struck me there was
something fair, open, and even generous in his mode of dealing, very
different from the fraudulent extortion which his countrymen generally
display in their transactions with foreigners. There was, too, an expression of good nature and intelligence on his countenance, which strongly
prejudiced me in his favour. In all my small dealings thenceforth I
resorted to Hamet Sherkin, and whatever I happened to want which he
did not himself possess, he procured for me on more favourable terms
than I could otherwise have obtained it. Hamet told me his history. He
was not wholly unversed in European knowledge, and he united to it a
natural intelligence of no common order. He described to me the most
remarkable scenes and occurrences of his travels—Bagdad, Mecca, and
Damascus—his sufferings in the Great Desert—the attacks made upon
his caravan by the wild Arabs, and a thousand hair-breadth escapes by
flood and field, to which those of the Moor of Venice were as nothing.
Hamet, though a Mussulman, was something of a *wet* one; for, though
he avoided the scandal of drinking wine in public, he had no objections
occasionally to discuss a bottle in company with Nazarenes. I believe he
entertained a sincere regard for me; and when, before our departure
from the Rock, I took leave of him, there was something like a tear in his
eye as he invoked the blessing of Allah and the Prophet on my head.

There was one scene in which Hamet played a conspicuous part, and
from which a coolness of some duration between Colonel Grimshawe
and myself took its origin.

The day had been fixed for an entertainment of more than common
splendour at the mess. The Governor—the General next in command
—the Admiral—the Naval Commissioner—a young nobleman on his
travels, and several other personages of more than ordinary calibre and
consequence, were to grace our festivities with their presence. Of course,
it was tacitly expected and understood, that the guests invited by the
individual officers, to meet so distinguished a party, should be of some

rank and prominence in society. Whether, under such circumstances, it proceeded from want of tact, or from mere wanton negligence of rule on my part, at this distance of time it would boot little to decide, but it is at least true in fact, that an invitation to dinner on that day was sent to my friend Hamet Sherkin. To this an answer from Hamet was duly received, in which he swore by the beard of Mahomet that he would not fail to gratify me by his presence at the appointed time.

The day came, and with it the expected congregation of official dignity, for whose suitable reception, splendid preparation had been made. With it, too, came Hamet Sherkin, in clean turban, and splendidly embroidered jacket, according to the fashion of the best circles in Barbary, but with bare legs and yellow morocco slippers, which being slipshod, displayed rather more of a broad horny heel than a nice and critical eye might have found pleasure in surveying. On the entrance of my Barbaric friend, I observed the eye of Colonel Grimshawe to lower in offended dignity, and when I proceeded to present Hamet as my guest on the occasion, he declined the proffered introduction by turning rapidly on his heel. However I might be affected by the awkwardness of such a reception, Hamet neither displayed nor felt the smallest portion of *mauvaise honte*, and joined in the good-humoured laugh that went round the assembly on his appearance, with the most enviable unconsciousness of its being excited by himself. What reason, indeed, was there, why honest Hamet, rich in true nobility of spirit, should have felt humbled or abashed in such a party? He knew, or, at least, might have known, that in power and grasp of intellect, he was inferior to none of those around him, while he felt, and could not but feel, the consciousness, that by a single blow of his sinewy and powerful arm, he could have levelled any one of the assembly, from the general to the lowest ensign, prostrate in the dust.

At length dinner was announced, and the guests paced forth into the hall, in due order and solemnity, and with the most precise regard to claims of precedence. The seat allotted to Hamet was, of course, next that of his entertainer, and none but Theodore Hook can fully understand my discomfiture, when I beheld him, instead of conforming to the sedentary habits of the Europeans, seat himself on his chair cross-legged, like a tailor. This unlooked-for circumstance occasioned considerable derangement of the gravity and decorum of the entertainment. The younger part of the company laughed outright, while it was impossible even for their seniors to repress a smile.

Unluckily, the eccentricities of Hamet did not rest here. The European fashion of knives and forks had not yet spread into Barbary, and notwithstanding my anxious recommendation of these utensils to the notice of my guest, I could by no means prevail on him to avail himself of the facilities, which these unwonted implements might have afforded. Nothing, indeed, could be more primitive than his mode of eating. His fingers made rapid and frequent voyages from his plate to his gullet, and whole platefuls of Hash or Harico disappeared with a velocity which it might have puzzled the most expert " Furcifer " to excel. The leg of a chicken, drawn through a double row of grinders, which evidently stood in no need of the skill of the Chevalier Ruspini, became instantaneously denuded of all esculent matter, and was returned a mere skeleton to his plate. Sooth to say, however, the appetite of Hamet being more than usually miscellaneous, his hands, after half an hour's continued dabbling among sweets and solids, became objects neither very gracious to the eye or the fancy; and it was not till the appearance of finger-glasses with the desert that he enjoyed an opportunity of even an imperfect ablution.

The total disregard of established routine which Hamet had displayed throughout the entertainment, set gravity and form at defiance. Never was there, to all external appearance, a merrier party assembled round a table, and Hamet was the cynosure of every eye. His name, too, was heard simultaneously reverberated by many voices. " Mr Sherkin, a glass of wine? "—" Thornton, the pleasure of wine with you and your friend Sherkin? "—" Hamet Sherkin, do me the honour? "— " Thornton, wine with your Oriental friend?"—" Happy to take a glass of Champagne with the worthy African on your right, " rung loudly and confusedly through the apartment, and all other sounds were drowned in the hilarious uproar. The prevailing epidemic spread even to the servants, who, though they were too prudent to incur the certainty of a broken head, by indulging in a laugh, yet might be seen discharging their ministerial duties, with countenances relaxed into a grin, which neither the awful presence of the Governor, nor even the more awful terrors of Colonel Grimshawe's eye, were adequate to repress. With the removal of the dinner, the encroachments on the programme of the entertainment did not cease, and the regular succession of loyal toasts was interrupted by one of the younger officers, who, after an appropriate prefatory speech, proposed the health of Hamet in a bumper, with all the honours. Never was any toast more loudly applauded; in short, Hamet Sherkin was the Lion of the night, and Governors, and Admirals, dock-yard Commissioners, and other puissant official dignitaries were, in the eye and thoughts of all, but secondary personages.

The Governor was far from feeling offended at this infringement of decorum, of which I had been the unthinking, if not the innocent cause. He enjoyed the party not the less that every one around him appeared happy and at their ease. But it was not so with Colonel Grimshawe. On the following day, he assembled the officers, and in a speech which dealt not leniently with my offence, in having caused the unwelcome intrusion of an improper person on so great an occasion, he proposed, that henceforward, on all great regimental entertainments, no individual should be invited, whose name and pretensions had not previously been approved of by a committee. This proposal, however, the younger part of the corps considered as conveying an insulting reflection not only on me but on themselves, and when put to the vote, it was negatived by a considerable majority. For myself, I regretted to think that I had been the cause of spreading even temporary dissension in a regiment always distinguished for the harmony and good fellowship of its members. This, however, did not last, but there remained a coolness between Colonel Grimshawe and myself, which long prevented any friendly intercourse between us.

CHAPTER VII

————Let us walk
With heads uncover'd, and with prostrate souls,
Unto the humbled city of despair.
Amid the roar of ocean solitude,
God hath been with us, and his saving hand
Will be our anchor, in this dreadful calm,
This waveless silence, of the sea of death.
                          The City of the Plague.

Oh, it is monstrous, monstrous!
Methought the billows spoke and told me of it,
The winds did sing it to me; and the thunder,
That deep and dreadful organ pipe, pronounced
The name of Prosper.
                          Tempest.

A SUMMER and a winter passed away, and we were still tenants of the Rock. During this interval, nothing had occurred to break the ordinary and monotonous routine of a garrison town. But Gibraltar, dull as we thought it, was not without its amusements. We boated, cricketed, and rode horse-races; during the carnival there were masquerades, and once a-week a ball was given at the Government House, to which all the officers had the privilege of entré.

To excursions on the water I was particularly partial, and though an unskilful, I was an ardent sailor. Often by daybreak were we abroad in our little yacht, cutting through the green waters of the bay, or stemming the current of the Straits, or stretching onward into the Mediterranean, till the grey twilight was gone, and the curtain of darkness was again spread upon the deep. Sometimes we crossed to Ceuta or Tangiers, at others lay along the Spanish coast to Tariffa, and once on a more extended excursion we visited Malaga, and amid the gaieties of that city, spent several pleasant days. In this manner did we endeavour, not always unsuccessfully, to tip with feathers the leaden wings of time.

Another year had begun, and rolled on from spring to summer, unmarked in each advancing step of its progression. The summer, though unusually hot, was healthy; that, too, passed, and the autumn came sultry and oppressive, and with heavy rains. Thick fogs hovered over the sea, and sometimes, extending even into the upper air, veiled the summit of the Rock in darkness. The rain-drops as they fell were hot and unrefreshing, and the sun, as he slowly sank behind the Barbary mountains, was white as silver. Such were the months of August and September in that memorable year: October came, and apparently with better auspices. The weather was cool and pleasant; there was keenness in the morning air, and the breeze that came at eventide from the sea, seemed loaded with restorative freshness to frames like ours, already languid and relaxed. The active sports and exercises, which the debilitating influence of the climate had for a time suspended, were once more resumed, and an increase both of physical and mental energy, was perceptible in all.

It was at this period, and under these apparently favourable circumstances, that the most fatal scourge of humanity, the yellow fever, made its appearance in the town. It came unknown and in silence, nor was it till many of the inhabitants had fallen its victims, that the medical officers of the garrison were aware of its approach. Every measure of safety or precaution was instantly resorted to, but in vain. Its progress would not be arrested, and the unshackled pestilence spread through the narrow streets and crowded houses, like a destroying angel, conquering and to conquer.

It is impossible to conceive a spot better fitted for the dissemination of infectious disease than Gibraltar. Had the town been doubled in extent, it could scarcely have afforded sufficient accommodation to the numbers which were even then crowded within its narrow limits. The rent demanded for the smallest house in Gibraltar equalled that of a splendid mansion in London. The consequence of course was, that a domicile which could afford comfortable accommodation for one family, became the residence of many; nor was it an uncommon circumstance that fifty, or even an hundred individuals were congregated beneath a single roof. The great proportion of these were foreigners; and when we consider how little attention was necessarily paid to cleanliness in such dwellings; the unhealthy atmosphere in which their inmates were condemned to live and breathe, we shall not feel surprised that all human endeavours to arrest the progress of the pestilence were in vain. I had been in such houses. In an apartment scarcely the size of an ordinary English bedroom, I had beheld the accommodation of twenty human beings, where, stretched upon a mat or carpet, they every night, even in the hottest season, retired to rest. In such *hives* of men, when fever once appeared, it of course spread like wild-fire; there the arm of death was raised to strike—Who could prevent its falling?

Weeks passed, and the fever-demon continued to stalk onward in his course, nor would stay his step even for a moment. The disease spread on all hands; the Lazzarettos were filled, and the number of deaths increased till it exceeded an hundred a-day. Our regiment were stationed in the town, but no time was lost in removing us from the focus of infection, and we went into camp on a very elevated part of the hill, which gave promise of exemption from the disease raging below, in the healthy freshness of its atmosphere. Had it been possible, indeed, to cut off all communication with the town, it is probable this promise might have been fulfilled. But the military duty of the place required the presence of soldiers, and it was necessary that every day a certain proportion should descend into what might almost, without poetical figure, be called " the Valley of the Shadow of Death." Under such circumstances, it was scarcely to be expected, that we should pass through the arrowy shower safe and unstricken; several of the soldiers caught the infection, and there was fever in the camp. The disease, whose ravages till then we had regarded with a sort of disinterested compassion, now came home to the business and bosoms of us all, and brought with it a sense of helplessness and depression, even now painful to remember. Men, who have since proved themselves incapable of shrinking from death in the field, shook with the terrors of this new and terrible assailant, and would gladly have fled from a contest which cost the vanquished life, but brought no honour to the victor.

I have always had an almost morbid dread of fever. In its slow and silent approach,—in the sudden and dreadful gripe with which it seizes on the very life-springs,—in the entire prostration of strength with which it is accompanied,—in the fearful tempest of delirium with which the spirit is at once cast down and overwhelmed,—in the horrid nightmare of the soul, the visionary yet dreadful phantoms that hover round the pillow of the sufferer,—in all these things, I have ever found matter of deep and unconquerable fear. There is no other phasis of disease which brings with it, to my imagination, an accumulation of terrors, so deep and awful. It is not the pain, for that I could contemplate calmly, and I trust endure patiently. It is not the death to which it leads, that could thus fright my soul from her propriety. But at once to lose all the powers and attributes of an intellectual being,—not to meet death calmly and collectedly, but, in the wreck of all the faculties, to be swept, as it were, by a hurricane into the grave—this it is, at which I still shudder—this it was, that I found it impossible to contemplate, with a resigned and resolute spirit.

There are melancholy associations connected with this portion of my narrative, from which I would gladly escape. I am unwilling, too, to attempt a description of scenes, to which, though indelibly imprinted on my memory, I could do little justice in words, and which have already given full scope to the powers and genius of writers, with whom I would not willingly be weighed in the balance : yet to pass them wholly by is impossible.

Deep gloom hung on us all. Melancholy was the daily meeting at the mess; for we had only to recount the still advancing progress of the pestilence, or the name of some companion who since yesterday had fallen its victim. But worse than all was it, when called by duty to descend into the town ;—to see the streets desolate and deserted,—to hear, as we passed the closed dwellings, the loud and terrible shrieks of some delirious sufferer within—and then the horn that gave signal of the approach of the dead-cart, as it slowly rolled onwards in its dismal circuit! Never has its wild dissonance passed from my ear—never, I believe, shall it utterly pass away, and be forgotten.

Many of the Europeans, on the first appearance of the fever, had quitted the town, and taken up their residence at Algesiras or St Rocque, or gone on board of the ships in the bay. This, however, could not continue. The Spaniards formed a cordon a few miles' distance from the fortress, in order to prevent any communication with the interior, and all avenue of escape from the danger was at once closed. The disease soon spread its havoc among the shipping, and the deep daily yawned over a new accession of its victims. There was death alike upon the land and the waters. In the camp, too, he was busy; and in the course of about three weeks, we had lost five officers, and above an hundred men. Among the former were Major Warburton and Captain Spottiswoode, to whose company I was attached. Popham, too, was attacked, but recovered. I was not coward enough to be prevented by my fears from attending his sick-bed; and the little, friendship could do, to allay his sufferings, was done. I mention this, I confess, with something of pride, for the conflict within was a severe one, and the struggle long.

The pestilence, which had hitherto despised the feeble efforts of man to obstruct its progress, was at length arrested by the hand of God. With no external or visible cause, to produce a change in its character or consequences, when it was already raging in its fury, and even hope was wavering in the stoutest heart, a sudden relaxation of its power became apparent. From that hour its gripe was loosened; day after day its victims were diminished in number, and in a few weeks all traces of its former ravages were to be found only in the grave. Then, as if a vast and overwhelming pressure had been removed, there was a sudden revulsion of our spirits, a rebounding of the heart so powerful and extraordinary, as to seem almost allied to madness. The lips on which no smile had been seen for months, now gave utterance to sounds of wild merriment, and downcast and heavy eyes were lighted up with more than their original gladness. Each individual felt as if he himself had been preserved from death by a miraculous interposition of Providence. Never at mess had I seen the wine-cup filled so high, nor heard the wild revelry of light and jovial hearts, echoed so loudly and so long.

Let us hope this was not all. Let us believe that in silence and retirement, there were knees bent in the humility of prayer, and that the sound of thanksgiving rose from many voices to that God, by whose almighty arm, they had been upheld and supported.

After this, we did not long remain in Gibraltar. An order came for our return to England, and our hearts beat high in the near prospect of once more revisiting our native land. The transports destined for our reception soon arrived, and we embarked. The Rock had become associated with too many melancholy recollections, to cause any feeling of regret, as we bade it farewell. The evening gun was fired as the fleet weighed anchor, and the commencement of our voyage was prosperous. We passed the Straits with a fair breeze, and ran down our distance in high style, till we reached the Chops of the Channel. There we encountered a gale, and thick darkness coming on, the ship in which I sailed was separated from the fleet, and driven in upon the French coast near Ushant. In the course of the following day, however, the wind abated, and the vessel once more lay on her course. Our appearance so near the enemy's coast seemed to excite the suspicions of the British cruisers on that station; and we were several times boarded, to ascertain our real quality and object, in having so far deviated from the usual track.

In the morning we had observed a suspicious-looking sail at a considerable distance on the weather-bow. During the day we had lost sight of her, but as evening closed, she was once more observed bearing down on us. We hung out our colours, but she displayed no flag, and, from the nature of her proceedings, the Captain reported to Major Penleaze, who commanded on board, that he had no doubt of her being a French privateer.

Instant preparations were made for her reception. The soldiers, who amounted to about three hundred, were directed to load, and being each provided with a cutlass, to be used in case of boarding, were arranged in their proper stations, and ordered to lie flat on the deck, but on no account to fire till the signal was given by the commanding officer.

Every proper step of precaution was adopted, in his department, by the captain of the ship. The tompions were taken from the guns, which were loaded, and placed under the management of such of the sailors, as could be spared from the duty of navigating the vessel. Each of the officers was assigned a post, and intrusted with a certain sphere of command; and every necessary arrangement having been concluded, we waited not without anxiety, for the commencement of hostilities.

The object of our precautions now neared us considerably, and, by the aid of the night-glass, we discovered her to be a large schooner. She passed us closely, sailing in a parallel course to our own, but on an opposite direction. When nearly abreast of us, she suddenly changed her direction, and crossing our stern, poured in a broadside, and continued on her course. Such of the guns of the ship as could be brought to bear on her, were fired, to revenge, if possible, this act of aggression, but, I believe, with little effect. The schooner, which had greatly the advantage in point of sailing, once more shot ahead of us, and then returning, crossed our bows, and poured in a raking broadside as before. Entertaining, perhaps, an exaggerated opinion of our weakness from the impunity of her first attack, she now drew up alongside, and the battle commenced in good earnest. Our soldiers still remained prostrate on the deck, and the action was confined to the great guns, on both sides, though, I believe, without much execution on ours. In fact, from the great disparity in the size of the vessels, our guns were too high, and were thus only able to do some trifling damage to the rigging of the enemy.

At length it was evident they were determined to board. Grappling-irons were thrown out, and attempts were made to lash the vessels together. This was no sooner done, than the word Fire was given, and instantly the men started up, and three hundred muskets were discharged down on the deck of the enemy, with dreadful effect. Their fire instantly slackened, and they were evidently in confusion. It is probable they had mistaken us for some rich homeward bound West Indiaman, and were by no means prepared for such a reception as they had encountered.

The fire from our deck now continued without intermission, till Stanhope, seizing a cutlass, brandished it in the air, and calling out, "Follow me, let us board them, my boys," sprang to the side of the ship, and followed by about a score of his own company, swung themselves down by the rigging to the enemy's deck. Memorable to me, indeed, was that moment. Even amid the bustle and confusion of battle, I gazed on him with surprise. There was a flush on his cheek, and a fire in his eye, which I had never before witnessed, which, alas, I was never destined to witness again.

When the boarders quitted the ship, of course, the firing ceased, and there was a hush on board of breathless expectation. It was too dark to see what passed on the deck of the schooner, but I leant over the side, and listened with intense eagerness. The clash of cutlasses was distinctly heard, mingled with shouts and groans. I heard, or thought I heard, the voice of Stanhope calling for assistance. My hand griped my cutlass instinctively at the sound, and springing up, I called aloud for the boarders to follow to the rescue of our companions. There was a cheer given, and springing down the side of the ship, I was in a moment engaged in the mêlée on the enemy's deck. The reinforcement I brought was decisive of the issue. The Frenchmen fled below decks, and we were left in possession of the schooner. She was the Espiègle of Brest, commanded by Monsieur Hypolite Podevin, carrying two long twenty-four pounders, and six smaller guns, with ninety-four men.

We had manfully fought and taken the prize, but what to make of her, now that our efforts had been crowned with success, was a point of some difficulty. We had no mariners to spare from the navigation of our own vessel, and had it not been for the opportune assistance we received on the following morning, from the Peterel sloop of war, it is probable we should have been obliged to relinquish all the advantages of our capture.

Where was Stanhope? I called aloud on him; I searched the schooner; I scrutinized the countenances of the wounded and the dead, but his I could not see. None knew what had become of him; from the moment he had sprung from our deck towards that of the enemy, he had been seen no more. Alas! this very ignorance afforded but too conclusive evidence of his fate. The vessels, by a sudden lurch, had increased the distance between them, and he had fallen into the sea, probably to be crushed to death by the returning concussion, or, what was scarcely less dreadful, after long and fearful struggling, to perish unassisted in the waters. By my entreaty, the ship lay to,—the boats were manned, and by the light of the moon, which had just risen, we searched around the scene of action for his body. In this manner several hours were passed, but in vain. No traces of him, except his hat, which was found floating at some distance, could be discovered. Hope at length died within me, the search was relinquished, and in a state of dreadful suffering and depression, I resigned my bosom friend to his fate, and returned to the ship. There was no song of triumph on board. No joyful congratulations were interchanged on our victory. We remembered the price at which it had been purchased, and were silent.

CHAPTER VIII

Now all the youth of England are on fire,
And silken dalliance in the wardrobe lies;
Now thrive the armourers, and honour's thought
Reigns solely in the breast of every man.
                                Henry V.

Have ye seen the tusky boar,
Or the bull with sullen roar,
On surrounding foes advance?—
So Caradoc bore his lance.
                                GRAY.

Charge, Chester, charge! On, Stanley, on!
Were the last words of Marmion.
                                SCOTT.

THE two years immediately succeeding the events I have just narrated, I shall pass lightly over. The life of a soldier in country quarters affords but few materials for the biographer, and these not of the most interesting description. Suffice it, therefore, for the reader to know, that shortly after our arrival from America, the —— were ordered to Ireland, and that during our residence in that country I was promoted to a company.

I have ever loved Ireland—I love it now—I shall love it till death. All Irishmen are dear to me; but in the wild men of Connaught do I delight the most. There is something about them at once piquant and interesting. Kind, warm-hearted, and ferocious; generous, hospitable, and bloody; the most amiable of incendiaries, the wittiest and most delightful cut-throats in the world. I have long ceased to read the details of Irish murder, for I found it impossible to do so, with a proper degree of moral indignation. In that country, arson and assassination are irradiated with a halo, to which in less favoured lands they are strangers. Outrage generally assumes the air of good fellowship. The jest and the pistol are pointed together, the trigger is drawn at exactly the proper moment, and the victim dies good-humouredly, in the midst of a guffaw. I declare, I never yet read of a tythe-proctor or an exciseman, losing his ears by a summary act of Whiteboy justice, without mentally becoming *particeps criminis*, and longing to throw in a kick. But a more melancholy note would become the subject better. Why is it, we may ask, that Ireland, bearing all the elements of a great and glorious people, has become a proverb and a by-word among the nations, whose very name suggests only the image of bigotry, persecuting and persecuted, of oppression and misrule? When shall the brand of her curse be obliterated from her forehead, and when shall she become, what God and nature intended, a happy and an united people?

During my stay in England I did not visit Thornhill, but I learned all that had passed there, from the letters of my sisters. A great and disagreeable change, they told me, had taken place in Miss Cumberbatch. The mild and unassuming deportment she had adopted on her first admission into the family, was now changed for one of patronage and authority. My sisters had complained to my father, but without obtaining redress. Miss Cumberbatch was too firmly established in her situation, to be removed from it, by any effort of theirs. The mild and gentle character of Jane, was indeed better fitted for passive endurance, than active resistance to oppression; and Lucy was yet too young, to oppose such usurpation with effect. Miss Cumberbatch had artfully wound herself into the good graces of my father, and bore, not meekly, the sceptre of her power.

Such had been the nature of my intelligence from Thornhill, when I received a letter, the superscription of which my eye instantly recognised to be in the hand of my father. I opened it, and found it was indeed from him, and was the messenger of strange tidings. It began by stating, that as I was now of age, it became proper that I should receive the patrimony to which I was entitled. That he had given directions for the necessary documents to be transmitted to me, by which I should be enabled to ascertain the amount of the sum to which I possessed claim, which per account (errors excepted) amounted to L.9373, 8s. 4d. This amount of stock, on my signing the proper discharge, should be transferred to my name.

My father's letter then went on to state, that he considered it the more necessary that an immediate settlement of my claims should take place, as he was again about to lead to the altar a lady, of whose amiable qualities and high accomplishments, he had already full knowledge and experience. That in doing so, he had sacrificed his inclinations to his duty, and thought only of securing the happiness of his daughters, by providing them with a mother, from whose tender care, and under whose affectionate guidance, they could not fail to experience the greatest advantages.

There was a certain *wordiness* in this letter so unlike the usual terseness and brevity of my father's style in addressing me, as to show pretty plainly that in writing it he did not feel very much at his ease. For myself, notwithstanding all I had previously learned from my sisters, of the state of matters at Thornhill, I read it with the greatest surprise. The possibility of such an event as my father's marrying again, had never for a moment occurred to me. It was with feelings of disgust—almost of horror, that I received the intelligence. In my eye, it seemed little less than a profanation, that the place of my beloved and sainted mother should be filled by another. But filled by Miss Cumberbatch! a person whom the world knew only in the character of a menial; a smooth, smug, smirking governess, companion or what you like, who made tea, embroidered purses, and ran up stairs for her mistress's pocket-handkerchief! Was it possible at once to regard the annunciation of such an event, with patience and resignation? At the very thought every feeling of my heart was ready to start up into tumultuous rebellion.

To my father's letter I returned no answer. To congratulate him on such a marriage, to say anything which could be construed into approbation of it on my part, would have been felt as a degradation, to which my nature would not submit. But in my letters to my sisters, I gave vent to all the vehemence of uncontrolled passion. I called on them to resist every act of oppression or encroachment on the part of their stepmother, and entreated them, if necessary, to quit their father's roof, and throw themselves on my protection. My protection! Of what folly are we incapable when in a state of high excitement? What protection, situated as I was, did it lie within the scope of my means to have afforded them? But passion never reasons.

In my calmer moments I wrote to Lady Willoughby, between whom and my mother a friendship had subsisted, which death only had broken, entreating her to extend her care and protection to my sisters, in the present altered circumstances of the family. To her I spoke openly, both of my own feelings, with regard to this new and hateful connexion, and of the consequences which I feared it might involve, to the happiness of Jane and Lucy. To this letter, I received a kind and affectionate reply, and my mind felt in some degree lightened of its burden of apprehension.

The effect which the intimation of my father's intentions produced on my sisters, was such as might have been expected from their different characters. Jane wept, and Lucy laughed. Jane, mild and gentle, bent like an osier to the blast. Lucy was of more gnarled and unwedgeable material,—a plant which the storm might rift or break, but could not bow. My fears were for the former. She inherited her mother's patient endurance of suffering, her warm and affectionate heart, but not her mother's energy of character and decision. In her, sorrow was mute and unrepining, and the gnawing of the worm could only be discovered, by the withering of the flower.

I am not aware that the period spent in Ireland was marked by any other event than those I have already narrated, of sufficient interest to merit record in these memoirs. In that country, military duty is always unpleasant. To be called on to spill human blood in repelling outrage, not always unprovoked, must ever be revolting. My duty was often deeply painful to perform, and is still to remember. All indeed that my mind now recalls or dwells upon with pleasure, is the hospitality which I uniformly experienced in that country most celebrated for hospitality. For my amusements, one sentence may suffice. I hunted and drank whisky-punch with the gentlemen, danced and flirted with the ladies, and, notwithstanding the charms of the fair daughters of Erin, when I quitted Ireland, as I am now about to relate, I did so

" In warlike meditation, fancy free. "

During the revolutionary war, and that which had succeeded to the peace of Amiens, the army had enjoyed few opportunities of distinction. In Egypt alone had they found a fitting field, and there, were the only laurels gathered, which, since the days of Minden and Quebec, had been added to their ancient wreaths. But brighter days were now about to dawn. The Spanish war broke out, and the heart of every freeman was at once enlisted in their cause. Never was enthusiasm more deep and general than that which animated the British nation at the period in question. Never was the unanimous voice of a mighty people poured forth with greater majesty and effect. It called on the government to assist, with heart and hand, a nation struggling for liberty, to cast off the chain of the oppressor. The government did not withstand,—no government could have withstood,—a call thus energetically made. In such an excited state of the public mind, if their rulers had dared to oppose themselves to the wishes of the nation, they would have been driven from their situations with scorn and ignominy. The path which ministers had to pursue was pointed out to them by the public voice. They had no choice ; their policy was dictated by the resistless acclamation of millions. It mattered nothing in such a case what party was in power, or on what peculiar principles their general measures were regulated. The ordinary barriers and distinctions of party were in a moment broken down, and Whig or Tory must have acted alike, in yielding instant obedience to a voice thus sublimely and irresistibly poured forth.

In June, 1808, an armament was accordingly collected, whose destination was known to be the Peninsula. It assembled at Cork, and was placed under the immediate command of Sir Arthur Wellesley. I shall never forget the delight of the regiment when the order for joining this expedition arrived. We were at mess. A packet was brought to Colonel Grimshawe, who, having hastily cast his eye over its contents, rose and stated that he had pleasant intelligence to communicate. He had just received an order for the regiment to proceed on foreign service, and join the expedition now assembling at Cork. This intelligence was received with three cheers—the health of Sir Arthur Wellesley, and success to the expedition, was drank with all the honours—and with temples throbbing with wine, and hearts panting for glory, did most of us that night retire to rest.

The order found us at Kinsale, and we had not a great distance to march. In a short time we were on our route, and on arriving were instantly embarked. A large fleet of transports and troop-ships were assembled in the Cove of Cork, in which the greater part of the force destined for the expedition were embarked before our arrival. A few days completed everything, and we waited only for a fair wind to proceed on our destination. That too came, and, on the 12th July, we sailed under a considerable convoy of men-of-war.

The immediate object of the expedition and the point of its destination were unknown. We only knew generally that it was intended to co-operate with the patriots of the Peninsula; of the *how* or *where* we were in utter ignorance. The orders issued to the fleet were, simply to obey the signals from the Admiral with regard to sailing; and, in case of unavoidable separation, to direct their course for Cape St Vincent's. It was known, that shortly after sailing Sir Arthur Wellesley had quitted the fleet; and to men immured on board of ship, such an occurrence of course afforded matter of abundant speculation and conjecture.

We proceeded on our voyage with light breezes, and in ten days arrived at the point of rendezvous. The general opinion now was, that we were destined to proceed to Cadiz, in order to co-operate with the Spaniards in their attack upon Dupont. It is probable, indeed, that such might have been our destination, had not any assistance in that quarter been rendered unnecessary, by the surrender of Dupont and his army. The conjectures, however, of the military Quidnuncs were completely set at nought, when, after laying-to for several days off Cape St Vincent's, the signal was made, to direct our course to the northward. It was now evident that Portugal was about to become the scene of our operations, and the force of Junot the more immediate object of our hostility. On the 28th, we were off Oporto, and on the day following the fleet anchored in Mondego Bay, where it was determined, if possible, to effect a landing.

The coast was not favourable for such an operation; and a strong wind from the north-west occasioned the surf to beat with such violence on the shore, as to render the attempt abortive. On the 1st of August, however, the weather became more moderate, and on that day the disembarkation of the troops commenced. It proceeded slowly. With a negligence of the authorities at home, of which it is impossible to say that this was a solitary instance, a sufficient number of boats had not been provided, and several days elapsed before the landing of the troops was completed. In the face of an enemy, such was the poverty of our resources, we could not even have attempted to disembark.

Never was anything more uncomfortable than our first night on shore. Tents we had none. There were no animals for the transportation of baggage, and it was therefore left on board. There were not even camp kettles to dress the rations of the soldiers, and we rested all night without cover on the ground, exposed to heavy rain and severe cold. The officers collected round a large fire, and merrily did the song go round, and the goblet pass, on that the first night of our campaign. There was no grumbling or complaining; and I believe we felt a pride in the very hardships and inconveniences, which, by the duties of the service, we were called on to suffer.

Before the commencement of our march from the Mondego, General Spencer, with a reinforcement of about five thousand men, had arrived from Cadiz, which he had quitted immediately on learning the surrender of Dupont. The disembarkation of this force, of course, occasioned some delay in our proceedings; but on the 10th, preparations being complete, we set forward in search of the enemy. As we advanced, the natives everywhere received us with enthusiasm, and we were greeted with a *viva* from every voice. On the 14th, we arrived at Alcobaça, from which the French had only retreated the preceding day. On the 15th, the first blood was shed. The brigade of General Spencer attacked the enemy at Caldas, and drove them from the village, though not without considerable loss. On the evening of the 16th, the army halted for the night in the neighbourhood of the heights of Roleia. It was known by reconnoisances, that these heights were occupied by the enemy, and, from the character of their demonstrations, it was evident that they intended, in that naturally strong position, to await our attack.

On these heights did we gaze that evening with intense interest. They rose before our eyes calm and bright in the splendour of the setting sun. On their summit, the main body of the French army was not visible; but here and there small bodies of horsemen, engaged, perhaps, in reconnoitring our position, were seen moving like mounted giants, in the upper air. This was the first time we had caught a glimpse of our enemy, and we remained watching his motions, till obscured by darkness from our view.

By the orders of that evening, the brigade of General Nightingale was directed to lead the attack at day-break on the following morning, and as our regiment formed the right of the brigade, of course the post of honour would be ours.

During the whole of our march from the Mondego, we had been clamorous for an opportunity of fleshing our swords,—yet maiden weapons, in war. When the French retreated on our approach, from Thomiere and Alcobaça, the event was lamented as a misfortune; our prayer was to meet them on a fair field, and the cry of battle was on every lip. Our wishes were now about to be granted; within half a league were the enemy,—within the compass of a few hours, we should meet them in deadly conflict. Yet there was no sound of exultation. A change had come over the spirit of the bravest. The voices hitherto loudest in clamouring for battle, spoke only in whispers, or were silent. There was a hush in the camp, but it would be injustice to believe it was the hush of fear. I knew those around me to be men who were prepared, at all hazards, to press forward on the path of distinction. Their silence proceeded from awe, not fear ; that awe, which even when the courage is most resolute, creeps over the human heart, when expectation is converted into certainty, and we are confronted with danger and death. In such a moment, we think less of the future than the past. A crowd of fearful memories, of ties now probably about to be for ever broken, of sins deep and unrepented, of hopes withered and withering, throng at once on the brain, and oppress the heart. Thoughts, which speech cannot utter, swell within us,—we seek solitude, and are silent.

No one overslept himself on the eventful morning. Instead of the usual call, we were warned by three small taps on the drum, sounded along the line, that the hour appointed was come. The signal was instantly obeyed, and, assisted by my servant in girding on my sword and sash, I issued forth to the parade-ground of my company. Twilight had not yet dappled the east, and it was dark as Erebus. The air was sharp and chilly, as the nights generally are in that climate, and fires had not been allowed in the bivouack, since the light they afforded might have given the enemy intelligence of our motions. A considerable time elapsed before the brigade was assembled and prepared to march. Through the darkness, the voice of Colonel Grimshawe, and the tread of his horse's hooves, rung on the ear, while both were yet invisible to the eye.

Before the regiment moved onward to take its station in the brigade, the word was passed for the officers in command of companies to assemble in the front. On reaching the spot indicated, Colonel Grimshawe energetically addressed us.

" I have assembled you, gentlemen, at the present moment, because I am anxious to address a few words to you, before we march to attack the enemy. I congratulate you, that the opportunity we have long wished for is at length arrived. I tell you plainly, that the service for which we are destined is one of difficulty and danger, for I know well that I address men of spirit and courage. The path of honour and distinction is now open to us all ; by God's grace we will follow it, wherever it may lead. I have no doubt the regiment will behave gallantly, but much will depend on the officers commanding companies. On your part no exertion must be spared ; you must check, by your vigilance and energy, the smallest appearance of disorder in the ranks. Suffer no man, on any excuse, to quit his place, and should any soldier be so lost to shame as to disgrace himself and his regiment by betraying cowardice, you will not hesitate to run him through the body on the spot. This is enough. You know your duty, and, I doubt not, will perform it gallantly. God bless you, gentlemen. Return to your places. "

Years—many years have passed, but not a syllable of this address has faded from my memory. Nothing could be more impressive than the tone in which it was spoken. It was still dark, and we could but dimly discern the features of the speaker; yet I knew then, and know now, the expression of his countenance as perfectly, as if the concentrated light of fifty suns had encircled it with a halo. The eye—the smile—the brows firmly compressed, as he directed instant death to be inflicted on the coward—the bend of courtesy—the air of command; these I saw not, and yet I beheld them all.

Day was just breaking in the sky when we were formed in brigade. By the first rays of morning, General Nightingale was seen slowly riding along the flank of the column, accompanied by his staff, and stopping as he reached the head of each battalion, to hold a short conference with its commanding officer. He at length placed himself at the head of the brigade, by the side of Colonel Grimshawe—the word " Forward " was given, and the column was instantly in motion.

As we advanced, I had leisure to take a nearer view of the heights of Roleia, about to become the theatre of action. They were steep and difficult of access, of very considerable height, and covered here and there with patches of thick brushwood. They presented no apparent demonstration of the presence of an enemy. A single horseman had been seen for a moment on the summit of the ridge, but he had disappeared, and everything was calm and undisturbed as when the shepherd tended his flock in peace and quietness, amid the green pastures on the hill-side.

When we reached the foot of the hill, up which our path lay, we halted for a brief space, and Sir Arthur Wellesley, attended by the Adjutant and Quartermasters-General, and his personal staff, came up nearly at the full speed of his horse from a neighbouring height, from which he had been making observations on the position of the enemy. After conversing for a minute or two with General Nightingale, at some distance on the flank of the column, an Aide-de-camp came up to Colonel Grimshawe, and informed him, that his presence, and that of the other officers commanding regiments, was immediately desired by the Commander of the Forces. The object of this conference was evidently to issue orders with regard to the plan of attack, for, as he spoke, he frequently pointed to the heights we were about to storm, and the ravine up which we afterwards advanced. When this was done, and the column stood with shouldered arms, once more prepared to march, Sir Arthur Wellesley approached, and standing in his stirrups, address-ed a few words to the soldiers. To our regiment he spoke as follows :—

" I know you well, ——. There is not a better nor a braver set of fellows in his Majesty's service. I have appointed you to lead the attack, and I have no doubt you will prove yourselves worthy of the honour. Go on, my gallant lads—Remember you are about to fight for your king and country. "

This was spoken with much rapidity of utterance, and vivacity of manner, and Colonel Grimshawe waving his hat at the head of the battalion, the command to advance pealed loudly through the welkin, and we commenced climbing the ascent. The path was so steep and rugged, that the other mounted officers of the regiment found it necessary to quit their horses, and ascend on foot; but Colonel Grimshawe, having greater confidence in his own powers of horsemanship, did not imitate their example. We had already advanced about two-thirds of the way, without annoyance or obstruction from the enemy, beyond that occasioned by an ill-directed fire from their artillery, when we were suddenly saluted with a shower of grape from a battery, which had been hitherto so successfully masked, as to elude observation. The loss it occasioned was great, and Hopkins, the adjutant, was killed in front of the battalion. A shot struck him on the head, and dashed his brains in our faces. The soldiers, who, but a moment before, had trembled at his frown, now trampled on his body. Such is war!

Colonel Grimshawe rode out to the flank of the column, to urge the men to increased speed, in order to reach if possible the summit of the hill, before time could be afforded for a second discharge from the battery. At that moment, a sharp fire of musketry opened on us from the brushwood on either flank, and from the top of the hill, on which the French lines were now partially visible. Both men and officers were falling thickly, and some of our soldiers fired into the brushwood in which their assailants lay concealed.

"Let there be no firing now," exclaimed Colonel Grimshawe: "They shall have firing enough when we crown the hill. Charge on briskly—follow me!" And putting his horse to his speed, he almost instantly resumed his place at the head of the battalion. He rode about twenty yards in front—sometimes wholly enveloped, at others only partially visible, in the clouds of smoke occasioned by the enemy's fire. The last words he spoke were addressed to myself.

"Captain Thornton, charge on at double quick with the grenadiers; the other companies will follow."

He had scarcely uttered them, when I saw him fall headlong from his horse. As we passed, he lay prostrate on the ground in the agonies of death. It was indeed a sight terrible to see. There was grass and earth in his mouth, which he champed with his teeth. His features were frightfully contorted, and his body and limbs were agitated by a convulsive tremor. In the impulse of the moment, I quitted my station in the ranks, and ran up to him. I raised him gently in my arms, but when I then gazed on his face, I knew, from his fixed and glassy eyes, that the last struggle was over. Never was the blood of a braver man shed on a battlefield. I laid him reverently with his back to the field, and sprung forward to my place.

In a few moments, another discharge from the battery carried destruction through our ranks, and the fire of musketry became still hotter as we approached the summit of the heights. The men now fell into considerable disorder. They were disheartened at suffering so severely from attacks which they had not the power to repel. Every exertion of the officers was necessary to check the progress of the panic. The command of the regiment had devolved on Major Penleaze, but his station till now was in the rear, and he had not yet advanced to the head of the battalion. It was evident, that to remain in our present situation was to encounter certain death, and that our only chance of success could arise from charging the enemy, and driving them from the heights at the point of the bayonet. We had no leader; in this respect, indeed, the loss of Colonel Grimshawe was irreparable. There was already some confusion in the ranks, and I felt almost instinctively—for in the hurry of such a moment, I could not reason—that instant steps were necessary, to reassure the sinking confidence of the soldiers. Calling, therefore, loudly on the Grenadiers to accompany me, I placed myself in the front, and advanced rapidly towards the enemy.

On reaching the top of the hill, I remember being immediately surrounded, and receiving the thrust of a bayonet on my side, which luckily did not penetrate deeper than the bone. Situated as I found myself, it is probable I should have been dispatched, but for the good-natured interference of a French *Sous-Lieutenant*, of gigantic stature, who exclaiming, " *C'est un brave Garçon, ne le tuez pas,* " seized my sword, and instantaneously twitched it from my grasp. " *Rendez vous,* " cried he, addressing me at the same moment; and on my signifying my assent as distinctly as the confusion of my ideas would permit, I was hurried off in charge of a non-commissioned officer and several soldiers, to the rear.

After marching about a league, my conductors, who, by the way, were by no means too civil or polite, lodged me in a chamber of a deserted house, over the door and windows of which they kept guard. My solitude was not long unrelieved. Four of my brother-officers soon arrived to share it, and there is comfort even in community of misfortune. Of the issue of the action they could say nothing, having been captured precisely under circumstances similar to my own. We had, indeed, the mortification to observe, that about an hundred of our men were taken prisoners. They marched along sullenly and doggedly, and bore a certain ruefulness of visage peculiarly characteristic of my countrymen in such circumstances. To the appellation of " *Bêtes Anglaises,* " which was plentifully bestowed on us all, without distinction of rank, they answered with a surly imprecation, which I do not think proper to record, but which seemed only to produce the effect of increasing the insulting merriment of their captors.

We had not long been tenants of our prison, when an officer of the Etat-Major came up, and gave directions for our instantly proceeding on our march. In obeying, we at least enjoyed the satisfaction of perceiving that the French army were in full retreat, and our joy at the cause of this movement, more than counterbalanced the inconvenience to which it subjected us. We proceeded without halting about five leagues, and bivouacked in the centre of a Cordon, which rendered escape impossible.

On the following morning, we were sent for by General Laborde. He received us politely, and after inquiring our rank, offered us the liberty of parole. This, after some consultation together, we agreed to accept; and General Laborde politely assured us, that he placed so implicit a reliance on our honour, that he would instantly withdraw the guard by which we had hitherto been attended, and allow us to proceed to Lisbon alone. He then invited us to partake of the refreshment of coffee, during which he conversed agreeably, and expressed his surprise that the English general, instead of attacking his position at Roleia in front, did not rather prefer to turn his flank, and thus force him to a retreat. He spoke, too, of the general state of affairs in the Peninsula, and considered the conquest of Spain as already achieved. Altogether, General Laborde struck me as being a person of uncommon talent and intelligence. His manner was less vivacious than that of Frenchmen commonly is, and he assumed none of that air of factitious importance by which the parvenus generals of Napoleon were usually marked. The repast being concluded, we took our leave, gratified at once by the character and issue of our interview. A state of surveillance is always disagreeable, and we rejoiced at being freed from it. Our journey was performed on foot, and in three days we were in Lisbon.

CHAPTER IX

Gow. Here he comes, and the Scots captain, Captain Jamy, with him.
Flu. Captain Jamy is a marvellous valorous gentleman, that is certain ;
and   of
great expedition, and knowledge in the ancient wars, upon my particular
knowledge of his directions : by Jesu, he will maintain his argument as well as
any military man in the world, in the disciplines of the pristine wars of the
Romans.

Henry V.

OUR time passed gaily in Lisbon. We were, in fact, prisoners, without
experiencing any of the evils of captivity. Our baggage was forwarded
under a flag of truce, and with the pleasures of a gay capital at
command, we did not think it necessary to play *Il Penseroso*.

My curiosity was interested in observing, at such a moment, the
temper of the people. At first all was silence and submission to the
tyrannical usurpation of the intruders, and the majority of the higher
orders carried the tricolor cockade in their hats. But this gradually
changed. The victory of Vimiera at length brought speech to the
tongue-tied Patriots ; the assistance of the whole army of martyrs was
invoked to aid in the cause of Portugese freedom, by the clerical saints-
militant, and confidential curses on their unprincipled invaders were
muttered audibly in the streets and coffeehouses. But at the first intelligence of the Convention of Cintra, the storm, which had been gradually
gathering in the horizon, burst forth in its fury. The creatures formerly
most abject in submission, were now the loudest and most clamorous for
vengeance ; and those who wanted courage to draw a sword or trigger
by daylight, took advantage of the prevailing impunity, and assassin-
ated in the dark.

Never was a great and glorious cause more disgraced by its assertors
—more deeply contaminated by cowardice and ferocity. It was perilous
for a Frenchman to be seen alone in the streets. On the first favourable
opportunity he was butchered. For myself, I had been well treated by
the French—I had formed acquaintance with many of their officers, and
it was perhaps excusable, may I not say natural, that I should in such
circumstances feel interested in their favour. Woe betides the cause,
however just, in which the conduct of its partizans causes the better
principles of our nature to revolt from fellowship or participation. I
know my feelings on this subject are not those of Mr Southey ; and I
know also it is, or at least was, the fashion, to laud these deeds of
cowardly barbarity as acts of just retribution. Let them pass, if possible,
as such. Let it be recognised as an established canon, that violations of

national law on one side, justify murder and assassination on the other. But let it be remembered, that these acts of vengeance were perpetrated by the Portuguese, not in a struggle for liberty, but when the conflict was at least temporarily decided; when their enemies were about to be removed from their territory, by a convention which, however disgraceful it might be to our arms, was at least beneficial to Portugal, in affording her time for preparation and defence. They were acts of mere gratuitous barbarity, leading to no result, but that of degrading and contaminating a cause in itself as pure and generous as any for which patriot blood was ever shed on field or scaffold.

Before quitting Lisbon, I had the good fortune to meet the Herculean *Sous-Lieutenant* to whom I had been indebted for my safety when I was taken prisoner. He was an honourable and worthy fellow, and I was glad of an opportunity to express my sense of the obligation under which he had laid me. He often joined our English mess, and no one ever did more honour to good cheer. On such occasions, he united all the qualities, distinctive both of his own countrymen and ours. He ate like a Frenchman, and drank like an Englishman, making a mere trifle of two bottles of Collares, a wine superior to any Burgundy I ever tasted, but which, unfortunately for English Gourmets, is too delicate to admit of exportation. He drank an additional bottle on the day of his embarkation, and we saw him safely on board—to meet no more.

On the ratification of the Convention of Cintra, we were again restored to liberty. On rejoining the regiment, I found that Major Penleaze had succeeded to the lieutenant-colonelcy which the death of Colonel Grimshawe had left vacant. But the loss we had sustained in that officer it was impossible for Colonel Penleaze to supply. No one, however, understood his duty better, even in its minutest details. Dundas was at his finger ends; and I believe he could repeat without book the Mutiny Act and Articles of War from beginning to end. To his predecessor he formed a contrast in many respects. He had none of that energy and decision of character so necessary to one placed in a station of command. Colonel Penleaze was not, what is called in military phrase, a *fire-eater*, and did not even make a secret of his aversion to all gratuitous danger. There were underhand whispers too, abroad in the regiment, about his backwardness in heading the column, on the death of Colonel Grimshawe; and although in his conduct on that occasion, there was nothing so palpable as to amount to cowardice, there was at least enough to acquire for him the general character of being a *shy cock*.

What, perhaps, tended more than any other cause, to render him more unpopular with his brother officers, was a certain selfishness of character, and exclusive attention to his own comfort. No sooner had the regiment halted after a long and severe march, than Colonel Penleaze proceeded to select his own billet, and left the rest of the regiment to shift for themselves. In punishment, he was severe and unrelenting, even beyond the example of his predecessor, and the soldiers did not fail to institute comparisons, in which he was not treated with much favour. The reader will readily imagine that I was no great favourite with my new commander. Nor will he err in so doing. I believe he never either forgot or forgave my American frolic of dressing Neptune as his representative, and there had never been any approaches to intimacy between us. Even had the case been otherwise, however, a circumstance which occurred shortly after I rejoined my regiment from Lisbon, would have been sufficient to have fanned into a flame, the sleeping embers of his dislike.

In our convivial moments, Popham and myself had amused ourselves by inditing a ballad on the battle of Roleia, in which the exploits, real or supposed, of the different officers of the regiment were duly emblazoned and set forth. The stanza relating to Colonel Penleaze, though containing no direct imputation, was perhaps, under the circumstances, ill-natured. I only remember two lines of it ; they run as follows :

> In rear of the regiment, not quite at his ease,
> On his high-mettled steed, rode brave Major Penleaze.

The whole thing, indeed, was merely meant as a convivial *jeu d'esprit*, and by no means intended to circulate beyond the range of our intimate associates. But the attempt of Canute to check the advances of the sea, was not more hopeless than the attempt to limit the circulation of a jest. It spread, and I received authentic intelligence that it reached Colonel Penleaze. The consequence was, not an open declaration of hostilities on the part of my commander, but a petty underhand warfare of annoyance. I do not know that in this contest I came always off worst. In point of comfort I certainly suffered a good deal, and my only weapons were a squib or a sarcasm. But I flatter myself I wielded those with tolerable effect, and did not fail to make my antagonist wince under their application.

Under such circumstances it may be supposed that Colonel Penleaze would neglect no favourable opportunity of ridding himself of the presence of one so disagreeable. This soon offered. Sir John Cradock, who had succeeded Sir Hew Dalrymple in the command of the British army in Portugal after the Convention of Cintra, was, in his turn, superseded by Sir Arthur Wellesley, who, by a fortunate vacillation of the ministry, was again intrusted with the direction of the military energies of the country. When Sir Arthur assumed the command, he found the army occupying a line of positions extending from Santarem to Coimbra, and forming a sort of cordon for the protection of the capital. The enemy, whose ardour had not sunk under the Convention of Cintra, had again advanced under the command of Soult, and the direction of their movements indicated their chief object to be Oporto.

In order to defeat, if possible, the views of the French General, preparations were made for the rapid advance of the British army to the northward. A general depôt of the army was formed at Belem, near Lisbon, and the —— was required to furnish an officer for this duty. By the rules of the service the officer first for detachment should have been selected, and as I did not stand in this situation, it may be supposed that I felt considerable indignation and surprise, on finding my name on orders, as the person destined to remain on this unpleasant and inglorious service. I lost no time in waiting on Colonel Penleaze, and remonstrating very strongly on this piece of flagrant injustice. The Colonel was alone when I was ushered into his presence. He received me politely, but not I thought without some symptoms of embarrassment. I began the interview by stating, that he was of course aware of the subject on which I was about to speak. That my name had appeared in orders for detachment, when I was not first on the roster for such duty. That imagining this had proceeded from mistake, I had spoken to the Adjutant, who informed me that my name had been inserted by the express order of the Commanding Officer, and I requested to know if I was to regard this as a true statement of the case.

He hesitated a little in his answer, and stated that the duty in question could not be classed in the ordinary routine of detachments. That it required an officer of talent—one who was qualified to conduct a considerable correspondence. That on this ground only—one certainly not unpleasant to my feelings, he had fixed on me as the officer best qualified for the duty.

This answer of course was anything but satisfactory. I was aware, I said, that on him I had no claim for anything but rigid justice, but my right to that I never would resign. That if he persisted in the order I should take the liberty of forwarding a representation on the subject to the General commanding the brigade, since I considered it necessary to my own character to show to the world that in the present circumstances of the army, the duty in question was forced upon me—not voluntarily sought or accepted.

When I stated my resolution in this respect, he relaxed a little, said that the arrangements were now concluded and could not be altered, but assured me that on the arrival of an officer shortly expected from England, I should be relieved from my command, and return immediately to the regiment.

The contest of a subordinate officer with his superior, is at all times an unequal match, and one of which the issue may be pretty accurately predicted. In my own case, notwithstanding my remonstrance with the General, I had the mortification to find, that all my exertions had been ineffectual. When the army commenced its advance, I remained with the depôt, brooding indignantly on my wrongs, and finding comfort only in the hope that the day might yet come, when an ample reckoning should finally balance the accounts between Colonel Penleaze and myself.

In the honours acquired by the army in the brilliant passage of the Douro, and subsequent expulsion of the enemy from Oporto, I had no share. During the period occupied by these operations, and the advance of the allied forces into Spain, I remained an inglorious prisoner at Belem. Never did prisoner pant more ardently for his release. I counted the days, nay, the very hours, till the arrival of my successor, watched every veering of the wind, and made nautical calculations of the probable period at which the fleet might be expected to reach the Tagus. At length he came. He was a married man, who brought his family with him, and was apparently not displeased with the pacific character of the appointment which awaited him. It enabled him to live in comparative comfort with his family in Lisbon, instead of being called on to partic-ipate in all the dangers and privations of a campaign.

The arrival of my successor, indeed, was fraught with a double pleasure. My old friend Conyers came a passenger in the same ship, on his way to join the army for the first time. He had grown into one of the handsomest men I ever saw, and in the gay caparison and trappings of a dragoon, he was a youth whose tale of love, even to the chariest maiden, it had been " perilous to hear. "

Years had passed since we parted, yet

> " Time had nothing blurred those lines of favour
> Which then he wore. "

Those years, indeed, had brought with them manliness of look, but had deprived him of no portion of that youthful vivacity which in former days had shed a charm on his society. The service which he had seen during the interval of our separation, was of a somewhat different character to that in which I had been trained. His duty, instead of withdrawing him from the gay world, had brought him into frequent contact with the court, and kept him constantly within the sphere and the attraction of the world of fashion.

Still, in my eye, he was nothing changed. There was the same joyous smile on his lips—the same laughing brilliancy in his dark eye—the same openness of heart, and careless generosity of character, which had marked him in those days, when the spirit of young life was stirring in our blood. Need I say, that encountering as we did, thus unexpectedly in a foreign land, our meeting was a happy one? It was indeed so. A rush of half-forgotten thoughts came over me as my eye first rested on his countenance and I felt the first warm pressure of his hand. By a trifling increase of similarity, I could almost have mistaken for a moment the Praça de Roseia (there it was we met) for the quadrangle of Glasgow College.

Conyers, too, was going to the army, and, with the boiling blood of a soldier to whom war had hitherto rather been a dream than a reality, he was eager to set forth on his route. In this respect it was impossible that two instruments could vibrate in more perfect unison. The few days we spent in Lisbon were only those necessary for preparation. To both of us, I think, they were happy ones—to me, the only happy ones I had enjoyed since my separation from my regiment.

When we set out on our journey, the party was increased by the addition of a veteran captain of a Highland regiment, bound on a similar mission to our own. Captain Campbell, or Cameron, (I am really not very certain in which appellation our Caledonian fellow-traveller delighted,) was a character in his way, and amusing in spite—perhaps in consequence of, his eccentricities. In point of age, he was certainly above fifty, and piqued himself on the possession of great military experience, from having, in the early part of the late war, partaken in the glory of capturing several of the French West India Islands, under Grey and Jervis. He possessed little of his countrymen's acuteness, and to a tolerably long, if not profitable experience of the world, he united a simplicity and want of discretion, somewhat un-common in a North Briton. Of the military knowledge of Conyers and myself, he made exceeding light, and he was distinguished by a certain opinionativeness, and obstinacy of character, which made him peculiar-ly unapt to be swayed or influenced by the dictates of any other judgment than his own. To Conyers, the society of such a person was an absolute mine of enjoyment, and it was impossible not to be amused at the skilful and ingenious manner, in which he contrived to evoke, into broad light, the eccentricities of our companion.

We crossed Portugal, and entered Spain, without encountering any of those parties of Brigands, by which both countries were infested, and nothing occurred to disturb the harmony of the party, till we reached Plasencia, where it had been our intention to halt for the night, in the expectation that another day's march would bring us up with the army.

At Plasencia, however, Captain Cameron unluckily received intell-igence, that a considerable body of the enemy had been seen about three leagues distant on our right, and, with his usual promptitude and decision of character, determined on making a reconnoissance to ascert-ain the truth of the report. It was in vain that I endeavoured to convince him of the folly of such a proceeding, or represented the danger to which it would inevitably expose him. " What the deevil, man, " answered he, " do you think I would join the regiment with a cock and a bull story about the enemy, without ascertaining if it be true ? "

In short, persuasion had no effect, and Conyers, whose fancy was tickled by the absurdity of the project, wickedly took part against me, and offered to accompany him on his wild-goose expedition. Seeing my companions both determined, I allowed my better judgment to be over-ruled, and agreed to join the party.

The plan of our operations being settled, little time was lost in carrying them into effect. After dinner, we mounted our horses, already tired by a pretty long march, and set out to reconnoitre the enemy. Nothing more thoroughly ridiculous than our party can well be conceived. The Caledonian, who, as senior officer, assumed the chief command, was in person somewhat gaunt and raw-boned, and, without exception, the worst horseman I ever saw in my life. He bestrode a jade as sorry as that of Don Quixote, was attended by an escort of four lame dragoons, who happened to be in Plasencia at the time, on their way to the rear, and whom he had unwillingly pressed into this hazardous service. My horse, which was one of the country, was certainly a few degrees better, but by no means an animal on whose speed, in a case of extreme urgency, I was inclined to place any unnecessary reliance. Conyers was the best mounted of the party, and rode an English horse, which, though considerably reduced both by the scarcity and quality of the forage to which he had recently become accustomed, gave him an immense advantage over both his companions.

We rode about two leagues without interruption, or gaining sight of anything that could possibly be mistaken for an enemy. Never shall I forget the figure of our leader, as he rode at the head of the party, brandishing a huge spy-glass, and the air of complacent generalship with which it was occasionally directed to every point of the horizon. At length a party of cavalry was descried at some distance, near a point where the road entered a wood of considerable extent and thickness. They halted for a moment, as if to examine our numbers and appearance, and speedily retired into the wood, by which they remained concealed from further observation. For myself, I had no doubt they were a party of French cavalry, and exerted all my eloquence and energy to persuade our commander to prosecute his observations no farther. But in vain. Captain Cameron insisted the cavalry we had observed were Spaniards, and assured us that, by the aid of his glass, he had distinguished the national cockade in their hats. In this opinion he was, unfortunately, again strongly fortified by Conyers, who, anxious for a still farther prosecution of the joke, brought forward many arguments in corroboration of the captain's opinion. It was in vain that I laid before him the whole extent of the responsibility he would incur, in case any of the party should be captured by the enemy in the execution of so absurd a project. I could gain no convert to my opinion, and at length gave up all farther attempt at argument, in a case where it was abundantly evident all argument would be wasted. Accordingly, we still continued to advance, and passed the spot on which the horsemen had been discovered, to the great triumph of our leader, without encountering any hostile obstruction.

But his Pæans were destined to be of short duration. We had scarcely reached the middle of the wood, when the tramp of horses' hoofs was heard advancing from the rear, and on looking round, we perceived that a party of French cavalry were charging in pursuit of us with their utmost speed. In these circumstances there was not the least occasion for the cry of " *Sauve qui peut.* " Every one of us, lame dragoons and all, scampered off, without paying the smallest attention to the motions of his neighbour. As I drove the spurs into my jaded steed, which, with great difficulty, I could now urge into a gallop, I could not help cursing the Scotch captain for an ass, and my own folly in submitting myself to his guidance.

The object of all the party, of course, was to gain the extremity of the wood, as, by separating in different directions in the open country, there was at least a chance that some of us might escape. But in this we were disappointed. The entrance of the wood was guarded by a detachment of cavalry, who waited our approach, and we thus found ourselves, caught as it were in a trap, between two parties of the enemy. The cries of *Rendez vous*, *Rendez vous*, accompanied by a few shots, and an abundant volley of French execrations, now rung loudly in my ears, and looking round, I perceived that our commander was already in the grasp of the Philistines.

For a moment I was irresolute. The trees on both sides were too thick to admit the passage of a horse, and I was in the act of throwing myself from mine, in order to escape, if possible, on foot, when a shot struck him in a vital part, and he fell beneath me. Before I had time to spring again to my feet, I felt myself grappled by several dragoons, by whom I was surrounded. Of course, resistance or escape were now equally hopeless, and exclaiming, " *Prisonnier,* " I delivered my sword to my assailants, and surrendered at discretion.

The whole party, I found, with the exception of Conyers, had been equally unfortunate. He had escaped. I remember, he passed me at the moment I threw myself from my horse, exclaiming, as he dashed onwards at full speed, " Bad work, Thornton, I'll charge through them, by Jove ! " And he did so, as I afterwards learned, at the expense of a sabre cut.

The officer into whose hands we had fallen, was a captain of *Chevaux Legers*, and treated us with civility. His regiment formed part of the army of Soult, by whom he had been sent forward to reconnoitre the country, and ascertain how far the way was clear for a junction with Victor. As we rode to the rear, he entered into conversation with Cameron and myself, probably with the view of extracting some intelligence, with regard to the army. But we had none to give ; and by telling, what is not very usual in such cases, the simple truth, that we were direct from Lisbon, and on our way to the army, which we had not yet joined, we exempted ourselves from farther importunity.

The party halted for the night, in a Quinta about two leagues off. Our condition here was miserable enough. Both my Scotch companion and myself had been robbed of our money, watches, and everything valuable; and it may be supposed, under such circumstances, we were not very agreeable company to each other. Under any circumstances, however, I could sympathise but little in the loss he appeared principally to deplore, viz. that of a horn snuff-box, with a huge Cairngorm on the lid, which he stated to have been a lineal heir-loom in the family, from the days of his great-grandfather.

I never passed a more unpleasant night. My military prospects appeared utterly blighted, and I could look forward to nothing better than a long and dismal captivity at Verdun. Had this misfortune occurred in the regular discharge of my duty, I felt I could have borne it better; but there was nothing in the absurd circumstances of my capture, to afford me any consolation. It was impossible, I thought, to narrate them, without exciting contempt for my own folly, and feeling shame for that extreme easiness and pliability of character, which frequently occasioned so wide a variance between my judgment and my actions. My companion, too, was spiritless and chopfallen. The discredit, which he felt the circumstances of our unfortunate expedition, had thrown on his military talents, added to the prospect of an indefinite captivity, and the loss of his great-grandfather's snuff-box, had thrown him into a state of depression at once ludicrous and pitiable.

In the course of the day following, an order came for our junction with another party of prisoners, and immediate march to Madrid. The party to which we were united, consisted chiefly of Spaniards, with a few of our countrymen, who had been recently taken prisoners on an out-picquet. Nothing more disagreeable that this march can well be conceived. We were about thirty in all, of whom my countrymen formed about a third. The party was under the command of a French sergeant, who delighted in the exercise of his authority, and showed no inclination to contribute in any way to our comfort. There was a striking difference, however, in his treatment of the Spanish and English prisoners committed to his charge. The former were bound together without distinction of rank, and were treated with a degree of brutality most painful to witness. Our marches were long and oppressive, and when any of the poor creatures were unable to proceed, either from fatigue, or want of necessary refreshment, they were shot *sur le champ*, without the smallest compunction. There was certainly more ceremony used in the treatment of the English; and in case of any of them betraying too strong an inclination to fall into the rear, no more energetic measures of propulsion were resorted to, than an occasional prick of the bayonet, or blow from the butt end of a musket. Our rations during the march, which lasted for ten days, were scanty, and very irregularly issued; and most happy were we when the rising towers of Madrid intimated that one portion of our sufferings was about to terminate.

On our arrival at the capital, a separation of the officers and soldiers took place, and we were lodged in a large convent, already tenanted by about fifty of my countrymen, many of them severely wounded, who had fallen into the hands of the enemy, in consequence of the retreat of the army after the victory of Talavera. Among the party to whom we were introduced, were twelve assistant-surgeons, who had been left behind by Lord Wellington, in consequence of a promise from Marshal Victor, that whenever their assistance was no longer necessary to the wounded, they should be suffered to return, without being considered in the character of prisoners of war : A promise afterwards violated, with that *Punica fides* for which Napoleon and his generals have throughout been remarkable. In truth, no difference was made between their treatment and that of the prisoners of war, on whom they exercised their vocation.

Our party in the convent, was a large if not a pleasant one, and there is always something in community of suffering, which serves as a link between those, who have nothing else in common. Men, whose society, in other circumstances, I should certainly have considered as conveying something of a tarnish, I now associated with on a footing of temporary intimacy, just as one chats familiarly with his fellow-passengers in a stage-coach, knowing, and caring to know nothing farther about them, than that they are embarked in the same vehicle, and travelling the same road.

In the situation in which Madrid then was, the very seat and focus of the French power in the Peninsula, of course there was little demonstration of political sentiment, adverse to the ruling power. Nothing could apparently be more subdued, than the temper and spirit of the people, and I would be understood only as speaking of the higher orders, when I bear testimony that no legitimate sovereign of the present day was ever apparently the object, of more submissive loyalty, and abject adulation, than the easy, good-natured, and much ridiculed King Joseph.

I saw him when at Madrid. He generally drove out daily in his carriage escorted by a guard of Spanish cavalry. In person, he appeared a middle-aged man, slightly inclined to corpulency, with a head somewhat bald, and an expression of countenance, at once mild and intelligent. Notwithstanding the *vivas* of the populace, and the external demonstrations of respect, with which on those occasions he seldom failed to meet, Joseph had not the air of one very much at his ease. There was about him nothing of that look of confident authority, by which, (I take for granted) more legitimate potentates are distinguished. The rôle of a king, even with regard to air and manners, requires perhaps a longer apprenticeship, than he had yet served to the craft, for when the loyalty of his subjects became more than commonly obtrusive and vociferous, there was nothing, I thought, autocratical, or even regal, in the civil and well-bred air, with which he acknowledged the salutation.

In the contour of his face there was discernible a strong family likeness to Napoleon. But it was a similitude in dissimilitude, for nothing could be more different from the quickness of eye, and ever-varying expression, by which the countenance of Napoleon was distinguished, than the unchanging and philosophical calmness, which marked that of Joseph.

It were bootless to recall the many annoyances and privations, to which the English prisoners were subject during their stay at Madrid, because their happiness or enjoyment was in a degree altogether inconsiderable, influenced by these. No possible aggregation of personal comforts, could have reconciled persons in our circumstances, to their situation, and the want of these, in any probable degree, could have added but little to the disappointment and bitterness of feeling, engendered by blighted hopes, and hopeless captivity. The tone of feeling, I think, must have been in all the same ; yet how varied was its expression! There, was the deep scowl of solitary moroseness, the calm yet settled gloom of melancholy, discernible in the look of downcast vacancy, the pale cheek, and an unwonted compression of the lips. There, too, were the laugh and the song,—the revelry of heavy hearts, that sought in wine for an oblivion of misfortune,—and found it. And there, though rarely, might be recognised, the expression of calm and unshrinking fortitude, in those spirits of happier and more enviable mould, prepared alike for the cloud or sunshine, by which the firmament of their life, might be brightened or overcast. A prison is the touchstone of character, by which the ore of pure gold is at once separated and distinguished, from the baser metal.

The garrison of Madrid was commanded by General Bellegarde, an officer of considerable distinction in the French service. In person, he was well formed, and apparently of great muscular strength ; in manner, rude, coarse, and overbearing. Nothing could afford a stronger contrast to the polite and well powdered *emigrés*, whom I had been accustomed to meet in England, than this bluff and vulgar general of the new school. His talents had raised him from the ranks ; he had seen much service, and had the character, even among his own countrymen, of being " *ipsis Germanis Germanior,* " in his appetite for plunder. I well remember having my English ideas of military propriety considerably shocked, by the incongruity of topped boots and blue pantaloons, the costume he generally wore in riding out, and to which he appeared particularly partial.

From a character like that of General Bellegarde, we had little indulgence to expect, and in fact experienced none. Indeed, in the very ticklish circumstances in which the French then stood, it may be supposed that a more than ordinary degree of vigilance and decision, was required from those in authority. Among the soldiers, the smallest symptom of disobedience or insubordination, was punished rigorously, by the infliction of heavy irons and a dungeon, and the officers were informed, that any infraction of prison discipline would not fail to draw after it a similar visitation. The principal officer among the prisoners in point of rank, was Colonel Guard of the 45th regiment, and through him all negotiation with General Bellegarde was directed to be carried on. It was not till we had been some time at Madrid, that the British officers were allowed the privilege of going at large on their parole, as a preparatory step to their being sent off, under an escort to France. Hopeless of enjoying any opportunity of escape, I did not hesitate to adopt the only means left me, of being once more at large, and joined the great majority of the officers, by whom this proposal was accepted. We were allowed the freedom of a certain quarter of the town, under a system of surveillance so strict, as would have done credit even to Fouché himself. Our liberty extended from sunrise to sunset, when we were compelled to undergo a rigorous muster at the convent, and to remain there till morning, when our prison doors were again unbarred, and we issued forth joyful as birds let loose from a cage, in which they had been unwillingly pent up.

I had thus been a prisoner at large about a week, when I happened accidentally to enter the church of St Isidore during the performance of High Mass. There has always appeared to me to be something solemn and imposing, in the august service and ceremonies, of Catholicism. I neither envy the heart nor the imagination of that man, who can regard the form, under which any portion of his fellow Christians offer up their adoration, to our common Deity, with cold and senseless ridicule. At the moment I entered, the congregation were kneeling with every external demonstration, of humility and devotion. The priest was in the act of consecrating the holy elements, and the gorgeous censers spread around the fragrance of frankincense. He elevated the host, and every head was bent in adoration of a present Saviour. I too kneeled. Partly, perhaps, from deference to the religious prejudices of those around me, but partly, too, from an instinctive feeling of devotion that arose within me. The religion whose ceremonies I beheld, had been that of my fathers,—of the whole Christian world. They were at least reverend for their antiquity; and though, in some points of doctrine and belief, I differed from those around me, yet these, at that moment appeared comparatively trifling, and certainly not such, as to induce me to shrink from a communion of worship, with a people acknowledging the same Saviour, and imploring forgiveness of their sins, at the same altar of grace. The prayers of the mass, though (unfortunately perhaps) clothed in a language not generally understood, are yet rich in a certain antique beauty, which has never yet been rivalled, and certainly will never be surpassed. At all events, I joined,—I hope sincerely joined,—in the worship of my fellow Christians.

At the conclusion of the service, the congregation dispersed, and I remained to inspect at leisure a magnificent altar-piece, by I know not what great master, which had attracted my attention. The officiating priests and choristers had departed, and a few inmates only remained in the late crowded Cathedral. One of these was a female dressed in the ordinary apparel of the better class of Spanish women, with her face shaded by a black Mantillo, which depended on both sides from her head. For some time I did not observe her, till, choosing a favourable opportunity when there was no risk of being overheard, she addressed me. I looked on her at first without surprise, for in the freedom of Spanish manners, such an occurrence was not uncommon.

She was a woman past the prime of life, who apparently had never been handsome. She bore, it is true, even in the sere and yellow leaf, towards which her May of life was evidently fast declining, the dark and expressive eyes, and the same profusion of black and beautiful hair, by which her countrywomen are generally distinguished. But such attributes were too common, to attract any particular notice, or admiration on my part; and having civilly replied to her civil salutation, I would have passed on, without desiring or expecting, any further communication. Gradually, however, I was led into conversation. Of course, she knew by my uniform I was an English officer, and asked many questions, concerning my situation and circumstances. In particular, she inquired if I were married or single, whether I had mother and sisters, whether I was a Catholic (*bueno Christiano*,) and, at length, whether, if opportunity offered, I should feel inclined to brave the danger of an attempt to escape.

I answered her questions,—told her all she wished to know about my family and myself,—and she then informed me of the motives which had stimulated her interrogatories.

Her only son, she said, had been taken in some naval engagement, and carried as a prisoner to England. During his captivity in that country, he had experienced the greatest kindness and assistance, from a family, I think she said, of the name of Bevill. They had succoured him in his necessity; and when the subsequent peace with England had restored him to his friends and country, he had returned full of the praises of the generous hospitality of my countrymen.

All this had sunk deeply into the heart of his mother. A burden of gratitude had been laid on it, under which her generous spirit was uneasy. She longed for some opportunity to diminish the load of obligation, she had incurred to that people, among whom her son had found succour in his adversity. With this view, she had determined if possible, to effect the escape of at least one English prisoner. Chance had thrown me in her way, and I found, to that alone was I indebted for the offer of assistance, she then made me.

It was impossible to listen to the detail of her motives, without at once understanding the character of the person who addressed me. In what she said, there was no attempt at heightening or embellishment. The gratitude she expressed towards my countrymen, evidently came from the heart; and as she spoke of the kindness her son had experienced among them, she was much moved; her voice became quick and irregular, and she seized my hand, and pressed it warmly between hers. The matter she proposed to me, however, took me wholly by surprise; and expressing to her my warmest thanks, I declined her offer, stating that as I was at that moment on parole, it would be dishonourable even to enter on the discussion of any project of escape. Before we parted, however, she gave me her address, and in case any circumstances should occur, in which her assistance could be useful, I promised to have recourse to her good offices.

From that moment, the offer made me by this kind and excellent matron, was one of which I never lost sight. My mind dwelt on it by night and day, and many an airy and unsubstantial fabric did I erect on its basis. But the illusions thus created by my fancy, were uniformly dispelled by my calmer judgment. I had already given my parole, and to withdraw it in future would certainly excite suspicion, and occasion my being subjected to rigid, if not solitary confinement. But an avenue to my hopes was soon opened, of which I did not fail to take advantage.

The doctors, whom I have already mentioned as being left in charge of the wounded, had been so, on the express understanding, that they were not to be considered in the light of prisoners of war. As such, however, they had been treated from the commencement; and having completed their duties, instead of being suffered to return to the British army, were ordered to accompany the other prisoners to France, and during their residence at Madrid were only suffered to go at large on parole. These gentlemen not being members of a belligerent profession, revolted naturally from this unprincipled violation, not only of the law of nations, but of the express stipulation, entered into by the French generals. In spite of their parole, therefore, they, in surgical conclave duly assembled, determined on attempting their escape. In this attempt they failed; principally, I believe, from the extreme timidity of one or two of their number, who, being fired on without effect by a French sentry, became alarmed by the extra-professional danger they had incurred, and once more surrendered themselves prisoners.

The consequences of this attempt were not confined to the medical department. The parole liberty of all the prisoners was discontinued, until a very rigid and minute examination of the circumstances had taken place. The offenders, however, had too strong a plea of justice on their side, to meet with any very rigorous punishment, in consequence of their abortive effort to escape from thraldom. Colonel Guard once more set about his negotiations with the French general, and in a few days, the liberty we had before enjoyed, was again tendered to us. The offer was accepted by all, with the exception, I think, of seven officers and myself. What their prospects of escape were, or whether they had any, I knew not; but we were all equally explicit and determined, in rejecting the proposal.

Our refusal tended considerably to disturb the harmony, which had hitherto subsisted among the prisoners. We were strongly urged by Colonel Guard, and several of the field-officers, who, with him, had taken a lead in the affair, not to persist in our resolution. It was stated, that our adherence to the line of conduct we had adopted, must be severely injurious to the other prisoners, and occasion harsher measures to be adopted, with regard to them. Colonel Guard even stated, that he had pledged himself to General Bellegarde, that the privilege of parole would be joyfully accepted by *all* the officers, and that it was only granted on condition of its being so. The meeting did not terminate, without high words on both sides, but the apprehension of spending the better part of my life a prisoner at Verdun, overbalanced the eloquence of Colonel Guard, and I remained firm in my resolution of declining to take advantage of the liberty, thus strongly pressed on my acceptance. The consequence was, that I, along with my brother non-jurors, were removed to a separate part of the convent, in which we were detained close prisoners. The apartments we occupied were up one flight of stairs, on the top of which a sentry was placed, with directions to fire on, or run through the body, any prisoner who should attempt to pass him on his post. Each entrance to the building (for there were two) was similarly guarded; and the rooms on the ground-floor were occupied by the guard and jailer, if I may so call an Italian sergeant in the French service, who officiated in that capacity.

I had taken the precaution, foreseeing the close imprisonment which awaited us, to write to the lady whose assistance had been so freely offered in the Church of St Isidore, informing her of the situation in which I was now placed, and my anxious desire to take advantage of her kindness. I did not think it necessary to inform the bearer of this letter, who was an officer on parole, of the nature of its contents; but extracted from him a promise, that it should be delivered, without question, into the hands of the person to whom it was addressed. Imagining it related to some love affair, the commission was readily accepted, and the envoy probably returned from the execution of his mission, with a thorough contempt for my taste, in addressing billets-doux to an object, so little calculated to inspire tender emotions.

To my letter no answer was returned, and immured as I was, and separated by an apparently impassable barrier from the rest of the world, hope died within me, and it required all my philosophy, to encounter manfully those evils, from which, there appeared no reasonable prospect of escape. Day after day passed on, and I was still a prisoner; night after night brought hours of comparative happiness, for in my dreams I was free.

Such was my state of mind when the means of escape were suddenly presented to me. Our prison, of course, afforded no convenience for cookery, and our meals were daily sent from a neighbouring hotel. The party thus supplied, including the twelve assistant-surgeons of whom mention has already been made, consisted of nineteen ; and as we were daily furnished, not merely with dinner, but all its concomitants, such as plates, dishes, table-cloths, knives and forks, seldom less than five or six servants were necessary for their conveyance. It was the custom, for these men to wait on us at table, and the meal being finished, to reconvey the articles above mentioned, to the hotel.

I have already stated, that above a week elapsed without my having received any message or intelligence from my worthy matron. I was therefore, it may be supposed, not a little surprised, when one of the servants who brought our dinner, informed me that he was provided with a disguise, in which he was ready to assist me in escaping from the prison. Very few words were sufficient, to render the plan abundantly intelligible. While my companions were at dinner, I was employed in changing my dress, and before the conclusion of the meal, I was equipped at all points, in a manner similar to the dinner-carriers. I wore a white cotton jacket and apron, dark-brown breeches, and stockings of blue and white cotton. The trusty emissary had come provided with a second basket, and placing this on my head, I, with palpitating heart, took leave of my companions, and walked down stairs with as much of the cool and *non-chalant* air of my coadjutors, as I found it possible to assume. The *ruse* succeeded. I had to pass two sentries, neither of whom opposed any obstacle to my egress, and in a minute, I had the satisfaction of finding myself, moving in freedom along the streets of Madrid.

I think if I were to select the happiest moment of my life, it would probably be that in which the first sensation of liberty, fell like a gleam of sunshine, on my spirits and my senses. I am sure, I must then have played my part badly. For I danced rather than walked along the narrow *trottoir*, jostling all I met, and elbowing my way, without regard to age, sex, or rank. The French soldiers, ill-disposed to tolerate such rudeness, saluted me with a curse, and occasionally a push with the butt-end of their musquet, as I passed, insults, which of course I did not stay to resent. My steps were directed to the house of Maria de Noronha, where I arrived safely, a welcome and an expected guest.

CHAPTER X

I am free.
Once more, dear England, on thy sunny land
Is my firm footstep planted. Who can tell
Whose limbs ne'er felt a manacle, the joy
That fills the heart of the released captive,
As he inhales the first breath of free air,
And treads with chainless limbs his native shore?
Duke of Verona.

I EXPERIENCED every kindness from the worthy Senora in whose house I had sought an asylum. There I remained for some days, unknown to the rest of the family, secluded in a small apartment, of which she kept the key. But my situation was one of some danger. A French officer was quartered in her house, and there was consequently continual risk of being discovered. My good hostess, therefore, was anxious that I should be removed to a situation of greater safety, and prevailed on her sister, who was likewise domiciled in Madrid, to receive me. One evening soon after dark, I effected my change of quarters, dressed in a suit of naval uniform, belonging to the son of my Patrona, without encountering any unlooked for obstacle, in my transit.

In my new abode I was not received with any great show of hospitality; both mine host and his wife, being evidently apprehensive of the unpleasant consequences, in which a discovery of the place of my concealment could not fail to involve them. The husband, I found, was proprietor of an estate about thirty miles from Madrid, and a considerable dealer in wool. There was indeed some excuse for his bad humour, for in the present circumstances of the country, his estate was uncultivated, and his flocks had been seized, without payment, as supplies for the French army. When I had been a few days in his house without prospect of discovery by the French police, his apprehensions, however, began to wear off, and he frequently became tolerably companionable over a bottle of Sherry or Malaga, and a cigar. I remained an inmate of his house about a fortnight, when some French soldiers were unluckily billeted upon him, and it was again necessary, that my quarters should be shifted. I therefore once more removed to the apartment I had formerly occupied, in the house of Maria de Noronha, where I was received as kindly as before.

A considerable time had now elapsed since my escape from prison, and there was every reason to hope, that the vigilance of the police had begun to slacken. I had become heartily sick, too, of the state of close confinement in which I had lately lived, and was fully aware of the risk of detection, to which in my concealment I was hourly liable. In short, my whole heart had become bent on making an immediate attempt to escape, since further delay could apparently add nothing to the chances of my success. I communicated my sentiments on this head to my benefactress, who perfectly agreed in my reasoning, and promised that no time should be lost, in facilitating my views. I had formed a project of escaping in the character of a French officer, but to this many insurmountable objections occurred, and it was relinquished. It was, however, more easy to detect the dangers and difficulties of any plan, than to suggest another less liable to objection. In vain did I torture my imagination, in vain did I put my ingenuity to the rack, and rally all the energies of my nature, in the cause of my freedom. I summoned spirits from the vasty deep, but they came not at my invocation. Had my escape depended on my own solitary invention, I feel convinced I should have spent six years at Verdun, perhaps some of them at Bische. Luckily a better and a cooler head than my own, was at work on my behalf, and on this occasion of my life, at least, the star of my fortune shone bright and unclouded.

One day, my generous Patrona entered my apartment, with a man in the dress of a muleteer, whom she introduced to me by the name of Jozé. She told me that she had engaged this person to see me safely to Corunna, in which direction he was at any rate going with his mules, that she would provide me with the disguise of a Spanish muleteer, and assured me I should find Jozé a very good and trust-worthy person.

Of course, I was enchanted with the proposal, and accepted it with gratitude. In fact, no plan could have been better or more skilfully devised. To have attempted a direct escape to the British army, would have been to encounter difficulties and dangers, which the chance of surmounting with success, was disproportionately small. On the route to Corunna, on the other hand, we should encounter few, if any of the French army, and at Corunna I had the greatest chance of meeting an English ship, that town being in the hands of the British, and a considerable depôt for British merchandize.

All preliminaries being therefore arranged with Jozé, it was agreed that we should, on the second morning, set forth on our journey. The intermediate time was occupied in preparation for my suitable equipment, and in acquiring as much as possible the external appearance and demeanour, of the character I was to assume. To assist in this, the good Senora proceeded to cut my hair on the back, crown, and sides of my head, as close and bare as possible, leaving a long tuft on the top of the forehead, such as I remember to have seen in a picture of Time, in a book which inculcated on the rising generation, the propriety of seizing him by the forelock. My complexion, which was naturally dark, was rendered still more so by a decoction of walnuts, a contrivance, by the by, rather too permanent in its effects, for it was some months before I found it possible, to restore my skin to its original complexion.

It was not without sensations of rather a disagreeable kind, that I equipped myself for the first time in the garb provided for me. It was not new, and yielded to more than one sense indications scarcely to be mistaken of having long encased the person of some gross and oil-fed Muleteer. The night previous to my departure, sleep did not visit my eyes. Hope and fear contended for the mastery within me, and my mind was alternately elevated and depressed. I was hot and feverish, and rose, and paced the apartment for an hour before the first streak of morning was visible. Then I commenced the business of my toilet. My new dress consisted of a jacket and breeches of dark coffee colour, plentifully garnished with buttons, a crimson-coloured sash, in which was stuck a cuchillo or knife, blue stockings and red garters at the knees, shoes of brown-coloured leather, a striped handkerchief rolled round my head, and the whole surmounted by a huge Sombrero, far outshadowing in diameter of brim even the most extended pretensions of ultra quakerism. Thus furnished forth, I flatter myself I made a very tolerable Muleteer, at least one whose external appearance would not probably afford ground of suspicion.

The hour came when I was to join Jozé, who waited my arrival at the Plaça de Cevada. Farewell! How often, with sorrow and bitterness of soul, have I been doomed to utter that word! Cold indeed must my heart have been, had I repeated it without emotion, in parting for ever with my kind and generous benefactress. She, too, was moved. She invoked for me the protection of the Holy Virgin, and the tears were in her eyes as she pressed me in a last embrace.

I found Jozé with his mules at the appointed place; and as the morning gun was fired from the Retiro, as the signal for opening the gates, we set forward on our journey. The tremulous anxiety with which I entered on my new character may be conceived. I rode on a mule, loaded, beside the supererogatory burden I imposed on her, with two jars of oil, which hung on either side of the pack-saddle. Fear sat heavy on me till we passed the barrier, and we found ourselves pursuing our course uninterruptedly towards St Augustino.

Jozé, however, marched onwards with the air of one perfectly calm and unconcerned, alternately singing a verse of a Spanish song, and swearing with true Spanish vehemence at his mules. The morning was raw and cold, and from the two sentinels at the barrier, comfortably wrapped up in their great-coats, we experienced no interruption. Jozé's oaths, indeed, became more and more vociferous, as we approached the point of danger; and one of the sentinels, annoyed by his stentorian imprecations, threw a stone at him as he passed, cursing him half in French and half in Spanish for a noisy blockhead. To this my conductor replied, when fairly out of reach, with something about a " *Picaro*

Françese, " which his adversary durst not leave his post to resent.

During the day, we met several parties of French cavalry, who once or twice asked us a few questions, in replying to which, Jozé always officiated as spokesman; but nothing occurring to excite suspicion, we were suffered to pass on. When examined with regard to our route, we answered that we were bound for Salamanca, under a protection from General Bellegarde; Maria de Noronha having, how I know not, contrived to procure us one. When our course was afterwards changed, however, this protection was destroyed; but being then out of the line occupied by the French army, it was in fact no longer necessary.

In our journey, we met with fewer dangers and impediments, than might have been anticipated. In fact, when ten leagues north of Madrid, we had little to fear from the French. It is true, that near Zamora we were stopped, and our cargoes examined by a party of French soldiers; but this was done, less from suspicion, than a desire of plunder, and the rascals carried off my only change of linen, which I flattered myself had been sufficiently secured from discovery by being thrust into the stuffing of the pack-saddle. Luckily they did not search our persons, and my money escaped. Jozé's chief fears, however, were directed not towards the French, but his own countrymen; and had we fallen in with a party of Guerillas, even supposing we had the good fortune to escape alive, there is no doubt we should have been left to pursue our journey, in a state of primitive nudity.

Never—never shall I forget the sensations with which, from a height about a league from Corunna, the blue sea opened to our gaze, and I saw a ship at anchor in the bay, carrying the British flag. It was on Sunday, the 31st of August, at half past one p. m. that this blessed vision gladdened my eyes. To me the day and hour are memorable. I gazed a while in silence on the broad expanse of waters, speckled here and there with the boats of distant fishermen, the red sails of which showed brightly in the sunshine. But most did I gaze upon the ship, of whose voyage I hoped soon to be a partaker, as if endeavouring to recognise among the crew moving on her deck the countenance of some old friend or acquaintance.

But this mood of meditation was soon changed to one of exuberant delight. I sprung into the air with the agility, if not the grace, of De Hayes, waved my Sombrero over my head, and then kicked it from me, and played a thousand antics, at sight of which, Jozé evidently entertained strong suspicions of my sanity.

Having given vent to this paroxysm, we lost no time in entering Corunna. My first business was to call on the British consul, to whom I made known my situation, and who afforded me every assistance in his power. He insisted on my making his house my home during my stay, and the kindness I experienced from him has left me under an obligation, which I shall be happy, should it ever be in my power, to repay.

I had here no difficulty in procuring money, with which I recompens-
ed honest Jozé, and enabled him to return to Madrid with his mules well
loaded with English merchandize. I wrote also to Maria de Noronha,
and transmitted a sum through the muleteer, which I imagined to be
sufficient, to cover all the charges of which I had been the occasion.
From inquiries I afterwards made, I was glad to learn that the commission had been faithfully executed.

My stay at Corunna did not exceed a week. The Leander, Captain
Porter, was about to sail for England; I embarked in her, and after a
pleasant, because a short voyage, landed at Dover.

CHAPTER XI

From Marlborough's eyes the tears of dotage flow,
And Swift expires a driveller and a show.
                                        JOHNSON.

———Shall I call *you* father?
                        Troilus & Cressida.

FOR some time before I left Lisbon for the army, and of course during my confinement, I had received no intelligence from my family. So long a time had never before elapsed without my receiving letters from my sisters, who, to do them justice, were excellent correspondents. This unwonted absence of intelligence—this long and dreary silence, had filled my mind with dark forebodings, and unreasonable anticipations of evil.

While abroad, I felt this but little. The excitement of the circumstances in which I had been placed afforded full occupation for my mind; and the suffering of present evils, had prevented it from dwelling with much intensity on possible, and more contingent misfortunes. But when these had passed away, and I trod once more securely on my native land, a crowd of apprehensions came, to embitter my repose.

There was nothing in the circumstances of any of my family, when I had last heard from them, to create any fears on their account. Jane's spirits, indeed, were evidently depressed; but considering the change in her home, which my father's marriage had occasioned, there was nothing in this to excite surprise. Lucy's letters too, had been more serious than usual; but Lucy was growing older, and could not always be expected to retain the light-heartedness of a child. Still fears, not the less terrible for being vague and indefinite, haunted and depressed my spirit, and would not, by any effort within the scope of my energy to make, be shaken off.

In vain did I marshal reason to combat these visionary Gorgons—in vain did I cleave them down and smite them to the earth. For a moment, they were dissipated and subdued, but, like the members of the giant dissevered by the sword of Astolfo, they once more united, and stood before me in all their former ghastliness and terror. Immediately on getting ashore, I wrote Jane, informing her of my arrival, and requesting her to address a letter to me in London, by return of post.

I hurried, therefore, to town, anxious as soon as possible to put an end to this state of anxiety and doubt. There, however, no answer awaited me. Not an hour was lavished on pleasure or dissipation; and I waited only the brief space necessary to procure leave of absence at the Horse Guards, and to obtain a dress in which I could appear without ridicule, to set out for Thornhill. In fact, the Corunna Schneider whom I had employed to replace the discarded garb of the muleteer, had given, in that with which he supplied me, but a sorry specimen of his skill. The waist of my coat commenced nearly at my shoulders, while its lower extremities hung down almost to my heels. This unwonted longitude of one garment, however, was compensated by an equally unprecedented brevity of another. My trowsers scarcely reached to the knee, and resembled not a little those worn by Dutch fishermen above the huge water-proof boots in which they exercise their vocation.

To do myself justice, there was not, I think, much of the fop in my character; but I had quite vanity enough to make me averse to return to Thornhill in a dress so exceedingly *outré* and unbecoming. Stulze, on the present occasion, did wonders; and under excitement of feeling, perhaps, produced by beholding a customer so utterly disfigured by professional ignorance and barbarity, supplied me (notwithstanding an approaching levee), in a space incredibly short, with a costume, in which, without discredit, I might venture to appear in the very gayest circle.

No farther time was lost in getting *en route* for Thornhill. Once more I passed the old lions at the gate, and gazed on the mutilated and benignant countenances of these venerable guardians. Once more I stood in my paternal halls, disinherited and a stranger. I looked around me as I passed through the vestibule, but strange faces met my eye; nor did it now rest, as formerly, on the aged, but still rosy countenance, of Jacob Pearson. He was gone. With a sorrowing heart he had quitted that mansion, of which, from his boyhood, he had been a tenant; that service, in which he had, by half a century of frugality, barely secured a small competence to keep penury from the gate.

The new mistress and the old servant, had not agreed. Jacob was an aged tree, which would break, not bend. Thornhill was no longer for him, nor he for Thornhill. He had gone;—but I am sure Jacob's prayer and blessing still lingered with his master, unkind as he was, and with those children whom in infancy he had dandled on his knee, and to whom, in their maturer years, he had been an object of affection.

Let me at once finish his story. He retired to a cottage at some distance, where in a few years he died. There were none, with whom he claimed kindred; and he left my sister Lucy, who had always been, from her light and joyous disposition, his especial favourite, heiress to his little property.

Worthy and excellent Jacob, farewell! Deep and dreamless be to thee the sleep of the grave, till summoned to receive that reward, which we have high assurance will be bestowed, at last, on an humble and an honest heart!

When I entered, the butler inquired my name. The question struck a chill through my frame, and answering it only by a wave of the hand, I continued to advance. The servant, though evidently surprised, opened the door of the drawing-room, and I entered. It was vacant. I advanced, and seated myself in a chair, half afraid to look around me, from the associations, with which I imagined every article around me, to be indissolubly linked. The chair on which my mother had been used to sit,—the table at which she worked,—the sofa on which, when faint or weary, she had been accustomed to recline,—the thousand little elegancies with which she had adorned the apartment,— could I gaze on these things without stirring up a countless throng of mournful memories and solemn thoughts? Slowly and fearfully did I raise my eyes, and look around as one who expected to discover a frightful fiend looking forth on him from some dark nook of the chamber.

Soon, however, all dread of painful association was dispelled. The apartment was newly and gaudily furnished in the fashionable taste of the day. Hangings of crimson silk, tables and chairs of rose-wood inlaid with buhl, splendid cabinets of shells and minerals, had been substituted for the more ancient furniture to which my eye had been accustomed. I gazed round the room, but there was nothing in it to recall the memory of former days. No, nothing. The beautiful antique mirror, which nearly covered the wall of one end of the apartment, had been newly framed, and in more modern taste. Even the room itself was changed. A bay window had been thrown out since I had last seen it; and the Gobelin tapestry, which had been the admiration of the whole country, and on which were represented the history and miracles of the apostles, had been displaced by a showy French paper and a gold moulding. All this delighted me. There was nothing here to remind me of the home of my early days. *That*, it seemed, was now gone, and I stood a stranger in a strange place, calm and indifferent.

Mrs Thornton at length entered the apartment. I rose on her entrance, and saluted her with a distant bow. She raised her eye-glass as she advanced, and soon recognised my features.

"Ah, Captain Thornton!" she exclaimed, with an easy and *nonchalant* air. "I am delighted to see you. You are welcome, most welcome to Thornhill. This is really such an agreeable surprise! I assure you both Mr Thornton and myself were so disappointed at learning you had been taken prisoner,—such a blighting of all your prospects in the army, and then to find you here so unexpectedly! What delight it will give my excellent husband. I must not lose a moment in letting him know the pleasure that awaits him. I am not selfish enough to deprive him of it for a single instant unnecessarily. Pray, excuse me, Captain Thornton, for I cannot suffer any one but myself to be the bearer of such pleasant tidings."

"I beg first to ask one question," I interrupted: "How are my sisters?"

"Both well—quite well. Jane is with her husband in Gloucestershire, quite gay and delighted with her change of condition; and Mr Hewson is so charming a person——"

"Her husband!" I exclaimed, staring with astonishment—"Is my sister Jane married?"

"Yes, to be sure, some months; I thought you must have known that. I remember some one or other talked of writing you about it; probably it was forgot; but I assure you it is a delightful match, and Mr Hewson has been most liberal in point of settlements. But, excuse me, I must run and tell Mr Thornton of your arrival. I hope you mean to make some stay at Thornhill? Pray, authorise me to say you will pass a day or two with us? Your father, I am sure, would be quite delighted. At all events, you shall positively not leave us today—I must at least insist on that. I assure you, nothing less will satisfy either Mr Thornton or myself." Having thus spoken, she left the apartment.

I had some difficulty in recognising, in the portly and loquacious personage who had just quitted me, the mild, pensive, and demure Miss Cumberbatch of former days. The insect which changes from a chrysalis to a full-grown butterfly, and flutters with painted wings in the sunshine, undergoes not a metamorphosis more complete, than that which had been wrought on my stepmother. True it is, we are but creatures moulded by circumstance,—clay from which the plastic hand of the modeller, may form at will, an angel or a demon. But there are certain changes of character, so marked and striking, so sudden and unexpected, as to make us forget at once, the previous deductions of philosophy, and look on them, with unmixed wonder and surprise. Of this nature was the revolution, if not in character, at least in its external demonstrations, which I had observed in Mrs Thornton. In her appearance, too, she was considerably changed. In person she was larger and fuller than formerly, and the increase of expansion had given her a certain portliness of presence, which consorted well with her recent augmentation of consequence. I think it possible, that in mixed society, she might be considered an agreeable woman; and she possessed a certain quickness of apprehension, and a decided manner of expressing her opinions, which would probably acquire for her the character of a clever one. She was generally considered handsome, but there was something unamiable and repulsive in her eye, which marred the expression of her countenance, and appeared to indicate a selfish disposition, and a heart callous to those finer feelings, which contribute at once to elevate and sanctify, the baser and more grovelling attributes of our nature.

In whatever haste my good stepmother might be, to communicate the intelligence of my arrival to my father, he, at least, betrayed no symptoms of haste, to take advantage of it. I waited for half an hour alone in the drawing-room. At length my father entered, leaning on the arm of his wife. I half started, as my eyes first rested on his figure. Time had evidently made deep inroads on his frame, since I had last seen him—deeper, indeed, than might have been expected from his age, which was little above sixty. His brow was furrowed, and his cheek hollow and wrinkled. His body was worn and emaciated; yet it was evidently a burden which his feeble limbs were with difficulty able to support.

Though the ravages of time, and perhaps of mental inquietude, were thus visible on my father, care had evidently been taken, to conceal as much as possible, the havock of the spoiler. In former days, he had been in a more than common degree, negligent of his toilet. A marked change in this respect, was now obvious. His dress, which, within my memory, had been uniformly black, was now composed of several colours, and there was a certain neatness and precision in its arrangement, which bespoke considerable attention to personal adornment. His head, which was formerly bald, except a few silver locks, which still afforded a scanty covering to his temples, was now adorned by a wig.—*Honi soit* to the man who first invented wigs,—who taught mankind the detestable art of disfiguring the noblest portion of the noblest work of the divinity—the human head. Nature had no charm for him; no eye had he for the beautiful and picturesque; never did high or bright imaginings dawn on his dull soul. *Anathema maranatha* on his vile calling!

My father's teeth, too, were gone, and the skill of the Chevalier Ruspini had evidently been called in, to contribute its quota of renovation. Those he now displayed, were far too white and regular to be mistaken for genuine, and they occasioned an unnatural elevation about the mouth, which affected disagreeably the expression of his countenance. Everything around me had undergone a change, but to me the most striking and impressive, was that I now beheld in my father.

Immediately on observing his entrance, I rose from my chair, and advanced to meet him. His gait was tottering and unsteady, and as I extended my hand, and inquired kindly for his health, he spoke in a feeble, tremulous, and almost unintelligible voice. There was no feeling depicted in his countenance, on our meeting,—their natural lustre had faded from his eyes, and he gazed on me as one gazes on a stranger, with whose features he imagines himself familiar, yet concerning whom, he can recall only few and uncertain particulars.

After the first salutations, I remained silent, for I was shocked by discovering, that my father had suffered equally from mental, as from bodily decay. He looked at me for a short space, and was evidently endeavouring to collect his ideas; at length he spoke.

" I think I have had the pleasure of seeing you before; and yet—, " he hesitated, and placed his finger on his head, as if making a strong mental effort, " excuse me, I cannot exactly recollect when or where. "

"This is your son, Captain Thornton," interrupted my stepmother; "you know, he has been abroad in Spain; and you heard lately of his being taken prisoner, which occasioned us all, great regret and alarm.— You see," said she, addressing me in an under tone, "your father's memory is a little gone; but it is only his memory, all his other faculties are quite perfect, and on most subjects, I assure you, he is wonderfully acute."

To what she said, however, I paid little attention, for I was occupied in observing what effect the intelligence of my presence produced on my father.

His eyes, which had been turned towards his wife as she spoke, were now keenly directed on me, as if engaged in the act of recognition. There was more of life and expression in them, than I had yet seen. "Cyril," he said, "you are altered, and I did not know you; but I might have expected that, for you left Thornhill a boy, and you have returned a man. You are welcome—I am glad to see you."

I was indeed considerably altered. Exclusive of the change wrought by the transition from youth to maturity, my face had become embrowned by exposure to a more southern sun, and the whiskers, which I had suffered in my character of a muleteer to cover the largest possible quantum of my cheek and chin, had not since my arrival in England been reduced to more moderate and civilized dimensions. Yet, however different I might be in appearance, from the smock-faced boy, who, seven years before, had solicited his blessing, and gone with joy and lightness of heart into the world, there was something bitter and melancholy in the idea, that I should not again be recognised by him to whom I owed my being. But the change, alas! had not been in me alone. I beheld before me the wreck of a stately vessel, from the summit of whose lofty mast, I had seen the pendant float proudly on the breeze—and but a wreck—her power, her glory, and her pride, were gone for ever.

The knowledge of my presence seemed to have the effect of collecting and condensing my father's ideas, and on everything connected with myself, he spoke connectedly and with perfect memory; but on other subjects his mind evidently wandered, and betrayed imbecility both of memory and judgment. Mrs Thornton seemed determined to make up, by the exercise of her own conversational talents, for the deficiency of her husband, who, apparently exhausted by the effort, he had felt himself called on to make, remained mute, with distressing vacancy of countenance. I passed a melancholy day. Lucy was at Bath with Lady Willoughby, and there was nothing to obliterate even for a moment, the sad spectacle of decay which I was called on to witness.

At dinner, however, our party was increased by the presence of three sisters of Mrs Thornton, who had, I found, established themselves as stationary inmates at Thornhill. I do not know what the previous situation of these ladies had been, but certainly their present one, did not seem very enviable. When my good stepmother addressed them, she did so with an air of patronage and authority, and they were frequently called on by their more fortunate sister, to discharge offices, which, although trifling in themselves, could not, I thought, but involve mortification, by being publicly demanded. The dinner was served with more attention to routine and display than had formerly been usual. The livery of the servants, which in my recollection had been always plain, was now garnished profusely with lace, and adorned with epaulettes. Splendid candelabras shed a glare on the dinner-table, and the observance of trifling points of minute punctilio was evidently magnified into a duty. This was vulgar. It was the error of one who, elevated to a sphere above her natural pretensions, wished to draw as marked a line as possible between her present station, and that in which she had originally moved.

The dinner passed cumbrously and slowly, and was succeeded by the wine and the dessert. Not by these only, for with them entered a nurse flounced and furbelowed to her middle, and bearing in her arms a rickety and squalling baby. Nothing could exceed the *empressement* displayed by the whole party, in soothing and caressing the little irritable darling. Miss Polly Cumberbatch whistled for its amusement; Miss Emma held down her nose to be grasped by its little fingers, and Miss Margery dangled her watch and trinkets before its eyes, and cried—Da, da!

I was not long suffered to remain ignorant of the relation in which I stood to the diminutive intruder, of whose existence I had not till that moment been aware. It was necessary that I should say some civil things on the beauty and engaging appearance of my little brother, but when its mother, taking advantage of my complaisance, proceeded to propose my taking it in my arms and kissing it, I gave a positive veto to the proposition, and assured her that, from a certain nervous awkwardness, to which I was subject in such circumstances, I had already dropped three children, one of which had broken its leg, and another fractured its skull, by falling on a marble floor. This declaration had the desired effect of relieving me from further importunities, at the trifling expense of becoming an object of detestation to all the females of the party. Never was a penalty more readily paid.

In consequence of my refusal, the bantling was transferred to the arms of its father, by whom it was joyfully received. There is always, I think, something melancholy in the contrast exhibited by the conjunction of infancy and old age—the decrepitude of exhausted powers, and the helplessness of those not yet developed. But besides this, there was something at once sad and disgusting in the spectacle before me. The tears of dotage and fondness flowed down the cheeks of my father, as he kissed the slobbering babe, and dandled it in his withered arms. Had his elder children experienced from him but one tithe of the fondness he lavished on this supererogatory offspring of his declining years, by what strong and undisseverable ties would he not have bound our hearts!

When the ladies retired, and I was left alone with my father in the dining-room, he was evidently uneasy, and embarrassed. I pitied his condition too much, to allude in conversation to any of those topics, which were likely to excite emotion, and soon afforded him relief, by repairing to the drawing-room. There I withdrew myself as much as possible from conversation, and spent the evening with a book. In the morning, I bade farewell to Thornhill, without any regret implied or expressed on the part of its inmates.

CHAPTER XII

But now I am return'd, and that war-thoughts
Have left their places vacant; in their rooms
Come thronging soft and delicate desires,
All prompting me how fair young Hero is,
Saying I liked her, ere I went to wars.
                              Much Ado about Nothing.

My destination was Bath. I was a homeless traveller—a leaf parted from its parent tree, which is wafted where the wind listeth. My sister Lucy was at Bath, and that determined my choice. A day and a night brought me to the conclusion of my journey, and I lost no time in proceeding to Lady Willoughby's. Sir John had died since my departure for the army, and she was now a widow. On inquiring for her residence, I was directed to a handsome house in the Circus; and on my arrival learned from the servant that the ladies were at home. My name was announced. Lucy and Laura were seated in the drawing-room when I entered.

Never did fawn spring more lightly from its lair in the mountains, when its ear is suddenly startled by the distant baying of the hounds, than did Lucy to embrace me. In a moment she was in my arms, and I felt the throbbing of her young heart as I pressed her to my bosom. For a few seconds she was breathless and overcome; then bending back her head, she gazed upon my face, as if anxious to read there an answer to questions, which she could not speak.

Never had I gazed on a picture of simple and expressive beauty, like that which then rivetted my eyes. From the position of her head, the ringlets of her dark brown hair, fell backwards, and left her forehead bare. Her cheeks were flushed, and her eyes, which were fixed on mine with looks of joy and love, were brighter than, till then, I had deemed it possible for human eyes to be.

Lucy, though by no means a delicate flower, had been overpowered by the unexpectedness of the meeting; but she soon recovered, and never was there a happier maiden, as she sat with my large and tawny hand clasped in both of hers, listening with eager interest to narratives of broil, battle, and escape.

But Lucy, dear as she was, did not wholly engross my attention. Laura Willoughby was there. She received and welcomed me as an old friend,—as one who had been her playmate in infancy, and of whom she still cherished a pleasing, though distant remembrance. As for me, it was natural that I should gaze on her with more than common interest and curiosity. I had left Laura Willoughby a child, and she had now grown up into a woman. She had been the Lady of my childish love; love in which my boyhood had felt the first foretaste of passion; perhaps too airy to be permanent, yet too pleasing to have faded from my memory. Her figure, as I now beheld her, was a little inclining to *en bon point*, but well and symmetrically formed. I do not know, that, considered in its individual features, notwithstanding its extreme sweetness of expression, her face would have been reckoned beautiful. Perhaps not, for the charm that hung around her, proceeded less from any distinct and peculiar perfection, of form or feature, than from a general harmonious combination of them all. When quiescent, her countenance generally bore something of that calm tranquillity of expression, that still, and almost death-like beauty, which is shed around the finer creations of Chantrey or Joseph, and mingles with the admiration of the spectator, somewhat of awe. But it was in speaking that she appeared most captivating; for then the eloquent blood mounted into her cheek, and the words breathed by one of the most musical of human voices, were rendered even more charming, by the sparkling comment of her eye.

In Lucy, too, a striking change was visible. From a fat and chubby child, she had sprung up into a tall and elegant girl. The flush of health was on her cheek, life in the sparkle of her eyes, and her dark-brown hair, yet innocent of *papillotes* and curling-irons, hung down in beautiful ringlets, nearly to her shoulders. The changes of time had been favourable to her beauty, and entirely removed a certain cock of the nose, which approached somewhat too closely to the character of *snub*, not occasionally to incur the application of that odious expletive. Altogether, there was something *riant* in the character of her countenance, and one might read in its expression, the lightness of the heart within. It was indeed a countenance which not even the nose of Slawkenbergius could have rendered other than delightful.

Lady Willoughby received me with kindness almost maternal; and to enjoy as much as possible the society of Lucy, I determined on making Bath my head-quarters during the period of my leave. The season then passing had been to Lucy the memorable one in which her career of gaiety had commenced, in which, according to common phrase, she had been *brought out*. I had never yet enjoyed an opportunity of mingling much in the gay world, and I was delighted at the opportunity now afforded me, of doing so, and of acting, in some respects, as a guardian and protector to my sister, on her first entrance into life. To me, as to her, the gay assemblies, in which I then for the first time formed an unit, were arrayed in all the charms of novelty. There is a freshness of spirit which one brings to the first enjoyment of such things which lingers but for a brief space, and then departs to return no more.

'Tis odour fled
As soon as shed ;
'Tis morning's winged dream ;
'Tis a light that ne'er shall shine again
On Life's dull stream.

I enjoyed Bath then, but I have never had the spirit to try it again. I am sure it would be insipid. The dull monotony of the pump-room promenades,—the eternal routine of balls and parties, different, yet the same,—varying in trifling accessaries, unvarying in essentials. Who would travel like a horse in a mill, eternally in the same track? And yet Bath remains the same,—it is *I* who am changed. The mountain still towers, but Mahomet has passed away.

The circumstances which I learned from Lucy, connected with Jane's marriage, were such as to excite strong fears for her happiness. Hewson, (I had heard of the man before,) was a wealthy profligate, who having run a career of more than youthful dissipation, had, with a heart rendered callous, and a head silvered by debauchery, determined on marrying. Jane, sensitive, delicate, and retiring, was not, it may appear, a person likely to captivate such a man ; and yet it was so. He admired her perhaps, for the contrast she afforded to the coarser class of females, with whom alone in the career to which his early years had been devoted, his taste had led him exclusively to associate. His character was known, and he was one of those persons whom prudent mothers took care to exclude from the society of their daughters. But he was master of a fine estate, and others were not wanting, who endeavoured to draw him into wedlock, in that most visionary of all expectations, that the attractions of a wife would convert the worn-out *roué* into a fond and respectable husband.

Vain hope ! The Leopard may change his spots, and the Ethiop his skin, but the leprosy of such a man reaches to the core,—it pervades his system,—his very vitals are contaminated,—his veins circulate venom,— Vice has set her signet on his heart, and the impression is ineffaceable.

Hewson, too, was a man of sporting celebrity, and possessed precisely so much honour and morality as is considered necessary in the circle of Newmarket. He was, indeed, an experienced economist in morals, and his supply of marketable virtue was always precisely proportioned to the " effectual demand. " The value of the commodity was never depreciated by any excess of production. Not good enough to excite one scintilla of esteem, and scarcely bad enough to be expelled from respectable society,—not so openly fraudulent in his dealings as to be considered a Blacklegs, and yet enough so to be distinguished as a " sharp fellow, " and " an old one, "—such was Hewson.

Was it possible for Jane to love such a person,—to marry him? To love him,—no. To marry him,—unfortunately, yes. Mrs Thornton was

too anxious to rid her establishment of a person, whose presence, retiring
and unassuming as she was, could not but frequently be felt as a check
and a control, not to back with all her influence the proposal of Hewson.
My father, I do him but justice in believing, would never, in the full
possession of his faculties, have consented to such a sacrifice of his
daughter. Then, alas! he could scarcely be considered, as a moral and
responsible agent, and at once governed and deluded by his wife, joined
his influence to her's in promoting his daughter's misery.

Deep must have been the cruelty and persecution by which poor Jane
was driven to seek for refuge even in so hateful an union. Yet Hewson's
manners had nothing in them, of the grossness of the debauchee. No one
knew better than he, how to cast a veil over his depravity, and cover a
rotten heart, with a fair exterior. That Jane knew his character, I do not
believe; for how could a creature so innocent and inexperienced,
conceive the existence of a being like Hewson? It was impossible. Beset
by importunity,—urged by parental authority,—suffering under daily
cruelty and mortification,—without enjoyment in the home, which till
then had been so dear to her, and in which present misery must have
been rendered more bitter, by the remembrance of former happiness,
with no friend to comfort or advise, is it wonderful—is it unnatural—
that she should sink under such difficulties, and become the wife of
Hewson?

It is at least *true*,—she did so.

I entered into all the gaieties of Bath, and it was delightful to me to
observe the effect of such scenes, on a spirit formed so naturally for their
enjoyment, as that of Lucy. Scarcely, as her light form passed down the
dance, did she seem to touch the ground, but like a winged creature,
skimmed along its surface, with her small feet twinkling to the sound of
music.

My eyes were not wholly occupied with this fair vision—often were
they turned to another, as fair and not less delightful,—Laura Willoughby. How, with looks rivetted on her countenance, did I not drink in
the tones of her silver voice, as they fell like snow-flakes, soft, pure, and
melting on my heart! It was, indeed, impossible for any one, to know
Laura Willoughby, as I did, and not to love her. To the world her
manner probably appeared cold and distant, but beneath that vestal
stillness of expression, I knew there dwelt a spirit of fervent feeling,—of
deep though quiet energy. Yet how different both in character and
degree was the tranquil affection she inspired, from that resistless tornado of passion by which I was soon destined to be overwhelmed!

The circumstances of my escape had blazed abroad, and I found
myself in Bath an object of curiosity and interest. My ear caught
whispers in the Pump-room as I passed, opera-glasses were levelled at
me in the theatre, and bright eyes beamed on me in the ball-room. It was
the period when military enthusiasm was at its height, when victory had

not yet satiated the strong appetite for glory which existed in the public mind. Then, every soldier who had fought in Spain was considered a hero, and a subaltern with a wooden leg attracted as much interest and attention, as Wellington himself, the hero of an hundred fights, in these days of more tempered enthusiasm and calmer feeling. To the vanity of a young man, this could not be but gratifying; and I felt with the Roman satyrist,

Pulchrum est digito monstrari et dicier, hic est.

Till then I was not conscious of anything peculiarly heroic in my own character; but in this matter I was not peculiarly bigotted to my own opinion, and soon brought myself to partake sincerely enough, in the general sentiment respecting my hitherto latent merits and achievements. In truth, I believe, our real value is generally that which the world puts on us. Let a man, however gratuitously, be irrevocably set down in public opinion as a scoundrel, and he is pretty sure to become one—let the courage of a martyr be lauded in another, and he will die bravely at the stake. Men's powers and passions, alike depend on surrounding circumstances for their development, nor is it impossible, had these been changed, that Sir William Curtis might have ruled the senate, while Canning stammered at a city feast. So true it is

Men's judgments are
A parcel of their fortunes; and things outward
Do draw the inward quality after them,
To suffer all alike.

Of all places in the world, Bath is perhaps the best for meeting odd figures, and as one calculates on being brought in contact with queer people, they are generally seen with little interest, and no surprise. But there was a party at one of the subscription balls, to which the attention of the company seemed peculiarly directed. It consisted of a mother and five daughters. In the morning, we had seen them at the Pump-room; but their veils, and the fashionable shape of bonnet then prevalent, were so successful in concealing their countenances, that nothing had been recognised but their costume. That, indeed, was sufficiently bizarre, and, joined to the general oddity of deportment which distinguished the party, had excited peculiar observation.

Their appearance at the ball was no less remarkable. The mother wore a gown of light purple, with a necklace of huge amethysts, the whole surmounted by a turban of the brightest yellow. The five young ladies (young by courtesy,) were gorgeously furnished forth, in dresses of Pompadour satin. The air and language of the party were singularly novel and outré. They partook in nothing of the manner and appearance of those around them. There was a certain rawness of bone, an indescribable air of sauvagerie, which marked them, as distinctly as Celt can be distinguished from Goth, even by the eyes of Mr Pinkerton, to belong to a different variety of the species from those among whom they mingled. One of them looked like a man in petticoats, and strode through the room with the air of a grenadier. Another might almost have passed muster, had her dress been long enough to have concealed feet about the length of a folio, and the breadth of an octavo volume. Two were disfigured by red elbows, and high cheek-bones, and the fifth was easily recognisable by a wreath of white roses intertwined with locks, whose brightness of hue, it was impossible for the grossest flattery, to reduce to auburn.

The faces of this singular-looking party, being displayed for conquest, I recognised them at the first glance to be those of my aunt and cousins, with whom I had parted at Balmalloch. I was not a little surprised at thus encountering my relations, in a situation and circumstances so unlooked for. My first object was to avoid recognition, but it was impossible. It was too plain by the direction of their glances, that I was already recognised, and that the impending calamity admitted of no escape. I lost no time, therefore, in preparing Lucy for the interview, by informing her of the name and quality of the strangers, to whom, I was aware, it would soon become necessary that I should introduce her. The drama, indeed, was obviously verging rapidly towards the catastrophe, for when I rose to dance with Miss Willoughby, I had the mortification to perceive that Miss Thomasina Spreull was led to the same set by Mr Archibald Shortridge, junior, son, as my readers may perhaps remember, to the worthy *ci-devant* chief magistrate, of the Commercial Metropolis of Scotland.

Mr Shortridge was dressed as superbly as rings, brooches, gold chains, and the skill of a Wapping or a Glasgow tailor, [certainly one or other,] could make him. His golden locks were spread out in the utmost amplitude of friz, of which the art of the peruquier could render them susceptible, and every eye-glass in the room was put in requisition, as with that sort of walk, generally known by the name of *heel and toe*, he led his fair partner to her station.

The astonishment of the company, however, did not reach its perihelion, till they began to dance. With agility, in Bath at least, quite unprecedented, increased perhaps, on the present occasion, by the desire of display, this gifted couple commenced, by springing at least three feet above the level of the floor, and whirling themselves in the air, with a command of muscle altogether wonderful; while their return to earth from these aerial saltations, was signalised by gestures and curvatures of the body, scarcely less worthy of admiration.

For the benefit of those readers, whom the facilities of steam-travelling have not yet tempted, to pay a visit to the portion of our island, north of the Tweed, I may here mention, that the steps danced by my fair cousin and her partner, were those of the *Highland Fling*, a dance which, although deservedly popular among " Caledonia's Mountaineers, " is probably still destined to remain a rare exotic in the South. I would have given—I know not what, but certainly a great deal, to have avoided the public recognition of acquaintances, whose appearance and deportment, were evidently objects of ridicule, to the whole assembly. But, *dis aliter visum,* it was otherwise decreed. In passing down the country-dance, it became necessary, by the figure, that I should turn Miss Thomasina Spreull. Mutual salutations of course passed between the fair *danseuse* and myself.

"Bless me, " said she, capering loftily as she spoke, " is this you! Mamma will be so glad to see you. She's been bobbing to you for the last half hour, but you would never look our way. "

I answered, civilly and briefly as possible, by inquiring for her health and that of her family, and darted off, happy that the mazes of the dance put a stop to a colloquy, of which there were too many listeners to be agreeable.

At the conclusion of the set, any further attempt at evasion being useless, I thought it better to make a merit of necessity, and advance with a good grace to pay my respects to my relations. On doing so, I was saluted by a clatter of tongues from the whole family at once. Their sojourn in the South had softened down none of their national peculiarities, either of accent or expression, and my welcome was pronounced in the broadest Doric of their native land. The first burst of recognition, having subsided, our dialogue became gradually more intelligible.

"Waes me, but ye're poor in the flesh, by when ye was at Balmalloch, " said the mother, eying me as a butcher eyes a calf, that he has some intention of purchasing ; " but nae doot, that's wi' campaigning. "

"Hoot, mother, " interrupted one of her daughters, "it's a' the fashion now to be slim and genteel, and in my opinion Mr Thornton's no a pin the waur o' the change. But, to be sure, he's sair freckled. "

"Whare are ye biding? " resumed the mother; " and wha's that auncient dooager o' a lady, that's matroneezin' the twa young anes? Yin o' them's yere sister, I ettle, and twa better faurt lasses I never set my een on, mair especially the douce-lookin' sonsy yin ye've just been dancing wi'. The ither, too, is very bonny, but she's young, and no just filled oot yet sae weel as she will be ; but, bless me, sic a lauchin' and kecklin' as she's keepin' up wi' her neebour, that seems o' a mair douce and composed character. "

I informed my new friends of the name and character of the different persons composing our party, and nothing could exceed the impatience expressed by them all to be introduced to their cousin. Wishing as much as possible to avoid attracting public attention, I proposed they should remain in their places, and that I should bring Lucy, to undergo the ceremony of introduction. This proposal, however, was rejected. They insisted on making the first advances, and simultaneously rose to traverse in a body, the whole length of the apartment, which intervened between them and the object of their search. This motion *en masse*, was effected amid the tittering and stare of the company, to my infinite discomfiture, and was not perhaps rendered less ludicrous, by the dismay expressed on the countenances of Lady Willoughby and her party, on observing, that this irruption of the Philistines was directed towards them. I endeavoured to regulate the introduction, with as much regard to decorum and propriety as possible.

"Mrs Spreull, Lady Willoughby—Lady Willoughby, my relation Mrs Spreull. Lady Willoughby, my cousins," pointing to the disorderly host coming forward like a party of Highland caterans; "Lucy, my dear, let me present you to your aunt and cousins."

No sooner were these last words uttered, than poor Lucy felt a pair of long bony arms clasped about her neck, and a huge bearded mouth in the act of kissing her cheek, which had flushed to the deepest crimson. The *Scot* did not stand more afflicted and aghast when

"The shadowy kings of Banquo's fated line
Through the dark cave in gleamy pageant passed—"

than did poor Lucy, as the fated and apparently interminable line of her aunt and cousins, successively came forward, at once claiming and enforcing the privilege, of an affectionate embrace. Then rose many voices of loud and discordant gratulation, more than half unintelligible, as she stood in the centre of a circle of her blood relations, all bent on demonstrations of most unwelcome kindness. One patted her neck, and assured her she was the gleggest and bonniest young thing she had ever seen. Another sadly deranged the economy of her hair, by pushing back the ringlets from her forehead, as she declared her inheritance of the *bree* of the Spreulls. Another admired prodigiously, a string of pearls which encircled her neck, from which hung a small diamond locket containing her mother's hair, and after a minute inspection, pronounced them beautiful and genuine.

I saw all this was perfect martyrdom to poor Lucy, and did everything in my power to create a diversion in her favour. Lady Willoughby assisted me with her usual good nature,—spoke to Mrs Spreull,—requested her and her daughters to be seated, and at length, with much difficulty and exertion, succeeded in reducing the mighty chaos into something like order. Poor Lucy's dress had suffered considerably, in the closeness of the engagement, to which she had been exposed, and she took the earliest opportunity afforded her, of an honourable retreat.

For myself, I was still exposed to molestation. Mr Archibald Shortridge, who had been overlooked in the brunt of the battle, now came forward, and insisted on making himself a prominent object in the group. Accosting me, with what he no doubt considered an air of elegant familiarity, with one hand in the pocket of his yellow breeches, and the other stretched forth in token of old acquaintance, he commenced his friendly greeting.

"Damme, Thornton, how's a' wi' you?—devilish glad to see you,—tired of the fighting trade, ey? that's but a poor business to embark in, all loss and no profit. I'm thinkin, it would have been a better spec to have turned merchant, and chirted yoursell into a snug birth with old David."

My countenance must certainly be one of no expression, for the look I endeavoured to throw into it must otherwise, I think, have had the effect of stopping this odious gabble. This look, and a cold bow of recognition were indeed the only answer it received; but not at all daunted, Mr Shortridge proceeded—

"I saw the old gentleman lately, but he's cursedly changed since you left Glasgow, quite failed; he can hardly jog his trotters along the Trongate, and goes to the coffee-room in a chair. Bless my soul, what a lot o' money he keeps in the bank! A capital old boy to fly a kite on. I suppose you sometimes touch him up with a fifty? if you don't, you're a fool for your pains, and were I in your shoes, I'd make the old codger trundle the mouldy blunt out of his money bags, to some purpose, I warrant you."

This was carrying the joke somewhat too far; and I instantly adopted what I thought effectual steps, for putting a stop to further outrage from this impudent babbler.

"Mr Shortridge," I replied, "I do not imagine you have any intention of insulting me, and am ready to attribute to your ignorance of the world, the extremely improper expressions you have thought fit to use, both with regard to my uncle and myself. I am not accustomed to hear such language, and request that it may not be repeated."

He was obviously a little what sailors call taken aback by this address, and apologized with a look of somewhat diminished assurance; but his vulgar audacity soon returned, and I was glad to escape from it by leading Miss Willoughby again to the dance.

Since I saw him last, he had become doubly detestable. He had been led by business, to a temporary residence in London, and thus, in addition to the indigenous vulgarity which still clung to him, he had acquired much of that vile Cockney slang and underbred assumption, which mark the beaux of Broad Street and Pudding Lane.

I was apologizing to my partner, for the annoyance to which she had been exposed, from my Vandal relations, when my indignation was suddenly roused to its utmost pitch, by observing this Glasgow Yahoo lead my sister Lucy, as his partner to the dance. The possibility of such an occurrence, had never for a moment been present to my thoughts, or I should have taken effectual means to prevent so unpleasant a consummation. Poor Lucy, I afterwards found, had at first declined dancing; but urged by the united clamour of her Scotch cousins, who declared it " both a sin and a shame sae young and bonny a creature should sit still wi' the auld folk, instead o' kicking her heels about wi' the young anes, " she had, with the infirmity of purpose natural to her age, suffered herself to be persuaded, to adopt what appeared the smaller evil, and danced with Mr Shortridge, in order to avoid the continuance of solicitations, at once urgent and disagreeable.

With what an air of self-complacent triumph the booby led her to the dance, and made it evident, by the alternation of his glances, that his admiration was nearly equally divided, between his fair partner and his yellow breeches ! Then, to see the villain, as he stood opposite to her, deliberately produce from his breeches-pocket, a huge silver snuff-box, and having tapped the lid with his knuckles, proceed to offer her a pinch ! One kick, one single solitary kick, inflicted on the monster, in the act of perpetrating such unheard-of enormities, would have been as balm to my spirit, and have lightened the burden under which it groaned. But, alas ! even this trifling consolation was denied me, and I was compelled passively to behold the inhuman barbarian lead my sister down the dance, jumping like a kangaroo, and followed by the ridicule of the whole assembly.

Mortified as Lucy was, her gravity could not stand the exhibition of her partner, and she found it impossible to refrain from laughing. But even this, the stupid savage seemed to consider as a compliment to his skill, and capered if possible even higher than before. On the whole, I found that " *digito monstrari,* " was not always so pleasant a thing, as I had imagined ; and I retired to rest that night, in no very amiable state of mind and feeling, firmly resolved to quit Bath forthwith, in order to escape any further mortification from the presence of these pestilent relations.

CHAPTER XIII

Knights and dames I sing
Such as the times may furnish. 'Tis a flight
Which seems at first, to need no lofty wing,
Plumed by Longinus, or the Stagyrite :
The difficulty lies in colouring
(Keeping the due proportions still in sight,)
With Nature, manners which are artificial,
And rendering general that which is especial.
BYRON.

WITH the morning, better thoughts came. These good people were simple and warm-hearted, and I was not ungrateful enough in my calmer moments, to forget the kindness of their welcome at Balmalloch. That estate had been purchased by my uncle, and the ladies were now possessed of a very considerable fortune in money, with the world all before them where to choose. A sudden desire of mingling in fashionable society, and becoming denizens of the *beau monde*, had been endemic in the family. They set up a gay equipage, and bidding " farewell to beggarly Scotland, " now blazed forth in native and reflected radiance, in a handsome tenement in Bath.

Their domestic circle had been increased by the marriage of one of the elder Miss Spreulls, and had the speedy prospect of being still more so, by its fruits; for Mrs M'Craw, wife of Major Gulliver M'Craw of Cockapistle, in the county of Aberdeen, was evidently in the way that women wish to be, who love their lords. The Major was a tall gaunt man, with enormous black whiskers, and a face the colour of Lundy Foot's Irish snuff, who had served with distinction in the Royal African Corps, and survived a residence of nearly twenty years in Sierra Leone. By the death of a brother, he had succeeded to the small paternal inheritance, to which his lady was now about to furnish him with an heir. The Major was solemn and taciturn, not addicted to light conversation, but partial to Sangoree and tobacco-smoking. It was made no secret in the family that Miss Thomasina Spreull was soon about to follow the example of her sister, and, at the suit of Mr Archibald Shortridge, become a votary of Hymen.

I received from the Spreulls much interesting information with regard to my uncle. He was fast declining into the vale of years, and had not escaped the infirmities of increasing age. The account of Mr Shortridge, which from its manner had excited my indignation, was true as to matter. My old and warm-hearted friend,—for friend, in the widest acceptation of the term, I knew him to be,—was beginning to pay the penalty of life extended beyond its usual limits. I learned that Girzy, too, (for my inquiries extended to that faithful domestic,) began likewise to show traces of incipient senility, yet was active and bustling as ever ; and though my uncle, as formerly, vehemently insisted on being king in his own establishment, the subdolous Girzy, by prudently resigning all external symbols of domestic power, still managed to secure its substantial enjoyment. Mr Spreull having become the purchaser of Balmalloch, was now proprietor of his ancestorial estate ; and I believe neither Major nor Mrs M'Craw were without hopes, that the expected produce of their union, might one day add the succession of Balmalloch, to that of Cockapistle.

I have already said, that I received occasional letters from my uncle. These were generally charged with friendly monition and advice, not always, indeed, very applicable to my situation and circumstances, but evidently dictated by strong regard, and anxiety for my welfare and prosperity. His was a heart of hard materials, and difficult to move to kindness ; but the impression once made, it was indelible. " There are some hearts, " says Crabbe, that great master of human character,

> " Which are like wax : apply them to the fire,
> Melting, they take the impression you desire,
> Easy to mould and fashion as you please,
> And again moulded, with an equal ease ;
> Like smelted iron, some the forms retain,
> But once impress'd, will never melt again. "

Thus my boyish freedom, and entire absence of artifice, and perhaps the discovery that I really loved him, and found pleasure in his society, had established me at an elevation in his good graces, from which I think scarcely any after misconduct on my part could have occasioned my fall.

On the day following the ball, the whole family of Spreull, escorted by Major M'Craw and Mr Archibald Shortridge, came to call at Lady Willoughby's. I was there when they arrived. They entered the drawing-room in long array, the *cortége* being headed by the Major, who appeared flanked by Mrs Spreull and his lady. The veteran advanced with an air of solemn dignity to the head of the apartment, where Lady Willoughby was seated on a sofa, and on being presented to her ladyship by his mother-in-law, he performed three separate salaams, with a formality and stiffness which would have done no discredit to Dr Pangloss.

Though the motions of the head of the column were thus unusually ceremonious, the same observation certainly did not apply to the centre and rear, which advanced in tumultuous disorder, like that of the Trojans in the third book of the Iliad. Miss Duncan and Miss Thomasina, the youngest and most loquacious of the party, seated themselves beside Lucy and Laura, with whom they instantly commenced a conversation, of which balls, lace, fashions, jewels, theatres, and dress, were the subject. When the party had become sedentary, and Mr Archibald Shortridge had wriggled into a chair, where he sat with crossed legs, coaxing his hair into an erect position, (which from its being naturally rather limber and oleaginous, seemed a matter of some difficulty,) and displaying a pair of enormous brass heel-spurs which adorned his boots; I had leisure to attend to the conversation, which commenced between Mrs Spreull and Lady Willoughby.

"I houp your leddyship," began the former matron, "wasna the waur o' the ba' last night. It was just extraordinar het and overpoorin'. I likit that kind o' amusement weel eneuch in my day, but I'm gettin ower auld for't noo. Though, when one has dochters to bring out into the world, it's really necessar, mair especially in a place like Bath, for a prudent mither to keep an ee ower them, to see they dinna fa' in wi' discreditable folk, that are aye on the look out for weel tochered lasses, and ready eneuch to tak a' advantage o' their youth and inexperience."

Lady Willoughby, who had been able to collect the drift of this address, though many of its expressions were unintelligible, answered by yielding a civil assent to the propositions of Mrs Spreull, on which encouragement that lady proceeded.

"It's a sair tax on me, I assure your leddyship, but it's one I houp that will no continue much longer to fa' on my shouthers. For there's my dochter David,—that's her sittin' there beside the gudeman—will soon be able to tak my place, and matroneeze her sisters. But you see she's near the downlying, and no just at present in a condition to appear in public.—Major, you had better get her a cod and a foot-stool, for, puir soul, she seems no that easy in that cane-bottomed chair."

The Major rose, with the stiffness of a church-steeple, to perform the task assigned him, and of course all eyes were turned on his interesting helpmate, to whose situation the attention of the company had been so pointedly directed. That lady, however, betrayed no symptoms of embarrassment, on finding herself thus suddenly the object on which the gaze and interest of the party, were concentrated. The truth, I believe to be, that a spinster who unexpectedly changes her condition, at that critical period of female life, when the horrors of antiquated maidenhood are felt to be nearly impending, is naturally led to think more highly than usual, of the honours of the *femme couverte*, and to display perhaps an overweening pride, in the prominent demonstration of approaching maternity.

The object of the Major's mission was rendered unnecessary, by two of the young ladies insisting on Mrs M'Craw taking their places on the sofa, where, with cushions judiciously adjusted to her back by the tender care of her spouse, she reclined in a pleasant and self-complacent consciousness, of the interest she had excited.

My attention, which had been hitherto otherwise engaged, was now turned to Mr Shortridge, who, drawing his chair nearer to Miss Willoughby, appeared determined to begin a conversation.—" Fine day, ma'am. "

A slight nod of acquiescence from the lady.

" Have you seen the papers this morning, ma'am? "

" No, sir; I seldom read newspapers. "

" No read the papers! That's astonishing; I could not live without them. There's an account in the Traveller to-day, of a horrid murder, that amused me so much this morning at breakfast. The brains of a whole family knocked out; the maid-servant with her throat cut from ear to ear, and a butcher's knife found sticking in the small ribs of an infant in the cradle. I'll be happy to send you over the paper, ma'am, if you wish to see it. "

The proposal was civilly declined, and the assailant, finding his approaches in this quarter not very likely to succeed, changed his point of attack.

" Have you been long in Bath, ma'am? "

" Some weeks. "

" It's very stupid, ma'am, isn't it? Terrible riff-raff set the company at the ball last night—very few of the right sort, but plenty of what I call tag-rag and bobtail—people one wouldn't choose to know, if one met them in Pall Mall or St James's Street. You've been in London, ma'am, haven't you? "

" Yes, sir. "

" Ah, that's the place to go it in style; Bath's nothing to London.— Tommy, " addressing his intended, " when we're married, I must have you to town, to show you a little of life; what do you say to that, my tight wench? "

Tommy, as he called her, expressed perfect acquiescence in the proposal; but observing how much poor Laura was annoyed, by the pertinacious continuance of this vulgar balderdash, I took occasion to cut short the conversation by stepping up between her and the object of her annoyance, turning on the latter what Lord Castlereagh would have called a *back front*. This had the desired effect, and the booby, if not silenced, at least directed his conversation to those, the meridian of whose taste it better suited.

From the samples of my relations which I have already exhibited, the reader may imagine that their society, which it was impossible wholly to escape, was an abundant source of annoyance and mortification. But these, after all, diminished in a trifling degree, the sum total of our enjoyment. With Laura Willoughby I experienced that sort of pleasure, which arises from the almost abstract consciousness of being an object of interest to a young and beautiful female. I loved her; but when I now calmly reflect and analyse the feelings by which I was moved at that period, I think my love was that of a brother, and I imagined it was in that light she regarded me.

The days flew by, as days of happiness ever do, on fleeting wings. The destined period of Lady Willoughby's stay at Bath had elapsed, and she returned to Middlethorpe. She carried with her the only inducements I had to a longer residence there—Laura and Lucy. They were gone, and notwithstanding I had formed a pretty large circle of such acquaintance as one generally contrives to pick up at a watering place, I felt that my chief objects of interest had been removed, and I roamed about the streets, with all the feelings of a solitary man. The gaieties by which I was surrounded, had lost their zest; I was like Jaques, in the mood of being " melancholy and gentlemanlike. "

In such a state of mind, I determined to quit Bath for London, in search of new objects of excitement, which might stir the sluggish current of my spirits, into more rapid motion. Having resolved on speedy departure, I was walking in the Circus, in a fit of blue-devils, and abstraction from Bath and its concerns, when a portly elderly gentleman, either from hurry or blindness, or a fit of musing like my own, ran up bolt against me. The shock was something like that, one has read of as occurring between two ships at sea, which have happened to run aboard of each other in the dark. For myself, being the lighter vessel, I was most damaged by the concussion; and on recovering my senses, which were at first somewhat deranged by the rudeness, as well as suddenness of the encounter, I looked towards my opponent, with no very amiable feelings. Had I known nothing of the man, it would still have been impossible to be angry. He sputtered out a thousand apologies, attributed the accident to his blindness, and bore himself as a person of consummate tact, and knowledge of the world, might be supposed to do in such unpleasant circumstances.

It was Lord Amersham. I immediately made myself known to him, and, of course, vied in assuming, for my own absence and awkwardness, the whole blame of our collision.

"Ah, my good friend Thornton, " exclaimed his Lordship, on learning who I was, " I can scarcely call this a pleasant meeting for old friends—not a pleasant mode of meeting at least—for to meet with you must always be pleasant. Ha, ha ! to think that so gay and gallant a man of war, should be run down, by an old, crazy, and heavy-sailing hulk like myself. Glad to see you, at all events,—hope your excellent father is quite well, and your sisters—Gad, I hear they are fine girls, very fine girls. Ah, and there's a marriage too, I hear, to congratulate you on. Wish you joy, with all my heart,—everything one could wish,—good family and large fortune. From the army, I suppose—not wounded, or on the sick list, I hope,—come home for a little pleasure, eh ?—I know what young men are—like to sweeten Mars with a little of Venus, and then run back to campaigning,—too young yet to change like me, the

sword for the plough—mustn't think of that, for the next twenty years. "
It was in vain to attempt stopping his lordship, in the full career of
speech, and I waited till he was fairly out of breath before I attempted a
reply. Having then with difficulty hitched in an answer to the more
prominent queries of his address, I expressed a hope that Lady Amersham and [my heart fluttered as my lips pronounced the name] Lady
Melicent were well.

"Thank you, thank you, Melicent quite well,—but poor Lady
Amersham—of course you know, very bad indeed—sadly changed
since you saw her—Sir Henry ordered change of air, and sent us to Bath
for a fortnight,—thought the waters might do her good. Here's my
card,—don't see company, but always glad to see you. Good bye, my
dear Thornton—Colonel, eh—Major—pardon my not giving you your
proper title—always in a hurry, you know—it's my failing, can't help
it—what's bred in the bone, eh—you know the rest—hope to see you
very soon. Good morning. "—So saying, this antiquated Mercutio set
off at a pace between a walk and an amble, while I stood gazing after
him, till, by turning the corner of the street, he was lost to my view. Then
I continued my walk, but in how different a frame of mind from that
which I experienced before this unexpected encounter.

What a strange piece of mechanism is the human heart! What a
revulsion of feeling had been excited in mine by the bare mention of a
name! But it was a name indissolubly linked in my imagination, with
beauty, grace, pride, splendour, and captivation, with days, the memory of which was flattering to my vanity, and therefore fondly cherished.
The gloom which had hung over Bath was gone, and to my eye it seemed
encircled by a zone of light and beauty.

Yet the transports I felt, were not those that swell the breast of a lover,
when the blessed vision of her whom he has long silently, and it may be
hopelessly adored, unexpectedly greets his eye. When even to breathe
the same air—to gaze on the same objects—to hear the same sounds
with her, from whom by time and distance he has been long divided, is in
itself a joy unspeakable, and sheds enchantment on them all. Raptures
such as these, mingled not at all in the delight, which the knowledge of
the near presence of Lady Melicent, had caused so abundantly to
overflow within me. I was spurred onward by a vague stimulus, and was
contented to swim with a current, which carried me, I knew not
whither. My pleasure was a blind one. The society of Lady Melicent had
been to me pregnant with greater excitement than that of any other
woman. She had piqued my vanity, and to become agreeable to one so
accomplished at all points, had roused within me, powers and energies,
which, till then, had lain dormant. I had been flattered, too, with the
belief of success. I imagined that I had succeeded, in rendering myself to
her, an object of more than common interest. I had done this, with no
hope of successful passion, with no definite nor distinct object in view,

beyond the immediate gratification of being pleasing in her eyes, whom all sought to please. This arena, I imagined, was once more opened to me, and I felt as a young and *preux chevalier*, about to enter the lists at a splendid tournament, and try a passage at arms with the bravest and noblest of the land; perhaps scarcely hoping to come off victor, yet conscious, in such a contest, it was pride to have been even a competitor.

The preparations for my departure were countermanded, and on the following day I presented myself at Lord Amersham's. I sent in my card, and in a few moments was admitted. Lady Melicent was the first object that met my eye as I entered the apartment. She was seated at her harp, but rose immediately on my entrance. There was a smile on her countenance, as she approached to welcome me, but I observed none of that hurried tremour, and nervous rapidity of motion, which, I think, must have been observable in myself. She moved slowly and gracefully, and extended towards me a hand unsurpassed for beauty and whiteness, which I grasped in mine, with somewhat more vehemence of pressure, than was perhaps quite suited to the occasion and circumstances. That she perceived this I know, for a slight and scarcely perceptible suffusion, overspread her cheek, but found there no resting-place, for in an instant it was gone.

The usual compliments, and nothing but the usual compliments of meeting, passed between us. At the head of the apartment, in an armchair, propped up by cushions, sat Lady Amersham. I had not observed her at first, but her figure soon caught my eye, and I approached to offer salutation. Eight years had barely elapsed since I had seen her last, and had I not been prepared, by the meeting with Lord Amersham, for a great and striking change, I certainly should not have known her. She was no more like the Lady Amersham, whose image was perdurably imprinted on my memory, than I to Hercules. Nothing of that fine and dignified form, which had formerly struck me with admiration, now remained. Her cheek was hollow, her eyes—those large, dark, proud eyes, twinkled small and dimly from beneath the forehead, by which they were now far overshadowed. It was evident, disease had made sad inroads in her frame; her form was thin and wasted, and she was suffering before the time of its natural advent, the debility of extreme old age. She spoke in a voice so feeble and tremulous as scarcely to be intelligible, and it seemed as if the exertion of speaking was not unaccompanied with pain.

Though it was impossible I should feel more than common interest for one into whose society I had been only once transiently cast, yet I could not regard the spectacle of decay before me without considerable emotion. It seemed as if I stood before the ruins of a splendid and gorgeous palace, fallen from its high estate—deserted—desolate. The contrast of the present and the past occupied my imagination. It was a striking one. I had not seen the gradations of the change; they might

have been slow and gradual, but to me she seemed as one brought low by
some awful and sudden dispensation—one whom the lightning of God
had scathed and smitten, in the very season of her pride.

This train of thought, however, was suddenly interrupted. A servant
entered, and announced that the Earl of Lyndhurst was below, and
solicited admission. " Not at home, " was the laconic answer, and the
menial made his instant exit.

There was something in the unhesitating and decisive manner in
which these words were spoken by Lady Melicent, which implied that
the person suing for admission was disagreeable to her, and there was
something in the circumstances of Lord Lyndhurst which made them,
perhaps, more than usually remarkable.

He was a young man, who had recently succeeded to an Earldom,
and a princely fortune, and his arrival at Bath had excited a " strong
sensation " among speculative mothers, and marriageable daughters. It
was understood that, like an Eastern Sultan, he had only to throw the
handkerchief, in order to concentrate on one happy female, the envy of
her sex. Such was the person to whom Lady Melicent had in so marked a
manner denied admission.

A minute or two had barely passed in that kind of conversation,
which, though not perhaps interesting in itself, frequently leads to that
which is so, when our dialogue was interrupted by the entrance of Lord
Amersham, accompanied by Lord Lyndhurst.

" Very pretty work this ! " exclaimed his lordship ; " at home to one
young gentleman, and denied to another ; very pretty, upon my honour.
Why, it seems that you young soldiers, Thornton, have only to cry,
Open Sessamé, to be admitted everywhere. Ha, ha, ha ! However, as the
Scotch say, 'Blood's thicker than water;' and as Melicent can plead
relationship as a sort of excuse in this case, I suppose it must be admitted.
Lord Lyndhurst, Captain Thornton—Captain Thornton, Lord Lynd-
hurst. "

The person to whom I had thus the honour of being introduced, was a
young man, apparently of three or four and twenty, with fair hair, face
round and full, not remarkable for expression ; figure well formed and
somewhat inclining to obesity, and marked altogether by that easy
confidence of manner in society, arising from a full and habitual sense of
his own consequence, and claims to distinction. On the whole, he was
good-looking, but there was a want of spirit and animation, both in his
countenance and manner, which in some degree derrogated from the
amount of his claims to personal attraction.

The ceremony of introduction being concluded, Lord Lyndhurst
threw himself on an ottoman, and with an air of easy *nonchalance*,
addressed occasionally a question or an observation to Lady Melicent. From the little I could gather of his conversation, in the moments of interval I could snatch between the voluble sentences of Lord

Amersham, it was of that light and uninteresting sort, which is the common vehicle of intercourse in well-bred society, and is the better fitted, perhaps, for its purpose, that it calls forth no latent difference either of sentiment or opinion. His manner in addressing her was free, and altogether unmarked by any of that diffidence of manner, which at once betrays an anxiety to please, and an apprehension of failure in the attempt.

Lady Melicent, on her part, listened to him with that sort of air, which betrayed consciousness of superior powers; such as a very clever person may sometimes be detected in assuming when conversing with one of inferior talents, with whom he feels it is some condescension to place himself on a footing of temporary equality. This, however, was unnoticed; Lord Lyndhurst had nothing about him of *mauvaise honte*, and was, perhaps, too conscious of his own value and importance to feel the slightest apprehension of a rebuff.

In this state of things, a servant entered, and announced to Lady Melicent that the carriage was at the door. On receiving this intelligence, she started up, and declaring she had a world of business before her, tripped out of the apartment, glancing a smile towards me as she departed. I also soon rose to take leave, and after accepting an invitation to dinner, from Lord Amersham, made my *congé* and exit.

CHAPTER XIV

———There, my father's grave
Did utter forth a voice.
Measure for Measure.

Vex not his ghost : Oh, let him pass ! He hates him,
That would upon the rack of this rough world,
Stretch him out longer.
Lear.

DURING the remainder of my stay in Bath, Lady Melicent was to me the loadstar of attraction. Yes, to me she was as some bright particular star, shining far above in the blue firmament of heaven, beautiful to gaze on, and to love, hopeless. Therefore it was, that even in the depth of my admiration, I enjoyed a dreamy and contemplative tranquillity. Never was homage more fervent and sincere offered as a tribute to beauty ; yet my heart was free from passion. I suffered none of that bitterness and depression attendant on a hopeless attachment. I could have tranquilly borne to see her in the possession of another ; even in my waking dreams—those moments of glory and of power,—I had built no fabric of love or of ambition, on a foundation so visionary and fantastic, as that of winning Lady Melicent, to be the lady of my love.

Indeed, in our relative circumstances, it was scarcely possible that such a hope could even for a moment present itself to my fancy. It was generally known that Lord Lyndhurst had already made proposals to Lady Melicent, which, from the continuance of their intercourse, had evidently not been definitively rejected. It was even said, all the preliminary arrangements had been settled to the satisfaction of both families, and that the marriage, which had been delayed only by the illness and precarious state of Lady Amersham, was positively to take place in the course of the following summer.

It may be supposed that an alliance between parties so distinguished afforded matter for abundance of comment and tittle tattle to the *bavardes* of Bath. Many, indeed, were the rumours and speculations, of which it was the daily subject. In one point alone, did all opinions appear to coincide, namely, that the union was one less of love, than policy and expedience ; that it had been concerted and matured, by Lady Lyndhurst and Lord Amersham, and the parties most interested had yielded an assent mutually cold and indifferent, to the project of older, and more calculating heads.

The intimacy, which at our first interview at Staunton, had sprung up, like Adam, full grown even in its birth, was at this our second meeting, a plant of slower, though perhaps of stronger growth. When I had last seen her, Lady Melicent was just emerging into the world, with high and buoyant spirits, conscious of her own pretensions, and eager to start forward into that world, which she felt she was alike calculated to enjoy and to adorn. With too much pride, and too much talent, to form herself on any model, she possessed that delightful freshness and originality of thought and expression, which, requiring a certain degree of nerve and innate power for its display, can only be expected from those who feel their consequence and pretensions to be above the censure and ridicule of the world. In ninety-nine cases out of a hundred, where this is tried it will fail; in Lady Melicent it succeeded. With nothing of sentiment or manner, which it was possible to censure, it was evident at the first glance that Lady Melicent was *singular*; that the impulse of her own spirit was to *lead*, not *follow*; and, without betraying any one very marked peculiarity, there was something in her most trifling speech and action to arrest the attention and interest the fancy. Such was the impression of the Lady Melicent which my visit to Staunton had left on my memory.

When I again met her at Bath, she had been abroad in the world. She was beautiful, but the character of her beauty was changed. When she spoke, the eloquent blood no longer mantled in her cheek, and the sparkle of her eye was somewhat dimmed of its brightness. I missed, too, that extraordinary vivacity, or rather enthusiasm of manner, which in former days had sat upon her with a grace so charming. Her smile, indeed, was beautiful and enchanting as ever, but it was no longer the smile of her youth—perhaps not less captivating—yet different.

I confess, that at first I was disappointed. Lady Melicent was not as I expected to find her. I had not allowed sufficiently for that influence on character, which intercourse with the world never fails to exert. Had not I too undergone a change? Had not ripened years, the gratification of debasing passions, and the lessons of worldly prudence, which I acquired in the interval, changed me from the light and open hearted boy, who had bent before the shrine of her beauty? Had my manhood been such as in the high aspirings of my youthful heart, I had believed and trusted it would have been? No. But the change which is continually taking place in ourselves, we pass unnoticed; while that in others, appears to our eyes with all the strength of contrast.

Whatever disappointment, the change of character perceptible in Lady Melicent, at first occasioned, soon wore off. Being the thing she was, it was impossible to wish her different. She was admired and beautiful; and possessed in an extraordinary degree,

——" that grace and ease,
Which mark security to please. "

Her friend, Mrs Masham, whom our readers have already known in
the character of Miss Pynsent, was at Bath with her husband, the colonel
of a regiment of militia, then stationed there, and it was under her
auspices, Lady Melicent generally went into public. I followed her
everywhere. There was an attraction about her, which I sought not to
analyse, while I yielded to its influence. Lord Lyndhurst was considered
by the world her acknowledged and accepted lover ; and my appearance in her suite, constant as it was, excited neither notice nor suspicion.

While the course of events was thus proceeding, my stay at Bath was
cut short by the death of my father. He had fallen from his chair in an
apoplectic fit, and survived but a few hours. This intelligence was
conveyed in a letter by post, from Miss Polly Cumberbatch, who assured
me, that my worthy stepmother had submitted with Christian resignation to the severe dispensation, but was too ill to write.

I lost no time in setting off for Thornhill. My father had never loved
me, and in the state to which he had been recently reduced, death could
scarcely be considered as an evil. He was not, and could not, be to me an
object of strong affection : yet the intelligence of his sudden death moved
me strongly, and I received it with a fearful awe. An old familiar face
had disappeared for ever. He whom, from the very dawn of life, I had
been accustomed to regard with respect and reverence—who had heard
the first prattle of my infancy—whom I had been early taught to love
and to obey—and whom I had obeyed, but not loved—was no longer
numbered among the living. Never again would his voice fall upon my
ear—never should I behold him but as a livid and lifeless corpse. Such
reflections may be trite, but they are natural, and they engrossed me till
my arrival at Thornhill.

It was winter. The trees were bare, and the snow lay· deep on the
ground. The cold was intense, and having travelled all night, I arrived
about mid-day. The sun was bright, and shed a sort of desolate, but
brilliant splendour, on the face of nature. For the first time in my life, I
returned to Thornhill without a palpitating heart. What did Thornhill
now contain that was dear to me ? Nothing.

As I approached, I gazed around me with a bitter sentiment of
wrong. The inheritance that should have been mine was destined to
another. Like Esau, I had forfeited my birthright, but not like Esau had
I bartered it away. No—As I gazed on my paternal demesne, I felt that
the wealth of the Indies, would not have tempted me to injure or
dismember, the succession of a far-descended line. That which came to
me from my fathers, should have passed to my descendants. But this was
not to be. There was a ban upon my name and fortune, and I, the head
of my family, was fated to endure even worse than the torments of
Macbeth, in seeing my natural inheritance, pass from me, and from my
line, for ever.

Occupied in such reflections, the carriage stopped at the door. I descended, and, on my name being announced, I was shown into an apartment, the windows of which were closed, where, seated by taper-light, I beheld Mrs Thornton and one of her sisters. The ladies were evidently in some bustle, as I entered. A white handkerchief was instantly applied to the eyes of my stepmother, while her sister was unsuccessfully, endeavouring to conceal below the sofa, an embroidery frame and a book, which I afterwards had the curiosity to examine, and found to be a volume of Tom Jones. There was nothing in this interview very moving or sentimental. *Ma belle mère* came forward to receive me, in the character of a disconsolate widow; but finding this part rather too irksome to be kept up longer than occasion required, her lamentations became gradually fainter, and before the conclusion of our interview, she professed a perfect resignation to the will of Divine Providence, and resolved not to yield herself up to sinful sorrow, and unavailing regrets.

Unwilling to mingle more than necessary in society that was disagreeable to me, I requested that two apartments might be made ready for my reception, and stating my intention of confining myself to these, till the time of the funeral, I wished the ladies good morning, and retired.

I found that Mrs Thornton had taken the necessary legal steps of sealing up, in presence of a man of the law, all those places in which either important papers, or valuable property, might be supposed to have been deposited. All suitable arrangements for the funeral had been likewise set on foot; and having written an affectionate letter to each of my sisters, and procured a stock of books from the library, I passed my solitary hours in reading, till the period fixed for the performance of the last obsequies, arrived.

That came, and with it a vast concourse of people to attend the ceremony. The representatives of the old families in the county, forgetting the differences to which the frequent unfortunate exacerbations of my father's temper had given rise, came personally, or sent their carriages, to form part of the procession, less, perhaps, from any personal regard to the deceased, than a desire to show respect to a family, with which most of them, in the course of a century or two, had formed connexions, the memory of which was not yet wholly eradicated.

Occupied by sad and solemn thoughts, I found myself in the carriage, moving slowly towards the place of interment. Once before, I had approached it, to lay the head of my beloved mother in the earth. My father had now followed her, and the awful sounds of dust to dust, were once more about to be pronounced in my hearing, over the remains of him, whom, next to God, she had most loved and honoured. At that moment my heart was softened; all thoughts of wrong had passed away, and tears, the only tears I had shed to his memory, flowed down my cheeks, and restored tranquillity to my spirit.

On opening my father's will, which had been executed only a few months before his death, it was found that he bequeathed his estates, both real and personal, to his wife, with remainder of the former to his son by the second marriage, the latter remaining entirely at her own disposal. Small legacies were likewise left to my sisters, and a trifling one to myself, as heir-at-law.

I could experience little disappointment from the contents of this document. So far as concerned me, they were what I had expected, and announced the completion of that parental enmity, which I had long learned to contemplate with fortitude. But its injustice to my sisters, I could not forgive. Under the circumstances of the case, however, I reflected, with all the calmness and deliberation I could command, on the steps most proper to be pursued. Knowing as I did the state of mental imbecility, to which my father had been reduced, for a considerable time before his death—knowing how perfectly his weakness was open to be practised upon, by a person whose influence over him was so great as that of Mrs Thornton, and knowing, likewise, how strong the motives were, to urge her to an interested exercise of that influence, and considering the strong internal evidence afforded by the tenor of the document itself, that such influence had, in reality, been exercised to the prejudice of his children, I at length resolved to dispute the validity of the will.

This resolution, too, was not a little strengthened by communication with the family physician, who had been in the habit of attending my father, for many years. He expressed his opinion, that, at the date of the will, my father's mind was not in the state necessary for the legal execution of such a document, and his perfect readiness to give evidence to this effect, in a court of justice.

Having formed my decision, I communicated it by letter to Mrs Thornton, and set off for London. There for a while I remained, immersed in business. Evidence was collected on all hands, and at length formed a mass so strong and overpowering, that I was assured, by counsel of the first eminence, there scarcely existed a possibility of an unfavourable result.

During my residence in town, I allowed myself but little participation in the pleasures of society, and none in that society, in which, in former days of youth and gladness, I had delighted to mingle. I was now, for the first time, engaged in business. I felt as if a great and important duty had devolved upon me, and as if called upon to stand forward as the champion, not merely of my own cause, but of that of my family. The interest of my sisters, particularly of Lucy, was deeply involved in my success, and in the new dignity, of knowing myself at once an object of hope and of fear, I felt my importance enlarged in my own eyes, and assumed a gravity both of mind and deportment, to which I had hitherto been a stranger. The charms of youthful dissipation, now exerted their influence in vain. The midnight revel, which called forth the glorious swing of spirits high and unrestrained, combining, in a temporary and mystic communion, beings altogether dissimilar, and united only in the pursuit and the enjoyment of one maddening delight, was now, in my eyes, but little distinguishable from the orgies of coarse and vulgar debauchery. In the change which the plastic influence of circumstances had wrought in my character, these pleasures were no longer for me, nor I for them. I was as a bird which had moulted the gaudy plumage of its youth, for one of stronger pinion, and more sober hue.

I had been several weeks in London, and had effected all the necessary arrangements for the successful prosecution of my suit, when I received a letter from Lord Amersham, of condolence on my father's death, conveying a very kind and cordial invitation, to spend the remainder of my leave in England, at Staunton Court, to which they had already returned from Bath. It mentioned also, that Lady Melicent had written to my sister Lucy, inviting her to accompany me, a request which Lord Amersham entreated I would back with my influence, as the state of his daughter's spirits, depressed by anxiety for her mother, made the presence of such a companion, peculiarly desirable.

For my own part, nothing could be more agreeable, than this invitation. It gave me the means of being again placed within the sphere of that attraction, to whose influence I was ever ready to resign myself, conscious only of the pleasure it afforded. I knew of no danger in thus exposing myself, and I feared none, for no one can appreciate the danger of love, till he has felt its sufferings. I wrote, therefore, to Lucy, expressing my desire that she should accept Lady Melicent's invitation, and desiring her to be in readiness in the following week, when I would myself escort her to Staunton.

In a few days I accordingly left town for Middlethorpe. My reception there was what I knew it would be, warm and cordial. There is a certain kindness of heart, and generosity of feeling, which is sometimes found to be characteristic not merely of individuals, but of families ; and so it was with the Willoughbys. Living in the world, they were nothing worldly, nor did increasing years, in them, appear to obliterate any thing of the warmth and vivacity of youthful feeling. Lady Willoughby had loved my mother, and loved her to the last ; she was gone, but her regard had survived the grave, and was extended to her children.

Frank Willoughby had been the friend of my boyhood. We had been long separated, and in the busy scenes of life, by me he had been forgotten. Time and absence, however, had, apparently, nothing diminished the warmth of his regard, and in the companion of my childhood, I found the friend of my maturer years. Laura, too, she loved my sisters, and extended a share of her affection even to myself. When we met, the blood for an instant forsook her cheeks. I extended my hand, and it received hers. My pressure was not returned ; her fingers were in mine, passive and motionless as those of the dead. Few and brief were the answers, which Laura Willoughby afforded to the kind inquiries of meeting. She seemed anxious to conceal by silence, the difficulty of utterance occasioned by inward emotion. Soon, however, did her cheek recover its bloom, and the power of breathing sweet sounds, was again restored to her lips. Lucy mingled in the conversation, and in a few minutes we were tranquil and happy.

There was certainly a striking contrast between the two females, by whom my feelings had been most deeply interested, and who seemed destined by turns to become the engrossing object of my thoughts and impulses. Yet, even in the influence they exercised over me, they were different. Lady Melicent had subdued my heart, by her power of exciting my imagination; Laura Willoughby excited my imagination, only from having touched my heart.

Lady Melicent was dazzling and brilliant. Wherever she moved there was light in her path, and she was encompassed by grace and splendour. Rank, talent, beauty, all contributed to aid the enchantment, and render the tenure of her power secure. She bore about her a certain air of pride and of distinction, which, even in the largest and most promiscuous assembly, could neither fail to attract the eye, nor engage the attention.

Very different from this was Laura Willoughby. She was not talented, in the common sense of the term, and she did not pretend to be so. Her strength lay in her very weakness, in possessing, in their highest perfection, all the tender, mild, graceful, and retiring attributes of woman. She carried about her nothing of that glare and display, which is perhaps necessary, to attract a large share of admiration in a public assembly. There was nothing brilliant or obtrusive about her. In the ball-room or the theatre, she would probably be overlooked; it was only in the intercourse of private life, that either her beauty or her character, forming, as they did, a delightful unison, could be appreciated as they deserved. She was, in truth, formed after the imagination of the poet:—

> " A creature not too bright and good
> For human nature's daily food,
> For transient sorrows, simple wiles,
> Praise, blame, love, kisses, tears, and smiles.

Such were the two most charming women whom I have ever known; nor was the character of their attraction less different, than those from whom it emanated. In the society of Laura Willoughby, I felt repose; in that of Lady Melicent, I was goaded on by a perpetual stimulus. With the one I enjoyed a delightful quiescence of mind, and the heart only, was active and awake. To render myself agreeable to the other, every faculty was called into action, and, in the belief of success, I felt that pride and elation, which is ever attendant on the successful exercise of power. To a person of my age and temperament, perhaps the latter constituted the more powerful charm; it aimed at a prouder triumph, if not a more valuable conquest.

I found, on the day of my arrival, that a family in the neighbourhood were expected to dinner. It consisted of Colonel and Mrs Culpepper, their son and daughter. Colonel Culpepper had, early in life, gone out as an adventurer to the East Indies, and, late in life, had returned with a large fortune. Mrs Culpepper had likewise been a sojourner in the East, and, in marrying the Colonel, had been equally successful in her speculations, as he had in his.

The great object of both Colonel and Mrs Culpepper having been thus happily accomplished, they returned to England, where the Colonel lost no time in purchasing a magnificent estate, and astonishing his country neighbours, by a style of living to which they had hitherto been unaccustomed. The ancient designation of this estate, one of the old baronial residences of the country, was, in rather questionable taste, changed to Culpepper Park. The mansion-house was pulled down, the park enclosed with a high brick wall, and a huge Chinese-looking building, plastered all over with stucco, afforded ample evidence to the admiring neighbourhood of the wealth and taste of its owner. It is one misfortune of so long an exile, as the acquisition of a fortune in India generally involves, that the gratified fortune-hunter is necessarily alienated, from the habits of the country to which he returns, and has seldom either tact, or versatility of character, sufficient to naturalize him in a new society, with whose manners and ideas, from the nature of things, he can have nothing in common. He has been all his life employed in growing indigo, or fighting black men. His entrance into polished society is only recent. In tastes and habits, he differs entirely from those around him. He has not, and cannot have, that tact and *savoir vivre*, without which no man in this country, can hold his place in the higher circles of society, and which early habits alone can supply. An Indian is an animal in the eyes of the beau monde *feræ naturæ*. He is excluded from the statutes. The laws of fashion afford him no protection ; he is without their pale.

I was riding along the road with Frank Willoughby, an hour or two before dinner, when a carriage and four, with two outriders, emblazoned with armorial bearings, which occupied nearly the whole breadth of the panels, drove past.

"Ah, there go the Culpeppers, " said Frank ; " you know they dine with us to-day : but I daresay you don't know my mother has cut out, in her own imagination, a match between Miss Culpepper and myself. Her fortune is large—a crore of rupees, or some such unintelligible sum ; and my old acres, you know, are not without some burdens. "

" Well, I hope you are not unreasonable enough to object ? "

" Object ? Not I. She has never mentioned it to me ; but I see her wishes, and shall be sorry to disappoint them. "

" Why should you disappoint them ? "

" For this reason, I do not like the girl ; and if I did, I should not like to be connected with her family. "

" What sort of girl is she ? "

" Don't ask me : I could never describe a young lady in my life. Her brother I will describe, if you like, and that briefly. He is an arrant puppy, who has lately, I think, showed strong symptoms of a *penchant* for Lucy. Will your brotherly sagacity approve of such a match ? "

This intelligence roused my curiosity, and, in the exercise of my functions, as next of kin to my sister, I inquired more particulars about the family than I should otherwise have been interested in knowing. The Culpeppers, Frank assured me, were vain, rich, harmless, flashy, and stupid people, with nothing about them of the *odeur de la bonne societé*. Living in a style of expense and profusion, with which none of their immediate neighbours could pretend to vie, they had at first been rather shyed in the county ; but by dint of playing the agreeable to all the old families around them—a large subscription to the county-hounds—and a splendid ball given annually on the birth-day of Miss Culpepper, they had gradually brought themselves to be considered in the light of at least a tolerable nuisance, and were admitted, *cum nota*, among the *elites* of the province.

On descending to the drawing-room, I found it only tenanted by Lucy, with whom I was not displeased to have an opportunity for a little private conversation. In the course of it, I endeavoured to probe the sentiments she entertained for young Culpepper. Lucy appeared, indeed, entirely unconscious of having ever been the object of any unusual attentions from the gentleman in question, though the singularity and pretension of his deportment had occasionally been the source of amusement. The entrance of some of the family put a stop to our colloquy ; and shortly afterwards Colonel and Mrs Culpepper made their appearance.

The Colonel was a little dapper man, who wore a wig *au naturel*, and came into the apartment with that air of strut and consequence, for which persons of diminutive stature are generally remarkable. His coat was of light-green, a colour which contrasted rather unfavourably with the yellowness of his complexion. His nether man displayed integuments of straw colour, joined at the knee by a diamond buckle ; and flesh-coloured silk stockings, with huge open clocks, adorned his inferior extremities. In her day, Mrs Culpepper had been handsome, and though fallen somewhat into decline, was evidently unwilling, to resign her pretensions to admiration. All that the milliner, the peruquier, and other professional contributors to female embellishment, could do, to establish a claim so dubious, had evidently been done. The pretence to beauty was indeed clearly made out, whatever hesitation might arise, with regard to the presence of the reality. Their daughter was a little swarthy girl, with fine eyes and a pretty foot, displaying chains and bracelets *ad infinitum* of Trinchinopoly gold. Mr Frederick Culpepper, the son, though, like the rest of his family, cast in a small mould, was evidently, in his own opinion, a beau of the first magnitude. Nothing could be more *recherché* than his dress, or more splendid than his rings and brooches. Redolent of perfume, and pointing his toes with the air of a dancing master, he advanced into the room in the evident expectation, that being, as he considered himself, the " Glass of fashion and the mould of form, " he was instantly to become " the observed of all observers. " Still, to one who knew the world, it was evident he was not quite sure of his ground. He had none of the calm and collected security of an experienced tactician in society. There was something restless and fidgetty in his manner, and he was obviously apprehensive lest the bills at sight which he drew on the admiration of the company might not be duly honoured.

To each member of this family I was successively introduced, and received by all with a certain indifference of manner, somewhat mortifying to my vanity. The truth was, I was no longer heir apparent to the Thornhill estate. The intelligence of my father's will had blazed abroad, and the Culpeppers were by no means anxious to form any intimate *liaison* with a disinherited son. When I say by *all* the Culpeppers I was so received, perhaps I am wrong, for the distance of Miss Culpepper's manner soon wore off, and her after *accueil*, at least, was sufficiently benignant and encouraging. The thews and sinews of a man formed an item, and a very important one, in her account of personal property ; and though for this inheritance I was perhaps indebted to my father, it was fortunately one of which I could not afterwards be disinherited. Though such possessions generally go for nothing in the catalogue *raisonné* of a lover's wealth, when estimated by parents and guardians, they are generally of some consequence in the eyes of the young lady, and often serve as a counterpoise, to his deficiency in more vulgar opulence.

Dinner was announced, and I handed Miss Culpepper to the dining-room. The style of living at Middlethorpe was without ostentation, yet in perfect harmony with the rank and character of the establishment. It is true, there was rather more of plenty on the board, than was quite consonant to the recent refinements of fashionable delicacy. The apartment, too, was very different from the ideas attached to a modern dining-room. It was, in truth, a large hall, paved with marble, and wainscoted with oak, at either extremity of which blazed a fire large enough to roast an ox. In the centre was spread a Turkey carpet ; and there was a massiveness and antiquity about the furniture, in perfect keeping with the character of the mansion. In the style of the entertainment there was evidently no catching at modern fashions, nor adoption of those recent innovations, which have by degrees succeeded in effecting a complete revolution in the ancient *programme* of an English dinner.

It was easy to observe, that Colonel Culpepper was an adept in the science of good living. On the soup and fish being removed, he raised his eye-glass, and took a leisurely survey of every dish on the table.

" Pray, Captain Thornton, may I inquire what dish that is immediately before you, which is hid from me by the centre of the plateau ? "

" Jugged hare. "

" And that immediately below ? "

" Stewed beef. "

" Oh, I see rice at the other end, and presume there's curry ? Bring me some curry. "

But the promise of curry, though thus given to the eye, was broken to the hope, the defective vision of the Colonel having metamorphosed a boiled fowl into that oriental esculent.

I was seated between Laura Willoughby and Miss Culpepper, and, as may be supposed, was led by the bent of my inclinations to bestow the larger share of my attention on the former. This division of my favours, however, I found scarcely practicable. Miss Culpepper was not one of those young ladies who throw the whole burden of conversation on the gentleman, and in case he is rather taciturn, sit moping and silent by his side, until restored to freedom and loquacity by the departure of the ladies for the drawing-room. Finding, perhaps, that I was engrossed with Miss Willoughby more than impartial justice required, she proceeded to enforce her claims to attention by such queries as the following :—

" Pray, Captain Thornton, is it long since you returned from Spain ? "

" About four months. "

" Pray, were you ever in a battle ? "

" I have had that honour. "

" And were you wounded ? "

" Very slightly. "

" But you were taken prisoner ? "

" I have been so unfortunate. "

" In what battle ? "

" Roleia. "

" Oh, pray, describe it to me. I cannot possibly understand what people do in a battle. Pray tell me all about it ? "

" I fear it would be rather a difficult task to make it intelligible. "

" Oh, not at all. I am very quick, I assure you ; now, suppose the table to be a field of battle, I am sure you can make it quite plain, and you will so oblige me. Come now begin. "

" Well, since you insist on it, I will endeavour. Suppose, then, that Sirloin of beef to be a height, on the top of which there is erected a battery. This, the English, who are represented by these dishes, wish to take, and the French, who are those dishes opposite, wish to defend.

Then the English send this Venison-pasty, which is a brigade of infantry, to attack the Sirloin of beef, which, as I said before, is a hill, with a fort on the top of it. The French seeing this, send up that dish of Maintenon cutlets as a reinforcement. That Capon is the Duke of Wellington, who immediately directs these Chickens, which are the light cavalry, to charge the enemy in flank. These Partridges are the French flying artillery, which that Calfs-head, which is the French general, orders forward to act as a *point d'appui* to that dish of Beef-à-la-mode, which these Maintenon cutlets—no, the Harico opposite is about to attack. Thus you see the battle is fairly begun. The Partridges, you observe, have opened a heavy fire on the Chickens and Stewed-duck, which are advancing with the courage of lions to the charge, and the French general is riding up and down the table—I mean the field, attended by these Butter-boats, which are his aides-de-camp ; and this Mustard-pot, which is the Quartermaster-general. But I fear, after all, I have not succeeded in making the plan of the battle quite intelligible. "

"Oh, perfectly, I assure you. Pray go on, I am quite interested I declare. "

Luckily for me, however, the dishes were in the act of being removed, and this change of the *materiel de guerre*, having thrown all the operations of the battle into confusion, a cessation of hostilities was found necessary.

I did not fail during the dinner, to cast occasional glances of observation on Lucy, who, on the opposite side of the table, was seated next Mr Frederick Culpepper. There was in her manner of addressing him no symptom of constraint or embarrassment ; and she had evidently no idea that there was anything implied in his attentions, beyond the homage, to which perhaps no young and beautiful woman can be unconscious of her claim. Still, however, it was evident to me, that a trifling stretch of that vanity, in which her admirer was certainly not deficient, might attribute her naturally gay and good-humoured reception of his advances, to a sentiment of prepossession in his favour, which I was very certain, she was far from entertaining. This, however, admitted of no remedy, for I could not think of imposing on one so artless and innocent, the task of schooling and restraining her words and actions, lest the folly or vanity of another, might be led to draw from them erroneous conclusions.

After the departure of the ladies, the conversation was dull enough. For want of a more interesting subject, hunting, that never-failing resource of a country dinner party, was brought on the tapis. This naturally led to the county pack of foxhounds, and these foxhounds, to certain extraordinary and unprecedented runs, which they had lately afforded. Though my military avocations had of late years prevented the indulgence of my sporting predilections, I still felt myself to be a foxhunter in *posse* if not in *esse*, and knowing the country well, felt some interest in Willoughby's narratives of perilous adventure by hedge and ditch.

But a Nabob is always a perfect Marplot in matters of this description; and the Colonel, who had never followed a fox in his life, dexterously introduced the subject of tiger-hunting in India, relative to which he insisted on telling us long stories; the shortest, and therefore the best of which, occupied at least a quarter of an hour, in the narration. Then came elephant-hunting, lion-hunting, boar-hunting, and jackall-hunting. On each of which subjects he had much information to give, and many anecdotes to relate. To get rid of this, Willoughby talked of the war in Spain, and inquired some particulars of my escape. He did not, however, gain any thing by the change. Fighting in Spain led to fighting in the East. Lord Wellington had fought in both, and the Colonel had unluckily been at Assaye, in the character of a commissary. All the details of Indian tactics were studiously explained and commented on, and the advantages of Gram, Bat-money, and Camp-kettle allowances in the Company's service, were laid open to the meanest capacity.

Politics were then tried, and politics failed. The Colonel had been employed as a diplomatist at some of the Eastern courts, and having jockeyed a Rajah to the complete satisfaction of the Company, the political relations of Europe were speedily merged in others, on which our Nabob could deliver his sentiments without fear of contradiction.

When we returned to the ladies, Mrs Culpepper was in the act of recapitulating the extensive improvements then carrying on at Culpepper Park, and strongly impressing on Lady Willoughby the propriety of inducing her son to knock down one side of the drawing-room, for the purpose of adding a conservatory, which she assured her, and appealed to the Colonel for corroboration of her opinion, would be a vast improvement. On this, indeed, she was sure there could be no difference of opinion in those who had ever seen her drawing-room at Culpepper Park. Lord R——, (an Indian, by the way, who had recently been created a peer from the weight of his purse,) had lately been there, and declared the drawing-room at Culpepper Park, to be the finest thing he had ever seen; the *beau ideal* of elegance, splendour, and comfort. As there was evidently no desire, however, either in Lady Willoughby, or her son, to convert Middlethorpe into any thing resembling Culpepper Park, the proposal having been coldly received, was not further enforced by its advocate.

Music was then introduced, and Miss Culpepper was handed very gallantly by Frank Willoughby to the piano. She was certainly a player of great execution, and united firmness and rapidity of touch, in great perfection. Nothing could be more facile or masterly, than her performance of the most difficult passages of Mozart or Beethoven. Then she sung. Her's was one of those clear, hard voices, possessing great power and little softness, and none of that mellowness of tone, which, judging from my own feelings, is essential to the excitement of strong musical delight. I felt this, perhaps, more strongly, when Miss Culpepper's performances were concluded, and I saw Laura Willoughby bending gracefully over her harp, and listened to the etherial sounds with which it filled the apartment.

When the song was finished, she rose from the instrument, and resumed her place on the sofa. Surely beauty is never more resistless, than when the heart has been softened by music, and prepared to feel the whole influence of its charms. Never had Laura Willoughby appeared more interesting in my eyes. The flush, which during the exertion of singing had risen to her cheek, had passed away, the sparkle of excitement had faded from her eye, but without diminution of her loveliness. I rose, and, crossing the room, seated myself beside her. Since my arrival in the morning, there had been no opportunity for unrestrained intercourse between us, and on the following morning I was to depart. We had both many questions to ask, and many to answer; and I looked upon her as an old and dear friend, from whom a long separation was about to divide me.

She received me with the same open and unembarrassed air to which I had been accustomed. At first we talked of Lucy, and her approaching departure. "Bring her back to us," said she, looking on me with earnestness, and speaking in a pleading tone; "for though Lucy must be loved everywhere, nowhere will she be loved, as she is loved here."

I promised this, and the conversation gradually changed to what was more immediately connected with myself.

I told her, for I saw she was interested, and loved to listen to me, all my plans, and all my hopes for the future. She was at that moment to me as a kind and loving sister. We spoke not the language of lovers, but of friends; and though she sighed when I told her, of my yet unsated thirst for military distinction, and spoke of the path of danger I was yet destined to pursue, she read in my words and looks the bias of my spirit, and she dissuaded me not from following the career, in which I had embarked.

Then we spoke of the Lady Melicent. Laura had never seen her, but the praises of her beauty were familiar to her ear. With eyes half averted, yet with a tone that bespoke a deep interest in the question, she asked whether her charms had been exaggerated by report; and whether she was, in truth, the captivating person which the world represented her.

At first, I spoke of the Lady Melicent indifferently and calmly, but warming with my subject as I proceeded, my description became gradually more glowing, and far outstepped those limits, within which alone, perhaps, it is ever pleasing to one woman to hear the praises of another. At length I stopped, when, looking at Laura, I perceived the blood had left her cheeks, and she was pale. In the impulse of the moment I exclaimed, "Laura, you are unwell. I hope——" By a sudden motion she raised her head, and, laying her hand on mine, she entreated me not to attract the notice of the company to her discomposure.

" It was but a sudden pain that shot through here, " said she, removing her hand from mine, and slightly pointing to her heart—" it was but the pang of a moment, and it is now gone. "

As she spoke she smiled in my face, but I saw there were tears in her eyes although her cheek was dry. Soon after she arose, and, mingling with the company, no traces of her emotion were discernible. I too rose, and observing that Mr Frederick Culpepper had once more succeeded in entangling Lucy in a tête-à-tête, I exerted the privilege of a brother, in rescuing her from what I imagined she could only regard as an annoyance.

As it is probable I may be too much interested in my own concerns, to notice it in its proper place, I may here take the liberty of anticipating an event, which did not take place till some time after.

Shortly before my return to Portugal, I received a letter from Colonel Culpepper, inclosing one from his son to Lucy, containing an offer of marriage. In the envelope, addressed to myself, the Colonel stated, that he would be happy to consent to such settlements as were suitable to my sister's fortune, should the match, to which he could anticipate, on our part, no objection, be agreed upon.

I delivered Lucy's letter, and found her not a little surprised at the proposal it contained. After much labour, and the consumption of a quire or two of paper, she succeeded at length in making her refusal sufficiently civil and decided ; and I inclosed it to the Colonel in a letter of my own, containing the usual professions of thanks, for the honour which it had been in his contemplation to confer on my family by the proposed alliance.

END OF VOLUME SECOND

VOLUME III

CHAPTER I

Take heed you steer your vessel right, my son;
This calm of heaven, this mermaid's melody,
Into an unseen whirlpool draws you fast,
And in a moment sinks you.

DRYDEN.

ON the following morning, Lucy and myself bade farewell to our excellent and kind friends, and set out for Staunton Court. There were wet eyes at our departure, and young and bright countenances were darkened with sorrow; yet there was no tear on the cheek of Laura Willoughby, no outward sign of inward agitation, when the words of parting kindness were exchanged between us. Her countenance was calm and unmoved as that of a statue, and but for one long and convulsive heave of her bosom, as she quickly turned from me to cast herself into the arms of Lucy, her figure, too, might at that moment, have been taken, for one wrought into the semblance of life, by the Promethean art of the sculptor. Then, however, and not till then, came the burst of grief; and never, I believe, were purer tears shed from angel-eyes, than bedimmed the cheeks of these innocent and lovely girls.

But, painful as it is, the moment of parting comes at last. The weeping Lucy was assisted to the carriage by Frank Willoughby and myself; and, after one kind pressure of the hand, and one kind look, poor Lucy's effort was over, and we were rapidly moving onward, to our destination.

For the first mile or two, she leant her head upon my shoulder, and was sorrowful and silent. But the change of scene and object, which every minute was presenting to her view, and the excitement of rapid locomotion to one little accustomed to travelling, wrought their usual effect, and, before the conclusion of the first stage, all traces of grief had been obliterated from her countenance.

There is a pleasure in travelling with a young and happy creature, smiling in the exuberance of her own innocent delight—to whom all that she beholds, comes clad in the charm of novelty. Lucy had a thousand questions to ask, and I to answer; and when at length fatigued by her long-continued task of observation, she warbled for me a sweet and lively song, often stopping suddenly, with a note half modulated on her lips, when any new object appeared to excite her curiosity, or interest.

We slept that night on the road, and the next day found us rapidly approaching the termination of our journey. It was about three o'clock when we drove through the splendid gateway into the large outer park, which stretched for miles on every side of the mansion. During the latter part of the journey, a change had come over the spirits of Lucy. External objects had no longer their former power, in swaying the mood of her mind. All her anxiety and inquiries, were now connected with the Lady Melicent; and the impression which she, a simple and inexperienced girl, could expect to make on one, so imposingly arrayed in all beauty and accomplishment. Poor Lucy knew not the charm she bore about her, in her own fair countenance, and guileless heart. I endeavoured to calm her fears, by all the assurances in my power, but her spirit was damped by apprehension of the new scene on which she was about to enter,—of mingling for the first time with strangers, to all of whom she was unknown, and by all of whom, of course, unloved. As we approached the house her anxiety increased; and in crossing the bridge, through the superb portal which I have already described, she clasped her arm in mine, as if clinging to me for support and protection, and her breathing was hurried and irregular.

We descended from the carriage, and were ushered into the library. We found there the Lady Melicent, and a very starched and dignified old lady, who was introduced to us, as her aunt, Lady Greystoke. The dowager rose from her chair as stiff as a poker, and scrutinizing poor Lucy with her keen spectacled eyes, dropped such a courtesy, as might be in vogue in the reign of Queen Anne, and resumed her work. I felt gratified by Lady Melicent's reception of Lucy. She seemed charmed by her appearance; and seating herself beside her on the sofa, spoke to her a thousand kind things, which were aided in their effect, by looks, if possible, yet kinder. The task of making Lucy happy, was never a very difficult one; and before half an hour had elapsed, all the fears which her imagination had conjured up, had vanished into thin air.

It was natural, that at first Lucy should be the principal object of Lady Melicent's attentions, and I was therefore not mortified, as in other circumstances I probably should, at finding myself thrown into the back ground. If it was impossible to extract any thing flattering to my self-love from the mode of my reception; there was, on the other hand, nothing in it, which could be mortifying to my vanity. Nothing indeed, but the height of coxcombry could have led me to expect, if I really did expect, to have perceived in the Lady Melicent any demonstration of peculiar pleasure on our meeting. Yet mine was an imagination, which, when fairly at work, was generally unshackled, either by reason or probability, and delighted in constructing, from visionary contingencies, gorgeous fabrics of future happiness, which, like the enchanted castles of old, a single breath sufficed, to dissipate and dissolve.

The conversation, which had become general was, however, soon diverted from the channel it had sought, by the entrance of Lord Amersham, accompanied by Sir Charles Greystoke, and Sir Cavendish

Potts. His Lordship entered the library in his usual extraordinary pace, and running, if so it can be called, up to Lucy, seized both her hands in his, and saluted her cheek, before she was aware of his intention. The blood, for a moment, mounted into her face ; but, when she had time to contemplate the figure of Lord Amersham, and listen to the compliments, which he pronounced in a voice, and with a volubility peculiar to himself, the suffusion gave place to a smile.

"Welcome, most welcome to Staunton Court, my dear young lady ; and you too, Thornton, how d'ye do ? glad to see you. Nay, don't blush, Miss Thornton, I'm an old man, you know, and a relation, and entitled on both grounds to a salute. Hope you've not suffered from your journey ?—Pleasant weather, but bad roads. Your sister—Mrs Hewson, I think—pardon me if I mistake the name—shocking memory for names—quite well, I hope, when you last heard ? Well, Thornton, when are you going to be a Colonel, ey ? Dont let 'em rest at the Horse-Guards, you know—that's the secret ; out of sight out of mind's, the rule there. Nothing like a monthly memorial, and a visit to the levee. Sir Charles can tell you that—ey, Sir Charles ?—old services apt to be forgot—a freshener of the memory always good in such cases—By the by, Sir Charles, let me introduce my young friends to you. Sir Charles Greystoke Miss Thornton ; Captain Thornton of the —— ey, am I right—that your regiment ? Ah ! I see Sir Cavendish and you are old friends, so I needn't go through the form with him. Sir Cavendish knows all the world, and, of course, you too. "

Lord Amersham was right. Sir Cavendish Potts was one of those people who never drop an acquaintance, nor forget a single person whom, in a very extended and promiscuous intercourse with the world, they ever chance to meet. To drink a glass of wine with Sir Cavendish, or sit next him at dinner, was to establish an acquaintance for life, for never after, would he pass you even in the street, without a bow of recognition.

On the present occasion he had accosted me as an old friend, though we had never met since I had last seen him at Staunton. Immediately on entering the apartment, he advanced towards me, retaining his eye-glass in its position, by the compression of his eyebrow, and exclaiming—

"Ah ! my old and excellent friend Thornton, I declare ; I trust I have the pleasure of meeting you in perfect health ? I am delighted once more to have the honour of taking you by the hand. I scarcely dared, from hearing you were abroad, to anticipate the pleasure of so soon again enjoying your agreeable society ; and it is now with sincere pleasure, I venture to congratulate you, on your return to your native land, crowned with laurels and distinction. "

Though Lady Greystoke has been already mentioned, as being in the library with Lady Melicent, on our arrival, I have thought it better, to defer introducing her more particularly to the notice of the reader, till the appearance of Sir Charles, in order that those, whom holy church had joined, should not be separated even in description. Lady Greystoke was uterine sister to Lord Amersham, by a former marriage, and was several years older than his Lordship. The illness of Lady Amersham, who was now unable to quit her chamber, and whose recovery was hopeless, had rendered it desirable, that a person of some standing and consideration in the world, should, by her presence, relieve Lady Melicent from that awkwardness of situation, which is sometimes apt to arise, in an establishment ungraced by the presence of a matron.

For this purpose, the person to whom Lord Amersham's eye naturally turned, was Lady Greystoke. She was indeed the very mirror of decorum ; and the fact of her countenancing any person or establishment, was considered by the world, as sufficient evidence of its perfect propriety, in the very widest and strictest acceptation of the term. Lady Greystoke was, indeed, one of those persons, the lustre of whose reputation, the breath of scandal had never dared to dim. Rigid and censorious in her judgment of others, and a perfect precisian in all observances of external decorum, she realized the *beau ideal* of a Duenna, and was at once shrewd, sharp, and unbending in exacting a scrupulous conformity to her opinions from all within the range of her influence.

Modern fashions, and modern innovations in manners, were her aversion. In dress she was at least half a century behind her age, and delighted in that style of antique and picturesque adornment, now considered only as historically curious. Her grey hair was drawn up straight from her forehead, beneath which, peered two keen grey eyes, the expression of which was in perfect accordance, with the sharpness of her other features.

Sir Charles Greystoke was exactly the sort of person, one would, *a priori*, imagine, to have selected such a woman for his wife. Sir Charles was a military man of the old school, who had been employed in several important commands, as a general officer, and had been rewarded for his conduct in them, by the insignia of the Bath. There was something professional in his dress and air, which betrayed him at once to be an old soldier. He wore a blue surtout, with the button of a Lieutenant-General ; high military boots, which were cut square at top, and reached in front above the cap of the knee ; and his hair, which was highly powdered, was collected behind into a club, to which the motion of his head generally communicated a sort of vibratory swing across his shoulders, not unlike that of the pendulum of a clock.

The hour of dinner found the party all assembled in the drawing-room. Lord Amersham was spruce as usual, and adorned with the never-failing Star of the Bath. His brother knight, though renovated likewise, by the cares of the toilet, was not similarly decorated. Holding the post of equerry to the King, he wore what is called the Windsor uniform, and the cut of his coat, the tails of which, when buttoned, nearly met in front like a petticoat, was of a fashion apparently contemporaneous with the dress of his better half. That, indeed, was sufficiently remarkable in these days of degenerate taste, to draw the attention of every eye, which custom had not rendered familiar with the appearance of Lady Greystoke. Her gown was of the old Florentine silk, the pattern of which displayed flowers of all sizes and colours. The sleeves, which were of an enormous size, terminated at the elbow, and were decorated with broad lace, the inferior part of the arm, being covered with gloves of white silk. The waist was of unusual length and slimness, and at the lower extremity, the skirt or petticoat bulged suddenly out in a rotundity and fullness of drapery, indicating to an unpractised eye, a plenitude of that inexpressible part of the person, altogether disproportioned to what above was more visible, and better defined. Her head-dress was something in the shape of a sugar-loaf, and from the summit, lappets of Brussels point hung down behind. On her bony hands she wore rings of an enormous size, and the handkerchief which covered her neck, and reached almost to her chin, was decorously pinned in front by a large diamond brooch, corresponding with the antique brilliant ear-rings which sparkled above.

When Lord Amersham approached to hand her to the dining-room, nothing could exceed the formality and stateliness of the whole proceeding. She tendered his lordship the tip of her gloved fingers, (for taking a gentleman's arm she held to be altogether a modern innovation,) and slowly led the way from the apartment, in all the grace and dignity of rustling silk, and high-heeled shoes.

The dinner passed—to me heavily enough, for I was *not* near the Lady Melicent, and *was* near Lady Greystoke. Of course, I was courtier enough, to give her no reason to complain, of any want of assiduity in my attentions. Her observations, which at first, to say the truth, were cold and haughty enough, were by me received as oracles, and before the second course was removed, I had drank Champagne with her, and evidently had gained some footing, in her good graces.

"Your sister, Captain Thornton, " said the Dowager, in the civil and benignant mood into which my attentions had brought her,—" your sister, Captain Thornton, " glancing at the same time, with her sharp grey eyes at Lucy, who was seated on the opposite side of the table, between Sir Charles Greystoke and Lord Amersham, (what a situation for poor Lucy!) "seems a very good, and a very pretty girl. I have been talking to her in the drawing-room, and find her to be very well informed, and really better educated than common. "

I, of course, bowed, and expressed my delight that Lucy should have obtained the good opinion of so accomplished a judge of female excellence, as Lady Greystoke. The old lady wreathed her lips into what was intended for a smile, and proceeded :—

"Your sister told me, I think, she had been educated at home.

Indeed, I should have known as much, without being told it, for public schools are sad things, Captain Thornton. I never would have allowed any daughter of mine, to be educated at a public school. Of the immorality acquired at these public schools, you can form no idea; besides, the girls are always pert, forward, ill-educated, and ill-bred. "

I answered, that although she was right in supposing that the immorality taught in public seminaries for young ladies, had not fallen within the immediate scope of my own experience and observation, my conviction must naturally follow any statement of opinion, from one so eminently qualified, to decide on such a subject as her Ladyship.

"Now, I'll give you an instance, Captain Thornton, in which it would have been fortunate, if my advice had been followed. Perhaps you know Tottenham—Colonel Tottenham, of the —— Ah! no matter; he was aide-de-camp to Sir Charles, when he commanded the Brighton district, and fell in love with some silly girl with a pretty face, whom he met with at a ball. One morning Captain Tottenham, for he was then only Captain, came to me, and said, 'My Lady Greystoke, I wish for the honour of your ladyship's advice on a point that concerns me very nearly.'—'You know, Captain Tottenham,' I replied, 'that my advice is always at the service of my friends.' Well, I soon found out he wished for my advice about his marriage. 'But how can I advise you, Captain Tottenham,' said I, 'till I know something of the lady.' 'Oh,' replied he, 'she is a very nice, elegant, accomplished, and pretty girl, of a respectable family, and only lately returned from a finishing-school at Bath.' 'Hold, Captain Tottenham,' I interrupted, 'not a word more. What, marry a girl from a finishing-school! Yes; I'll warrant she's finished enough; young ladies are generally tolerably well finished before they quit such seminaries. Are you mad,' said I, 'to think of marrying such a girl? Have nothing to say to her. Give up the connexion instantly, or if you don't, take my word for it, you'll repent it all the days of your life.' Well, Captain Thornton, in spite of all he married her, and mark the sequel. In less than two years she eloped wth Major Farebrother, of the Shropshire militia, whom Tottenham shot afterwards in a duel. "

I soon found, Lady Greystoke's character was not a very difficult one to fathom. She, in truth, was one of those people, kind and friendly enough at bottom, who insist on managing everybody and everything. Submit yourself to the guidance of such a person, and she will do everything in her power to promote your interest. Dispute her authority, or neglect her advice, and the kind friend becomes at once a determined enemy.

On the departure of the ladies, the conversation would have been stupid enough, but for Sir Cavendish Potts, who, though rather inordinately loquacious, was furnished with such a store of anecdote, as to render him, occasionally, an amusing companion. The authenticity of most of these might, perhaps, be disputed, but if not *vrais*, were at least *vraisemblables,* and that, for all common purposes, is enough.

Lord Amersham introduced farming, and began an explanatory dissertation of his own recent improvements in the art agricultural. This, I found, was coldly received by his auditors, who had probably been too often caught by the same bait, to nibble at it very freely again. Farming being discarded, then came the war in Spain and Viscount Wellington. At first, I was not without hope of profiting by the military knowledge and experience, of the two Generals, and listened to their observations in a spirit of respectful attention. But the old fable of the Mountain and the Mouse, could not have been more fully illustrated. To me, who, from personal observation, knew something of the facts and circumstances of the war, nothing could appear more puerile and jejune than their remarks, and the plausible *sottises* of Sir Charles Greystoke, were, in reality, little better, than the more violent absurdities of Lord Amersham. I discovered, indeed, that both of these veterans, but especially Sir Charles, in common, I believe, with most officers similarly situated, felt not a little jealousy of their younger rivals, whom the circumstances of the Peninsular war, had suddenly called forward into action and distinction. They felt that their own fame had diminished, in comparison with that of officers, of standing far junior to themselves. The Generals, whose greatest achievement consisted in the capture of a fort, or the defence of a sugar island, could not but perceive, that they were no longer looked up to, as the heroes of their age. Those whose fame, a few years ago, had been second to none, were now become second to many, with the imminent prospect, from the occurrences which were taking place around them, of sinking still lower in the scale.

In such circumstances, a little bitterness of feeling is perhaps pardonable, and the merit which a man cannot see without pain, he may be excused for shutting his eyes, and refusing to see at all. Sir Charles gravely maintained the impossibility of permanently supporting an army, in the interior of Spain, from the impossibility of procuring supplies, and both he and Lord Amersham joined in considering the retreat of Lord Wellington, after the battle of Talavera, to be a proof of utter and hopeless failure. The opinions of these distinguished officers were not singular, and probably not original. They were in strict accordance with the sentiments of a very large portion of the British nation, by whom Lord Wellington was at that period regarded with jealousy and distrust; nor were they finally relinquished, until he had succeeded in crowning the British arms with a series of victories, unsurpassed in our annals, and his fame had become, alike beyond the reach of envy or detraction.

In the drawing-room, I enjoyed no opportunity of particular conversation, with Lady Melicent, nor did I seek for such. I saw her, I heard her, and this in itself was happiness. Perhaps she was to me more attractive, that she now resembled more what I remembered her to have been, on my first visit to Staunton. Her spirits were certainly better, than when I had seen her in Bath ; her step was more elastic, and her manner more airy. Lovely she was, indeed, in all her phases, but to me most delightful in this, in which she had at first impressed my young imagination.

A week flew past at Staunton, and found the same party still assembled within its walls. Once a day, Lady Melicent generally walked with Lucy in the Park, or drove her in a pony carriage. On these occasions, sometimes alone, sometimes with Sir Cavendish, I formed their escort. Often, when tired by the length of her walk, Lady Melicent would lean on my arm for support. At first, by the very privacy which this afforded, I felt embarrassed. That to which my wishes were most eagerly directed, when obtained, brought with it no enjoyment. But by degrees this wore off. There was nothing of reserve about Lady Melicent ; her manner was ever free and unconstrained ; and open in the expression of her sentiments, she was vehement alike in her partiality and aversion. Thus were the artificial barriers to our intimacy broken down, and now for the first time did hope dawn on my spirit, and whisper of high destiny, and successful love. The seeds of passion, which had hitherto lain dormant in my bosom, by degrees burst out into life and vigour. Its roots became gradually twisted with every fibre of my heart, and I felt and knew, that the tree to which my life-blood lent its nourishment, could not wither, till that heart had perished. I was a being no longer under the sway of reason. In all that concerned my love, or its object, my judgment had no share. I acted under a vehement and commanding impulse, which it was alike impossible to oppose or to restrain.

CHAPTER II

The house which was my father's, is mine own ;
I am the lord of all this fair demesne.
Montalto, a Tragedy.

FROM the period of her marriage, both Lucy and myself, had received occasional letters from Jane. Those written immediately after that event, were not couched in the established phraseology, which new-married ladies generally employ, to convey their first blissful experience of the wedded state. She did not profess herself the happiest of women, nor bless Providence in the exuberance of her gratitude, for having given her an angel for a husband. This I did not expect. She had given her hand to one who I was well aware could never touch her heart. But I was not without hopes, that, unpromising as the character of Hewson certainly was, he might be led, in a great degree, to relinquish his former habits, by the allurement of domestic pleasures, to which he had till now been a stranger. Jane's fortune, though considerable, was not such, as to hold out any strong inducement to a man like Hewson. Love alone, I imagined, could have led him to seek an union with one, whom it appeared to me, so natural to love ; and little pleasure, as I could promise myself in his society, I deemed it right, for Jane's sake, to cultivate the acquaintance, and, if possible, to secure the friendship, of a person with whom, I had become so closely connected.

On our arrival at Staunton, I had therefore written to Jane, offering a visit from both Lucy and myself, which had been joyfully accepted. I felt it would be unkind to quit England, without seeing her. It would seem, as if her own family declined affording her either countenance or protection, and left her to depend solely, on the kindness of those, among whom she might be cast, when, by the disseverment of all former ties, she was but as a waif amid the troubled waters of the world.

When we reached Feltham, for so Hewson's place was called, we found Jane there alone. Hewson had gone to Newmarket, and was not expected for some days. I was not displeased at this.

It gave us an opportunity of enjoying that confidential intercourse with Jane, to which Hewson's presence must have been a bar. The meeting was, as might be expected, an affecting one. Since we had last met, our only surviving parent had been laid in the grave ; and in the situation of us all, great changes had taken place. I endeavoured to support Jane's spirits, which I saw were strongly agitated, by rendering the meeting, as little as possible, the vehicle of painful remembrance, and smilingly congratulated her on her recent change of condition. Jane too smiled, but her smile was a faint one, and certainly not a smile of gladness. My presence, indeed, had but little share in exciting the deep emotion, which the meeting had evidently caused her. The two sisters clasped each other in a long embrace, and wept bitterly. From infancy to womanhood, never had they been separated for a single hour.

> " They with their neelds created both one flower,
> Both on one sampler, sitting on one cushion,
> Both warbling of one song, both in one key ;
> As if their hands, their sides, voices, and minds,
> Had been incorporate. So they grew together,
> Two lovely berries moulded on one stem ;
> So, with two seeming bodies, but one heart.

But the vows which Jane had breathed at the altar, had been to them the fiat of separation, and then, they first had been divided. They spoke not—they could not speak ; but well did I know, at that moment, that their hearts were full, even to bursting, with the memory of *Home*.

What an infinity of mournful recollections had not that single word the power to conjure up within them ! They thought at that moment of all their childish happiness and love—of love unbroken—of happiness, perhaps no longer so. Even to those, whose days have been unclouded by sorrow, the memory of past delight brings with it a pang. But, happy as their days of youth and innocence had been, they had not been unmarked by storm and darkness. Their joys had been the same, and the same clouds had overcast them.

There exists between sisters a confidence too sacred, even for the ear of a brother to partake. Nature herself, has placed a barrier in the difference of sex, to that perfect sympathy and communion of feeling, that guileless out-pouring of the heart, which knits still closer the ties of blood, and alike alleviates the sorrows, and heightens the enjoyment, of young and innocent sisters. It was natural, that in such a meeting I should form but a secondary object. They embraced, they wept in each other's arms, but sunshine came again, for in their tears there was comfort.

Perfect confidence, even between sisters, can exist only before marriage. Thus far can it go, but no farther. Different feelings, and separate objects of interest, then inevitably spring up, and the ties by which female hearts till then had been bound together, are either loosened or snapt in twain. The love may still remain, but the confidence is gone.

Thus I found it was with Jane. When I questioned her on the situation in which she was now placed, and, pressing her hand in mine, inquired if she was happy, she answered evasively, and was evidently anxious, to turn the conversation into another channel.

" Do not, my dear brother, " she at length said, " believe me to be

unhappy, till I complain of being so. Do you not see me surrounded by all the comforts and elegancies, which wealth can bestow? and if——"
She paused for an instant, for a sigh mounted to her lips, and struggled for utterance. "And if—there are some drawbacks to my happiness, these can, and ought to be known only, to God and myself, and must be borne unrepiningly, and in silence."

I forbore, therefore, any further entreaties, on a point to which allusion was evidently painful.

Jane, since I saw her last, had not in appearance, undergone any remarkable change. Her figure was thin and graceful, as it had been in the days of her maidenhood. Her countenance bore the same sweetness of expression, but its vivacity had been dulled, by an acquaintance with the new cares and duties, of a married life. The cheek was paler, and the eye more dim, than my memory told me, they had been of yore. I regarded these external demonstrations with interest, for it was in a great measure from these alone, that I could draw any conclusion with regard to the effect which her union with Hewson, had produced on her happiness.

In speaking of her husband, she used neither the language of complaint nor reproach. I read the delicacy of her feelings, and felt their propriety. Whatever Hewson might be, she was now his wife; and she was resolved to shrink from no duties, whether of action or sufferance, which that relation imposed on her. His failings, whatever grief they might have caused her, were things, of which it was painful to think, and impossible to speak; and of whatever sorrows, her union might have been the fatal cause, they were treasured in the secrecy and silence, of her own heart.

While I was still at Feltham, and before Hewson returned from Newmarket, a letter reached me, which had been forwarded from Staunton, having arrived there the day after my departure. It was from Mrs Thornton, informing me of the death of her son, and stating her willingness, now that her own interests alone were concerned, to enter into a reasonable compromise, in order to avoid the unpleasant family disclosures, to which the legal prosecution of my claims could not fail to give rise. She invited me, therefore, to grant her an immediate interview at Thornhill, by which the preliminaries of our agreement might be arranged, and the lawsuit brought at once, to an amicable termination.

Nothing could possibly be more consonant to my own wishes, than such an arrangement. I was willing to give up much, in order to avoid the humiliation, of a public disclosure of a father's weakness and prejudice. The idea that the sanity of my father's mind, should become the subject of investigation in a court of law; that the privacy of his domestic life should be exposed to the public gaze, become the subject of newspaper comment, and furnish matter of amusement, to every coffee-house in London, was to me inexpressibly painful. With the most perfect conviction of having both law and justice on my side, I felt this, and felt it strongly; and to escape from such an alternative, there was scarcely any demand, short of the entire alienation of the hereditary estate of my family, with which I was not fully prepared to comply. I determined, therefore, to lose no time in seeking the proposed meeting; and having already spent a day or two with Jane, I left Lucy with her till my return, and on the following morning set off for Thornhill.

There was nothing remarkable in my journey, and on my arrival, I was instantly ushered into the presence of Mrs Thornton. She was alone, and apparently, or (why should I question the sincerity of a mother's sorrow for the loss of her only child?) really absorbed in deep and violent grief. I offered her such condolence, as it was natural for one, peculiarly circumstanced as I was, to feel and express—neither suffering the expression of my sympathy to exceed the modesty of nature, nor to sink below, what one, in any case, may be expected to feel, for the bereavement of a mother. My little brother, I learned, had always been an unpromising and sickly child; and at last had fallen a victim to one of those fevers, to which children are peculiarly liable.

The conversation, which had begun in this melancholy strain, however, gradually converged to the point, which constituted the more immediate object of the interview. I stated, that I now waited upon her, in compliance with the desire expressed in her letter; that I was fully prepared to enter into any reasonable terms for an accommodation, which would obviate the unpleasant necessity, of determining the extent of my rights, in a court of law. In case she wished it, I was ready to submit to her, the opinions of the very eminent counsel, by which I had been guided, in the legal steps I had taken. By these, she would at least be convinced, that in uniting in her wish, for an amicable adjustment, I was prompted, not by any fears of the issue, but by those motives of delicacy, and proper feeling alone, for which I was prepared to give her full credit in making the proposal.

It boots not, however, that the reader should be troubled with the details of a negotiation, of which it is sufficient that he be made acquainted with the issue. Waving, therefore, all minor details, be it known, that our approaches having been mutually made, in a style that would have done credit to the most experienced diplomatists, I requested my worthy stepmother to name her terms. These were, first, that the jointure of five hundred pounds a-year, settled on her by the contract of marriage, should be doubled. Secondly, that all the furniture which had been purchased for Thornhill, since her marriage with my father, should be assigned over to her. Thirdly, that out of the personal estate, she should be paid the sum of two thousand pounds, to defray the expenses attendant on change of residence, and fitting up a new establishment. To these conditions I instantly acceded, and in the presence of old Humphreys the steward, and of an attorney, whom the providence of

Mrs Thornton had caused to be in attendance, the proper missives were instantly written and exchanged, and directions given, for the preparation of the deed of settlement.

The joy of Humphreys, at finding the natural heir of Thornhill, thus undisputedly in possession of his natural rights, was the most affecting incident of the scene. Tears filled the eyes of the old man as he pressed me to his bosom, and uttered broken ejaculations of thanksgiving to God. My own heart, too, was full, as I cordially returned his embrace, and heard myself hailed as the lord of that inheritance, to which I had never expected to succeed.

The objects of the meeting being thus accomplished, I bade adieu to Mrs Thornton, and accompanied Humphreys to his house, where I intended to remain for the night. I had much information to receive, and many arrangements to make, with regard to my newly-acquired property, and I was anxious to devote every possible moment of my necessarily short stay, to receiving the one, and communicating my wishes on the other.

The house, in which the aged steward had dwelt for nearly half a century, was situated at the extremity of the Park. We walked at a slow pace, for the limbs of my companion were stiff and feeble, and he leant heavily on his staff. With difficulty I prevailed on him to accept the additional support of my arm, and we advanced in silence, for I was too much occupied in reflection to speak.

I looked around me on the rich landscape that spread on every side,—the noble oaks, beneath whose shadow we passed, and in whose topmost branches, the rook had fixed its airy dwelling,—the hill, the woods, and the fair valley watered by the Severn,—and a thrill of pride passed through my heart, as I thought—Of all this, I am now the master. The pride, however, soon gave place to feelings of a different character. I remembered it was to the hand of death that I was indebted for the inheritance. These oaks, which my progenitors had planted, had seen many generations pass away around them,—had beheld their progress from infancy to youth, from youth to manhood, from manhood to decrepitude and death. They were gone, and the face of nature had remained unchanged. The spring came again, the trees had blossomed, and the birds carolled from their branches, the summer had been gay with flowers, and the merry song of the reapers had been heard in autumn, even while the worms were yet busy with his body, who had called these things *his own*. The eyes that wept for the possessors of this fair demesne, as they successively dropped into the grave, were long since closed for ever; the hearts that loved them were undistinguishable from a clod of common earth, and were cold and senseless as that.

I, too, had seen a generation pass away; had laid my parents in the dust; and what was I but an insignificant link between the future and the past in the great chain of creation; a creature doomed like them, to live, die, and be forgotten.

This train of reflection, more melancholy perhaps than may appear suited to the occasion, was interrupted by our arrival at the domicile of old Humphreys. He was a widower. My father had procured his only son an appointment in India, where he then was, and a maiden sister, nearly as old as himself, officiated as mistress of his establishment.

Though my appearance as a guest could not have been anticipated by either of these worthy people, yet I was not troubled with any verbose apologies for the plainness of their fare.

" Had we been apprized of the honour you have been kind enough to confer on us, " said the lady, as we seated ourselves to such a substantial repast as is generally seen on the board of the wealthier class of English yeomen, " we should have been better provided. "

To say this much, was perhaps due to the pride of her character as a housewife ; but on my assuring her I was an old campaigner, and accustomed to fare a thousand times worse than that I saw before me, I was not annoyed by any farther prosecution of the subject.

After dinner, Humphreys and myself were left alone, and over a bottle of admirable port, which with his own hands he brought from the cellar, we proceeded to business. Humphreys explained to me very clearly the state of the property. There were no mortgages, and the rent-roll amounted to about L.2700 a-year. So that after paying my stepmother her stipulated allowance of L.1000 a-year, there would still remain a surplus, adequate, and more than adequate, to all my wants. He then informed me of several minor arrangements, which he thought would be conducive to my interest, and which I gave him full authority to carry into effect ; and, aware that my profession would again soon render my presence necessary abroad, I committed the estate to his management during my absence. I directed likewise, that such of the old servants, as wished to resume their former situations at Thornhill, should be engaged, and that those who were now too old for service, should be allowed such trifling pensions as might be required to make them comfortable in their old age.

Perfectly satisfied that my affairs were committed to the hands of a faithful steward, well qualified by experience for the charge confided in him, and whose attachment to my interests was sincere, I, on the following morning, set out on my return to Feltham.

Hewson had returned in my absence, and received me on my arrival. I had never seen him before. He was a man, whose manners in general society would be considered pleasing. They were manners which, expressing nothing, might be called conventionally good, and were such as a person, long used to the mingling in the bustle of the world, might be expected to acquire. He received me with an *empresse-ment* evidently without meaning, and poured forth a torrent of common-place civilities, like a man whose cue it is to play the agreeable, for some underhand purpose of his own.

There was something in the expression of Hewson's countenance, too, to me extremely unpleasant. There was a coldness of eye, which was changed occasionally for a certain cunning twinkle, and there was a curvature of the lip, and something generally about the region of the mouth, which indicated a licentious man, and one given to sensual indulgence. In his expression, there was nothing in the slightest degree intellectual, though it conveyed the impression, of considerable shrewdness, and worldly sagacity.

The joy of my sisters, on learning that I had now become the possessor of Thornhill, was sincere and warmly expressed, nor was Hewson deficient in his congratulations, which were only cut short, by the entrance of a party of gentlemen he had brought with him from Newmarket. These, it was easy to gather from their conversation, were what is called sporting characters, second or third-rate betters on the turf, and first-rate betters on a cockfight, or a boxing-match. Among them was a clergyman, who was generally addressed by his companions by the name of Jack, and was certainly altogether a bad specimen of his cloth. After dinner, betting and horse-racing formed the principal topics, both of interest and conversation. Pocket-books were in every hand, and whoever ventured to express an unguarded anticipation of any contingent event, was generally pulled up by an inquiry, whether he had courage to back his opinion. As I certainly wanted inclination, if not courage, to back mine, of course I was a mere cipher in such a party.

The bottle circulated freely, and the pleasures of the table being concluded, the party sat down to cards. I was not a gambler, in the strict sense of the word, because I had never yet been thrown into a situation where I was assailed by the temptation of high play. But I always experienced a degree of pleasing excitement from games of chance, even with the very moderate stakes, which my circumstances had allowed me to venture. Little fellowship as I felt with any of the company, I was weak enough to suffer myself to be prevailed on to engage in play. The stakes were high, my opponents were all experienced players, and the consequence as might be expected was, that when we rose from table, I was a loser to a very considerable amount. It was late when the party broke up, and on going to the drawing-room, I found my sisters had retired. In no very pleasant humour I followed their example, moralizing on my pillow, till sleep closed my eyelids, and brought oblivion of my folly.

It gave me sincere pleasure on the following morning to witness the departure of the guests. They had left on me no very favourable impression, of Hewson's character and habits; and what I afterwards saw of his conduct to Jane, did not tend to raise him in my opinion. The manner in which he addressed her, betrayed nothing of the affectionate intercourse which marks a happy marriage. Towards her, his manner was cold, plausible, and unfeeling; and there was even in his perfunctory observance of the decencies of politeness, something which forced the conviction, that in different circumstances, he would not hesitate to violate them all.

I had intended to court this man's friendship, but I could not. I shrunk from him, as from something loathsome; and it was with difficulty that even my regard for Jane, made me consent to remain his guest for a few days. These at length expired, and after a mournful farewell, Lucy and myself returned to Staunton, filled with pity for Jane's irremediable misfortune, in having become the wife of Hewson, and indulging melancholy forebodings of the future evils which awaited her.

CHAPTER III

I've seen the day
That I have worn a visor, and could tell
A whispering tale in a fair lady's ear,
Such as would please. 'Tis gone—'tis gone—'tis gone!
Romeo and Juliet.

On our return to Staunton Court, we found that some change had taken place in the party since we had quitted it. Lord Lyndhurst and his sister Lady Eleanour had arrived. The former was in the library when I entered it. He lay extended on an ottoman, engaged in the perusal of the Morning Post newspaper, and his faculties were so deeply absorbed in the task, that he did not perceive my entrance till I stood opposite the fire. Then casting towards me a languid glance, he exclaimed—

" Ah, Thornton, is that you! Monstrous glad to see you, 'pon my honour, " slightly raising himself at the same time, and extending two fingers of his hand as a token of welcome. " Hope you've come to enliven the dull scene ; for it is monstrous dull, upon my honour. "

" Whatever effect my presence may have, whether of enlivening the scene, or rendering it still duller, here I am, at your lordship's service. "

" Duller, that's impossible, " indulging in a long yawn ; " I do believe my jaws will crack if I stay here much longer. There's old Potts last night bored me for two hours with his long stories ; and I had scarcely dropped asleep in an arm chair, when Lady Greystoke knocked me up to make a fourth at half-crown whist, for it seems she never plays higher. Half-crown whist, Thornton, wasn't that good? "

" Well, I hope you played the agreeable, and consented. "

" Why, what could I do? I refused at first, but Lady Greystoke's a stiff old dowager, and talked of the young men of her days, and moralized upon me ; and Lady Melicent quizzed me, and called me the Sleeping Beauty, so I was obliged to consent. But, after all, she was monstrous angry, for I was her partner, and made all kinds of mistakes and revokes, and she grumbled so confoundedly, because she lost two guineas. She can't bear losing her money. "

" Not a singular failing. But where are the ladies? "

" Gone out, I believe. Eleanour wanted me to go too ; but old Amersham had just been hauling me all over his vile farm, and I was knocked up. You've no idea, Thornton, what a bore it was. Would you believe it, he pulled me about to see ploughs, and great fat bullocks, and fields of turnips, and monstrous pigs, and sheep, and threshing-machines ! I'm sure I wished him to have the benefit of one, with all my heart, for dragging me about so. Can you conceive a greater bore, Thornton?"

"Not easily, I confess."

Just then the ladies entered from their walk. Lady Melicent (for had there been an angel in company, she would first have caught my eye,) was blooming from exercise, and looking, I thought, more lovely than I had ever seen her. Her companion, too, was a pretty girl; but her beauty was of that dull and inanimate sort, which attracts no deeper admiration, than that of the eye. The ceremonies of introduction and salutation had scarcely passed, when Lady Melicent, glancing her eye round the apartment, inquired for Lucy.

"You have not, I hope," said she half smilingly, and half seriously, "dared to return without her? If you have, I shall exercise the authority I possess over all the gentlemen in this house, and charge you, on your fealty and allegiance, to set out instantly to bring her back."

"That were indeed to evoke a spell of power," I answered; "and one I could not choose but obey. But it is unnecessary. Lucy returned with me, and is now in her chamber."

She gave me a smile of kindness, and turning to her companion, she said,

"Come, Eleanour, I must introduce you to my dear Lucy;" and the two damsels vanished from the apartment.

To any one but myself, the tone of the party was little if at all changed, by the arrival of the new guests. To me, however, all was changed. I saw that Lord Lyndhurst was regarded by every one, as the destined husband of Lady Melicent. That he had made proposals to Lord Amersham, which had met an encouraging reception, I had no doubt. I thought, nay, I was sure, Lady Melicent did not love him; but the very indifference—nay, stronger—the dislike she often manifested to his society and attentions, served but to provoke the conviction, that, urged by worldly motives, she had given a cold, perhaps even a reluctant consent, to be united to a man, in all the qualities of an intelligent being, a thousand degrees beneath her.

But my mind was not fixed. We are slow to believe anything, which would give a death-blow to our hopes; and though sometimes the conviction was strong and irresistible, and the storm of jealousy raged within me, at others, one glance of her bright eye, one whisper of her sweet voice, would banish doubt and suspicion from my heart.

She knows, I thought, she must know I love her. It is impossible that the deep devotion I bear to her, should not be made intelligible by a thousand indications, minute perhaps, but not to be mistaken. And knowing that she is thus adored, can she make a sport of my feelings, and lead me on, by cruel encouragement, till she beholds me at last irrecoverably lost and entangled, in the labyrinth of a hopeless passion? Oh no. To cherish even such a suspicion for a moment, what was it but foul treason to the lady of my love. Doubt and fear, at all events, had come too late, for I had set my life upon a cast, and I felt that I must stand the hazard of the die.

Weeks passed on, and everything proceeded as formerly at Staunton. Our morning excursions still continued, and though Lord Lyndhurst generally formed one of the party, watchful and engrossed as I was with only one subject, it still fell to my lot to render any little act of gallantry or attention to Lady Melicent. That, compared with my rival, I was to her an object of preference, was what I could no longer doubt, and I longed for an opportunity of putting a period to the state of suspense, in which I suffered—of knowing the best or the worst, that could befall me—of becoming at once supremely blest, or more, if possible, than supremely miserable.

Well do I remember sitting whole hours in my chamber, meditating on fitting words in which to embody the declaration of my love, and pouring forth, in its solitude, the eloquence, (for so I thought it) of deep, fervent, and overpowering passion. Thus, I thought, would I speak, thus would I lay bare my heart before her, and she should read at once its pride, and its humility, its hopes, its aspiring hopes, its fears, that seemed to fall cold and witheringly, on the very springs of life. I would, at least, give voice to my passion. I would, at least, not die, a silent and despairing lover.

But how different it is, to meditate a declaration like mine, in the confidence of solitary communion, and to utter it to the adored object. It was in vain. Days rolled on—she leant as formerly upon my arm—I sat beside her in the library—I listened to her sweet music, when I was the only listener, and might have spoken the words that burned for utterance within me, when no ear but her's could have caught the sound.

But I did *not* speak them. My lips refused their office. A glare as of the noontide sun was in my eyes, and a sound like the rush of mighty waters in my ears; and my knees trembled, and I gasped for breath, as I vainly attempted to syllable her name. After such scenes, I would rush forth, half-frantic, into the Park, or bury myself in the solitude of my own apartment. There, in all the bitterness of self-reproach, I would curse myself for a coward, in having shrunk in silence and trembling from the trial I had courted.

Spring was now fast melting into summer, and reviving nature had once more brightened into life and love. The blossom was on the bush, and the bird on the bough. The sound of gladness came from above, and re-ascended from the earth unto the sky. Who could then wander forth into the woodlands, or the bright green meadows, and gaze on the gay and glorious face of nature, without feeling thankful that his lot had been cast, in a world so beautiful and happy? Yes. In bitterness of soul, I beheld the scene of glad revelry around me. I contributed not to swell the mighty diapason of gratitude and joy, which rose in one grand and universal voice from all created beings. I was as a discord in the harmony of Nature, a blot on her fair escutcheon. There was but one object in my soul, and the whole world beside appeared a vast interminable blank.

The hopes which in their youthful vigour had blossomed in my heart, faded before the full expansion of the flower. The ecstatic dreams of bliss in which I had delighted to indulge, visited me no longer. I shrank even from the presence of the Lady Melicent, and as the destined period of my return to the army, drew near, I anticipated, with a gloomy satisfaction, the opportunity which would be then afforded me, of finding—an honourable grave. Yes; in another month, I would quit my country, never, never to return. Then, perhaps, the memory of my folly would be washed away by its retribution, and she would not refuse a tear to the memory of one, who had loved her, not wisely, but too well.

While my ideas flowed on in this melancholy channel, I was indeed an object to be pitied. I loathed society, yet, when forced to mingle in it, my spirits were unnaturally high. I laughed, I talked, I sang, and was perhaps, in the common acceptation of the term, delightful company. I rivalled Sir Cavendish Potts in loquacity, and was as frisky, and apparently as light-hearted as Lord Amersham. Lady Greystoke, it is true, called me a foolish young man; but Lady Eleanour declared me a charming creature, and in the vivacity of a heavy heart I rattled on. But when, after an evening thus spent, I retired to my chamber, who knew, or could know, the suffering that awaited me! There, when the temporary excitement had passed away, and in the weariness of exhausted nature I cast myself on my pillow, then came the hours of dread and agony, and that dismal sinking of the heart, compared with which all other pains are but as dust in the balance. To such sufferings were added the pangs of self-reproach. The fatal temptation had not found me, I had sought it. In the pride and vanity of my heart, I had been buoyed up by visionary and foolish hopes, and could I complain, that these had now deserted me?

In this melancholy mood of mind, I was walking one morning in one of the least frequented portions of the Park, when I met Lady Melicent alone. She was going to a neighbouring cottage, and invited me to accompany her. Her spirits were high, and she talked of several recent occurrences in a strain of animation, even more vivid than usual. The cottage was at no great distance, and we soon reached it. On our return, the conversation continued in the same strain. She rallied me on the late accession to my spirits.

"Since the arrival of Lady Eleanour," she said, "you have become quite a different creature. You are no longer a moping meditative young man, like Jaques, melancholy and gentlemanlike—in manner solemn and sententious, and philosophizing with the air of a cynic, on all the foolish people about you. I congratulate you both on the improvement and its cause. "

"And you attribute this change to the presence of Lady Eleanour? "

"Certainly. The miracle commenced the very day you first met. I am pretty accurate about dates, and we women, you know, are tolerably sharp-sighted in each other's affairs, whatever we may be in our own. "

"And yet you are mistaken. I admit the charms of the Lady Eleanour, but she is, and can be nothing to me. Do *you* think her a person likely to inspire a deep and lasting passion? "

"Really, I think Lady Eleanour a very lovable person indeed. She is pretty, amiable, and not too clever, and what more could any reasonable man desire. As for your deep and lasting passion, I imagine it to be altogether a thing of romance,—a mere fabulous creation of the poets. "

"You do not, then, believe in the existence of such love? "

"Why, to say the truth, I have no settled belief on the matter. Such love may have been, and may be again, in some strong and peculiar circumstances, just as ghosts have appeared, and may, for aught I know, appear again, though, having never met with the one or the other, my judgment with regard to both rests in abeyance. "

"Oh, why is Lady Melicent so unjust, at once to our sex, and her own! Most of all, why is she so unjust, to her own noble nature, as to doubt her power of exciting, and ours of feeling such love as alone is worthy of its object,—deep, fervent, and eternal,—or, if perishable, perishable only with the heart that gave it birth! "

I would have proceeded, but my voice here faltered, and I stopped. But I had already said enough. I felt that the Rubicon was past, that I had reached the awful crisis, when my fate must in a few moments be decided. As I pronounced the last words, I looked upon her face, with such concentrated intensity of gaze, as that with which a criminal endeavours to read his chance of mercy, on the countenance of his judge.

Her eye met mine, and a blush deep as crimson suffused her cheek. As she answered, she looked upon the ground, and a faint smile was on her lips.

"The love you talk of, is the love not of real life, but of romance. It is the love one reads of in a novel, of some high-born heroine in a cottage among the Welsh mountains, or in the south of France, preceded generally by something about the cooing of doves, and followed by a copy of verses, or a serenade from some noble lover in disguise. This is but the fanciful theory of love, not the dull and vulgar reality. "

"Oh, breathe not, " I replied, "such treason of the human heart. *You*, indeed, have never felt such love, for where is he who is worthy to be its object! But, believe there is at least one bosom—— "

I paused, for agitation choked my utterance; my limbs refused their office, and I stood, with every fibre quivering, rooted to the spot.

She too stopped.

In a few moments my powers were restored, and I knelt before her.

" Yes, " I exclaimed, " I have *dared* to love you; turn from me with disdain—I know my crime, and I ask only for its punishment. I know you are above my sphere—I know such passion is folly, is madness—I know its fate, and I am prepared to meet it. "

As I spoke, her frame too trembled, and she stood silent, and with downcast eyes.

" Oh, speak, " I continued ; " one word, not of anger, but of pity, is all—all I require. "

She stood still unmoved before me ; there was no motion of her lips, but in a faint, and scarcely audible voice, I heard the word —

" Rise. "

I obeyed, and stood once more beside her.

" I know,—I feel that I have given you pain, and would not willingly prolong it. Command me from your presence—bid me quit you for ever, and you shall be obeyed. My lips shall but breathe one farewell, and henceforward I shall be to you but as a dream. "

She was silent. I know not what there was in her look, for I saw it undergo no change, but hope dawned suddenly on my heart, and I took the hand that hung motionless by her side.

Her face, which had till now been pale, became in one instant the colour of carnation. Her very fingers reddened as I raised them to my lips, but they were not withdrawn. Words cannot express the blessedness of that moment, for then my heart told me I was beloved.

For some seconds, perhaps minutes, (for who in such a situation could take note of time ?) we stood silent and motionless. No—not motionless—for the bosom of the Lady Melicent heaved tumultuously, and her heart even visibly beat itself against the walls of its prison, as if struggling to be free. I felt the small quick pulses of her hand, which still lay passively in mine, and encircling her with my arm, I drew her to my bosom with a pressure as soft and gentle as a mother's first embrace to her new-born babe.

She started convulsively as she felt this, and her eyes, which till then had never met mine, were raised to my face, with a gentle look of fear, and of reproach.

It was understood. I asked for no declaration of passion, no avowal of love, and, releasing her from my scarcely perceptible embrace, I placed her arm within my own, and we walked on silently, in a path sheltered by shrubs and underwood, from the chance of observation.

Long did we wander that morning, and swiftly fled the winged hours ; and ere the sound of the dinner-bell had warned us of the necessity of our return, I had imprinted the first kiss on the glowing lips of Lady Melicent.

At dinner, we met again. Never did conqueror advance to a triumph with lighter step, or prouder heart, than those with which I entered the drawing-room. Lady Melicent was there, and never had she seemed in my eyes so transcendently lovely. All the radiance that elegance of adornment can lend to beauty had been contributed, as if to barb the arrows of her charms, and render their wounds incurable. In everything connected with Lady Melicent, there was something pre-eminently refined and *recherché*. On that day she wore jewels. They were few, but rich and beautiful; and I could have exclaimed, in my enthusiasm, as I gazed on her—

> Up, up, fair bride! and call
> Thy stars from out their several boxes; take
> Thy rubies, pearls, and emeralds forth, and make
> Thyself a constellation of them all.

The colour on her cheeks was more brilliant than usual, and her eye, though restless and unfixed, was if possible brighter. Once, and but once only, it met mine, and it was instantly withdrawn; but her glance, transient as it was, had spoken what volumes would have been insufficient to express.

For myself, though my mind was, by the events of the morning, freed from a burden, which had pressed on it almost to madness, I was even less capable than formerly, of entering into the spirit of society. So perfect was the enjoyment I derived from the concentration of my own thoughts, that I found it almost impossible, to divert any part of my attention to the scene in which I mingled.

I had the misfortune, again to sit next Lady Greystoke at dinner, and my conduct must have certainly formed a striking contrast, to what it had been on a former occasion. Lady Greystoke talked a great deal, but not one particle of her discourse, did I either hear or understand; and when the expression of her countenance made it palpable that an answer on my part, was become necessary, it was generally so little apropos to the subject, as to excite in the old lady, serious doubts with regard to the perfect sanity of my intellects. To do her justice, I do think she bore with me very patiently; but when my absence of mind extended so far, that, instead of port, the wine she preferred, I ordered the servant to fill her glass with porter, and in place of chicken, sent her plate back loaded with the leg of a goose, her choler was very pardonably roused, and endurance could extend no farther. I never afterwards recovered her good graces.

Of what passed in the dining-room, after the departure of the ladies, I have not the slightest recollection. Till the gentlemen returned to the drawing-room, I was as completely cut off, from all communication with the external world, as a new-born puppy. All the avenues of my senses, were blocked up. I neither saw, heard, smelt, touched, nor tasted, and partook more of the nature of a pure and abstract *Ens*, than I recollect ever to have done before, or since.

Corporeal life again, dawned with the presence of the ladies. One look of bashful consciousness from Lady Melicent, as I entered the drawing-room, recalled me once more to the material world. In my then state of excited feeling, I durst not trust myself to approach her. I was jealous of observation, and imagined that every look and word, was scrutinized by those around me. I dreaded lest the secret confined to two conscious bosoms, might be laid open to profane eyes.

Aware as I was of the necessity of present concealment, reserve towards Lady Melicent was palpably dictated by prudence. But what weak and inconsistent creatures we are! How few of our actions are guided by reason, how many by impulse! Lord Amersham, who was fond of music, asked his daughter to sing.

" Don't ask me, papa, " she answered ; " indeed I cannot. "

" Come, Lyndhurst, and you, Thornton, do you try your influence. Two young men may succeed, when one old one fails, " said Lord Amersham, laughingly. " Now, Lyndhurst, you try first. "

Lord Lyndhurst, who was lolling in an easy chair, slightly raised himself on this appeal, and in the letter, though scarcely in the spirit of his instructions, yawningly joined in the request for music.

Lady Melicent instantly declined, even more decidedly than before.

" Come, Thornton, you're our forlorn hope ; exert yourself, or all's lost. "

" Where the request of Lord Lyndhurst and your Lordship has been denied, it were vain, indeed, to hope that mine would be granted. "

" Ah, who knows? " said his lordship ; " make the experiment at all events. "

Vain and senseless as I was, I could not resist the silly and dangerous triumph which I saw before me. I approached Lady Melicent, who was seated alone at some distance, and in a voice low and inaudible to the rest of the party, I added my entreaties to those which had already been ineffectual. She answered—

" If you ask it, I will try ; but I fear I cannot. " And a glance of fond reproach accompanied her words.

I then, to avoid suspicion, addressed her in a louder tone.

" You have heard, Lady Melicent, that I am deputed to beg of you, in the name of Lord Amersham and Lord Lyndhurst, to oblige the company by singing. What I durst not presume to ask in my own character, I now humbly solicit as their deputy. "

Lady Melicent sang. Her voice was weak and tremulous, but never did it sink so deeply into my heart. That indeed was to me a moment of pride, which kings might envy!

I was soon, however, awakened to a full sense of the danger I had incurred, by observing the look of strong displeasure that marked the countenance of Lady Greystoke. That Lady Melicent should have been influenced by my entreaties, to grant a favour which she had already denied to her father, and the man selected by her family as her future husband, seemed in her eyes a flagrant violation of that propriety, for which she was on all occasions a rigid stickler. Even Lord Amersham, I thought, was not much gratified by the success of my mission, but I could never discover that any serious suspicions had been excited by my folly.

CHAPTER IV

Hope is a lover's staff; walk hence with that,
And manage it against despairing thoughts.
Two Gentlemen of Verona.

I LOVED, and if there be truth in woman's words, I was beloved again. Yet not with the consciousness of reciprocal affection, ceases a lover's fear. Seldom calm and unruffled, are the waters of his spirit. There is a tide of dread and apprehension, which is continually ebbing and flowing in his soul. Even in the very excess of my good fortune, there was something which had a tendency to excite fear. Could I look on the Lady Melicent—all that nature,—all that rank and fortune had made her—and at once undoubtingly and confidingly believe, that, being all I saw and knew her to be, she was, she could be *mine?*

Yes, often I did so believe, and then indeed I was happy. Yet how many obstacles to our union, still remained. Could I hope for the consent of Lord Amersham? What had I to offer, which could serve as a counterpoise, in his estimation, to the high rank, and immense fortune of Lord Lyndhurst, who had already declared himself her suitor? How small, how utterly insignificant, were my worldly claims, when put in competition with his? If I excelled him in personal qualities—and, without vanity, I felt I might assume such a superiority—what was this, in the calm and calculating eye of a father, compared with the splendid settlements, the influence, and the distinction, which belonged to an union with my rival? Under the circumstances, indeed, it seemed as if there was something even ridiculous, in my venturing to make proposals to Lord Amersham for an alliance with his daughter. What could I expect, but that they would instantly be rejected, with scorn and contempt? I was too proud to encounter such a rejection. A mortification so humiliating, was one, to which I felt that all my philosophy, could not enable me to submit with patience.

The interviews of Lady Melicent and myself, were rare, for the circumstances in which we were placed, rendered it necessary that they should be arranged, with the greatest prudence and caution. Our intercourse was secret, and on that account perhaps more sweet. It was seldom that we met alone, and then it was with beating hearts. Oh! these blessed but fleeting moments, within whose narrow limits the delight of centuries was concentrated and compressed, it is with a throbbing pulse that I even now recall them to my memory!

But at other times, I at least enjoyed the privilege of beholding her, and though my lips were silent, my eyes were free. Her presence was indeed, become as the life-blood to my heart. Sometimes I would sit with a volume in my hand, one line of which I never read, secretly watching her motions, and drinking in, even the most trifling word her lips might syllable. Then at night, when I retired to my chamber, not calmly was my head laid upon my pillow, not gently and serenely, did sleep descend upon my eyelids, for there was fever in my blood, and a burning in my limbs, and I could not rest.

Often did I rise from my sleepless couch, and throwing open my window, sit for hours in the moonshine, and gaze on the light that twinkled from the lattice of her chamber window. And if a shadow fell but for a moment on the curtain which shaded it, I knelt as in the presence of a superior being, till it had passed away. Neither waking nor in sleep, was she absent from my thoughts. By day I gazed on her, and by night she visited my dreams.

In our interviews, I communicated to her, all my hopes and fears, and told all the obstacles, that presented themselves to our union. Our hopes, indeed, were in unison, but she partook not of my fears. In her glowing imagination, difficulties vanished, and the horizon of our future destiny, contained no cloud to darken its beauty and serenity. She told me, indeed, that the heart of her father was set on her union with Lord Lyndhurst, and that the latter had already made an offer of his hand, which he was urgent she should accept. In the present situation of affairs, therefore, it was too evident, that any proposals I might make to Lord Amersham, would have the effect of putting a complete and final stop to our correspondence, or at least of rendering its continuance a matter of great and almost insurmountable difficulty.

For the present, our engagement was to be secret. It was better, indeed, that in rejecting the addresses of Lord Lyndhurst, her father should not imagine that she was influenced by any previous attachment. But this done, on my return to England, which would certainly be in the course of the following year, we would go to Lord Amersham, and lay before him the truth. We would tell him that the happiness of both depended on our union, that our troth was already plighted, and in such circumstances, she, who knew him well, assured me, he could not—he would not refuse his consent. But even if we should be deceived in these fond hopes, still, still she would be mine. She loved her father; she had always loved him. She was an only child, and in her had centred all his love. But there are holier ties than even those, which link together the hearts of parents and their offspring. By these, she was bound to me, and no exercise of paternal authority should induce her to violate those vows of constancy, and unswerving love, which in the presence of God, we had sworn to each other.

Thus assured, in those blessed and happy hours, doubt was banished from our bosoms. What doubt, indeed, would not the sight of that countenance—the glance of that eye, have dissipated in a moment?

But love, though the sweetener of life, cannot constitute its business. In whatever relation we may stand to society, we are bound to the performance of certain active duties, inconsistent with a life of contemplative indulgence. The world is our creditor, and a hard one, for it will relax nothing of its claims. A life devoted to love, though one of the staple fictions of poets and romance writers, is incompatible both with the natural character of man, and his social relations. Our bodies and our minds are alike framed for action, and he who could merge all his duties, in the indulgence even of the purest passion, would in so doing, prove himself to be an object not of love, but of contempt.

The hour which was to tear me from the presence and society of her I loved, approached, and came. We had met the evening before my departure, (for it was then summer,) once more to repeat our vows of constancy, and say—if our lips could speak it—Farewell.

Well do I remember the spot, where, seated with her head resting on my bosom, I kissed away the bright tears that flowed fast down her cheeks, at the prospect of our separation. It was beneath a huge tree, whose branches spread higher and wider than those of its surrounding brothers, and which, from some ancient tradition, was known by the name of "The Wizard Oak." It stood deep in the woodlands, in a solitude rarely disturbed, save by the footsteps of the woodman.

Here it was that we parted.

We had met to speak, yet we spoke not. The deep silence of the tranquil evening, was broken by no vows, or protestations of fervent and unchanging love. Were they needed? No. I read her truth in the convulsive heaving of her bosom, in the tears which my lips drank up, as they trickled from their bed.

At length we rose, and supported by my arm, we walked together to the extremity of the wood, and our hearts told us, that the moment of the final struggle was come at last.

I cast myself on my knees before her. I invoked blessings on her head, for the proud gift of her love to one so unworthy. She extended her hand to me, and I arose.

"Oh, grieve not thus!" I exclaimed, for I saw she was much agitated—"The pang of parting is bitter, but it is short. I go happy, for if I fall, I know there is one faithful heart to deplore me; if I return, it will be to enjoy the unspeakable reward of your love."

Lady Melicent spoke not, she could not speak.

"I see,—I feel, that my lingering here but adds to your distress, and I will tear myself away."

"Oh, no, no!" she exclaimed, clasping my hand between both of her's, as if to prevent my departure—"Not yet."

I waited silently till the paroxysm was past, then gently releasing her from my embrace, and imprinting on her lips one long last kiss, murmured Farewell, as I sprung forward with the speed of an arrow, and we saw each other no more.

On that evening Lady Melicent was visible to no eye, and Lord Amersham reported, that she was confined to her chamber, by a severe headach. I passed the night in gazing on the light that shone from her chamber window, but it was crossed by no shadow, nor could I detect the smallest indication that the apartment was occupied by a living tenant.

In the morning I descended to the breakfast-room—the party had already assembled, but Lady Melicent was not there. Breakfast passed, and my carriage was at the door. My heart smote me as I bade farewell to Lord Amersham. I felt as if I had taken an unfair advantage of his hospitality, to seduce the affections of his daughter. I felt, that the simplicity and openness of his character, had not been met with the reciprocal qualities in mine. He had welcomed me to his house as a friend and a relation—had I acted the part of one?

A still small voice within me answered, No.

Nothing, however, could exceed his kindness. " Good bye, Thornton, my boy, " said the old nobleman—" Good bye, and may God bless you. I hope to see you come back with a red ribbon at least. Let me know if they ill use you, at the Horse Guards. I have not much interest there, but I'll do what I can. I am sure Melicent is sorry she is unable to bid you farewell, and give you assurances of her good wishes before you set out on your campaigns. Take care of yourself, you know. No volunteering on Out Piquets or Forlorn Hopes, but get distinction in the regular course, and then come back and marry a pretty girl, and settle down as a country gentleman at Thornhill. "

In reply, I thanked his lordship, and begged him to convey my acknowledgments to Lady Melicent, for the more than ordinary kindness I had experienced at Staunton, which, I assured him, should never be obliterated from my memory.

My parting with Lucy (for at the earnest request of Lady Melicent, I had consented to her remaining at Staunton some time longer) was melancholy, yet, compared with the parting of the preceding evening, it cost but a trifling pang. The dear and loving girl clasped her arms around my neck, and hiding her face in my bosom, wept bitterly. There were many spectators of the scene, but poor Lucy, in yielding to her natural emotion, forgot them all. She clung to me, as to one from whom she would not be parted, and her sobs were violent and hysterical. Nature became gradually exhausted—I felt the grasp with which she still held me, relax, and after a mental blessing, I kissed her lips, and consigning the almost fainting girl, to the arms of Lord Amersham, I sprang into the carriage, and drove off. For the first few minutes of my journey, I was confused and stupified; then I gazed from the carriage window, to catch, in the windings of the avenue, an occasional glimpse of the house, as its summit rose above the trees, or was visible in their intervals. Within its walls, was contained all that I most loved on earth, and my eyes were still turned towards it, long after I had emerged from the demesne, and it was no longer visible.

London was the object of my destination. I had lingered at Staunton till the last moment, and there was barely time, before the expiration of my leave, to make the necessary preparations for the voyage, and to equip myself for the field. In my escape from Madrid, I had lost all my baggage; and rapid as London tradesmen proverbially are, under the excitement of the *auri sacra fames*, my wants could not be supplied in a day. On my arrival, however, I lost no time in taking measures for my full equipment. The exertions of tradesmen of every denomination were put in instant requisition; and Prosser, that most facetious and urbane of accoutrement makers, promised to defer the execution of an order, he had just received from the Prince of Wales, in order to supply me, *quam primum*, with sash, gorget, epaulettes, hair-trigger pistols, and a sword, in comparison with whose temper, a Damascus blade was as nothing.

While these preparations were in progress, I had a few days of leisure, which I found myself at liberty to devote to certain necessary arrangements in my affairs, and to entering a little into the amusements of town. By the latter, I endeavoured to dissipate a certain gloom, which, in spite of the brightness of my prospects, hung occasionally on my spirits.

In order to prevent my being utterly forgotten at the Horse Guards, I adopted Lord Amersham's advice, and determined, before quitting town, to attend the levee of the Commander-in-Chief, and personally solicit the promotion, which I thought was due to my services. With this view I waited on Colonel Torrens, and having informed him of my claims, and their object, I was directed to attend on the following Tuesday, at two o'clock, when I should have the honour of an interview with Sir David Dundas.

I was punctual in my attendance at the appointed hour, and, on my arrival, was ushered into a large antechamber, filled with officers of all ranks and descriptions. The levee was already proceeding. General after general was admitted into the presence-chamber, and after a longer or a shorter audience, was dismissed, to make way for a successor.

Three tedious hours did I wait before my turn for admission came. They passed, however, less heavily than might have been expected, for, in the crowd which filled the antechamber, I had the good fortune to meet with an agreeable companion. He was a Major O'Shaughnessy, a captain of seventeen years' standing, who had only recently received a brevet majority. The Major was most vehement in the exposition of his wrongs. He had endured all varieties of climate—he had fought in the East, and in the West—had been taken prisoner by Tippoo Saib—and shot through the body, at the capture of Guadaloupe. In his return from India, the ship in which he sailed, had been wrecked, and his wife and two children drowned. With all this series of service and suffering, he still remained a captain, nor had even the promotion of brevet, been given to him till it had become his right, from being bestowed on every other officer of similar standing in the army. Still the veteran's spirit was unbroken, and he that day attended the levee for the first time of his life, apparently less from the hope of any beneficial consequence to himself, than from a certain abstract pleasure, which he felt in the detail of his wrongs. When I compared my own claims and services with his, I could scarcely help feeling a little ashamed, of the errand on which I had come, and was even disposed to demur to my own right to advancement in the service, when such officers as my grey-haired companion, were suffered to remain unrewarded with promotion.

While engaged in these reflections, I heard my name pronounced by the usher in a loud voice, and starting up, I passed immediately through a folding door, and stood in the presence of the Commander-in-Chief. He was an emaciated old man, apparently in the very last stage of physical debility, and evidently altogether unequal, to the arduous and important duties of the office, to which he had been recently appointed. Still the air of a soldier had not deserted him; age had not descended lightly on his head, but he did not bend under the burden of his years. His person was erect, and one might in his gait and deportment, still discern some remnant of the man, who had studied discipline and tactics, under the immediate eye of Frederick the Great. To that monarch, indeed, as he is represented in his later years, Sir David Dundas was not without some personal resemblance.

On my entrance, Sir David bowed, and requested me to inform him of my claims and wishes. I did so. I stated, I was now a captain of nearly five years' standing. That I had served in America; that I had twice been taken prisoner in the Peninsula; that I had once the cleverness and good sense to escape; that I was now about to return to my regiment abroad; in short, that he then saw before him a most excellent and praiseworthy officer, whom it would be highly creditable to his own judgment, and beneficial to the service to promote. In fact, having cast off the modesty, which encumbered the eloquence of Othello, I prudently did everything in my power, to

" Grace my cause in speaking of myself. "

Sir David, to do him justice, heard me out with the most imperturbable patience, then assured me that my claims should be noted, and that it would give him pleasure to promote my views, whenever a favourable opportunity might occur. He concluded by two or three bows, then ringing his bell, the door was thrown open, another name announced, and I took my departure. Such was the conclusion of the only levee I ever attended at the Horse-Guards.

In the course of a week, I found nothing further remained to detain me in England, and getting into the Falmouth Mail, soon found myself at my point of embarkation. A packet was about to sail on the following morning, and I went on board the evening of my arrival.

CHAPTER V

Thou hast talk'd
Of sallies, and retires; of trenches, tents,
Of palisadoes, frontiers, parapets,
Of basilisks, of cannon, culverin,
Of prisoners' ransom, and of soldiers slain,
And all the currents of a heady fight.
Henry IV.

ONCE more upon the deep. With a flowing sheet, we ran rapidly on our voyage, and on the fourth day had skirted the mountainous waters of the Bay of Biscay, and were to the southward of Cape Finisterre. We saw the Burlings on the evening of the seventh, passed Fort St Julian in the night, and at day-dawn, beheld the towers of Belem, gilded by the radiance of the morning sun.

I have never seen Naples or Genoa, but when viewed from the sea, I can conceive nothing more beautiful than Lisbon. It rises on the side of a magnificent amphitheatre of hills, gradually heightening as it recedes from the shore, and widening its expanse, till the eye in gazing on its palaces and convents, becomes almost confused in the mighty wilderness of dwellings.

I had known Lisbon before, and the eventful period which had intervened since I last quitted it, had produced little change on the city or its inhabitants. Apparently no people could be more loyal, the national cockade was in every hat, and those who had formerly been peaceful citizens, now donned their weapons, and went forth arrayed in the pride, the pomp, and panoply of glorious war.

The grand depôt of the army was at Belem. Thither were sent the sick and the wounded, and perhaps scarcely fewer in number, those who found in sickness, a convenient excuse for avoiding the fatigues and hazards of a campaign. The streets were crowded with British officers, apparently in the full enjoyment of youthful lustihood and vigour, who, though unequal to encounter the duties of the field, were perfectly equal to mingle in all the gaiety and dissipation of Lisbon. Such characters were usually contemptuously distinguished by the title of *Belem loungers*. I was not at all disposed to swell their numbers, and having purchased such cattle and stores as were necessary for my field equipment, no obstruction remained, to delay the moment of my departure. A detachment of about fifty men, belonging to several regiments of the second division of the army, was placed under my command; and my horses and baggage having been sent forward by land, I embarked with the party on the Tagus.

The Tagus and its golden sands! What dull soul is he, who says there is no magic in a name? It is not true, that "a rose by any other name would smell as sweet," if all the associations connected with its fragrance, be lost in the change. At all events, I embarked on the Tagus, prepared to admire both the river, and its scenery.

When we had lost sight of Lisbon, I sat in the stern of our little vessel, recalling all that history or romance had connected with its waters, as the poles of the boatmen, slowly and lazily propelled us forward. After all, I have seen finer rivers than the Tagus. There is seldom anything beautiful, and never anything grand, in its scenery. It is true, its banks are occasionally clothed with vineyards and olive groves, and such things sound well in description. But the woods of old England are finer objects than the latter, and a cottager's garden quite as pretty a feature in a landscape as a Portuguese vineyard.

Five weary days did we journey on the Tagus, counteracted in our progress, by the united influence of wind and stream, running ashore on sand-banks, at least a dozen times a-day, and encountering all those "moving accidents by flood," to which fresh-water travellers are liable. On the fifth night we reached Punheté; and the river becoming shallower and more difficult to navigate, the higher we advanced, on the sixth morning we quitted the boats, and commenced our march across the country, towards Almeida, in the neighbourhood of which, by the latest accounts before our departure, it was most probable we should fall in with the army. The intelligence we received from the country people with regard to the movements of Lord Wellington, was at first vague and contradictory; but in proportion as we approached nearer to the scene of operation, it became more definite. We learned, on testimony impossible to be doubted, that Almeida had fallen, and that the allied forces were in full retreat, closely followed by the enemy, and accordingly changing our course, we endeavoured as soon as possible to intersect the line of march, on which it was probable we should fall in with the retiring army.

The situation of our little detachment, indeed, was not without its difficulties. On quitting the boats, we had only four days' provisions; and had we been too late in arriving at our destined point, there was every chance of our falling into the hands of the enemy, who were rapidly advancing in pursuit.

Our fourth day's march brought us to Penalva. There we learned that a division of the British army, were retreating towards us, and that we should probably fall in with them, on the following day. We learned likewise, that a party of French cavalry had, in the course of the day, been seen hovering in the neighbourhood of the village, in which we then lay. On the following morning, we were early on our march, and had proceeded several leagues, without being able to detect any indication of the proximity of an armed force. At length, upon the summit of a hill, as far distant as the eye could reach, a gleam of unusual brightness was discernible, which gradually extended down its side, in one long and unbroken line. It was the glancing of arms, though those that bore them were yet invisible. As they drew nearer, the sight of the scarlet uniform, put a stop to any apprehensions which might have lurked within us, and we joyfully recognised friends and countrymen, in the advancing body. It was the division of General Hill, to which we belonged. On its approach, I rode up to the Hon. General Stewart, who led the advance, and reported my own arrival, and that of my party, and had once more the satisfaction of joining my regiment, as it passed on the line of march.

There is never anything melancholy, in the meeting of soldiers. With them, the present is everything, the past a point, the future a blank. The greeting of surviving friends, is seldom embittered by recollections of those who are no more. In a life of danger and casualty, this is natural. Death is too common an occurrence, to make any very vivid or lasting impression. His presence is but an every-day event. Soldiers become accustomed to the terrors of his eye, and from frequently regarding him, lose their fear in their familiarity. They love their living friends not the less, that they mourn not for those who are departed.

There was certainly no want of warmth in the greeting of my companions. They thronged around me, and kind inquiries, and cordial pressure of the hands were exchanged, as my eyes rested on those who had been endeared to me by communion of pleasures, and perhaps still more, by the fellowship of danger and privation. Some, indeed, I missed from the circle, for during my absence, war had claimed its victims. They were gone, and a word of praise, a passing thought of regret, was all the tribute offered to their memory.

The British army continued their retreat, without annoyance from the enemy, and, after a halt of a day or two, which a series of severe marches rendered almost necessary, took up their position on the heights of Busaco. Our division, whose route had hitherto been on the left of the Mondego, crossed that river on the 26th, and formed the right wing of the army. Our position on these mountains seemed admirably chosen. The ridge of which it consisted extended in a northerly direction about eight miles, affording a complete command of all the roads to Lisbon, and the road to Coimbra, which passed on its extreme left. On the low ground, in front, was collected the main body of the enemy's army, whose intention of forcing our position soon became evident. Never before had I seen so large a force collected, as it were, into a single focus. It was, indeed, a sight stirring to the spirit. The officers stood singly, or collected in groups, on the summit of the hills, gazing on the fires that blazed in the camp beneath them, and the peaceful occupations of those with whom they were so soon to be engaged in deadly contest.

While I was thus engaged, the sergeant of my company came up, and presenting the orders of the day, I found, on reading them, that I was destined that evening for the duty of Out Piquet. I confess, that the first ideas which the knowledge of this circumstance inspired, were not pleasant ones. The duty of Out Piquet was always one of danger, but in the existing situation of the armies it involved peculiar peril. It was certain—next to certain, that we should be attacked and driven in during the night, preparatory to a general engagement. I returned the orderly book to the sergeant in silence, and continued gazing on the scene around me. If possible, the interest it excited had become more vivid, in proportion to the increase of hazard, to which I now saw myself exposed.

But the hour of evening approached, and the necessity of preparation roused me from my reverie. I returned to my tent, and gave directions for the instant packing of my baggage, and having finished a solitary meal, repaired to the spot appointed for the parade of the Piquets. As night closed in, we descended the brow of the hill, and marched in deep silence to our station, distant but a few hundred yards from the advanced posts of the enemy. It was pointed out to me by the Quarter-master-general, who accompanied the party, and having received the necessary directions, which were spoken in a whisper scarcely audible, and the expression of his good wishes for our safe return, he retired.

The Piquet under my command, consisted of a subaltern, two sergeants, and sixty rank and file. In our front, and on either flank, videttes were pushed up as closely to the enemy, as was found practicable, without occasioning a discovery of our position. A short distance in rear of the videttes, were placed a sergeant and six men, and between this party and the main body of the Piquet, was stationed the subaltern and fifteen, thus forming a connected chain of communication from front to rear.

Independently of the feeling of insecurity, which naturally attached to our situation and duty, I have seldom spent a more uncomfortable night. It was dark and gusty, and the wind came at intervals, accompanied with heavy torrents of rain. We were without shelter from the inclemency of the weather, and the soldiers, wrapped in their great-coats, lay down in the ranks, their hands still grasping their firelocks, and prepared, in case of alarm, to spring instantly to their feet.

Heavily and slowly did the hours that night flow by. The sounds of song and merriment, that came by fits upon the wind from the enemy's camp, by degrees died away, and the occasional neighing of horses and braying of mules, alone gave indication of its vicinity. Aware that the safety even of the whole army might be endangered by any negligence in the discharge of my duty, I passed the night on foot, visiting occasionally the different detachments and videttes, and endeavouring to detect, by ear or eye, indication of an advancing foe. Sometimes I would advance on tiptoe towards a point, from which some suspicious sound appeared to proceed, and then hurry back on finding I was deceived. When tired by fruitless watching, I would sometimes cast myself on the ground, and gaze for a few minutes on the dark canopy of clouds, which hung loweringly in the sky, then spring again upon my feet, at the fancied sound of human voices, or the approaching footfalls that rung upon my ear.

Often, too, at intervals, did the thought of England—of my sisters, and of one bright object even dearer than they, steal unawares into my heart, in the silent watches of the night. Often did I see the beloved forms, floating towards me, beautiful in the darkness; but when, with extended arms, I would have pressed them to my bosom, I knew they were but shadows, for they flitted past me, as if borne onwards, by the viewless winds.

Thus did the night wear on, and at length the first streaks of morn, were seen dappling the edge of the horizon. No form of danger had approached us, and we were already with joyful hearts, preparing to return with the dawn to our encampment.

Suddenly a shot was heard, which, after a silence of a few moments, was succeeded by the irregular firing of a larger body. Every instant it became more frequent, and between the intervals was heard the tramp of many feet, and the murmur of voices. It was but the work of a moment in the men to rouse themselves, and stand prepared for the impending attack, and scarcely had they done so, when the advanced parties appeared, driven back breathless, and in confusion from the front. They re-formed in the rear of the main body, and were ordered instantly to prime and load. Before time was afforded to effect this operation, the enemy had advanced within a few yards, and giving them a volley, the retreat instantly commenced. Our fire was returned with interest, and it was evident the enemy had attacked us in overwhelming numbers. We had now retreated some distance, and were still closely pursued, when a quick but desultory firing suddenly arose on our right. This proceeded from a detachment of a Rifle battalion of the 60th, which had been thrown in advance, in order to support the Piquets in case of attack. The pursuit of our assailants was instantly checked, and we continued to retire, with little further molestation from the enemy, who, in their turn, were driven back on the main body of the army. In this skirmish four men of the Piquet were killed, and seven wounded.

My regiment, when I rejoined it, was under arms. The sound of firing was yet heard occasionally from below, which showed, though the enemy were still hid by the mist-wreaths of the morning, that they were on the advance. As day gradually brightened, general officers were seen anxiously reconnoitring from the summits of the ridge, the movements of the hostile army, and aides-de-camp and adjutant-generals rode past at full speed, delivering orders to the different parts of the line. The dreadful voice of the artillery, which had been hitherto silent, then rent the air with its thunders, and the fire of musquetry became evidently heavier and more continuous. At this moment, my attention was arrested by the appearance of Lord Wellington, who rode up, with foam on his bridle, in front of the division. Upwards of two years had elapsed since I had last seen him. These had been to him, certainly, years of mental toil and anxiety. But there was little change discernible in his appearance. There was the same fire in his eye, and animation in his countenance, and his air betrayed even more of that confidence and self-possession, with which I had formerly been struck. He delivered his orders to Sir Rowland Hill, with promptitude and rapidity, and instantly setting spurs to his steed, again vanished from our view.

The point which the enemy selected for his attack, was on our left, in front of the station occupied by the 3d division. Their advance up the hill had been made under a severe fire, and on their attaining its summit, they were instantly charged with the bayonet, and driven back with heavy loss. Our division moved to the left, to support the part of the line thus assailed, but our assistance was unnecessary, the troops already engaged having proved themselves fully adequate to the repulse of the enemy. The firing, which had now ceased in our part of the line, was still warmly kept up in the centre, and on the left, both of which points, had been made the scene of formidable attack, by the enemy. From our station on the right, little of the action was discernible, and our gaze was principally directed to the large masses of the French army, which were now visible in the plain beneath, and whose motions we watched with curiosity and interest. These were soon observed to be retiring, and the only firing heard was that of the artillery and of the light division, which still continued to follow the enemy, and harass them in their retreat. By degrees this too died away, and all was silent.

During the remainder of the 27th, no farther attack was made by the French on our position. Tired with the fatigues of the night, and the excitement I had since undergone, I threw myself on my pallet, and slept soundly. Towards evening I awoke. Willingly would I have slept again, for visions of tranquil beauty had visited me in slumber, and it was painful to exchange the bright world of dreams, in which I had been ranging, for that less lovely reality, to which I was again awakened.

The night passed undisturbed, and two hours before the dawn of day, we were under arms. It was the general expectation of the army, that the attack would be again renewed. It was not. The hours passed on without alarm, and when the sun rose, the enemy were observed in motion, on the road leading to Coimbra and Oporto, which passed on the extreme left of the Sierra. In consequence of this, we were ordered instantly to march, and again crossing the Mondego, Sir Rowland Hill's division continued their retreat towards Lisbon, by the road leading through Thomar and Santarem.

Till our arrival at the lines of Torres Vedras, we saw nothing further of the French army. Our march continued for ten days, and it was indeed a melancholy one. The roads were crowded with thousands of families, driven from their homes in a state of utter destitution, and presenting images of squalid misery, never to be effaced from the memories of those who witnessed them. On these I shall not enlarge. They have often been described, and, I believe, never exaggerated ; and he who trusts to his imagination for a picture of the miseries of war, need scarcely fear, however dark his colouring, that, his limning will exceed the truth.

I believe it was on the 9th of October, that we reached Alhandra, a village on the Tagus, which formed the extreme right of the line we were about to occupy. On the night of our arrival, one of those events occurred, which, in the eyes of foreigners, contribute more than any other, to affix a tarnish on the character of our arms. By some culpable negligence, the wine, of which the town contained a great quantity, had not been destroyed ; the soldiers broke into the cellars, and a scene of unparalleled drunkenness ensued. It was a truly fortunate circumstance that the enemy did not attack us on that night, or on the following morning. Had they done so, I am convinced there would not have been found, in the second division, a thousand men capable of bearing arms. The possession of Alhandra, would have afforded the means of turning our position, and the war in Portugal, might thus have been brought to a sudden, and abrupt conclusion.

On the morning after our arrival, General Stewart harangued the men on the parade, and drum-head court-martials being instantly assembled, several severe, but, in the circumstances, not unnecessary punishments, were inflicted.

By the arrival of some French prisoners, we learned that a pretty severe rencontre, between our cavalry and that of the enemy, had taken place that morning at day-dawn. A trumpeter of the 13th bore at his saddle-bow, the *spolia opima* of a French officer, whom he had cut down in the charge. I examined the helmet, which was of brass, and found that it had literally been divided in two. Such a blow was not unworthy the arm of Roland the Paladin, or the most stalwart knight of the Round Table of our own King Arthur.

As night set in, the drum beat to arms, and we were unexpectedly ordered to march. The rain fell in torrents, and the darkness was extreme. I know nothing of the direction in which we marched, but the roads were literally knee-deep, and we proceeded several hours before halting. The night was passed on the road. It was impossible to distinguish any object a yard off, and I and several of my companions remained seated till morning, at the foot of a rock, a projecting ledge of which afforded a slight shelter from the pelting of the storm. Thus on

> This night, wherein the cub-drawn bear would couch,
> The lion, and the belly-pinched wolf,
> Keep their fur dry,

did the division remain exposed to all the fury of the elements. Even the men's knapsacks were wet through, and the rain penetrating their cartouche-boxes, nine-tenths of their ammunition was destroyed.

The morning at length dawned, and the joyful order to advance, was sounded in our ears. A weary journey of two leagues, brought us to a small village in the mountains, where we remained two days. Here better precautions were taken to prevent the repetition of the scene, which had taken place at Alhandra. Before the billets were issued to the soldiers, every house was examined, and the wine which they contained poured out into the streets. This work of destruction was carried on, amid the rueful looks of the natives, and the curses, not loud but deep, of the shivering soldiers.

Our next movement was to Bucellus, famous for the wine which bears its name. It is situated in a hollow, on one of the principal roads to Lisbon, a short distance in the rear of the second line of defence. The town, which is not a large one, was crowded with soldiers, and was the station appointed for two brigades of infantry, and one of cavalry. Here the chances of the service threw me again in contact with my friend Conyers, now a captain of dragoons. Those who have never met a friend of their youth in similar circumstances, know nothing of the glow of feeling which such a meeting excites. In seasons of danger, the heart is peculiarly open, to the impressions of old-remembered friendships. The mind delights to turn from present difficulty and privation, to those who were associated with our former happiness, whose voice recalls to our memory the dream of former days. Conyers was delighted to see me; for he, of course, knew I had been taken prisoner, but had not heard of my escape. Seated at evening, over our canteen of wretched *Ordinaire*, we told the story of our lives, since we had last parted. I learned, that at the time of our capture he had escaped, at the expense of a slight wound, by charging boldly forward, and trusting afterwards to the speed and mettle of his horse. Nor did we fail, while we laughed at his eccentricities, to crush a wine-cup to the health of the old Scotch Captain, who had been our leader on that occasion, and who was now paying the penalty of his generalship at Verdun.

Another goblet, and it was a bumper, was crowned to the health of my worthy uncle; nor was even Girzy unremembered in our potations. Then rose the memory of those days of youthful hope, when, with panting hearts, we had longed for that moment, when our feet would be free to follow the career of pride and honour, for which we felt ourselves to be destined. The hopes of neither of us had been blighted by fortune. The path we panted to pursue we had since trod. Yet we felt that our boyish aspirations were yet unfulfilled, and, too probably, were ever destined to remain so.

Conyers stayed but a few days at Bucellus, nor did we remain much longer. The brigade went into camp about a league in advance, from which, after a sojourn of about ten days, our regiment was ordered to occupy the Quinta de Cunha, a large and solitary chateau among the hills. It was fortified with a few pieces of light artillery. Embrasures were cut in the walls for the action of musquetry; and protected as it was by the surrounding batteries, the Quinta might be considered a place of some strength. Owing to the severity of the duty to which we had hitherto been exposed, I had been seized, before quitting the camp, with an attack of ague. This was so violent, as to render me, for some time, unfit for duty. From a Quotidian, however, it gradually subsisded to a Tertian; and though considerably enfeebled by its continuance, I was enabled once more, to play my humble part in the great game of war.

During the weeks that we remained thus stationed, nothing memorable occurred. Yes, there was one occurrence, the relation of which may perhaps serve to diversify a little the monotonous tissue, of this portion of my memoirs.

The gallant conduct of the Portuguese troops at the battle of Busaco, had induced the ministry, to confer on Marshal Beresford the Order of the Bath. The occasion of his investment with the insignia, Lord Wellington determined to celebrate by a grand party, and an invitation to all the officers of the army, who should be off duty on the appointed day, was inserted in the General Orders.

Although our Quinta was fully twenty miles distant, from Mafra, which was to be the scene of the destined festivity, my friend Popham and myself determined to relieve the dulness of our mode of life, by accepting the invitation. At daylight, we set forward on our way, and after riding for many hours, on the most villainous roads that were ever trod by the foot of either man or horse, sometimes ascending to the mountain-tops, and at others sinking to the very bottom of the valleys, about two o'clock we reached the palace of Mafra. On inquiry, we found there was neither stabling nor forage for our horses; but observing some ruinous and deserted cottages at a short distance, we selected the most weather-proof for a stable, and returned to the palace.

We were ushered through a handsome suite of apartments into a splendid saloon, which we found already filled by a large and miscellaneous assemblage. There, were generals in their stars and ribands, and their staff, all tags and embroidery; and there, too, was the humble subaltern of a marching regiment, his coat the colour of brick-dust, and patched at the elbows, staring about him, as if in wonder how the devil he got into such company. There, too, were Portuguese generals and officers of the higher ranks, some with gold keys on their pocket-flaps, parading the apartment with an air of self-complacent dignity, and grinning their little compliments, whenever " *El grande Lord* " happened to approach them. The party altogether amounted to between two and three hundred; and considering the circumstances under which it assembled, struck me on my entrance as forming rather a brilliant *coup d'œil*.

Of course, the principal object in the group, " the observed of all observers, " was Lord Wellington. There was no assumption of state or dignity in his demeanour. He wore the uniform of his rank, with the star and riband of the Bath, and laughed and talked with those around him, in a tone of freedom and familiarity, which showed his disregard of all ceremony and punctilio.

We had been there about an hour before the grand ceremony of the day commenced. There was nothing about it remarkably imposing. Marshal Beresford advanced, supported by Sir Brent Spencer, and Sir Rowland Hill, and kneeling down, the ceremony of installation was performed, with all due pomp and solemnity. This done, the Neophyte shook hands with his brothers of the Order, and received the congratulations of the company, on the acquisition of his new honours.

But however august the spectacle might have been, I believe the majority of the party were in little humour to enjoy it. My own appetite had been excited to an unpleasant degree, by a ride of twenty miles, over a mountainous country; and Sir William Curtis himself never looked to the hour of dinner with more anxious anticipation. Our fare, indeed, had recently consisted of the common rations of the army, there being no market from which it was possible to derive any additional supply. The prospect of this day's dinner, therefore, rose before us like a green oasis in the desert, a star in the surrounding darkness, on which the fancy loved to linger.

Never did lover pant more ardently for the hour of meeting with his mistress, than did the hungry crowd assembled at Mafra, for the annunciation of dinner. " Time and the hour, " as the old proverb hath it, " wear out the longest day ; " and our ears were at length greeted by the anxiously expected sounds. The more distinguished portion of the guests " paced forth into the hall, " in the due order of their rank and seniority in the service, and were followed by the *profanum vulgus*, whose order of advance was regulated by the no less intelligible principle, of " Devil take the hindmost. " The reader may conceive our consternation, when, having with difficulty, obtained entrance into the crowded *salle-à-manger*, it was evident that the table would not contain one tithe of the company, and we heard it announced, that dinner was provided only for the general officers.

Never was blank discomfiture more forcibly depicted, than in the countenances of the disappointed guests. They suffered the agonies of Tantalus. A splendid dinner was before them, yet with the savoury fumes of the viands in their nostrils, the sentence of famine had gone forth against them. As the unwelcome sounds met their ear, a murmur of anger and disappointment ran through the assembly. No dinner! exclaimed an hundred voices, in accents of indignant astonishment. No dinner, was pensively echoed by an hundred more.

The doctrine of passive obedience, however, was by no means exemplified in the conduct of the excluded guests. Some by dint of impudence, still endeavoured to secure places at the table, and others gazed around, in hopes of an opportunity of securing unobserved some portion of the spoil. An officer of the Buffs was detected in the act of taking improper liberties with a turkey, and another arrested in his attempt to escape with a Giblet-pie. Decisive measures were evidently become necessary, and the generals appeared perfectly aware, that their generalship was never more emphatically called for, than on the present occasion. Orders for our instant departure, were loudly vociferated, but without effect, and the dinner would certainly have speedily disappeared from the board, but for the opportune arrival, of a party of the 79th Highlanders who had been introduced by General Cameron, and proceeded by his directions, to expel us from the apartment, at the point of the bayonet.

When the process of summary ejectment had been completed, by this unusual act of hospitality, we returned to the saloon, where we were regaled with music by the fine band of the Guards. Great as the power of music is admitted to be, its soothing influence certainly did not extend, to the mitigation of that complaint under which we all so vehemently suffered, and never did sweet sounds, fail more completely of their effect.

There is a certain brotherhood and free-masonry in misfortune; we felt ourselves linked together by one common calamity, and stranger addressing stranger, poured forth the most unmeasured expressions of anger and invective, on the subject of their common wrongs.

While thus employed, an aide-de-camp of Lord Wellington entered the apartment, and apologizing for the disappointment under which we suffered, announced, by way of consolation, that supper would be provided for the whole party. The reaction of feeling excited by the simple enunciation of the word *supper*, was really a psychological phenomenon. The brows that had been knitted closely together, suddenly expanded, and dull, heavy, and spiritless eyes, were once more lighted up with the sparkle of animation. There were even smiles in company, though these were few, and the approximation to a growl in the tone of our conversation, was now certainly less remarkable than before.

But the balmy impression, even of this welcome intelligence, soon very sensibly diminished. Ten o'clock was the hour of supper, and we knew from the consentaneous information of an hundred watches, that four dreary hours had yet to elapse, before the advent of that blessed consummation. During these long hours, we were still destined to receive internal evidence, of nature's cordial abhorrence of a vacuum.

For nearly half that period, indeed, we stood wedged together in one solid mass at the door of the supper-room, waiting to burst in like a torrent, whenever it should be opened. Opened it was at length ; but on entering the apartment I found to my inexpressible dismay, that those before me, had swept every dish away from the bottom of the table, leaving nothing in the shape of an esculent, for those who followed. I shall not attempt to describe the scene of wrangling and confusion which ensued. Those who have seen a whole squadron of half-starved dogs, snarling, quarrelling, and fighting for a single bone, may conceive something of its character. At first, poor Popham and myself were in despair. But instant action was necessary, and we set out foraging in different directions, agreeing to return and share together, the produce of our exertions.

With great difficulty, and a large bribe to one of the servants, I at length procured a bottle of Madeira, and found Popham had been equally successful, in obtaining a loaf of bread. On this we supped, and afterwards retired to our appointed dormitory, which was in an un-inhabited wing of the mansion. There, wrapt in our boat-cloaks, we passed the night on the floor, and with the dawn of day, mounted our unfed horses to return to our cantonments.

CHAPTER VI

Her vine, the merry cheerer of the heart,
Unpruned dies. Her hedges even pleacht,
Like prisoners wildly overgrown with hair,
Put forth disordered twigs. Her fallow leas,
The Darnel, Hemlock, and rank Fumitory
Doth root upon ; while that the coulter rusts,
That should deracinate such savagery.
Henry V.

ABOUT the middle of November, Massena broke up from his cantonments, and retired. The English army advanced instantly in pursuit. During the day of our first march, the rain fell heavily, and without intermission, and our route lay, through villages desolate and deserted. It was not till long after dark, that we arrived at Villa Nova where we halted for the night.

The filth and brutality of the French army, can only be conceived by those, who saw as we did, the state of the villages they had occupied. There was something revolting and even degrading to human nature in the extreme uncleanness of the dwellings, they had just quitted. In the village, where we were now to take up our quarters, there was not a door or window remaining, and we were left to grope our way, into any house we might think proper to occupy. Our baggage, owing to the badness of the roads, was still far in the rear ; it was therefore impossible to procure any refreshment, and the night was one of almost impenetrable darkness. In selecting quarters under such circumstances, there was only one of our senses which could assist in guiding our choice, and after a *nasal* reconnoissance, I at length fixed on my residence for the night. I groped my way into a room, at one end of which there was a heap of dry straw, and tying up my horse at the other, I cast myself upon it, cold, wet, and weary as I was, to rest till morning.

Sleep, that

——upon the high and giddy mast,
Seals up the ship boy's eyes, and rocks his brains
In cradle of the rude imperious surge,

seldom witholds his anodyne from the tired soldier. I never enjoyed deeper or more tranquil slumber than on that night.

When I awoke in the morning, my servant (though by what means he had found me out, I know not) stood beside me, with a countenance on which horror was strongly depicted. As I knew him to be a blockhead, I did not at first think it necessary, to inquire into the cause of his emotion, but desired him to lay out my dressing things, and provide water for my toilet. Still he did not move, and I more peremptorily repeated my orders.

"For the love of God," at length ejaculated the booby, "does your honour know what sort of bed you're lying on?"

"No," I answered, "but I find it a very comfortable one. But no talk—execute my orders instantly."

"Your honour's lying," he exclaimed, "on a heap of dead men!"

He had no sooner uttered the words than I sprang to my feet, and found to my horror and consternation, that his assertion was true. An arm and a livid hand at one part protruded from the straw, and a griesly head was visible at another. After making this discovery, I remained not another moment in the house, but ran out into the street, determined to enter it no more.

On my departure, an examination took place, and it was discovered, that I had slept on the bodies of nine dead Frenchmen, which were covered by the straw. As these men had died a natural death, some of them probably of contagious disorders, I was not at first without some dread of infection. But my apprehensions were soon forgotten, and no bad consequences ensued.

On our arrival at Villa Nova, we had expected to march again, on the following morning. But in this we were deceived. The morning passed, and we received no order to proceed, nor did we move from our quarters till the day following. While we remained there, a circumstance occurred, which showed how little, even Lord Wellington was at that time aware, of the plans of the French General.

I was standing engaged in conversation with some other officers, in the street, when Lord Wellington, accompanied by Sir Brent Spencer and a numerous suite, rode past. The cavalcade stopped within a yard or two of us, and I distinctly heard him, deliver the following order, to the Adjutant-General.

"You will write to Admiral Berkely, and tell him that my advanced-guard are to-night within a league of Santarem, and they will enter it early to-morrow morning."

It was undoubtedly true, that the advanced-guard of the army, were that night within a league of Santarem, but nearly *four months* elapsed, before they entered it. In fact, next day it was generally known, that Massena had established his army in a strong elevated position, of which Santarem formed the right, and which he had been some weeks engaged in fortifying, by numerous batteries and redoubts. This occasioned a change in the destination of the second division, which was directed to cross immediately to the south bank of the Tagus. For this purpose, men-of-war's boats, had been brought up the river from Lisbon, and the passage was effected, with little delay, and no difficulty.

The dismal scene of desolation, on which we had lately been compelled to gaze, was now changed for one more pleasing and cheerful. This part of Portugal, had comparatively suffered nothing of the evils of war. It had been invaded by no hostile army, and the husbandman had, undisturbed, pursued his peaceful occupation, reaping where he had sown. Here all was peaceful and quiet, and the war, which had for years agitated their unhappy country, had been to the natives of the Alentejo rather a rumour than a reality. They witnessed now, for the first time, the presence of a foreign armed force ; and soldiers who spoke a different language, and professed a different religion from their own, became peaceful inmates, of their domestic circles.

It was evident, from the labour he had bestowed in strengthening it, that Massena contemplated more than a transient occupation, of his position at Santarem. Our division, therefore, went into quarters for the winter, in a series of small towns and villages, which, within the space of a few leagues, bordered upon the Tagus. General Houghton's brigade, of which the —— formed a part, were stationed at Chamusca, where Sir Rowland Hill established his head-quarters. Here we led an easy and a pleasant life. The inhabitants were kind and hospitable ; the army sutlers brought copious supplies of all the comforts, and even luxuries, we could desire, and the toils and dangers of war, were for a time forgotten.

Near Chamusca, the Tagus was scarcely broader, than the Thames at Richmond. On our side, it was guarded by the Portuguese Ordenenza, for whom huts were erected at convenient distances. It was a favourite morning amusement for the British officers, to ride down to the banks of the river, and hold parley with the French, who came for a similar purpose to the opposite margin. In these dialogues, offence had been taken, probably at some national reflections, and the meetings in question at length came to assume a more hostile form. The daily routine was as follows :—A Frenchman would advance close to the river, while an English officer, taking the musquet of the neighbouring sentry, deliberately took aim at him and fired. The Englishman, after waiting to receive the fire of his antagonist, then yielded his place to some other competitor for the honours of the *duellum*. This sort of contest was idle and absurd enough, and on reaching the ears of General Hill, was very judiciously put a stop to.

On the 6th of March, intelligence was received, that the enemy had evacuated his position on the preceding night, and was in full retreat. Our brigade received instant orders to cross the Tagus, and join the pursuing army.

Once more we entered upon scenes which displayed the ravages of war, in all their darkness and atrocity. Never was a country more completely devastated, than that through which we now passed. Not a blade of grass—nothing that could afford food either to men or animals, remained. It was evident, that the impossibility of longer procuring the supplies, necessary for so large an army, had been the cause of the retreat of Massena. We pursued him closely; and though our brigade formed, in fact, the rear of the British army, the enemy were evidently but a few leagues in advance, and we halted for several days successively, on the very ground they had occupied, on the preceding night.

The road along which we travelled, indeed, afforded abundant proof of the cruel necessities, to which the French army had been reduced. It was literally strewed, with the carcases of mules and horses, which had fallen on the march, from famine or fatigue. From many of these, the French soldiers, as they passed, had cut large slices of the flesh; an expedient for satisfying hunger, to which its extreme pressure, could alone have induced them to resort. Even the sight of human bodies, left to rot unburied by the road, or form the repast of the region kites, was not wanting, to complete the dismal character of the scene. Some of these were the bodies of French soldiers, who had sunk exhausted by disease or famine, and had been left by the rapacity of their comrades to perish naked and miserably. But by far the greater number, were those of Portuguese, who had fallen victims, to the gratuitous barbarity, of the invaders. Many of these were shockingly mutilated, some were hanging from trees, others had been run through the body by the bayonet.

The fourth day's march brought us to Thomar, a town of considerable magnitude, and the seat of an episcopal see. Here a portion of the French army had likewise been stationed, and they had left similar proofs of their occupancy, to those, I have already mentioned. Here, too, I was witness of a scene, which has left an ineffaceable impression on my memory.

We had marched before daylight, and about noon we reached Thomar. An hour or two after our arrival, I found I had been unfortunate in the quarters I had chosen, and went out, in hopes of being able to provide myself, with a better lodging. In passing through the streets, my notice was attracted by a large convent, which I entered, in order to ascertain what sort of accommodation it afforded. The gate opened into a large court-yard, from the other extremity of which, ascended a stair, which led into a range of cloisters. I passed through these, and suddenly found myself in a large gallery, which, it was apparent, had been used by the French as an hospital. Most striking and terrible, indeed, was the sight which my eye then encountered. Round the apartment, some stretched on wretched truckle-beds, some on a little dirty straw upon the floor, lay about fifty dead soldiers. Each was in the attitude, in which he had expired. On some, death seemed to have fallen like a tranquil sleep; in others, the struggle with the death-agony had evidently been strong, from the frightful contortion of limb and feature, into which they had been thrown. One man sat bolt-upright against the wall, and the hideous expression of his countenance rises at this moment before me, as the words flow from my pen. Never, never shall I forget it. There was something so striking to the imagination in the scene, terrible as it was, that I could not immediately quit it. I walked slowly round the gallery, gazing with a sort of awful fear on the objects as they successively presented themselves—then the spell was broken, and by a sudden impulse of horror, rushing hastily down the stair, I quitted the mansion of death, scarcely venturing to breathe, till I found myself once more beyond its dismal precincts.*

Some indication of a change in the intentions of the enemy, was the occasion of our halting a day at Thomar. Early in the following morning, we were again in pursuit. The spectacle of mortality which the roads exhibited, seemed to deepen as we advanced, and our marches became longer, and more severe. Since we commenced our advance, no engagement had yet taken place between the retreating and pursuing armies. But on the third day's march after leaving Thomar, the distant roar of cannon and volleys of musquetry were heard, which became evidently louder and more frequent, as we advanced. An aide-de-camp of Marshal Beresford shortly after came, riding at full speed from the front, with orders to General Houghton to advance as rapidly as possible, with his brigade. The order was instantly obeyed, and we hurried on, with all possible speed, towards the scene of action. As we proceeded, I remember passing a village, which had that morning been the theatre of an engagement, between our light troops, and a party of the rear-guard of the enemy. The appearance of a British force had been wholly unexpected, and, on their approach, the French soldiers were seen running forth, from the houses of the village, in great confusion. They were instantly fired on, and charged by the English, and among the number killed, was the commander of the party, a colonel in the French service. As we passed, his body lay naked on the road. He was a young man, with a countenance, even in death, handsome. The orifice of a bullet, which had passed through his body, was visible on his chest. I looked steadfastly on his face as we passed, and read, or thought I read there, that he was a man of high birth and breeding, brave, gifted, and accomplished. The hope—the only surviving one, perhaps, of some fond and anxious mother,—the beloved of some fair maiden in his own beautiful land, who would now vainly, and in sickness of heart, expect his return. Yet here he lay, an outcast in the public road, his body soiled, spit upon, and trampled by the feet of vulgar men.

The firing, which had intermitted for a brief space, was again

---

* I once communicated this occurrence, to a writer of distinguished genius, who has since made it the ground-work of a paper, of singular interest and power, which appeared in one of the periodical publications of the day. The facts were simply as above stated; the brilliant colouring, and striking accessories, with which he invested them, were the additions of his own fine imagination.

renewed, before we arrived at Redinha. There we halted in rear of an
eminence, over which the road led, and remained in readiness to bear a
part in the action, should our services be required. This, however, was
not the case. The firing gradually became slacker, and more distant, and
it was evident the enemy were again in full retreat. I rode to the top of
the ridge in our front, in hopes to catch a glimpse of the French army. I
succeeded, but the glimpse was a distant one, as they were in march
along the side of a hill about a league off. The action had been fought, in
order to cover the passage of their army, across the Soure. Their purpose
having been effected, they instantly destroyed the bridge, and continued
their retreat. Our brigade halted that night on the field of battle, which
was covered by the dying and the dead.

Never was greater generalship displayed than by Massena, in the
conduct of this memorable retreat. Retreating under every disadvantage, unable to collect more than ten days' provisions for his army, and
consequently debarred from risking the chances of an engagement, and
closely pursued by the British army, he made no sacrifice, either of
baggage or artillery, and reached the frontier of Portugal with an army,
which, though it had suffered much from famine and privation, had, in
fact, lost nothing, from hostile attack. The only place, where Lord
Wellington was enabled to bring his army into collision with the enemy,
was at Redinha. There a partial engagement took place with the rear,
while the main body were employed in passing the river, but from that
time forward, his retreat was unmolested.

This praise is of course confined to his retreat. The conduct of
Massena in the preceding campaign, was certainly not marked by great
military talents, and in strategy, he decidedly showed himself throughout, inferior to his great antagonist. His policy manifestly was, to have
immediately attacked the lines of Torres Vedras. Had he done so, with
his vast superiority of force, there was at least a strong probability of
success. In the attempt, he would undoubtedly have sacrificed a large
portion of his army, but certainly not more, than afterwards fell inglorious victims to famine and disease, from his wintering in the very heart of
a country, which he must, or should have known, was unable to furnish
supplies, for so large an army. But these are matters, on which it would
ill become me, to offer more than a very diffident opinion; if, indeed, to
do even this, be not to diverge too widely from the narrow walk of
personal adventure, to which I have hitherto been studious to confine
my steps.

On the following day, we continued our advance, and after a march
of five leagues, again bivouacked for the night. Thirty thousand of the
British army, were here collected within the space of a mile. No sight, I
think, can be more picturesque, than the encampment of a large army
by night. The blazing fires—the shadowy figures moving in the red and
flickering light,—the busy hum of a thousand voices, with which the

wind is loaded on its passage, lost for a moment in the sound of the bugle or the trumpet, but again heard in its intervals,—these, independent of the associations to which they are naturally linked, form an aggregate of sight and sound, striking when present, and when past, not to be forgotten.

This was our last night with the army. Lord Wellington, in the course of it, received intelligence, that Soult was advancing against Badajos, intending by that route, to enter the Alentejo; and General Houghton received orders, on the following morning, to retrace his steps, and crossing the Tagus, once more to unite his brigade, to the second division, which had not joined in the pursuit.

Our march back, was doubly dreary and disagreeable. In advancing, we had the stimulus of a flying enemy, the chances of a battle, the hope of victory, all floating before us. But on our return, the excitement had ceased, and even the soldiers in the ranks, seemed dull and spiritless. The carcases which lay along the road, had, since we formerly passed, become putrid, and we breathed an atmosphere, tainted, and redolent of corruption. The raven and the vulture, had been busy with their prey; the kites hovered over us in the air, and the eagle poised himself high up among the clouds, waiting only for our departure, to return and finish the repast, in which he had been interrupted. If we were formerly awe-struck, by the bare perception of mortality, what were our feelings, in thus beholding mortality, invested with all those hateful and disgusting concomitants, from the sight of which, nature shudderingly recoils.

I remember nothing of note, connected with our march back to the Alentejo. On the 18th we crossed Zezere, at Punheté, and reached Abrantes on the 20th, where a bridge of boats had been established across the Tagus. On the 21st, we joined our division, which we learned had only been prevented by our absence, from commencing active operations against the enemy. It was known that Badajos had surrendered without a siege, owing either to treachery or cowardice, and that the enemy had likewise obtained possession of Campo Mayor, a town, of which the works were in too dilapidated a state to be capable of any effective resistance.

Sir Rowland Hill having, to the regret of the army, been obliged to return to England for the recovery of his health, the command of the second division, at this important juncture, when it was about to play a distinguished part in the war, had devolved on Marshal Beresford. The fatiguing marches which our brigade had lately undergone, rendered it necessary that before the commencement of operations on the south side of the Tagus, they should be recruited by a halt. We rested for two days in the neighbourhood of Arronches, and on the 23d, commenced our advance towards Badajos.

It was evident, from the slowness and caution with which we proceeded, that Beresford had no very accurate intelligence with regard to the enemy's movements. We advanced, when the nature of the country seemed to require it, with the skirmishers extended on our flanks, and the cavalry in front, engaged in what is called "feeling the way."

For the first few days of our march, we proceeded without any intelligence of the French army, and we observed, in the appearance of the country, no marks of their having penetrated "thus far into the bowels of the land." On the 26th, however, a party of cavalry were observed on an eminence at some distance, over which our route lay, who, after reconnoitring us, instantly disappeared. The front of the division immediately halted until the rear had come up, and our advance was then cautiously continued, with the cavalry and light infantry in front.

When the infantry passed the height on which the enemy had been observed, the appearance of a few prisoners of the French cavalry, whom a party of the Thirteenth were conducting to the rear, and several wounded men who lay bleeding by the road, gave us the first intelligence that a collision had taken place. We now advanced as rapidly as possible, and the road commanded a view of Campo Mayor, which lay about half a league distant, in the plain before us. The French, who had apparently just received intelligence of our approach, were seen running from the town, and forming hastily on the plain, in order of retreat, protected by their cavalry in the rear.

Never did any army profit more by superiority of tactic, than did the French on the present occasion. They certainly amounted to not more than three thousand, and were commanded by General Latour Mauberg. The road from Campo Mayor to Badajos, which is about three leagues distant, lies over a flat and sandy plain. We enjoyed, therefore, in our advance, a perfect view of the operations in front. The thirteenth Light Dragoons made a most gallant charge on the enemy's cavalry, and drove them back on their infantry, which halted, formed rapidly in square, and firing a volley in turn, forced their assailants to retire. Their cavalry having again formed, returned once more to the rear, and the infantry resumed its march. This fine manœuvre was frequently repeated, our cavalry displaying and maintaining an evident superiority over that of the enemy, but unable to derive from it any material advantage. One charge, I remember, was made by the Portuguese, who were emulous of sharing the honours of the day. The issue, however, was not precisely that which I have described as following the attacks of the British. They rode on most gallantly, till they came within pistol-shot of the enemy, who knowing, apparently, with whom they had to deal, spurred on to meet them, when the Portuguese, without waiting for the "tug of war," retreated with even more rapidity than they had advanced. It is, indeed, a curious fact, for which I shall not pretend to account, that though the Portuguese infantry behaved on many occasions with great gallantry, both charging and defeating the enemy, this distinction was by no means predicable of their cavalry.

In this manner the French continued their retreat, and reached Badajos, without sustaining any considerable loss. Certainly all the honours of the day were theirs. In the face of an army of five times their number, they effected their retreat without suffering any loss, either of baggage or guns, and I believe we did not, on the whole, make twenty prisoners. The fact was, that even our heavy cavalry were never engaged, and the infantry, during the whole day, did not fire a shot. This specimen of Marshal Beresford's talents as a general, certainly did not lead to any congratulation on our good fortune, in being placed under his command.

When the enemy were evidently fairly beyond our reach, we retrograded to Campo Mayor, where we halted for the night. We questioned the inhabitants with regard to their treatment by the French, and found the conduct of the enemy on this side of the Tagus, had been less marked by atrocity than on the other.

On the following day, we marched to Elvas, certainly the strongest and best fortified city in Portugal. Fort de Lippe, which stands on the summit of a high cone-shaped hill, is, I should think, nearly impregnable. It must be admitted as a practical proof of its strength, that after the English army had withdrawn from the Alentejo, and the place was defended only by a Portuguese garrison, Marshal Soult never even attempted to lay siege to it, although it is unquestionably the key to that province.

From Elvas we advanced to Borba, where we halted for a few days, while the engineers were engaged in constructing a bridge, by which we crossed the Guadiana. The stream is extremely rapid, though not broad, and the operation was found to be one of some difficulty. On the opposite bank of the Guadiana we remained encamped for some days. Here the whole country seemed covered with Gum Cistus, the fragrance of which was so strong as to be absolutely oppressive.

I remember one morning, when standing on our alarm-post, observing some soldiers of the thirteenth Light Dragoons approaching the camp, covered with blood, and severely wounded. We soon learned that an Out Piquet belonging to that regiment had been surprised in the night, and taken prisoners by the enemy. With a want of caution certainly censurable, they had unsaddled their horses, and the French, who, in their advance, had contrived to elude the observation of our videttes and outposts, left them, by the suddenness of their attack, no time for preparation. The officer in command was taken prisoner, and the lieutenant had only escaped by throwing himself on his horse like a second Mazeppa, without either saddle or bridle, and leaving the direction of his flight to the choice of the animal.

Not satisfied, however, with this successful *coup de main*, the enemy

rode forward even to the village in which Marshal Beresford had his
head-quarters, and breaking open his house, the Marshal only escaped
capture by leaping out of a back window in his shirt and cocked hat,
and, in this uncomfortable trim, making the best of his way across the
fields to the camp, where the unexpected and grotesque appearance of
their commander was beheld with merriment and wonder by the troops.

Quitting this station, we marched towards Olivença, a fortified town, in which the French had left a garrison. On being
summoned, the governor refused to surrender, and the rest of the army
continuing its advance, General Cole and his division were left to
conduct the siege. On the following night, we slept at Albuera, yet a
bloodless field, and not destitute of a wild and romantic beauty. The
ground was prettily variegated by little ranges of hills, and a bright and
peaceful stream murmured on its way through banks clothed with
woods. It was a quiet and pastoral scene, such as one might look for,
rather amid the green mountains of Scotland, than where we found it.

The heavy battering train had not yet arrived from Lisbon, and this
circumstance occasioned a considerable delay in our operations. It was
impossible to begin the siege of Badajos without it; and, in the meantime, the army was cantoned in villages a few leagues in front, covering
all the roads by which Soult could possibly advance to the relief of that
city. Our station was a town called Almandrelejo, about six leagues
within the Spanish frontier. Thither we accordingly marched, and
remained there about a month.

CHAPTER VII

Count. Brother John Bates, is not that the morning which breaks yonder?
Bates. I think it be; but we have no great cause to desire the approach of day.
Will. We see yonder the beginning of the day, but I think we shall never see the end of it. Who goes there?

Henry V.

I HAVE not interrupted the details of the military events, with which the story of my life is naturally linked, by allusion to incidents, which, although they materially affected my own happiness, had nothing in common with the character of the narrative in which I have been recently engaged. I would take advantage, therefore, of the interval of peaceful occupation which we enjoyed in our new quarters, to supply the blank which has been thus occasioned.

It has been said, that absence subdues passion. I have never found it so. Never was she, to whom my troth was plighted, the object of a love more fervent and engrossing, than when seas rolled between us, and the cloud of danger hung deepest and most loweringly in my horizon. Then, indeed, love became not a passion, but a madness, and reigned in my heart a single, solitary despot. Like the Rod of Aaron, it swallowed up all other sentiments and passions. The future contained but one object, for which I panted; the past, but one object of memory.

I had hitherto been fortunate. Every packet had brought letters from England, and such letters as would have cheered and consoled me under privations far greater, than any I had been yet called on to endure. My sisters were well, and Lady Melicent—still loved me. Dear and precious to me as the light of Heaven were those letters. The intelligence of the arrival of a packet brought with it a tumult of emotion. I calculated the course of the winds, by which the voyage might be shortened or prolonged, and prayed that the vessel, in which so many hopes were centered, might be wafted to her port with fair breezes, and on a summer sea.

I also wrote frequently. Often, when jaded and overcome, my companions cast themselves on the ground to rest their wearied limbs, and forget in sleep their troubles and their dangers, did I seize the pen, and pour forth to my beautiful betrothed, all my hopes, my fears, and all my love. Never, never was her image absent from my thoughts. It went with me into battle,—it forsook me not in pain and suffering, and when beneath the cloudy canopy of Heaven, my head rested on its stony pillow, it mingled with the sweet slumbers that descended on my eyelids.

During our stay at Almandrelejo, for the first time since my arrival in

Portugal, a packet came from England, and brought no letter from her I loved. A thousand fears came over me, and my fancy devised sad, though visionary causes for this unlooked-for silence. Was she not ill? Had not some dreadful misfortune happened? Might not she whom I adored be stretched, at that very moment, on a bed of sickness and suffering—the bloom faded from her cheek—the lustre gone from those eyes—those beautiful eyes, that, by a single glance had made my blood to gush onward like a cataract through my tingling veins? My spirits were low, my heart anxious and depressed. Something,—I knew not what,—but something of evil omen to my happiness, had befallen, and my fears, though vague, were overpowering.

Such was the state of mind in which I opened the letters brought me by the packet. The superscription of the first I knew; it was from Frank Willoughby. He was in London. Since I quitted England, he had become an M.P., and his new duties demanded a residence of some months' duration in town. From this letter I derived at least a partial relief from the dark forebodings that oppressed me. Lady Melicent was well. Willoughby knew she had been the object of my admiration, though not of my love, for to no human ear had that holiest of secrets been confided; but he had often heard me speak enthusiastically of her charms, and he mentioned her in his letter as one of whom, far distant as I was, he imagined it would be agreeable to receive intelligence.

I learned that Lady Melicent too was in London, that she moved in the gayest circle of the metropolis, and was the star of first magnitude in the hemisphere of fashion. When she appeared at the opera, the box in which she was seated, was that to which all eyes were turned. When she mingled in the dance, grace hovered round her, and she moved peerless and pre-eminent amid the circle of surrounding beauty.

She was, he said, the gayest of the gay, seen everywhere, and everywhere attracting homage. Lord Lyndhurst too was in town, and the world still considered him, as the affianced lover of the Lady Melicent.

Willoughby's letter told me all this, and had the immediate effect of relieving my mind from much of that burden of anxiety, under which it laboured. At first, something of a pang shot through my heart, and I was moved by a sort of vague jealousy, at the thought that Lady Melicent, during the absence of one whom she loved—whom she knew to be encompassed with perils in a distant land, should have felt equal to the prominent part she was then playing in the great theatre of fashion. Was that love, which in me was all pervading, all engrossing—which was the very anchor of my hope, nay, almost the condition of my being—was that love, which to me was everything, to her so little—so very little, that her heart required other objects of interest and excitement, her mind other thoughts, than those which the memory of him who loved her could inspire?

Such thoughts and feelings disturbed me for a while, but not long. I soon brought myself to believe that the distinguished part she occupied in the world's eye, was the consequence not of choice but of necessity. How could Lady Melicent de Vere appear in society, without stepping forward into that high station, for which the gifts both of nature and fortune had evidently destined her. Whose veins bounded richer blood than Lady Melicent's? Who to so noble and extended an inheritance, united so rich a dowry of beauty, grace, and talent? How could she, the synthesis of attractions so rare and numerous, cease to become the cynosure of admiring eyes, unless by withdrawing altogether from that world which she adorned, to solitude and seclusion? Could I expect this? No. I had no right to claim or to expect so great a sacrifice; perhaps I scarcely wished it. I felt pride in the idea, that she to whom my heart told me I was bound by indissoluble links, on whose faith I rested implicitly as on gospel truth, should thus stand forward to receive the guerdon of the world's homage and admiration. There was vanity in my thoughts, for I felt a reflected consequence and honour in the remembrance, that *I* was the man by whom the prize of this fair creature's love had been won.

While occupied in such reflections, a letter from Lucy lay before me unopened. From her I heard frequently, but from Jane, since I quitted England, I had only received one letter, and that was of a character rather to excite, than to allay apprehension on her account. It was evidently written under strong feelings of depression, but it breathed nothing of the language of complaint. She was ill, she said, very ill, and spoke of sufferings acute, but indescribable; a mortal sickness of the heart, for which there was no balm but death. " Pray for me, my dearest brother, " she said; " pray that God, who in his mercy tempers the wind to the shorn lamb, may soon vouchsafe me this relief. Pray, and your petition will be a kind one, that in this world we may never meet again. "

There was in the tone of this letter an occasional wildness and incoherence, even more alarming than the intelligence it conveyed. In answer to it, I entreated her not to give way to that depression and despondency of spirit, which her letter betrayed, and assured her, should the conduct of her husband require her to throw herself on the protection of her family, she would find my heart and hand, ever warm and ready in her defence.

To these offers and assurances, she had made no reply, but the letter from Lucy, which I have already mentioned, left no room for doubt with regard to the nature and causes of poor Jane's illness. Till now, Lucy informed me, Jane, even to her, had maintained a strict reserve, with regard to the conduct of her husband, and the sources of her domestic disquiet. But the outrages of Hewson had at length exceeded even the bounds of Jane's patience and meekness of sufferance. The very worm, when trod on, will turn on its oppressor; and I knew that under any ordinary,—I had almost said any conceivable aggression, Jane would have pined in secrecy—suffering, yet silent. The substance of what I learned was as follows :—

Hewson, though he had never been a kind husband, had at least, for some time after his marriage, treated his wife with some degree of consideration and respect. He probably felt proud of her elegance and attractions, and gratified by the admiration she excited when she appeared in public, he received the praises bestowed on her beauty, as an indirect compliment to his own taste. But the zest of this wore off with its novelty ; a man, palled like Hewson by a long course of licentiousness, could scarcely revert to the calm and peaceful enjoyments of domestic life. He required something more poignant and racy, than he found in the society of the simple and retiring Jane. He treated her first with neglect, then with harshness. He filled his house with rude and boisterous company, who with their filthy and abominable slang, offended her ears, and insulted her delicacy. Females, too, who having lost the reality, thought it scarcely worth while to retain even the semblance of virtue,— creatures from whose profligate audacity she shrunk with loathing and disgust, were the companions, with whom her husband wished her to associate. But even these were not the limits of his brutality. He introduced into his house, a woman taken from the very lowest order of society, who was publicly known to be his mistress, and endeavoured, by a course of barbarous and inhuman treatment, to make his wife submit to the daily outrage of her presence.

But his tyranny and his cruelty were in vain. Jane, meek and submissive as she was, could not bend so low. She would not stoop from the dignity of her virtue, and her whole soul revolted from this most cold-blooded and cruel consummation of insult. In a state of despair, closely verging on insanity, she fled from his hated mansion, and sought the protection of Lady Willoughby. There did this wretch pursue her. There did he drag her from the arms of her sister, to become again the victim of his hellish outrage.

My own feelings, on receiving the letter which contained this intelligence, it would be impossible to describe. There was fury in my soul. I was agitated by a tornado of conflicting emotions. One moment, I determined instantly to return to England,—to sacrifice my military rank, nay more, my honour, for the sake of inflicting instant and signal punishment on this cruel and cowardly assassin. Then, again, I shrank from my resolution. To return to England, a disgraced and dishonoured man, what was it but to baulk the very vengeance I contemplated,—to place myself on a level, in the eyes of the world, with the wretch I was about to punish,—to pluck out the sting from my revenge? I knew it would be fruitless,—and as we were then situated, almost disgraceful, to apply for leave of absence. Nine months had barely elapsed since I had joined the army ; to have requested so soon to quit it again, in the very middle of my first campaign, I felt would be to subject my character to observations, which I could not brook.

Here, therefore, I was chained by fetters, in comparison with which, the strongest iron bonds were light and frangible, and from which I knew that no human power could set me free. But the fury of my passion was not diminished by my consciousness of its present impotence. All benevolent and charitable sympathies were for a time dried up within me. What would I not have given at that moment to have struck the villain to the earth, to have seen him slowly expiring in long and lingering agonies, to have spit on him, as he faltered forth his vile spirit, and have watched the vultures as they made their unclean repast on his loathsome carcase!

Under the influence of such feelings, I seized the pen, and wrote to him as follows:—

"HEWSON,

"Think not that the hour of reckoning comes not, because it is delayed. I know your conduct to my sister, and if I live, as there is a God in heaven, you shall answer it in this world, as well as in the next.

"CYRIL THORNTON."

As my reason slowly emerged from the cloud which the receipt of this melancholy intelligence had spread around it, I did not neglect to take such inadequate means as were in my power, for the immediate protection of my sister. I wrote to my solicitor in London, to employ any legal measures that might be conducive to the object, of forcing Hewson to observe the common decencies of life, (from such a man I could not hope for more) towards his unhappy wife, and having done this, I had to endure the mortifying reflection that I had done *all*.

A life of danger and activity is unfavourable to the indulgence of grief. New objects and difficulties continually excite our attention, and call for exertion, and produce at least the fortunate effect, of diverting the mind from dwelling too long and unceasingly on hidden sorrows. A soldier cannot long abstract his thoughts from the world in which he moves. In him there are no slumbering energies, for his duty requires them all, to be in constant action. The part of *Il Penseroso* must be played by idler men. And so it was with me. My vows of vengeance slept, but they were not dead. Time might yet rouse them from their slumber.

We remained at Almandrelejo till the beginning of May, and Soult did not appear to disturb our repose. The army then returned to invest Badajoz, and the siege instantly commenced. We were encamped in an olive grove, about a league from the town, where we lay completely concealed from the observation of the enemy. On our part, though the duty was abundantly harassing to the troops, the siege was not very vigorously prosecuted. For some days, Marshal Beresford appeared undecided with regard to the point against which his first advances should be directed. Operations were repeatedly commenced on different sides of the town, and abandoned before any effective progress had been made. At length, however, he appeared to have finally arrived at a decision. The covered way was commenced, and batteries were erected, as the works proceeded nearer the town.

There was a small fort at some distance from the walls, which interrupted our progress, and which it therefore became necessary to storm. A party of two hundred men was appointed for this duty, under the command of a major, whose name I have forgotten. Next in command to this officer was my friend Popham; and having received from him information with regard to the arrangements, my curiosity made me anxious, if possible, to be a witness of the attack. The hour at which the party were to be assembled in readiness, was eleven o'clock. Popham and myself were messmates, and before his departure, a bumper was crowned to his success, and we shook hands, in the uncertainty of ever meeting again.

Before the appointed hour, I had stolen alone through the darkness, to a neighbouring height, on which I stood, waiting with quickened pulses, for the issue of the impending conflict.

All external circumstances were in favour of the assailants. There was no moon abroad, and not a star twinkled in the murky sky. The enemy, however, were vigilant. Ever and anon, blazing fireballs rose from the town, illumining the heavens with an arch of brilliant flame, and when quenched, leaving the darkness more palpable than before. All was silent, save the sound of a distant drum, caught up by the night-breeze, as it swept over the ramparts of the leaguered city.

The road by which I knew our brave party must pass, wound round the base of the eminence, on which I stood. I had watched long and anxiously for the sound of their footsteps, before it met my ear. There was deep silence in the ranks as they passed onward, and even the noise of their tread would have been inaudible, to an ear less tremblingly awake than mine. But in a minute the sound was gone, for they had already passed my station, and I knew they were fast approaching the scene of struggle. My heart beat quick in my bosom, as, with straining eyes, I endeavoured vainly to penetrate the darkness, and waited for the first signal of the attack having commenced. I knew the party were yet undiscovered by the enemy, for their fireballs had hitherto been fortunately thrown in a different direction, from that in which they were advancing.

At length, however, when they were already close to the fort, a fireball fell within a few yards of them, and for a few seconds they were visible, as distinctly as in the glare of the noon-day sun. All again was darkness. The sound of drums and bugles rung from the ramparts of the town, and a heavy fire of musquetry, mingled with the roar of artillery, was heard from the fort.

The excitement of my feelings at this moment, had reached the highest possible pitch, and I waited in awful suspense for the result. Another fireball came blazing like a comet through the air, and the English were seen scaling the walls of the fort, on which the enemy were visible, some hurrying to and fro, others firing down on their assailants, or thrusting at them with their bayonets, as they attempted to ascend. Again the scene was hid from my view.

By the light of a third fireball, as it ascended from the town, I observed the garrison were under arms, and already collected on the ramparts. It fell in the very middle of the fort, and there was my interest concentrated. Our brave fellows had already effected their entrance, and were mingled with the enemy. The contest was bayonet to bayonet, and I huzzaed and waved my hat in the darkness, for I then knew that our arms would be victorious. The next fireball showed my anticipations to have been correct; and a few of the enemy, who had escaped by springing from the walls of the fort, were retreating rapidly to the town.

So soon as the fort was observed to be in our possession, a tremendous fire was opened on it from the ramparts. The shot and shells flew thickly, but the darkness was in our favour, and they occasioned little loss. The enemy did not attempt by a sortie, to deprive us of our conquest, and before morning, the guns of the fort had been carried off, and its walls levelled with the ground. The commander of the party was severely wounded, but Popham escaped unhurt; and most sincerely did I congratulate him, when we again met, on the issue of the truly gallant attack, of which I had been witness.

By the capture of the fort already mentioned, all external obstacle to the progress of the siege had been removed, and it was now carried on, more vigorously than before. Each brigade took it in turn to work by night in the trenches, and harassing as the duty was, it brought with it a certain novelty and excitement, which made us unrepiningly submit to the labour it imposed. On the night of the 12th of May, our brigade was on duty. The Marshal's plans had apparently undergone some change, for we were ordered to break ground within point-blank distance of the walls, at a point considerably distant from that, on which the advances had hitherto been made. This was indeed a service of peril. Had we been discovered by the enemy, it was certain we should be swept off by his guns; to say nothing of the consequence to be apprehended from a sortie of the garrison, made on men who had laid aside their arms, and were busy with the shovel and the pick-axe.

Luckily for us, neither of these contingencies occurred. The night again was in our favour, for it was profoundly dark. The attention of the enemy was principally directed to the quarter, which had hitherto been the scene of our operations, and our advance was fortunately not detected. It was absolutely necessary, however, that we should be covered before break of day; and the soldiers, conscious that their own safety depended upon the progress of their labour, plied their toil unremittingly.

I was sent forward with a party of light infantry, to act as a corps of observation, and prevent surprise. The orders I received from General Hamilton, who commanded for the night, were to advance as closely to the walls as possible; to listen attentively for any indication of movement in the town; and in case of observing the advance of any armed body, to dispatch a messenger to announce the intelligence to the general, and then, by opening our fire, to delay their progress as much as was compatible with our own safety.

In pursuance of these orders, we crept forward on all fours, till we came within fifty yards of the walls, where we lay flat on the ground, endeavouring to catch even the smallest sounds that floated in the air, and to penetrate the darkness with our gaze. The night was still, and favourable in all respects for our object. We heard the hours sounded by the clock of the great church in the city. The sentinel on the wall above us, in his solitary walk, whiled away the time in singing catches of a French song, which he interrupted to challenge the advancing officer on duty, as he passed along the rampart on his rounds. Again we heard the challenge of the sentinel, and the sound of approaching footsteps. It was the relief. Words of command were given, the motion of arms heard, the very instructions of the new sentinel were distinctly audible; this passed; the party were again in motion, and the sound of their retiring footsteps was soon lost in the distance.

These are, perhaps, insignificant circumstances to relate; but to men in our situation they were full of interest. They gave rise to a far-extending train of fancies, which relieved the tedium of our long night-watch. There was something pleasing, too, in our thus becoming spies on the unconscious enemy,—in being so near as to hear their very whispers,—and to know that the smallest signal of our presence would call instantly to arms the sleeping garrison, and rouse the loud thunder of their artillery.

I had been directed to return, on observing the first streak of daylight; but while the darkness was yet unbroken, a messenger brought orders from the general for the instant return of the party. Marshal Beresford had become alarmed at the prospect of the destructive fire which could not fail to be opened on us by the besieged on the return of day; and abandoning our works, after a night of fruitless labour, the brigade returned to the camp.

I was awakened from a sound sleep, into which I had fallen immediately on our return from the trenches, by the sergeant of my company, who brought orders which had just been issued from headquarters, for the army to hold themselves in instant readiness to march. Intelligence of this sort is the best antisoporific in the world; and on that morning I slept no more. There were rumours in the camp, that Soult was advancing with a large army to the relief of Badajoz, and it was evident, from the order now issued, that these rumours were well-founded. On the following morning we raised the leaguer of the town, and marched to Valverdé, in the neighbourhood of which, we halted for the night. The whole army felt aware, that we were now on the eve of a battle, and the discontent, which the vacillation of our commander had caused to lower on every brow, quickly vanished in the prospect of terminating by a victory, our hitherto inglorious campaign. We encamped on the heights of Albuera on the 15th, in order of battle; and it was evident, that Marshal Beresford intended here to await the approach of the enemy. The Spanish army, under Blake, arrived during the night, and occupied the right of the position; in the centre were the British, and the Portuguese were posted on the left.

Heavily rose the sun on the eventful morning of the 16th of May 1811. Dark volumes of clouds obscured his disk, and his rays lost more than half their brightness in penetrating the dense masses of vapour which on all sides overspread the horizon. We were under arms two hours before day-dawn, and thousands of eyes, which that morning watched his rising, were destined never to see him set. The morning, though still and dark, was not misty. Objects, even at a considerable distance, were distinctly visible. There was not a wind to stir a leaf upon the smallest spray, and the scene before us, though gloomy, was peaceful. It was seven o'clock before we returned to our tents, and at that time no enemy was visible. Two of my brother-officers that morning shared my breakfast; and of the whole party, including the three servants who ministered to our wants, I was, in the course of two hours, the only individual alive.

While we were at breakfast, a few shots were fired by our artillery, which did not at all influence our meal; but that concluded, my curiosity led me to advance a considerable distance in front of the line, to observe the motions of the enemy, who was reported to be fast approaching. The report was correct. Their advancing masses covered the road for several miles, and their cavalry, formed in column of squadrons on the plain, had already menaced an attack on the bridge of Albuera. Fast as their infantry came up, they halted in column on either side of the road, without indicating by any demonstration, what part of our position was about to become the chief object of their attack. I spent about half an hour,—it might be more, in thus gratifying my curiosity, and when I returned, the tents were struck, the baggage sent to the rear, and the whole army drawn up in line of battle.

The pain I felt at this sight was excruciating. To have been absent from my post at such a moment, when the sound of the artillery, which had already opened on the advancing enemy, showed that the battle had even now begun, was to incur the possibility of an imputation, which I could brook no lips to utter. I ran madly to the rear, and found with some difficulty the place where my tent had stood. I was in dishabille, and it was necessary, on such an occasion, to appear in uniform. My coat, hat, and sash, had been left on the ground ; but in the hurry, my sword had been removed with the baggage. I changed my dress as speedily as possible, casting from me those I wore, for plunder, either to our own soldiers, or those of the enemy, and having supplied the place of my own sword by that of a sergeant, I joined my regiment.

My old enemy, Colonel Penleaze, was not displeased, on the present occasion,to have an opportunity of venting his long-suppressed resentment.

" How does it happen, Captain Thornton, " he exclaimed in front of the battalion, " that when the regiment has, for the last half hour, been instantly expecting to be called into action, *you* were absent from your company ? "

I was proceeding to answer this question, but he interrupted me.

" Make no reply, sir, for your conduct admits of no excuse. *Nothing* can justify your absence from your duty, at a moment like the present. Had you been a minute later, sir, I should have sent you to the rear in arrest ; and, as it is, I may yet possibly think it proper to report your conduct to the General. "

My blood boiled in my veins as he spoke, and had death been the consequence, I must have answered.

" Colonel Penleaze, I am ready to account for my conduct anywhere, or in any manner, and shall repel, as becomes me, either in public or private, whatever charge you, or any man, shall dare to make, affecting my honour. "

Just at that moment a heavy firing commenced on our right, and the Adjutant-General rode up, with orders for our brigade instantly to advance.

In order to render the subsequent account of this, to me most eventful and memorable battle, more clear and intelligible, I shall here take leave to say something of the relative situation of the hostile armies.

Our position was a chain of eminences, along the front of which flowed the river Albuera, a shallow stream, and in many places fordable. Through the centre of it ran the road to Badajoz and Valverde, crossing the river by a bridge, which Beresford evidently expected would have been the main object of the enemy's attack. To the left of the road lay the village of Albuera, apparently deserted, and in ruins. Near this was stationed our artillery. The enemy, however, merely menacing this point, crossed the river about a mile higher up, where its course was nearly at right angles with that which it subsequently took in front of our position. By this movement, our right flank, consisting of Blake's army, was laid completely open to attack, and instantly driving the Spaniards from the heights they occupied, Marshal Soult drew up his army in a commanding position, which completely raked the line of the allies : Thus an immediate change of front, on our part, became necessary ; and the object to which our efforts were directed, of course, was to dislodge the enemy from the very important heights of which he had already gained possession. In truth, on the success of these efforts depended the whole issue of the battle, for, if the French succeeded in maintaining *their* position, *ours* became untenable, and no resource was left but a retreat, which, situated as we then were, could not fail to be both disgraceful and calamitous.

Such were the circumstances in which both armies stood, when the order, which I have already mentioned, arrived for our brigade to march instantly to attack the enemy on the heights he occupied.

The morning, which had been overcast, " and heavily with clouds brought on the day, " had now changed to one of storm and rain, so heavy, that less than forty days of it, would have sufficed for a second deluge; and it was, with every part of our apparel perfectly saturated with water, that we commenced our movement. The enemy soon opened on us a tremendous fire of artillery, which did considerable execution in the column, and dashed the earth in our faces, as we advanced. One cannon-ball struck close to my foot, and bounding onwards with terrific velocity, passed through the body of the officer commanding the company immediately in rear of my own, and killed two soldiers in its further progress.

As we approached the spot, where the courage of both armies was about to be tested, a sight of the most dispiriting description presented itself, at some distance on our right. The first brigade, in the act of forming line, was charged by a large body of Polish lancers, and thus taken at a disadvantage, were thrown into disorder, which it was found impossible to retrieve. By this attack, nearly the whole of the Buffs, and second battalion of the forty-eighth, were made prisoners.

We had reached the bottom of the heights, which we were about to ascend, and for that purpose were deploying, by an echelon march, from column into line, when Sir William Stewart, the second in command, rode up to us at full speed. His appearance arrested my attention. The day, as I have already said, was cold and wet, but the perspiration stood in large drops on his forehead, and ran down his cheeks. He was always a man of martial appearance but at that moment particularly so. There was strong agitation visible in his countenance and manner, but there was a striking expression of high courage in his eye, and as he spoke, his utterance was quicker, and his voice more animated, than I had ever heard it. He addressed us as follows :—

" Men of the third brigade, you are about to fight for the honour of your country, and I am not afraid to tell you, that the fate of this army is in your hands. I have committed a great and unfortunate error with the first brigade, but I am sure you will repair all. You will crown the height, and then charge the enemy with the bayonet. Go on, my brave fellows, and may God bless you ! "

To this inspiriting address, the men answered by a loud and hearty cheer, and General Houghton, waving his hat, led the way up the side of the hill. On reaching its summit, we were instantly assailed by a dreadful fire, both of musquetry and artillery, and the men fell thickly in the ranks. For a moment, the line first wavered, and then recoiled for a pace or two, but General Houghton, again waving his hat, spurred on to the front, and we advanced once more, in double-quick, to the charge.

The other regiments of the brigade, being in rear, had not yet taken up their position in the line, and we enjoyed the honour of leading them into action. As we advanced, I remember passing Marshal Beresford on the height. He was on foot, with no staff near him, and in a situation of extreme exposure; his look and air were those of a man perplexed and bewildered.

Our intention of charging the enemy was unfortunately defeated, by the intervention of a small ravine, on the opposite bank of which the French were stationed, and were enabled, by the acclivity on which they stood, to fire on us eight deep. It was on the edge of this ravine that we halted, and opened our fire. The carnage in our ranks was dreadful. General Houghton had been killed in the advance, and bullets flew like hailstones. I saw my friends and brother officers fall around me, and it seemed as if I bore a charmed life, and that I alone moved secure and scathless amid the surrounding havock.

Such had been our situation for some time, when the sergeant-major came to inform me, that the command of the regiment had devolved on me, all the officers senior in rank having been killed or wounded. In the rear I found the horse of the adjutant, who had been killed, and mounting him, I rode along the ranks, and saw that I had indeed succeeded to a melancholy command. We had taken upwards of seven hundred men into action, of whom not a third remained, and it was evident, if we continued much longer in our present situation, few even of those could expect to escape the fate of their companions.

The firing, which had somewhat slackened on the part of the enemy, had, from the exhaustion of ammunition, almost entirely ceased on ours, yet we had received no orders to retire. In this situation, a brigade of artillery was advanced to the front, and instantly opened their fire. It was charged by the French cavalry, and we had the mortification to observe the artillerymen driven from their posts, and the guns remain in possession of the enemy. The regiment were already retiring when this unfortunate event took place, but even destitute as we were of ammunition, I determined to make an effort to recover the guns, thus disgracefully sacrificed, at the point of the bayonet. Once more we faced the enemy, and calling on the small remains of the regiment to follow me, I led the charge, trampling, as we advanced, on the bodies of our dead and dying companions. The charge was successful. The enemy were driven back, and the guns were once more in our possession.

The Fusileer brigade was seen at that moment advancing to our support, and everything seemed to indicate a happy termination of the contest. Before the arrival, however, of this seasonable reinforcement, we were charged by the Polish lancers, who had already done so much execution in the commencement of the action, supported by a heavy column of infantry. At this moment I received a shot in the body, but did not fall from my horse. I was immediately surrounded by the lancers, and remember receiving a dreadful sabre-cut on the face, and a pistol-shot in the left arm. I fell to the ground, and of what passed afterwards, my memory gives me no intelligence.

CHAPTER VIII

She is my essence, and I leave to be,
If I be not by her fair influence
Foster'd, illumined, cherish'd, kept alive.
                                        Cymbeline.

How like a younker or a prodigal
The skarfed bark puts from its native bay,
Hugg'd and embraced by the strumpet wind ;
How like a prodigal doth she return,
With over-weather'd ribs and ragged sails,
Lean, rent, and beggar'd by the strumpet wind !
                                Merchant of Venice.

My return to consciousness was accompanied by acute bodily suffering.
I was in a tent, and the surgeon of the regiment, with one of his
assistants, stood beside the pallet on which I lay. My feelings were those
of a man on whom death had set his gripe. I gasped convulsively for
breath, yet at every respiration, was nearly suffocated by the blood,
which gurgled from my throat, and obstructed the action of my lungs.
Had relief not been administered, it was impossible I could have
survived many minutes. Fortunately, the surgeons, in examining my
body, found a small protuberance below my left shoulder, which they
immediately opened ; the bullet and a mass of coagulated blood issued
from the wound, and the dreadful feeling of suffocation was instantly
relieved. The blood, which had hitherto flowed through my throat, now
found another channel, and from that moment I date the full and
unimpaired restoration of my senses.

The difficulty of breathing, that primary of the vital functions, had
absorbed all other sense of suffering, and that removed, I awoke only to
pain, of which I had hitherto been unconscious. Stimulated by their first
success, and the slight hope which it held out of their skill being
efficaciously exerted, the doctors proceeded to examine my other
wounds more minutely, than in my apparently hopeless state, they had
at first deemed necessary. This done, they consulted a few minutes
apart, then Holford approached, and taking my hand, thus addressed
me :—

"Thornton," he said, and I saw the tears rise to his eyes as he spoke,
"you are a man of courage, arm yourself with it."

"You mean to tell me my wounds are mortal. Speak, do not fear
me."

" Not so. There are hopes of your recovery, and by God's blessing, we shall have you once more among us. But an operation is necessary. You must lose your arm. "

" And is this the only means of saving my life ? "

He answered, in a low but decided tone of voice, pressing my hand between both of his—" In our judgment it is. "

On receiving this intelligence, I at first made no answer, but closing my eyes, endeavoured to collect my energies for the scene of sufferance, through which it was necessary I should pass. To do so, was no easy task. Weakened as I was by loss of blood, my mind partook of the feebleness of my body. I was distracted and irresolute. A cold and clammy perspiration overspread my forehead, and there was fear and shrinking in my heart. At that moment I would have preferred death, but I felt, that to incur death for the mere avoidance of bodily pain, would leave an indelible imputation on my courage—what was it but to conclude my short, and hitherto not dishonourable career by dying like a coward ? The struggle was long and severe, but it passed, and I told the worthy Doctor that I was prepared. He again pressed my hand in strong emotion, but was silent.

Sympathy for mere physical suffering, ranks in the very lowest class of mental emotions, and I ask it not for mine. In the operation which followed, I bore only what thousands have borne before me, many with greater fortitude, and a more resigned spirit ; for I know by experience, that a sick-bed may afford occasion for the exercise of a higher courage, than is required, under the influence of strong extraneous excitement, to brave death in the field ;—that the humble and inglorious sufferer, may display a spirit more truly heroic, than his who perils life, for human honour and applause, in the imminent deadly breach.

A few days afterwards, the march of the army, which being re-inforced, returned once more to resume the siege of Badajoz, made the removal of the wounded a measure of necessity. I was in too miserable a state to be able to bear the jolting of an hospital-waggon, and by the exertions of my kind Doctor, a litter was procured for my conveyance to Olivença. But even the slightest motion of my shattered frame, made every muscle quiver with agony ; and though the distance was little more than two leagues, such was the accession of fever occasioned by the journey, that long before its conclusion, I was in a state of violent delirium.

At Olivença I remained about three weeks, during a considerable part of which I was dead to every object of the external world. Often, I have been told, during my madness, did I rave of the Lady Melicent. Sometimes, as if bending at her feet, I poured forth the most impassioned oaths of constancy and love, and called on her to redeem her troth, irrevocably plighted in the sight of God. Then would I accuse her of perfidy and falsehood, and invoke heaven and earth, and all the unseen beings of the air, to bear witness of her treachery. Sometimes, in more violent mood, I made the walls to ring with the name of Hewson, and with clenched teeth, and fiery eye-balls, called on him to stand forth and defend his villainy, heaping, when I found he came not, loud and burning curses on his head. In such paroxysms of my disorder, I would tear the dressings from my wounds, till the very agony I occasioned, found a cure in its excess, and I sank fainting on my pillow.

I would not tire the reader by any account of the various alternations of amendment and relapse, by which the slow progress of my recovery was marked or impeded. Suffice it, that when intelligence arrived that the British army had raised the siege of Badajoz, and were about to retire from the Alentejo, it found me reduced to the very lowest state of debility and exhaustion. The wounded were immediately ordered to be removed from Olivença to Elvas, the only fortress in the province of which possession was to be retained by the allies. I heard the news with indifference, for all energy, both mental and bodily, had departed from me, and I lay a helpless and a passive creature, alike incapable of thought or action. A litter was again procured for me, which rested on two poles, like those of a sedan-chair, and was carried by mules. The awning which covered it, afforded little protection from the heat of the noontide sun, and the air I breathed, was scorching to my wounded lungs. I lay gasping, and unable to move, in speechless anguish, finding relief only in occasional fainting fits, for insensibility was then indeed a relief.

I did, however, reach Elvas alive, and there I remained for three months. Weary and dreary months they were to me. Day after day passed on, and the voice of kindness never reached my ear. I was without books, without a friend,—nay, an acquaintance,—a sick and solitary man. Night after night came silent and sleepless, another yet the same.

And yet I wished for darkness. The apartment in which I lay, and every object it contained, had become odiously familiar to my eyes. Everything around me was associated with the memory of suffering. The table—chairs—the huge oak chest that occupied one corner of the room—the print of the Holy Virgin that hung opposite to my bed—the dark building which threw its gloom across the street upon my window—the huge rafters of the roof, every speck and spot on which was rooted in my memory, what would I not have given to have had them blotted from my sight—to have even enjoyed the privilege of gazing on vacuity !

But worse than even these, was the eternal ticking of a clock that hung beside my chamber-door. From the detested objects of vision I enjoyed some respite in the darkness of night. But *this* was ceaseless. By night and day its hateful voice was in my ear, ever recalling to my memory how slowly the hours of pain and weariness went by.

These were the feelings of a suffering body and a diseased mind ; but even now, that the circumstances which occasioned them have passed away, I find evidence of their strength in the vividness with which they almost, unbidden, present themselves to my memory.

It was during my stay at Elvas that I received intelligence of my having been promoted to the Majority of the regiment, which became vacant by the death of Colonel Penleaze. It had been my intention, on my recovery, to have noticed, even, if necessary, at the expense of my commission, the insinuations which I considered to have been cast on me by that officer, before our advance at Albuera. But death settles all differences, and Colonel Penleaze was no more. He had received a dangerous wound, of which, about three weeks after the battle, he died.

Gratifying as the intelligence of my promotion was,—for, even in the miserable state to which I was reduced, there was yet ambition in my heart,—another still greater pleasure awaited me. I received letters from England. But it was a pleasure, alas, not unmixed. The letters were from Lucy—there were none from Lady Melicent. When the servant brought them to my bed, vigour for a moment returned to my wounded frame, and, starting from my pillow, I snatched them with my only hand, and pressed them to my lips. Then I fixed my eyes upon them, in the hope of recognizing the hand I most panted to behold.

None were in the writing of Lady Melicent. I knew her small and beautiful characters,—I was not,—I could not be deceived.

Three months had elapsed, and I had received no letter from Lady Melicent. The very hope had been sufficient to buoy my sinking spirits, in the moments when they had most needed support. More than food or sleep to me had been this fond—this visionary hope. The anticipations of long days and nights had centered in this, and it was now broken. The dreams of solitary and suffering hours had vanished in one instant. The blow was a severe one. Disease for a time had conquered the manliness of my spirit, and, brooding in the loneliness of sorrow, I wept as a child.

Let no one in the palmy pride of unbroken and unbending manhood, sneer at this confession of my weakness. He knows not—he cannot know, till tried by circumstances, what which is within him. The tide with him is full, but the waters may yet ebb from beneath his bark, and leave it dry upon the sands.

Disappointed as I was at the silence of Lady Melicent, my heart still recoiled from the idea of accounting for it by any decrease of affection. It was not—it could not be. Hearts joined as ours, so short an absence could not have divided. Could I not appeal to the confession of her lips,—nay, to the bright tears by which our parting had been hallowed, for evidence of her love? Might she not be ill? Might not her letters have miscarried? Might she not be in circumstances, when to write was impossible? Oh! all, or any of these might be; but *not*, that her silence proceeded from fickleness of heart. There was treason even in the thought, and I cast it from me.

Poor Lucy! little was there of her natural joyousness of heart discernible in these letters. I had not written, I had been incapable of writing, and she only knew that my name had appeared in the Gazette among the list of the "severely wounded." But this was enough to people the warm world of her bosom with terrible fears. The time of Lucy's greatest trial had come. Her sister and her brother, the beings she most loved on earth, had become to her the sources of grief. One lay wounded in a foreign land, and the other—alas, how much more melancholy was her lot!

Of Jane, Lucy could give me no information. She had received no tidings of her, from the moment when Hewson had separated the sisters in their last embrace, and claimed the victim of his tyranny. It was evident that Hewson was determined to prevent all intercourse with her own family—to darken the last faint gleam, which, till now, had lightened the gloom of her condition.

Not unaccompanied with pain, therefore, was the enjoyment I derived from the perusal of Lucy's letters. With regard to Jane, I had already anticipated the worst. In her case, I had no ground on which to found a hope for future happiness. I knew she had been sold to a demon, and was in his power; he would exact, to the uttermost, the penalty and forfeit of his bond. But even the simple kindness, and fond anxieties of Lucy were as balm to my spirit. Cut off as I then was from the world, I felt desolate and deserted, and there was something soothing in the proof these letters afforded, that I was not yet wholly forgotten,—that I was still, in one kind heart at least, the object of fears, hopes, prayers, tears, wishes, and regrets. Oh! this, in a situation like mine, was much to know and to remember.

My wounds gradually healed, and I was at length pronounced to be in a state when I might, without danger, be removed to Lisbon. The wounds on my head and face had now cicatrized, and the bandages were removed.

I remember the day, when, curious to observe the change they had produced in my appearance, I ordered a looking-glass to be brought, and gazed upon my countenance, as reflected on its surface. Heaven and earth, what did I behold, ere it dropped from my relaxing fingers, and I sank back half fainting on my couch! I felt as if a frightful Gorgon had looked forth on me from the mirror. It was not, I at first thought,—it could not be my own face, that had thus hideously glared on me,—Alas, my doubts were shortlived. A dreadful truth, of which, till then, I had been ignorant, was at that moment revealed. I knew that I was thenceforth destined to be in men's eyes but an object of pity or aversion.

There may exist philosophers, on whom such a change of external appearance, might make but a trivial impression; who, devoting all their energies to brightening the jewel, care little for the casket, in which it is enclosed. Such men I envy, and admire. They are formed to play a nobler and a better part, and they will find at least one portion of their reward, in being exempted from the chance of such sufferings as those to which I was a prey.

In my constitution, however, there was but a small leaven of original power. What I was, education and the world had made me. Mine was not a mind of strong internal resources, and alike by my ambition and pursuits, I was bound closely to society. In such circumstances, a sudden change had come upon me. What I had been, I was no longer—I could never be again. The prepossessions excited by personal appearance, were, in future, not to be *for* me, but *against* me. I must enter society under disadvantages which it was impossible to overcome. I was to labour under the conviction of being an object, whom *men*, indeed, might tolerate, but from whom *woman* would instinctively shrink back.

It was not the loss of mere personal advantages which excited my regret; these might have departed, uncared for, and disregarded. I would have been but as thousands are, and the course of my life would still have flowed on, calmly and unruffled. But to be different from my fellow-men, to be singled out among them, as an object of remarkable deformity, whom pity and aversion were doomed to follow as his shadow,—to be a creature offensive to all,—was more—far more, than I could calmly bear.

Several days had elapsed before I again had courage to gaze on the reflection of my features. When I did so, the vehemence of my emotion had passed, and my feelings were calmer, though not less deep. Such a creature as I gazed on! My face was pale and haggard, my eyes sunk deeply in their sockets, and my features were frightfully distorted by a wound, reaching from the temple to the mouth, by which my upper lip had been divided, and the extent of which was indicated by a long red scar. The whole expression of my countenance was changed, and the very features I beheld, seemed those of a stranger.

Happy, however—comparatively happy, at least—was the moment when I quitted Elvas, and found myself on the road to Lisbon. Oh, that bed, which had for months been to me the unchanging theatre of pain, how did my heart leap, when I knew that I had quitted it for ever! The memory of all the cheerless days and weary nights I had passed in it, vanished in a moment, as my eye once more gazed on the blue firmament, and I felt my throbbing brow bathed by the first gushing of the free air.

I was obliged to be assisted, almost carried, into the cabriolet; for reduced as my body was, it was still more than my limbs were able to support. The jolting of the carriage was painful to my wounds, which were yet tender, but my spirits were comparatively light, when I found myself winding slowly along the level but beautiful country of the Alentejo, interspersed with pretty villages and antique towns. The journey was performed slowly, for I was unequal to length of travel; and though the distance was only ninety miles, I did not reach Lisbon till the fifth morning.

As we drove through the streets, I thought there was more bustle and business apparent than before. The citizens, considering themselves now free from all danger of invasion, had laid aside their arms, and returned to their peaceful avocations, adorned only by the national cockade, as a signal of their loyalty. The number of British officers in the capital, great as it had formerly appeared, had evidently increased. They were to be met with in every street, some on crutches, some with an arm supported by a sling, some evidently suffering from sickness, and many, in the perfect enjoyment of all bodily functions, stood conversing in groups, or loitered in the shady places, endeavouring, by demonstrations of gallantry, to win the eye and favour of some fair Donna, who might be seen singing over her embroidery at a neighbouring lattice.

I drove to the Town-Major's office, and demanded a billet. It was given me, and I was pleased, on arriving at the domicile of my *Patrone*, to find it situated in the highest and most beautiful part of the city, called Buenos Ayres.

Nothing could be finer than the view commanded from my windows. From one, I beheld the suburban prospect of the whole city, stretched out beneath on an inclined plane, reaching down to the very margin of the Tagus, on whose quiet waters lay a large fleet of British men-of-war. From another window, I beheld, in the near ground, the towers of Belem; and afar off, the eye rested on the vast interminable ocean, with here and there a distant speck, seen slowly moving athwart its bosom.

Nothing, in short, could be more delightful than the situation of my residence. While, in the lower parts of the city, the intensity of the heat was scarcely endurable, in the more elevated region, in which I dwelt, the temperature of the air was cool and pleasant, and the breeze came pure and untainted from the sea. Here symptoms of reviving strength again visited my limbs; and though I felt my constitution had received a shock, too violent to admit the hope of a perfect restoration to vigour, there was at least the prospect before me, of a gradual recovery from that distressing state of debility, under which I then laboured.

The only alarming symptoms that now remained, proceeded from the wound in my chest. I had still a violent cough, and suffered much after any unusual exertion, from an extreme difficulty of breathing. These were indications of an internal disorder, from which there was no chance of an early recovery; and to avoid the unpleasantness of a long residence at Lisbon, I determined to apply for the sanction of a Medical Board to my return to England.

This conclave of the faculty was held once a fortnight at the Estrella Convent, and thither came the sick, the wounded, and the idle, soliciting, though from very different motives, a continuance of exemption from military duty. I found a very large party assembled on the stated day in the convent. One portion of the company, among whom I formed no unconspicuous unit, was pretty similar to that which is recorded in Scripture, to have annually assembled at the Pool of Bethesda.

It is at a meeting of this sort that one obtains a compendious view of the more immediate and direct evils of war. There were men in the very pride of youth, whom nature had endowed with constitutions of iron, whose bodies were maimed and mangled—whose very looks told of sufferings, on which their lips were silent. I could not gaze on them, without a feeling of brotherhood and interest. We belonged to the same profession, we had been animated by the same hopes, we had fallen martyrs to the same cause. How many of the ties which contribute to bind societies together, are less strong than these! And there was, I thought, a sort of *esprit de corps* among us; the Shibboleth of suffering was common to us all, and though strangers to each other, we naturally spoke in the language of friendship and regard.

The Medical Board, after a minute examination of my case, without hesitation, granted me the leave of absence it was my object to obtain.

While yet at Lisbon, I received a letter from Lady Melicent. She at length had learned that I had been wounded, and expressed many fond fears, and flattering anxieties, on my account. In the delightful emotions which the perusal of this letter excited, all other thoughts and feelings were for a time absorbed. After so long a silence, the most indifferent words traced by her pen, could not be otherwise than precious. Yet when the first glow of gladness had subsided, I imagined there was something in its tone and character different from that by which her former letters had been marked. Why I thought so, I cannot tell. I could detect no coldness; the sympathy it expressed for my sufferings, was deep, and apparently sincere. I weighed every word of the letter; I analyzed each expression; I pondered long and deeply on every sentence. Criticism lent no aid to my conclusions, yet the instinctive consciousness within me, though unsupported, was unshaken. It came not from reason, nor at the voice of reason would it depart. It was something to be felt, not proved—a conviction—shadowy, perhaps, yet firm and immovable.

I felt, however, that no change of sentiment on the part of her I loved, could now influence my destiny. Fortune had cast an impassable barrier betwixt us. Love! what a creature am I, I exclaimed, in bitterness of soul, to think of love! As I spoke, I cast my eyes on a mirror that hung in the apartment, and gazed on the reflection of my own miserable form. Is this the remains of the gay and gallant youth, who had won the guerdon of a lady's heart, for which the proudest had striven, and in vain? This poor maimed, defaced, and wasted object, can thought of passion still linger in his heart? Where now are the strong and glorious pulses, with which it once beat, as if, in the fulness of passion, it would have burst its prison-bonds to have throbbed in freedom? Is this the countenance on which ladies have smiled? Are these the eyes, dim, cold, and hollow, which have exchanged glances of love with the proudest and most beautiful of her sex? And are these thin and distorted lips, those that whispered a tale of burning love in the ear of the Lady Melicent?

I dashed my clenched hand on my forehead, as I turned from the mirror. No! I exclaimed, I may excite pity, my fate may draw tears from her eyes; I may be to her an object of tender,—nay even of fond regret, but of love—Oh never, never, never! Farewell for ever all thought of passion. In woman's eyes I am become a fearful and a loathsome thing. I will give back to the Lady Melicent her vows; I will free her from her plighted troth; I will resign my claim to the dearest blessing of Heaven. Yet never shall the love I bear her pass away. It shall go down with me to my grave, and her name shall be mingled in my latest prayer.

These resolutions were made when my feelings were under the influence of high excitement, but I did not swerve from them in my calmer moments. Lady Melicent should be free, or rather in justice, she was already free. I was not the man to whom her heart had yielded. The blow that smote me to the earth, had widowed her first love, and she again was free and unshackled as the blackbird in the summer trees, or the lark upon the hill. But even if in the constancy of her heart she still desired to unite her fate to mine, never, never would I consent to the sacrifice of one so generous and noble. It fitted not, that beauty should be linked, to the maimed and the decrepid. Such an union was unnatural, it was revolting. Even to wish it, was to become contemptible in my own eyes—and in the eyes of the world—no, the world never should despise me.

Violent, however, was the effort, and long the conflict, before I was able to give effect to my resolution. For hours I remained seated at the table, the pen in my trembling fingers, but it traced no characters on the paper. A multitude of feelings were struggling within me for expression, and struggling in vain, for they were inexpressible. I wished that my heart should be understood, yet could find no words to shadow forth its emotions. I sought in language, what language does not afford, the power of painting the wild tumult of vehement and conflicting passions.

Days elapsed before I could command sufficient calmness for the execution of my task. But that at length came, and the letter was written. Deep and poignant were my sufferings, as my fingers traced the words by which I renounced the hope that was dearest to me on earth; but strength came as I proceeded, and the struggle passed away. I told her of the condition to which the fortune of war had reduced me, and painted myself as the wretched creature I was. I thanked her—fondly, fervently, and gratefully thanked her—for her love. That I had been its object, would still be the pride, as it must now be the only consolation of my heart. I absolved her from her engagement, and assured her, that her happiness would ever be the object of my fondest prayers. Fortune had dealt me perhaps a hard measure, but I was resigned. Henceforward she would think of me as one severed from her for ever, but as one whose love would only be exhaled in his latest gasp. Then I bade her,—and there was a long pause ere I could write the word—

Farewell.

Such was the substance of my letter. As I wrote it, there was a heavy and stupifying pressure on my brain; yet I was calm, for at the time there was an awful stillness of passion within me, like the silence that intervenes between the sweeping gusts of a hurricane. A casual spectator, I think, would have discerned in me no external symptoms of emotion. I addressed, sealed, and dispatched the letter, locked the door of my chamber, and then came the swoop of the tempest, perhaps the more violent for having been so long repressed. Such were the circumstances connected with the most severe trial of my life.

Nothing remained to detain me in Lisbon, and I was soon prepared for my departure. I returned in the Daphne frigate, and was landed at Portsmouth.

CHAPTER IX

Am I so changed by suffering, so forgot,
That love disowns me ; Zillah knows me not ?
                              MONTGOMERY.

Then what must woman be ? * * *
* * * * * * * * * * * * * * * *
They're like the winds upon Lapanthae's shore,
That still are changing. Oh then love no more.
A woman's love is like that Syrian flower,
That buds and spreads, and withers in an hour.
                              Thracian Wonder.

I HAD never before returned to my native land without buoyancy of
spirit. It was with dull and sluggish feelings that I now first beheld it,
looming in the extremity of the horizon. Every eye but mine sparkled
with pleasure ; every heart beat quicker with the thought of home. What
a multitude of dormant sympathies did not the sight of old England
awaken in the ship ! The songs that rose that night from the forecastle,
were merrier than usual, as with outspread wings, the vessel flew
onward amid the darkness, triumphing in her way.

The passage had been a rough one, the weather,—for it was
winter,—boisterous and cold, and it was in a state of great weakness and
exhaustion, that I at length found myself housed in a Portsmouth hotel.
I remained its inmate for a week, during which I never quitted my bed. I
laboured under a general sinking of the system ; all energies, both
mental and physical, were dead within me, and life presented no object
of sufficient power to stimulate me to exertion. Mine was become

A grief without a pang, void, dark, and drear,
A heavy, drowsy, unimpassion'd grief,
Which finds no natural outlet, or relief,
In word, or sigh, or tear.

Even affection for my own family, which till now had ever tenanted
my bosom, appeared for a time to have become extinct. I wrote no
letters, and wished to receive none. The well of every emotion was dried
up. Earth contained no spell to rouse me. The chords of feeling were
slackened, and refused to vibrate, and though the current of bodily life
yet continued to flow, my spirit was torpid and exanimate.

Death is a blessing, when compared with such an existence as mine
then was. I thank God, it did not continue long. Green places once more

arose amid the desert, and the springs of human sympathy again bubbled up in the fountain of my heart. I was again a being bound by the same ties, and influenced by the same motives, as my fellow men. Even in the cares and anxieties which assailed me, I found pleasure, for any suffering was preferable to the dull, cold, and deathlike torpor of the soul, which had sat on me like a night-mare. I would have braved the fury of the storm, to escape from the stagnation of the calm.

When I reached London, I wrote to Jane and Lucy, informing them of my return. I told them I was ill, and much changed, and promised Lucy soon to visit her at Middlethorpe, where she was again residing with the kind and excellent Willoughbys.

For a man who wishes to enjoy society, or for one who wishes to avoid it, London is alike the place. It was my intention to remain there for some time, and after visiting my sisters, to retire and bury myself in the solitude of Thornhill, if possible, the world forgetting, very certain of soon being by the world forgot.

I had scarcely been in town a week, when one morning, the door of my apartment was thrown open, and in a moment I found myself in the arms of Frank Willoughby. He had learned my address from Lucy, and had hurried up to town to welcome my return, and render me any service in his power. I had resolved to avoid all society, yet the meeting once past, I felt comfort in the presence of a friend. Willoughby was evidently much shocked, though he endeavoured to conceal his emotion, with the change in my appearance; indeed, I knew it could not be otherwise, but I had already begun to learn the hard, though necessary lesson, of submission to my fate. I felt it was cowardice to sink beneath a blow, which human courage could surmount. I was unhappy, yet resigned.

In spite of my urgent entreaties, Frank would not leave me, and the continual flow of his cheerfulness, and a certain characteristic humour which marked him, had, I believe, the effect of preventing the return of that wretched mental depression, to which, perhaps, I had an hereditary predisposition, and which occasionally came like a sudden blight upon my spirit.

We were seated at breakfast a few days after his arrival, when my servant, to the astonishment of us both, announced " Mr Lavender of Bow Street, " and that gentleman entered the apartment. After several polite bows had been interchanged, I addressed him :

" A visit from you, Mr Lavender, is an unexpected pleasure, and has, I fear, originated on the present occasion, from some mistake. "

" No mistake I think, sir. I have been sent here by the magistrate on a small piece of business, and shall be happy to await your leisure, to accompany you to Bow Street. "

" This, Mr Lavender, is Sir Francis Willoughby, and I am Major Thornton, of the —— at your service; pray, with which of us may your business lie ? "

" With you, Major Thornton. "

" Then, pray, be so good as to acquaint me with its nature ? "

" A small warrant, that is all, sir. A gentleman has sworn that you have put him in bodily fear, and it is necessary you should be bound over to keep the peace. "

Though at first exceedingly surprised by this intelligence, a little reflection convinced me, that Hewson must be the person at whose instance this proceeding had taken place, and it served to increase, if that was possible, the contempt and hatred which I already entertained for his character and conduct. I, therefore, dispatched a messenger instantly, desiring my solicitor to meet me *quam primum* at Bow Street, whither Mr Lavender accompanied us.

On my arrival in town, I had taken legal advice as to the best mode of proceeding, with regard to Hewson, and was strongly advised to refrain from all personal violence, which could only injure my sister's cause, and render the attainment of the object we had in view, more distant and uncertain. I had, therefore, resolved to await calmly the issue of the legal proceedings, before I sought any interview with Hewson, or inflicted on him that vengeance, of which it was now evident he stood in awe.

On arriving at Bow Street, I found the case was as I supposed. Hewson had made affidavit that he was apprehensive of personal violence, from the letter I had written, and the magistrate informed me it was necessary that I should be bound over to keep the peace, myself in L.2000, and two sureties in L.1000 each. This was accordingly done, and we departed.

During my stay in London, I met likewise with an old friend, who has been already mentioned in the early portion of these memoirs. It was William Lumley, whom I had not seen for many years. He now belonged to one of the Inns of Temple, and had become a barrister of considerable practice. Of course, we met often. He was still a bachelor ; and in telling old stories, I found my sister Jane had been the object of his youthful and ardent love. Circumstances had not favoured his passion. He was poor, and had to push his way in the world, and his attachment remained unknown, even to its object. The flame smouldered, but was not extinguished ; and amid his slow and toilsome progress in his profession, it had served to light him on his path, and animate him in his labours, with the prospect of a reward, still within the pale of his ambition. But the course of true love never did run smooth. Jane married, and poor Lumley's long-cherished hopes were dashed rudely to the ground. The *Château en Espagne* was gone, but the solid benefit of the exertions to which it had stimulated him, remained, and his character as a sound and able lawyer stood high.

I told him Jane's melancholy story, and it deeply affected him, and I was glad to find one, at once so able and so zealous, to whose management her cause might safely be committed. The good old man his father, he informed me, now an Octogenarian, still lived, and felt pride in the pupils he had sent into the world, stored with his instructions, several of whom had already attained to distinction, in their different walks of life.

Before I quitted London, an incident occurred, which once more stung my feelings into an agony almost insupportable. One morning, I had gone with Willoughby to the Exhibition of Ancient Pictures, which we were engaged in examining. The exhibition having been open for some time, the number of spectators was few, so few at least, that one might look at the pictures without being jostled in a crowd. I have no technical knowledge of painting, but I have a taste,—of course an uncultivated one, for the art, and I was standing opposite a fine landscape of Gaspar Poussin, when the noise of a party advancing from the bottom of the room, for a moment diverted my attention from the picture. What were my feelings, when turning round, the first object that met my eye was Lady Melicent! She was the leading star of a gay group, and advanced from the bottom of the Gallery, leaning on the arm of Lord Lyndhurst, whom she occasionally addressed in that half-whispering tone, which indicated a considerable change in the footing of their intimacy. It was evident she was in high spirits; I had never seen her countenance more gay and animated, and I observed her eyes glance occasionally round the apartment, as if to enjoy the homage, which the gaze of the bystanders paid to her beauty. Pleasure was written legibly on her countenance, no inward care disturbed its serenity. The fabled smiles of Euphrosyne were not more beautiful and joyous, than those which adorned her features.

Still hanging on Lord Lyndhurst's arm, Lady Melicent advanced slowly, and stood near the centre of the apartment, right opposite to the spot, to which, from the moment my eye first rested on her, I had been rooted. Then a sudden failure of strength came over me, and I sank into a chair, literally gasping for breath, for there was a choking in my throat, and every muscle of my frame became rigid as those of a corpse. Language cannot express the agony, or if torture be a stronger word, the torture of these moments. At length her full, dark, beautiful eyes rested on my countenance. She evidently did not know me, but as if willing to avoid the contemplation of a disagreeable object, hastily withdrew them.

Just then my situation became such as to attract the attention of the company.

" Here's a sick gentleman, " cried one, " give him air. "

" Bring a glass of water directly, " cried another.

" Assist the gentleman down stairs, " cried a third.

" He's dying, " ejaculated another.

" Give him time, and he'll recover, " exclaimed a fifth.

I heard all this, for my senses had not forsaken me. I was the object of universal attention, and I believe of pity. Willoughby, on hearing the noise, came running up, and found me in the situation I have described.

"Good God, Thornton, you are ill—very ill!" he exclaimed loudly, in the first paroxysm of his anxiety.

At the word "Thornton," Lady Melicent turned her face towards me, with a sudden and almost convulsive motion, and again gazed for a moment on my haggard and deathlike countenance. I imagine she recognized me, for I saw her become pale as ashes, then whispering something in the ear of Lord Lyndhurst, she turned suddenly away, and I saw her no more.

One of the servants brought me a glass of water, with which Willoughby bathed my temples, and accepting one of the dozen smelling bottles, which the surrounding ladies offered for my use, [woman is ever kind and compassionate] Willoughby held it to my nose, and I recovered, though slowly.

At length, I was able to quit a scene, in which I had played a part so involuntarily conspicuous. Leaning on Willoughby's arm, I with difficulty staggered out of the apartment, and, getting into a coach, drove home to the hotel.

On our arrival, I thanked him for his assistance, and entreated him to leave me. To this he at first demurred, but on my more strongly urging the request, he complied, and I was left alone.

For some time I continued walking up and down the apartment, in a state of pitiable mental confusion. The elements of thought and feeling within me were conglomerated into confused and inextricable masses. There was anarchy in my brain, and chaos in my heart. All impulses of soul and sense had been awakened, and in their very multitude lay the cause of my disorder.

More enviable, perhaps, was even this condition, than that by which it was succeeded. Was it possible, I thought, that this woman had ever loved me, when, even at the moment when she must have thought, that I lay mangled and suffering, in a foreign land, (for I had not mentioned to her, my intention of returning to England,) she was thus happy and regardless of my fate?—yes, the fate of one who had received the maiden vows of her eternal love, whose bosom at parting had been moistened by her tears, by whose arms she had been encircled, whose lips had imprinted kisses on her burning cheek! And yet within one month— one little month—this being had been forgotten. She had no sorrow for his fate, no tear for his memory. His misfortunes had not banished the smile from her lips, nor dimmed, even for a season, the sparkle of her eye. No grief had paled her cheek, no melancholy remembrance lingered in her heart. *He* had been whistled down the wind a prey to fortune, unsorrowed for, and unloved.

True, indeed, she was free. I had given back the proud promise of her love. That precious gift had indeed been mine, but it was mine no longer. I could accuse her of no wrong ; I had suffered no injustice. But to be *so soon* forgotten ! It was there my flesh quivered, and the iron entered into my soul.

I expected not that she should pine in unblest maidenhood for my sake. But I did expect,—why should I conceal my vanity ?—that she would have wept for my loss, and lamented, at least for a season, the unhappy fate by which we had been eternally divided. Surely the memory of fond and unhappy love claimed more than was compatible, at such a moment, with a light heart and an unclouded brow.

For the first time, I felt tired and disgusted with the world. I felt myself solitary and deserted—a being cut off from all human sympathy, for his sorrows and sufferings. On whom, did I now possess any claim for commiseration ? On my sisters ? Was there not one dearer than they, to whom I had been bound by ties yet closer, and by whom that claim had been denied ? But what, after all, was the commiseration of sisters ? Was that alone sufficient to sweeten life, and reconcile me to the weary burden it imposed ? Was my cup not empty, because a single drop might still remain in the goblet when its contents had been dashed upon the ground ?

Not by day alone was I the victim of these mournful thoughts. They came to me by night, and mingled poison in my dreams. I loathed society ; even that of Willoughby was a burden to me, but he would not forsake me. What had happened he knew not, but he saw that something pressed heavily on my mind, and my health had become evidently worse. Every symptom under which I laboured was aggravated, and all his kind endeavours to relieve the oppression which weighed me to the earth were employed in vain. The spell that bound me was a strong one, and would not for a time be broken.

Willoughby urged me to accompany him home ; I was glad to flee from London, and consented. The unhappy are seldom stationary, for there is some relief, even in mere locomotion, to the dull monotony of settled sorrow. Lucy, too,—I would again embrace my sister ; and that was something. To me, indeed, it was now *all* ; for what more of pleasure had the world in store for me ?

We set out for Middlethorpe, and arrived there. As we passed the farm, Willoughby stopped to give some orders, and left me to proceed to the house alone. I descended from the carriage, inquired for the ladies, and was ushered into the drawing-room. Laura was there alone. The servant had announced my name, and she was deadly pale, as I entered the apartment. She rose, as if she would have advanced to meet me, but yet remained rooted to the spot, with both her hands extended towards me, in token of welcome. I could but take one of them, and I pressed it warmly in mine.

It was natural that I should be considerably moved, but the sight of her emotion, which all her efforts to be calm could not conceal, added greatly to mine. I endeavoured to address her cheerfully, but, though her lips moved, she answered not. The tears which had collected in her fine eyes, rolled down her cheeks slowly, and in large drops, as she gazed on me. There was no sobbing, or convulsive agitation of the features. The current of her emotion might be strong and deep, but there was calmness on the surface.

Laura Willoughby had resumed her place on the sofa, and I was about to seat myself beside her, when a sound of joy was heard in the apartment, a soft rushing of feet, and, scarcely had my eyes caught a glance of Lucy, ere I felt myself clasped in her arms, and she hung about my neck. Light as was her slender form, the burden was too great for my strength, and I staggered back a pace or two. She felt this, I think, for her grasp became lighter, and pushing herself gently from me, she bent her eyes upon my face, then, uttering a faint scream, hid hers in my bosom.

The emotion of this meeting brought on an attack of that suffocating oppression which my wound had occasioned, and, unable longer to support it, I sank exhausted into a seat. Laura Willoughby observed my condition, and approaching gently, she clasped Lucy in her arms, and the tears of these two kind and beautiful creatures were mingled in their sorrowful embrace. Lucy's sobs came loud and convulsively; Laura shed tears, but they were silent ones.

This scene was interrupted by the entrance of Lady Willoughby and Frank. The countenance of the good old lady showed that she partook considerably of the emotions by which the party on her entrance was pervaded.

" We have all suffered much on your account, Cyril, " she addressed me ; " but, thank God, we see you once more restored to your country and friends. I have felt for you as I would for my own son, and as a son you must allow me to welcome your return. " So saying, the Dowager bent forward, and, for the first time in her life, kissed my cheek.

I looked my gratitude, but could not speak.

" Come, come, young ladies, " cried Frank, willing to relieve a little the sombre character of the scene, " don't give my friend Cyril so dismal a reception. He has brought home, you see, some honourable badges of his gallantry; a few scars, for which a militia officer would give a thousand pounds, in order to look like a veteran. To be sure, he's rather weak, but now we've got him amongst us, it will go hard but we'll set him on his legs again. Depend upon it, a month of your good nursing, and my pleasant society, will make him another man. But don't throw him at first into the blue-devils, by crying, as if he had come home to you a mere Rawhead and Bloodybones ; smiles, not tears, are what are wanted for his recovery.—Ah, there's the dinner-bell, so run away up stairs, and mind you come down with pleasant faces. "

Laura and Lucy, perhaps glad of an opportunity of recovering themselves, withdrew, the latter kissing me as she passed, though, I observed, she closed her eyes as she did so.

There is something soothing and gratifying to a man to find himself the object of woman's tears. It is to woman we naturally look for consolation in affliction; from her alone it is not mortifying to receive compassion. Man's pity hurts our pride; woman's, like oil shed upon the billows, stills the heart.

When the ladies descended to dinner, Lucy's eyes were still red, but she had mastered the violent emotion which the unexpected change in my appearance had excited in the morning. She sat beside me with her hand clasped in mine, as if desirous to receive stronger evidence than her sight afforded her of the reality of my presence. I saw she had resolved to be calm, and made strenuous efforts to be so, yet every now and then, when she thought herself unperceived, she stole a glance at my countenance, and I saw again that the tears were brimming in her eyes. Laura Willoughby, I thought, looked paler than I had seen her of old. She sat with downcast eyes, but when she spoke, she raised them on me, with a melting expression of kindness, melancholy yet soothing, and there was tenderness in every tone of her finely modulated voice.

At Middlethorpe I was the engrossing object of interest to all. Willoughby was partial to field-sports, in which I was too ill to partic-ipate, and his pursuits led him to be much abroad. My exercise did not at first extend beyond a walk in the park, or a short ride on a favourite shooting pony. Even these, however, I was not suffered to make alone. When on foot, Lucy walked with me, and was unhappy if I accepted not the support of her arm. When I rode, her hand was on the bridle, guiding the steps of the docile animal, on the smoothest path. Nor was Laura less assiduous than Lucy in rendering me all those little offices of kindness, trifling perhaps in themselves, yet deeply prized, because they evidently proceeded from a warm and an affectionate heart. Cold is his spirit who feels no flattering emotion in knowing himself the engrossing object of the ministering cares of two young and beautiful women. Their hands were ever ready to arrange the pillows on my couch; and there were moments, as I beheld their graceful forms hovering around it, when my heart almost ceased to be forlorn, and its pulses beat as they had once been wont. Never, indeed, for a moment, was I absent from their thoughts. My wants required no expression, for they anticipated them all. When dull and dispirited, they soothed me by their kind sympathy. On our return from walking, when my weary limbs required repose, Laura Willoughby would sing, for me, to the accompaniment of her harp, or read aloud a novel of Miss Austen or Miss Edgeworth, while Lucy sat at my feet, watching every look, and imagining little offices of kindness.

Frank Willoughby's prediction was in some measure verified. Before a month elapsed, my health was, indeed, greatly improved, but there was a barbed arrow in my heart, that could not be withdrawn.

CHAPTER X

Did I but purpose to embark with thee
On the smooth surface of a summer's sea,
While gentle Zephyrs play in prosperous gales,
And Fortune's favour fills the swelling sails?
And would forsake the ship, and make the shore,
When the winds whistle and the tempests roar?

PRIOR.

I HAD been some weeks at Middlethorpe, when I received the following letter from Lady Melicent. It was addressed to me in Lisbon, and from thence had been returned to England :—

"YOUR last melancholy letter, my dearest Cyril, has cost me many tears. The thought of all you have endured, and the evident depression of your spirits when you wrote, have caused me deep uneasiness, and must continue to do so till I receive happy tidings of your recovery. Believe me, I deeply sympathise in all your sufferings. Would to God, that, by any sacrifice of mine, I could assuage your pain, and restore you to happiness!

"I know and appreciate the generous motives that prompted you to resign all thoughts of our union; and, believe me, though I consent that our engagement should cease, the reasons of my consent are altogether unconnected with the personal misfortunes you describe yourself to have suffered. Oh, no. To me you will be always the same, and no loss of personal attractions could ever alter my affections.

"But perhaps we were rash in forming that engagement. I confess, that difficulties, which appeared small at a distance, seem almost insurmountable on a nearer approach. I could never hope to obtain my father's consent to our union; nor, were I to marry against his wishes, could I ever hope for his forgiveness.

"It is for these reasons, and these alone, that I now consent to break off our correspondence. Let us no longer think or write as lovers; but, believe me, I shall never cease to feel a deep interest in your happiness; and when time, as I trust it will, has softened the ardour of our feelings, we may yet meet as friends,—warm, unchangeable, and sincere ones.

"You may believe, that to write thus has cost me a severe struggle. Alas! that it should have been a necessary one. Farewell. And believe me ever, my dearest Cyril,—for so I must still call you,—with unchanging affection,

"Yours,

" M. DE VERE. "

I know not that the perusal of this letter produced any new feelings of bitterness and disappointment, but it certainly added new pungency to those from which I already suffered. Its tone, I thought, was cold, heartless, and unfeeling. It was evident she had never loved me. The cords of a love, that deserved the name, could not thus have been broken by a sudden wrench. When I remembered the tearless agony in which my last words to her had been addressed, and read the answer which these words had called forth, I felt that it never could have been written by one who loved as I had done. I felt that there had been, on my part, a needless waste of unparticipated suffering. I had been led to play a dangerous game, and had been a loser; for that, indeed, I had myself to blame. But the players had not hazarded equal stakes. She had played but with counters; I had set my all upon a die. Love, which, to her, had been but as a toy or an amusement, was to me the very food of life.

But to what purpose were these reflections? Be her faults what they might, my heart still clung to her. She was still destined to be to me the object of fond and devoted passion. Her empire had been established too firmly to be reconquered; but even were it otherwise, I would have remained a voluntary bondsman: I willed not to be free.

The Lady Melicent thus still remained the engrossing subject of my thoughts. I suffered unutterable pain, whenever I heard her name even casually uttered in conversation. In this respect, poor Lucy was continually inflicting pangs, of which she was unconscious. The kindness of Lady Melicent, during her stay at Staunton, had excited her warm regard; and there was no theme on which she was more eloquent than the grace, the beauty, and the thousand claims to admiration, of her, whose very name pierced me like a dagger. Lucy had not been a confidante. She knew nothing of our attachment; she saw only what lay on the surface, and had not attempted to penetrate beneath it.

About a fortnight after the arrival of the letter, we were seated one morning at the breakfast-table, when Lucy, who had just taken up the newspaper, attracted the attention of the party, by her exclamations of pleasure and surprise.

"Well, this is extraordinary," she said, half speaking to herself, and half to the company. "How blind I must have been, never to have observed what was going on. Indeed, I always thought she positively disliked him. The courtship must have been carried on very slyly, to escape my notice; but I'm so glad she's married, I must write her a letter of congratulation. I daresay, she has not forgot to send me gloves and bridecake."

Lucy's soliloquy, of course, attracted general attention, and I asked, whose marriage it was that had excited so strong an interest?

"Nay, guess if you can," she answered, playfully; "but on second thoughts, I don't think you ever could guess right; so I'll relieve your curiosity by reading it:—

" 'Married, by special license, at Staunton Court, by his Grace the Archbishop of York, the Earl of Lyndhurst, to the Lady Melicent de Vere, only daughter of the Earl of Amersham. The celebration of the ceremony was strictly private, none being present but the near relatives of the two noble families thus happily united. In the evening, a splendid entertainment was given, to which all the rank and fashion of the county were invited. Nothing could be more interestingly lovely than the appearance of the bride. She wore a splendid dress of Brussels lace, magnificently adorned with diamonds. After the ceremony, the happy pair set out, in a new travelling carriage, ordered for the occasion, for Battiscomb Park, the seat of the noble bridegroom, to spend the honeymoon.' "

This, or something similar to this, was what Lucy read. In a sort of convulsive stillness, I heard it to an end. The cup, which I was raising to my lips, as she began to read, was still held untasted when she concluded. Then in a moment, a violent and irresistible impulse seized my frame, and dashing it, rather than dropping it, from my hand, I sprung up, and ran from the apartment. As I passed, the hall door stood open, and I rushed forth into the park.

It was a winter's day. The snow lay upon the ground, and the wind, which blew from the north-east, was accompanied by violent showers of hail. There was an unaccustomed vigour in my limbs, I felt a wild desire of motion, and I hurried on, I knew not, cared not, whither. Often, indeed, was I obliged to stop, and pant, like a dying man, for a mouthful of breath ; but then, the fiend from which I fled overtook me, and again I rushed on. My reason, which had withstood many assaults, had yielded at last. The hailstones, driven by the wind, beat painfully on my face, but I thought not of this, and quitting the park, I ran madly for the uplands.

The hare started from my foot, and fled from me afar off; and the flocks of sheep, as I approached them, ran, in wild confusion, from their food, as if scared by the approach of some unholy thing.

This could not last long. I sunk at length, overpowered, amid the snow, and lay shivering and helpless. Then, for the first time, did my anguish find vent in words.

" Oh God, " I exclaimed, " why hast thou made a thing, so eminently lovely, thus merciless and cruel ? Does she not know, that the poor, maimed, and mangled creature, on whom she tramples, can feel a pang as great as she, in all her beauty and her pride ? Oh, why does she thus outrage the feelings of a heart that would have died for her ? Yet is not her nature soft ? She could not plunge a dagger in my bosom,—she would shrink from the sight of a fellow-creature broken alive upon the wheel, —and yet inflicts an agony, to which such sufferings are but mercy. Oh, how long must I endure the grievous burden of life, and suffer under the weight of madness and misery that presses upon my soul !

"Almighty God, to whose behests all nature ministers, grant that in these cold and wintry elements, I may find the only balm for wounds like mine—Death. Leave me not a desolate and wretched being, in the hell of this unfeeling world!"

Thus madly, impiously did I rave, and the wind, as it covered me with the snow-drift, swept on, loaded with the sound of my frantic imprecations. By degrees, my limbs became icy cold, and at length I was silent, for the muscles of my throat refused their office. The numbness gradually extended to my vitals, and I lay, a living being, yet without the power of motion. My faculties seemed to have recovered from their temporary derangement, and were again clear. I felt as if the union between mind and body had been dissolved, and my free spirit waited only for a signal to take its flight.

In this state I had lain for some time, dying, and wishing to die, when, at the bottom of the hill, I observed Frank Willoughby, and some of the servants in search of me. They had tracked my footsteps to the extremity of the park, but there, from the drifting, they had been lost; and, extended in a line, the party were now advancing towards me, hallooing at short intervals as they proceeded.

They saw me not, for I was already white with the snow, and I watched their progress with an anxious eye. I prayed they might be delayed but for a few minutes, for my heart beat languidly, and at long intervals, and the blood was freezing in my very bosom.

"Let but their footsteps linger a little longer, let the snow-drift blind their eyes but for a short space, and all my earthly sorrows will be over."

My petition was not granted. I was observed, and in a moment, Frank Willoughby had thrown himself on the ground beside me, and pressed me in his arms. I could not return his embrace, nor answer his kind words. I had no power to move a single muscle of my frame. Never was a spirit united to a body, by a smaller or more fragile link.

They raised me on their shoulders, and carried me to the nearest cottage, where I remained, till the arrival of a carriage to convey me to Middlethorpe. Before it came, the efforts to restore animation to my limbs had been partially successful, and the sense of feeling had been excited. When we reached Middlethorpe, Lucy's grief, at beholding me lifted from the carriage, and with difficulty supported across the hall, was violent and excessive. Laura, too, was there, but Niobe was not more still.

I was put instantly to bed. The doctor, who had already been sent for, soon arrived, and pronounced that I laboured under a violent inflammation of the chest. All the progress to convalescence which I had hitherto made, was in one moment gone. Copious bleeding was declared necessary, and carried into effect. The violence of the disease was thus conquered, but I was reduced by it to a state of even more than infantine weakness.

Never were the labours of love around a sick bed more zealously performed. Under what different aspects, even in my short experience, had I already beheld woman. I had known her, in the hours of elation and joy, shedding grace and beauty on life, and gilding the horizon with light and splendour. But clouds had gathered on the surface of the sky, and the star had hid its light.

Then I had known her in hours of pain and anguish, soft, tender, generous, loving, and compassionate, charming the eye, and pouring balm into the heart. Trite, indeed, but only trite, because the heart of universal man has acknowledged them to be true, are the exquisite lines of our mighty minstrel.

> Oh woman, in our hours of ease,
> Uncertain, coy, and hard to please,
> And variable as the shade
> By the light-quivering aspen made,
> When pain and anguish wring the brow,
> A ministering angel thou !

My recovery was slow, for the stamina of my constitution, originally firm, had at length given way, and its elasticity was gone. I was pressed down by deep and settled dejection. Perhaps, till now, even unconsciously, a germ of hope had lain buried in my heart; if so, it was now crushed for ever. I knew at once the worst and the best, that could befall me. To all the future arrows of fate, I was invulnerable. Henceforward, hope and fear were to be eradicated from my nature. One dull unvarying shadow hung over my future life, neither to be brightened into sunshine, nor darkened into deeper gloom.

Weeks wore away, and the effect of time, and the warmth of the advancing summer, had restored as much of a shattered frame and constitution, as appeared destined ever to be restored. The affection of my lungs still continued, and the doctors spoke of my chance of recovery, as doubtful and remote. This moved me little, for though I sought not for death, I was yet indifferent to life.

Another and more interesting conviction had reached my heart; I knew that I was beloved by Laura. Gradually and slowly had this knowledge dawned upon me. In no look or gesture had her love betrayed itself, no word of passion had been spoken, no written thoughts had unconsciously told the secret of her bosom, yet I knew, and felt it to be so.

The conviction was to me a sad one. It brought with it no feeling of triumph, no thought of pride. The time was past, when it might have goaded on the sluggish current of my blood, and have lit up the flashes of my sunken soulless eyes. Alas, it came no welcome intruder, for it was accompanied by deep and bitter self-reproach.

Hitherto, in the sad story of my love, I had been more sinned against, than sinning, and I had felt the dignity of suffering wrong. Towards the Lady Melicent, whatever might have been my errors, they had been followed by more than the full measure of expiation. The love that had been sown in rapture, had been reaped in agony. *I* alone had suffered— there had been no partner in my pangs—*one* victim only had bled.

Now it was otherwise. I had ever regarded Laura with strong affection; but she had never been to me the object of vehement and engrossing passion. The regard I felt for her had not been incompatible with the deeper and more powerful sentiment, inspired by another. I had lived with Laura, in habits of unrestrained confidence. In brighter and happier days, how many sweet hours had I passed in her society! Our regard had begun almost in infancy, and never had the shadowy chain that linked us together, from childhood to maturity, been broken. Had I never known Lady Melicent, she would, I think,—she must have been, the object to attract the whole undivided strength of my affections. As it was, I had given Laura cause to think she knew my heart, and I had deceived her. My lips had never breathed the secret of my passion for another. I had led her, in the blindness of undoubting confidence, to the brink of a precipice, and I felt that *her* sufferings were *my* guilt.

Often, in moments of incredulous depression, would I start back, from the conviction that I was, or could be the object of love. But not as that of the world, had been the love of Laura Willoughby. It had stood the ordeal of time and of misfortune, and what I had been to her in the days of prime, I now was in those of my decay. My star had become pale, yet her love had not waned; amid the darkness of my misery, it had shone shadowless and unchanged.

I felt it a paramount duty that she should no longer be deceived. Tardy and inadequate as such a reparation was, it was now all I had to offer. It was necessary that she should at length learn, the story of a blighted and a withered heart. To speak was painful, but to be silent— guilt; and I had already become too familiar with suffering, to care for the retrenchment of a pang.

One morning, when we were seated alone in the drawing-room, I determined to execute my task.

" Laura, you remember the morning when, after hearing the account of, Lady Lyndhurst's marriage, (the words half stuck in my throat) I ran from the apartment like a madman. Did you not think me a strange and unaccountable being? I am sure you did. "

She did not answer, but gently raising her eyes, cast them on my face, and a smile,—a faint one,—passed like a sudden gleam of light over her countenance.

" I am sure you must, even if your own conjectures led you to divine the cause. "

" Yes, " she answered in a low and soft voice, " the cause of your agitation could not be mistaken. I think I already know *all*. "

" No, not *all*, not all. God, the Searcher of hearts, alone can know all ; but something of my story—enough, perhaps, for your kind heart to compassionate, I would, if you will permit me, now tell you. "

She again raised on me her moist and beautiful eyes, with a look that sank into my soul.

" Nay, Cyril, " she said, taking my hand as she spoke, " do not now enter on a subject, on which it is impossible for you to speak without agitation. I, too, know that memory is painful, and it were perhaps wiser not to break the slumber of past sorrows. Think rather on the future, *that* at least may be gilded by the fancy ; the present, and the past, are beyond our power. "

" To me, Laura, there is no future, or, at least, such as the present is, the future will be—must be. True, my eyes may gaze on new scenes, and my own circumstances, and those of the world around me, may be changed. But that wintry world that is within, no second spring can ever renovate. I feel that to be changeless as the grave. For me, futurity has nothing brighter or darker than the present. Such as I am, death must find me. "

" You talk sadly, Cyril ; you ought not,—you must not indulge in such gloomy presentiments. It is wrong, Cyril, very wrong, to despair. Even in this world there is a balm for every wound but dishonour. I speak to you as a friend, for I have ever looked upon you as my best, "—she hesitated, " my dearest one. Give not way to this sinking of the spirit, I entreat you. It is ungrateful—it is sinful. "

" I have, I fear, talked more sadly than I intended, " endeavouring as I spoke to smile, " for I meant not to distress you. I will now speak calmly."

" You have never, I think, seen Lady Lyndhurst ; but the fame of her beauty,—of her fascination, has of course reached you. "

Laura bowed slightly, without raising her head, and her face was hid from my gaze.

" I loved her. With what love, I will not speak. You think, perhaps, this was madness, but I did more than even this. I told her of my love. I will not say it was returned, but our troth, at least, was mutually plighted. I quitted my country a proud and happy man, bearing within me the full treasure of my happiness, in the confidence of being loved. Her image went with me. It forsook me not on sea or on land, in the tent, in the siege, or on the battle-field.

" In a moment, I became the creature you now behold me. The struggle between life and death was a long one, but in pain and suffering it was still with me, and I recovered.

" Then I released her from her promise. For worlds, I would not have bound her to a thing like myself. I received a cold answer to my letter ; I saw her, on my arrival in London, happy and careless of my fate, and, in less than two months, she was married to another.

" Tell me not to banish her from my heart. It were but a waste of words to do so. Believe me, I have striven strongly, fearfully, and vainly, and I know it cannot be. "

At first, when I had done speaking, Laura bent her head forwards to the table, and, pressing it with her hands, remained in that posture for about a minute, then, as if suddenly acquiring strength to command her feelings, she once more turned her face towards me, and it was calm. I say calm,—for, although deep pity and interest were never more legibly expressed, her countenance retained no trace of more violent emotion.

" Cyril, " she said, " your's is indeed a melancholy tale. I know,—at least, I think I know, your character, and can imagine through what sufferings you have passed. I would comfort you, Cyril, but what have I to offer but tears ? you see they are yours, " pointing at the same time to my hand, already moistened with them, " take them, they are my all. "

" Yes, Laura, I receive them, and, believe me, with a grateful heart, " raising at the same time my hand to my lips, and kissing away the drops that lay on it. " Earth can now afford nothing more precious, than these tears. The wounds for which *they* afford no balm, must indeed be incurable. "

" Though I cannot comfort you, " she resumed, " I would yet entreat you, by all you hold dear on earth,—and surely, Cyril, there is still much to which your heart grapples,—not to yield yourself to despondency. You have been, and are perhaps yet destined to be tossed on a stormy sea. To your eye no haven may be near,—no ray of hope may shine in the surrounding darkness—but you are alike called on by reason and religion, to buffet with the waters to the last, and, at least, not to sink a supine and willing victim in the abyss.

" Let your trust be in that God, who raised the tempest, and can again calm it. Cast yourself on Him, with a full reliance on his mercy, and He will not forsake you in the struggle. "

I was silent, and she proceeded.

" I fear I am a bad preacher, Cyril, and I weary you. I have touched on a subject, perhaps, too sacred to be even alluded to by one like me. Pardon me, for I have indeed spoken in the fulness of my heart. "

Most beautiful and benign was the expression of her countenance at that moment. Never had her eye gleamed more brightly ;—never had the music of her sweet voice fallen so meltingly on my ear. But the tears, which, as she spoke, had ceased to flow, again fell fast, and bending down her forehead, she covered it with her hands.

" Do not think, Laura, " and I took her unresisting hand as I spoke ; " do not think, Laura, though my heart be not now fitted to receive them, that your words have fallen on a cold and an ungrateful soil. They have been treasured here—they may long lie dormant, but they shall not die, and it may happen that, like bread cast upon the waters, their consolation may be found after many days. Forgive me, Laura, for the pain which it is too evident I have occasioned you. There is no other being on earth to whom I could have disclosed the secret that preys on me. It concerns not me alone, but with you it is safe. "

She answered only by a look, that spoke plainly as words, " can you doubt it ? "

Much did we talk of on that morning, and the voice of her sweet soothing was not without its influence, on my irritable spirits. She spoke comfort to me, and I was comforted, for I knew that she shared my sorrows; and the thought stole through my heart, as we parted, that if, in my brighter days, I had loved Laura Willoughby, happiness might yet have been mine.

CHAPTER XI

Though hills were set on hills,
And seas met seas to guard thee, I would through ;
I'd plough up rocks steep as the Alps in dust,
And lave the Tyrrhene waters into clouds,
But I would reach thy head.

BEN JOHNSON.

Nor sleep nor sanctuary,
Being naked, sick ; nor fane, nor Capitol,
The prayers of priests, nor times of sacrifice,
Embarquements all of fury, shall lift up
Their rotten privilege and custom, 'gainst
My hate to Marcius. Where I find him, were it
At home upon my brother's guard, even there,
Against the hospitable canon, would I
Wash my fierce hand in his heart.

Coriolanus.

ON the morning following this conversation, the post brought me two letters. The first I opened was from my uncle. I had written to him since my return : but as it was probable we might never meet again, I had not thought it necessary to inflict on him the pain, of learning the nature and consequences of my wounds.

This letter was to desire, if possible, I would again visit him. He was old, he said, and his decreasing strength told him, that if we were again to see each other in this world, our meeting must be a speedy one. Had his infirmities been less, he would have spared me this journey, and have come to me, but he was now unequal to travel, and hoped I had still regard enough for an old man that loved me, to visit him once more before I again went abroad, if that was my intention. At the end of the epistle was inserted, probably by stealth, the following characteristic note from Girzy :—

"Noo, Maister Cyril, mak nae havers aboot the matter, but just pit yer fit in the coach, and come yer ways doon, to gladden the een o' yer auld uncle wi' a sight o' ye, afore he gangs the way o' a' flesh. Puir man, he's had a sair dooncome sin' ye parted; but he's aye toddlin' aboot, and canna get his heart awa' frae the coontin'-house. Ye mind, ye promised to come back afore ye gaed awa'; but dinna negleck to gie me a day or twa's notice o' yer comin', that ye mayna find the house ower bare o' provisions, and that I may hae yer bed weel aired.

" Your loving servant,

" GIRZY BLACK. "

The other letter awakened feelings deeper and more violent. It was from William Lumley, to whose management I had intrusted the legal measures which were in progress in Doctors Commons against Hewson, for a separation *a mensa et thoro*. Miserable indeed was the intelligence it conveyed.

It had been ascertained, he said, that poor Jane, under the brutal treatment of her husband, had become insane, and was now in confinement in a private mad-house in Gloucestershire. By a sudden impulse, I crushed the letter in my hand as the words met my eye, and ringing, ordered the carriage to the door as soon as possible. I did not make Lucy a partner in the suffering, which this intelligence occasioned; and without stating the object of my journey, I merely informed her that unexpected business had rendered my presence necessary at some distance; and requesting Frank Willoughby to accompany me, I told him in a whisper, that my motive in making the request should be explained to him on the road. My portmanteau was soon arranged for the journey, and in less than an hour, Frank Willoughby and myself were rolling rapidly on our way to Feltham.

I then communicated to him the nature of the intelligence which had occasioned this sudden journey, and my firm resolution no longer to delay calling Hewson to account, for his base and inhuman conduct. My blood boiled as I proceeded in the narrative, and vain was every disuasive argument, with which my companion endeavoured to temper my rashness.

True, I was bound over to keep the peace to Hewson. What then? Had every shilling I possessed in the world, or might hereafter possess, depended on my forbearance towards this wretch; nay, more, had the infliction of just punishment on his head been attended with disgrace as well as beggary, it would not at that moment have changed one iota of my resolution. I would have sacrificed all, to the gratification of this one ruling purpose of my heart. Had he been separated from my vengeance by a wall of fire, I would have gone through flames to reach him. The wrongs of my sister called aloud for retribution, was it in my nature to prove deaf to the cry?

Willoughby soon saw that dissuasion was hopeless, in the state of extreme morbid excitement under which I laboured, and limited his endeavours to moderating rather than opposing the impetuous current of my feelings. Though rejected as a counsellor, he remained with me as a friend.

We slept on the road, and on the following day reached Hewson's. I wished to have an interview with him alone, and for this reason Willoughby consented to remain at a little inn a few miles distant, while I proceeded unaccompanied to the house. Hewson was at home. The servant announced my name, and I was shown into an apartment, where I found him seated alone. He rose hastily from his chair, with an air of mingled fear and embarrassment, as I entered, and bowed. His salutation was not returned, and an interval of silence ensued. Hewson, who at first had been taken by surprise, was too much a man of the world not soon to recover sufficient self-command to address me.

" Major Thornton, " he said, " I should be happy were I suffered to look on this visit as a prelude to the return of that good understanding between us, which I regret has ever been interrupted. Pray be seated. "

" No, sir—in your house, never. My business with you is short, and may be settled standing. Our account has been allowed to run too long, and the balance has become a large one. It must now be wiped off. "

" If you allude to anything pecuniary,—the fortune of your sister,—I am always ready—— "

" No. Such matters I leave to the law. I come, as the brother of a wife, whom your brutal outrage has driven to madness, to bring you to a reckoning of a different sort. "

Weak and irritable as I was become from long and severe illness, my agitation every moment increased, and I was acted upon by impulses over which I could exercise no control. The whole volume of my blood seemed sent upwards into my brain, and I spake the words, not of reason, but of passion. Hewson saw my emotion, for my whole frame shook with it.

" I do not understand you, sir, " he replied. " If your intentions are hostile towards me, you could not presume to violate the sanctuary of my own house ? "

" Yes, the sanctuary of God's house ; and were you snatched from my living vengeance, even the sanctuary of the grave. I would go there, even for the sake of trampling on the corrupting remains of a scound-rel. "

" Sir, I will bear such language from no man, and least of all in my own house ; " rising at the same time, and hastily approaching the bell, as if to ring for assistance.

I intercepted him, and pushing him back, produced a small pair of pistols from the pocket of my greatcoat, which, after he retired, I threw upon the table.

" You will not bear it ! I congratulate you. I rejoice to be spared further experiments on the limits of your sufferance. There, sir—the means of redress are before you. Take one of these pistols, and use it with the spirit of a man. "

The face of the craven grew pale as death.

" Are you aware of the consequences of such mad and bloodthirsty conduct ? " he asked, in a voice with some tremor in it. " You are bound over to keep the peace in a large penalty. "

" Were I bound in penalty of my salvation, " I interrupted, " the bond should be estreated. It is only because I know from your conduct, that you want courage to meet me in the field, that I am forced thus to deal with you. Will you fight? Speak—is there even one dormant spark of courage in your heart? "

" I will not fight,—not now, at least,—not in this manner, and without witnesses. "

" Nay, nay, " I answered, " think on it again. Do not suffer yourself to be buffeted and spit upon—to be proclaimed a coward in the highway. "

I took the pistols from the table, and advancing close up to him, as he stood the figure of a corpse, and holding them by the muzzle, extended them towards him. He shrunk back.

" Villain, miscreant, despicable coward! you can wreak your brutal ferocity on a weak and helpless *woman*—outrage the sanctity of her pure, and innocent, and confiding heart, and goad her, till, in the very madness you have caused, she finds a refuge from your inhuman persecution! How does your dastard spirit shrink before a *man!* How tamely and submissively do you now stand, trembling before me, bearing contumelies which you *dare not* resent! Raise my opinion of human nature, let me not believe the earth holds a reptile so vile and so degraded! Take a pistol, and signalize a life of vice and meanness, by at least one faint glimmering of manhood. "

I again extended the pistols towards him, and he took one.

" Hah, this is well. I will cross the apartment, and the signal to fire shall be given by you. "

I turned about for this purpose, but had scarcely gone a pace or two, when he fired. The bullet passed through the collar of my coat, but without injuring me, and lodged in the opposite wainscot. When I turned round, he had flown to the bell, and was ringing furiously for assistance.

" Vile and wretched assassin! " I exclaimed, " I will not defraud the gibbet of its prey; I will not fire on a thing so utterly despicable, " and hurling my pistol, with all my strength, at his head, it struck him on the mouth, and dashed out several of his teeth. Just then the door opened, and servants entered the apartment: I lost no time in quitting the hated roof, and returned to my carriage.

The occurrence I have just described, would undoubtedly have forfeited my recognizances; but Hewson was too conscious of his own turpitude, to take any steps which might elicit the particulars of his dastardly conduct.

I found Willoughby waiting my arrival, and I related to him those particulars of my interview with Hewson, of which the reader is already in possession. I had brought him with me, because I foresaw that circumstances might have occurred, in which the presence of a friend might have been necessary. Now there was no occasion to impose a further burden on his kindness, and on the following morning we parted; he to return to Middlethorpe, I to proceed on a melancholy errand, in which the society, even of Willoughby, would have been painful.

It was to visit the poor unhappy Jane, that I now bent my footsteps. A shuddering came over me, at the thought of the sad condition in which I was about to behold her. I, too, had been unfortunate, but when I compared my situation with her's,—the burden under which my stronger shoulders had bent, with that which had pressed her fragile frame to the earth, I felt as if I had been guilty of ingratitude in repining at my fate. In duration, if not in intensity, her's had far transcended mine. Jane's had been the sufferings of years, mine but of months. My reason had survived, her's had sunk in the conflict.

During my journey, however, I thought not of myself, I remembered only Jane, and her unhappy fate. Her countenance, as it had been in former days, rose vividly in my memory. Her mild, bright, and dove-like eyes, beamed on me with more, if possible, than even a sister's love. I saw her fair, pale countenance shaded with its bright ringlets of sunny hair. The smile of joy was on her lips, as it had been when, in youthful days, she came to welcome my return. My ear drank in the silver tones of her glad voice, as I pressed her in my arms.

Such was the creature on which my memory had ever dwelt. Good God, what was she now! Was this the desolate and deserted maniac whom I was about to behold? Oh, would that she had died! I could have laid her in the earth, as I had laid others as dear; but to find her thus! My own dear, loving, and beloved sister, the inmate of a mad-house! There may be philosophy enough to enable a man to bear such a thought, but I did not possess it.

Occupied by sad reflections, the hours passed slowly on, and I at length approached the object of my destination. It was a large building, situated at some distance from the road, gloomy, I thought, but perhaps this arose only from the sad associations which were linked with it. The house was surrounded by a high wall, and we drove through a massive gate, which was opened by a middle-aged man of sinister and forbidding aspect. In a large court-yard before the house, the windows of which were secured by iron bars, like those of a prison, there were a considerable number of men, some of them rather prepossessing in appearance, playing at bowls, chuckfarthing, and other games of a similar description. The passing carriage, however, seemed to arrest both the eye and attention of all, and I heard several voices call out, "Here's another come,"—"another poor devil, to be confined as we are,"—"let us see him."

We had already stopped at the door of the house, and I had inquired for the head of the establishment, when a respectably dressed and grave-looking personage stepped up to the door of the carriage, and addressed me with those customary salutations, with which strangers in this country generally preface an attempt at conversation.

" Good morning, sir. I hope you've had a pleasant journey. Have you come far to-day ? You like what you've seen of your new abode, I hope ; you'll find in it very pleasant society, I assure you. "

I answered, that my stay would be too short to enable me to judge of such particulars. I should probably be gone in an hour.

" Ah, sir, don't believe them, " answered my grave friend, with an incredulous shake of the head. " They told me so too when I first came, but I've already been here seven years, and I now believe I shall never quit it till death. " Then turning to his companions, I heard him say as he retired, " Poor fellow, he tells me he is not going to stay above an hour or two ; " and peals of maniac laughter rang loudly from his auditors.

The servant, who had been in search of the Doctor now returned, to say that he was at home ; and alighting, I was shown into his presence. He was a little squinting man, dressed in black, with a powdered head, and received me with a profusion of bows. The apartment in which I found him was in character something of a non-descript. One end of it gave indication of its being a library, and displayed a book-case, the shelves of which seemed tolerably filled. Another was fitted up like the shop of an apothecary, with rows of glass bottles and gallipots, and drawers, and compartments, all duly labelled in golden letters, according to the formula of the Pharmacopeia. The sides were hung with anatomical preparations, interspersed with stuffed animals, and prints of John Hunter, Dr Boerhaave, and other eminent professors of the healing art. The most striking object on the chimney-piece was a child with two heads, preserved in spirits, flanked by sundry other specimens of *lusus naturæ* equally pleasant and interesting. Over the Doctor's table, suspended in a cage, hung a large grey parrot, and a fat and pursy poodle lay snoozing before the fire upon the rug.

On my entrance, the Doctor after a profusion of bows, requested me to be seated, displacing, at the same time, for my accommodation, a large brass pestle and mortar, which occupied the only arm-chair in the apartment. I sat for some time silent, unable, or unwilling to make the effort necessary to enter in words on so painful a subject, as that which occupied my thoughts.

" May I request, sir, at length, " said the polite Doctor, " that you would be good enough to state, to what cause I am indebted for the honour of this interview. "

This roused me.

" I am so unfortunate, sir, as to have a sister at present under your care. I am Major Thornton of Thornhill, in the county of——, and my sister's name is Mrs Hewson. I shall feel obliged to you to give me what information you can, with regard to her present condition, and the prospect it affords of recovery. "

" Why, Major, she is certainly better, considerably better, since she was placed under my charge, " taking down at the same time a large folio volume, and turning over the leaves. " I always keep a record of the state of my patients. Let me see—brought here by Mr Hewson's house-keeper, and bailiff, on the 17th of November. Pulse quick and feverish, eye dilated, mind high, uttered loud screams when touched, raved of her brother (that's you, I suppose, Major,) and family. Bled and administer-ed an anodyne. 18th. Same state. 19th. Symptoms the same, though somewhat diminished, and so on, I see, till the 23d of December. Change of symptoms, great depression, eye sunk and heavy, no appetite, never speaks. Prescribed change of diet, fifty drops of Tinct. vol. Valer., to be taken three times a-day, diluted in water. All January no change. 12th of February, higher than usual, talks much and loud, seems frightened at some object she imagines to be before her; let me see, this continues till the 19th. Spirits again low, rejects food, was observed yesterday to shed tears, and since that time to the present, no material change has taken place. "

Having extracted all the information I could from the Doctor, with regard to poor Jane's condition, I next desired to see her, and that the interview should be without witnesses. The feelings with which I regard-ed the approaching meeting may be conceived, but not expressed. I was conducted by a matronly and respectable-looking woman through long passages, in our progress along which, the loud shriek of madness, and voices hideously discordant, reached my ear.

We at length entered a chamber, where, seated at the window, from which she looked with a vacant gaze, I beheld Jane. She was paler, and thinner, than when I had last seen her, and I missed those beautiful ringlets, by which till now her countenance had ever been shaded and adorned. She did not turn her head as I entered, nor change the direction of her eyes, and I stood some time gazing upon her, before she saw me.

At length I was observed, and with a look that betrayed something of fear, she sprang from her seat. I had now a full view of her face. Not a feature had lost its beauty. Even the eyes were the same, but there was resulting from the whole—an indescribable change of expression, for which, from mere examination of the features, it would have been difficult to account. Jane looked on me, but evidently without recognit-ion.

" Oh, Jane! " I exclaimed, approaching her as I spoke, " Do you not know me ? "

She started back from me with a slight scream.

" Do not fear, Jane, " I went on, " it is Cyril—it is your brother, who has come to embrace you. Will you not welcome him ? "

Her eyes, which till now, notwithstanding my presence, had been wandering and unsettled, were fixed stedfastly upon me, as if scrutinizing the truth of my assertion, by a survey of my person. At length, bursting into a laugh, every note of which pierced me like a dagger, she exclaimed—

" No, no, you think I'm mad, and therefore I'll believe anything. *You* Cyril Thornton,—*You* my brother, you, you ! " and again the chamber rung with her laugh.

" Oh, yes, Jane, I am your brother—your unhappy brother ; do you not remember my voice, the happy days of our childhood, how on summer evenings we roamed together in the Cromer wood, and with my brother Charles, who died by my hand, we knelt side by side at the knee of our angel mother, to receive her blessing ere we retired to rest, with innocent and happy hearts ? "

The scenes which I wished to recall to her memory, rushed back with overwhelming force upon my own. The tears fell fast from my eyes, and I could not proceed. Jane looked on me again, if possible, with a keener gaze than before, as if half hesitating in her belief.

" No, no, " she at length exclaimed, " I will not,—cannot believe it. What a creature are you to tell me you are Cyril Thornton ! Well do I remember his fair face, and his glad blue eyes, and do you, with that scarred and hideous visage, declare you are my brother ? Go. You are gaunt and haggard, and hateful to look upon ; get from my sight, you cannot deceive me. I am not mad enough. "

Her countenance flushed up with anger as she spoke, and the brilliance of passion shone in her eyes. She averted her head when she had done speaking, as if the sight of me aroused unpleasant feelings ; but when she turned it again, and saw that I still stood unmoved before her, she stamped in vehement passion, with her small and beautiful foot upon the floor.

" Begone, I say, why do you still haunt me with your frightful presence ? Go—I am *not* your sister ; my brother is not mutilated as you are, his face is a fair and a happy one ; but I shall never see him more. He knows not that his sister is confined in a common madhouse. No, no, he is far away, or they durst not keep me here. "

Glad was I to behold the tears that sprung into her eyes, for, as I saw them, my heart whispered to me, " there is yet hope. "

" Jane, dearest Jane, do not turn thus from a brother, to whom you are dearer than his life-blood. True, I am sadly changed since you last saw me. Look at this scar upon my face ; it is by this,—by deep sorrow, and by long and grievous sickness, that my countenance has been changed. I have been in the wars ; you know I was a soldier—my arm too is gone—I am but a wreck of what you remember me ; but believe me, Jane, I have brought home a heart that loves you fondly as ever, an arm that, while life remains, will protect you. Nay, doubt me not. I will

P

tell you of old times,—of our mother,—our father,—Charles, and little
Lucy, the delight of all our hearts. I will speak to you of Thornhill—of
the swans upon the little lake—their nest on its woody island, and the
bower that Charles and I built for you on its margin. I will recall to you
the happy hours that we spent in the summer-house on the hill, where
our young eyes used to gaze with wonder and delight upon the setting
sun, and the sound of your sweet music often mingled with the song of
the nightingale. Do you see those tears, Jane? Do you hear the choking
utterance, with which I speak to you of days of happiness now long gone
by? Do you see how this hand trembles, as I stretch it towards you, and
do you still doubt that I am Cyril, the brother whom you love, and by
whom you are beloved, and who swears, as there is a God in heaven,
never, never to forsake you?"

" Oh, yes, " she exclaimed, " you are indeed Cyril! I remember your
voice—I know you now, " and she fell forwards upon my bosom. I
clasped her with my arm, and pressed her half lifeless form to my heart,
kissing as she lay her pale and motionless lips.

She soon recovered, but a long silence ensued, which I wished not to
interrupt. Wrong, indeed, was I, when I said there was no joy in store for
me in this world. Never, even in my happiest days, did I experience a
moment of more exquisite delight, than that in which Jane recognised
me for her brother, and fell into my arms. It was a joy so pure, and
unalloyed by earthly dross, as even beatified spirits might have partaken
of, without contamination of their purer nature.

When she again opened her eyes, and cast them on the face that was
bent over hers, it seemed as if doubt had again seized her, for she pushed
me rudely back, and recoiled from my embrace.

" Nay, I am deceived; this is not the face of Cyril; wretch that you
are, thus to torture the heart of a poor mad creature. Speak—speak
again, that I may hear your voice; but dare not to impose on one so
desolate and friendless,—for God, who is the shield of the helpless, the
friend of those that have no friend on earth, the husband of the widow,
the father of the shivering orphan, from whose protection even the poor
maniac is not an outcast,—*He* will avenge my cause, and visit cruelty
and falsehood like yours with a terrible punishment. "

Again I spoke to her of old times, and again she was calm, and knew
me for her brother. She clasped me in her arms, and, dropping her head
upon my shoulder, wet my bosom with her tears.

" You will take me from this hateful house,—you have not come to
me, again to forsake me—you will not leave me to the care of cold and
heartless strangers. True, I am mad, but I am harmless,—why, oh why
should I be confined in a place like this? Why am I debarred from the
pure air of Heaven, from the sight of the clear blue sky? Why am I not
suffered to roam on the green meadow, or sit by the purling brook, as we
were wont in the days of childhood, listening to the blackbird in the

bush, and the ring-dove in the tree? Why am I shut out from all that is gay and beautiful in the world, immured by dark walls, with terrible voices in my ear, and glared upon by frightful faces? Oh! if you *are* my brother, you will not leave me here. Never would Cyril have suffered a rude hand to touch me; were *he indeed* here, I should be safe,—I know—I know I should."

"Be calm, my dear,—my beloved Jane; agitate not your mind with vain fears. Not all earth's treasures, or Heaven's blessedness, would tempt me to forsake you. Not long shall you remain an inmate of this house. You shall return to Thornhill—you shall once more wander on the meadows and in the wood, and sit by the side of the brook that murmurs through the shady glen, downwards to the fair Severn. Never shall your person be profaned by the touch of rude hands, and no voice, save that of kindness, and of love, shall meet your ear."

Unused as poor Jane had been to tenderness, my words, and perhaps the deep feeling that governed my voice, seemed to produce a strange revulsion of her frame. I supported her to a seat, and she remained pale, and with closed eyes, and motionless, save a scarcely perceptible quivering of her lips. I sat at her feet, with her hand clasped in mine, but not venturing to interrupt by speech the current of her emotion. At length she opened her eyes, and rising, but still holding her hand, I again addressed her.

"Endeavour to collect your mind, my poor Jane, and listen to me. Though it is necessary that I quit you now, think not that I have forsaken you. I go only to prepare for your deliverance. Believe me, though you see him not, that your brother is active in your cause.— Scarcely shall these eyes know sleep, or these limbs rest, till he beholds you once more in your father's house. Be calm, my dearest sister; think not you are friendless and forsaken while I live. Farewell—and may the blessings of a God, infinitely merciful, rest upon you."

I kissed her lips, and pressed her to my bosom as I spoke, but she remained still as marble till I had quitted the apartment. The matron, who had formerly conducted me, stood waiting at the door, which she immediately locked. A loud shriek reached me as I retrod the long passage, and the words—"My God, has he forsaken me!" thrilled through the very marrow of my bones.

I again saw the Doctor before I departed, and directed that poor Jane should be treated with every kindness till my return, holding out, at the same time, a promise of reward if I found my instructions were complied with. The Doctor having solemnly engaged it should be so, I stepped into the carriage, and quitted the melancholy mansion.

The horses' heads were turned towards Thornhill, and my journey was made as rapidly as possible. As I approached, the house appeared deserted, no smoke rose from the chimneys, and the windows of the principal apartments were closed. I had given no intimation of my coming, and of course was not expected. In the place, too, all those little observances, and that attention to minute adornment which indicates the presence of the master, had been neglected. The gravel roads were over-run with weeds, and as the carriage stopped, I remarked, the steps that led to the vestibule were covered with grass. The door-bell was rung, and though its hollow tinkle was heard reverberating through the empty chambers of the mansion, no servant came at the summons. Again and again was the signal repeated, and with similar success. The opening and closing of distant doors was at length heard, the sound of footsteps approached, the key grated in the lock, and I stood again beneath the roof of my fathers.

The door was opened by a house-maid, who, on learning my name, soon ran off to spread the news in the distant apartments occupied by the servants. The old housekeeper, who had been dismissed by my step-mother, had since been restored to her office, and soon came bustling forward to welcome my arrival, and make a thousand apologies for my reception.

Thomas Jones, a grey-headed footman, was, in the present case, made the scape-goat for the rest of the establishment. Thomas, it seemed, was good for nothing, he was grown old and stupid, and thought only of smoking and guzzling ale, in the public-house of the village. It was Thomas's duty, she said, to have opened the door, but Thomas, as usual, was not forthcoming, and if Marjory, the house-maid, had not accidentally heard the bell, we might have rung till doomsday. I told Mrs Parkyns, for so the good housekeeper was called, to give herself no concern about a matter of so little importance, and requesting a fire in the library, and dinner to be got ready as soon as possible, I crossed the park to the house of old Humphreys, with whom I wished to have a short interview.

He was at home, and I explained to him my views with regard to the preparations that might be necessary for the reception of my sister Jane at Thornhill. Poor old man! He was shocked at the change in my appearance, but more deeply so at the intelligence I gave him of the melancholy condition of my poor sister; and it was with a sad though zealous heart that he entered on the duties of the task assigned him.

On my return, I found the household had not been idle during my absence. A huge fire was blazing in the library, and old Thomas gave proof of having returned to his duty, by receiving me in the hall. As I passed through it, melancholy memorials met my eye. There was my father's hat hanging on its accustomed peg, his gold-headed cane yet stood in the corner, beside his long silver-tipped riding-whip, with which, I well remembered, he had once beat me when a boy.

Dinner was speedily announced as ready, but I did not partake of it, till I had dispatched a letter to William Lumley, requesting him to meet me at Thornhill as soon as possible. This done, the shelves of the library, and my own reflections, afforded me abundant occupation, if not amusement, till I retired to rest.

CHAPTER XII

Oh! I have lost a sister,
Whose worth, if praises may go back again,
Stood challenger on mount of all the age,
For her perfections.

Hamlet.

It was some days before Lumley arrived. The mornings I spent partly in business, and partly in visiting the haunts of my youth, and such of the old tenants as had survived the lapse of years since my departure.

When Lumley came, I explained to him all the particulars of Jane's situation, and my own determination to take instant measures for removing her to Thornhill, and getting her definitively placed, beyond the reach or influence of Hewson. In effecting this, he appeared to anticipate no difficulty. Hewson's character gave every reason to suppose, that he would be glad of any scheme, by which he would be relieved from the expense of the maintenance of his wife. But, in the event of his refusal, Lumley advised that steps should instantly be taken, to obtain, both for her person and fortune, the protection of Chancery. If possible, however, this step was to be avoided; and I authorised Lumley to propose, that if Hewson would consent to give up all right to the custody of his wife's person, that not only, no demand should be made on him for her support, but that he should be suffered to enjoy the life-rent of her fortune.

In case of his refusing this offer, Lumley was to apprise him, that a petition on her behalf would immediately be filed in Chancery, which would involve the consequence of his being instantly compelled to refund her fortune, a necessity which, embarrassed in pecuniary matters as he was, could not fail to be abundantly unpleasant. Armed with these powers, Lumley lost no time in departing to seek an interview with Hewson, and I awaited his return at Thornhill, with the deepest anxiety for the event. All went as we expected. Hewson, who never lost sight of his own interest, made no difficulty in accepting the proposal, and Lumley brought with him the necessary legal documents, duly executed.

Once more, and under happier circumstances, I returned to my poor sister. On my arrival, I had an interview with the Doctor, settled all his demands, and did not visit poor Jane, until I was apprised that every preparation was made for our departure.

Since I had quitted her, the Doctor informed me, the symptoms of her mental disorder had varied considerably, both in character and intensity. Sometimes she had been calm and collected, expressing her confidence in my love, and reliance on my promises. At others, she had been wild and violent, accusing me of having forsaken her, and then sinking into the deep lethargy of despair. As we approached the door, I heard her (it was impossible I could mistake her voice,) singing a wild and melancholy song.

She stopped as the sound of the key turning in the lock, informed her of our approach. She was at the other end of the apartment when I entered, and screaming as she beheld me, she rushed forward, as if to cast herself in my arms, but ere she reached me—fell senseless on the floor.

I raised her gently, and carried her to a couch, on which I seated myself, with her head resting on my bosom. She lay there without motion; once—once only, she opened her eyes, but their gaze was vacant. Then closing them, she breathed one long sigh—it was her last.

Assistance was immediately procured, and a vein opened, but without effect; my beloved and unhappy sister was unhappy no longer.

For some time I remained kneeling by the couch, on which the lifeless remains lay extended. I closed her eyes. I crossed her white hands upon her bosom, and as I did so, her marriage-ring caught my eye. " Accursed symbol ! " I exclaimed, as I drew it from her finger, and dashed it on the ground ; " last and only memorial of a hateful and unhappy union, of chains, which death at length has rent asunder, instrument of cruelty and baseness, begone ! I cast thee from me, to furnish food for the famishing beggar, or to be trodden under foot by villains, less mean than he, by whose hands thou wert bestowed. "

It was with a solemn calmness of heart, that I imprinted the last kiss, on the lips of my departed sister, and turned to behold her no more. Her death cost me no tear. What, alas, was there to weep for, in the scene I had been contemplating ? Not surely that a creature had been snatched from life, to whom life could have brought but suffering—that she, whose only refuge was death, had found it. No. It was with dry eyes that I sprang into the carriage, and as I journeyed homewards, my heart, though awed by the merciful demonstration of divine Power that had passed before me, was calm.

The body was conveyed to Thornhill, and I laid the head of another of my family in the grave. Four had been already sepulchred—two had died in my arms—and cut off, as I was, from all the enjoyments of life, the prayer rose within me, that *I* might be the fifth. Yet the last solemn offices of religion were not heard in a cold and repining spirit, and it was with an humble and a chastened heart, that I turned once more from the dead to the living.

After the funeral, I remained about a month at Thornhill, in solitude and comparative tranquillity. My mind, I think, had already assumed a somewhat healthier tone, for I was able calmly to deliberate, on my future plans. The doctors told me it was necessary that I should seek a warmer climate, and my own feelings told me so too. I felt convinced, that to remain in England was to die, yet I felt an invincible aversion to foreign travel. I could not loiter up and down the world, sick, spiritless, forlorn, seeking health, yet carrying disease, a wandering stranger in a strange land, to become at last the tenant of a foreign grave. Better than this, I thought it were to die at home, to mingle my ashes with those of my fathers, to sleep in death with those whom I loved in life, to be incorporated with kindred earth. But best of all it was, to die as a soldier. If death will not be cheated of his victim, rather let me fall in the field, than faulter out my feeble spirit in the slow languishing of a sickbed. Who so brave as he for whom life retains no charm? Where was the danger from which I would now shrink? What peril was there, which my heart would now flutter to encounter? To such a termination of my life, I found pleasure in looking forward. My soul revolted from the idea of dying in a corner; like Ajax, I would at least perish in the light of day.

My resolution, therefore, was decidedly taken, at all events, to return to the army. It was true, there was little prospect of my health being sufficiently restored, to enable me successfully to encounter the fatigues of a campaign; but I would at least make the effort; it could cost nothing, for death, come as it might, was a cheap remedy and efficacious one.

Before I quitted England, however, I determined, once more, to visit my uncle. I felt that to quit England, without bidding him farewell, would be unkind—ungrateful. The old man loved me, and me alone of all his family, and there is something flattering in being the sole object of attachment, even to the meanest of God's creatures. Little suited as we were, to each other, from dissimilarity both of age and pursuits, I felt strongly grateful for the warmth of his regard. At first, I thought of making Lucy the companion of my journey, but on reflection, I abandoned the idea. The *menage* of my uncle, I well knew, was not calculated for the reception of a lady, and Lucy's presence, I feared, might cause more bustle and derangement in the establishment, than might well comport with that quiet and regular routine, to which the old gentleman was accustomed.

Having completed my arrangements at Thornhill, I returned, for a few days, to Middlethorpe, to bid adieu to Lucy, and my kind friends, before starting for the north. Since poor Jane's death I had not seen her. When we met, she was pale and sad. The loss of her dear sister, under circumstances of misfortune so peculiar, following the agitation, of which I had been the unhappy cause, had proved too much for her spirits—gay as they naturally were—and she had sunk under it. It is in a creature of her happy temperament, that sorrow stands out in strongest relief. It shows, like a dark shadow in the sunshine, more gloomy, from the contrast of the surrounding light. I felt much for poor Lucy, yet I did not waste words in attempting to comfort her. I told her not, to dry her tears, for I knew, that for such grief, time brings the only balm. Yet my tears mingled with her's, for I remembered, as I gazed on her, that we were now the last of all our race.

At length I set forth upon my journey; but travelling by easy stages, it was not until the fifth day, that I beheld the high black towers and spire of the Cathedral, overtopping the dense volumes of vapour that lay spread like a canopy above the city. Glasgow had evidently received a great increase of population since I had last seen it. The dirty and miserable suburbs by which it is surrounded, now extended a mile or two further into the country, and the smoke of innumerable coal-works and factories, which had sprung up on all hands, infused a new and uncalled for pollution into the atmosphere.

In the character and appearance of the city, little apparent change had taken place. The crowd and bustle in the streets had perhaps increased, but altogether the place was precisely as dirty, dingy, and detestable, as I remembered it of yore. The carriage stopped at the Buck's Head; and I remembered the jolly dowager, who received me smiling on the landing place. I was shown into the very apartment I had occupied ten years before, and again looked out upon the same scene of business and bustle, which had then arrested my attention, and of which the impression was yet uneffaced.

With what dull uninterested feelings did I again behold it! I regarded the beings I saw moving before me, as belonging to a different species. I had nothing with them in common. I had never felt the stimulus, by which all around me were so powerfully actuated. Love of gain had never been the motive, of any thought or action of my life. True, I had been a slave, but it was not to Mammon.

I might probably have philosophised on the scene around me, had not the current of my thoughts been diverted into another channel, by observing the words " Cyril Thornton, 13th September 1802, " scratched on a window-pane, in a half schoolboy hand. The characters were my own. I did not remember to have written them, but there they still remained—a memorial of former days.

Lightly did my memory at that moment pass over the intervening years, as it returned to call back the thoughts and feelings of the time when these characters were traced. I had then known but one sorrow, and though I had for a time bent under it, the elastic spring of youth had speedily rebounded, and the winds carried with them the cloud, which, in passing, had cast its shadow on my spirit. Alas! the boy of one grief, had become the man of many.

The train of sombre reflection, into which memory was about to lead me, was interrupted by the entrance of the landlady, who politely curtseying, inquired whether I was to remain her inmate for the night. Till that moment I had not given the subject a thought, and looking at my watch, I found it was already evening. My uncle's dinner hour was past, and it was, I thought, on the whole, better to delay my visit till the following morning. I therefore declared myself stationary in the Buck's Head till the next day, and feeling at the moment a more proximate and cogent want, than that of sleep, for during my day's journey I had tasted no refreshment, I requested a sight of the bill of fare.

" Bill o' fare, " replied the jolly and facetious dowager, " troth that's puttin' the cart before the horse, for ye maun hae your fare first, and syne it will be time enough, to speer for the bill. "

" Perhaps you do not understand me, or it may not be your custom in Scotland, to keep one. "

" I understand you weel aneuch, Major, and it's what you fine Englishmen often ca' for ; but I never trouble mysel' to put pen to paper aboot the matter, for I was aye glegger at the speaking than the writing ; and weel I wat, a supple tongue comes better speed than the best pen that ever came out o' a goose. You'll be for soup, I'se warrant ; and there's baith stot's tail and hare-soup in the house, besides barley-broth, gin ye like that better. Then, in the way o' fish, there's haddocks, partins, and herrings, fresh from the Broomielaw. For meat, ye can hae a chop, a stake, or a nice veal cutlet, for ye'll maybe no like to wait for the roasting o' a joint ; or ye can get a spatch-cock made o' a chicken in ten minutes. Then there's game, patricks or muirfowl, wham o' them ye like best ; and gin ye like nane o' thae things, I daursay there's mair in the house, though I canna just mind them at the present moment. "

I assured her there was not the smallest occasion to tax her memory any further, and made my selection from the delicacies, of which she had already indicated, the local habitation and the name.

This dispatched, the pursy matron appeared still further inclined, to indulge in a little conversation, and instead of quitting the apartment, advanced to the bell, and ringing it, a waiter answered to the summons, to whom she issued orders, for the speedy preparation of my repast. For my own part, I did not object to continuing the conversation, for it amused me, and I was glad of any resource, to escape from the gloom of my own solitary meditations.

" May I take the freedom to ask, Major, if ye're going to the Highlands to shoot, or if ye're come on a toorin' expedition, as they ca't, to Staffa, or the Trossachs, as is noo a' the fashion wi' you gentlemen o' the south ? "

I answered, that neither of her conjectures were right, and that I had no intention of proceeding farther north than Glasgow.

" Maybe, then, ye're come on a visit to some gentleman in the neighbourhood ; it will be either to Pollock House, or Cumbernauld, or Blythswood, or I daursay—— "

" No, " interrupted I, " it is a gentleman of your city, who is the object of my visit. Do you know old David Spreull ? "

" That's a daft-like question, Major, to speer at onybody in this town. Ken David Spreull ! I wonder wha, within thirty miles o' the Heigh Kirk, doesna ken him ? He's a man o' mair siller than ony in the haill county of Lanrick, though that's a wide word, Major. But surely ye're no come on a visit to him—at least ye're no thinkin' o' pittin' up at his house ? It's now twenty years since I came frae the Black Boy in the Gallowgate, to the Buck's Head, and no yae stranger, in a' that time, has ever found hack and manger wi' David Spreull. "

" How is the old gentleman ? " I asked ; " hale and stout, I hope, and bearing his declining years as lightly as can be expected ? "

" Atweel, Major, " replied my landlady, glancing, at the same time, at her own portly and capacious figure, " time tells upon us a'. For my part, I think I get fatter and sonsier every year o' my life, though, to be sure, I'm a hantle younger than Mr Spreull ; but he, puir man, seems just dwindling awa' to a perfect atomy. It's no aboon a month sin' I saw him hirple past on the Trongate, for he still gangs on foot when the weather's gude, baith to the countin'-house and the coffeeroom ; there he was, hirplin awa' wi' his staff in his nieve, naething mair nor less than a rickle o' banes. It's easy aneuch seen he's no lang for this world. "

The arrival of a carriage put a stop to the dialogue, and the loquacious landlady bustled down stairs to receive her new guests, with as much celerity of motion, as lay within the scope of her volition to communicate, to the voluminous mass of matter, by which she was encumbered.

Dinner was duly served, and after spending a quiet and solitary evening, I retired to bed. On the following morning, after breakfast, having lounged an hour or two in an arm-chair, from a dread, perhaps, of a scene, which would scarcely fail to bring with it some painful emotion, I set out for the residence of my uncle.

CHAPTER XIII

I am old, I am old. I love thee better than e'er a scurvy young boy of them all.
Henry IV.

That is not forgot
Which ne'er I did remember; to my knowledge,
I never in my life did look on him.
Winter's Tale.

As I walked through the well-known streets which led from the Trongate to my uncle's residence, I recognised, as old friends, the picturesque, dark, and somewhat venerable-looking buildings by which they were flanked. The external crust of smoke, which coated their surface, had been somewhat deepened since I had last seen them; in other respects, I could detect no change. The names, indeed, on the large signboards, displayed in front of the houses, I thought, were generally different from those which had formerly become familiar to my eye. In some cases, I knew this to be so, for several names, which yet lingered on my memory, were gone.

The dwelling of my uncle soon came in sight, and on that alone, my gaze was rivetted. I paused right in front of it, and looked up to the windows, endeavouring, if possible, to catch a glimpse of its inmates. There were none visible. I knew my uncle's parlour, but the window-panes were so deeply embrowned by smoke and dust, as to baffle the penetration of the keenest eye.

For a few minutes, I stood thus occupied, then slowly crossing the street, ascended the well-remembered stair, and reached the landing-place. Here I again paused, as if in a momentary fit of irresolution, with the raised knocker in my hand, which I wanted courage to let fall. My uncle's name was still, though not without difficulty, legible on the brass-plate, and bade fair soon to be entirely erased by the friction of the brick-dust, with which, for so many years, it had been daily brightened by the fingers of the housemaid. No paint had touched the door since my departure, and age had told on that, as it had done on the living inhabitants within.

At length the knocker fell. The sound, I thought, was a hollow and a mournful one, and I waited, not without some palpitation, for an answer to my signal. After some time, the door was opened, and I bent a keen glance on the countenance, which presented itself to my view. It was not that of Girzy, and had it even been Jenny's, it could not, I thought, have escaped my memory. But the person that awaited my demands, though not Jenny, was clearly another individual, belonging to the same variety of species. She was dirty as her predecessor, like her was without shoes or stockings, and wore on her head, a soiled and rumpled *mutch*, the flaps of which hung down like dog's-ears on either side of a countenance, evidently not often washed, but to which all the cosmetics in the world could have lent no charm.

The damsel, to whom my minute examination of her person, appeared by no means pleasing, soon lost patience, and was the first to break silence, holding the door scarcely half open as she spoke, and eyeing me somewhat askance.

" Weel, sir, what do ye want ? "

" Is Mr Spreull at home ? "

" Ay, he's at hame, " replied she, still guarding the aperture of the door, and not at all offering to open it for my admission.

" Then I wish to see him. "

" Naebody can see him the day, for he's no weel, and in his bed. "

" Not seriously ill, I hope ? "

" I kenna what ye ca' sariously ; but he's been laid on the braid o' his back sin' last Wednesday come aucht days, and Doctor Cleghorn comes to veesit him aye yince, and sometimes twice, i' the day. "

" Is Girzy within ? I should like to speak with her. "

" No, she's no in the now. "

" Will she be long absent ? "

" I dinna ken, but it's no likely she'll be out lang. She's gane to the market in the Candlerigs, for a howtowdy to the maister's denner, and to get some pheesic for him at the laborawtory. "

" Then I shall wait her return ; show me into the parlour. "

She whom I addressed appeared to hesitate about the propriety of acceding to this unexpected proposal, and still remained holding the door, as if unwilling to admit me.

" Ye had better gang awa the now, " was the inhospitable answer ; " and gin ye're passin', ye may just gie anither ca' in hauf an hour, for I've nae orders to admit onybody. "

I was not, however, thus to be rebuffed, and without more parley, advanced to effect an entrance. The damsel did not think it necessary to carry measures of resistance so far as to shut the door in my face, and she retreated slowly before me to open the parlour door, muttering, as she went,—" I'se warrant, Girzy will be the death o' me for lettin' him in. " I entered the parlour, and the maid, sulkily slamming the door after her, left me to my own reflections.

I looked round the well-known chamber, and remembrances of the past came thick and fast upon me. There was my uncle's arm-chair by the fire. That, too, was a veteran in the service, and the stuffing protruded at many apertures, which time and use had worn in the covering. Sofa, table, (many a good bowl of punch had I drank on it,) carpet, chairs, book-case, grate and gardevin,—there were separate memories attached to all of these, and they rose upon me tumultuously, and at once.

The room was cold and chilly, for winter had already set in, and there was no fire. I walked to the window, and looked out upon the street. There, all was bustle. There, I beheld the scene of activity and business, amid which, he who now lay sick and solitary in his chamber, had spent a long and anxious life. *Cui bono?* To accumulate wealth, which he could not enjoy, to die unloved, unregretted, and neglected by all——but me.

I turned from the window, and approached the book-case. There stood my old friends, the well-remembered volumes; but his library, since I had last seen it, had received considerable additions. These were chiefly religious. Among them I recognised Leighton's Works and Haliburton's, Watts on Devotion, Baxter's Call, and several others, which, from the hasty glance I threw over their pages, appeared to contain much of mystical divinity. I presumed, from this circumstance, that the mind of my uncle had become more tinged with religion than formerly. My reveries were just then interrupted by the sound of voices in the passage, and I overheard the following dialogue :—

" There's a gentleman in the parlour wantin' to see you. "

" A gentleman wantin' to see me! The lass is surely demented ; wha is't ? "

" I kenna wha he is ; but he speaks like the Englishers, and didna seem very gleg at the uptake o' what I tell't him. He first spier't for the maister, but when he fand he couldna see him, he askit for you, and though I tell't him ye wasna at hame, naething wad fen him, but waitin' in the parlour till ye cam back, and in he gaed, in spite o' a' that I could say. "

" Troth, whaever he be, he's no blait to come rampagin' in folk's hooses, whether they wull or no. I daursay it's just that glaikit neer-doweel creature Baldy Shortridge, that they've been makin' a bailie o'. Bonny on sic bailies ! Ever syne he married that muckle tawpy Tammy Spreull, he's been a perfect torment wi' his ca', ca', ca'in at a' times, and at a' hoors, in houp o' a legacy. But he may just as weel stay at hame, I can tell him that ; and I'll take care, frae this day, that he never gets his ugly neb ayont the door. Let me ben to him ; I'se warrant, I'll send him awa' wi' a flea in his lug. "

These last words had scarcely reached my ear, when the door opened, and with a stately step, and most vinegar aspect, Girzy stalked into the apartment. She was evidently somewhat put out, when her eye first rested on a person very different from the one she expected to encounter. She stared at me for a few moments without any symptom of recognit-ion, and while she was thus engaged, I looked on her not without interest. Girzy was still a hale woman, and her years sat lightly upon her, though there were more wrinkles in her cheek, and deeper furrows in her brow than formerly.

I held out my hand to the old woman.

" Girzy, " I said, " I am glad to see you ; do you not know me ? "

" It's no very likely, I should ken yin I never saw in a' my life, till this blessed minute. "

" Yes, Girzy, you have seen him often. I am Cyril Thornton. "

" Ceeral Thornton ! It's no possible. Gin ye're Ceeral Thornton, my een's good for naething, but ye speak like him too. Stop till I put on my specs. Waes me, but I ken you now,—atweel, ye're just him after a' ; " and, running up to me, she threw her arms about my neck, while tears, and a most discordant blubber, somewhat like the grunting of a pig, spoke the depth of her emotion. I did my best to shorten this unpleasant part of the scene, and after a kind expression or two, inquired for my uncle, and intimated a wish to know the particular character of his disorder, but it was some time before I could elicit an answer.

" Dear me, " she ejaculated, " I never wad hae kent ye, " releasing her grasp, and eyeing me from top to toe. " Oh, but it gies me a sair heart to look at ye. Lord saf us, but ye've lost yin o' yer arms. Cuttit clean off by the oxter, as I'm a living woman ! " Here the tears of the kind creature flowed faster than before, and her voice became inarticulate.

" Why, Girzy, " I said in a cheerful voice, " you did not surely expect me to come back the same smooth-faced boy you remember me at College ? You know I've been a soldier, and, though I've lost an arm in fighting the French, I assure you I have come better off than many of my companions. A man in this world may meet with heavier losses, than either leg or wing, so let me pass as you find me, and tell me about my poor uncle, who, I am sorry to hear, is unwell. "

" Ay, he's unweel ; but waes me, ye're sair hashed about the chafts. It's a sorrowfu' sight to me to see ye come back sic an object. As I live by bread, and there's a lang scaur frae yer gab to the corner o' your ee, just as if ye had gotten a claut wi' the haggin knife. Bless and preserve me, was that done wi' a swurd ? Thae French maun be perfect deevils incarnate—did ever leevin' woman see or hear tell o' the like o't, for them to daur to sair ye that gait, and you sic a douce and weel-faur'd laddie—Oh, it gars me grue to think o't. "

There was no stopping the overwhelming torrent of Girzy's affection- ate regrets, and after several ineffectual efforts, I gave up the attempt, and waited patiently till its strength had become somewhat exhausted.

" I aye kent, " she proceeded, " thae Frenchmen were a set o' salvages, though I find now, I aye thought ower weel o' them. Foul fa' baith them and the mithers that bore them, and the howdies that brought them into the warld, Satan's limbs as they are. Oh, that I had twa or three o' them here, and a good Scotch rung in my hand. Little wad I care for their swurds, ay, or their bagnets either ; and gin I didna crack their crowns, and gie some wark for Doctor Balmanno, my name's no Girzy Black. They're a neerdoweel race a'thegither; and when Belzebub gets a grip o' them, as he's sure to do at the hinder end, gin he doesna haud them baith tight and fast, he's a deil no worth a button. And there's some o' them in this toon too, " continued she, with the air of a person who suddenly recalls to memory an important fact; " there's some o' them—think o' their impudence—in this very toon. There's that Degveal the dancing-maister, an emigrant they ca' him, that comes loupin' down the street every day like a puddock, wi' his wee cockit hat on his head, and silk stockings on his windlestrae shanks; my certy, but he shall hae a jaw o' dirty water on his green coat and his powdered pow, the very neist time he passes this hoose. Oh, Maister Ceeral, but it's a sight o' doul to see ye come back in siccan a sair condition. What for did ye no stay at hame, instead o' gaun stravaigin' outower the warld fechtin' wi' thae French deevils, for deevils they are, and naething less? "

" But, Girzy, don't you think it would be better to let my uncle know of my arrival? he may think it unkind that I should have been so long in the house without his knowledge. "

" There's maybe something in that, " replied Girzy, " for he's gayan fanciful sometimes aboot sma' things, and, I daur say, it will be as weel to let him ken; but, poor man, there's a heavy heart waitin' on him, and I'm sure the sight o' you will gar him grue maist as muckle as mysel. Hech! this world is fu' o' sair trials! But just tell me afore I gang, how ye are in yer health. Oh! but there's a hantle o' hills and hows in yer chowks. Ye're poor in the flesh, and look as if ye were but silly. I'm fear't yer stamach's no that gude, sae just tell me what ye wad like for yer dinner, and I'll get it, gin it's to be had in the coonty o' Lanrick. "

I assured her that I was an old campaigner, and begged that, in the matter of catering, she would consult my uncle's taste or her own, without reference to mine.

" Weel, " replied Girzy, " gin ye leave't a' to me, ye see, I'll just get what I think's best for ye in yer present weakly condition; sae, for yae thing, ye shall hae, the day, a guid dish o' cocky-leeky, than which, Doctor Cleghorn assured me, there was naething mair disgestable to the stamach, or mair—— "

Here I interrupted her, for, to say the truth, my patience began to be somewhat exhausted, and I dreaded the prolixity of the dissertation on the medicinal virtues of cocky-leeky, on which she was about to enter. " Now, do go, Girzy, to my uncle, like a good woman, as you are, and inform him of my arrival. Tell him too, Girzy, the creature you have found me, " pointing as I spoke to the remains of my dilapidated arm; " tell him I am not as I was; for I know he loves me, and the surprise of finding me so changed, may have evil influence on his health. "

" Weel, I'll gang, " rejoined Girzy; " but it's a sair task ye've pitten on my shouthers; " and uttering something between a sigh and a groan, she left the apartment, casting back a sorrowful glance on me as she departed.

I was again left alone, but my solitude was not long, for in the course of a few minutes Girzy re-entered the room.

" I've tell't Mr Spreull ye're here ; but I'm thinkin' I've no succeeded in gettin' him to undertand ony thing mair ; for the moment he heard your name, and kent ye were here, he ordered me to haud my peace, and tell ye he wad be glad to see ye direckly ; and when I insisted, as ye wushed, on gangin' on to tell him a' aboot ye, he up wi' a volume o' Erskine's Sermons, and swore he wad ding it at my head, gin I didna leave the chaumer instantly, and deliver his message to you. "

On hearing this account of matters, I desired Girzy to lead the way, and followed her to my uncle's chamber.

It was with some internal trepidation that I entered it. I found the old gentleman sitting up in bed, with his head enveloped in a red Kilmarnock night-cap, the colour of which contrasted strongly with the sallowness of his countenance. His body was clothed in a flannel jerkin, or shirt, somewhat like those worn by sailors, which reached about half way up his scraggy throat, leaving the upper part bare. As I approached him, I could detect no change of expression, no lightening up of the countenance, but he regarded me with the same grim and saturnine lock, which had remained for long years imprinted on my memory. He did not at first speak, but when I approached, he stretched out his two long and bony arms, somewhat like lobster claws, and seizing the hand I extended towards him, drew me to the bed.

I sat down on it, beside him. The old gentleman continued to gaze on me for some time in silence, with one hand placed on the crown of my head, with which he gently turned it, first to one side then to the other, as if hesitating with regard to my identity, or anxious to ascertain the full extent of the metamorphosis I had undergone. At length he broke silence.

" Cyril, I'm glad—no, God forgie me, there's nae gladness in my heart, to see you even beneath my ain roof-tree, sae maimed and broken down. "

This was spoken hurriedly, and but for a convulsive twinge of the features, with a calm countenance. I answered, by expressing my sincere regret that the state of his health should be such as to render necessary, so close a confinement. This, however, had not the effect of changing the current of his thoughts, of which I was the engrossing object.

" Speak na o' me, Cyril, for little matters it what becomes o' a withered and a barren trunk, the seasons of whose flower and fruit (alas ! when were they ?) are gone for ever. But this is a sad welcome to my poor laddie ; I'm grown weak, I fear, in mind, as weel as body ; leave me a minute in silence to mysel, and I'll soon be better. "

I did as he desired, and remained seated on the bed some minutes, silent and motionless. The old man threw himself back on his pillow, and lay with closed eyes. His features were still as those of death, but his hands afforded evidence of the working of his spirit, by being alternately clenched and opened. After some interval, he once more raised himself in the bed, and turned his face towards me.

"This jaw o' sorrow, I find," said he, once more taking me by the hand, "is the heaviest I have long felt, and will not pass away sae soon as I thought it would hae done, frae a heart sae worn and cauldrife as mine. I look upon this, Cyril, as God's last, as surely it is his sairest judgment upon me, in this warld. I had hoped to see you—and it has lang been to me a solitary hope, standing, as I now do, wi' yae fit in the grave,— blythe and happy as you ance was,—kind and affectionate as I still ken ye to be. It's lang since we parted, yet, often sin' syne, hae I seen your black pow and laughin' countenance baith by night and day, floatin' like an airy vision before my e'en, rising like a thing o' glamour, and then vanishing awa'. Like a father for an only son, hae I petitioned the Almighty, for your happiness and welfare. Ay, I hae prayed for you, when I couldna pray for mysel; but the wind scatters the prayers o' a sinner, and I see now that mine hae never reached the throne o' divine grace. I maun bear in my auld age the punishment o' the sins of my youth."

There were tears in the old man's eyes as he spoke, and deep dejection might be read, in his countenance and voice.

"Why, my dear uncle," I said, endeavouring to throw vivacity into my tones, in order, if possible, to raise his spirits, "this is more like mourning for a dead nephew, than welcoming a living one. I have come to see you,—to be happy with you, as I used in days of old. Pray, do not look on me as an absolute *memento mori*. Mine is something of a death's head to be sure, but though the husk be changed, you will find the kernel the same. But *you*,—I hope you are not seriously ill, and that before I have been here long, you will be able to take my arm, (for I have still one, at your service,) and walk as we used to do in the Green, or down by the sunny banks of Clyde."

I was pleased to see that the melancholy impression which my first appearance had made on him, in some degree wore off, and that his spirits were slowly remounting from the extreme pitch of depression to which they had fallen. The conversation had continued about an hour, and I had told something of my own history, and something of that of my family, when we were interrupted by the entrance of Girzy.

"I ken naething o' the ways o' you red-coated offishers," she said, addressing herself to me, "sae I just came to spier at what hoor ye wad like yer denner. It's nae great matter about the cocky-leeky, for that will keep het by the fire lug as lang as ye like; but I maun ken afore I pit on the saumon, for that's a mair kittle commodity, and wad a' drap to pieces if left five minutes ower lang in the pat."

"What cares he, you auld gowk," answered my uncle, "aboot either yer salmon, or yer cocky-leeky? Get them at the usual hour; and, do ye hear, lay plates for twa, and rax ower my claes afore ye gang, for I'm gaun to get up directly."

"Bless me," replied Girzy, "but the man's gane clean wud a' thegither. Doctor Cleghorn, when he was here on Tuesday, tell't baith you and me too, that ye was to keep your bed, and no think o' gettin up for the neist week at soonest. And 'noo, Girzy,' said he to me, in his ain coothy way, as he gaed down the stair, 'dinna let that maister o' yours be getting oot o' his bed till the weather's warmer, or ye'll be haein' him laid up on yer haunds a' the lave o' the winter, and what's waur, he may be a lameter a' his life wi' the rheumateeze.'—'Weel, Doctor,' said I, as he raxed his leg oot ower the back o' his horse, 'depend upon't, that deil a fit shall he pit ower the door o' his chaumer, till ye come back.' Sae ye'll just lie still where ye are, and I'll get Maister Ceeral his denner in the ither room by himsel."

"Do ye offer to contradict me?" rejoined her master, apparently more irrate than the occasion required; "Doctor Cleghorn may ride to the deevil gin he likes, and if the beast carries double, he may take you on a pillion ahint him; but up I shall get this moment, so steek your gab, and lay my claes directly on the chair by the bedside."

"Ye's get nae claes to pit on the day," answered Girzy, resolutely, "sae just lie still where ye are, and be content."

The words were no sooner out of her mouth, than, after an ejaculation of anger, which I do not deem it necessary to record, one of my uncle's long and bony legs was seen to be protruded from the bed, and he was obviously in the act of rising, to provide himself with those habiliments which the contumacy of his attendant refused to supply. It seemed as if Girzy's maidenly delicacy was somewhat outraged by this summary proceeding of the old gentleman; but whether this was so or not, it was evident, that further opposition on her part, to the resolute determination of her master, was hopeless. Like a prudent general, therefore, she thought it better to capitulate with a good grace.

"Weel, weel," said she, "it's easy kent that a wilfu' man maun hae his ain way, sae lie still where ye are, and I'll get yer claes frae the kist."

My uncle, though his eyes still glittered with passion, complied with this desire, and slowly withdrew the gaunt and unshapely limb, which had thus succeeded in frighting Girzy into her propriety. She was clearly determined, however, to have at least the privilege of a little talk, as she performed the unwelcome office of arranging her master's integuments by the bed.

"Hech, sirs," said she, addressing me, "saw ye ever the like o' this, Maister Ceeral? there's nae use in threapin' wi' him, for he's just as deaf as Ailsa Craig to onything that copes his ain whigmaleeries." Then turning to my uncle, "He that will to Cupar, maun to Cupar; whether will ye hae yer velveteens or corduroys?—mind it's no my faut, gin ye're

keepit grainin' on the bread o' yer back for the neist twa months,—ye'll
surely clap a pair o' gamashins on yer cuits?—Hech, but there's thrawn
folk in this warld—nae doot ye'll wear yer flannin' wrapper—I'll hae a
sair time o't wi' ye—Ye'll be the better o' twa couls on yer pow, for the
room's cauld—Little wad I be surprised to hae the straiken o' yer corp
afore lang, frae this daft-like proceeding. "

The caloric of my uncle's wrath, which, during the last few minutes,
had been every moment increasing in intensity, now burst forth with the
vehemence of a volcano; and Girzy, as if aware of the coming explosion,
prudently desisted from further irritating remark, and hastily quitted
the apartment. Notwithstanding this, however, the choler of the old
gentleman vented itself, in objurgation, loud and long, on the impudence of his attendant. Having experienced some relief from this discharge, he requested to be left alone, to perform the duties of the toilet,
and I returned to the parlour.

CHAPTER XIV

I do suspect I have done some offence,
That seems disgracious in the city's eye.
Richard III.

ON entering the sitting-chamber, I found the maid, under the superintendence of Girzy, engaged in the preparatory decoration of the
dinner-table, which, on my account, was perhaps destined to display,
somewhat more than its usual bravery. The latter, on my entrance,
desisted from her occupation, in order to adjust what she called the cod
in the easy chair, for my comfortable accommodation.

"Come yer ways," said the matron, as I entered; "come yer ways,
and crook yer hoch in the chair by the chimley lug. Oh, but ye look silly,
after a' the sair troubles ye hae gane through in foreign parts. Weel I
wat, Mr Ceeral, ye hae lost a hantle o' yer birr sin' ye last sat in that
chair. Weel, weel do I mind the time when you and that funny callant
they ca'd Conyers cam to tak' yer kail wi' us, the day before ye gae'd
awa. An' what's become o' him noo? Hae thae French deevils been
cuttin' and hashin' him as they have din you? Oh, ye a' gang out wi'
light hearts, and fu' o' smeddom, but, waes me, what do ye come
hame?"

Here the increasing huskiness of Girzy's voice gave notice that she
was fast sinking into the melting mood, and unwilling again to become
the subject of her pathetic lamentations, I endeavoured, by the cheerful-
ness of my reply, to direct the current of her ideas into another channel.

"I believe Conyers is well, Girzy. He is now a dashing major of
dragoons, and I have no reason to fear that, since I last saw him, he has
either been *hashed* by the French, or lost any of the *smeddom* of his younger
days."

"A major o' dragoons ca' ye him! and what, I wonder, were he and
his dragoons aboot, that they allooed thae rampagin' idolators the
French,—for I'm tell't they worship graven images, in spite o' the
commandments,—to sair you in sic a fashion, as they hae done? Had
they nae swords to help ye? What for did he no come wi' his gallopin'
dragoons, to lend ye a helpin' haun when he saw ye in the grup o' the
Philistines? Hech! I fear he's but a ne'er-do-weel after a', though I am
loath to think it o' him."

I had some difficulty in vindicating Conyers from these unmerited
imputations of Girzy, and in making her comprehend, that being, as he
was, about an hundred miles distant with another branch of the army, it
was scarcely reasonable to blame him, for not having seasonably

appeared, to the rescue of his friend.

Our conversation, however, was soon interrupted, by the approach of my uncle. A clattering was heard along the floor of the passage, and Girzy, who was still engaged in venting her indignation, against the authors of my disfigurement, left her diatribe unfinished, and running to the door of the apartment, hastily opened it, and the old gentleman entered. He could walk with difficulty, and only by the assistance of a staff. His limbs were stiff and feeble, partly, perhaps, from the remains of an attack of acute rheumatism, under which he had recently suffered, but principally, I thought, from that most incurable of all diseases—old age. His progress was slow, and some time elapsed before he reached the easy-chair set apart for his peculiar use, and still more before, by the aid of the sedulous Girzy, who arranged the cushions for his accommodation, he was comfortably settled in it. During this operation, the activity of her other members was at least equalled by that of her tongue.

"Weel, ye've ta'en yer ain way o't," exclaimed she: "but mind, whatever comes o't, ye've naebody to blame but yoursell. Ye care nae mair what I say till ye, than if I was as big a tawpy as Meg there, that canna pit the dinner down right on the table.—Pit the kail at the tap, ye negleckfu' limmer that ye are, and the saumon at the fit, as I tell't ye.—Ay, ye may grain awa'," continued she, taking advantage, with true oratorical promptitude, of an expression of pain to which my uncle at that moment gave utterance; "I'se warrant, ye'll get sma' pity frae me, grain and pech as ye like.—The deevil's in the woman, I declare, can ye no clap the sparrowgrass down forenent the howtowdy?—And I'll tell Doctor Cleghorn the morn, that this daft-like proceeding was nane o' my doing; but I'm done, and in a' time comin' I'se neither mak' nor meddle.—What for are ye stravaigin' aboot the room wi' that mustard-pat in yer nieve? Set it doon, I say, direckly, and draw the porter there by the fire-lug, and then gang ben to the kitchen, and comena back here without I ring for ye."

While such a continuous volume of sound was produced by Girzy, the double object of her cares and her invectives, appeared to be suffering considerable pain, from the motion which the change of his apartment had rendered necessary; but the expression of his countenance showed, that he was by no means so entirely engrossed by it, as to be unconscious either of the meaning or the prolixity of her oratorical display. At first, his rheumatic twinges appeared to follow in such rapid succession, as to leave no time in the short intervals which divided them for anything more than the application of a single emphatic expletive to the object of his wrath; but these, considered abstractedly from all ideas of decorum and propriety, as vivid though unconnected vehicles of the mental emotions of the speaker, could not have been more happily chosen. They were indeed of a character so little complimentary, that even the chariest maiden might have pardonably found ground of offence, in being made the object of their personal application. Nothing, however, could be more philosophical, than the spirit with which Girzy appeared to listen to the *opprobria* of her irate master. They evidently passed by her as the idle wind, and when, by his satisfactory adjustment in the large high-backed armchair, the decrease of his pain enabled him to pour forth a more connected, though not less fervid strain of vituperation, she interrupted him by pushing forward his chair towards the dinner-table, exclaiming as she did so,—

" Come, just haud yer bow-wowin', and tak yer denner, that's gettin' cauld on the brod wi' waitin' for ye. It's a bonny like swatch o' yer discretion ye've been gie'in' Maister Ceeral the day. Weel I wat, better things might hae been expeckit frae a man o' your years.—Come awa', Maister Ceeral, and tak yer place forenent him. And noo," she continued, again addressing her master, and pulling off his night-cap as she did so, " there's your coul aff yer pow, sae just ask a blessin' and fa' to. "

The suddenness of both Girzy's words and motions had evidently taken the old gentleman by surprise. He at first gazed on her with an expression, which seemed to indicate that he was about to pour forth on her head, the whole vials of his wrath, in one relentless and unmitigated discharge ; but I was already seated opposite to him, and when his eyes rested for a moment on my countenance, a change seemed suddenly to have taken place in the whole character of his emotions. Girzy and her impudence were forgotten, and mournful memories connected with myself, appeared to have become the engrossing subject of his thoughts. A minute or two elapsed, during which the old man did not speak, and Girzy, who was already engaged in decanting a bottle of Madeira at the sideboard, by a somewhat unusual coincidence, did not interrupt the silence, into which the late storm had thus unexpectedly subsided.

Whatever my uncle's feelings might have been, he did not express them. " Cyril, " he at length said, " let us ask a blessing ; " then closing his eyes, he again was silent for a few seconds, as if collecting his thoughts for the duty of prayer and thanksgiving. The consequent grace, though long, and somewhat miscellaneous in its petitions, was pronounced in a low and almost inaudible voice, and, at its conclusion, having again adorned his head with its former covering, we commenced our meal.

I leave the pressing cares and hospitable anxieties, with which it was attended on the part of Girzy and my uncle, to be shadowed forth by the imagination of the reader. It passed as such a meal may be supposed to pass, and the departure of the viands was followed in due order of succession, by the introduction of the punch bowl.

To a native of Glasgow, there is, even in the sight of a punch bowl, something of exhilaration and excitement. It brings with it no mournful associations. It is linked to a thousand bright and pleasing remembrances, of youthful and joyous revelry, and of the graver intoxications of maturer years. Within its beautiful and hallowed sphere, are buried no "thoughts that do lie too deep for tears." In its very name there is delightful music, and it comes o'er his ear

> Like the sweet south,
> That breathes upon a bank of violets,
> Stealing and giving odours!

There was,—or at least I imagined there was,—something of all this discernible in my uncle. He regarded Girzy, with a mollified look, as she placed it on the table, and issued his directions in an accent somewhat softened. In his tone of addressing me, too, there was more of vivacity, than he had yet displayed since our meeting; and that dull heaviness of heart, by which hitherto he had been evidently oppressed, seemed to have become lighter, and at least not utterly overpowering.

The punch was made, and Girzy appeared glass in hand, claiming from her master a bumper " to the health of Maister Ceeral." The toast, indeed, as drank by the venerable virgin, was somewhat prolix; for, though in part dedicated to its professed purpose, it concluded by an imprecation on those worshippers of Baal, the neerdoweel French landlowpers, who had been the occasion of my thus returning to my uncle's house the mutilated object she beheld.

Girzy departed, and we were left alone. Then it was, for the first time, that the old gentleman gave expression to that torrent of warm and affectionate feeling, which had hitherto been pent up in his bosom. He was desirous of learning the story, of my not uneventful life. Much of it I told him, but there was much likewise which *he* could not have understood,—which *I* could not tell. In my nature, circumstances had awakened sympathies into strong and terrible action, which in him, during a long life, had lain in torpid slumber, from which they could not now be awakened. In all my physical sufferings, his kind heart was ready to participate; of my mental ones, he knew, and could know nothing.

We did not, however, long enjoy an uninterrupted colloquy. While in the act of detailing to him such portions of my life as I imagined might be most interesting, the door opened, and Girzy came bustling into the apartment, followed by a gentleman of somewhat portly presence, and canonical appearance.

"Here's Doctor Balfour come to see you," exclaimed she, drawing another chair towards the table, and dusting it with her apron as she spoke. " Come yer ways, Doctor, " she continued, addressing the stranger, who had stopped on finding Mr Spreull was not alone, as he had expected;—" there's naebody wi' him but Maister Ceeral, and a bonny like sight he's come hame frae the wars, as ye may see. Waes me! Little wad the mither that bore him ken him, honest woman! were she to clap een on him the now. Just come ben, and crook yer legs aneath the mahogany, and tak a preein o' the bowl. "

My uncle, being seated with his back to the door, and unable to rise from the rheumatism which still affected his limbs, having learned the name and quality of his guest, now added his invitation to that of Girzy, for the worthy Doctor to come forward and be seated. The stranger accordingly advanced, and having shaken hands very cordially with the old gentleman, seated himself without further ceremony in the chair, which Girzy had provided for his accommodation.

Doctor Balfour, (for by such title was the respectable divine distinguished,) was one of the leading members of the High or Calvinistic party of the Scottish Church, and certainly one of the most powerful and energetic preachers of his day. From the period of the French Revolution, deistical principles, or at least a general lukewarmness and indifference to religious observances, had, I think, become more peculiarly endemic in Glasgow than in most places in the kingdom. During my former residence in the city, gentlemen were not much in the habit of frequenting public worship, and the congregations, which were always thin, consisted chiefly of ladies. In such a state of things, to have succeeded in rivetting the attention, and exciting strong religious emotions, in those so little prepared for their reception, was certainly indicative of some power in the preacher. In truth, Dr Balfour was a man of considerable mental energy and shrewdness, and possessed a native though somewhat homely eloquence, which he exerted with much salutary efficacy in his vocation. In the present day, it requires perhaps some courage to preach the stern and uncompromising doctrines of Calvin, without veiling their consequences with somewhat of varnish and disguise. Doctor Balfour, however, did this. He followed the tenets of his founder to their legitimate conclusion, was startled by no difficulties that met him in his path, and would, I believe, have died a martyr at the stake, for the doctrine of supralapsarian election, and irrespective decrees. Perhaps, some such strong and spirit-stirring medicaments were necessary to rouse his hearers, from that state of torpid indifference to religion, into which they had fallen. Certainly something more powerful, than the gentle anodynes hebdomadally poured forth by his weaker brethren, was required to rouse them from the deep sleep, into which their eyelids had been lulled. This, Doctor Balfour provided ; and even those, whom mere curiosity had brought together to listen to the preaching of this great cannon of the city, generally returned with less zest than usual, to their Sunday's sheep's-head, and found that on that day the contents of the punch-bowl had lost something of their savour.

Such was the person who formed the unlooked-for, and to me unwelcome addition to our party. My uncle, I found, had become one of the flock of this zealous pastor, who frequently "dropped in," to administer spiritual consolation to the old gentleman, or to enjoy the exercise of a little theological disputation on questions of polemical divinity. In person, the divine was stout, and somewhat inclining to obesity, and his face was marked by a certain ruddiness which bespoke no ascetic abstinence from the good things of the world. His head was covered—certainly not adorned by an unpowdered scratch-wig, which in many places had become threadbare from age, and displayed here and there considerable portions of the Doctor's skull, shining through the net-work from below.

Having shaken hands with my uncle, the reverend gentleman proceeded to compliment him, on the change for the better, which had evidently taken place since his last meeting.

" I was just passing, Mr Spreull, " he continued, " and thought I couldna do less than give you a ca', to see how you was getting on in your tough warsle wi' your sair fleshly enemy the rheumatism. Troth, I didna expect you would have gotten so soon clear of this thraw, I'm really glad to see you so far recovered. "

This address elicited a cheerful reply from my uncle, who concluded, by requesting his spiritual comforter to push in his glass, and become a participator in the nectareous contents of the bowl. With this request, the Doctor instantly complied, while his entertainer, in the act of dealing forth with scrupulous exactitude the stated measure of liquor to his guest, thus proceeded :—" Cyril and mysel have already taken a glass or twa frae the bowl, but it will no taste the waur, if you, Doctor, would ask a blessing on this our sober enjoyment of the present mercy. "

To the desire thus expressed, a cheerful acquiescence was yielded by his guest, who, closing his eyes, and holding up his right hand, pro-nounced a long grace, or rather prayer, to which my uncle having again divested himself of his night-cap, listened apparently with reverent attention.

The interruption which this devotional exercise gave to the cheerful-ness of the conversation was only temporary. It was no sooner over, than the meeting resumed its former character, and the Doctor proceeded obligingly to congratulate me on my return to my native country, from the dangerous service in which I had recently been engaged. He asked many questions concerning what he termed " the idolatry of the poor benighted race, " in whose land I had been a sojourner, and when I spoke of the splendour of the Catholic ritual, its penances and absolut-ions, its magnificent altars and altar-pieces, its images and gorgeous processions, he expressed infinite astonishment at the details of such heathenish proceedings, and turning to my uncle, " Surely, Mr Spreull, " he said, " we canna be thankfu' enough to divine Providence, that has cast our lot in a land in which the pure waters of the gospel trickle, though maybe but in a sma' stream, rather than in one where the folk get naething to drink but the puddles o' corruption that come frae the dirty jawholes o' idolatry, the Popish priests. "

This sentiment, of course, met with a cordial concurrence from my uncle, and the conversation gradually diverged to such clerical matters, as came more immediately home to the business and bosoms of the interlocutors, than those already mentioned. There was much discourse anent Presbyteries and Synods, and Elders, and Overtures to the General Assembly, and parochial occurrences, which were considerably beyond my fathom to understand. The dialogue, however, was interrupted by the entrance of Girzy and Meg, the former of whom advanced to the table, and placing before the divine a large quarto Bible and Psalm Book, again retreated towards the sideboard, where she took possession of a chair, near that which Meg already occupied, as if waiting for the commencement of family worship.

The Doctor having adjusted his spectacles, began by reading a chapter of the Bible, at the conclusion of which, the whole party, with the exception of my uncle, stood up during the delivery of an extemporé prayer, of at least half an hour's duration, in several of the petitions of which, the present circumstances of the family were specially noticed, and thanksgiving duly offered in their name, for my safe return from the idolatrous country of the Cushites, and the Amorites, and the Gergashites, to the land in which the God of Judah was worshipped in purity and peace.

Both in the substance of the prayer itself, and in its singularity of style and delivery, I found something moving and impressive. In my uncle's countenance there was every external demonstration of sincere devotion. He sat with closed eyes and clasped hands, and at those petitions of the prayer, which came particularly home to his own bosom and condition, he bent his head downwards towards the table, in token of his deep and fervent participation in the supplication thus put up on his behalf to the throne of Divine Grace. Had a stranger entered the apartment at that moment, he might at first, perhaps, have found something ludicrous in the appearance of the party; and it must be confessed that the unfinished punch-bowl on the table, surrounded by the other instruments of carousal, did not exactly harmonize in the imagination with the devotional exercises in which they were engaged. But all ludicrous associations, I think, must have speedily subsided, and in the energetic words of the pastor,—in the spirit of humble and pious supplication, legible in the look and manner of the aged and infirm old man—perhaps even in my own melancholy countenance, and mutilated form, he might have found matter for other thoughts, and he that came to scoff, might have remained to pray.

But the solemnity of the worship certainly ceased with the prayer. In the psalm which succeeded it, it was with difficulty that even I could prevent the indulgence of a smile. Girzy, who apparently had some taste, if not talent, for music, enacted the part of precentor to the household, and led the tune in a voice, to say the least of it, not remarkably melodious. My uncle joined in this, with apparently as much sincerity and fervour, as he had done in the preceding part of the service, sending forth with the full force of his lungs, a stentorian cacophony, which certainly left Girzy no cause of apology, for the vociferous discordance of her psalmody. The Doctor sung well, and evidently did his best to reduce the discord of the party into something bearing at least a faint and distant resemblance to music. In this, it is almost needless to say, he was eminently unsuccessful. Had Mozart or Rossini been present, neither could have gone alive from the apartment. Physic could not have saved them—they must have died on the spot.

For myself, having an ear by no means remarkably sensitive, I did not suffer any material inconvenience from the prevailing want of harmony; but my constitutional gravity did suffer some involuntary derangement by the interjections in which Girzy, during the intervals of the tune, deemed it necessary to address her fellow servant. Of the tenor of these, the following specimen may give the reader some idea:—" Ye're ower heigh, Meg. "—" What for do ye skirl that gate—hae ye nae lug for the tune? "—" No sae loud, ye limmer. "—" Mak less sough wi' yer skreighin. "—" Haud yer timmer-tuned thrapple. " From the moment these sentences reached my ear, I confess, I found it impossible again to join my voice in the exercise of praise.

At the conclusion of the psalm, the worthy Doctor pronounced a benediction on the family, and the servants having retired, the glasses were again replenished, and the conversation proceeded as before. The compotation, however, did not extend beyond due limits, and the bowl being finished, Girzy and Meg, bearing the apparatus for tea, again entered the apartment. The former, who possessed but a small share of the national talent for silence, took advantage of the privilege of *entré*, which her occupation afforded her, to address the doctor in a strain of familiarity, at which a dignitary of the English Church would certainly have been somewhat astonished.

" Weel, Doctor, yon was a bonny-like chiel ye got to preach for ye last Sabbath's afternoon. What ca' ye *him*, now? Hech, but he was a puir fizzionless stick, as ever I heard in a' my life. "

Here my uncle imperiously ordered her to be silent, but without effect.

" He's but a preacher, I ettle, " continued the incorrigible Girzy, " for he had nae bands on; and weel I wat sic a smeddumless tike is no very likely to get a kirk in a hurry. He wasna like yersel, Doctor, and drave nane o' the dust frae out the cushions o' the poopit wi' the true birr o' the Gospel. "

Girzy would probably have proceeded yet further with her animadversions, had she not been again interrupted by her master, who, in a tone which showed that his anger was now fairly roused, commanded silence.

" Haud yer peace, ye impudent and misleart limmer that ye are; is that a way to speak o' ony friend o' the Doctor's in my house? Gang but the house immediately, and learn when ye come back to keep a calm sough and a steekit gab. "

"Ye needna set up yer birses at me, Mr Spreull, " rejoined Girzy; " for the Doctor kens weel enough I meant nae offence; and gin a's true that's said, waur folk hae preach't for him afore now; for it's weel kent in the town that

> The deil gat power,
> For half an hour,
> To preach in the poopit o' Rab Balfour;
> But soon the gospel began to fail,
> And the elders pookit him oot by the tail.

And had that windlestrae creatur that preached last Sunday been sairt as he deserved——"

Here my uncle became too irate for further sufferance, and reaching out his staff, aimed a blow at his attendant across the portly person of the divine, which fortunately prevented it from taking effect; and Girzy, finding matters had put on so serious an aspect, prudently retired, without affording any further cause of provocation.

The Doctor, who had felt something of the weight of the blow which had been intended by my uncle for his contumacious handmaiden, deemed this a suitable occasion for a little ghostly remonstrance on the subject of those ungoverned fits of passion to which the old gentleman was constitutionally subject.

"There's nae doubt, Mr Spreull, " observed he, " that Girzy has maybe gotten somewhat mair of the gift of the gab than might just hae been desired; but ye ken she's a clever, managin', and faithfu' servant, and her extraordinary gift of speech was likely ordained by Providence to afford you occasion for the exercise of Christian patience; a virtue, Mr Spreull, ye'll excuse my freedom in telling you, wi' which you are no overly stocked. I was really quite sorry to see you so wrathfu' and put out wi' her rampagious tongue, instead of just letting her words gang in at the tae lug, and out at the tither, like a wise man, as the world kens you to be. Tak my word for't, had ye been married, ye would afore this time o' day hae learned to bear better wi' the clatter o' a woman's gab. "

"It's very true what you observe, Doctor, " meekly answered my uncle; " and I ken weel I'm to blame; but the sound o' her voice just gaes through me like a knife, and it's no to tell what I hae suffered for the last three-and-thirty years frae the tongue o' that woman. Yet, as you say, Doctor, it ought to be mair patiently tholed, as an ordinance—though it's a sair yin—o' divine Providence intended for my edification. "

At length the divine took his departure, and afraid of the effects which the unusual excitements and exertions of the day might produce on the enfeebled health of my uncle, I, too, soon intimated my intention of returning for the night to my quarters in the Buck's Head. Though this proposal met with vehement and indignant opposition, I was so well aware that fixing my abode beneath the roof of my uncle would necessarily involve the complete sacrifice of my own privacy and comfort, without proportionally contributing to his, that, in spite of all opposition, I remained resolutely fixed in my determination.

"Isna this bonny-like behaviour, Maister Ceeral," exclaimed the irate Girzy, "no to sleep in yer ain uncle's hoose, when ye've come sae far to see him? There I've had yer sheets hanging a' day by the fire, and I've gart Meg sleep in the bed for the last fortnight to keep it weel aired for you; and after a', to think o' you gaun awa' stravaigin' at this time o' night, to waste yer siller at an inn—Yin wad hae expeckit better things frae you, Maister Ceeral, than the like o' that."

I had never before observed in my uncle any symptom of approbation of the eloquence of his loquacious functionary; but on the present occasion, he evidently listened to her strenuous endeavours to revolutionize my intentions, with complacency and satisfaction. He had sufficient tact, however, soon to discover that I was obstinately bent on adhering to my plan of returning to the inn; and addressing Girzy, under whose troublesome though kind importunities I was still suffering,—"Weel, weel," he said, "it's nae use plaguing him ony mair about the matter; ye ken he has some o' the blood o' the Spreulls in him, and likes as weel as ony o' us to hae his ain way; and after a', it's maybe but reasonable he should; sae clap a bung in yer gab, and hae done at yince wi' yer deavin."

Even when the main point of my return to the inn had been carried, some difficulties still arose with regard to the mode in which it was to be effected. I proposed walking.

"Atweel, ye'll no walk the night, without Mr Spreull's big-coat; but ye had better let Meg rin for a noddy," exclaimed Girzy.

And with this latter request, in order to avoid a repetition of the penance I had endured on a former occasion, I thought it more prudent to acquiesce.

Shortly afterwards, the noddy was reported to be in waiting for my conveyance, and having faithfully promised an early visit on the following morning, wished the worthy couple good night.

CHAPTER XV

———Thou old and true Menenius,
Thy tears are salter than a younger man's,
And venomous to thine eyes.

Coriolanus.

FROM the details,—given, I fear, with somewhat too much prolixity,—in the preceding chapter, the reader will, I imagine, have acquired sufficient insight into the circumstances, and domestic relations of my uncle, at the period of my visit. In appearance, he was considerably changed by the years which had elapsed since my former visit. He was no longer the hale and vigorous old man, my memory depicted him; his frame had suffered much from the inroads of time, as well as of disease, but the stamina of his naturally strong constitution were not yet utterly broken down, and I rejoiced in the hope, that years,—if not of happiness, at least of tranquillity and comfort,—might yet be in store for the kind and warm-hearted old man. In contributing to his recovery, indeed, I believe my presence and society did more than all the medicines of the doctors. After my arrival, his complaints gradually subsided, and leaning on my arm, with the assistance of his staff, he was soon able to repair to that place where merchants most do congregate— the Exchange Coffee-room. There, seated in an arm chair, he every day spent several hours, transacting business with his usual acuteness, or with spectacled nose, poring over the newspapers of the day, or, when interrupted in his occupation, listening for a few moments, with contemptuous gravity, to the political speculations of some communicative Quidnunc.

I generally dined with the old gentleman, and, over a bowl of his favourite beverage, the evenings went by more rapidly and pleasantly than might have been expected from the apparently impassable gulf which utter dissimilarity of age, habits, and pursuits had set between us. But the mornings were my own; these my uncle divided between the counting-house and the Exchange, and my society, at such times, was regarded only as an idle interruption to business. The intervals of liberty thus afforded me were gladly welcomed. I took advantage of them, to escape from the smoky atmosphere of the city, and sallied forth into the country to inhale the balmy air of spring—to gladden my eye, wearied by the dismal monotony of the town, with the sight of the bursting blossoms, and my ear with the melodious rejoicings of bird and insect.

Once, and once only, were my steps directed to the College. Effacing and barbarous hands had been at work, since I had last beheld it, and much of that antique grace, which had lingered over and around it was gone. One side of the venerable Gothic quadrangle had been pulled down, and a detestable building, utterly anomalous in point of architecture, now occupied its site. Behind, too, my eye was shocked by the appearance of a large Grecian edifice, erected since my departure, for the reception of the Hunterian Museum. Abstractedly considered, there was little in the building to excite admiration; but, situated as it was, nothing more barbarously discordant with the prevailing character of the place, can well be imagined. It almost seemed to have dropped from the clouds, and stood staring on the dark and time-honoured masses, by which it was surrounded, as if wondering by what extraordinary chance, it had been thrown into such company. Verily, I thought, as with feelings of regret and disappointment, my eye rested on the confused architectural jumble, by which the remains of venerable antiquity had been defaced,—" Verily, this university *may* be the seat of learning, but too surely it is not the receptacle of taste. "

Occupied with such thoughts, I passed onwards, and entered the once beautiful pleasure grounds, which, in my younger days, had been the scene of healthful recreation, and manly exercise to the students. These, too, had been curtailed and disfigured. Streets now covered the ground, where, beneath the shade of venerable trees, I had wandered, buried in the dreams of young philosophy, or meditating on the prospects of my future life, as they rose bright and unclouded to my ardent imagination. As I beheld the havoc which the *auri sacra fames* had carried, even into these academical retreats, unpleasant feelings were awakened, and willing to escape from them, I turned hastily, and retraced my steps. As I retrod the courts, they were filled, as of yore, with students, and the loud voice of gaiety and merriment rung from the aged echoes, as it had done in the days of my youth. Since then, years had gone by; many of the excellent and estimable men, to whose instructions I had been indebted, were no more. The flood of generations was rolling on its eternal course, and I, a waif upon its waters, had already been carried far onward to the grave. Once, in these very courts, I had mingled in a crowd of joyous and happy beings, such as I beheld around me. Now I stood unknown and a stranger, my very existence had passed from all hearts and memories, and when I asked the aged Janitor, with whom I had been an especial favourite, if he remembered Cyril Thornton, who about ten years before formed an unit in the youthful throng? he answered in the negative.

" There may hae been sic a yin, " he said, " for aught I ken, but I really canna say that I mind onything about him. "

My steps did not linger long in the College, and never were they again planted within its precincts.

Though in the external aspect of Glasgow, little change was apparent from the lapse of years, which had intervened since my former visit, yet a great change was certainly observable in the manners and mode of life of its inhabitants. Wealth had evidently increased, and exotic luxuries and fashions had taken root in the soil. At the epoch of my former visit, the city boasted but one carriage; now gay equipages, with servants in gaudy liveries, were to be met with in every street. Formerly a few clumsy and quakerlike buggies, drawn by horses better fitted for the plough than the shafts, might be seen lumbering along, conveying a physician on his rounds, or an elderly gentleman and his wife to their cottage in the suburbs; now vehicles of the smartest and most fashionable description, whether designated in the nomenclature of the day as Dennet, Stanhope, Whiskey, Tilbury, or Drosky, glittered past with almost meteor-like velocity, in all the great avenues of the city. The ideas of the generation, which had been springing up during my absence, evidently differed widely from those of their fathers, and least of all did they seem disposed to imitate them, in those habits of parsimony and frugality, in which, perhaps, the chief source of their increasing prosperity was to be sought. Several new and elegant streets had sprung up to the westward of the city, and the gayer and more wealthy part of the population had deserted their former small and smoky residences, for the more elegant and commodious mansions which these afforded. Nothing, in short, could be more striking than the almost total revolution, which a few years had effected in the tastes and habits of the community. The spirit of improvement was evidently abroad. There was less of that narrowness of mind with which, young as I was, I had formerly been struck. Their wants and ideas had evidently been enlarged, and of the truth of the axiom, that wealth and civilization are indissolubly connected, Glasgow might be cited as a striking and irrefragable instance.

In other circumstances, perhaps, these changes might have attracted little of my attention. But separated from the world, as I felt myself to be, during my sojourn with my uncle, I was glad to find in external objects, anything to withdraw my mind, from brooding on its own solitary griefs. On the whole, I think there was something in the entire novelty of scene and objects in which I moved, and by which I was surrounded, favourable to the restoration of my mental tranquillity. The storm of violent emotion, by which the very foundations of life and reason had been shaken to their centre, found there no mournful association, to excite its dormant fury into action. Memory, indeed, was not idle; yet the keenness of the agony it occasioned had been somewhat diminished. The meridian of glowing passion had already subsided into twilight, and the shadows of time and distance had already partially shrouded, the poignant sources of my sorrow.

The morbid sensibility, with which I had at first regarded my personal disfigurement, had now been displaced by sounder and more reasonable thoughts. It was—or at least I imagined it was, more trifling

Q

than I had at first supposed. Those whose love I still valued, loved me
not the less for my misfortunes. What then had it cost me? The love of
the Lady Melicent? Oh, no. My calmer judgment told me it could not
be. There were other and deeper causes of alienation, of which I could
scarcely be unconscious, but on which I wanted courage to reflect.

The impression I might make on the inhabitants of Glasgow, at all
events, cost me no uneasiness. I was nothing to them, and they to me
were as nothing. I went abroad; I mingled in the crowded assembly of
the Exchange; I daily encountered the stare of rude and vulgar men
with the most philosophical indifference. I wished not to attract, I cared
not to repel. I was as a star moving onward in its own erratic orbit,
uninfluenced in its course or its velocity, by the constellations of the
surrounding firmament.

One day, in walking the Trongate, I was accosted by a very grave
and dignified-looking personage, who had often before attracted my
notice, from the singularity of his air and appearance, though unaccompanied by any personal recognition. He was dressed in a suit of sables,
wore knee and shoe-buckles of Bristol stones, and walked the streets with
an air of magisterial authority, with one hand buried in the folds of a
black satin waistcoat, over which hung a massive gold chain, indicative
of his rank as a bailie, and the other flourishing a large bamboo cane
with somewhat of the grace of a drum-major. His hair, which was highly
powdered, and gathered behind into a pig-tail, was surmounted by a
large three-cornered cocked hat, not unlike those worn in field days by
Scottish doctors of divinity. The reader will not probably be surprised,
that in this imposing personage, I did not at first recognise my old
acquaintance Mr Archibald Shortridge. Yet he it was. Since I had seen
him at Bath, he had been joined in holy wedlock to Miss Thomasina
Spreull, and having returned to his native city, had there become a
person of sufficient prominence and consequence to be elected to the
honours of the magistracy.

Under a metamorphosis so complete, some seconds elapsed, during
which there remained in my mind some lurking doubts as to his
identity; but his voice was not to be mistaken, and he had not articulat-
ed a sentence, ere hesitation, though not wonder, was at once banished.
In his manner of addressing me, and in the tone of his voice, there was an
expression of conscious dignity, which amalgamated harmoniously with
his official gravity and importance. Vulgar and unprepossessing he still
was, yet by no means so in a degree unsuitable to the character of a
Glasgow bailie.

"Ah, Major, how's a' wi' you?" exclaimed he, extending at the
same time towards me one of his ungloved hands; "I heard of your
being in town some time ago, but really the official duties of the
magistracy—Take a pinch, Major," producing his snuff-box as he
spoke—"really the official duties of the magistracy have been so

weighty lately, that I have never yet been able to snatch a moment to call on you. I met Meg yesterday on the street, who told me you put up at the Buck's Head; and you may depend on it, I shall seize the first leisure moment I can command to call upon you."

I answered merely by an inquiry for the health of Mrs Shortridge and her family.

"Thank you,—Mrs Shortridge is keepin' pretty well; but I'm sorry to see you in sic a changed condition. I daresay you thought it very odd I should pass you in the street, as I have done several times, without speaking, and I houp ye'll no attribute it to any pride on my part, for I really did not ken you from that ugly slash on your chowk, which has gien you a thrawn look about the mouth, really far from becoming."

I assured him in reply, that I had by no means attributed his silence to any such cause, and was in the act of passing on, when he seized me by the coat, and compelled me unwillingly to continue a listener to his conversation.

"And how's our worthy uncle? We called on him several times lately, but that Girzy always takes care that I never get a sight o' him. I was glad to hear that he has lately been recoverin' frae his trouble. Honest man! drap aff when he may—and in the course o' nature he canna be expected to haud out much langer—he will be a sair loss to a' his relations, but mair especially to Mrs Shortridge—to say naething o' the town o' Glasgow, that canna houp to look on his like again in a hurry. You may tell him what I say, for it will maybe be a consolation to him in his illness to ken he's sae weel loved and respected by us a'."

I here made a second effort to depart, but the Bailie still kept firm hold of my coat, and my intention was defeated.

"And, Major, could ye no induce him, do ye think, to get a decenter housekeeper than that Girzy? She's really no to be trusted, wi' sae much in her power as she has. She seems to me naething better than a randy, and I warrant a puir account o' things will be gotten at the old man's death. She's taken care to feather her ain nest brawly, I'll be bound. Ye might just drap a hint or twa in the auld man's lug, though not from me, for I would neither be seen to make nor meddle in the matter, but just as · if it came from yourself."

I declined the task thus assigned me rather peremptorily and briefly, and bidding the magistrate good morning, we parted, with reiterated assurances on his part, that his first leisure moment should be devoted to calling on me at the Buck's Head.

In a few days the projected visit of the Bailie was carried into effect, and though I took all necessary precautions to prevent his admission, it became, of course, incumbent on me to return the unwelcome civility. The house of the Magistrate, to which my steps were accordingly directed, I found to be situated in a new and elegant street, which had sprung up since my former residence in Glasgow. Every thing in its

external appearance gave evidence of an opulent proprietor. My application to the door-bell was not at first attended to, nor were my second
and third attempts to attract the notice of the family more fortunate. At
length, after waiting about a quarter of an hour, I lost patience and
departed; but I had not proceeded farther than a few yards from the
door, when I was arrested in my progress by a voice calling after me
from the vestibule—" I say, you gentleman, wha was ye wantin'?" and
turning round, I observed that the door had been at length opened by a
foot-boy, from whom this somewhat free and unceremonious address
proceeded. A more complete lout can hardly be conceived. He wore a
dirty apron, his stockings, which were of grey worsted, hung down in
large folds about his ancles, and his shoes, which betrayed no traces of
either brush or blacking, were without latchets. Above the dress I have
already described, he wore a coat of pea-green livery, with scarlet
facings, which had evidently but a moment before been donned for the
nonce. Of this hopeful scion of the establishment I inquired for Mrs
Shortridge, and being informed she was at home, I was ushered up a
splendid stair-case to the drawing-room, which was without fire, and
betrayed no sign of recent habitation. The furniture of this apartment
was handsome and costly; yet there was something in the assortment of
colours it displayed, glaring and unpleasant to the eye. On one side of
the apartment, stood a harp and a piano-forte, and confronting each
other, at either end, hung full-length portraits of the master and the
mistress of the mansion, displaying all that stiffness of figure and *stariness*
of look, which bad artists generally contrive to infuse into their resembl-
ances.

I had been several minutes in the drawing-room, when a servant
entered and requested my name. The request was complied with, and I
was again left to my own solitary meditations.

These were at length broken by the appearance of Mrs Shortridge,
who entered the apartment evidently fresh from the toilet, in all the
splendour of feathers and gros-de-Naples.

In her air and manner there was, as might have been expected,
something more sedate and matronly than in the days of her maidenhood, when her unparalleled agility in dancing had been the admiration, if not the envy, of the fashionable assemblies in Bath.

The reader will perhaps excuse me for not affording him the minute
details of a conversation, which consisted chiefly of felicitations on her
own change of condition and condolences on mine. I learned that two of
her sisters were married since we last met. One to a respectable country
curate of the English church, the other to a gigantic kettle-drummer of a
regiment of dragoons, with whom she had eloped, to the great grief and
scandal of her family.

While still engaged in conversation, a nurse entered, bearing in
her arms a little carroty-headed boy, with a snub nose, and a most

insufferable squint. The appearance of this heir of the accumulating honours of the Shortridges, of course, diverted our colloquy into the channel most agreeable to the feelings of a mother. I was told the story of all his infantine pranks, and preternatural precocity of talent, and having heard him repeat his letters, and sing a song, of which the tune was somewhat indistinguishable, I did not neglect to take advantage of the earliest opportunity of escape. From the Bailie and his lady I afterwards received several invitations to dinner, but these I declined.

The time now approached, when I was about to quit Glasgow. I hesitated long before I could bring myself to state my intention of departure to my uncle. I knew it would give him pain, and I felt a sort of nervous anxiety to delay the intimation of its necessity as long as possible. I did so ; but the moment at length came when it was necessary to speak, and I told him that a few days were destined to be the limit of my stay. While I spoke, the old man listened in silence ; but a sigh broke from him as he stretched out his long and bony hand, and grasped mine, with an intensity of pressure indicative of the warmth of his feelings.

"What you have now tell't me, Cyril, " he at length said, " hasna ta'en me by surprise. I kent ye couldna bide here long, wasting the prime o' your days wi' an auld and feckless man, waiting to see him hirple by inches into his grave. O' that fearsome journey, Cyril, I hae little left to gang ; for frae what I feel within, " here he laid his hand upon his breast, " I ken the spade's already bought, and the mattock in the gravedigger's hand, that's to howk my bed in the kirkyard. Great as the comfort of your presence would be to me in the struggle that is fast approaching, I dinna ask ye to bide, for when the spirit's gane, it matters little by what hand the een may be closed. Yes, gang your ways, Cyril, and though my body's ower auld to move, my spirit will gang with you. "

I returned the pressure of his hand, but spoke not. He resumed.

" Cyril, rax down the Bible frae the skelf, and read out a psalm and a chapter. It's good, when the shadowy and fading objects of this world are engrossing ower much of our thoughts and our affections, to turn them on God—the God whose almighty hand has upheld us in times past—on whose saving grace alone all our hopes for the future can rest for their completion. "

I did as the old man desired, and not with heedless ear did he drink in the words of holy inspiration. They calmed the tremor of his spirit, and he became again tranquil.

I did not tell my uncle the particular day fixed for my departure, for I had not courage to take leave of him. I dreaded too much the effect of strong agitation on his enfeebled frame, not to feel anxious to spare him every pang of which our separation—too probably an eternal one— could be divested. The evening preceding my departure came, and I at length rose to depart. I advanced towards the old man, who, uncon- scious that he then gazed on me for the last time, stretched forth his hand, and wished me, in a calm and untroubled voice—Good night.

At that moment, the gush of feeling overpowered me, and I wept—I confess it—like a child. His hand was bedewed with my tears, and surprised at this unexpected ebullition of feeling, he addressed me in an anxious yet a soothing voice.

" Wae's me, Cyril, your spirits have been low the night, and I fear ye're no weel. Gang to your bed, and I hope you'll get a good sleep, and be better the morn. "

" Yes, uncle, " I replied, " I am well, but my spirits are indeed low. Give me your blessing ; I shall then feel calmer, and sleep, when it descends on my eyelids, will be more refreshing. "

" My good laddie, the blessing o' a sinfu' man like mysel' is but little worth—yet ye shall hae't. "

I knelt down before him much moved, and he proceeded :—

" May the blessing of an all-merciful God be ever on you and around you. May his grace be a lamp unto your feet, and a light unto your path. May it guide, strengthen, and support you in all the troubles and adversities of this life, and bring you, through faith in our Redeemer, to eternal blessedness in that which is to come. Amen. "

With a sad and softened spirit, did I reverently listen to the affecting benediction which he had poured forth in the fulness of his heart, and I rose not from my knees, without a mental prayer, that grace might descend abundantly on his grey and aged head,—that all his errors and frailties might be mercifully forgiven,—and that the last days of his earthly pilgrimage might be hallowed by a blessing. No word passed my lips, but pressing the hand of the old man in one last and almost convulsive grasp, I hurried from the apartment.

When I returned to my hotel, I did not retire to rest, but seizing a pen, wrote a letter to my uncle, in which I bade him farewell, and gave utterance to the feelings of affectionate regard with which his kindness had inspired me. On the following morning I quitted Glasgow.

CHAPTER XVI

When I said I would die a bachelor, I did not think I should live till I were married.

Much Ado about Nothing.

If souls guide vows, if vows are sanctimony,
If sanctimony be the gods' delight,
If there be rule in unity itself,
Then this is she.

Troilus and Cressida.

ONCE more my steps were turned southward, and having crossed the border, in a few hours, I found myself in the green and sunny land of my nativity. My sojourn in Scotland had certainly, by abstracting my mind from those objects which might have retarded the restoration of its composure, been favourable to my health. I had regained strength, and my spirits were firmer and less variable, than they had been since my return from abroad.

As I approached Middlethorpe, it was not without some palpitation of the heart, that I reflected on the painful task, which there awaited me. My resolution of again joining the army remained unshaken, and I was about to bid farewell—an eternal farewell, to Lucy, who had ever regarded me with fond affection, and to Laura, by whom, I knew, that I had, at least, *once* been beloved. I was about to break the last links that bound me to earth; to gaze *once* on the beings to whom my heart still clung with fondness, and then to behold them no more.

Laura Willoughby! How often since we last parted, had her image started up, like a thing of light and life, amid the darkness of my memory! With how many dear associations, tranquil, yet serenely beautiful in their tranquillity, was not her image in my imagination, indissolubly connected! From her fair eyes it was, that my heart had first learned its rudiments of love. It was when breathed from her soft voice, that the spirit of sweet music had first sunk meltingly into my soul. Not from the painter's or the sculptor's art, but from Laura, young, beautiful, and joyous, as I remembered her, had I drawn my first conceptions of female beauty, which time had never afterwards obliterated from my heart and fancy. And yet I had loved another! I had been false and recreant to all the finest and the holiest impulses of my nature. Why was this? Why had I suffered my heart to be led astray, from its allegiance to one, on whom, I now felt, it might have rested, and been happy? In which of the ennobling and peculiar attributes of woman, was Laura

Willoughby inferior to the highest and the proudest of her sex? Had I
not, in forsaking her for another, been misled by ambition? Were all the
sufferings I had incurred,—all the torture and the anguish which had
brought me to the brink of the grave, more than a just retribution for my
offence? She had loved me. I had sacrificed her peace of mind, but had
not secured my own. The victims had, indeed, bled, but the demon had
not been propitiated.

What a multitude of tender sympathies and affections, lingered over
and around her! Often did I think of her bathed in tears, as at the
moment of our parting, when, with marble cheek and closed eyes, she
stood before me, and I knew only by the tremulous motion of her lips,
that she strove, though in vain, to pronounce the word Farewell. Oh,
that in my happier days, I had made her the object of my love! But alas,
I thought, it is now too late. Could I now offer her—would she stoop to
receive, the homage of a heart, which had already been rejected by
another? Could I, who in my days of prime had worshipped at another
shrine,—could I now, maimed and broken down, widowed in heart,
and bankrupt in affection, presume to speak of love to Laura Willoughby? Could I, indeed, love at all? Was my heart not seared and callous?
Had my feelings towards Lady Melicent been changed? I knew not; she
was still to me an object of emotion; yet pride mingled with my pain,
when I thought of those days of almost more than mortal beatitude, in
which I had won and worn the high guerdon of her love. I had suffered;
I had been miserable; I was still unhappy. There was poison mixed with
the intoxicating contents of the goblet, and I had drained it to the dregs.
Fortune had done her worst. Physical and mental anguish had wrung
my body and my soul. Yet fortune could alone influence the present and
the future,—it could not obliterate the past.

Of such a character were the confused and multitudinous thoughts
that stirred, and were stirring within me when I reached Middlethorpe.
It was night. The carriage had been rolling on for several hours amid the
darkness, before I was awakened from my reveries, by the sudden
stopping of the vehicle. In a moment I had sprung into the hall, and
rushed onward unannounced into the drawing-room. The family were
assembled there, and I appeared suddenly in the midst of them an
unexpected guest.

I leave my reception to the imagination of the reader. Let it shadow
forth for him all that is warm, kind, and affectionate, and he will not
exceed the truth. Lucy had recovered her looks since my departure.
Never on maiden's cheek was seen a richer bloom, never did maiden's
eyes dart brighter effulgence, than Lucy's as she gazed once more upon
her brother. It was not so with Laura. She was paler and thinner than I
had ever seen her. Sadness was on her brow, which the smile of her
colourless lips could not obscure from observation. No joyful light came
dancing from her eye, and in the expression of her countenance, there

was an indefinable something that told of secret suffering and sorrow. Laura was not now, as I remembered her; yet no ray of loveliness that had lingered round her was gone. The character of her beauty was indeed changed, but it was beauty still.

My heart smote me as I gazed on her, for I entertained a vague consciousness, that but for me, she had been happy.

When I inquired anxiously about her health, she answered she was well, yet I learned from Lady Willoughby and Lucy, that, from some withering impulse, for which medicine afforded no cure, they saw her, with deep anxiety and alarm, gradually fading.

During my stay at Middlethorpe, Laura, in such sad circumstances, was the engrossing object of my cares and anxieties. In her presence, all sadness was banished from my brow; I endeavoured to raise her spirits by a forced elevation of my own. The effort was seldom successful, and yet I believe a melancholy and dreamy happiness—a calm, not bright, but untroubled—a waveless stillness of all painful emotion—a soothing and tranquil quiescence of heart and mind frequently stole over her in my society.

The week which I intended to pass at Middlethorpe carried with it much of sadness of spirit; for it was felt by all to be the prelude of a parting, and that parting—an eternal one. In the course of it, Frank Willoughby, who had been in town, on my arrival, came to accompany me to the place of embarkation, and bid me farewell. The week soon passed, and I was still at Middlethorpe. When I talked of departure, Lucy, with streaming eyes, would throw her arms about my neck, and implore me not to leave England in the feeble and precarious state to which I had been reduced, and call on Laura to join in her entreaties. Laura was silent, yet raised her eyes on me, with a look of pity and of kindness, which spoke more than words could have conveyed. But my resolution was taken, and I would not be moved.

" Nay, Lucy, " I answered, " why should I remain in a country, in which life has lost for me all charm. In the excitements of the field, I may yet find something to stir my sluggish spirit into action; and if I die—alas, what loss do I create to any one but you ? "

Laura bent down, and hid her face as I spoke, that I might not read her emotion.

Though my determination was unshaken, it was difficult to be carried into effect. Lucy, in the fulness of her heart, would beg but for a single day, and could I refuse her ? No. Yet this could not last for ever, and delay it as I might, I knew that the moment of the final struggle must come at last.

At length it came. I had made my arrangements unknown to any of the family, and the carriage was at the door, before I had announced my intention. Then I sought Laura, for with her, I felt it necessary to my happiness, to have a short interview before my departure, to tell her, on the eve of an eternal separation, that I did not part from her in cold indifference of heart. She was not in the house. I learned she had gone out an hour or two before, and had not yet returned. I went forth into the park in search of her, I visited her favourite walk, beneath the spreading arms of the gigantic beeches, and I called aloud upon her name, but received no answer. Then I sought her in her flower garden, but that had long been neglected, and she was not there. I remembered her favourite bower, on the banks of a shady dell, in which she delighted to seek retirement, when the sun was high. This bower was peculiarly her own, and here, even by her own family, her solitude was held sacred from intrusion. Thither my steps were bent. As I approached, no sound was heard but the murmuring of the brook beneath, and the carolling of the birds from the branches of the leafy wilderness, in which it stood embowered. When I came within a few yards I stopped, unwilling to intrude suddenly on her privacy, and in a low, but audible voice, I pronounced her name. No answer was returned, and uncertain whether it contained the object of my search, I at length approached the door.

When I entered, she was seated at a rustic table, with her face buried in her hands. A bunch of wild flowers was before her, and a book lay open upon the table. She did not move on my entrance, and I again addressed her.

" Laura, " I said, " I am come to bid you farewell. "

She raised her head quickly and suddenly, as if surprised by my presence. She rose as she beheld me.

" You are going, " she said, and extending her hand towards me, she sunk back upon her seat, as if exhausted by the effort. Her face was pale as death, and her eyes in a moment became lustreless and glassy.

" Oh, Laura, you are ill ; excuse me for having thus intruded on your privacy, but I felt I could not depart without seeing you once more. "

I saw she was struggling to speak, but could not, for her lips moved, yet they produced no sound. At length the word farewell, in deep and suffocating tones, was faltered from her lips.

" Ere I bid you farewell, Laura, I have something to say, which I could not be happy were I to leave unspoken. I would not have you believe me unkind—ungrateful. Alas, could you read my heart, you would know, I am neither. "

As I spoke I seated myself beside her on the mossy bench—her head fell upon my shoulder, and in a few minutes the power of utterance was restored to her lips.

What passed at that interview, words shall never tell.

The carriage was countermanded. I did not return to the army.

CHAPTER XVII

Whither is he vanish'd?
Into the air, and what seem'd corporal
Melted as breath into the wind.

Macbeth.

But where is he, the pilgrim of my song,
The being who upheld it through the past?
Methinks he cometh late, and tarries long.
He is no more. These breathings are his last.
His wanderings done, his visions ebbing fast,
And he himself is nothing.

Childe Harold.

ONCE again, in spite of all my sufferings, my mind was happy and at rest. The man who says, "I will sorrow, and will not be comforted," is ignorant of the laws of his own nature,—he knows not that which is within him. He cannot dedicate his days to unavailing regrets. Comfort will visit him in a thousand unknown shapes, and unsuspected forms. Sometimes it will steal unawares into his soul, and, brooding like the Halcyon on the billowy waters of his spirit, they will become calm. Sometimes, like a thing of life and beauty, it will start up before him in his path, and he will welcome it to his arms. If joy is transient, so is sorrow. The chariot of Time, though its wheels be noiseless, is ever rolling onward in its course. The world may remain unmoved, but *to us* it is ever changing. The mountain, which in the morning, hid half the firmament from the eye of the mariner, when seen at eventide from the deck of his receding vessel, seems to have shrunk into a molehill.

Hitherto, gentle reader, I have made you the depositary of my confidence. I have laid bare to your view my actions and my motives. You know my errors—I have told you the secrets of my life. These were my own, I had a right to reveal them, and I have done so. The time has at length come—I write it with regret—when this confidence must cease. I married; and from the moment I did so, the secrets of another became indissolubly connected with my own. A barrier has sprung up between us, which cannot be overpassed. I would not deceive you; thenceforward the workings of my bosom can be known but to God, and one only of his creatures.

Yet, separated as we are ever destined to be, I would willingly indulge the hope that there are some kind natures at least, who are not utterly indifferent to the future fate of one, whose career through infancy and in manhood they have already followed. To such—if such there be, the few and brief particulars I have yet to relate may not be without interest.

In a few months from the period referred to in the last chapter, bloom had again visited the cheek of Laura Willoughby, and she became my wife. Never, perhaps, was there a more complete and sudden revolution in a human heart, than the conviction that I was still to one fair being, the object of fervent and devoted love, created in mine. The discordant jarring of its elements was in a moment hushed, and the chords of my spirit, when moved by her gentle breathing, gave forth symphonious music. I was happy, but my happiness was of a different nature from any I had before conceived of. It was in nothing like the glorious swing of rapture, which in former days had thrilled every fibre of my frame, and shot like wild-fire through my veins. Yet it was better than that, deeper, less troubled, more serene, less variable, and more enduring.

After my marriage, I wished not again to mingle in the world. I had already experienced my share of its vanities, its dangers and its disappointments. The full capacity of my affections was filled at home, and what need was there that I should seek enjoyment abroad. I quitted the army, and retired to Thornhill. Twelve tranquil and happy years have since passed, during which I have found no reason to doubt the wisdom of my resolution. My life, indeed, has not been one of idleness ; and, I trust, that in discharging the duties of my station with zeal and fidelity, I have not served my country less effectually than I could have done in the more active services of a military life.

At first, Thornhill was to me the source of many painful remembrances. Every object I beheld there, was linked with sad associations of those whom I had loved, and who were gone for ever. Every spot of the ground—almost every tree was connected with the memory of youthful days, and stirred my heart with melancholy thoughts. This, however, by degrees wore off. The associations, indeed, still continue, but the pangs which they excited are gone. My regrets have been softened, not deracinated by time. Of those I have committed to the grave, I now think with tender memory—not with poignant sorrow.

There is a healing medicament in nature for minds that delight to dwell too fondly on the past. When I gaze on my children, the sources of a thousand fears and hopes, my thoughts are either fixed on the present, or projected to the future. Yet how frequently, do even these awaken the sleeping remembrances of my youthful days. The sunny hair, and blue eyes of Charles, recall the brother of my youth whose name he bears, and Laura—little Laura—is she not the image of that Lucy, who came dancing in the glee of her childhood to welcome the return of her brothers to their home ? Yes, in her sylph-like form, in her dark and laughing eyes—even in that nasal tendency to *snub*, which time has so happily removed from Lucy, the resemblance is perfect. But I would turn from circumstances exclusively connected with myself, to others in which the reader may perhaps take deeper interest.

From the period of my quitting Glasgow, the infirmities of my uncle continued to increase. I wrote him of my marriage, and received a letter of kind congratulation in return. I entreated him to quit Glasgow, and make Thornhill his future residence; but the old man felt and knew that the habits of a long life were not thus to be broken by a sudden wrench. Business, which had been the labour of his early life, was become the pleasure of his later days. He was sensible, he said, of the kindness of the motive which prompted the invitation, but he would not lay on me the burden of a querulous and infirm old man. He was too old a tree to be transplanted; he would die where he had lived, and lay his bones with his father's. He survived about five years, during which period I paid him several visits.

At length, a letter came from Girzy, informing me that he was very ill, and the physicians despaired of his recovery. In half an hour I was on the road, and travelled day and night, in the hope that I might yet be in time to close his eyes. I thank God I was so. He was dying when I arrived; yet when Girzy told him of my presence, in a voice which sobbing rendered almost inarticulate, he gazed on me with a look of kindness, and I felt the pressure of the hand I held in mine. His death was easy. No one knew at what moment his spirit had departed. He appeared to sink into a slumber, from which he never woke. May we not believe of this kind and generous old man, that, dying in the sincerity of his faith, " he fell asleep in the Lord. "

At another moment, I might have laughed at the expression of the countenances of the numerous relations who were present at the opening of the will. Never perhaps was hope, and fears that kindle hope, more variously and ludicrously depicted, than on the faces of those who listened with breathless anxiety, to each succeeding bequest of the important document, when read aloud by the slow and drawling voice of the solicitor. By this it appeared, that the old gentleman had left legacies to each of his brother's children, but the bulk of his large fortune, including the estate of Balmalloch, to me. By this large accession I have been enabled to purchase back all that portion of my ancestorial estates, which, from the extravagance of my grandfather, it had been found necessary to sell. Thus have the shorn honours of the family been unexpectedly restored.

To his old and faithful domestic, my uncle bequeathed an annuity of a hundred a-year—to her, wealth as great as the mines of Potosi. Yet long was the kind and faithful creature inconsolable for the death of her master. She did not cry, but she wandered up and down the house, in a vague but sad consciousness that, like Othello, her occupation was gone. Often would she start up from her chair in the kitchen, in forgetfulness of the sad event, and run towards the chamber in which the body was laid, anxious to administer to the wants of him, who could feel human wants no more. Thus did her time pass till the day of the funeral, but when she saw the mournful assemblage, and the coffin, that contained the remains of one, who for forty years had been the engrossing object of all her ministering cares, carried forth to be committed to its last home, the poor creature seemed utterly broken-hearted and bent down by the weight of her affliction.

I accompanied the funeral into Dumbartonshire, and laid the old man by the side of his brother.

On my return, I did what I could to comfort Girzy and soothe the violence of her grief. Her relations I found were all dead, and there was no tie, since the departure of her master, that bound her to Scotland. So Girzy went with me to Thornhill, where she has remained ever since.

Knowing the natural activity of her constitution, and her aversion to quiescence, I at first endeavoured to find scope for her energies, by placing her in a situation of authority. The English servants and the Scotch housekeeper, however, did not agree. The flames of civil war broke out in the establishment, and all was discord and confusion. Girzy, who carried her zeal for my interest, a point or two further than was desirable, came to me with loud complaints of the waste and the extravagance of my domestics.

" Thae wasterfu deevils o' servants, Maister Ceeral, " she would say in the fullness of her heart, " will eat you out o' house and hame. It just drives me demented to see the galravichin that's gaun on at a' hoors in the servants' ha', to say naething o' the loupin and rampagin o' thae neerdoweel cutties, wi' the bardy flunkies, that are nae better than themsells. I'se warrant we'll hae some o' them sittin' in the kirk, on the black stool, afore lang. And then they maun hae meat three times a-day, and the strong beer gangs ower their thrapples like sae muckle water ; set the like o' them up, indeed, wi' their yill and roasted meat! This very morning, when I made a haill pat-fu' o' parritch mysel', and set it afore them for their breakfast, wad they sae muckle as look at it? Na, they turned up their noses at the very sight o't, and tell't me to tak my Scotch dishes to the pigs! Heard ever leevin woman the like o' that? But I'se bring down their proud stamachs, and gar them pike their banes better, before a's done, or my name's no Girzy Black. "

In short, Girzy seemed determined to set up as the Joseph Hume of the establishment, and her labours met with pretty much the same reception, with those of that distinguished economist. The servants came in a body, and declared they could no longer remain in office under that Scotch skinflint of a housekeeper. Resignation was the order of the day. I was briefly, but decidedly, informed, that I must either seek a new housekeeper, or a new establishment of servants. The steward talked of resigning the seals, and the house-maid of laying her mop at my feet ; the butler would not draw a cork without a change of ministry, the groom gave up his curry-comb, and even a Flibbertigibbet of an errand boy, hesitated on the propriety of carry my letters to the post, without an immediate prospect of a satisfactory adjustment. Under such appalling circumstances, I was compelled to yield. Girzy was transferred to the nursery, where she reigns with undisputed authority, teaching the children to speak Scotch, and spoiling them by over indulgence.

From Lucy, now Lady Willoughby, I scarcely consider myself separated. Middlethorpe is not beyond the limits of a morning's ride, and the intercourse between the families is cordial and constant. Frank has become almost as domestic as myself, and makes an excellent husband. Time has deprived Lucy of none of her attractions. She is neither less gay nor high-spirited than formerly, though, with respect to all the duties of a wife and mother, I confess I do not know a more exemplary matron. Frank's companions sometimes joke him, indeed, on the change of his taste and habits, which has become apparent since his marriage, and I have remarked that he is generally silent in conversation, when allusion is made to the domestic circumstances of families, in which the grey mare is known to be the better horse.

The society of Conyers, now a K.C.B., with about a dozen foreign orders dangling from his button-hole, I also frequently enjoy. He married Miss Culpepper, a young lady to whom I have had the honour of introducing the reader in the course of these Memoirs, but with whose good qualities I enjoyed no opportunity of becoming acquainted. By the death of her brother, who died from bolting ice when heated by dancing at a ball, she succeeded to the estate of Culpepper Park, which Conyers now possesses in right of his wife. Age has somewhat moderated the extreme vivacity of his spirits, but by no means diminished his attachment to old friends, and our regard, begun in youth, is likely, if I may judge from my own feelings, to continue unbroken till death. Sir Charles and Lady Conyers are the gayest people in the county. No one rides better horses, or is a keener sportsman, than my old friend ; no one drives a smarter equipage, or gives more splendid parties, than her Ladyship. We are but sober people at Thornhill, yet Conyers always spends a fortnight with us about Christmas, a visit to which we make a regular return.

William Lumley went some years ago to India as a Judge. He writes me, he is there engaged in a ponderous book on Indian Antiquities, with which he means to astonish the learned on his return to Europe.

Lady Lyndhurst (I really beg pardon of the Lord Chancellor, but mine is the older creation) continues to fill that prominent station in the world of *haut ton*, to which by her rank, beauty, and talents she is so eminently entitled. Since my marriage we have twice met, and she received me with the cordial welcome of an old friend. Though I have never ceased to feel a deep interest in her happiness, these meetings were not the cause of any very painful or violent emotions. The season of these has passed away, and when I gaze on Laura and my children, I can bend in grateful acquiescence to the decrees of Providence, and say, from the bottom of my heart, " It is better as it is. "

READER, it is time that the drama of my life should close. The curtain must now fall, and the puppets, which for your amusement have strutted their little hour upon the stage, are about to vanish for ever from your view. If, in following the vicissitudes of my career, you have occasionally felt sympathy for my joys or sufferings, accept my thanks; and should your early days, like mine, have been overcast with storms, may these too pass away, and leave the sunset of your life serene and unclouded as that of

CYRIL THORNTON.

FINIS.

NOTES

In the page references in the notes below, the letters within brackets indicate the part of the page to which the note applies: *(a)* signifies the first quarter of the page, *(b)* the second quarter, *(c)* the third quarter, and *(d)* the final quarter.

Half-title. Shakespeare, *The Taming of the Shrew*, I.ii
Page 1(a). Thomas Heywood, *Challenge for Beauty*, I. i
Page 1(b). from Shakespeare, *Coriolanus*, V. ii
Page 1(c). Johnson, *The Vanity of Human Wishes*, line 222
Page 1(d). 'an orielle-d'ours-coloured silk gown': the colour of a bear's ear, i.e. brown
Page 3(a). Thomas Campbell, *The Pleasures of Hope*, part 2, line 375
Page 3(a). 'Twas Greece, but living Greece no more', untraced.
Page 5(a). Felicia Hemans, *The Graves of a Household*
Page 6(c). 'propria quae maribus': what is suitable for a man—man's work
Page 7(c). This quotation, from Shakespeare, *As You Like It*, I. iii, was deleted from the second edition, possibly because of its mildly incestuous suggestion.
Page 8(a). Gustavus Adolfus (1594–1632), King of Sweden; Prince Francois Eugène de Savoie Carignan (1663–1736), youngest son of the prince of the Savoy Carignan and a niece of Cardinal Mazarin; Charles Mordaunt Peterborough, 3rd Earl of (c.1658–1735). All three won great fame through their military exploits.
Page 8(a). Sebastian Le Prestre De Vauban (1633–1707), a Marshal of France who developed a system of fortification, the 'systeme de Landau perfectionné,' outlined in his posthumously published *Memoire pour servir a l'instruction dans la conduite des Sièges* (Leiden, 1740).
Page 8(d). From Wordsworth, 'The Two April Mornings.'
Page 9(a). *Royal King and Loyal Subject*: play and quotation untraced.
Page 13(a–b). Wordsworth, Ode: 'Intimations of Immortality', lines 1–6, 182
Page 13(c). Shakespeare, *The Winter's Tale*, IV.iv.118–22
Page 14(a). Wordsworth, 'A Poet's Epitaph'
Page 14(c). Scott, *Rokeby*, 4, xi. This quotation was deleted in the second edition.
Page 15(a). 'And shew'd no signs of life, save his limbs quivering'; untraced.
Page 16(c). 'Professor R—': Professor William Richardson, author of *Essays on Shakespeare's Dramatic Characters*.
Page 16(d). 'Ballmalloch, in Dumbartonshire': a fictional estate, possibly derived from Baldernock or Balmore, both villages to the west of Glasgow, or Balmulloch, to the east. But Hamilton's Balmalloch is clearly situated near the head of Loch Long.
Page 17(a). Cock laird: 'a landholder who himself possesses and cultivates all his estate' (*Scottish National Dictionary*).
Page 17(a). George Combe and Richard Poole were Scottish followers of the German phrenologist Dr Spurzheim.
Page 20(a). Shakespeare, *Comedy of Errors*, I.ii
Page 20(c). The Latin quotation (Plautus, *Merc.*, I. ii) may be translated as follows. 'If anyone comes in your way on the crowded pavements, drive them right off, give them a shove, tumble them on the road. What a vile practice this is they have here. If you're running, in a hurry, hardly anyone deigns to give way. So when you've started one thing, you have to tackle three all at once — run, fight and curse en route.' Plautus (born circa 254 BC) was a Roman comic poet, twenty of whose plays have come down to us.

Page 23(a). Spreull's Land: built back from Glasgow's Argyle Street, on a site then lying between Shawfield Mansion and the original Hutcheson's Hospital, in 1783/4 for City Chamberlain Spreull, head of a firm of muslin merchants. The building was designed to have shops on the ground floor and superior dwelling-houses above. Its spiral 'hanging staircase', beneath an oval cupola, was for long regarded as one of the outstanding architectural features of the City. Money was lavished on its construction because it was inalienably entailed upon Spreull's family, of which Cyril Thornton's uncle was a member. In spite of the entail, it had been split up into offices by 1845. Eventually, it came into the hands of the Royal Bank of Scotland. As the last eighteenth-century Glasgow 'land', it should, of course, have been conserved. The present editor visited it in 1974, shortly before the Bank had it demolished to make way for new development.

Page 23(c). Hoggets were large casks or barrels; muscovado was unrefined sugar.

Page 26(a). Shakespeare, *Coriolanus*, V.i

Page 26(b). Thomas Middleton (1580-1627), *A trick to catch the Old One*, II. i

Page 26(c). The Goosedubs: a lane connecting Stockwell Street to the Briggait, named after a goose-keeping Glasgow baillie who had a house with a lang rigg (long garden) in Stockwell Street, adjacent to the lane.

Page 26(c). Ramshorn Church: the original Ramshorn Church was built in 1720. It was replaced by Thomas Rickman's St David's (Ramshorn) Church in 1824/5.

Page 28(c). Kilmarnock nightcap: probably a 'Kilmarnock hood,' a knitted woollen conical skull-cap worn as a nightcap by indoor workers such as weavers.

Page 31(c). George Cruickshank (1792-1878): English artist, caricaturist and illustrator.

Page 31(d). Wordsworth, 'The Fountain'

Page 37(a). Untraced.

Page 38(b). Richard Porson (1759-1808), Professor of Greek at Cambridge. He played an important role in establishing sound textual criticism.

Page 38(b). Joseph Addison (1672-1719), essayist, poet and statesman; his fame rests on his two hundred and seventy-four *Spectators*.

Page 39(a). 'Professor Y—': John Young

Page 39(b). 'the Digamma': the sixth letter of the original Greek alphabet. It was a consonant, probably equivalent to the English *w*. It was obsolescent by Homer's time and vanished in classical Greek.

Page 39(c). Edmund Burke (c.1729-77): though a considerable orator, he never achieved high political office.

Page 39(d). 'Odes of Tyrtaeus': Tyrtaeus was a seventh-century B.C. Greek elegiac poet of Sparta, whose work survives only in fragments.

Page 39(d). 'Professor J—': George Jardine, Professor of Logic

Page 40(c). From 'waste its sweetness on the desert air', *Elegy Written in a Country Churchyard* by Thomas Gray (1716-77).

Page 41(a). From Jim Belcher, pugilist, who made popular parti-coloured hankerchiefs, blue with white spots, worn round the neck.

Page 41(d). 'Robin Carrick's Bank': Robert Carrick (1737-1821), known as 'Robin', was a dour but polite Lowland Scot and a lifelong bachelor. He was the leading figure in the Glasgow banking world around the turn of the century. His Ship Bank withstood the crisis of 1793 which brought down several Glasgow banks, the Ship 'standing firm as a rock while other banks foundered.'

Page 42(b). 'the second city of the Empire': in 1811, Glasgow realised that it was not only larger than Edinburgh, but larger than any other place in Britain apart from London. So it began to call itself the Second City (adding, later, of the Empire). C. A. Oakley, *The Second City* (third edition, 1975).

Page 43(a). Shakespeare, *The Merry Wives of Windsor*, I. i

Page 43(a). Dr Johnson quotation untraced.

Page 49(b). Wordsworth, 'Ruth'.

Page 50(a). Thomas Heywood, *English Traveller*, II. 1–4

Page 51(a). 'Mores hominum multorum vidit et urbes': he saw the manners and cities of many men. Horace, *Ars Poetica*. The Latin quotation is itself a paraphrase of Homer, *Odyssey*, I. iii, said of Odysseus.

Page 52(c). George Washington (1732–99), Commander-in-Chief of the American forces in the war which secured the independence of the United States, and later the first President of the United States.

Page 52(c). Sir John Burgoyne (1722–92) was defeated by the Americans at Saratoga in 1777.

Page 52(c). Charles Cornwallis, 1st Marquess (1739–1805). He served as a major-general in the American War.

Page 52(c). James Wolfe (1727–1759) was given command in an expedition to wrest Quebec from the French. The British seized the Heights of Abraham on the northern shore of the St Lawrence river, bombarding the city. Before the battle ended, but with its probable victorious outcome apparent, Wolfe was mortally wounded by a musket-ball.

Page 52(c). Thornton's use of 'harquebuss' is an anachronism. His exclamatory paragraph bears no relation to the course of the battle of Minden, 1759, in which the British cavalry conspicuously failed to charge.

Page 54(a). Shakespeare, *Richard III*, I.iii

Page 57(b). 'De non apparentibus, et de non existentibus, eadem est ratio': 'Of that which does not appear to the senses, and of that which does not exist, the account is the same.' i.e. what you don't see, isn't there.

Page 60(a). George Crabbe, *Tales (1812)* 'The Parting Hour'. Hamilton misquotes: the original reads 'forty years'.

Page 60(a). Shakespeare, *Henry VIII*, IV.ii

Page 60(d). 'Honest Jehu': a coachman, a fast and furious driver. 2 Kings 9.

Page 60(d). Giovanni Belzoni (1778–1823) was an hydraulic engineer, six feet seven inches tall. He was also a pantomime player and professional strong man. He was the first person known to have excavated in the Valley of the Kings, in Egypt. He sent a colossal bust of Rameses II to the British Museum.

Page 61(d). 'galligaskins': a kind of legging

Page 62(a). 'a succedaneum': a substitute

Page 63(b). A Cicerone is a guide who shows places to strangers.

Page 63(b). The so-called Wallace sword, allegedly lying by his side when he was taken by the English, was for many years housed in Dumbarton Castle. According to Irving's *History of Dunbartonshire* (1860), it was sent for repair to the War Office in London in 1825, when it was decided that it did not date further back than the 18th century. After the Wallace Monument on the Abbey Craig, near Stirling was built, the sword was transferred to Stirling in 1888.

Page 63(c). The lines quoted are from John Finlay, *The Sword of Wallace*.

Page 63(d). 'the river Leven ... immortalised in tuneful song': Tobias Smollett, 'Ode to the Leven'

Page 65(a). 'passibus æquis': step by step

Page 65(a). 'longo intervallo': by a long span

Page 66(c). 'bound each to each, by natural sympathy': Wordsworth, final line of 'My heart leaps up', but with 'sympathy' in place of the poet's 'piety'.

Page 66(d). Wordsworth, 'The Fountain'

Page 70(a). Sir John Denham, *The Sophy*, V

Page 70(c). Auchterfechan is a fictional name.

Page 70(d). Drumshinty is a fictional name, perhaps from Drumchapel, then a village to the north-west of Glasgow.

Page 70(d). Garscud and Glenscadden are fictional names combining the parts of Garscadden, a district of Glasgow.

Page 71(b). Lamlash is a village on the Island of Arran, in the Firth of Clyde.

Page 71(c). 'drystane dyke': a wall built without mortar

Page 72(b). 'enormous queue': a long plait of hair worn down behind, like a pigtail.

Page 72(c). Auchentorlie is an estate between Bowling and Dumbarton.

Page 73(b). The 'very amusing personage' was no doubt Provost Pawkie, in Galt's novel *The Provost*, supposedly based on the character of Baillie Thomas Fullerton of Irvine. Dumbarton has never had a Provost Aulay MacAulay.

Page 73(d). 'never ending, still beginning': Dryden, *Alexander's Feast*

Page 74(a). 'ne plus ultra': unbetterable

Page 74(d). Arncraik is a fictional estate.

Page 76(c). 'in puris naturalibus': stark naked

Page 77(c). 'Apicius or Dr Kitchiner': Apicius was the name of a notorious gourmet (probably more than one). One such, M. Gavius, lived at the time of Augustus and Tiberius; but the cookery book *De re coquinaria*, surviving with his name as author, was compiled later, probably in the fourth century A.D. William Kitchiner was the Eton-educated son of a coal merchant. He became 'a gourmand, a wit, a musician and a man of science,' (according to the *Cornhill Magazine*, 41 (1880)), and, around 1820, published a popular cookery book, *The Cook's Oracle*.

Page 77(d). 'the force of fancy could no further go': untraced.

Page 78(a). Shakespeare, *Comedy of Errors*, I.ii

Page 78(a). Shakespeare, *The Merchant of Venice*, IV.i

Page 79(a). Glencroe is the glen between Loch Long and Loch Fyne, through which ran the old 'rest and be thankful' road.

Page 80(d). 'Cui bono?': to what purpose?

Page 80(d). Regency tavern: no such tavern is known to have existed.

Page 81(c). Shipping lists were posted in the Exchange, attached to the Tontine Hotel, where they would commonly be discussed.

Page 83(c). Glenlivet is a famous malt whisky, still produced

Page 84(a). 'howdie': a midwife

Page 85(a). 'Bell Geordy': the town crier

Page 85(d). 'status ante bellum' (usually 'status quo ante bellum'): the condition (i.e. of military boundaries) that existed before the war.

Page 86(a). Byron, *Childe Harold*, Canto IV, c.xxxvi

Page 86(a). See Pope, *The Rape of the Lock*, Canto I, 84/85.

Page 86(b). 'time passes o'er us with a noiseless lapse', and 'hopes, and fears that kindle hope': both untraced.

Page 86(b). 'the first of May is the day fixed by immemorial usage in the University, for the distribution of the prizes': this custom, described in Murray's *Memories of the Old College of Glasgow* (1927), began in 1792 and was related to the ending of the session on 1st May. This was altered in 1892, so the 'immemorial usage' ceased.

Page 87(c). 'had a borough or two at command': prior to 1832, certain Parliamentary boroughs in England were at the disposal of rich landowners.

Page 88(d). 'the Carlisle mail': it left daily from the front of the Post Office in Nelson Street, Glasgow. Hamilton, when living in the Lake District, frequently used it on its return journey to send manuscripts to the publisher Blackwood in Edinburgh.

Page 91(a). Inigo Jones (1573–1651), the great English architect, modelled his style on that of Andrea Palladio (1518–1580).

Page 91(b). 'A gladio et per gladium': by the sword and through the sword

Page 93(a). Friedrich, Freiher von der Trenck (1726–94), the son of a Prussian general, entered the Prussian army and soon became an orderly to Frederick the Great. But Trenck carried on a love affair with Frederick's sister, Princess Amalie, and suffered imprisonment as a result.

Page 93(c). 'La distance n'y fait rien; il n'y a que le premier pas qui coûte': the distance is nothing; it is only the first step that is difficult. (Mme du Deffand, in a letter to d'Alembert dated 7 July 1793, regarding St Denis's legendary two-league journey carrying his head in his hands).

Page 94(c). 'babbles of green fields': Shakespeare, *Henry V. II. iii*

Page 95(b). 'scope and tendency of Bacon': presumably a pun on the name of the learned Sir Francis Bacon, Lord Verulam.

Page 95(c). 'adscripti glebæ': bound to the soil

Page 96(a). Pitt's reference was to 'emporiums of trade'.

Page 97(a). Shakespeare, *King John*, II. i

Page 103(c). 'like quills upon the fretful porcupine': Shakespeare, *Hamlet*, I. iv. But Shakespeare wrote 'porpentine'. Hamilton later repeats this misquotation.

Page 103(c). 'limbs stiff as those of Niobe': Niobe boasted of her large family in comparison with that of the Titaness Leto, who had only two children, Apollo and Artemis; whereupon Leto killed all Niobe's children and turned Niobe herself into a rock, which still sheds tears on Mount Sipylus (Homer, *Iliad*, 24, 603–17: Ovid *Met*, vi 155–312).

Page 104(b). 'the Irish Giant': Finn Mac Cumheill (fl. c. A.D. 250) the general to whom Cormac mac Airt, King in Tara, entrusted an army to establish suzerainty over the whole of Ireland. He attracted a vast body of legend to himself in Ireland, Scotland and the Isle of Man. The growth of the Finn legend is traced in Kuno Meyer's *Fianaigecht* (Royal Irish Academy, 1920).

Page 104(b). 'divide et impera': divide and rule

Page 104(c). The Greek phrase means 'winged words'; a common Homeric expression.

Page 105(a). 'the Rosicrucian process': the Rosicrucians were a mystical fraternity, founded around 1410, the early followers of which devoted much time to the study of alchemy, and to experiments in transmutation, as well as to the transmutation of base humans into more spiritual beings.

Page 105(a). Thomas William Coke of Holkham (1752–1842), a pioneering agriculturalist, particularly interested in breeding Southdown sheep and Devon cattle.

Page 105(a). John Russell, sixth Duke of Bedford (1766–1839). Practised agricultural improvements and was an enthusiast for sheep-shearings.

Page 105(c). 'on dits': scandal

Page 106(d). 'say unto the trumpets': Job 39.25, but garbled

Page 107(a). William Godwin (1756–1836), an English thinker and writer whose *Inquiry concerning Political Justice, and its Influence on General Virtue and Happiness* (1793), in which the sentiment referred to by Hamilton is expressed, influenced many young people, including Shelley and Bulwer Lytton.

Page 107(a). 'Alnaschar in the eastern story': Alnaschar was the brother of the talkative barber in the *Arabian Nights* (cf. Brewer).

Page 107(d). 'partie carrée: a game of four players

Page 107(d). 'invita Minerva': literally, 'against the will of Minerva', against the grain. It is in Horace's *Ars Poetica*. Cicero explains the tag in *De Officiis* (I.110) as 'in direct opposition to one's natural genius', the goddess Minerva standing for one's natural wit or propensities.

Page 108(b). *Marmion* (1808): narrative poem by Sir Walter Scott (1771–1832). *The Pleasures of Hope* (1799): long moralising poem by Thomas Campbell (1771–1844). *The Mysteries of Udolpho* (1794): Gothic novel by Mrs Ann Radcliffe (1764–1823).

Page 110(a). Prior, 'To the Honourable Charles Montagu'; Southey, *Thalaba the Destroyer*, 7. 31.

Page 110(d). 'Golconda mines': Golconda, a fortress and ruined Indian city once ruled by the Shahi dynasty, stood five miles west of Hyderabad. It was taken by Aurangzeb in 1687 and annexed to the Mogul empire. Golconda has given its name in literature to the diamonds which were found in other parts of Kutb Shahi's dominions and simply taken to his capital to be cut.

Page 111(a). Sir John Sinclair (1754–1835), established in Edinburgh a society for the improvement of British wool and was the first President of the Board of Agriculture.

Page 111(b). Lucius Quintus Cincinnatus (b. circa 519 BC) a patrician Roman hero who twice thwarted the proposals of Trentilius Arsa to draw up a code of written laws equally applicable to patricians and plebeians. Twice, however, he refused to become dictator of Rome, preferring life on his farm.

Page 113(c). 'noli me tangere': 'touch me not', occurring in the Vulgate, John 20.17.

Page 113(d). 'damned with faint smiles,' 'with civil leer': Pope, *Epistle to Dr Arbuthnot*, 201

Page 113(d). Sir William Edward Parry (1790-1855) published *Nautical Astronomy by Night* (1816), *Journal of a Voyage to discover a North-West Passage* (1821) and *Narrative of the Attempt to Reach the North Pole* (1827).

Page 118(a). *Forest Sanctuary*: play and quotation untraced.

Page 121(a). The Reverend Charles Wolfe (1791–1823), Irish poet, author of 'The Burial of Sir John Moore'. This quotation, however, comes from a song, 'If I had thought thou coulds't have died,' eventually collected in a' very slim volume, *The Poems of C— W—* (1903), edited by Litton Faulkner. Hamilton must have known the song from its magazine publication.

Page 122(a). 'a wiser and a better man': Coleridge, *The Ancient Mariner*, but garbled.

Page 123(c). 'Fishing, hawking, hunting country gentleman': untraced.

Page 124(a). Aboukir: a village with a bay, on the Mediterranean coast of Egypt. On 1 August 1798 Nelson fought the Battle of the Nile near the bay. On 8 March 1801 the British Army under Sir Ralph Abercromby landed at Aboukir in the face of fierce French opposition.

Page 128(a). Anonymous, sometimes attributed to John Webster and William Rowley, *The Thracian Wonder*, I.ii; and Thomas Heywood, *English Traveller*; the lines by Heywood are deleted in the second edition and replaced by lines from Byron, *Childe Harold's Pilgrimage*, IV.x; The thorns which I have reaped are of the tree

I planted,— they have torn me and I bleed;
I should have known what fruit would spring from such a seed.

Page 129(a). 'She was as sportive as the fawn,' etc.: Wordsworth, 'Three Years She Grew in Sun and Shower' [a Lucy poem], lines 13–15, with a change of tense.

Page 130(a). 'the true Amphytrion': a host or dinner-giver; but Hamilton refers to that part of the legend where Zeus took Amphitryon's appearance in order to seduce the latter's wife, Alcmene. There is a heavy sarcasm in the application of this to the frigid Miss Cumberbatch, though in the end she does seduce Cyril's father.

Page 130(c). 'it might have puzzled Lavater himself to determine': Johann Kaspar Lavater (1741–1801), Zurich-born poet, mystic, theologian and physiognomist, was the author of a once much-admired but unscientific treatise, *Physiognomische Fragmente zur Beförderung der Menschenkenntnis und Menschenleibe* (1775–78).

Page 132(b). Shakespeare, *Othello*, I. iii

Page 133(a). Shakespeare, *Much Ado About Nothing*, IV. i

Page 133(b). 'She could not bear their gentleness', etc.: untraced.

Page 135(a). Scott, *Quentin Durward*, Chapter 4

Page 138(a). Erebus: darkness, son of Chaos and Homer's name for the dark passage from Earth to Hades.

Page 139(b). Scott, 'Lochinvar'

Page 144(a). 'in the —— regiment of foot': later details confirm that this is the 29th (Worcester) Regiment, in which Hamilton himself served.

Page 145(a). *Wonder of a Kingdom*: play and quotation untraced.

Page 152(a). The 'Swan with two Necks' appears in the London directories from 1839 to 1893, though it probably existed before these directories were first issued. It stood at 6 (later 19) Great Carter Lane. In 1839 the licencee was John Kingston.

Page 152(d). 'the leaves that strew the brooks in Valambrosa [*sic*]': Milton, *Paradise Lost*, I, 302–303

Page 154(a). 'Dundas on the Eighteen manoevres': Sir David Dundas, *Principles of Military Movement, chiefly applied to Infantry* (1788), then the standard work in English on tactics.

Page 157(a). *Henry V*, I.i.55 (not *Henry IV*).

Page 157(b). Edward Augustus, Duke of Kent and Strathearn (1767–1820), fourth son of George III and father of Queen Victoria, was Commander-in-Chief in British North America, 1799–1800, and Governor of Gibraltar in 1802, whence he was recalled after a mutiny. He was, as Hamilton says, a martinet and notoriously pedantic about military dress and etiquette.

Page 160(a). Shakespeare, *Love's Labours Lost*, I.i

Page160(c). 'Lord Kinnaird': probably George William Fox Kinnaird, 9th Baron (1801–1876), who succeeded his father in 1826. An agricultural reformer, he introduced steam-ploughs and steam-threshers to Scotland. His uncle, Douglas Kinnaird (1788–1830), whom Hamilton may have meant, though he was untitled, was a friend of Byron and is mentioned in *Don Juan*.

Page 161(d). Antinous, famed for his manly beauty, was a favourite of the Emperor Hadrian.

Page 162(b). The firm of Stulz, tailors, existed from 1818–1915, by which time it was Stulz, Binnie and Co. Tailoring was continued thereafter, but with the German name dropped. In Hamilton's time the premises were at 8 Clifford Street, off Bond Street, London.

Page 163(a). 'The condition of Polyphemus': one-eyed

Page 163(c). '*selon les règles*': according to the rules

Page 164(a). Sir Francis Legatt Chantrey (1781–1842): English sculptor.

Page 164(a). John Flaxman (1755–1826): English sculptor and one-time designer for the Wedgwood factory.

Page 165(d). *'ainsi va le monde'*: that's just the way things are (literally, And so goes the world).

Page 168(a). Miss Baillie quotation untraced.

Page 178(b). 'The Roast Beef of Old England': words by Henry Fielding adapted to a tune composed by Richard Leveridge about 1728 and first published in Walsh's *British Miscellany* (1740).

Page 179(d). Captain Charles Morris (1745–1833), a soldier, a wit and a beau. A two-volume collection, *Lyra urbanica or the Social Effusions of Captain Morris* (London, 1840), was published posthumously, containing 'The Toper's Apology', from which Hamilton's quotations come.

Page 180(d). Drawcansir is a blustering, bragging character in George Villiers's burlesque *The Rehearsal* (1667) who, in the final scene, enters a battle and kills all the combatants on both sides.

Page 180(d). *The Legend of Roland* (transferred as Orlando to the Italian), was based on the achievements of Charlemagne in the eighth century. The oldest form of the poem was written by an Anglo-Norman scribe about the end of the twelfth century.

Page 180(d). *Amadis de Gaul*, a chivalric romance surviving only in a Castilian text, is claimed by both Spain and Portugal. The probable author was Joao de Lobeira, who served the Portugese court between 1258–85. Its record of fantastic gallantry, wonders and adventures led Cervantes to call it the 'best of all the books of its kind ever written'.

Page 183(a). Shakespeare, *Measure for Measure*, III.i; Shakespeare, *Measure for Measure*, III.i; Shakespeare, *Cymbeline*, II.ii

Page 186(d). Pierre Terrail Bayard (1473–1524), a French soldier of noble descent who accompanied Charles VIII to Italy and was knighted after the Battle of Fornova (1495). Known as *le bon chevalier*, he died in action.

Page 189(b). Thomas Campbell, 'The Battle of the Baltic'

Page 190(c). Shakespeare, *As You Like It*, II. viii

Page 190(d). See Shakespeare, *As You Like It*, II.i

Page 191(a). John Dyer (1700-58), *The Fleece*, Book IV

Page 192(a). Coleridge, 'The Ancient Mariner', part I

Page 192(c). John Benbow (1653–1702): English Admiral who served in the West Indies, but when chasing the French in 1702 was mortally wounded. His name has attracted much naval mythology, including erroneous association with the ship 'Arethusa'. For the anonymous song 'Admiral Benbow' see *Augustan Lyric*, edited by Donald Davie (1974), p.47. 'Arethusa' was a popular song by Prince Hoare (1775–1834), commemorating (inaccurately) a naval engagement of 1778 (also in *Augustan Lyric*, p.133) regularly played at the last night of the London Proms.

Page 193(e). Santa Cruz de Tenerife, the capital of Tenerife, was bombarded by Nelson in 1797, during which unsuccessful engagement he lost an arm. Some British flags captured at the time hang in one of the churches.

Page 195(c). Tenerife, the largest of the Canary Islands, is dominated by a double-pointed volcanic peak, Pico de Teyde, or Mount Teide. In 1798, a vent on the North-Western side ejected 'much lava and other volcanic matter.'

Page 196(c). Galen (c. A.D. 130-c.200): Greek physician and writer who pioneered research in anatomy and physiology. The standard twenty-volume edition of his works, edited by C. G. Kohn, appeared at Leipzig in 1821–33.

Page 198(c). re infecta: without accomplishing the matter

Page 202(a). *Hydaspes*: play and quotation untraced.

Page 204(d). General Charles O'Hara (1740-1802): illegitimate son of James O'Hara, 2nd Lord Tyrawley, the General became aide-de-camp to the Marquis of Granby. He served as a Brigadier General in America, where he was taken prisoner of war. He was a close friend of Horace Walpole.

Page 204(d) 'Granby and Ligonier': John Manners, Marquis of Granby (1721–1790), Lieutenant-General, commanded Cumberland's army and left a description of the devastation wreaked at Culloden by that army. He was painted by Reynolds twelve times. John Ligonier (1690-1770), of Huguenot extraction, became a Lieutenant-General in the British army in 1743, fought in the Flanders campaign and was recalled to defend Lancashire during the Jacobite rising.

Page 204(d). The Kevenhuller hat was 'a Swiss military headdress ... named after the Austrian Field-Marshal Kevenhuller. Really a bicorné it was built high in front and back, with a spout-like crease in the middle. It was worn by George Washington.' It was also known as the continental or cocked hat, in French *androsmane* according to *The Dictionary of Costume* by R. Turner Wilson.

Page 209(c). Theodore Edward Hook (1788–1841): English author and son of the composer James Hook. When only sixteen, Theodore collaborated with his father in a comic opera, *The Soldier's Return*. By charming the Prince Regent, he got himself appointed Accountant-General of Mauritius, but five years later came under investigation for embezzlement. He was a virulent detractor of Queen Caroline. A prolific writer, his novels include *Jack Brag* (1837) and *Gilbert Gurney* (1838).

Page 210(a). 'Furcifer': a nonce-word for 'fork-bearer'

Page 212(a). First line misquoted — 'Let us onward walk' — in passage from John Wilson's *The City of the Plague*, Act I (*The Poems of John Wilson*, 1825); Shakespeare, *The Tempest*, III. iii

Page 219(a). Shakespeare, *Henry V*, II. i; and Thomas Gray's translation of a fragment of the *Gododdin*, first printed in 1775 (*The Poems of Gray, Collins and Goldsmith*, edited by Lonsdale, 1969); Sir Walter Scott, *Marmion*, Canto VI, xxxii.

Page 222(a). Parody of Shakespeare's 'In maiden meditation, fancy-free', *A Midsummer Night's Dream*, I. ii

Page 222(a). The Peace of Amiens was signed in 1802 between Britain, France, Spain and Holland.

Page 222(a). As a result of Napoleon's victory over the Turks at Aboukir in 1799, and internal warring Egyptian factions, Sir Ralph Abercromby landed with an army in March 1801. Though mortally wounded, he succeeded in driving the French out of Egypt. There was another expedition in 1807, (which ended in evacuation) during the struggle between the brutal but victorious Mehemet Ali and the beys.

Page 223(b). Count Pierre Antoine Dupont de l'Etang (1765–1840), French general.

Page 223(c). Androche Junot, Duke of Abrantes (1771–1813) took part in the Italian and Egyptian Campaigns, served in the Peninsula from 1808 to 1811 and commanded a Corps in the Russian Campaign.

Page 224(a). General Sir Brent Spencer (1760-1828) commanded the 1st Division of Wellington's army 1810/11, and was frequently mentioned in despatches by Wellington.

Page 224(c). General Sir Miles Nightingale (or Nightingall) (1768–1829) served under Lord Cornwallis at the Siege of Bangalore and subsequently became his aide-de-camp. In 1807, he went on a secret expedition to Cadiz with General Spencer, and then joined Wellesley's forces in Portugal, where he commanded the 3rd Brigade in the 1808 Campaign.

Page 227(a). The attack Hamilton describes is that of the 29th Foot at Rolica, in which their commander, Lt. Col. Lake, was killed.

Page 228(b). C'est un brave garçon, ne le tuez pas: He's a good boy, don't kill him.

Page 229(a). General Henri Francois de Laborde (later made a Count of the Empire), who commanded the 1st Division of Junot's army in 1808, the 3rd Division of Soult's at Corunna in 1809 and a division of the Young Guard in the Russian Campaign.

Page 230(a). Shakespeare, *Henry V*, III. ii

Page 230(d). Robert Southey (1774–1843): the Poet Laureate who, in his younger days, had strong, if eclectic views on social reform.

Page 232(d). Sir John Francis Craddock (1762–1839) fought in Portugal, where he was superseded in command by Sir Arthur Wellesley.

Page 232(d). General Sir Hew Whitefoord Dalrymple (1750-1830) commanded the garrison at Gibraltar before taking command in Portugal. He was created a Baronet in 1815.

Page 232(d). Nicolas Jean de Dieu Soult, Duke of Dalmatia (1769–1851) was appointed a Marshal of France in 1804. Though he despised Napoleon, he commanded a Corps at Ulm and led the decisive attack at Austerlitz. He was created Duke of Dalmatia in 1808 and the following year was given a command in Spain, pursuing Sir John Moore at Corunna. He fought through the Peninsular War, though after Wellington's victory at Salamanca, was recalled by Joseph Buonaparte, with whom he habitually disagreed. He took command of the French army at Vitoria, but was thereafter repeatedly defeated by Wellington.

Page 234(c). Quotation untraced.

Page 235(b). General Sir Charles Gray and 1st Earl (1729–1807) was nicknamed 'no flint Gray' because he ordered the flints to be removed from his men's muskets to prevent any accidental betrayal of their advance. He co-operated with Jervis in the taking of Martinique and Guadeloupe.

Page 235(b). John Jervis, Earl of St Vincent (1735–1823), had a distinguished naval career. After capturing Martinique and Guadeloupe with Gray, Jervis played so successful a part in engaging the Spanish off Cape St Vincent that he was promoted Admiral of the Fleet.

Page 237(d). Claude Perrin Victor, Duc de Belluno (1764–1841), made a Marshal in the field by Napoleon in 1807 and later Duke of Belluno. From 1808–12 he commanded in Spain but after initial successes, lost the Battles of Talavera and Barrosa.

Page 238(d). 'shot *sur le champ*': shot then and there.

Page 239(a). Talavera de la Reina is a town in central Spain where Wellesley defeated the forces of King Joseph Buonaparte in July 1809, but was forced to retreat into Portugal instead of marching on Madrid. The French lost 7,268 men out of 44,138, the British 5,363 out of 20,641 and the Spanish 1,201 out of 36,000.

Page 239(a). 'Punica fides': with Carthaginian faith — i.e. faithlessness, treachery. Sallust (86–34 B.C.).

Page 239(c). Joseph Buonaparte (1786–1864), Napoleon's eldest brother, was a claimant to the throne of France. He became King of Naples in 1806 by his brother's decree and King of Spain in 1808, but had to leave Madrid hastily after the French army ignominiously surrendered at Baylen, giving the Spanish the first real success against a Napoleonic army anywhere. On Napoleon's surrender, Joseph went to the United States, but later lived in Florence and Genoa. Though he resembled his brother physically, by temperament he was too 'mild, supine and luxurious' for the tasks put upon him.

Page 240(c). General Bellegarde: Hamilton perhaps never saw this name in print. The real name was Count A.D. Belliardé, second-in-command to Louis Desaix, who campaigned successfully in Egypt against Murrad in 1799. Belliardé pacified Upper Egypt, capturing the port of Kosseir, on the Red Sea. In 1801, however, he was caught between two British forces and a Turkish force and forced to surrender Cairo. With Menou's capitulation at Alexandria a few months later, French resistance in Egypt was at an end.

Page 240(c). 'ipsis Germanis Germanior': more German than the Germans themselves.

Page 241(a). The official records have now no trace of a Colonel Guard.

Page 241(b). Joseph Fouché, Duke of Otranto (1759–1820) was an opportunist Jacobin politician who effected the overthrow of Robespierre, he supported Napoleon who, however, did not entirely trust him. Fouché was elected President of the Commission that briefly governed France on Napoleon's second abdication. He retired to Prague, then moved to Trieste, where he died.

Page 246(a). *Duke of Verona*: play and quotation untraced.

Page 251(a). Johnson, *The Vanity of Human Wishes*; Shakespeare, *Troilus and Cressida*, II. iii

Page 251(d). Astolfo: an English knight in Ariosto's *Orlando Furioso* (1532).

Page 252(a). 'Schneider' is German for tailor.

Page 255(b). *Anathema maranatha* on his vile calling: the biblical phrase is taken from I Corinthians 16.22. Hamilton naturally followed the Authorised Version taking the two words to mean a severe curse. 'If any man love not the Lord Jesus Christ, let him be Anathema Maranatha'. But the two words must be separated. 'Anathema' is Greek, and means 'accursed'. 'Marana tha' is Aramaic, and means 'Come, Lord.' It forms a separate sentence in Paul. The *New English Bible* and Lorimer's *New Testament in Scots* both got it right.

Page 255(c). Ruspini, Chevalier Bartholomew (1728–1813) was an Italian-born dentist who lived in London, and became a highly-acclaimed surgeon-dentist and freemason, whose *Treatise on the Teeth* (1768) ran to thirteen editions. His son, Chevalier James Bladen Ruspini, who succeeded to his father's title (1768–?) became a partner in his father's practice at 32 St Albans Street, London, in 1787. Both father and son were the surgeon-dentist to the Prince of Wales. There is some dispute as to which Ruspini invented the dental mirror. See also 'Chevalier Bartholomew Ruspini' by James Menzies Campbell in *The Dental Magazine and Oral Topics*, December 1953.

Page 259(a). Shakespeare, *Much Ado About Nothing*, I.i

Page 260(b). Samuel Joseph (1791–1850): a British sculptor who studied in London but moved to Edinburgh in 1823. In 1826, he returned to London.

Page 260(c). Hafen Slawkenbergius: a character in Sterne's *Tristram Shandy*, according to Sterne the author of a treatise on *noses*.

Page 261(a). ''Tis odour fled', etc.: untraced.

Page 263(a). 'Pulchrum est digito monstrari et dicier, hic est': It is a fine thing to be pointed out and have it said 'That's him'. Persius I.28.

Page 263(b). Sir William Curtis (1752–1820), third son of Joseph Curtis of Wapping. Sir William became Lord Mayor of London. He inherited his father's seabiscuit factory and established his own bank, but his stoutness made him an object of ridicule in Peter Pindar's *The Fat Knight and the Petition.*

Page 263(b). George Canning (1770-1827): British statesman. Under-Secretary of Foreign Affairs in 1796; Treasurer of the Navy under Pitt, 1804–06; Secretary of State for Foreign Affairs, March 1807–September 1809; Prime Minister from September 1827 until his death later in the year.

Page 263(b). 'Men's judgements' etc.: Shakespeare, *Antony and Cleopatra*, III. iii. 31–34

Page 263(c). John Pinkerton (1758–1826): Scottish man of letters, born in Edinburgh, but settled in London in 1780 and in 1802 moved to Paris. His twenty-four books include *Origin of the Scythians or Goths* (1827), which displays a strong anti-Celtic prejudice.

Page 265(a). 'dis aliter visum': the gods decided otherwise. Virgil, *Aeneid*, II. 428

Page 266(b). 'The shadowy kings of Banquo's fated line', etc.: William Collins, *Ode on the Popular Superstitions of the Highlands of Scotland*, 181–2

Page 269(a). 'Knights and dames I sing', etc.: Byron, *Don Juan*, XV. xxv

Page 269(d). Sangoree: a West Indian drink of wine, diluted and spiced.

Page 270(b). 'Which are like wax; apply them to the fire', etc.: George Crabbe, *Tales* (1812), no. 17, 'Resentment', 11–16

Page 270(d). Dr Pangloss: the optimistic philosopher in Voltaire's *Candide* (1759).

Page 272(c). Lord Castlereagh: Robert Stewart, 2nd Viscount (1769–1822), was responsible as Secretary of War for the despatch of a British force to Portugal in 1808 and for ensuring that Wellesley was eventually made Commander-in-Chief. As Foreign Secretary (1812–1822, when he committed suicide) he organised the final coalition against Napoleon, and dominated the Congress of Vienna after the latter's defeat.

Page 273(a). 'melancholy and gentlemanlike': the reference is to Jacques in *As You Like It.*

Page 278(a). Shakespeare, *Measure for Measure*, III. i; Shakespeare, *King Lear*, V. iii

Page 279(d). Untraced.

Page 281(a). *Tom Jones*, a novel (1749) by Henry Fielding (1707–54).

Page 284(c). Wordsworth, 'She was a phantom of delight'

Page 285(c). Savoir vivre: literally, 'to know how to live': manners, tact

Page 285(c). The remarks on Miss Culpepper's taste in men gain point when we learn in the last pages of the novel that she marries Thornton's friend, the Irish dragoon, Conyers.

Page 287(c). 'feræ naturae: of wild nature

Page 290(a). Nabob: governor of a town in India, the word transferred by usage to mean 'a person of great wealth,' usually got by exploitation, especially in British India.

Page 290(a). Marplot: one who mars or defeats a plot.

Page 290(b). Assaye is a village in Hyderabad, southern India, where, on 23 September 1803, Wellesley secured the most overwhelming victory ever achieved by the British in India, when a force of 4,500 defeated the Mahratta army of 50,000.

Page 293(a). Dryden: untraced.

Page 301(a). *Montalto*: play and quotation untraced

Page 302(a). Shakespeare, *A Midsummer Night's Dream*, III. i; 'needls' is an obsolete term for needles.

Page 309(a). Shakespeare, *Romeo and Juliet*, I, iv

Page 309(b). *The Morning Post and Daily Advertising Pamphlet* appeared, with several changes of title, between 2 November 1771 and 30 September 1937, when it was incorporated in the *Daily Telegraph*.

Page 315(a). 'Up! Up! fair bride' etc.: source untraced.

Page 318(a). Shakespeare, *Two Gentlemen of Verona*, III. i

Page 322(b). John Prosser, accoutrement maker and sword-cutter, was in business at 9, Charing Cross, London, from 1816 to 1853, when the firm moved to 37, Charing Cross.

Page 322(c). General Sir David Dundas (c.1735–1820), a member of the family of Dundas of Dundas, abandoned the study of medicine for an army career in 1752. He fought in France and Holland, and became Commander-in-Chief of the forces in 1809, in which capacity Thornton no doubt saw him.

Page 323(d). Shakespeare, *Othello*, I. iii

Page 325(a). Shakespeare, *Henry IV*, II. iii

Page 325(b). Lisbon, the capital of Portugal, on the right bank of the Tagus, near its entrance to the Atlantic, suffered in the great earthquake of 1755, and from a huge fire in 1788. The French invasion of Portugal in 1807 led to the removal of the Portugese court to Brazil and brought on the Peninsular War.

Page 327(a). Sir Rowland Hill (1772–1842) proved himself one of Wellesley's ablest commanders.

Page 327(a). 'Hon. General Stewart': Major-General the Hon. William Stewart (1774–1827) commanded the 1st Brigade of the 2nd Division in 1810, and the Division itself in 1811, at Albuera, where he was wounded.

Page 328(b). Quarter-Master-General: George Murray (1772–1846)

Page 332(a). 'This night, wherein the cub-drawn bear would couch', etc.: Shakespeare, *King Lear*, III. i. 12–14

Page 333(b). General William Carr Beresford (1768–1854), the illegitimate son of the 1st Marquess of Waterford, reorganised the Portugese Army for Wellington (being made a Portugese Marshal), and took part in the Battles of Salamanca, Vitoria, the Nive and Orthez, among others. He was made a Baron at the end of the Peninsular War and created Viscount in 1823. Later, he served Wellington in a political capacity.

Page 335(b). There were two Camerons involved in the Peninsular War, and it is not clear to which one Hamilton refers: i) General Sir Alan Cameron (1753–1828), head of a branch of the Clan Cameron, accompanied Sir John Moore to Sweden and Portugal: ii) General Sir Alexander Cameron (1781–1850), a younger son of Cameron of Inverailort, Inverness-shire, who covered Sir John Moore's retreat, distinguishing himself at Corunna. On the other hand, Hamilton may have invented this officer, naming him after the regiment he mentions, the Cameron Highlanders (79th Foot).

Page 337(a). Shakespeare, *Henry V*, V. iii

Page 337(d). Shakespeare, *Henry IV*, III. i

Page 338(c). Admiral George Cranfield Berkeley, the second surviving son of the 4th Earl of Berkeley, entered the navy serving under his cousin, Rear-Admiral Keppel, and was with Captain Cook aboard the *Resolution*, surveying the coast of Newfoundland and the Gulf of St Lawrence. He served in Gibraltar and was promoted Admiral in 1810. From 1783 to 1810 he also represented Gloucestershire in Parliament.

Page 339(b). Major General Daniel Houghton commanded the 2nd Brigade of the 2nd Division at Albuera, where he was killed.

Page 342(a). 'across the Soure': Hamilton seems to be describing the clash between the Light Division of Wellington's army and Massena's rearguard (commanded by Ney) as it retreated across the river Ceira on 15 March 1811.

Page 344(c). Marie Victor Nicholas de Fay Latour-Maubourg (1768–1850) fought at Albuera, where he inflicted heavy losses on the Allies. He also fought with Soult at Marmont and Badajoz. He lost a leg in the Battle of Leipzig, 1813.

Page 346(a). General Sir Galbraith Lowry Cole (1772–1842), second son of Willoughby Cole, 1st Earl of Enniskillen in the peerage of Ireland, commanded the 4th Division in the battle of Albuera, in which he was wounded. He was wounded again at the Battle of Salamanca.

347(a). Shakespeare, *Henry V*, IV. i

Page 347(b). In one of his unsuccessful attempts to free the Israelites from the Egyptians, Aaron, Moses's spokesman, threw his rod down in front of Pharaoh and it at once turned into a serpent. The other magicians at the Court did likewise, with similar consequences. Aaron then caused his serpent to eat all the others. Exodus 7: 8ff.

Page 354(a). Probably Major General John Hamilton (b. 1755), who commanded the Portugese Division, 1810-1813, and was with Beresford in the Albuera campaign.

Page 355(a). Hamilton's account of Albuera is, of course, from the point of view of the 29th (Worcester) Regiment.

Page 355(a). General Joachim Blake (1759–1827) of Irish extraction and a soldier of fortune, commanded the Valencian army and surrendered under the French onslaught on Valencia by Suchet.

Page 359(a). The Fusileer Brigade: the 1st Brigade of the 4th Division, comprising two battalions of the 7th (Royal Fusiliers) and one of the 23rd (Royal Welsh) Fusiliers.

360(a). Shakespeare, *Two Gentlemen of Verona*, III. i (not *Cymbeline*); Shakespeare, *The Merchant of Venice*, II. vi

Page 367(a). The pool of Bethesda, reached by Jerusalem's Sheep Gate and surrounded by seven porches, was the place where crowds came to be healed. It became troubled when its healing properties were about to be activated. John V. 2ff.

Page 370(a). James Montgomery (1711–1854), *The World Before the Flood*, Canto Third; *Thracian Wonder*: play and quotation untraced.

Page 370(d). Samuel Taylor Coleridge, 'Dejection: An Ode'

Page 379(a). Matthew Prior, 'Henry and Emma', lines 387–92

Page 383(b). 'O Woman, in our hours of ease' etc.: Scott, *Marmion*, XXX

Page 388(a). Jonson quotation untraced; Shakespeare, *Coriolanus*, I. x

Page 389(a). 'a mensa et thoro': from bed and board

Page 400(a). Shakespeare, *Hamlet*, IV. vii

Page 403(a). The population of Glasgow in 1801 was 77,385: in 1811, 100,749: in 1821, 147,043, and by 1841, 255,650. The figure for 1827 cannot be traced.

Page 403(b). The Buck's Head Hotel: built on the corner of Argyle Street and Dunlop Street about 1750 as a residence for Provost Murdoch, a brewer, the building was converted to an hotel in 1790, its sign, a gilt stag's head. Robert Southey and Thomas Telford stayed at the Buck's Head in 1819. It closed in 1863, was demolished and replaced by 'Greek' Thomson's office block, which still stands.

Page 404(d). Pollock House: built 1747–52 to designs by William Adam. Wings were added by Sir Rowand Anderson. The home of the Maxwells, later Stirling-Maxwells, it is now in public ownership.

Page 404(d). Cumbernauld House: built in 1731 by William Adam for the 6th Earl of

Wigton. The interior was destroyed by fire in 1877. The exterior survived as an outstanding building, superseding an older castle which passed from the Comyns to the Flemings in 1306. Later the seat of the Burns of Kilmahow, it is now a public building in the 'new town' of Cumbernauld.

Page 404(d). Blythswood House: late eighteenth-century seat of the Campbells of Blythswood, demolished to make way for Blythswood Square, Glasgow, circa 1815.

Page 405(a). The Black Boy, in the Gallowgate, was so called because of the eighteenth-century aristocratic craze of employing black page-boys (a custom enshrined memorably in Richard Strauss's opera *Der Rosenkavalier*). By the 1830s, the tavern had fallen into disrepute as the result of a series of notorious robberies and murders that took place in the adjacent Black Boy Close.

Page 406(a). *Henry IV*, II. iv; *Richard II*, II. iii (not *A Winter's Tale*)

Page 408(b). Robert Leighton (1611–1684) was successively Bishop of Dunblane and Archbishop of Glasgow. The first near-complete edition of his works was published in London in 1692, a second two-volume edition in Edinburgh in 1748.

Page 408(b). Thomas Hallyburton (1674–1712): Professor of Divinity at St Andrews University. His works were first collected in 1833 and published in Glasgow. His *Memoirs* appeared in 1715.

Page 408(b). Isaac Watts (1674–1748): a non-conformist hymn-writer. Hamilton's reference is to his *Guide to Prayer*, first published in 1715.

Page 408(b). Richard Baxter (1615–1651): an English Puritan divine, whose *A Call to the Unconverted to turn and live* was first published in 1658.

Page 409(d). John Balmanno (?-1840) occupied the Chair of Materia Medica in the Andersonian University and was a physician at Glasgow Royal Infirmary, with intervals, from 1804. He lived latterly in St Vincent Place. He did not marry.

Page 410(a). Degveal, the dancing master: no such person can be traced. Hamilton may have mis-spelled the name, only hearing it said.

Page 411(a). Ebenezer Erskine (1680-1751): founder of the Scottish Secession Church. His sermons went through many editions, as did those of his brother, Ralph (1685-1752), who also published them. Hamilton could have meant either divine.

Page 413(d). 'as deaf as Ailsa Craig': Robert Burns, 'Duncan Gray'

Page 413(d). Scots proverb: 'He that must go to Cupar' (a town in Fife) 'must go to Cupar'.

Page 414(a). 'gamashins on yer cuits': galoshes on your ankles

Page 415(a). Shakespeare, *Richard III*, III. viii

Page 418(a). 'Like the sweet south' etc.: Shakespeare, *Twelfth Night*, I.i

Page 423(a). 'The deil gat power' etc.: untraced.

Page 425(a). Shakespeare, *Coriolanus*, V. i

Page 425(d). The Exchange Coffee Room was situated on the ground floor of the Tontine Hotel, in Argyle Street, and was added to the hotel in 1781. It was entered from the piazza of the Exchange itself and was an oval room seventy feet long. It was supplied with all the imported English, Irish and Continental newspapers as well as the Scottish ones. A regular subscription cost £1–12s. per annum. Strangers were admitted for a limited period without charge. Dorothy Wordsworth described the readers on the circular bench in the window at the end of the room as having the appearance of 'figures in a fantoccine, or men seen at the extremity of the opera-house, diminished into puppets'. The Tontine

Hotel building ended its once-glorious days as slum housing and was demolished early in the nineteenth century.

Page 426(a). Hunterian Museum: the medieval College of Glasgow, whose demolition in 1870 was probably the City's greatest ever architectural loss, had bequeathed to it by William Hunter (1718–83), an East-Kilbride-born but famous London surgeon, physician and teacher, his large collection of coins, paintings, prints, books, zoological specimens, fossils and minerals. The building had a handsome Doric portico of six columns and an Italianate dome. The facade stood at the eastern extremity of the College grounds.

Page 427(a). Dennet: a German three-wheeled cab. Stanhope: a light open one-seat carriage of a type first made for Fitzroy Stanhope (1787–1854). Whiskey: a light gig. Drosky: also a light gig. Tilbury: a light gig for two, said to be named after its first maker.

Page 430(c). 'gros-de-Naples': a kind of feathered ruff

Page 433(a). Shakespeare, *Much Ado About Nothing*, II. iii; Shakespeare, *Troilus and Cressida*, II. iii

Page 437(a). Shakespeare, *Macbeth*, I. iii; Byron, *Childe Harold*, Canto IV. clxiv

Page 439(d). 'mines of Potosi': Cerro Potosi, Bolivia, a mountain of silver ore discovered in 1545, the source of most of the world's silver and Spain's wealth for two centuries.

Page 440(d). Joseph Hume (1777–1855): British politician born in Montrose, who became 'the self-elected guardian of the public purse' and caused the word 'retrenchment' to be added to the Radical programme 'peace and reform'. He opposed flogging in the army and the impressment of sailors for the navy, and became an expert on lighthouses and harbours, securing greater efficiency in the operating of the former and saving useless expenditure on the latter.